BLACK
lace

Omnibus

The Top of Her Game
Emma Holly

Stand and Deliver
Helena Ravenscroft

Taking Liberties
Susie Raymond

Doubleday Direct, Inc.

GARDEN CITY, NEW YORK

BLACK LACE OMNIBUS IV
A 3-in-1 Edition including The Top of Her Game,
Stand and Deliver and Taking Liberties

Black Lace novels are sexual fantasies. In real life,
make sure you practice safe sex.

First published in 1999 by
Black Lace
Thames Wharf Studios,
Rainville Road, London W6 9HT

Published by arrangement with the authors and copyright
holders of the individual works as follows:

The Top of Her Game © 1998 Emma Holly
Stand and Deliver © 1999 Helena Ravenscroft
Taking Liberties © 1999 Susie Raymond

ISBN 0-7394-0713-9

Printed in the United States of America

CONTENTS

The Top of Her Game

Emma Holly

Chapter One

New York: Thursday night

*A*ll her life Julia Mueller had been searching for a man she couldn't master. It seemed she wouldn't find one tonight.

The open gift box sat on her lap, tissue paper blossoming over its edges like a fallen angel's wings. A custom-made riding crop nestled inside. Julia lifted it out, her mouth pursed in admiration for its workmanship. She'd say one thing for Durbin: he had exquisite taste in toys. The handle was thicker than the whip and dotted with small brass studs that pressed cool and smooth against her palm. She ran the flexible length under her nose, inhaling the scent of resin. Her pleasure centres fired. She shifted in the deep green chair. Silk rasped silk as her thighs brushed together. They were strong thighs. A sense of health and power filled her awareness. Her heart rate slowed. Her sex warmed.

A knob swelled from the base of the whip like the

1

head of a good-sized penis. Julia pressed her thumbnail into the bulge and smiled. If Durbin had been watching her, instead of being stuck in a meeting, he would have shuddered at that smile, shuddered and hardened with delight. Durbin loved a threat almost as much as he loved the execution of a threat.

She opened the accompanying gilt-edged card. 'I think it's time we moved to the next level,' it said. 'I adore you. D.'

Julia stood so abruptly that the box spilt from her lap. The next level. Beyond play-acting and spanking, beyond a harsh voice and a velvet blindfold. She paced to the balcony window, her heels clacking on the marble floor, the whip swinging beside her impeccably tailored skirt. The lights of Manhattan twinkled in the off-black dark. Like blood through a stiffened cock, the city's energy thrummed through the walls. She flattened her fingers against the glass as if it were a too-tight skin she needed to escape.

But there was no escape, not even when she closed her eyes. She was there again, frozen at the door to the general's office, her face stained with tears from some forgotten school-playground trauma. The door was open only a crack. They didn't see her. The general was bent over his government-issue desk, his uniform trousers shoved to his knees. Beneath the hair of his thighs muscles tensed, some thick, some narrow. Julia's mother stood behind him. She'd unbuttoned her jacket and she held something in her hand, something long and dark. Julia watched her arm rise; heard the breath she took to gather her strength, the huff as it rushed back out. The doubled belt descended with an eerie whistle. When it struck the general's ass, he bit his wrist to muffle his cry.

Even at fifteen Julia interpreted it as a cry of

pleasure. Her instincts did not mislead her. The shadow of his cock jerked beneath his khaki shirt-tails. Its head was large, the proverbial baby's fist. She recalled the plop, plop, plop of his pre-come hitting the brown carpet. Back then she thought the drops were sweat, but the sound was no less enthralling. The belt fell again, and again. The dripping silhouette jerked higher, vibrating with the force of pleasure-pain. Julia clutched the door, her body humming with a strange excitement. The general's legs stiffened. His chest swelled. The belt cracked once more and he came in milky, twisting spurts. They rolled down the army-green drawer. The general sighed. 'I adore you,' he said.

Then the strangest thing of all happened. Her mother bent down and licked the sweat from the back of the general's neck: her mother, that model of Swiss propriety, who buttoned every blouse to its neck and never slept without a nightgown, who said, 'Rule yourself, Julia, and you rule the world.'

The whip rolled now beneath Julia's palm, trapped between her hand and the glass. Her mother hadn't ruled herself. The game had seduced her, just as – two years ago – Julia had been seduced by the chance to play dominatrix to her boss. He was the up-and-coming director of Durbin-Moore Investments. She was his executive assistant, his whipping girl until the day she'd thrown his espresso in his face and told him to get his own damned lemon peel. He'd stared at her, coffee dripping on to his starched white collar. A current sprang to life between them, shockingly new to him, old as sin to her. She'd locked this tiger in its cage too long. Now it was too strong to resist. Energy prickled her skin like static; tweaked the flesh between her legs. As one, their eyes fell to his cock. It rose swiftly behind his trousers, a thick, unruly bulk. She didn't stop to think. She touched his hand. He clutched her wrist. One wild and desperate kiss later they were both lost.

She bent him over the desk and spanked him until her wrist ached. He shot a river of come, then dropped to the floor and kissed her shoes. It had been so long since she'd played the game. Once a year she allowed herself to; no more. His slavish kiss sent a spasm through her sex. When he lifted her skirt and mouthed her there, she came in seconds.

She promised herself she'd only take a taste. She wouldn't succumb to the spell the way her mother had. But even now, when she caught herself falling into the old seductive pattern, hot, thick moisture seeped from her core. She wanted to go to the next level. She wanted to go as far as Durbin could bear. Farther. She wanted to annihilate him.

She rolled her forehead against the glass and moaned. Like mother, like daughter, she thought. Except that her mother had loved the general. What she felt for Durbin was nothing like love.

Her reflection mocked her from the window. She was tall and strong and elegant; Grace Kelly with muscle. Her cheekbones were high and wide, her skin smooth as ivory. No hint of emotion shadowed her grey-green eyes. Her carriage was regal, her composure flawless. No one could fault her manners, but a woman would be no happier to find Julia Mueller seated next to her husband than to meet her in a dark alley. Nor would the husbands care to confront her there. She was a formidable creature. Looking at her, no one would guess she had any vulnerabilities at all.

But she did. She longed to fall in love. She was thirty-two years old and she had never come close. She

4

wanted the freedom to be tender as well as cruel, not as part of a game but in truth. She was never going to find that with Richard Durbin. She was going to have to break it off with him. Soon. Before it was too late. Maybe tonight.

The outer door thudded against the hallway wall. Her heart leapt. Durbin had arrived.

'Julia,' he roared, not yet shed of his public persona. 'Julia, where the fuck are you?'

She did not answer. She turned from the window and composed herself. He would see her as he saw her in the office, cool and competent in her dove-grey business suit.

He rounded the corner of the spacious living room. With an air of satisfaction, his gaze traversed the lacquered green walls, the recessed lighting, the elegant glass and steel. He stopped when he saw her. His respiration increased. His face coloured. He was a big man, six foot four inches to her six foot, and at least fifteen years older than she was. He ran his own company, was responsible for more than a billion dollars in assets, and she still had the power to halt him in his tracks.

Her cunt tightened with pleasure, but she did not lose her presence of mind. She saw that his tie was askew, his iron-grey hair ruffled from running his fingers through it. Something must have happened after she left the office. Normally he was as meticulous in his dress as she was. He tossed his overcoat on to the leather sofa, then his six-hundred-dollar suit jacket. His crotch bulged impressively. The ride up the lift could do that to him, or sometimes just the sight of this building from a distance. Neither of them lived here. This astronomically expensive art-deco penthouse was their playroom. They fucked here when Durbin could

5

escape his wife and family; when Julia decided he had earnt an escape. Two weeks had passed since their last visit and the flush that coloured his broad, brutal face declared his impatience to end the wait. They stood on opposite sides of the room, an expanse of black marble shining like the sea between them.

'Jesus,' he said, aroused by her icy silence. 'I could fuck you where you stand, Jules.'

She tapped the whip against the side of her leg. 'You know better than to call me that.'

'Right. Ms Mueller. Sorry.' He ran his hand through his mussed hair, then retrieved a spiral-bound folder that had fallen on to the sofa. 'But you won't believe this, Jules. We lost the Go-Tech account to Capital Edge. That bastard Santorini underbid our fees by one quarter per cent. One quarter! And you know what they were pushing? A mix of conservative growth and A-rated bonds. In the same fucking proportions as our proposal.' He pointed the rolled-up papers. 'It can't be a coincidence. Somebody leaked our strategy. DMI has a traitor.'

Just saying the word proved too much for him. He slammed the folder down and turned to the well-stocked bar. Ice cubes rattled as he threw them into a glass. 'It's either that *shvartzer* Isaacs or Prentiss. Frigid bitch.' He poured a generous slug of bourbon over the ice. 'She's been shitting bricks ever since I made Marty a senior VP.' He snorted. 'As though she deserves a promotion.'

He lifted the tumbler towards his mouth. Julia stopped him with a quiet cough.

'Oh, God,' he said. He strode across the room and offered the drink to her. 'Please forgive me, Ms Mueller.'

She should have made him kneel, but that would

wait. She brought the heavy glass to her lips. The liquor burnt her throat until that passage was as hot as the one between her legs. She filled her mouth again, grabbed the back of his neck and kissed him. He choked as she pushed the alcohol into his mouth, then swallowed and moaned, opening himself to her invasion. The change was on him, the spine-tingling transformation from her boss to her slave. Julia loved this moment more than any other. He was passive under her kiss, his neck limp, his hands fisting and unfisting at his sides.

But he had to misbehave. That was part of the game, too. He sidled closer, brushing her hip with the ridge of his swollen cock. She pushed him away.

'Down,' she said, a low, soft order.

He knelt so swiftly his knees cracked on the hard black floor. At once he began removing his clothes. He knew what she wanted. Always they began like this, a ritual. His hands fumbled with his shirt buttons, shaking with arousal and apprehension. From the first she'd inspired this cocktail of emotion in him. She watched impassively but inside she was drinking it in. He had to have her, would die to have her, but – oh – to suffer first was best. Eyes flickering from her face to her hands, he ripped off his shirt, then undid his trousers and shoved them down. He wore no underwear. She did not allow it. His cock was hard and red, its glans shining with eager juices. She was glad she'd made him wait a full two weeks. He was like a teenager now, thrusting thick and potent from the jungle of grey hair at his groin. He was a hairy man. When he got excited, sweat ran down his body in streams. He was sweating now.

He sat back to remove his trousers and shoes, then crawled to her feet. 'I'm sorry, Ms Mueller.' He kissed the toe of her three-inch grey heel. 'I shouldn't have been discussing business. It was very wrong of me.'

'Yes, it was.' She ran the tip of the riding crop down his naked spine. He was strong and firm, much firmer than when they'd met. She'd ordered him to use the company gym every weekday; told him that if he did a good workout he could masturbate afterwards and think of her. No one but she understood why he'd immediately installed doors in the men's showers. Smiling to herself, she stroked the leather over his hairy buttocks. He quivered.

'Does my mistress like her present?' he dared to whisper.

Rather than answer, she swung the whip sharply across his bottom. He jumped at the stinging blow, but made no protest. A line of pink appeared on his flesh. The whip had a good reach; she barely had to bend. She gave the weal a mate, then another and another, then judged she'd better stop. This crop was fiercer than anything she'd used on him before. Durbin had not cried out, but his back was bathed in sweat and a small puddle of pre-come had formed on the marble beneath his belly. Worse than hurting him would be allowing him to come too soon. He could do that, she had discovered, without her ever touching his cock; domination affected him that strongly.

'Turn around,' she ordered, then prodded him on hands and knees towards the bar. To speed him along, she pressed her shoe between his thighs. His scrotum was heavy, pendulous. It warmed the top of her foot as she separated his balls with her shoe. The toe was sharp. She dug it in just hard enough to suggest a threat.

He whimpered through tightly closed lips. Without waiting to be told, he opened the bar's bottom cabinet, then shifted aside for her. Julia knelt. His shoulder brushed her hip, hot and damp, but she didn't scold. She had enough in store for him. Reaching towards the back of the shelf, she extracted a jar of lubricant.

Durbin winced and looked away. Anal play made him nervous. He was no homo, not Durbin. But only an idiot would imagine he'd be using that blatantly phallic whip-handle on her! Whether he cared to admit it or not, by giving her the whip he had invited this very torment.

'Now, now.' She stroked his head before forcing his face around again. 'Do you want to move to the next level or not?'

'Yes,' he whispered. His eyes caught on the whip-handle, the same cold brown eyes that made his employees – and most of his competitors – quail. He licked thin, dry lips. Julia suppressed a shiver of delight. Yes, indeed, she thought. The mighty had fallen.

'Kiss it,' she said and thrust the whip in his face. He complied with a shudder. 'Now put the lube on it, slave. Nice and thick. We want it to go in easy, don't we?'

While he did as she asked, she pushed lubricant into his ass herself. The ring of muscle puckered, then gaped with a greed he would have denied if he could. She adored his panicked squirms, his heat, his deep-seated fear of the pleasure she was giving him. She rubbed the lube in slowly, gently, working dollop after dollop into his smooth dark passage. By the time she finished he was gasping for breath and whimpering with excitement. She took the whip from him, then hiked up her skirts. He watched her position the whip between her stockinged thighs, knob end out. It wagged there like a phallus.

'It won't fit,' he gasped, eyes riveted on the thick, shining pole.

The words sent a thrill through her sex. He might have been the virginal heroine from a novel. She flicked her hand across his cheek, a light, admonitory smack. 'Turn your head, slave. And grab the edge of the bar.' She kneed his thighs wider; big, hairy thighs, heavy with muscle but powerless to resist her will. 'Prepare yourself,' she growled. Using her hand to guide the whip, she pressed the handle past his sphincter.

He moaned and pushed, instinctively trying to expel the intrusion, but that made it slide in all the easier. Lube gushed out and ran down his legs like a woman's cream. Julia tightened her thighs. His passage was so slippery she could pull the whip back and forth with the strength of her leg muscles. She could fuck him, fuck him like a man.

She had to bite her lower lip to contain her moan.

The end of the handle pressed hard against her panties, easing between the soft, juicy split of her sex. Each time she thrust, the leather-covered wood mashed her clit. Delicious. She draped herself over him, still clothed in her prim grey suit, still completely in control.

'Do you know who I am?' she asked. 'Do you know who's fucking you?'

He shook his head and gulped for air. His knuckles whitened on the edge of the bar.

'I'm Marty, Richard. I'm Marty and I'm fucking you the way you always wanted me to.' She had a gift for mimicry. It was easy to infuse her voice with the senior VP's distinctive Bronx drawl.

'No,' he protested, head wagging. 'Don't.'

She laughed. 'Go on, Richie-boy, you know it's me. I'm fucking you, mister, and I ain't gonna stop till we both blow our wads to Kingdom Come.' He should have laughed but he couldn't. To him the thought was horrible: his protégé, his golfing buddy, taking him in the ass. Marty Fine was the office stud; always had a female co-worker loitering at the door to his office. He had a full head of curly black hair and a five o'clock shadow that started at two. If Durbin weren't attracted to him, at the very least he'd been jealous. And now she was forcing him to consider whether there might be something more.

Pushed to his limit, Durbin tried to pull away. Julia manacled his wrists in an iron grip. For all his hours at the gym, she knew more about overpowering people than he did. She'd wrestled with army grunts, after all. She could take Durbin down in a minute. She brought her mouth to his ear. 'Come on, buddy. You know you want it. You've watched my cock, haven't you? Seen me shake it dry. You know it's a big one. I bet you've wondered if I know what to do with it. I know you've wondered how it would feel, in your mouth, up your ass. You can't lie to me, buddy. You want it so bad you're dripping on the floor.'

She shifted her angle, catching his prostate on the handle's bulge. He moaned with anguished pleasure. The muscles of his back were rigid, bathed in sweat. She pulled back and stopped. He hesitated, but then his hips tilted towards her, mutely begging. He wanted what she was giving him. He wanted more. Yes, she thought, tightening her thighs and sliding in again.

'Cold,' he gasped, and she knew he meant the little brass rivets that studded the leather.

'Cold as ice,' she agreed, taking up a rhythm now. 'Cold as fucking ice, Richie-boy.' In and out she went, not hard but steady, knowing the effect of her thrusts was cumulative. His body stiffened beneath her, tensing for orgasm even as he tried to resist it. She could hear his teeth grinding. 'Oh, yeah,' she said. 'It's coming. I'm gonna shoot you full of spunk, Richie. You better get ready to take my load.'

'No,' he said, head shaking, spine arching.

She knew he was going through the roof.

He spasmed in climax just as hers began to rise. The air hissed from his lungs. His seed hit the marble floor, four splashes, five. He groaned at the sixth and shivered like a wet dog. Julia pushed back from him and stood. She pulled her skirt down. The whip handle was still embedded in his body. The lash end shook with his tremors.

She drew a slow breath to still her own shakes. She hadn't come. She should have been furious, or pretended to be. Instead, she eased out the whip and offered her hand to help Durbin to his feet. He dragged on it heavily, then staggered to the leather sofa and collapsed. He threw one arm over his eyes and released a languid sigh. Once upon a time they would have snuggled together in the aftermath. Once upon a time he would have wanted her to. But he'd got what he wanted tonight, all he ever wanted these days.

'You should move in here,' he said as if unaware of the distance, both literal and figurative, between them. 'No point paying for your place when this is here.'

A bitter heat turned in her belly. How dare he treat her like some tart to be housed at his convenience, available at his demand, especially when she was inches from leaving him flat!

'I don't think so,' she said. The ice in her voice made him sit up. He blinked at her, wary.

She began unbuttoning her fitted jacket, then her blouse. She slipped both from her shoulders and stalked towards him, her breasts bouncing in their cage

12

of fine white lace. Her steel-tipped heels clacked an unspoken threat. She didn't often let him see her naked, but not from insecurity. She knew her body was a dream most men had forgotten they had. No rake-thin model, hers was a body of firm, generous curves, of melting soft skin that smelled of baby powder and lust. The muscles beneath provided the necessary hint of danger. She was stronger than her lovers. She could enforce her will with more than feminine wiles. Not that she scorned feminine wiles. She didn't scorn anything that gave a woman power.

She undid her bra and tossed it on to a chair. Her nipples were peaked with arousal and as pink as a fresh spring rose. She ran one finger around each swollen areola. The pink deepened. The centres lengthened. Entranced by the display, Durbin's recently sated cock twitched and began a wavering ascent. She planted her shoe on the couch.

'Do you honestly think I would allow a lowly slave the privilege of paying my expenses?'

'No, of course not. I just –'

She backhanded his cheek. 'I am not moving in here. In fact, little man, you and I will soon be parting ways.'

He gasped. His penis leapt under the shock of her words, as if this were a new and better form of playacting. He slid off the couch and fell to his knees.

'No,' he pleaded, kissing the smooth, bare skin of her belly. 'Anything but that.'

She gripped his ears and shoved him back. 'I'm serious. I'm leaving you, Richard.'

'Of course you are,' he said, but she knew he didn't believe her. His hands slid around to the back of her skirt. He lowered her zip. His movements were tentative, respectful, as if he feared being stopped and desperately hoped he wouldn't be.

13

'I didn't give you permission to do that,' she said, but the protest was weak. Ignoring it, he dragged her skirt down. Within moments she stood before him in stockings and heels and a short double strand of South Sea pearls. His eyes slid shut at the picture she made. For a moment her eyes drifted, too. His expression . . . His hunger . . . Her blood felt thick, drugged with her own power.

'I'm such a bad slave,' he soothed. 'But I'd die without you, Ms Mueller. You must let me make it up to you.' He dragged his face, open-mouthed, across her belly, over her golden thatch. His lips slid lower, finding her unappeased clit. She couldn't stifle a tiny cry as he caught it on the tip of his tongue. 'I came without you, didn't I? That was wrong of me. So wrong.'

His mouth was clever and warm and avid. His subservient murmurs rose like smoke from a hookah, dizzying silver-blue spirals. She swayed. He eased her from her shoes and tipped her on to the couch. He burrowed between her legs amidst the dark, skin-soft leather.

'I adore you,' he said.

Memory jarred her. The general. Her mother. The sticky-sweet trap that had caught them both. She gripped the cushion, torn between desire and anger. Had she forgotten everything she meant to do? She took Durbin's arms in a bruising grip, meaning to shove him away for good. He lifted his head. His breath panted hot across her sex. His face was flushed, his eyes glassy with need. Truly, he was her creature, her slave. Her pussy squeezed itself in longing.

The ache was unbearable. One more time, she thought. Just one more.

'Turn around,' she said with a sternness that made

him quiver. 'I want to watch your cock while you worship me.'

He repositioned himself so that his cock and balls swung above her face. He was good with his mouth. Twice she almost came, but she held off by relaxing her muscles and controlling her breath. His jaw would be aching but that was for the best. He needed to suffer, loved to suffer. His cock was so hard now it defied its own weight, angling towards his belly. She ran her hands up his trembling thighs and on to his buttocks. She found the heated stripes that her new riding crop had left. She pinched one between forefinger and thumb. His small, pained cry vibrated through her pussy. He would come soon if she kept this up. He'd never had her discipline.

Rule yourself and you rule the world, her mother had said. It was so true.

But now she had earnt a reward. She rocked into his mouth, imposing her own rhythm. The tight, hard heat curled inside her, an aching coil of pleasure preparing to burst. He didn't deserve it but she would bring him with her. His pleasure intensified hers. It was proof of her mastery. She gave his balls a quick, threatening squeeze, then slid her fingers up his swollen shaft. She bent it downwards until she could see the deep red slit. His mouth paused, slack with enjoyment, then redoubled its efforts. She gave in to her urge to purr. His veins throbbed beneath her fingertips. She wouldn't stroke him, though; that wouldn't inspire the kind of explosion she craved. Instead, she set all ten of her nails into his glans and let them bite.

He cried out and jerked from her hold, his body obeying a reflex he could not control. A second later, he jerked straight back.

'Oh, yes,' he cried as she pricked him again. 'More, please, more.'

He returned to his duties, lapping and suckling with the knowledge that he bought his pleasure with hers. Again she pricked him and again he moaned, his flesh whitening and reddening beneath her nails. The coil of climax heated between her legs. She tugged his hips lower until she could catch his heavy scrotum with her teeth.

'Yes,' he hissed, his words muffled by her flesh. 'Bite it.'

She licked him, twice. Crisp silver hair tickled her tongue. He growled. This was too gentle for him. She gave him a taste of the edge, a tiny bite, a delicate tease of pain. His cock struggled against her grip, fighting to rise higher. Moisture welled from its tortured cap.

'Not yet,' she ordered. 'Not fucking yet.'

He groaned, the sound reverberating through her cunt. He slid his thumbs into her slit, pumping her, desperate to bring her off before he lost control. His efforts were not in vain. Her tension rose, the sweet almost, almost there. Her thighs tightened around his ears. The signal of her coming climax put him over the edge. His cock jerked, spewing in her hands, and then she lost her sense of him. The belt fell, a flashing image on the screen of her mind. The general bit his wrist to muffle his cry and her orgasm broke in a surging red wave, rolling through her sex, through her limbs, blood and pleasure, anger and satisfaction and then a great, empty peace.

Afterwards, they lay together on the leather couch. Julia was bone-weary, her head so heavy she wasn't sure she could lift it from his shoulder. Durbin stroked her fallen hair, absently, territorially, with no more sentiment than a man stroking his tie.

16

'I am leaving you,' she said, though she didn't usually repeat herself.

His hand stopped moving. His fingers tightened on her skull. 'Where would you go, Jules? There aren't many bosses who'd pay their secretaries what I pay you.'

Her weariness increased. Two years together and he still didn't understand her. Concern for her financial future was the last thing on her mind. He had indeed paid her generously. Given Durbin's spending habits, her liquid assets were many times his own. But even if money had been a concern, it wouldn't have swayed her from her course. She would never permit herself to become a slave to a job or a person or, she vowed, to a way of life that no longer fulfilled her.

Tonight's events forced her to admit she was as much of an addict as Durbin. She had meant to resist, but she hadn't. She'd sucked up the power high and then she'd crashed. If she had loved him, she might not have regretted the obsession, but she never had and she no longer respected him, either. They had worked too closely for too long. She'd had too many opportunities to see how selfish he was, how short-sighted and how petty. Even his ambition, once so admired, was revealed as no more than ego. He didn't care about Durbin-Moore Investments, only about how its success reflected on him.

She shifted on to her back, her head cradled on his upper arm, her gaze on the geometric ceiling frieze.

How could she persuade him to let her go? The crueler she was, the more he liked it. If she left him, he would hound her, would convince himself it was part of the game. There would be scenes. He did not realise he had lost his ability to behave in a rational manner. He knew only that the pleasure she brought him was more intense than any he'd known and he did not want to lose it. She doubted he could do her any lasting harm, but he might do himself a great deal. If he did, she would share the responsibility. She had set him on this road. She might not like him, but she wouldn't let him crash and burn if she could help it.

Overcome with frustration, she sat up, swung her legs to the side and leant over her knees. Any other man would have asked what was wrong. Durbin merely spread his hand across the small of her back. He stroked his thumb over her skin.

'I'm sending Ben and Carolyn on a retreat with Marty this weekend. I told them they can't return until they come up with ten good ideas for increasing business. I want you to go with them.'

Julia looked at him over her shoulder. 'Why?'

His eyes followed the motion of his hand. 'I want you to watch them. I want you to unmask the traitor. That bastard Santorini will rue the day he crossed swords with me.'

Julia fought a sigh. She hardly wanted to spend the weekend babysitting three squabbling portfolio managers. In her opinion, Durbin's fast-talking golf buddy Marty was the likeliest candidate, not that he wanted to hear that.

'You'll like it,' he said. 'It's a dude ranch in Montana. Gorgeous country. It'll warm even your cold heart. Bob Kingsley over at Alliance takes all his big clients there. Fishing, hunting, steaks the size of dinner plates. The owner is about to go private. You'll be his last paying guests.'

'An honour, I'm sure.'

Durbin seemed oblivious to her sarcasm. 'I need to know who slipped Santorini our proposal. If anyone can find out, it's you.'

Julia squeezed her knees in annoyance. But maybe she should go. Maybe a weekend far from New York, far from Durbin, was just what she needed. She could walk in the mountains and clear her head, set her priorities, devise a plan of action. Revealing the culprit's identity could be her parting gift, the dominatrix's version of a diamond kiss-off. The thought of treating Durbin like a discarded mistress brought a tiny smile to her lips. She stretched her back until it cracked, then got to her feet.

'Where are you going?' he asked with a hint of injury. 'I don't have to be home for another hour.'

She reached for her discarded skirt. 'I need to pack,' she said. Her smile was still in place.

She headed for her exercise room as soon as she reached her apartment. Forty minutes split between her weights and her rowing machine worked off most of her disgust with herself.

Still sweating, she mopped her face with a towel and reached for her cordless phone. Montana was two hours behind New York. It wasn't too late to reserve another room at the ranch. At least, she didn't think it was. But the phone rang twelve times without rolling over to an answering machine. She draped the towel around her neck. Perhaps, out there in cow country, they didn't believe in such newfangled contraptions. Finally, on the thirteenth ring, a male voice responded.

'Taylor,' said a husky baritone.

After waiting so long, the answer caught her by surprise. 'Oh,' she said, uncustomarily flustered. 'This is Julia Mueller. I work at Durbin-Moore Investments. I need to reserve an additional room for this weekend's retreat.'

'Hm,' said the man called Taylor. 'I've been meaning to call you folks about that. I think you'd better cancel.'

Julia swiped the towel across her sweaty chin. 'Cancel?'

'Yep,' he said. 'Snow's a-comin'.'

Snow's a-comin'? Who taught this character to talk? 'Nonsense,' she said. 'I was watching CNN weather at lunch today. There's no precipitation anywhere near the Rockies.'

'Still,' he said, the way other people said 'nonetheless'. She expected more, but that single word was all he had to offer: 'still', as if he knew more than a million-dollar satellite.

She found it surprisingly hard to argue with a man who spoke in monosyllables.

'The arrangements are made,' she said in a slow, clear voice. 'Do you have accommodation for an additional guest or not?'

'Yep,' he said. 'But you'd better plan on staying more than a weekend.'

Then he rang off. Julia stared at the phone in disbelief. Snow or no snow, this retreat was shaping up to be a long one.

Chapter Two

Somewhere over Montana: Friday afternoon

D MI's private jet bumped gently over the turbulent air. Julia sat in solitary splendour at the front of the cabin, soothed by the hum of the engines and her sense of escape. A wide stretch of country lay between her and temptation. She intended to burn some bridges while she was here, to which end she had a trunkful of toys guaranteed to light the match.

But it was time to take stock of her suspects. They sat at the rear, safely out of hearing range, or so they must have thought. Allowing herself the faintest smile, Julia folded her hands over her seat belt and closed her eyes. She had learnt to exploit the deceptions of appearance from a drill sergeant at Fort Benning. Old Hothead Hopkins had used her to embarrass new recruits. See what this girl can do, he'd say. Turn your back on her and she'll whup your mangy butt. He taught her to fight dirty and he taught her to fight smart. Then he taught her a few tricks he'd picked up on a tour of Asia.

She clocked her breathing just as he'd trained her: four seconds to inhale, eight seconds to hold, four seconds to exhale, eight to hold again. Her pulse slowed to sixty beats a minute, fifty-five, fifty. Her senses sharpened. She could smell the solution that the flight crew used to clean the carpets, a stick of gum the pilot was chewing, the cigarette Prentiss had sucked back five hours earlier. Glass ticked in the window at a slight change in temperature. She pictured a white-gold funnel leading from the three portfolio managers to her ear.

'I don't know why he sent her,' Carolyn Prentiss was saying. 'Except it's obvious he doesn't trust us. Shit, it's like big sister is watching. Her face would crack if she had to smile.'

A seat creaked as someone pushed it back and stretched. 'Look at it this way,' Marty Fine said. 'Now we've got someone to take notes and make coffee.'

'Like hell. The Ice Queen only makes coffee for senior VPs.'

'Jealous, Prentiss?'

'Fuck you, Fine.' Her necklaces jingled as she changed position. 'Christ, I need a smoke. How long till we –'

Julia started as a hand settled on her shoulder. She'd been concentrating so hard she hadn't heard Ben Isaacs come up the aisle. She looked up at him and experienced a familiar twinge of awe, the same she felt on seeing a Rodin or a Michelangelo. He had to be one of the most beautiful men she'd ever met. He was a light-skinned African American of mixed descent, part Jamaican, part white and part Asian, she suspected, from the slant of his clear green eyes. Everything about him was elegant, from the shape of the skull beneath his close-cropped hair to the simplest gesture of his

22

hands. He smiled at her now, a shy smile, though there was pride in it: the defensive pride of an outsider. Few African Americans held management positions in the hallowed halls of high finance.

'Do you mind if I sit with you?' He cocked his head towards Marty and Carolyn. 'Those two are at it again.' Rather than point out the existence of ten other empty rows, she lifted the unread copy of *Forbes* from the seat beside her. He settled in with another quick smile, flashing his teeth this time. 'Thanks,' he said. 'I've had all the "did so, did not" I can stand.'

'I can imagine.' Her tone was pleasant but not encouraging. She flipped open the magazine. Unfortunately, attempting any more eavesdropping was pointless. Ben's presence was too distracting. Hell, his cologne was too distracting. Whatever it was, it had formed an intoxicating bond with his natural body chemistry. The tissues of Julia's sex began to swell.

After a moment of silence, he turned in the seat. 'Do you mind if I ask you something?'

'Be my guest,' she said.

'Why are you here?'

She shrugged. 'To take notes and make coffee.'

'Bullshit.'

She was startled into revealing her smile. 'I'm sorry that isn't the answer you wanted.'

'It doesn't matter.' He shook the fall of his trousers down long, slim legs. She realised he was nervous. The timbre of his voice had deepened. 'I'm glad you're here.' His head turned and he pinned her with his exquisite green eyes. 'I've been meaning to get to know you better. I have a feeling you're not at all the way you seem.'

She blinked once, taken completely by surprise. Before she could respond he laid his hand over her wrist where it rested on the magazine. His palm was warm and dry, his skin strangely smooth. His eyes showed his awareness of the barriers he was crossing, between co-workers, between races, never mind the barriers he was crossing unawares. He probably knew she slept with their boss, but she sincerely doubted he guessed what they did together. Their games would have shocked him. He had too much simplicity of character for it to be otherwise.

She turned her hand under his, meaning to pull away, but he immediately wove their fingers together. He was making sure she could not mistake his touch for a simple, friendly gesture. Arousal fluttered through her groin, hot and soft. She swallowed. 'I'm not in a position to get to know anyone better right now.'

'Are you sure?' His voice was warm oil with a hint of island music. His thumb stroked her palm, sending another fountain of sensation through her sex. 'If Durbin is stopping you . . .'

'No.' She eased free, perilously close to laughing, or crying. Did this quiet, decent man think she needed rescuing from Durbin? If only he knew! 'No, it's not that.'

'I see,' he said, though she hadn't given him any answer at all. He stared at the wall that separated them from the cockpit, probably wishing he could sink through the floor of the plane. Embarrassment prevented him from speaking, pride from leaving, and Julia couldn't think of a single thing to say that wouldn't have made him feel worse. He shook his trousers straight again and she noticed they were tented at his groin. Their brief touch had aroused him as fiercely as it had her.

24

Hell, she thought, sweat prickling beneath her arms. This trip was getting more complicated by the minute.

Julia's breath caught as she descended the stairs to the tarmac. Mountains surrounded the little airport, huge craggy green mountains capped with creamy white. The sky was so deeply blue it seemed more a night sky than day. Incredible. The colour beat through her eyes, through her body, as though it had the power to root her to the ground. She turned in a slow circle to take it in. Fluffy clouds swam through the ocean of blue, like sheep wandering among the peaks. Tears pricked her eyes. She'd travelled this country from coast to coast, and never in her life had she seen anything so breathtaking.

But there was not, she saw, a speck of snow on the ground.

'Welcome to Big Sky,' said a husky masculine voice.

She turned, still transported, and looked into a lean, smiling face half-shadowed by a dusty cowboy hat. A light brown moustache curled upward with the smile. The man was tall, taller than her, and solidly built but not fat. He shoved the brim of his hat back and his eyes twinkled at her. Before she could respond to his greeting, Carolyn Prentiss clattered down the stairs.

'Good Lord, what a view!' she exclaimed. Carolyn was a rail-thin, foul-mouthed, born victim who honestly thought she was a ball-buster. When it came to relationships she never walked if she could run. The ladies lounge at DMI had witnessed many of her Monday-morning crying jags. Men are bastards, she liked to say, never seeing the KICK ME sign that drew the worst of the lot like magnets. Now she fluffed her gamin-short hair and tugged her ski jacket over her tiny waist.

The stranger crossed to her and shook her hand. 'Welcome to Big Sky,' he said.

Her eyes gave him a quick once-over before she flashed a brilliant smile. 'Well, thank you, sir. I appreciate a warm welcome.'

The stranger retrieved his hand and tipped his off-white hat, shyly, as if he wasn't used to such effusion. 'Zach Taylor, ma'am.' He nodded at Marty and Ben, now blinking in the bright sunlight. 'Zach Taylor,' he said again. 'Glad you all made it. Hope you don't mind about the snow.' He waved towards the belly of the plane. 'I'll just get your luggage and we'll be off.'

'Well, yippee-ki-ay,' Marty muttered, sidling up to Julia. 'You ever hear such a drawl in your life? "I'll jist git yer luggij."'

Julia tried not to laugh but it was a struggle. She realised this must be Mr Snow's a-Comin'. He didn't look as stupid as she'd expected; the eyes under the brim of that stetson had been sharp. But he was a bit much. His shearling coat was so worn it might have been unearthed from an archaeological dig. And his boots had flames shooting up their sides! She turned to get another look just as he reached into the luggage compartment to pull out the first bag. His coat rode up. The view improved. Well, well, she thought, admiring the fit of his jeans. Apparently, everything people said about cowboy butts was true. His glutes were rounded and firm, a true sight for sore eyes.

She went to help him retrieve her steamer trunk.

The cowboy seemed surprised to find himself shoulder to shoulder with a woman. 'Big girl, ain't you?'

'Yes, I am,' she said, and hefted the trunk out herself. Idiot, she thought, watching him scratch his head over that. She forced herself not to let her arms drag. Luck-

26

ily, there was only one place the trunk could be stowed and it wasn't far. A dusty red sports utility vehicle sat by the edge of the tarmac with its back door popped open. Julia heaved her luggage inside and slapped her hands together.

Marty and Ben followed, each having grabbed their own bags.

'Jeez, Mueller,' said Marty, catching sight of the trunk. 'You planning on moving in?'

Julia didn't deign to answer and in a moment there was no need because Carolyn came tripping over with the cowboy, already hanging on his arm.

'I just love four-wheel drives,' she gushed. 'You can roll the windows down, hang your head out in the breeze. You don't mind if I sit up front, do you, Zach? I don't want to miss an inch of this gorgeous scenery.'

I'll bet, thought Julia, climbing into the back between her two male co-workers. She had a pretty good idea what scenery had caught the female VP's eye.

'Oh, dear.' Carolyn batted her lashes at the cowboy. 'I can't seem to fasten this seat belt. Do you think you could –?'

'Sure thing, ma'am,' he said, and leant across her to do it.

'That's funny,' said Marty. 'You didn't have any trouble with the belt in my truck.'

'Oh, stow it,' Carolyn snapped.

Julia saw the cowboy's moustache twitch before he ducked his head to start the ignition. Amused or not, he did nothing to shake off his new friend. He chuckled when Carolyn draped her arm along the back of his seat. Julia suppressed an urge to grind her teeth.

He swung them on to a narrow mountain road, explaining that they were heading north towards Glacier National Park. That seemed to exhaust his

27

conversational repertoire. Unfazed, Carolyn played with the hair at the nape of his neck. The cowboy patted her hand. Resigned to watching this love-fest all weekend, Julia craned past her seat-mates to catch the scenery. To the left of the road, a scarp of lichen-splashed rock towered over their heads. To the right, the land fell sharply to rolling grassland. A river ribboned through it, its placid surface reflecting both the sapphire sky and a copse of trees in full autumn dress. She leant closer to the window, causing Marty to grunt and steady her shoulder. Brown humps were moving amidst the glowing foliage, like small, shaggy tanks.

'Bison,' said the cowboy, who must have been watching her in the rear-view mirror. 'A few of the ranchers hereabouts raise them for meat.'

'They're adorable,' Carolyn said before Julia could respond. With a too-sharp laugh, the VP removed the man's hat and plopped it on to her own head. He took that liberty with equanimity.

'Looks good on you,' he said. 'We'll have to pick one up for you in Taylorsville.'

Julia's mouth softened in amusement. Apparently the cowboy drew the line at giving up his hat. Not that Carolyn noticed. She simpered with pleasure.

'Taylorsville?' she said. 'Any relation to you?'

'Great grandaddy,' said the cowboy and scratched his unsheltered hair. A nice honey-brown, it was receding at his temples. It was clipped short, though, so he wasn't trying to hide its retreat. 'We'll be stopping there before we head up to the ranch. I need to get some feed.'

Marty pressed one hand over his grin.

'For the horses,' Zach clarified. 'In case it's a big snow.'

Marty whispered in her ear. 'Why does he keep talking about snow?'

Julia was struggling so hard not to laugh she couldn't answer. If she got through this ride without busting, it would be a miracle.

Zachary Taylor thought of himself as a simple man. Whether he was or not was another matter, but he had his own notions about himself and this was one of them. He loved horses and cow dogs. He loved to stand in a snowfall at midnight. He loved to kiss. He loved to fuck. He loved the sound of a woman's laugh. He loved being naked. He loved the smell of leather and hay, and just-washed babies, though he wasn't entirely sure he wanted any of his own. Of all those things, he probably loved fucking the best, though cantering Starlight across a field of wildflowers came close.

Thing was, he needed to fuck: every day if he could get it, all day if he couldn't. He'd started early, barely old enough to shave, and his body had been greedy from the first. He'd never had the knack of coming quickly. His body clung to its pleasure, and clung and clung, until he sometimes thought he'd sell his soul for an orgasm.

He was popular with the ladies. This was a good thing because, as his mother put it, Zach was a shy 'un. Not just a little shy, either; Zach had the sort of shyness that stuns a man to silence. It wore on him hard. Seemed to him the whole world knew how to talk; just opened their mouths and let whatever was in their heads fall out. Sometimes he had things to say, but he'd look around and think: there isn't a soul in this room who'd understand a word. Even in the

29

bosom of his family he'd think that. So he'd keep his mouth shut.

In all the world there were two places he felt completely at home: in the saddle and between a woman's legs.

Today he'd caught sight of a pair of legs that had his six-shooter bucking in his jeans. They were long legs, wrap-around-your-neck long legs, and the woman they were attached to . . . she was something all right. She had skin like cream dusted in rose. Her eyes were real steady, as if she'd ridden some rough trails in this life. She didn't talk much, which might pose a problem, given his own lack in that area, but her voice was as smooth and cool as a dish of vanilla ice cream. That voice had given him a hard-on the first time he heard it. Now that he saw her, he had an itch that wouldn't quit. He couldn't imagine when he might be allowed to scratch it, either.

For all that, he was happy to have her sitting in the back of his vehicle, within spitting distance, as it were. He hummed under his breath, an old Bonnie Raitt tune about not being the only one, the lonely one. He liked that Bonnie Raitt. She was all right.

He pulled into the newly paved lot of the Taylorsville Coffee Stop. The genuine gold-leaf lettering in the window looked nice. That artist fellow from Butte had done a good job. Zach didn't mind spending money, but he liked to see it well spent.

'Stay and have a cup,' he said, when his passengers climbed out from the truck. 'I got to see a man about some oats.'

Flo poked her head out of the door as he was crossing Main Street's second lane. 'Hey, Sev,' she called. 'Stop in when you're done. I've got a rent cheque for you.'

He touched two fingers to his hat brim. Flo would see to his guests. Flo knew how to be friendly. When he hit the pavement in front of the feed shop he couldn't resist turning for another look at the blonde; Julia, she called herself. Flo had seated the easterners by the window. Julia had the profile of a queen and, despite the brisk mountain breeze, her hair was barely mussed. If a cock could have moaned, Zach's would have. It was pressed up tight against his zip, aching to be freed. He let his breath out in a sigh and thanked God for the length of his coat.

The cowboy was staring at her. Julia could feel it clear through the window. Annoyed and unsettled, she left her seat and moved to the counter instead.

The café was surprisingly attractive, 1950s vintage but not too kitsch. Miniature juke-boxes sat on the tables. Two songs for a quarter. The waitress-owner had 'Flo' stitched across the pocket of her uniform. She was a nice-looking older woman, soft around the middle and worn at the edges, but pretty. Her bouffant hair was an improbable shade of red.

'Howdy,' she said, as Julia slid on to a stool. 'You look like a double-espresso type to me.'

Julia confessed that she was. Flo winked and tipped a scoop of fresh grounds into the machine. 'Bet you're surprised you can get fancy coffee in a little place like this, but we're up to the minute here. Sev sees to that.' She nodded sagely. 'All sorts of rich folks are moving to Montana these days: Californians, Hollywood types. Got to have someplace to spend their money. Our galleries are every bit as good as Whitefish and, if I say so myself, our coffee puts what they pour in Missoula to shame.'

31

As good as that, thought Julia. But all she said was, 'Sev?'

Flo laughed and slid a small, steaming cup across the counter. '"Sev" is what the women round these parts call Zach Taylor, on account of his limit.'

Julia dipped a spoon in her cup and made what she hoped was a disinterested noise. She did not want to know the cowboy's life history. Flo, however, was not to be discouraged. She propped her forearms on the counter and lowered her voice. 'Never sleeps with a woman more than seven times. Want to know why?'

'I'm sure it's none of my business.'

Flo pushed back from the counter and chuckled. 'Because by the seventh time they all want to marry him! It's true,' she said, though Julia had made no protest. She crossed her arms and nodded. 'Wanted to myself.'

Which was far more than Julia needed to know. 'I'll just take this back to the table,' she said. 'Thanks for the chat.'

The table wasn't much better, though, because Carolyn was full of budding romance jitters, jiggling her knee and playing with her assortment of silver chains until Julia wanted to rip them from her neck. Every five minutes she looked around as if expecting Zach to appear. Julia wondered if it would do any good to send her to Flo for the low-down on her prospective beau. She doubted it. Carolyn didn't have the self-protective instincts God gave a flea.

Finally, the hyperactive VP popped up from her chair and muttered something about checking the view from the back. Wanted to light up, more likely. Carolyn knew better than to smoke in front of a new man before she'd discovered where he stood on the issue.

Her perfume hadn't faded before Marty peered at

the juke-box. 'Say, Mueller, you got a quarter? I see a song here for Prentiss.' He grinned from Ben to Julia, both of whom stared at him blankly. 'Right here, see: "Working on My Next Broken Heart".'

Julia shuddered. Country and Western. Her favourite. She decided it was time to retreat to the ladies'.

Zach dumped the feed in the rig and returned to the Coffee Stop by the back way. Flo had a view of the Swan Range that was pure poetry. High black mountains rose from a grassy plain, their shadows stark and purple, their peaks dusted with white, as if the earth were baring her spine to mortal eyes. He breathed in the sight for a long moment. Behind him, from the west, he could smell the coming storm, a strange, pale scent, a mixture of mothballs and fragile alpine flowers. The smell was stronger than yesterday. Yesterday he'd been annoyed at the thought of being snowed in with his last batch of paying guests. Today he was happy.

He wondered if he might be in love. The idea was pretty crazy but, in truth, he'd never met a woman like Julia before. It didn't matter that he didn't know a thing about her; he could feel her, smell her, like the coming snow. She was mysterious and powerful, but real, a thing of the earth. His body yearned to join up with her until his very marrow echoed the aching beat. Fuck her, said the bone-shaking pulse. Fuck her, fuck her, fuck her.

He shoved his hands into his back pockets and thrust his erection towards the mountains, as if the rocks would see his need and answer it. A hand touched his shoulder. The moment seemed so magical, he thought it must be her, but when he turned he found the other woman, the bird-like one with the brittle smile. She smelled of expensive perfume and cigarettes.

She slid her hand around his shoulder and up his neck. His jacket was still open from the heat of the feed shop. When she tucked herself against him, her skinny thigh slid between his legs and pressed the swell of his balls. Good news, said his cock. The rest of him wasn't so sure.

'Fresh air make you horny, too?' she said, low and sugared against his neck. Her lips opened. She tongued his racing pulse.

With a sex drive like his, Zach didn't often turn a willing female away. Force of habit made his hands settle on her waist. Lord Almighty, it was small. He could just about span it. She squirmed closer and gave his cock a nice firm rub with her hipbone. Her hands wandered down his shirt and took hold of the metal button that fastened his jeans.

Oh, yeah, said his cock. 'I'm not sure this is a good idea,' said his mouth.

'It's a very good idea.' She raked him through the denim with her nails, drawing circles round his scrotum and up his shaft.

His eyelids started to slide downward about the same time as his zip did. She lifted him free and stroked him lightly from root to crest. She had little hands, little bird bones under baby-soft skin. It felt as if he were being given a hand job by a child, creepy and exciting at the same time. His chest went up and down a little faster. He was so hard his skin hurt.

She wrapped her fingers around his shaft and tugged him. 'Walk back this way,' she said. 'I don't want anyone to see us.'

He wasn't too clear on where she was heading until he heard her back hit the aluminium siding of the building. She dropped to her knees in the grass and rubbed her face across his thighs.

'Want me to suck it?' she asked.

'Oh, yeah,' he said, too lost to think. He grabbed the windowsill to support his weight and eased his cock down to mouth level. He closed his eyes when she took him. Her mouth was as small and tender as her hands. She didn't swallow much, but she played a symphony on the bulging crown, a combination of tickle and rub and suck. She gripped his thighs for balance and he swung his knees to either side of her torso so that he could brace them on the siding. He wanted to thrust in the worst way but he didn't dare. She was like a glass ornament hung from a tree, too delicate to touch.

'Mm, you're so big,' she said, pausing to grab a breath.

He wasn't really, just a bit more than average, but it was something women said and he appreciated the sentiment. Good manners, Grandpa would have said. He looked down and stroked her short, feathery hair, marvelling at the cat-like neatness of her skull.

'Is it good?' she asked, a shy whisper.

He smiled and rubbed the tip of his cock around her little mouth. 'It's great,' he said, and she took him in again, resuming that wonderful-awful teasing suck. He wasn't sure he could come from such soft, slippery torment but he was willing to try. He closed his eyes again, his mind wandering deliciously. He saw Julia descending the metal stairway from the plane; saw her face turn to his in that first moment, her mouth open in wonder, her eyes shining. He'd wanted to kiss her, to lick those incredible Nordic cheekbones.

He'd lay her across the engine of the plane, he thought. The metal skin would be hot from the sun and maybe somebody would fire it up, so it would rumble through her sex while he shoved up her skirt and yanked down her panties. He bet she'd have a nice, meaty bottom. He bet a man could hold it in both hands as he eased himself inside. She'd be warm there, that coolness all for show. God willing, she'd be greedy. God willing, her soft little cunt would suck his penis dry.

His knees began to tremble, and he thought: maybe this little lady can make me come.

'A little harder,' he said, his voice thick and husky. 'Sweetheart, just a little harder.'

The mouth tightened on him and the tongue dug in, tastebuds rasping his slit. His grip on the windowsill tightened. He let his hips swing towards the mouth, just a little, just enough to push the kill spot under the head over that flicking tongue. Pressure spiralled up from his balls, turning, swelling. His neck sagged back. Oh, yeah, he thought. Oh, Julia.

He opened his eyes. He didn't know why. He hadn't heard anything, hadn't smelled anything, but when he did, he met a mocking, grey-green gaze. The window was open and the object of his fantasy was leaning on the sill, cool as you please, her jaw propped in her hand, her index finger bracing her temple. Her bare pink lips curled in a sneer that seemed to say this was no more than she'd expected. The only sign that the show moved her at all was a faint flush across her cheeks.

None of which mattered to his cock. It swelled up fit to burst and his balls nearly crawled into his body. The ache was more than he could stand. Lord, he needed to come.

Carolyn whimpered. He realised the polite roll of his hips had turned to a thrust. Her nails dug into his thighs, holding him off even as she sucked harder.

Julia's mocking grin deepened, but he couldn't look

away from her mouth any more than he could stop pushing. Her lips parted. Her tongue crept out. The wet pink tip touched the little valley between the peaks of her upper lip. That was the last straw. Stars exploded up Zach's spine, as if a mule had kicked his tailbone. He slammed forward, come shooting from him like a train from a tunnel. He groaned and shook, only pulling back when he felt Carolyn's throat spasm around his cock. He finished in the air, in the cold.

Carolyn fell to her hands and coughed, come spilling from her lips in a thin, glistening stream. Their audience started a slow, resonant clap. Carolyn gasped and looked up.

'Very impressive,' Julia said, clearly meaning the opposite. 'But I think you two had better be more careful in the future. I'm betting a town like this has laws against indecent exposure.'

'Fuck you, Mueller,' said the little lady. She swiped her lips with the back of her hand. 'Why don't you get your own man and stop spying on people who have a life.'

Julia's mouth pursed in a wry moue. 'As you wish,' she said.

Despite her mild response, Zach had a feeling Carolyn was going to pay for that crack.

Julia had nothing to say about the glorious technicolour sunset. Nor did anyone else. Only the truck's engine broke the silence, rattling up a mountain whose pine-studded peak was wreathed in red-gold clouds. Taylor's Mountain, the sign at the start of the gravel switchback had stated. 'Your own mountain!' Carolyn had exclaimed. Zach had grunted. Then Marty tried to needle Carolyn with his rendition of the mournful

Country-and-Western tune. When that failed to provoke a response he, too, fell silent.

Ben was no better. Julia could tell he felt awkward about the pass he'd made on the plane. He kept glancing at her from the corner of his eye. His thigh rested against hers from hip to knee, jiggling in the bumpy ride. He didn't press it closer but he didn't pull it away. Its warmth added to the heat she already carried, a dull but insistent throb at the meeting of her legs. She wedged her shoulder against the door and attempted to push the memory of Zach's climax from her mind. It was impossible. She could picture every detail. His lips had pulled back from his teeth. The lines of his face had deepened. She hadn't been able to look away from his eyes. At the final moment, tears of sheer, primal feeling had glistened in their corners.

Here was a man who put his whole heart and soul into his orgasm. Here was a man who really loved to fuck.

Of course, he didn't have much else to recommend him. Poor Carolyn had nearly gagged when he tried to deep-throat her. Julia's eyes narrowed. Carolyn was going to pay for that crack about finding her own man. Not in the way she expected, though. Julia knew how Carolyn's gears turned. She'd expect Julia to make a play for Zach herself, and clearly believed she'd triumph in a battle of the cunts. To her simple mind, any woman who'd let a dick near her mouth before the hundredth date had to have an advantage over the rest of the female population. Besides, what man in his right mind would choose a size sixteen over a size eight?

Julia smoothed her skirt over her knees. She felt, more than saw, Ben's eyes follow the motion. A muscle in his thigh jumped. He'd folded his coat over his lap.

She knew if she looked beneath it, she'd find him hard. Carolyn, that poor misguided stick, didn't understand the lure of rich flesh and an indomitable will.

But she would when Julia was through with her.

Chapter Three

Taylor Ranch: Friday evening

Zach could tell the ranch wasn't what Julia expected. She stood in the entrance to the great room, hands arrested in the process of removing her long leather coat. He moved to help her as the other woman exclaimed how darling everything was.

'Darling' wasn't the word he'd have chosen. It was a big place, despite being neatly tucked into the landscape. Eight guest rooms filled a wing on the ground floor, the basement housed a gym, and skylights flooded the main rooms with clear mountain light. The conference room could seat twenty at a pinch and the barn had every amenity that a pampered dude horse could desire. In the office that led off the great room, four computers, each with its own modem, awaited the demands of busy executives who'd had their fill of fly fishing. Thanks to his grandmother's business savvy, everything at the Taylor Ranch was first-rate. Zach had always been proud of it.

His chest warmed as Julia's head tipped back to take in the vaulted ceiling. His grandfather had built this place of solid pine, from the polished floors to the slanted cathedral roof. The sun's last rays slanted through the windows, and in that golden light, the peeled log walls glowed like honey from a comb. This ranch had been Zach's sanctuary from an early age, the home he'd wished was his, until one day it was. Soon he'd have it all to himself.

Julia must have shared his pleasure because he caught an appreciative sigh as he eased her coat from her shoulders. The leather was buttery soft, the construction Italian. It must have cost a bundle. Carolyn had made a point of telling him that Julia was 'only a secretary'. Zach sympathised with the impulse behind the put-down; a woman like Julia could inspire insecurity, but clearly there were secretaries and then there were secretaries. In any case, Julia sure seemed like the lead bull of this herd.

Not that she didn't have her soft spots. The hair at the nape of her neck was silky fine. She smelled of baby powder, surprising, but nice. His cock jumped up to take a sniff, worse than Gracie after a bone. He draped her coat over his arm to hide his sudden erection. The whole world didn't need to know what she did to him.

'This is a lovely place,' she said, her face serene.

'My grandfather built it.' He sounded strangled. He cleared his throat. The removal of her coat had revealed a severe grey suit that fit as if it had been sewn on to her body. It skimmed her generous curves, all six feet of them. She was ripe and firm and strong. As she strolled towards the stone hearth, she trailed her hand along the back of the leather couch. He immediately pictured that hand trailing down his

41

spine, one vertebra at a time. She was a sensualist, he decided with a tiny shiver, a creature of touch and taste and smell.

'Where should we hang our coats?' asked one of the men.

Reluctant to turn from this vision, Zach waved behind him. 'There are pegs in the hall.'

Maria must have turned up the heat before she left. The room was warm. Julia began unbuttoning her snug grey suit jacket. A flush prickled across his groin with an intensity he hadn't felt since he was a teenager. The sides of her jacket parted and through her starched white blouse he saw the curve of her breast. His palm itched to weigh the luxuriant flesh, to shape it, to squeeze it. Her bosom rose as she lifted her arm to touch the photograph his grandmother had hung above the mantel.

He shook himself. It was an old rodeo picture. In it he was getting the tar bucked out of him by a bronc called Sunfish, so named for his habit of turning his belly towards the sky. That horse had helped him win the world championship five years ago, his best ride and his last. By the time the pick-up men dragged him off that fool bronc, his wrist had been busted bad enough to require a metal pin. He'd earnt more than a hundred thousand dollars in prizes that year, which he'd used to stake his first real-estate venture. His eyes crinkled at the memory. He'd been proud to add his acquisition to those of his grandparents.

He wondered what Julia thought of his former occupation. Did it dampen her panties, the way it did the rodeo groupies, or did she think he was as loco as that horse?

Before he could interpret her expression, Carolyn grabbed his arm. The two men stood behind her, the tall black man and the shorter, curly-haired one with the funny accent. That one had the devil in his eyes. Even now he was grinning about who knew what. Zach noticed everyone but Julia wore jeans and expensive sweaters. Seemed his Julia could stand to loosen up.

Carolyn tugged on his hand. 'Come on, Zach,' she said. 'Show us around.'

He gave them the grand tour, sort of. It lasted a lot longer when Maria led it. All Zach could think of to say was 'kitchen, bedrooms, exercise room' and 'out back there's the stable'. The curly-haired man, Marty, was amused by the fact that there were windows in every wall, even the walls between the bedrooms.

'This dude ranch must be popular with peeping Toms,' he joked, pretending to peer into the next room.

Zach yanked down the shade. 'My Grandpa Joe liked windows. First time he saw my grandmother she was walking past the window of her father's house. He said he wanted to frame her like that for always.'

Carolyn pressed her hands to her heart. 'That is so romantic.'

'Mm,' said Julia.

Zach turned away, his face heating. That mocking hum told him, clear as day, that she thought his grandfather was an idiot. Well, fuck her, he thought. A second later his mouth lifted in a rueful grin. Fucking her was, of course, exactly what he wanted.

Carolyn sat at the end of the table, playing lady of the house to Zach's gent. Julia watched her look from the platter of meat to the handsome man who held it, her face a picture of dismay. Apparently, the latest Mr Right was teetering on his pedestal.

'Steak?' she said faintly.

Seated to Carolyn's left, Julia hid a smile behind her hand. Someone named Maria had been given the weekend off, due to the much-threatened snow. As a result, the cowboy had prepared their meal. Steak, potatoes and an overcooked vegetable medley were hardly fare to tempt a borderline anorexic like Carolyn. He'd made gravy, too, which Marty was happily ladling over his baked potato.

Taken aback at Carolyn's protest, Zach froze with a huge slab of meat dangling from the serving fork. 'Nobody said there were vegetarians coming.' He sounded as if vegetarians were akin to international terrorists.

Carolyn hastened to assure him she was nothing of the sort. 'I do eat meat, of course. It's just, well, red meat is so unhealthy.'

Zach looked even more horrified. Julia decided it was time to administer the first light tap of the whip. She speared the steak with her fork, plopped it on Carolyn's plate and cut it in half. The meat was beautifully prepared, lightly charred on the outside and blood-rare in the middle. Mouth watering, she slid half the portion on to her own plate.

Carolyn bent towards her. 'I don't want any,' she hissed. 'I'm watching my cholesterol.'

Julia snorted and pitched her voice just as low. 'Try selling that bridge to someone else. If you were concerned about your health, you'd quit smoking and go to the gym once in a while.' Carolyn's mouth opened to deny the charge, but Julia's sword was fully drawn. 'You and I both know you're calorie-counting and, frankly, you're crazy to do it. If you were to take your clothes off now, you'd scare somebody.'

'Oh, really?' she said, but her face was pink with

doubt, and with guilt; on some level she knew she'd taken her weight-consciousness too far.

'Really,' Julia insisted, more kindly this time. She reached under the table and squeezed Carolyn's knee. 'Twenty pounds would do you a world of good. You have no idea how beautiful you could be.'

Confusion deepened the colour of Carolyn's cheeks. The two women had always been antagonistic, more by Carolyn's choice than Julia's. She begrudged the respect Julia got from Durbin, and from her own clients. Plus, with Julia around, her tough-girl act rang false. Julia was the genuine article. Carolyn was at best a wannabe. Naturally, she detested her rival, but she craved her approval, too. Julia could tell she didn't know whether to thank her for the compliment or tell her she must be kidding. Satisfied she'd achieved the effect she wanted, she released her co-worker's knee and took a bite of steak.

'Excellent,' she said to the cowboy, who'd resumed his seat.

He was staring at them with the concern peculiar to the slighted cook. 'My daddy raised this cow,' he said. 'Free-range. No hormones. Good clean forage. I promise you, this cow lived well and died happy.'

Julia burst out laughing before she could stop herself. Her co-workers gaped, but even so little snorts of merriment escaped her control. Lived well and died happy! A claim to hearten diners everywhere. She covered her mouth with her napkin. 'Forgive me, Mr Taylor,' she gasped, 'but you do have a way with words.'

'It's Zach,' he snapped, and he sounded very angry indeed.

Her laughter died as suddenly as it started. She noticed his eyes were very blue, and when he frowned, even his moustache turned down. A funny feeling began in the pit of her stomach. For a moment she couldn't put a name to it. When she did, it intensified. It was shame. She was ashamed of herself for laughing at him.

'I am sorry,' she said, sincerely this time.

The cowboy busied himself with splitting his baked potato. A cloud of steam rose to obscure his face. 'That's all right,' he said gruffly. 'I imagine we seem pretty strange to you city folks.'

Marty glanced from her to Zach, his eyes wide with interest. Julia gave him a quelling look, but he merely shook his head as if to clear it. 'So, Zach, how long have you owned the ranch?'

Zach looked up from his plate. 'Just a year, since my grandma died and left it to me. But I've worked here since I was seventeen. My grandpa and I, we didn't like cows.'

Julia's throat jerked convulsively, but this time she managed to contain her amusement. 'I take it the rest of your family raises cattle.'

'Yep.' His eyes turned warily to hers. 'Got a big outfit down in the valley. My brothers and sisters all help out.'

There seemed to be a story behind this, but Zach wasn't saying any more and, ashamed or not, Julia wasn't sure she wanted to draw him out. After all, he had nothing to do with the purpose behind this week-end; at least, nothing to do with her purpose.

'We should get to work after dinner,' she said. All three portfolio managers groaned. She ignored them. 'We check out at noon on Sunday, so that only leaves you tonight and tomorrow to brainstorm.'

Marty laced his hands behind his head. His grin was

an unabashed challenge. 'I'm too jet-lagged to brainstorm. I say we start in the morning.'

Julia stared down her nose. 'Durbin wasn't happy about the loss of the Go-Tech account. If you three don't generate some good ideas for improving business, he may decide it's time for heads to roll.'

'Roll-schmoll,' said Marty. 'Rich likes to bluster.' He reached out and slapped Ben and Carolyn on the shoulder. 'But he's not going to do anything to break up his best team.'

'He will if he's given cause,' Julia warned, but Marty merely shrugged and returned to his steak.

'Ben would rather start tomorrow, too,' he said.

Ben looked startled at being put on the spot, but he nodded in agreement. 'I have some notes I'd like to go over tonight.'

'It's settled then,' Carolyn crowed. 'We start tomorrow.'

From the way she was twinkling at the cowboy, Julia could guess how she intended to spend the night. This annoyed her more than she cared to examine, but she knew better than to argue with the three of them ranged against her. Apart from calling her authority into question, this battle wasn't important. Moreover, what she failed to win by frontal assault, she would certainly gain by more subtle means. She'd already learnt one important fact: Marty Fine would be a tough nut to crack.

Zach knew he owed her. She was not what he was hankering after, but he owed her. Julia thought so, too. The memory of her smirk as she leant out the window of the Coffee Stop stung his pride. Not only did she consider him a hick but a ham-handed lover as well,

47

which simply wasn't the case. He could prove it, too, if only to himself.

He knocked lightly on the door.

'Just a minute,' said a light feminine voice. A second later Carolyn swung it open.

'I, uh . . .' His words dried up like trail dust when he saw what she was wearing, a light silk robe with a cherry blossom print, and nothing else. Through the sheer cloth, he could see both the colour and shape of her nipples. She had delicate breasts, less than a handful, almost a mouthful. His body reacted predictably and he forgot what he'd meant to say.

'You, uh, what?' she said with a girlish giggle. She shifted her weight and a pale length of thigh appeared between the flaps of her robe.

He scratched his head and stared at this new revelation. 'I, uh, I was going to invite you to my rooms, but I can see you're not dressed for wandering around.'

'No, indeed.' Her eyes tilting with her smile, she caught his hands and set them on her tiny waist. 'I guess you'll have to stay here.' His gaze cut to the little window between her room and her neighbour's. The shade was pulled down on the other side, but not on Carolyn's. She tugged him closer to the bed. 'Don't you worry about the Ice Queen, Zach. She's off pumping iron in your basement.'

The Ice Queen, he thought, then realised she must mean Julia. Was she that cold? She didn't seem so to him. Controlled, yes, but molten, like lava bubbling underground. This was not, however, the moment to argue. Carolyn was shrugging her robe off her narrow shoulders. Her right breast appeared, then her left. Both were pale and round. With a quickening of his pulse, he saw she'd rouged her nipples. Their tips were elongated, and as shiny as if they'd been kissed. The robe fell to the tie that bound it at her waist. He inhaled sharply. Her collar bones stood out with painful prominence. He could count her ribs.

'You're so thin,' he said before he could think better of it.

She blushed from her belly to her brow and turned away. She fumbled for the chain to the bedside lamp. 'I'll put out the light.'

'No,' he said, but the light was out and the damage done. He reached through the dark for her and pulled her against his body. Words couldn't help now. He crossed his arms beneath her breasts. He rubbed the swell of his cock between her silk-clad bottom cheeks, soothing her with his warmth, letting her know he still wanted her. After a minute she relaxed and began to rub back at him.

'That's nice,' she said, and turned in his arms. Her breasts were warm, her nipples hot. When she caught his thigh between her own, her pussy lips spread wetness over his leg. That put one fear to rest. In his experience, skinny women tended to be slow to rouse. Not enough hormones, he reckoned. This one at least was ready to roll.

'Help me with my shirt,' he whispered and shivered as her tiny hands moved over the buttons. He unzipped his jeans and shoved them down before she'd finished, wanting to feel her fragile body against his own, skin to skin, pussy to cock. With admirable skill, she rolled a condom down his shaft. The feel of it sliding on increased his impatience. She laughed when he ripped his arms free of his sleeves. She was a slender shadow in the dark, but his hands moved unerringly to the tie of her robe. The silk fell to the floor with a teasing hiss. Her palms slid up his chest, grazing his nipples before twining behind his neck. She pressed against him full length, her skin wonderfully smooth.

'You're too tall,' she said, laughter in her voice. 'You'll have to lift me up.'

He lifted her. She was so light it shocked him, but she clung with surprising strength, winding her legs around his waist as she searched for his mouth with her own. Her kiss was as wet and open as her pussy. Her juice ran into the crease of her buttocks where it met the upward arch of his cock. He gripped her bottom and shifted her until the tip of his penis met her wet, warm entrance.

'Sh,' he said at her quick intake of breath. 'Don't you worry. I'm a slow goer, sweetheart. You'll get yours this time. I promise.'

'I'm not worried,' she said, but he knew she had been.

He carried her to the bed and laid her gently down, using the descent to slide fully into her. Her easy acceptance pleased him. He'd been afraid she'd be too small. Despite the way she'd taken the lead before, it seemed natural to command her now. She was so pliant, so soft. He stroked her pussy with his cock, a steady thrust and withdrawal intended to comfort as well as arouse. When she began to purr at each insertion, he rolled her on top of him. She tensed.

'It's all right,' he said. 'I'm doing the work tonight. This is for you.' With one arm bracing her spine, he sat up until they were face-to-face. She kissed him and began to rock but he stilled her. 'No, no work for you.'

'But I need to move.'

'Not yet.' He slid his hand down her flat little belly and curled his thumb over the rise of her clit. Her groan was delicious. Her pussy pulled at his shaft. See, he said to Julia in his mind. This is what I can do to a

50

woman. He rubbed firm circles over the seat of her pleasure and nuzzled her breast in search of a nipple. He chuckled when he found it because whatever she'd painted on it tasted of cinnamon. He sucked one peak clean, then the other, then drew nearly the whole of one breast into his mouth. She came with a shuddering moan, her hands clutching his shoulders, her thighs tightening round his hips.

A promising start, he thought, but only a start. Sitting back on his heels, he cradled her head and eased her on to her back. His thighs supported her bottom. The position forced him hard against the front of her vagina. He pushed down on her mons to intensify the pressure on her G-spot. She was laid out before him, barely able to move except to roll her hips a little. The sense that she was entirely at his mercy sent a quiver through his sex. He kneaded her soft lips around the root of his cock

'Oh, yes, that's good,' she said, her head thrashing. 'But aren't you going to come?'

He smiled. 'Why do you ask, sweetheart? Are you sore?'

'Oh, no. I feel lovely, but you – oh, God.' She squirmed again and tightened on him hard. 'I want you to fuck me. Please, Zach, please, fuck me.'

'Not yet,' he said, even softer than before. Though he'd hardened further at her plea, he continued his slow, deep massage at the junction of their bodies. 'I like feeling you come around me. I like the sounds you make. I like the way your pussy creams just before you moan. You can feel how big it makes me, can't you? You can feel how hard it makes me pound.'

'Please,' she panted, but he wouldn't relent. He massaged her until she came again, then began a shallow rocking motion, just as far as tightening his

51

buttocks would take him. She gripped his wrists in an attempt to sit up. Rather than let her, he ran his hands from her hips to her shoulders, holding her down with pleasure. His palms slipped easily over her perspiring skin, long strokes, like a carpenter planing wood. He caught her budded nipples on every pass. She liked that. Her back arched into his touch. She would come again, he knew, and this climax would be the sharpest.

At the sight of her restless movements, the signals that his nerves were sending finally shifted from pleasure to need. He knew his body well. It had reached the pitch of lust where he could come. He ceased his slow massage.

'Stay,' he ordered, fearing she'd try to sit up again. When he saw she'd obey, he slid his left hand beneath her buttocks and gripped the top of her thigh with his right. He could control her movements completely then, pulling and pushing precisely as he wished. What he wished was to give her the greatest pleasure possible. A woman's pleasure always intensified his own. His cock pushed hard against the sensitive pad of tissue behind her pubic bone. It was swollen from her orgasms, juicy and soft. She whimpered as he quickened his thrusts, then groaned when he deepened them. Her hands fisted in the coverlet. Her heels dug into the bed behind his hips.

'Yes, yes, yes,' she cried, the sound rising in pitch and volume as she spasmed around his swollen cock. Unfortunately, the contractions weren't enough to tip him over. He knew she'd be sore if he went on much longer, so he drove as hard as he dared until she collapsed with a final sigh. As soon as she did, he pulled free of her body, ripped off the condom and squeezed his cock. Urgently, hand over hand he pulled it away from his body, hard tight strokes that stretched his shaft and drove the air like fire from his lungs. He tugged until his skin stung, until his balls grew heavy and tight. He closed his eyes and remembered her squirms, her sighs, the way her back arched off the bed.

Come on, he urged his stubborn penis. Come on, you bastard, let go. He squeezed the head of his cock, his palm sliding over a slick of gathered fluid. Julia's cream. No, not Julia's. Not anyone's. But his mind had slipped where it wanted to go.

Please, Julia said in the unruly regions of his imagination. Please fuck me. The sudden pang of longing alarmed him, but not enough to pull back from the fantasy. Her nipple was in his mouth. Her silky blonde hair swept his shoulder. She was wet. She was coming. Julia was twitching around his cock, tight, tighter. Oh, God. He was going to blow. He groaned, a sound like bulls make when they're roped off their feet: animal shock, animal pain. Julia, he thought, and his climax exploded, an aching rush of heat and fluid.

Carolyn murmured in confusion as his seed hit her belly.

On the other side of the wall, Julia turned away. She hadn't seen but she'd heard plenty, as Carolyn had assuredly intended. No wonder she'd chosen the room next to hers. She'd wanted to rub Julia's nose in her triumph.

It should have been an empty triumph. Julia rolled off the bed, cursing her own stupidity. Listen and learn, she'd told herself. And she had. She'd learnt she'd got to Carolyn with her admonition about her weight. She'd learnt Carolyn liked to be controlled. She'd learnt Zach wasn't as bad in bed as she'd expected. Neither was Carolyn, if the cowboy's orgasmic bellow was any

53

indication. She didn't believe she'd ever heard a man make quite that noise before.

None of these revelations would have bothered her if she hadn't also discovered something about herself. She wanted the stupid cowboy. She wanted to call that sound from him. She wanted to feel him striving between her legs. Her cunt was swollen with arousal now, pulsing, twitching, positively running with desire. She dug her nails into her palms, willing the pain to calm her. She couldn't afford this distraction. Her future depended on this weekend proceeding as planned. If she wanted to break free of Durbin, she had to keep her wits about her. She couldn't afford to fuck the help!

The murmur of foreplay resumed in the next room. Julia gritted her teeth. Didn't Carolyn know she was using up her quota with 'Sev'? Two down and five to go. At this rate she'd be history in a single night. The thought pleased her more than it should have. Muttering a curse, she grabbed a robe and left her room.

A dim light drew her through the great room to the kitchen. The tiny bulb above the stove was on. She found Marty seated at the table in his boxer shorts, moaning over a piece of the departed Maria's pecan pie. He liked to eat, that Marty. But he was stocky, not fat, the kind of man who ate what he pleased and burnt up most of it. The only time she'd seen him sit still was in front of a full plate.

'Hey,' he said, grinning through pleasure-slitted eyes, 'that caterwauling keep you up, too?'

'What do you think?' she said, annoyed to have been caught listening but too proud to deny it.

'I think if those two fools can get laid, there's no reason we shouldn't.'

Marty had been propositioning Julia since they'd

met. She'd never deigned to answer him with more than a cold stare. But perhaps this weekend demanded a change of strategy. Perhaps her throbbing sex did, too. She folded her arms and lounged back against the big stainless steel refrigerator. 'What did you have in mind?'

He set his fork down as if his muscles had gone numb. 'I'll be damned. Are you saying what I think you're saying?'

'That depends.'

He swiped his mouth with the back of his arm and approached her, slowly, like a dog stalking a cat. I just want to play, said his dark, laughing eyes. Please don't scratch me. She remained as she was even when he braced both hands beside her head in a classic gesture of dominance. His chest was broad, his arms well muscled. She'd gathered her hair in a simple braid and now he nuzzled the fine strands at her temple. His gold wedding band clinked against the refrigerator. The sound didn't make either of them flinch. As far as Julia was concerned, Marty's marriage was his business. She wasn't his first adulterous affair, and she doubted she'd be his last.

Obviously untroubled by guilt, he tipped his lower body closer and settled into the cradle of her hips. He sighed with pleasure and rolled his cock from side to side. He wasn't fully hard yet, but he was getting there. He bent his arms and nipped her ear. 'What does it depend on, Julia?'

'On what you've got in mind.'

'Honey, I've got so much in mind for you, it would take years to do it all.'

She wove her fingers through his curls and pushed his head back from her ear. 'You'll have to make a choice. This is strictly a one-shot deal.'

'In that case –' he wagged his bushy brows '– I've had my eye on this jar of home-made caramel sauce I saw in the pantry.'

'Perhaps you should get it.'

His eyes widened, then narrowed. Clearly, he thought this was too easy. It was, though he didn't need to know that yet.

'All right,' he said. 'I will.'

He returned with a wide mason jar, a wooden spoon and an impressive erection. Half of it stuck through the placket of his shorts, bouncing merrily with his steps. She found herself thinking of the game she'd played with Durbin, where she'd pretended to be Marty. Durbin must have seen this fat, shiny cock many times: over the urinals, showering at the club. Had he lusted after it the way she did? Did it make Durbin lick his lips?

Screw Durbin, she thought. Tonight was for her. She returned her attention to his grinning protégé.

Marty gestured at her moss-grey velvet robe. 'You'll have to take that off, along with whatever you've got underneath.'

Julia undid the tie and let the robe drop to the floor. She was naked. Marty clutched the mason jar to his chest and pretended to stagger. 'Good Lord, woman, you should warn a man before you do that.'

She couldn't help but smile. Marty was good for a woman's ego, even a healthy woman's ego. She nodded towards his boxers. 'Don't you think you should strip off, too? You wouldn't want to get sticky.'

He wrenched his shorts off with flattering speed, then patted the sturdy kitchen table.

Julia advanced one swaying step at a time, her hand behind her back to hide the tie of her robe. She watched his eyes rove her body; watched his cock bob in

56

admiration at what he saw. His lips were parted for his shallow breaths. His hands clutched the jar of caramel like a lifeline. She hopped on to the table and spread her thighs. The scent of pussy rose between them, musky and rich. His eyes fell to the shining flesh of her sex. He sighed.

'You're blonde,' he said. 'You're really blonde.'

Fighting a laugh, she pulled the jar from his paralysed hand. 'I think you'd better set this down.' She unscrewed the cap and stuck her pinky into the sticky sauce. His eyes followed as she brought it to her mouth and sucked it clean. 'Mm. Very good.'

'Oh, yeah,' he growled and reached out with the wooden spoon.

She let him dip it in the jar. She let him pull it out coated in sauce. She let him hold it above the slope of her breast until the first heavy golden drop began to form . . .

Then she whipped off the table, hooked her foot behind his ankle and downed him. It wasn't easy to trip a grown man without hurting him, but Julia caught his head with one hand and managed to send most of his weight on to his posterior. He gasped a sharp curse, too shocked to yell, too stunned to struggle. In a matter of seconds, she'd lashed his wrists to the table leg.

'What are you doing?' he demanded, trying to lift the table and get free. 'Damn, this thing is heavy.'

Julia allowed her laugh to bubble free. She patted his heaving chest. 'Come on, Marty. I bet you're always in charge. Wouldn't you like a change of pace?'

'Wouldn't you?' he fired back, eyes glittering with fury.

She shook her head. 'No, Marty, I wouldn't.'

'You crazy bitch,' he said, but he was half-laughing himself.

She drew the jar of caramel sauce off the table, and the spoon. He stopped struggling then, curious, his cock beginning to recover from its shock. As it rose, she dribbled a spoonful of sauce over his right nipple.

'It's cold,' he complained, but his toes curled in anticipation.

In silence, she coated his left nipple, then his breastbone, then drew a rippling line down his belly. She stopped short of his thatch. His erection pointed skyward now, wavering with the flow of his blood and the periodic clenching of his buttocks. She looked at his balls, a neat plump package between strong, hairy thighs. He followed the direction of her gaze and started breathing faster.

Good, she thought, her own blood flowing strongly. She gripped the base of his balls between the fingers of one hand and squeezed, forcing them forward until the skin pulled taut around their heavy bulk. She poised the laden spoon above them and waited for the drip.

'Use your hand,' he gasped, then bit his lip. 'Please.'

Since he asked so nicely, she set the spoon aside and dipped her fingers in the jar. He groaned as she slathered the cool, sticky mass over his upthrust testicles. His thighs quivered as if her touch tickled, but he pushed himself closer with every swipe. When she released him, his sigh held both relief and longing.

'Now your cock,' she said. The word made him shudder, as did the slow trail of caramel up his raphe. She coated the underside first, then the upper, then gently, slowly dabbed the sticky mess over his glans. His eyes squeezed shut when she touched him there and she realised he must be very sensitive. Her pussy clenched and wept. She adored knowing a man's vulnerabilities.

His eyes were still shut when she straddled him. She

did not touch any part of his body, just loomed above him, his conqueror. His lids rose slowly. She put her fingers to his lips and, one by one, he sucked them free of sauce. He had a surprisingly gentle mouth. She was going to have to reward him. He shivered as she pulled the last finger free.

'Shall I lick you clean?' she whispered.

'Please,' he whispered back, earning a smile for his manners.

The caramel was sweet on her tongue, and salty with his perspiration. His heat was beginning to melt it. She suckled his sharp, tiny nipples, which inspired a series of long, breathy sighs. They deepened as she lapped down his chest, and quickened when she crouched over his balls. Again, she squeezed his testicles within their pouch, lifting them towards her mouth. He groaned at the first dragging lick.

She knew he'd need an incentive to hold on as long as she wanted.

'I'll make you a deal,' she said, between firm, slow licks. 'If you hold off coming through the rest of this, I'll untie you and let you fuck me.'

His thigh muscles tightened. 'You will?'

'My word of honour.'

He seemed to believe her because he set his jaw and clenched his bound fists. 'Do your worst,' he said.

'I will,' she promised. 'My very worst.'

His balls were clean now. Wanting the skin of his shaft as taut as she could get it, she made a V of her thumb and fingers and pressed his testicles down over his perineum. Most of the caramel sauce had melted off his cock but a thin glaze remained. She moved until she knelt perpendicular to his body. She pressed her mouth sideways across his under-ridge. With wet, sucking kisses she drew the swollen flesh against her tongue. Marty gasped, his thighs jerking and trembling. When she'd kissed her way to the flare of the head, she swept her hand down his belly and depressed his cock until it pointed towards his feet. Again she kissed the full length of him, stopping when she reached his glans. He squirmed against the checkerboard linoleum.

'Julia,' he said. He tugged at his bonds, testing their strength, but she'd secured them well.

She petted the tangle of hair beneath his arm. 'There's nothing you can do, Marty-boy. You're at my mercy. I can tease you all night if I want to. I can tease you till you cry.'

He gasped when she yanked one curly hair out by the root. 'I'm ready to cry now.'

'Your eyes are tearing,' she agreed. She blew the hair free. 'But your cock just got thicker under my hand. You know what that tells me?'

Marty blinked rapidly and shook his head.

She squeezed him until the skin beneath her fingertips turned white. 'It tells me you like this game. It tells me you especially like the fact that I'm running it.'

'Uh,' he said: not a denial.

His cock sprang upward when she released it, a column of hot, pulsing flesh. A network of veins gnarled the shaft. Only the cap was smooth. Even in the stove light she could see it was darker than the rest of him, a deep, russet red. She poised her mouth above it. Her braid fell over her shoulder, its end striking the pale skin beside his thatch. He grunted in reaction, delightfully sensitised. He was watching her with strained but eager eyes.

'Ready?' she asked. He caught his lower lip between his teeth. She knew the head games she'd been playing had him wound as tight as her massage. She kept him

60

hanging a second more, then sank down on his shaft. She relaxed her throat as she descended, letting him see how much she could take. All of him as it turned out, though her jaw ached from his girth. His reaction was worth it. His cock quivered like a harp string in her mouth.

'Oh, God,' he moaned. 'That is so fucking hot.'

She began to move. Her pulls were slow and tight and she turned her head at the end of each rise, adding a little corkscrew to the motion. She cupped his balls against the base of him. That earnt a whimper, as did the hand she wrapped around his shaft to follow her withdrawals. She would surround him in feeling. No inch of genitalia would go untouched. Deep-throating made a good visual, but a clever pair of hands were a fellatio artist's best friend.

Marty seemed to agree. His head rolled from side to side on the floor. She sucked faster, wanting to bring him to the very edge of panic. No moment was wasted. Every pause to catch her breath was an opportunity to run her tongue over the sensitive head. Her guess had been correct. Each time she lavished attention on his glans, his thighs widened and thrashed.

'I can't,' he finally said. 'Julia, I can't hold back.'

'You can,' she promised, pressing the words into his deep, shining come-slit. 'Breathe.' She kissed the slippery dome. 'Breathe slowly. That's it. Relax.'

He tried but, two pulls later, he was tensing again. 'I can't. I'm running fucking bond rates through my head but I can't.'

'Don't try to distract yourself. Concentrate on what you're feeling. I'll slow down. And don't hold your breath.'

She gave him a minute to slip back from the brink before she began again, slower now, lingering over the nerve clusters in the head and neck. He moaned in time to her thrusts but he held on; and moaning was an improvement over holding his breath. Finally, when he was trembling like a rabbit and bathed in sweat, she let him slip free of her mouth. Then she freed his wrists from the table leg.

At first he didn't move, but then his eyes opened and his fingers flexed. She smiled down at him. He could only blink.

'Want to fuck me now, Marty?'

He struggled on to his elbows and sat up. His chest rose and fell as his eyes moved over her naked body. He shook his head in disbelief. 'Mueller, you are so fucking gorgeous you bring tears to my eyes.'

Still sluggish, he wrapped his hands over her shoulders. He rose to his knees and pushed her on to her back. She parted her legs for him, waiting, wanting. He kissed her mouth first, his tongue working deep, his groans heartfelt. Obviously, he'd been wanting to kiss her for a while. His weight settled on to her breasts. He rubbed them with his furry chest. He strafed them with his nipples. They both caught a sharp breath.

She slid her hands down his back and cupped his broad, hard buttocks. 'I've got something for you in the pocket of my robe.'

Without so much as a curse, he reached over her head to grab the trailing hem, his cock springing up and down against her belly. He made quick work of the cellophane packet, then lowered himself between her legs. He pulsed against her lips again, thick and ready.

'Come inside,' she said. 'It's nice and warm.'

'No kidding,' he said. He wrapped his hand around

his shaft, adjusting his aim. 'I wish I could drag this out. I really do. But I fucking gotta fuck you.'

She laughed as he pressed inside, then groaned at the hot throbbing stretch of him. His cock was stocky like the rest of him, not so much long as wide. She writhed with an unaccustomed impatience. 'Give it to me,' she said, pushing up at him. 'Give it to me hard.'

Her order demolished his restraint. He lunged deep and gripped her bottom.

'Remember,' he said. 'You asked for it hard.' The words hadn't died before he was pumping into her, deep, swift thrusts that sent pleasure lapping outwards with every jolt. He seemed frantic to get deeper, as if more than pleasure depended on his penetration of her mysteries. But perhaps he feared she'd change her mind before he came. Every few strokes, he changed position, gripping her bottom to pull her more forcefully into his thrusts. She'd expected lots of 'fuck' and 'bitch' from him, but he muttered compliments as he drove himself in and out.

'Oh, yeah,' he said. 'That's good. What a sweetheart. What a gorgeous pussy. Oh, you're so good to me' and more of the same until she would have laughed if she'd had the breath for it.

Soon he was rocking in and out so fast she feared he'd beat her to the finish. She slipped her hand between their bodies to finger her clit.

'No,' he said, getting his hand under hers. 'Let me. You're so good. You're incredible.' His touch was firm and sure, a hard shimmying agitation that shoved her quickly to the edge of orgasm. The manipulation had little finesse, but it was effective. Her pussy tightened, her longing sharp and heavy. She blew out hard and rode the gathering wave.

'Hold on,' he panted, thrusting faster yet. 'I'm almost

there. We'll come together. That's it. I feel you. I feel you. God, you're so fucking wet. It's coming. Hang on. Not yet, I'm still – now, Mueller, now!'

Somewhere in the recesses of her mind a belt whistled and struck flesh. But she was laughing when she came. It bubbled up through her cunt and gripped his cock and shook them both into a cauldron of sensation. His hips jerked convulsively, drawing her orgasm into a second stab of pleasure. They sighed in unison and then he settled against her, his joints popping as he relaxed.

Julia kissed his raspy cheek. 'Thank you. That was lovely.'

'Oh, no,' he chuckled. 'Thank you. And it wasn't lovely, it was in-fucking-credible.' With a gratified sigh, he rolled her on top of him. 'Don't let go yet. I'm afterglowing.'

She rubbed her face across his meaty shoulder, unexpectedly touched. He was a nice sex partner, much nicer than she'd expected. But that didn't mean he wasn't a traitor. She drew a lazy circle around the small of his back. 'You know,' she said, 'Durbin really was upset about losing the Go-Tech account.'

'Was he?' Marty didn't tense a muscle, not even the one that nestled inside her pussy. 'I'm sure you could handle his disappointment. You never seem to get ruffled, no matter what he throws at you.' He yawned. 'To tell the truth, Mueller, I don't know what you see in him.'

'But he's your friend,' she said, her ears pricked for every nuance.

He shrugged. 'As much as he's anyone's friend. He's done a lot for me and I'm grateful. But if push came to shove, I know he wouldn't hesitate to stab me in the back.'

Did that mean Marty did it first? Did Santorini offer him something he couldn't resist? Money? A better title than senior VP?

'So tell me.' Marty gave her bottom a friendly smack. 'What do you see in that bastard?'

'Not what I used to,' she said, and let him make of that what he would.

Chapter Four

Friday night

Marty shuffled back to his room, the image of a happy man: well fed and well fucked. Julia tidied the remains of their play and slipped on to the covered porch behind the kitchen. The air was frigid. She shivered in her velvet robe, but the stillness of the night was so seductively foreign she couldn't resist it. Gone were the rumble of traffic, the sirens, the hum of unknown machinery. Instead a soft rustling met her ears, the sound of feathery clumps of snow striking the eaves.

I'll be damned, she thought. The cowboy was right. As she peered through the fall, a flash of movement caught her eye. She leant over the smooth pine railing. Half-hidden behind a screen of evergreens, a deer lifted its head, its mouth working on something it had found beneath the snow. It appeared to be staring straight at her.

A tingle crept up the back of her neck. She stepped

on to the path that led through the yard from the kitchen stairs. The snow was cold and soft under her feet, an inch thick already. In the cloud-muffled moonlight she could see how hard it was coming down. The flakes melted on her skin and collected in her lashes. She laughed softly. The deer flipped its white tail and bounded away.

Goodbye deer, she thought, watching it disappear into the trees. She felt peculiar, as if a door were creaking open before her to reveal a strange and unexpected vista. Her encounter with Marty had been milder than her usual. She had laughed – with pleasure, not mockery – and so had he. She wondered whether having an affair with Durbin's protégé would anger him sufficiently to cast her off. Marty would certainly make a simpler partner. He wasn't obsessive. He didn't take life seriously enough for that. She hugged herself. Could breaking free be that easy? She had admitted what she wanted; had sent that desire winging into the universe, and here the ways and means were falling into her lap.

No. She shoved her hands under her arms. That was nonsense, wishful thinking. But she couldn't deny she felt lighter tonight, easier in her skin – and cold, of course. She was about to return to the warmth of the kitchen when she spotted a light in the stable. Zach had mentioned that he had horses. The closest she'd ever got to a horse was the mounted police who patrolled Central Park. She could change that now if she wanted. Surely there'd be no harm in taking a peek while they slept.

Zach had been brushing the same stretch of Starlight's withers for the past five minutes. Not that the mare was complaining. She loved being curried, especially now that her winter coat was growing in. No, he was the only one troubled by his distraction. He shook his head at himself. Twice now Julia's face had hovered before him as he shot his load, three times if he counted the fiasco behind the Coffee Stop. He'd come to the stable to puzzle out why he wanted this woman so badly. He'd wanted plenty of women over the years, but never with an eye towards keeping one. Usually, as soon as they got serious, he was ready to cut them loose. He shifted the brush to Starlight's back. He didn't think he wanted this one just because she didn't want him. As a rule, he wasn't so perverse, though some might call him harebrained, considering how slim the prospect of roping her seemed. She was a proud one all right. The memory of her scornful looks stirred a mixture of admiration and dismay. But as to why he wanted her . . .

His hand stilled at the mystery. Starlight shifted on her hocks, a gentle reminder to keep brushing. 'That's right, old girl,' he murmured, resuming the stroke. 'I haven't forgotten you.'

Maybe he wanted her because she gave off an air of live and let live. City girl or not, she wasn't a woman to crowd a man. She wasn't nosy. She was barely curious. Out here in Montana people sometimes lived so cut off they got starved to know every little thing about a person. Zach's family had given him a horror of too much closeness. From dusk till dawn, from birth till death, they did everything together on that blasted ranch: ate, slept, rode cattle, even fucked within a stone's throw of each other. Three trailer homes sat behind his parents' ranch to house his siblings and their mates. He could identify any family member by the sounds they made when they came. They thought he was crazy for closing the dude ranch now that he

68

could afford to; said he'd go nuts rattling around with no one to talk to but Starlight and Buck and Gracie. But Zach was counting the minutes till he had the place to himself, which made the thoughts he was having about that tall drink of city water very strange indeed.

The stable was large and, while not warm, at least warmer than outdoors. The earthen floor had been swept and a queue of stalls marched down either side, all shipshape and empty as far as Julia could see. Clean as they were, the stalls seemed to be waiting, as if new tenants were expected at any moment. When she was halfway down the row, a scruffy black and white dog trotted out to greet her. She didn't bark, which Julia found strange, just snuffled a wet nose over her feet. She sat quietly when Julia knelt to pet the long fur between her ears.

An image of her younger self scrolled across her mind. She was reaching through the bars of a cage in a pet shop while an ecstatic Labrador puppy licked her fingers. Her mother stood behind her, patient but silent. Julia hadn't dared say please, but she knew her eyes said it for her.

'It would not be fair,' her mother had said in her crisp Swiss way, 'moving around the way we do.'

Julia had known she was right. The general always did the best he could for them, but sometimes they had a house with a garden and sometimes an airless apartment with barely enough room for the two of them. A healthy young dog couldn't live that way. Nonetheless, it hurt to leave that puppy behind. He'd never turn away, she'd thought. I could love him all I wanted.

Shaking off the memory, she gave this funny-looking dog a final scratch and stood. The dog padded after

Julia as she continued her journey past the neat, empty stalls. Finally, in a double-sized box near the end, she spotted a young horse – a colt, she supposed – curled up on a pile of hay. He was a rich chestnut brown with one white sock and a black mane and tail. His head was narrow, his legs gangly. They twitched as if he dreamt of chasing foxes. Julia wished she could climb inside and pet him, but she didn't have the nerve. Worse than getting kicked would be doing anything to harm the little horse.

She'd almost turned to go when she noticed a soft rhythmic noise, like an old-fashioned razor being stropped. Curious, she peeked over the wall into the next stall. There she found Zach stroking the sides of a large brown horse with what looked like a boot brush. His back was to her, but the loose fall of his shirt suggested it was unbuttoned. The plain blue cotton draped his shoulders, which rippled with muscle as he worked. His hair was damp from his exertions with Carolyn and a line of white skin marked the nape of his neck. He must have got his hair cut since the end of the summer. Her fingers curled with an inexplicable urge to explore the vulnerable stripe of skin. In fact, his whole neck was beautiful, tanned and strong, tendons moving beneath the close-cropped surface. She wanted to place her lips against it, to press her tongue to the shifting cords. Immune to such temptations, the horse half-closed its eyes, its ears flopped out from its head as if it were too relaxed to hold them up. It breathed out in what sounded uncannily like a human sigh.

'That's a sweetheart,' Zach said in a low, soothing tone. 'You don't care if I'm harebrained, do you?'

Julia didn't understand the words any more than the horse did. Zach had large, rough hands, red and chapped around the knuckles, but surprisingly clean around the nails. His strokes were so caring and steady that her chest tightened with emotion. The man and animal were at peace with each other, at one. The games she'd played with Marty, on which she'd so recently been congratulating herself, seemed worse than meaningless when set against a communication as honest as this.

A person like her didn't belong in this place. She was an artificial construct, a blight on the landscape. Never in her life had she used her touch as a straightforward expression of love. She had ordered others, whipped them, tied them, spanked them, made them cry tears of excruciating pleasure, but never had she touched another creature, man or beast, simply because she loved it.

She had no doubt Zach loved this horse. He declared it with his voice, with his hands, with the endless patience of his strokes. She wanted to turn away but the sight held her captive. Her lungs ached and her eyes stung with unsheddable tears. A sound caught in her throat. The horse jerked its head, ears plastered along its skull, teeth snapping the air.

'Hey there,' Zach soothed, catching its muzzle in a gentle hand. The horse snapped again and rolled its eyes. Julia's face heated, as though someone she admired had called her a bitch in the middle of a board meeting. She stepped back. Zach turned.

'Hey,' he said, surprised. The horse's head tossed between his hands, but its agitation didn't seem to alarm him. His eyes travelled down her velvet robe, warming with admiration. He broke into a smile that lifted his moustache and deepened the lines around his mouth. 'You must have crept up quiet as a bug.'

His twang made the words comical but she did not

laugh. She took another step back. 'Sorry. I didn't mean to scare your horse.'

'Aw, you can't scare Starlight here.' He patted the diamond-shaped star between her eyes. 'She's kid-broke.'

Julia didn't know what kid-broke meant but she could tell the horse didn't like her. 'I shouldn't be here,' she said, and turned to leave.

'Hold it right there,' he barked. Normally she was immune to the voice of authority, but something in his voice stopped her. 'You aren't going back outside dressed like that. No, ma'am.'

He took her wrist and led her towards a door at the far end of the stable. His hand was callused but warm. Its light clasp sent heat pouring to the soft, tender flesh between her legs, making her pussy feel heavy and full. She stumbled and he caught her elbow. He smiled at her, his eyes as blue as the Montana sky. His expression was so kind, so ordinary, that once again she had a sense of having stepped outside her rightful sphere.

'You're lucky I just mucked out,' he said. 'A stable is no place to be wandering around barefoot.' He wore a disreputable pair of cowboy boots, caked with mud and straw. Perhaps he saved the flame-sided boots he'd worn to the airport for formal occasions. He pushed a door open and flicked on a light. 'We keep extra duds for the dudes in the tack room.'

His tone suggested he meant to be humorous, but Julia was too dazed by her surroundings to smile. Leather filled the musty room: leather reins, leather saddles, leather crops. A worn bridle lay on a small desk, obviously awaiting repair. His stetson sat next to it, the crown scuffed and dented. She pictured him wearing that and nothing else. Oh, Christ, she thought, overwhelmed by a surge of lust. There was no escaping the arousal. The cramped room reeked of her favourite fragrance in all the world. Her limbs trembled. She pressed her thighs together and a trickle of warm, silky moisture squeezed between the lips of her sex. She'd loved the feel and smell of leather since she was a child playing dressing-up with her mother's shoes. The first time she masturbated, she'd been dragging a belt she'd stolen from the general between her legs. Sick, but true, and what's more she still had that belt. Over the years, so many erotic memories had become associated with the scent of leather that her response was very strong. She touched the bridle that hung from the nearest hook and ran her fingers over the curve of the brow-band.

Did Zach have any idea what a roomful of toys he had?

With an effort, she shook herself from her trance, though she didn't let go of the reins. 'You've got so much gear,' she said. 'Where are the rest of the horses?'

She almost jumped when he laid his hands on her shoulders. His chest grazed her back, warm and hard against her robe. 'My grandma and I hired horses from the neighbours if we got a big riding party. But there's no point keeping them around all the time, eating their fool heads off.' His hands stroked down her arms and up again. It was a liberty she shouldn't have allowed. His crotch brushed her bottom and for a second she thought she felt the ridge of a strong erection. 'I want to build a herd when I get a chance. Train 'em and sell 'em, you know. But for now I've got too many pots on the fire.'

'Pots on the fire?' she asked, her voice shamefully weak.

'Property management. I own a few lots in town. Here –' He reached above her head to pull something

73

from the highest shelf. His groin touched her bottom again, and again her sex heated. He was hard. She was sure of it now. The knowledge unnerved and enflamed her. He handed her a pair of neatly folded, butter-coloured buckskin trousers. 'Try these on. I think you'll find they're more comfortable than those suits.'

She had to turn around to step into them. She expected Zach to look away but he didn't. Eyes focused on her hands, his lips tightened as she thrust her long bare legs into the trousers. In other circumstances she might have ventured a crack about cheap thrills, but his attention and the glove-soft feel of the leather joined forces to completely liquefy her insides. The cloth cupped her bare mound. She was going to get it wet. She was going to add her scent to the scent of the leather. Her hand shook as she pulled up the zip.

'Perfect,' he said, stroking his moustache. 'Those fit great.'

'I'm so gratified you think so,' she said, but the biting edge she meant to give the words was spoilt by their huskiness.

The sound brought him to attention like that funny dog of his. His moustache jerked up on one side. She ground her teeth. The stupid cowboy was grinning at her. He stepped closer. She lifted her hands to fend him off, but he'd already backed her into a wall of wooden shelves. He was heavier than she was, and broader. His chest wasn't bare as she'd expected – hoped, damn it – but covered by a thermal underwear top. Soft from many washings, the navy cotton hugged slabs of iron-hard muscle. They weren't the useless gym-bred sort Durbin and Marty sported, which did not excuse her complete lack of resistance. She'd let him back her into the shelves. She'd let him overwhelm her.

He slung his left arm behind her neck and pulled their heads closer. She meant to turn away but she was mesmerised by the approach of his eyes, his laughing, Montana blue, lash-starred eyes. She opened her mouth, one last chance to protest. He captured it before she'd made a sound and drove the wet spear of his tongue deeply, firmly inside.

A hum of pleasure escaped her control. He tasted of nothing but himself, slightly sweet, subtly metallic. His moustache was softer than she'd expected, almost silky. After the first deep thrust, his kiss softened, still greedy but playful, too. It was a kiss of surprising skill and charm. It reminded her of a square dance. Not that she'd ever been square dancing. But it had that sense of fun: light feet, light tongues. She responded almost without realising she'd done so, curling her tongue up the soft underside of his and sucking it gently deeper.

At once his kiss changed, like switching to a tango mid-dance. He made a hungry male noise, grabbed her waist and ground his hardened crotch over hers. He was taller than her but not by much. Their bodies fit together without a squirm. Oh, it felt good. The heat streamed out of his cock and up her cunt like sunshine in July. When he pulled his hips away she murmured in protest. Happily, the withdrawal was temporary, just long enough for him to fumble open her waistband and shove his hand between her legs. Her labia parted before his fingers, their rough length sliding through her lust-oiled folds. He groaned to find her wet, so wet his finger made a sticky, squelching noise as it eased inside her sheath. He drew it out and added a second, that entrance even noisier than the first.

She minded him knowing how aroused she was, but her body wouldn't let her pull back. Her body wanted more. Her body wanted to fuck him blind.

She breathed hard through the kiss, taking in the scent of leather, of man. Her knees began to give. She reached up to clutch his shoulders. Zach cursed softly against her mouth. He kneed her thighs wider and lifted one around his hip. Now his fingers moved freely, a steady, wet in and out. His thumb found the soft hood that covered her clitoris, pressing it over and around the little shaft. A ragged piece of skin scratched her with every pass. It felt so good she wanted to scream.

'Is that all right?' he whispered, the question panting hot against her lips.

She couldn't bring herself to answer, to participate any further in this stupidity. Besides, if she opened her mouth, she would order him to free that long thick cock and drive it between her legs. She closed her eyes and shuddered, her nails digging into him through his shirt, her head falling limply back.

She saw her mother's arm rise; heard the belt fall. The general cried out against his wrist and then, abruptly, the image was gone. The present jumped into focus. Zach's breath rasped in her ear. His legs sidled hers, the denim soft as velvet, the bulge of his cock pulsing on her inner thigh. She whimpered, a sound she couldn't recall making before. She was so close to coming that her sheath fluttered in anticipation.

'That's the way,' he said, cradling her neck more firmly in the crook of his arm. The pace of his fingers quickened, their rough spots jangling her nerves. 'That's the way. Ride it to the finish.'

Her stomach tightened and she gasped. So close. She seemed to ride a foaming wave, the anticipation as pleasurable as coming. Tingles swept her skin, hot alternating with cold. He licked a tendon at the side of her neck. His cheeks were damp, his mouth hot. He pressed his cock hard into the lee of her thigh. He rubbed it in tight, hungry jerks, not as if he were trying to come, just helpless to resist. Then he set his teeth against her skin and bit down.

She cried out at the love-bite but he didn't let go. His fingers worked her slippery flesh, lightning quick, diamond firm. Her cunt swelled, then drew in on itself. Her clit pulsed beneath the callused pad of his thumb. She quivered, her body escaping her control, and then she came, hard stabs of feeling that shot from her sex to the top of her head. The orgasm was better than anything she'd experienced lately, at her hand or any-one else's. The waves were hotter, more penetrating. They left an aftertaste of sweetness she could not deny.

He murmured endearments as she descended, the same way he'd murmured to the sleepy horse. The comparison returned her to her senses. No doubt he expected it was his turn now, but she was no dumb beast to be won over with a pat on the head and a handful of carrots. She was Julia Mueller, the hidden power at DMI.

She pushed him away so roughly he had to catch his balance on the battered metal desk. She yanked the edges of her robe together and cinched the tie.

'Very nice,' she said in her most condescending tone. 'I can see why that horse is so fond of you.'

His face darkened but he didn't say a word, merely folded his arms over his chest and rested his hips on the desk. His erection formed a monster arch she could barely tear her gaze from. As she strode from the room, his eyes followed her, prickling a spot between her shoulder blades. Despite the put-down she'd adminis-tered, she couldn't help feeling he'd got the best of the exchange.

He'd unsettled her.

'Damn,' she muttered, irritation warming her second barefoot trek through the falling snow. She didn't have time for this nonsense. She had less than two days to discover the culprit who'd betrayed DMI, less than two days to devise a sure-fire way to wrench herself free of Richard Durbin. Yes, she was interested in, some day, forming a more romantic attachment with a man, but not some stupid cowboy with hay in his hair and shit on his boots.

She stomped into the kitchen and shook the snow from her clothes. Her teeth were chattering, but she was too angry to care. She doubted the cowboy was looking for romance in any case. As far as she could tell, he'd screw anything that moved. He hadn't even waited to dry off from fucking Carolyn.

But it wouldn't happen again. From here on in she would focus on her purpose.

Her good feelings of half an hour earlier were history.

Zach's return to the house took him past the guest wing. He told himself he wasn't hoping for another glimpse of Julia, but in the end it didn't matter: her room was dark.

He shook his head at his own foolishness. But who could blame him? That kiss had been so promising, a sweet, aching, sinking together of mouths and bodies. She'd tasted so good. She'd fit him so well. Tall women were the best, tall meaty women with hair of gold and eyes like a mountain stream.

He rubbed the tightness at the centre of his chest. The imprint of her breasts and belly might have been burnt into his skin, so clear was his memory of it. He barely registered the light shining from the last window of the wing, except to wonder why one of the guests chose to sleep so far from the others. Then he drew up short. Had Julia changed rooms for some reason? Had she heard him and Carolyn making love? The possibility spurred a twinge of guilt. But the elegant young black man sat inside, his head bent over a scattered assortment of papers.

Few black people lived in Montana and he stood staring for a moment, rooted in place by curiosity. What was it like to walk in his boots? He'd barely said a word at dinner; barely looked up. Why was there such a distance between him and the others? Was the colour of his skin the cause, or some difference in temperament that none of them knew how to bridge?

He stroked his moustache in thought, jerking back to himself when he found snowflakes melting between his fingers. It sure was coming down. At this rate they'd get a foot, at least. This afternoon he'd welcomed the storm, but now he wondered if getting snowed in would do him a bit of good. He didn't know what he'd done wrong. Julia had enjoyed his kiss. She'd come so hard she'd squeezed his fingers to the bone. But as soon as she'd finished, she'd shaken him off like something she'd found stuck to her shoe.

She didn't strike him as the selfish kind, and he had reason to trust his instincts. He could always spot the yearling who'd hog the trough, who'd never be an equal partner to a man. But maybe her looks and manner had blinded him. Maybe her wrappings were so attractive, he hadn't looked hard enough at what lay inside.

No, he thought. I can't be that wrong. She is warm underneath. She is giving.

One thing was certain, though. Gentling a thoroughbred like Julia Mueller would not be a trot in the park.

* * *

Julia dreamt of the opening door. This time it lodged in the centre of her chest like a surrealist painting, full of clouds and mountains. A man on a horse rode down a distant peak and galloped towards the threshold. 'Yippee-ki-ay,' he shouted, waving a cowboy hat over his head. 'Crept up quiet as a bug!'

Julia bolted upright and pressed a fist to her pounding heart. Ridiculous. Utterly ridiculous. But she had a feeling the nightmare wasn't over yet.

Chapter Five

Saturday morning

Julia woke to a pearly grey light. Her body languorous, she indulged in a spine-warming stretch.
Despite the dream that began the night, she'd slept
soundly. Now a bone-deep relaxation weighted her
limbs. If she hadn't had so much work to do, she might
have lazed in bed, which was not a particularly productive impulse. Frowning at herself, she threw off the
down-filled coverlet and padded to the window. Snow
had blown against the panes during the night, leaving
small portholes in their centres. Outside, white fes-
tooned the world. The ponderosa pines that bordered
the guest wing were coated so thickly they looked as if
they'd been dipped in meringue.

She pressed her nose to the glass. The snow continued to fall, slantwise now that the wind had picked
up. This was nothing like snow in New York, which
dirtied as soon as it fell, more nuisance than beautifi-
cation. How wild this landscape seemed, how exhilar-

ating and clean. A craving for hot cocoa made her stomach rumble. Definitely time to get dressed. Her glance fell on the buckskin trousers Zach had lent her the night before. If she wore them, would he take it as a peace offering? If she didn't, would he think her childish? She glared at the fan-backed chair on which they sat. To hell with it. Those trousers were more comfortable than her suits; he could think what he damn well pleased.

She dragged them on with a sense of rebellion, though what she rebelled against she couldn't say. Fortunately, she'd packed a turtleneck. Zach had left a hickey the size of Boston on her neck.

When she reached the kitchen she found everyone there except their host. The hour was early, but Carolyn and Ben were accustomed to being at work by eight. In recognition of his seniority, Marty generally arrived at nine and left at four. She deduced he'd been kicked out of bed by his stomach.

Her entrance provoked a wolfish whistle.

'I'll be damned,' Marty said, taking in her cashmere and suede. 'This makes twice in twenty-four hours I've seen you without your executive armour.'

Ben's gaze jerked from her to the senior VP, obviously jumping to the correct conclusion. He found his voice after a jaw-hanging pause. 'That outfit is flattering.'

Julia pressed her hand to her heart. 'Gentlemen, your approval overwhelms me.'

'Now if you'd just let your hair down,' Marty said, 'you might not frighten every man you meet.'

The banter would have continued if Carolyn hadn't cleared a circle in the window over the sink and announced she wanted to see the barn. Julia presumed she'd spotted Zach out there. Her stomach tensed. She dreaded seeing him again, though she'd be damned if she'd let cowardice dictate her behaviour. Perhaps she had put herself in the wrong by taking her pleasure and leaving him unrequited. She had not, however, asked him to kiss her in the first place, or do anything else for that matter.

She tugged the hem of her soft grey sweater over her waist. 'Yes,' she said. 'Let's all go see the barn.'

Marty led them into the hall. Of the four, Ben seemed the sleepiest. He rubbed his palms over his face and shook out his arms.

Julia handed him his coat. 'Up late reading?' she asked.

His exotic eyes warmed at the friendly question. 'Not too late. I'm afraid I'm not much good before I've had my coffee.'

'I guess the cowboy isn't used to early risers.'

'I guess not.' He smiled and Julia's heart tripped at the sheer force of his beauty. Such a lovely man. What a shame he was too nice to get nasty with. But at least he'd forgiven her midnight rendezvous with Marty. Ben was one of very few people whose good opinion mattered to her.

'Stop dragging your heels,' Marty urged, flapping Julia's coat behind her. 'I want to see the horses.'

'There's only two,' she said. The coat paused in its slide up her arms.

'Is that so?' He smoothed the collar around her neck. 'And when did Fräulein Mueller discover that?'

Julia didn't answer and Marty didn't press, though he did leer at her all the way to the stable. Unlike Ben, he seemed to relish the idea that she got around, as though in some convoluted way her conquests reflected well on him. She snorted to herself. She supposed that, to another male, the cowboy might seem a status-enhancing tumble: all that salt-of-the-earth, bucking-bronco brawn. Her relationship with Durbin, however, was a questionable addition to her cachet. But who knew what kink her bed habits had triggered in Marty? He had his secrets, too.

The scruffy dog met them at the door to the barn. She sniffed furiously at everyone's shoes, then barked once and plunked herself at Julia's feet. From there she stared adoringly up at her, wagging her feathery tail. Julia couldn't help feeling pleased at being remembered, though it was, perhaps, a silly thing to take pleasure in.

'That,' said Carolyn, 'has to be one of the ugliest dogs I've ever seen.'

Marty jostled her shoulder. 'Take care, Caro. Lots of men live by "love me, love my dog".'

Carolyn frowned, but he had worried her sufficiently to send her to her heels before the animal. 'I'm sure he's very bright,' she said, and reached out to pet it.

The dog growled at her. To Julia's surprise, Ben was the one to laugh. They all stared at him.

'Sorry,' he said. 'It's a she, though, and maybe she's jealous.'

Zach forestalled whatever quip Marty was going to make by appearing with a bucket of oats in each hand. He wore his grubby shearling jacket and a pair of equally grubby work gloves. His breath made clouds of white in the chilly barn. Carolyn waved, but his eyes went straight to Julia. She braced herself to face the questions in them, but whatever he wished to ask was hidden from her. His gaze slid down her legs and up again. She damned him silently for giving her a gift she couldn't resist. He didn't smile, but he nodded as if he, too, approved of her outfit.

'I see you've met Gracie,' he said, tilting his head towards the dog. 'Best cow-dog north of Bozeman.'

'She's adorable,' Carolyn said, and stepped forward to plant a kiss on Zach's startled mouth. She put some tongue into it, stroking the back of his neck with her slender, long-nailed hands.

Julia sighed under her breath. She suspected Marty's 'love me, love my dog' remark accounted for the public display of affection. Carolyn wanted to prove that this romantic encounter should be taken seriously and that she, Carolyn Q. Prentiss, had the power to drive men mad.

Her assertion would have been more credible if Zach had actually put down the buckets while she kissed him. Worse, Julia's sharp hearing caught the tail end of the plaint she murmured in his ear, something about not spending the night in her bed.

'Got my own room' was his matter-of-fact response.

Carolyn backed away. Cheeks flushed, she hid her embarrassment by making a fuss over the colt, which caused the little horse to dash around his box in what looked to Julia like panic, though Carolyn merely clapped in delight.

'Come away from there,' Julia said, braving the mare's teeth to pull her back. True to her fears, the older horse did try to take a nip at her, but got only air for her pains. 'You're scaring him.'

'Me?' Carolyn huffed. 'He's excited. He's playing.' She turned to Zach for support, but he shook his head and eased out of the mare's stall.

'Buck probably is a bit anxious, Ms Prentiss. He hasn't been around many strangers. Once he gets used to you, I'm sure he'll want to play.'

If Zach's failure to back her up disappointed her, his calling her Ms Prentiss was a slap in the face. She turned and walked stiffly towards the door, already patting her pockets for a smoke. Apparently, rejection had a bad effect on abstinence. Too focused on the horse to notice her departure, or her hurt, Zach stepped into the oversized stall. At once the colt stopped racing around. He crept towards Zach on trembling legs and butted his chest. He reminded Julia of a toddler clinging to his mother's legs. Zach stroked his glossy brown neck and spoke kindly. Seconds later the horse's nose was in the bucket and he was chomping away as if nothing had ever been amiss.

Julia was amazed and, though she fought it, entranced. No doubt the horse had known him since its birth, but even so the connection between them was magical. Zach's gaze caught hers as he left the stall. He stopped, struck by whatever he found there. His gloved hand rose to his moustache and for a second Julia felt his fingers between her legs again. The memory inspired a strident throb of arousal. She pressed her lips between her teeth, willing the feeling away, but her cheeks grew hot even as she did. She couldn't believe it. Of all people, Julia Mueller was being put to the blush by a five-minute hand job.

He touched her shoulder. 'You OK?'

Before she could stop herself she flinched.

'I'm fine,' she said. Flustered, and aghast at her loss of control, she turned to find Marty climbing the side of the colt's box. He reached down to pat its shoulders. A protest hovered on her lips, but the horse merely snorted and went on eating.

Marty flashed a delighted smile. 'You should try this,' he said to Julia and Ben, but Ben was peering into the tack room and Julia didn't dare, not even to overcome her disgust with her own spinelessness. Nor did Zach encourage her to approach the horse.

86

He crossed back into the stall lugging a bale of hay on a hook. 'Buck here has a partiality for men,' he explained. 'But I'll let him and Starlight into the pasture after breakfast and you can watch them run if you want.'

'You let them out in this?' Ben asked, nodding at the driving snow.

'You bet.' Zach forked a second load of hay into Starlight's feeding rack. 'I let them out in most anything. Horses get ornery if you keep them stabled all the time. They need to run.'

Just like people, Julia thought, then rolled her eyes at her fanciful turn of mind.

Finished with his chores, Zach slapped his hands against his thighs. 'Hope you're hungry,' he said. 'I've got a real ranch spread planned for this morning.'

As they left, he touched the small of Julia's back to usher her out. It was more a gentlemanly gesture than a pass, but she couldn't stop herself from jerking away again. He didn't take offence, though. In fact, he broke into a brilliant boyish grin. He looked as if he knew a secret: her secret.

Julia didn't relish that possibility one bit.

Zach's ranch-style breakfast provoked another of Marty and Carolyn's squabbles. She took him to task because he, the son of kosher parents, was eating pork sausage and bacon; he, in turn, accused her of cutting her food into such tiny pieces that her new boyfriend would conclude she had lockjaw. Since Zach had left them alone to their meal, Carolyn didn't pull any punches.

'Don't you worry,' she snapped, 'my mouth is big enough to cut you down to size.' Marty patted his crotch and volunteered to test her claim. Carolyn turned bright red and pointed her fork at him. 'You do that one more time and I'll have you up on sexual harassment charges.'

'Ooh.' Marty wiggled his hands. 'I'm trembling in my teeny-weeny jockstrap.'

Ben spit his eggs out on a laugh. Marty slapped his back.

'Watch out there, Ben,' he teased. 'Pretty soon we'll be thinking you've got a sense of humour.'

'You leave him alone!' Carolyn cried. 'He's twice the man you are.'

They were still sniping when Julia herded them into the conference room. The window-lined space contained an assortment of comfy chairs and low tables, all in shades of green and brown and gold. The effect was masculine but cosy, especially with the veil of snow falling outside. Marty immediately kicked off his shoes and stretched out on the couch. Julia knew the pose was deceptive. The others might resent him playing the grand pasha, but Marty's mind was as keen as it was ambitious. Of them all, he was likeliest to pull this strategy session out of the fire, which didn't mean the others couldn't help. They would help if Julia had anything to say about it. With that in mind, she handed each portfolio manager a leather-bound notebook.

'This is a collection of marketing ideas the three of you have run by Rich this year. They've been rejected for one reason or another, but they all have merit. Together you should be able to whip at least some into shape.'

Marty imitated a snapping cat-o'-nine-tails. 'Break out the whips,' he said.

Carolyn was not so sanguine. She tossed her copy on to the burled walnut coffee table. 'What's the point if Durbin has turned them down already? Besides –'

her cheeks pinkened '– you're not our boss, Julia. You're Durbin's secretary. Why don't you go make coffee or something?'

Ben gasped at the affront. Julia shrugged. A flyweight like Carolyn wasn't worth getting angry over.

'You can do as you wish,' she said. 'But I think you'll find this saves you time. Some of these ideas were never submitted formally, but merely mentioned in passing and perhaps not as persuasively as they might have been.'

'You've been collecting our ideas?' Ben asked, eyes wide.

'Only the good ones.'

'And just how would you know what the good ones are?' Carolyn demanded, still trying to put her in her place.

Marty sat up and clapped his hands to his forehead. 'Don't you get it, Prentiss? Don't either of you get it? Who do you think handles Rich's clients when he's golfing? Who interviews new hires before anyone else sees them? Who sets salary grades and decides what software our traders will use next year? Do you honestly think Durbin would waste his time on anything so unglamorous? Or, God forbid, bother to listen to any idea that doesn't come with a money-back guarantee?' He pointed a finger at Carolyn. 'Julia is the reason you weren't fired last month for slapping Mrs Harrington's nephew; never mind that he had his hand down your dress. And –' he shifted the finger to Ben '– she's the reason you were hired in the first place. Durbin didn't care how smart you are. He thinks black people belong on the basketball court.'

He sat back in his chair then, obviously embarrassed by his fervour. With a smile she couldn't contain, Julia kissed his raspy cheek. 'Now that you've whipped them into shape,' she murmured, 'I think I'll make coffee.'

As she made her way to the kitchen, she heard him call the others to attention.

'Let's get cracking,' he said. 'I know I can't afford to get sacked. I've got a mortgage payment you wouldn't believe.'

She was still glowing from his defence and it took a moment for the words to sink in. When they did, her hands stilled on the coffee maker. Did Marty have money troubles? Had he been vulnerable to a bribe from Santorini? She realised that her attitude towards him had changed. Marty might have his faults; he might even be her prime suspect, but she wouldn't enjoy turning him in.

After supplying her charges with adequate caffeine, Julia went in search of her second favourite tension-reducer. The cowboy claimed to have a gym. She hoped he didn't mean a broken Exercycle and a set of dumbbells.

Her expectations low, she descended the basement stairs. She found a surprisingly Gothic space. The walls and ceiling were constructed of smoke-stained brick, arranged in pointed arches like the vault of an old church. Some of the bricks had crumbled and been replaced. Zach's grandfather must have built his dream on the ruins of something older.

Don't we all, Julia thought, with a twist to her mouth.

The first door she tried opened on a wine cellar. Cool, dusty bottles lay in tall wooden racks. Curious, she stepped inside. To her surprise, the vintages were not restricted to Californian, and they were all first-rate. She touched a yellowing label, trying to adjust her presumptions. She didn't know which would have shocked her more: if Zach had amassed this collection, or if his grandparents had.

A laundry occupied the bay next to the wine cellar, followed by two communal showers. COLTS and FILLIES stated their heavy steel doors. That, she wagered, had to be Granny Taylor's doing. She peeked inside. The shower floors were tiled, but here, too, she found tall Gothic arches, their brick protected by a shiny, clear sealant. The effect was intriguing: debauched monastery meets sleek modern plumbing. A shiver of imagined possibilities raced down her spine. She'd return to this room, she decided, and she wouldn't return alone.

The next door opened on the exercise room. Julia's eyebrows rose. Zach had enough equipment for a professional gym. In addition to a wall of free weights, he had three kinds of bikes, a rower, a treadmill and a full complement of Nautilus machines. Her lips twitched as she envisioned his dear departed granny dusting these contraptions.

But perhaps his grandmother was the mastermind behind their purchase. You don't know, she reminded herself. You simply don't know.

She'd stretched upstairs so now she stripped down to her exercise clothes and did a quick set of pull-ups on the chinning bar. A few minutes on the rower got her pulse going, after which she switched to weight work. Her body began to hum under the workout, a sensual feeling that flowed outward from her sex in warm, blood-tingling waves. Julia was no body builder but she loved being strong; loved the sight of her body sheened in sweat or her muscles swelling into prominence as she worked.

She moved to the leg machine and watched herself

in the wall-length mirror, her eyes slitted with a mild endorphin haze. She wore a red sports bra and a matching pair of skin-tight, hip-high shorts. Her stomach muscles rippled with each disciplined breath, her thighs clenched, her calves rounded.

'You look as if you're enjoying yourself,' said a drawling baritone.

Julia's breathing faltered, but this time he did not make her jump. 'I am,' she said. She continued pushing, determined to finish out the set. A pair of long, callused fingers feathered over her shoulders. She shivered.

'I could put on some music,' he offered.

'No, thank you.'

He chuckled at her vehemence. 'Just a little jazz, Julia. I know how you city folks feel about the local tunes.'

She didn't answer and he left to turn on the audio system. Something sultry filled the room. It had a strong backbeat, but it wasn't fast. It made a tendon jump between her legs. She rolled her head against the padded bench, trying to stretch the tension from her neck.

Before she knew it, he was on her, swinging his leg over the bench so that he could straddle her belly. She immediately let the weights fall.

'What do you think you're doing?'

The cowboy grinned and that made her pulse race, too. Something had happened since last night to make him more aggressive, more confident. A considerable portion of his weight rested on her hipbones. She could feel the soft crush of his balls flattening across her pubis. He leant forward and braced his hands above her head. 'I'm just giving you a little extra resistance, darlin'.'

92

'Don't call me that.' She pushed at his chest but he wasn't budging. 'I want you off me.'

'But we have unfinished business, you and I.' He bent lower and nuzzled her sweaty collar bone. 'Mm, your pulse is racing, but I don't think you're afraid of me. No, I think you want to finish what we started last night as much as I do. You're just too proud to admit it. That's all right, though. I don't mind giving a skittish lady a little gentling.'

So that's what this was about. She'd shied away from him this morning, and he'd decided to treat her like his pals from the stable. She gritted her teeth. 'I am not a horse.'

'Maybe not.' He sat back and pulled his hands down her front. 'But I bet you could use a good rub-down.'

'You mean you could.' She stared pointedly at the ridge behind the fly of his jeans. She shouldn't have looked. Her mouth went dry at the thickness of the bulge, at the way it pulsed beneath the faded cloth.

'Oh, I definitely could,' he agreed. His thumbs brushed her nipples. From the twang that went through her, she knew they were hard. 'But I think you could, too.'

'I am not interested.'

His gaze moved from her breasts to her eyes. He smiled, a lazy crinkling of skin and lips. 'That was my first mistake, believing what your mouth said instead of your body.' He caught her nipples between his fingers and plucked them outward. A strangled sound escaped her throat. 'Glory be, Julia, was that a whimper?'

His teasing pushed her temper over the edge. Julia heaved hard and dumped him on to the floor. He hit the mat with a curse. She should have quit while she was ahead but she couldn't resist following him down to complete his humiliation. Too bad it turned into her own. All too easily he twisted free of her attempts to pin him.

'Oh, no,' he laughed. 'You can't pull that on me. I used to wrestle steers for a living.'

Then he sat on her and trapped her wrists.

'Fuck,' she said.

'My pleasure,' he responded, and swooped down for a kiss.

His mouth was as sweet as she remembered. 'No,' she moaned, tearing away, but her legs were parting for his hips.

His breath came faster. He pushed his crotch at hers. She pushed back. 'That's it, darlin'. Work with me. I ain't trying to break you. I just thought we'd both enjoy a ride.'

But they wouldn't enjoy anything if he didn't cut out the horse talk.

'Shut up,' she said, and buried her fingers in his hair. They writhed together, rolling back and forth between the machines. Their kiss was noisy, more greed than style. She clutched his back, then his buttocks. Her shorts were thin and she wore nothing beneath them. The shape of him branded her through denim and Lycra. He wriggled like a fish, trying to reach the fastening of his jeans. Too perverse to let him, she tightened her thighs.

'My zip,' he gasped.

'Aw, does it hurt?'

'Doesn't it hurt you?'

'I like it,' she breathed, and nipped his lower lip.

He winced, then nipped hers back and dragged her hands above her head. He rocked her hard, his erection mashing her clit dead on. He knew what he was doing to her. He watched her eyes as she climbed. She held off, not wanting to give in, wanting to force him to come before she did. She kicked off her shoes; caressed his calves with her feet. His eyes narrowed. She craned forward and nuzzled his flannel shirt. She found his sharpened nipple on the second try.

'Oh, God,' he said, and she knew this was one of his sweet spots. His hold on her wrists slackened. She pulled them free and wrenched his shirt open. Buttons flew. 'Ah,' he sighed as she latched on to the tiny bud. She ran both hands around the curve of his buttocks and squeezed his balls. His cock jumped in its denim trap. He dug it into her, worked it over her, putting all his strength into each brutal jerk.

In spite of the vigorous treatment, she came before he did: twice. She'd never known a man to last so long. She lay under him, limp, drenched with sweat, and wondered what sort of a machine he was.

He didn't look triumphant, though. He looked desperate. He was shaking. His pulse beat visibly in his throat. He sat back on his heels as if unsure of his muscles' ability to hold him. When he rubbed his hands down his thighs, he left streaks of sweat on the worn blue cloth.

'Touch me,' he said, his thumbs stroking either side of his distended fly. 'I can't come unless you touch me.'

The confession perplexed her but, dom or not, she couldn't short him twice. She trailed her fingers down from his breastbone, savouring the firmness of his flesh. Every part of him was solid. He had a working man's muscle, a big man's bulk. Sweat sleeked the skin of his belly, matting the light covering of hair. She dipped a finger beneath his waistband to explore the hollow of his navel.

95

'Open the button,' he said, his voice rough, but vulnerable, too. 'Don't leave me hanging again.'

'I wouldn't do that,' she said and pressed the metal disk through its slit. She slid her hand behind the zip to protect him as she lowered it. His cock was hot against her skin. It pulsed with eagerness, then fell free. He sighed when she caught the heavy weight. She almost sighed herself. His cock was genuinely beautiful. Large enough to impress, but not to intimidate, it rose straight and tall from a bush of deep brown hair. She explored him slowly, finding her way through this lovely new territory. His skin was satiny smooth, and flushed a colour between old rose and russet. A single branching vein wound around the shaft, a graceful decoration, as if a Japanese painter had dashed it there for the sake of design. The crown was full, almost round, the two halves forming one mouth-watering whole.

Given his claim that he needed touching to come, she was surprised to find him so hard. She wondered if he had a problem with sensitivity, but as she began to stroke him in earnest it became apparent this was not the case. If anything, he was more sensitive than most men. The lightest touch provoked a dramatic response. He seemed alive to every nuance of every caress. She brought his inner thighs into her strokes, scratching up their hair-roughened skin. That made him quiver too.

A tiny thrill rolled across her shoulders as she imagined how he'd respond to a blow job. Very well, she thought. Very well indeed.

But touching him this way was a pleasure in itself. He was a fine, sensitive instrument and it was a joy to play on him. He shivered as she rubbed her thumbs in slow opposing circles over the hot zone beneath his glans. His neck sagged.

'Good Lord,' he said. 'You've got a sweet pair of hands.'

Still stroking with her thumbs, she added a rhythmic squeeze by compressing his shaft between the heels of her palms. His chest muscles tightened. He bit his lower lip so hard that the skin turned white. Any other man would have been coming. Any other man would have come twice over.

'What's wrong?' she asked softly. He focused on her with an effort. His face was dark with blood, his pupils dilated. 'Why can't you come?'

He groaned then pulled in a breath. 'My body's greedy,' he said. 'It likes to hang on to its pleasures. I –' He huffed again. 'I never did have the knack of coming quick. Not even as a boy.'

'Hm.' Julia's smile was just short of a laugh. 'I'm beginning to understand why you're so popular.'

'Are you? Well, that's something.' He closed his eyes at a subtle change in her stroke. 'Lord, that's perfect.' His buttocks tightened on her belly. He covered her hands with his own, more feeling their motion than guiding it. 'Yeah, that's – that's – ah, you've got such nice, big hands. Can you curl your fingers over the head? Can you? Oh, yes.'

He groaned his approval, his body rocking with pleasure, gently, dreamily. His expression was beatific. He wet his lips and rolled his head. His cock swelled between her hands and her pussy clenched in sympathy. Soon, she thought. Any second.

'Julia,' he said. 'God.' Then he came. The contraction was so slow his seed didn't spurt from his penis, it oozed. It flowed over her fingers and down his shaft and still he came, the pulses so pronounced she could count each one. They lasted a long time, at least a minute. Julia's mouth was hanging. Tantrists trained for years to come like this. How did an ignorant cowboy stumble on to the mystery, unless he came by it naturally . . .

His orgasm ended with a low sigh. He looked ready to keel over, so she tugged him forward, on to her. He was heavy but she was sturdy enough to support his weight. It seemed natural to put her arms around his back, necessary even. He was nice and warm and all this sweat was giving her a chill.

'Wow.' He turned his face into her neck. 'I've never felt anything like that. What did you do to me?'

'I – nothing.'

His chuckle rumbled against her throat. 'I understand. A woman like you needs her secrets.' He shifted higher and kissed the delicate hair that curled in front of her ear. 'You realise we're going to have to do this again, don't you? And next time –' his tongue crept out to wet her cheekbone '– I'm determined we'll both be naked.'

A sudden panic tightened Julia's chest. She should have fought it, but she didn't. She pushed him hard and squirmed out from underneath him. 'I need to shower,' she said. 'I'm getting cold.'

He was too sluggish to follow, though he did call out for her to wait. She didn't listen. The door to the ladies' shower had a lock. She used it.

There was only so much temptation a red-blooded woman could withstand.

His hand gripped the barred door so hard his palm hurt. He swore up a blue streak. He thought he'd had her this time; thought he'd finally found the answer. But here she was, shutting him out like before. He was hard again already. He wanted to slide inside her so bad he could taste it. She was naked behind this door. The water was pounding her lush pink flesh and he couldn't do a damn thing to join it.

He rolled his forehead against the metal. Patience, he told himself. Patience and courage were the primary qualifications of a good trainer. He was making progress. All he had to do was stick with it and eventually she'd come round. Eventually.

He tilted his head and stared at the arch above his head. If you love me, God, he mouthed, you keep that snow a-comin'.

Chapter Six

Saturday afternoon

Julia curled up by the fire with her biography of Alexander the Great, determined to spend a quiet and solitary afternoon. Alas, it was not to be. The wind picked up at one, wailing around the mountain like an army of lost souls. At two the power flickered. At four it died. Laughing and joking, the three portfolio managers joined her in the great room. Marty handed her the yellow legal pad on which he'd been taking notes.

'I've got writer's cramp,' he complained.

Julia took one look at his illegible scrawl and decided it was just as well.

Zach passed by with a torch and toolbox. He stuck his head in the entryway. 'Don't worry,' he said. 'I'll have the generator running in no time.'

Two hours later they were still working by firelight. Against her will, Julia found herself worrying about Zach. The cellar had to be freezing without any electric heat. She set her notes aside and stood up.

'Where are you going?' Carolyn asked.

'To rescue our host,' said Marty.

Carolyn popped up in her seat. 'I'll get him.'

'You're working,' he said, and tugged her back with one hand. He turned his eyes to Julia. 'Tell that cowboy to screw the generator. There are hungry people up here.'

As she'd expected, the cellar was icy. Zach had the generator in pieces on the floor. His lips were blue and the torch was dimming, but he was clearly reluctant to leave the enemy unvanquished. Such perseverance was admirable, she supposed, but stupid. A memory caught her blindside: the general sitting in the back yard repairing the chain on her bike. She couldn't have been more than twelve. He'd looked up at her and smiled. He had a dimple in one cheek and a cowlick where his hair parted. He'd seemed so normal, so much like any girl's father . . .

Rather than examine the sudden tightness in her throat, she planted her hands on her hips. 'Marty says he's hungry.'

Zach took one last reluctant look around. 'Guess this will have to wait till morning.'

'Guess it will,' she agreed.

They moved together to the stairs. As he had that morning, he ushered her up by laying his hand in the small of her back. Most men she knew wouldn't have dared. He had big hands. The chill of his fingers seeped all the way through her sweater. She fought an urge to either shake him off or chafe his cold extremities between her own. Rule yourself, she scolded, and managed to do neither.

But her control failed when they reached the kitchen. He'd been up since dawn, he'd spent the afternoon slaving in a frigid cellar, and now he had to cook dinner for four spoilt New Yorkers. Going soft was one thing. Being fair was quite another.

She followed him into the darkened room. 'I'll help,' she said.

He squeezed her shoulder, his smile brightening the gloom. 'Stove runs on gas, darlin', though I'd love the company.'

'I'm not company. I'm an extra pair of hands.' And I'm not your darlin', she almost added, except that she would have sounded snippy. Besides which, there was a tiny corner of her psyche that welcomed the endearment.

So I'm human, she thought, trying to throw off her irritation. This was not a surprise. The only surprise was that this particular man had inspired the weakness.

'I'd like to help,' she said more smoothly. 'You shouldn't have to do everything yourself.'

He laughed, the sound oddly joyous. 'Come on in then. We'll fire up this chuck wagon.'

He lit candles, more than they needed, and spread them across the tables and counter tops. Despite her resolve to remain aloof, she couldn't quite resist the mood he set. Even to a woman of her unorthodox experience, candles spelt seduction. When he handed her an icy German beer, her barriers wavered.

'Got to drink it before it thaws,' he said, and clinked her bottle with his own. 'Now.' He stared at the refrigerator as if reading its contents through the door. 'What do you think about three-alarm chilli?'

'I think very highly of it.'

He winked sideways at her, obviously attuned to her deadpan humour. 'Me, too. Especially on a snowy night. You can chop, can't you?'

'I can,' she said, 'and stir and measure, too.'

'Whooey.' He slapped his thigh. 'I knew you were a find.'

She laughed in spite of herself. The cowboy was cute when he loosened up. They worked in companionable silence until her curiosity got the better of her.

'Tell me about the rodeo,' she said as she stirred the cornbread batter.

He looked up from his pan of frying meat, his eyes shining with pleasure. 'You don't want to hear my ancient history.'

'I do,' she insisted. 'Tell me how many bones you've broken.'

'No more'n half a dozen.' He rotated one wrist in demonstration. 'Only got one pin. I know a rodeo clown who sets off metal detectors at the airport.'

'A clown?'

He tossed a bowl of onions into the ground beef. 'Clowns are the rescue workers of the rodeo. They pry riders loose if they get tangled in their gear. If somebody falls off, they distract the bulls so they don't get gored. They're the bravest, craziest men you'd ever want to meet. Braver than firefighters.'

She supposed this was high praise in a state with so much forest land. His hand stalled in the act of pulling a can of beans from the cabinet above his head. He was smiling faintly, his admiration for the men and his love of the sport written in his face.

After a moment, he looked back at her. 'You sure you want to hear this stuff?'

She nodded, feeling like a child waiting for a bedtime story. He must have read the sincerity of her interest, because he told her. He told her about bulls that tossed grown men over arena walls. He told her about horses that bucked so hard they'd go over backwards. He told her about roping calves with Starlight, and how Gracie the cow-dog once saved a junior rodeo champ from getting trampled by a sheep. Acts of bravery peppered his tales, and stupidity, and sorrow.

Finally, he covered the chilli pot and leant back on the counter, his thumbs tucked into the belt loops on either side of his crotch. 'You know what handlers say when you're waiting in the chute and you've drawn a hard ride, the kind of bronc that comes blowing out like Satan's minion?'

She shook her head.

'They say "cowboy up", which basically means grab your balls and hang on.'

'Gird your loins?' she suggested.

'Precisely.'

'But you want to draw a horse that bucks hard, don't you? So the judges will give you more points?'

He nodded in approval. 'A good stock contractor treats his animals better than his children. He won't ever try to break a rodeo bronc. A tame ride is a bad ride, and a bad ride won't bring in the crowds. Some folks say rodeo is hard on the animals and I don't deny that might be true in some cases. But I've drawn rides I knew were having as much fun as I was. When they toss you off, they'll prick up their tails and prance. King of the world. Bell rings after eight seconds, you know, and most riders have been bucked off long since. Cowboy might get the prize buckle, but the animal always wins.'

Julia paused in the act of chopping broccoli. 'You loved that life, didn't you?'

Zach grinned and blotted his forehead with his sleeve. The gesture half-hid his rosy cheeks. 'Yes, I did. But I've grown some since then. Now I'd rather have the horse working with me. Whew.' He coughed into the checkered flannel of his shirt. 'I haven't talked this much in years. You'll make me hoarse.'

'You tell a good story,' she said. 'I could listen all night.'

He looked down at his work boots, his cheeks flushing darker. Julia's heart beat out of time. He was going to ask her to spend the night with him. She could feel it. I want to make love to him, she thought, taking stock of her body, how warm it was inside, how easy and oiled.

He looked up and her heart stopped altogether. Could eyes really be that blue? Could they hold wisdom and simplicity and fondness all at once? The fondness surprised her the most. She didn't know what she'd done to earn it. She was sure he'd had avid listeners before. Unless, as he claimed, he didn't often talk this much. She could hardly hold his gaze it was so intense. Emotion glittered in his eyes. His hand moved. She knew he was going to touch her cheek; knew he was going to kiss her. What's more, she knew she was going to enjoy every second.

'Hey,' said Marty from the door to the kitchen. Zach's hand fell. Julia stepped back. 'What's all this laughing I hear? Who said you're allowed to have fun without the rest of us?'

'That's right,' Carolyn seconded, only her complaint wasn't so jovial. The gaze she sent from Zach to Julia was hard.

Zach patted Julia's shoulder. 'Julia here has been pitching in. She's earnt a laugh or two.'

Carolyn drew in a sharp breath. Before she could say she would have helped, too, Zach offered everyone a beer. Julia shook off her disappointment. The moment was over and good riddance. She had no reason for regrets.

* * *

105

They ate on their laps before the fireplace, washing the spicy chilli down with bottles of icy beer. Julia relaxed into the mellow mood. The VPs had progressed at their mission and the blizzard made everyone glad for shelter and company. Marty had thirds of everything and Carolyn actually emptied her bowl.

'This is nice,' said Ben. He sat on the braided hearth rug at Julia's feet, his long legs crossed, his elegant head resting on the couch cushion beside her knee. 'We ought to leave the generator off all weekend.'

Marty cracked another beer and passed it to him. 'I don't know, Ben. You may be singing another tune when you toddle off to your icy bed.'

'Guess I'll have to recruit a bunkmate.'

For a second everyone was speechless.

'Ben,' Carolyn giggled, too drunk to realise how silly she sounded. 'I didn't know you could be so naughty.'

Ben tipped his head back and winked at Julia. 'A lot of people didn't.'

Oh, Ben, she thought, stroking his temple with her thumb. If you only knew how tempted I am. She heard Zach shift in the opposite corner of the couch and knew he was watching her. She sat Indian style, but his legs were stretched out, his white-socked feet mere inches from her thighs. She fought an urge to check his reaction or, worse, reassure him that she had no intention of sleeping with the beautiful young man. Slowly, she pulled her hand back from Ben. She felt preternaturally aware of her own body, of the embrace of the leather couch, of her sex pulsing inside the soft buckskin trousers. She shouldn't have worn them again. She could still feel his fingers dipping inside her; could still taste his kiss. She curled her hand into a fist. She had to stop obsessing on Zach. She had to pull herself together.

'We should tell stories,' Marty said. Carolyn groaned but, as usual, he ignored her. 'Hey, what better way to warm up a cold night? We'll trade firsts.'

'Firsts?' Carolyn was curled into an armchair by Zach's end of the couch. Marty sat at her feet even as Ben sat at Julia's. 'You mean sexual firsts?'

'Exactly.' Marty's grin was pure mischief. 'And everyone has to tell something really intimate, so we'll all be equally easy to blackmail.'

'Hm.' Ben sounded doubtful. 'What if everyone tells their most embarrassing first and the last person chickens out?'

The senior VP had an answer for that, too. 'The least trustworthy person goes first.'

'Well, that would be Julia,' said Carolyn.

Marty and Ben both laughed. 'Like hell,' said Marty. 'That would be you.'

'Me?'

Marty squeezed her knee. 'Yes, little miss I-couldn't-keep-a-secret-if-you-paid-me.'

The fire wasn't the only thing turning Carolyn's face pink. 'I can too keep a secret.'

Marty shrugged. 'Now's your chance to prove it.'

'Fine. I'll tell you something so outrageous you'll have to work hard to top it.' She sat up straighter and stuck out her narrow chest. 'All right, listen and learn, Marty. This is the story of the first cock I ever saw.'

'Big deal,' he scoffed.

Carolyn smacked the side of his head. 'For your information, it happened to be my Uncle Biff's.'

Ben squirmed. 'Are you sure you want to tell us this? You have been drinking and maybe tomorrow you'll regret it.'

'Don't be silly, Ben. I can hold my liquor. Besides –'

she flicked a lock of hair from her brow '– someone has to get the ball rolling.'

Marty lifted his beer. 'Here's to rolling balls.'

'Stow it,' said Carolyn, and composed herself to begin. 'OK. When I was growing up, my family had a big beach house on Martha's Vineyard where we spent the summers. Between grandparents, parents, cousins and my six uncles there were almost thirty of us. Grandpa Herbert had married four times and had children by every wife, so by the time Uncle Biff came along, there were only five years' difference between him and the eldest child of Grandpa's first son, which was me.'

'Oy,' said Marty. 'My head is spinning already.'

'Ahem. Do you want to hear this or not?' Marty pretended to zip his lips. Carolyn resumed. 'Despite the measly five years' difference between us, Biff liked to lord it over me, never letting me forget that he was a member of the ruling generation. For sixteen years he made my summers hell until, lo and behold, the means to torment him fell into my lap.'

'When you blossomed?' Marty suggested, leering in anticipation.

Carolyn smiled down her nose at him. 'Yes, I blossomed and Biff noticed with a vengeance. He was mortified that I, his former victim, suddenly possessed the power to make him jump in his jock just by walking into a room. The fact that his desire was forbidden only made it worse. But even if he'd wanted to bully me into gratifying his unnatural longings, he couldn't with all those relatives around.

'So I could torture him as I pleased. I could wear my shortest shorts and my teeniest tops. I could sit on his lap when we piled into the car to go to the drive-in, and I was forever brushing against him "accidentally".

Unfortunately for Biff, on top of being a young man in his prime, he'd inherited Grandpa Herbert's sex drive. My cousins and I started placing bets on how quickly I could drive him to the bathroom to masturbate. Five minutes was the record, but I preferred those times when he could make no escape and I could force him to suffer for hours.

'This might have gone on all summer were it not for my staying home one day to nurse a younger cousin who'd taken a bad case of sunburn. The poor thing had finally fallen asleep when who should wander back from the beach but dear Uncle Biff. He pretended he'd returned for a book, but in truth he couldn't stay away from me.

'We sat in the kitchen talking about the universities I might go to. He wanted me to attend Harvard, like he did. I preferred Princeton, but I let him chatter and, as I did, I drew one foot up on my chair and pretended to scratch my knee. I had my usual short-shorts on. To make matters worse, for Biff at least, they were loose in the leg and I wore nothing beneath them.

'All of us girl cousins had taken to grooming our bikini hair that summer. I'd trimmed mine so close that poor Uncle Biff barely had a veil of smoke to shield his gaze from my bare pink pussy. His eyes kept sliding down my thigh to make sure he was really seeing what he thought he was seeing.

'Now Biff was a slim, lanky guy: good-looking in a preppy way and hung like a horse. All he had to restrain his giant organ was a pair of yellow Speedos. You can take it from me they weren't up to the task. He was so hard I could see the slit of his cock where it pressed the stretchy cloth. My sixteen-year-old eyes were popping, but I wasn't about to be distracted from my goal. I spread my legs a little wider and trailed my finger down the cleavage of my halter top. I was getting off on teasing him, of course, so my nipples stood out like bullets.

'As soon as Biff caught sight of them he stood, mid-sentence, and scurried off to the bathroom, so hard he was bow-legged.

'Well, the house was virtually empty and my curiosity was roused beyond resistance. I tiptoed after Biff and flung open the bathroom door. He had his dick in his hand and was pumping like mad, his face as red as if he'd been a sunburn victim. He turned when he saw me, said something like, "Oh, God, Caro" and dropped his quivering pole.

'It didn't drop far. In fact, it stood a little higher as I watched. I couldn't believe how huge he was. His dick was longer than my hand and thick around. The head was dark, almost purple, and a bead of clear fluid was rolling down the groove between the halves. The sight made my heart pound. Biff's, too. I could see a vein throbbing in his belly where he'd shoved his swimsuit down. His pubic hair was honey gold and not very thick. He was breathing hard. The noise of it filled the whole bathroom except for the sound of the tap dripping: drip, drip, like cream dripping from my pussy.

'His hand flexed at the top of his thigh and I knew he wanted to touch himself again; knew he could hardly bear not to. I was sure he wanted me to watch, but I had something even better in mind.

' "I could help you with that," I said, strolling into the room like a pint-sized Queen of Sheba. "But it would have to be a trade. You see, I need some help with this." I slipped my hand up the leg of my shorts and into my pussy. He moaned when he saw my fingers disappear. Before I knew it, he was on his knees eating me out. He was so sloppy it made me laugh,

110

but it was exciting, too. He ate me as if he really loved the taste, just sticking his whole face in there, you know? It didn't take me long to come and when I did there was no mistaking it. My body stiffened like a board and I moaned so loudly I could only hope our little cousin was a deep sleeper. Beads of sweat popped out on Biff's brow at the sound.

'"Now me," he said. I wasn't what you'd call sated, but what did I know about being assertive back then? What he'd asked seemed fair enough and I did want to touch him. Other boys had tried to get me to do it but, oddly enough, I never felt as safe with them as I did with Uncle Biff.

'"Like this?" I said, and took him in a grip better suited for opening pickle jars. Biff yelped and said, "Easy. Rub it easy. That's it." He clutched his balls with one hand and dragged my hand up and down his pole with the other. It was love at first touch, I think. I adored how hard I could make him, how he jumped in my hand and how, just by rubbing his dick, I could make my enemy beg for mercy. "Ooh, rub the head. Please, please," he said, sounding as if he'd sell his soul to have me do it. I wrapped my second palm over the helmet. It was slippery from all the pre-come he was leaking. He shuddered as soon as I moved. "Yes," he said. "Right there." Around and around I went, loving the satiny hardness of it, the fruit-ripe swell. Biff's knees started to twitch and his head fell to my shoulder. "So good," he said. "So fucking good."

'Poor Biff tried to make it last but his hormones were up and I'd been pushing his buttons for weeks. He started to whimper like the family dog when it needs to go out. He put his hand around mine again and squeezed it tighter. "Faster," he said. "Twist your palm on top. Oh, Christ." Then his cock got even hotter and stiffer, and he started to thrust really fast through my grip.

'"Are you going to come?" I asked, because I didn't want to miss anything. But he could only groan because he was shooting into my palm already and dripping on the floor. I'll never forget how those little pulses felt, all warm and slippery. I'd always thought there'd be more but, even so, watching him come was very cool. I especially liked the way his body tensed, as if that much pleasure was hard work. He made noises, too, grunting like weightlifters do. As soon as it was over, I knew I couldn't wait to do it again.'

'So did you?' asked Marty, craning his head around to look at her.

Carolyn curled her hands over her knees and smiled. 'That,' she said primly, 'would be another story.'

Julia clapped, sincerely this time. 'Very nice, Carolyn. Marty will be hard-pressed to match that.'

Carolyn flushed with pleasure. Marty rolled his eyes and rubbed his stubbled cheeks. His knees were drawn up, but the shadow between them could not hide the bulge that Carolyn's account had inspired. A quick look around told Julia the other men were in similar straits. She felt nicely steamed herself. Someone was going to get lucky when this gab-fest ended. She could personally guarantee it.

'Well,' said Marty. 'I admit that was an arousing little anecdote, but it's nothing to the tales I could tell.'

'Oh, bull,' said Carolyn. 'Put your money where your mouth is.'

'I'd be happy to, my dear, if you'd be kind enough to reach me another beer.'

Carolyn grumbled, but she pulled a bottle from the snow-filled cooler. She opened it, too. Julia hid a smile beneath her downturned face. Carolyn really was born to serve.

Marty took a long swig and cleared his throat. 'I'm not going to tell you what kind of first this is because I'd hate to ruin the surprise. But this first came into being because my wife took a liking to the new pool-boy. We bought a place on Long Island last year. As some of you know, Didi has a competitive streak as long as the Great Wall of China. When she heard the neighbour ladies cooing over what a studly specimen the pool-guy was, she decided she would be the first to seduce him.

'It wasn't an unrealistic expectation. Didi's a good-looking woman: pretty face, great tits. Plus, she knows how to chat a guy up. Pretty soon the pool-guy's giving her special discounts on chlorine and shit, drinking her lemonade, staring at her breasts – all of which I gotta hear about *ad nauseum*, so I can be jealous, of course. Being the bastard that I am, and knowing my wife pretty well, I pretend I don't give a shit. But she's still got the neighbour ladies to impress, so she doesn't give up. Finally, she manages to lure the pool-guy into the house where he sees our wedding picture. "Ah, you're married," he says and naturally she uses that as an excuse to tell him what a skunk I am; how I cut up her charge cards the month before; how I go at her in bed till she feels like a hamburger, which isn't true, mind you. OK, once she got this cramp and I was, uh, too caught up in the moment to stop, but I swear it's not a regular thing. I would never –'

'We're sure it was only the once,' Julia assured him. 'You may continue.'

Marty rubbed his temples and sighed. 'OK, enough of the domestic discord. The thing you need to know about Didi is, she may be devious, but she couldn't pull off a plot if Mussolini came back from the dead to hold her hand. Rather than *shtup* the pool-guy while she's got him oozing sympathy, she decides she's going to set up an assignation and then arrange for me to walk in on it. Then I'll be sorry, she reckons. Then I'll know she means business.

'Well, God knows how she convinces the pool-guy to come at the appointed time, but she does. Then she calls me at work saying the hot-water heater burst and I need to come home to help mop up. I'm not happy about it, but she's crying, so I say OK and head for my car. So far, so good – only Didi's forgotten it's not rush hour, which cuts my drive in half. She decides she has just enough time to run to Victoria's Secret for something to wow the pool-guy. Thing is, her luck being what it is, on the way back she gets stuck in traffic.

'Meantime, I get home, throw off my jacket, roll up my shirtsleeves and call out her name. No answer. Then I hear a voice from the bedroom. It doesn't sound like her but, who knows, she's been crying. Maybe she got froggy. I walk in and there's the pool-guy lying across my bed, stark naked, with his big, meaty *schlong* pointing at the ceiling. I see why the neighbour ladies think he's a stud. He's built like a swimmer, big chest, narrow hips, muscles so lean you'd think they were painted on. And that thing in his fist is nine inches, easy. He's working it kind of lazy, as if he's got all day and isn't worried about losing his edge. He's also got a dozen of my favourite Pierre Cardin ties scattered around the mattress. Well, I don't understand the ties, but I can add two and two, except I'm not adding it quite the same as the pool-guy.

'"Where's Didi?" he says. Well, if he doesn't know, I sure don't. Then he waves his hand. "That don't matter," he says. "I'd just as soon start without her."

Turns out, ever since this guy saw yours truly in the wedding photo, he's had a yen for me. For me, hairy old Marty Fine. Didi promised him a threesome. Guess she reckoned I'd walk in on them, blow a gasket, and she'd never have to pay up.'

'So what did you do?' asked Carolyn.

'I didn't know what to do. I'm standing there, my jaw hanging, kind of pole-axed, and the pool-guy – Barry was his name – rolls over and puts his hand on my crotch. That's when I realise I'm hard. I've got the Eiffel fucking Tower in my trousers and I don't even know it till he touches me. He smiles and his teeth are so white against his tan that he just about blinds me. "You know," he says, "you really haven't had a blow job until you've had a blow job from a guy." The words send this weird shiver through my cock. This Barry's no dummy. He can see I'm nervous but he knows there are plenty of guys who won't turn down a blow job, no matter who's offering, and, God knows, I guess I'm one of them. But "Is it really better?" I say, trying to sound sceptical. "It's better," he assures me. "A guy's mouth is harder and bigger. I can swallow you whole, Marty. And I won't be pissing and moaning about my jaw getting tired because I'll be loving every minute." "Well," I say, while what feels like a rumba band plays in my dick. "If you do me, I gotta do you. I may be a skunk, but I have my principles." "This is not a problem," says Barry, and he flashes that grin again, like an ad for a good orthodontist.

'So we get me undressed and we lie on the bed and he goes for it. It's everything he promised, only better. His mouth isn't just hard, it's soft, and – swear on my mother's grave – loving. I never felt as if anybody loved my cock before, but this guy worships it. He's got me so wet I'm dripping and I've only met one other person, who shall remain nameless, who used her hands the way this guy used his hands. He gave me a full cock-and-ball massage. Every time I got close to shooting, he'd back off and start again. I'm not ashamed to say that after the first couple of times I was crying like a baby. "Please," I finally say. "Please let me come." Then I see what he means by having a strong mouth. He sucks me so hard I can feel my skin stretching. He's got his thumbs on my balls and his fingers kneading my thighs, and I feel this tingle start in my toes. It races up my legs and into my tailbone and, whoom, I'm shooting my load down his throat. The orgasm is so strong I feel as if my eyelashes are coming. "Oh, God," I think as I'm lying there like a dishrag. "Now I've got to do him."

'But he don't want me to. He wants me to kiss him which, to me, seems harder than giving him a blow job. But I believe in fair play so I give it a go and, what do you know, soon I'm getting into this, too. He's a beautiful kid. Maybe it's a narcissism thing or maybe I'm not as straight as I thought. Whatever, I'm liking the feel of him in my arms. It gives me a kick that I can arouse him, as if I've got this power I never suspected I had. I mean, I'm used to turning women on, but men, this is new to me. Anyway, after a bit of rolling around and kissing, I'm hard again myself. "Take me in the ass," he says. Whoa. My eyes are bugging at this. I've never even taken a woman that way. But Barry's a persuasive guy and between the novelty of it and the second massage that he gives me rubbing the KY jelly over my cock, I'm pretty well up for it. So he lies down on the bed with his butt in the air and his legs bent up like a frog's. "Take it slow," he says. "You're thicker than I'm used to."

'Damned if I don't feel flattered. It takes ten minutes

116

to get me in and we're both laughing. That's weird, too, 'cause it's like two guys laughing over beers or something. A new twist on male bonding. I didn't expect it to be fun and I feel, I don't know, excited as hell, but relaxed, too, 'cause it's just us guys and who cares if I fuck up. He's feels incredible down there. It's smooth and tight and it moves like a woman moves inside. I guess Barry likes the way it feels, because he's groaning and saying, "Thrust, Marty, thrust!"

'I do, of course, and it's incredible. Soon we're huffing and puffing and sweating like pigs. The bed is making this God-awful racket and I'm praying Didi won't come back from wherever the hell she is, because I really want to see this to the finish. Barry's starting to sound pretty desperate himself, so I reach under him and grab his cock. He's hard the way only twenty-year-olds get hard and hot enough to burn my palm. He shoves himself into my hand and on to the mattress with so much force my wrist goes numb. "Yeah," he says. "Oh, fuck, yeah," and a second later we're both blasting off. I mean, the first time we ever screwed and we're coming together like Romeo and fucking Juliet. "That's the first time that ever happened to me," he says. "But I hope it won't be the last." God help me if I know what to say to this. I'm still shaking. I don't know what I want, so I say: "Tell me one thing, Barry. What are the fucking neckties for?" "Ah," he says. "That was your wife's suggestion. She says you like being tied up."'

'Do you?' Carolyn asked.

'Hell, no. That was probably Didi's idea of a joke.'

Ben turned and draped his elbow over Julia's leg. 'So what did Didi do when she got home?'

'Nothing. Barry was long gone by then. Didi probably decided he'd never showed, so she made up some story to explain why she'd lied about the hot-water heater. I pretended to believe it and we went out for a nice dinner.' Marty grinned. 'As you might imagine, I'd worked up an appetite.'

Carolyn couldn't contain her curiosity. 'So did you see Barry again?'

'That,' Marty said with an echo of her own finish, 'would be another story.'

Carolyn glared at him, then reached over to pat Zach's arm. 'You next, Zach. We want to hear your story.'

'Um,' said Zach. The leather creaked as he shifted in discomfort. Julia looked at him, wondering if he'd open up to everyone the way he had to her in the kitchen. She wanted to hear his story, but she also wanted those moments to be special. His eyes lifted and found hers. His smile woke a hidden fan of wrinkles. Something hot and sharp pricked her breastbone. A flush crept over her cheeks. He couldn't know what she was thinking. He couldn't.

'I'm just an observer here,' he said.

'No, no,' said Marty. 'You've broken bread with us. You're one of the gang now. You've got to spill your guts.'

Zach shook his head, his eyes still warm on Julia's. 'I don't mean to be rude, and I appreciate your letting me sit in, but I don't have it in me to tell a story like that.'

Julia knew he did but she didn't say a word, not even when Carolyn and Marty set up a chorus of pleas.

'I'll go,' said Ben, probably more out of sympathy for Zach than any desire to be the centre of attention.

His offer distracted Marty. 'Ben-ster!' he said. 'Reveal your mysteries. Invite us into the seamy, steamy world of the private Ben Isaacs.'

Ben's chuckle sounded embarrassed, but not painfully so. 'I don't know how seamy this story is, but it definitely was a first for me.' He drew his long legs up and wrapped his arms around them. His eyes glowed in the firelight, green as glass. Ben's mother had come from Jamaica and his faint, second-hand accent made the words flow like music. 'All right,' he said. 'A few months ago I went to a club in my old neighbourhood. It's not a bad neighbourhood, but it's not a great one, and the Blue Note is strictly low rent: the kind of place you don't want to see in the light of day. At night, though, with candles on the tables and fans turning the smoky air, it can stake a claim to ambience. Sometimes the floor is sticky, and sometimes the smoke isn't all tobacco. But the food is always good and the music . . .' Ben shook his head. 'The music is a beautiful secret whispered in the dark.'

'Old timers play there, old jazz greats no one ever heard of and no one ever will, because they can't get out from under bad breaks and worse habits. Sometimes, in the middle of a set, one of the musicians will nod off under the influence of his personal poison. Nobody's surprised. The manager walks over and shakes him awake. No big deal. It's a sad place, I guess, but when those old guys play you can hear devils and angels falling in love. I go there to remind myself where I came from; of the pitfalls I want to avoid and the riches I can't bear to lose. I never hear the same riff twice at the Blue Note, but I always know what I'll find.

'Not this night, though. This night there's something different. A woman is dancing in front of the stage, a customer, not a performer. Everyone's watching her because people don't dance at this club. They drink

119

their drinks and they smoke their smokes, and they sit real quiet and listen.

'I can see this woman is stoned out of her mind: drunk, it looks like. She's wearing a skin-tight red satin dress and a couple of carats' worth of diamonds around her neck. She's got the body of a geisha, slim, firm, girlish curves. And, man, can she dance. It's a slow, snaky kind of dance, with her body curling out and pulsing back like Eve in the garden. Her eyes gaze off into the distance. She's the only white woman in the place and I know there's going to be trouble. It's not a bad crowd, but it's not Sunday school and she stinks of too much money and booze.

'The crowd knows there's going to be trouble, too. They're holding their breath as if they're waiting for a car wreck. Then the woman turns and I realise I know her. I can't remember her name, but she's the wife of someone I met at an office party. She's got the eyes of a wounded doe, like bruises in her face. You know how some women seem to ask for trouble just by breathing? As if there's a sign on their forehead that says: I've been hurt before and now it's your turn?'

Ben paused. The fire crackled in the hush. He pressed his fingers into his thighs, steepling them until the pale ovals of his nails turned white. He didn't look at Carolyn, but the omission required such force of will that both Marty and Zach turned their eyes to her. If she noticed any parallels to her own character she didn't show it. She was listening so raptly her delicate pink lips were parted with anticipation.

'What next?' she whispered. 'Did you go to her?'

'Well, I couldn't just stand there and watch. I squeezed through the tables and said, "I'm Ben Isaacs. Do you remember me?" "Oh, Ben," she says in this whispery, girlish voice. "You'll dance with me, won't you?"

'I guess I got mad, or maybe I was afraid she wouldn't listen if I was polite, because I said, "Don't be a stupid cunt, Mrs X." I remembered her name then. I remembered it as soon as I heard her voice.

'She looked like a little owl blinking at me, as if she'd never dreamt anyone would call her a stupid cunt. Before she could get into any more trouble, I grabbed her arm and dragged her out of there. Nobody stopped me. I guess they didn't want to see a car wreck after all.

'When we got to my Audi, she wouldn't tell me where she lived. "Take me to your place," she kept saying. "Take me to your place, beautiful Ben, and we'll fuck until the sun comes up." She thought this was funny. She had this husky little laugh with a catch in the middle. The sound of it was making me hard. She'd squirmed over to my side of the seat and she ran her hand up and down the inside of my thigh. She didn't touch my cock, but that was worse somehow, because then I wanted her to touch it even more.

'She was gorgeous with her hundred-dollar haircut and her red satin gown and some stinging sweet perfume, like a hothouse orchid set by a fire. I couldn't drive around for ever so in the end I did take her to my place.

'Cute, she called it, and I knew she had bigger closets. I wouldn't let her drink any more so she started to undress. I couldn't take my eyes off her. She was so fucking pale she glowed. I'm going to touch her, I thought. I'm going to put my black hands on her pale white body. Stupid, but that was all I could think of: how my hands would look on her; how her hands

121

would look on me. I was so hard my teeth were chattering.

'"You've never had a white woman before, have you?" she said. I shook my head. She beckoned me closer. Then she undressed me. I didn't lift a finger. I watched her. When all my clothes were gone she drew me down beside her on the fake Persian rug. She put my hand on her breast and sidled her leg between my thighs. "Aren't we beautiful?" she said. "Aren't we the most beautiful thing you've ever seen?" When she said it, it seemed to me we were. Her skin felt different from what I was used to, and it smelled different: more fragile, less rich. Shivers ran down my spine when she trailed her long white finger down my cock. "Fuck me," she said, and I knew I was going to.

'She didn't have a condom. I knew she wouldn't. I got one of mine and made her put it on me. She thought that was cute, too. Dudley Do-Right, she called me; said a man like me could reform a woman like her. I knew better but I didn't care. I'm going to fuck her lily-white pussy, I thought. I wanted to stop myself from thinking that way but I couldn't, like a song that's stuck in your head.

'"Ride me," I said because I wanted to watch and because you can't trust a woman like that not to go round the bend if you make a wrong move. Let her make the moves, I thought. It's worked out fine so far. She lowered herself on to me real slowly, as if she knew I wanted to see my cock disappear inside her. It was something to see. I'd never felt so big, so dark. She rode me in waves, one curving rise at a time. Her movements were so much like her dance at the Blue Note, I thought she must be hearing the music in her head: the musky smooth sax, the throaty, thrumming bass.

122

' "Put your hands on my tits," she said. Her breasts were round and high and small. I could cover them when I splayed my fingers. I squeezed the peaks between my knuckles and she moaned. That must have been all she wanted because she didn't say anything after that. She rode me until I saw stars, little flashes of white popping in the air before my eyes. I tried to wait for her to come, but I thought I'd die if I didn't let go soon. I slid one hand to her pussy and rubbed her clit. She still didn't go over. I guess she was too drunk.

' "I can't wait any more," I finally said, feeling as if my skin were going to split. "I've got to come." She just smiled and nodded, and the feeling rushed out from my cock like a rocket shooting through the night, a velvety whoosh of air and fire. It was sweet and sad and when it was over I almost wanted to weep.'

Ben rested the back of his head against the couch and closed his eyes. 'She made me breakfast the next morning. Burnt the toast and boiled over the coffee. We fucked in the shower and I found out she bites her lip when she comes. She never makes a sound until she's finished and then she sighs, as if Christmas is over for another year.' Ben sighed himself and opened his eyes. 'And that,' he said, 'is the story of my first white lover.'

'That was beautiful,' Carolyn said, without her usual gush.

Julia stroked the tightly curled hair of his head. 'Yes,' she said. 'Thank you for sharing that.'

He reached up and squeezed her hand. His palm was warm and slightly damp, his grip too intense for anything but intimacy. Julia's insides quivered. He hadn't given up on her. He still wanted her. Part of her didn't know how to be sorry.

'Your turn,' he said, his gaze steady on hers.

'Yes,' said Marty. 'Last but we hope not least.'

Julia turned her gaze from Ben's glowing green eyes to Zach's brilliant blue ones. She found no jealousy there, merely interest and warmth. Nothing threatened in that calm, weathered face: no expectations, no hopes; none that she could see, anyway. There was no earthly reason for her to be disturbed and yet the back of her neck tightened all the same. Maybe his calm was patience. Maybe he was so sure he'd win her in the end he didn't need to be jealous.

She withdrew her hand from Ben's hair. Marty threw another log on the waning fire. As he bent forward, orange light licked his blue-black curls. She watched the flames leap up, greedy and beautiful, flickering over the rough, river-stone hearth. She couldn't recall experiencing a moment like this before. The combination of camaraderie and isolation, of fear and desire, of hope and dread, was unprecedented. Almost without conscious thought she decided on a course of action. This once she would bare her soul, but not for the purpose of strengthening ties with these people.

Burn your bridges, she thought, and never look back again.

Chapter Seven

Saturday night

Julia settled more comfortably into the corner of the couch. Deep inside she was shaking, but she knew it didn't show. 'Do you mind a long story?'

'Not at all,' Marty said. 'The longer the better.'

She permitted herself a smile. 'Very well. This first begins with the general. He was not my lover, but my mother's. My father was an army aviator, a dashing, handsome fellow. He was my mother's last hope for escaping the general's allure, but twelve days before I was born his plane took a nosedive into the Arizona desert and that, as they say, was that.'

Ben and Zach gasped, surprise and pity mingling in the sound. Marty, however, nodded as if he'd expected something of the sort. His reaction was by far the more comfortable for her. She smoothed her hair back with both hands. Her father was a shadow figure to her. She'd never known how to acknowledge sympathy for his loss, and she didn't now. She continued.

'The general was a bluff, kind man; the best sort of army man: competent, hard-working, punctilious in matters of ethics, but not without mercy when the situation called for it. He was fifteen years older than my mother. They met when he was stationed in Heidelberg. She was a Zurich schoolgirl, of legal age but barely. At the time, he was only a lieutenant-colonel, though to her that seemed lofty indeed. Their acquaintance was brief, but during his leave in Switzerland they discovered they had interests in common that were near and dear to their hearts.

'The general, you see, was a sexual masochist. My mother, while not a sadist in the strictest sense of the word, had a dominating personality. Even at the age of seventeen, her gift for mastery was so pronounced that the general was unable to forget the experiences they'd shared. She became the benchmark against which all women were judged. Needless to say, the others fell short, both in skill and in trustworthiness.'

Julia bent forward, her hands locked together in one joined fist. The others leant closer as well.

'I should explain that the code of the army officer prohibits intemperance of any kind: drinking, gambling, fraternisation with officers of the opposite sex; even foul language is considered a transgression. How much more the general's particular vice! Fortunately, being Swiss, my mother was as close-mouthed as she was self-controlled. Even if the general had been capable of forswearing the whip, my mother's reserve proved too great a temptation. With her as his partner, he could indulge without fear of betrayal. As soon as he was in a position to do so, he arranged her passage to the States and established her as his secretary.

'You may imagine what indulgence followed her arrival; their appetites were all the stronger for being

126

repressed. Things reached such a pitch of depravity that my mother, despite her pragmatic nature, began to fear for her soul. This fear led her to marry my father, a decent man, if lacking in imagination. The marriage was not a resounding success for either party, but amicable enough to result in my birth a year and a half later. From a survey of my mother's papers I have deduced that her affair with the general resumed when she was four months pregnant, so it may be said that I made the general's partial acquaintance early on.

'In any case, such were the undercurrents with which I grew up: the starched khaki discipline of the army coupled, or coupling if you prefer, with the secret sybaritic discipline of the whip. I did not discover the truth of what was going on until I was fifteen, but there were hints: doors locked against my entrance; strange objects kept in boxes at the back of my mother's closet; their banked excitement whenever they were together. For years I, and many others I'm sure, thought the general must be prodigiously well hung. He was invariably erect in her presence and had to wear binding cloths around his genitals to avoid giving himself away. The constant swelling misled people as to his size, though in truth his size was not inconsiderable. The bindings may also have been part of their game. One can only imagine the discomfort involved. Of course, to a man of the general's bent, discomfort gave as much pleasure as relief. Intentionally or not, I have no doubt those bindings became, in the end, as eroticised as his belt.

'He had a particular belt, you see, that my mother used to punish him. He wore it with his army-green service uniform, which is the normal duty dress. It was thus available on a daily basis for whenever they were able to steal a private moment during the long army day. I developed a fascination for the belt myself; it seemed to hold such power, as did the general. He was the closest thing I had to a father figure and, despite his sexual obsession, there was much to admire about him. By the time I was sixteen, he was spending nights at our house. My mother and he had realised I knew what was what. Since I was no more confiding at that age than I am now, they trusted me to keep my mouth shut. I imagine they relished the added time together, though their continued need for discretion saved their passion from any diminution by being over-gratified.

'Sometime during this occasional cohabitation, I snuck into my mother's room while they slept and stole the general's belt. I'm not sure I can describe the thrill it inspired in my dewy sixteen-year-old breast. Anger played a part in it. The devotion they gave each other could not compare to the mild affection they seemed to feel for me. On top of anger was added a fear of discovery, a sense of triumph at my own daring, and a deep vibratory lust I did not completely understand. What others feel for a first lover, I felt for that belt. Quivering with excitement, I returned to my room and stripped off my clothes. Over my now naked body I rubbed the well-worn leather. I smelled it; I licked it; I wrapped it around my waist and shook so hard I could barely stand. Finally, I knelt down by my bed with my forehead resting on the mattress and drew the belt between my legs.

'The first touch of that thick brown tongue sent a jolt of sexual energy through my cunt. Its intrusion into my private flesh was more intimate to me than a human hand, more emotionally penetrating, more forbidden. With a moan I attempted to muffle in the covers, I jerked the belt taut and pulled it back and forth between my cream-drenched lips. Back and forth I worked it, back and forth, ever harder, ever faster, until I thought I would die from the intensity of the sensations ricocheting through my body. But I would not stop. Indeed, I could not. I bit the edge of the mattress and groaned. I spread my legs wider. I wrenched the belt closer to my clit and gyrated against it as if that strip of leather were something I could fuck. Fuck it I did until I feared someone must hear my ecstatic groans.

'I did not know how to come back then. I barely knew what coming was, except what I'd read in various novels. I did not believe I'd achieved orgasm yet, though, because the suspense was unbearable. I closed my eyes and re-created the most arousing image I knew: that of the general leaning over his desk with his khakis shoved to his knees while the belt, doubled over in my mother's hand, swept through the air towards his ass. His poor, happy, tortured organ had been freed from its bindings. It thrust through the tails of his shirt like a policeman's baton, jerking higher with every slash, reddening, swelling and finally jetting out a forceful spray of white.

'I came to the image of his seed dripping down the drawer that held his pencils, came like the drawn-out wail of a bugle playing "Taps". The orgasm was a revelation, a violent squeezing together of muscle and bone. I came for minutes, it seemed, shaking under the sweet attack of the nerves between my legs.' Julia drew a deep breath. 'And so ends the story of my very first orgasm.'

'No, no, no,' Marty cried, his face both red and pale, his hips shifting under the bulk of his erection. 'You can't leave it there, Mueller. That wasn't a long story at all.'

'No, not long at all,' Ben agreed. He looked far more composed than Marty, though the bulge in his crotch was equally large. Even Carolyn was pink in the face, her nipples forming distinct protrusions beneath her snug angora sweater. She looked as if she wanted to hear more, though it would have galled her to admit it. Their eagerness surprised Julia, their seeming lack of disgust.

'Very well,' she said. She risked a brief glance at Zach. He was stroking his moustache in what appeared to be bemusement. At some point during her account, he'd resettled so that his feet brushed her leg, as if she needed support, as if she deserved it. Against her will, her eyes slid downward. He was as hard as Marty or Ben. His thigh muscles were tense with it, his breathing carefully controlled but clearly altered by arousal. Why wasn't he horrified? Had she not been frank enough? Had she told the wrong story? 'Very well,' she repeated. 'I'll tell the tale of the first time I used the general's belt on someone else.'

'I knew it,' Marty said with the sharp chuckle of someone who's won a bet with himself. Carolyn backhanded his shoulder and he motioned for Julia to go on.

'There was a drill sergeant at Fort Benning,' she said, 'who was known as Hothead Hopkins. Not long after my discovery of the general's belt, he discovered my skill for fighting. When you work for the military you move around a lot. When you move around a lot, you get to be the new kid on a regular basis. I was never small, never an easy mark, but my mother had taught me to hold myself with pride; with arrogance, I suppose, and there was always one kid, usually an older boy, who wanted to put me in my place.

'One day, after watching me bloody three noses in

succession, old Hothead decided he could make use of me. He asked if I wanted to learn to fight like a soldier. When I convinced him I did, he gave me my first taste of disciplined combat. He taught me how to take someone down without spilling blood; how to get back on top when any normal person would give up. Balance was his secret, cultivated through a mélange of martial arts. Size means nothing, he would say. The fighter who controls the balance controls the outcome. Then he turned me loose on the new recruits. The administration didn't know about it, of course; they'd have tossed him out on his butt. But Hopkins thought it worth the risk. He wanted to use a pussy to beat the pussies, as he liked to call his charges; the theory being that if you break a man's pride before building it up, he owes his pride to you.

'Hopkins did not, however, realise that young men entering the military, going through basic training, sometimes discover things about themselves the army would just as soon they didn't. Even today, the military is an intense and intensely male culture. Sometimes the experience forces soldiers to acknowledge latent homosexual tendencies. Sometimes it brings out the sadist in a man. And sometimes it teaches him that being the object of rigorous, authoritarian discipline affords a thrill far beyond the thrill of measuring himself against adversity. In my case, a pair of rangers in training discovered they enjoyed being whipped by a pussy best of all. For them, my gender heightened the sexual component of the process because it introduced the possibility, however remote, that their frustration might one day be consummated.

'Hopkins ran these unorthodox pussy-whipping sessions in the back of an old supply depot. He had a wrestling mat and a chalked circle, outside of which we could not step without admitting surrender. There were no rules except that I could not break bones. Given my aptitude and his training, there was little chance of anyone breaking mine. I was permitted to draw a small amount of blood if it appeared that my opponent was pulling his punches. Some did. They could not get beyond their childhood training. I was a female and they would not hit me, no matter what I did. Their attitude was impractical, but I admit I admired them for it. Hothead could be a vengeful bastard. Refusing to fight me took as much courage as agreeing.

'I had no such trouble with the two rangers. I'd noticed they kept being singled out by Hopkins for my special brand of discipline, as if they'd screwed up on purpose in order to face me. Both were a good match for me. They fought well enough to prolong their defeats and both, especially the larger of the two, liked to get me in a clinch so that I'd have to wrestle them to the mat. This predilection proved their undoing. Old Hothead wasn't blind. Even in camouflage trousers and jockstraps, it was hard to hide the level of arousal they were experiencing.

'He called an end to the fun soon after our fourth match. He didn't say why, but I knew. I'd seen the glitter in the rangers' eyes when we faced off, the flush in their cheeks, the near sexual squirm if I pinned their bodies under mine. I'd seen these responses in the general, as I'd seen my own heightened excitement in my mother. A new flow of vitality seemed to run through my spine. I stood taller and straighter. I felt invincible.

'I wasn't surprised when the rangers began following me, discreetly, of course. I'd spot them outside the commissary or the post exchange. If their duties permitted, they'd drive by the local high school when classes were let out. They'd offer me a ride and drop me at the door to our house. They were very polite, very well behaved, but I knew why they were dogging me: I had something they wanted, something that by now they needed. They just didn't know how to ask for it.

'Unfortunately, time was of the essence. Ranger training lasted nine weeks. Once it ended, they might be posted anywhere and who knew when they'd get another chance to explore this dangerous thrill? The question was, could they trust me not to report them? That would have ruined their careers almost before they'd begun.

'I let them sweat for seven long days after Hopkins stopped the matches. Then I invited them in.

'Our house was ideally situated for private games, located off the base and separated from its neighbours by a thick screen of magnolias. It was a hot May day, insects droning, pavements baking under the Georgia sun. I offered them a glass of lemonade, freshly squeezed. We sat in the kitchen as they drank it down. We spoke of inconsequentials: school, life at the base, the last films we'd seen. Despite the calmness of the conversation, the men grew increasingly agitated, fidgeting in their chairs and reddening each time my gaze swept theirs.

'Finally, one of them, the tall redhead who liked to make me pin him, said, "We were wondering . . ."

' "I know," I cut in. "And I'm prepared to give you what you want, now, today, if you think you can take it."

'Their mouths fell open. The smaller, dark-haired one, recovered first. He had the face of a sullen angel, and a taut, wiry body. He emptied a small paper sack on to the table. Out spilt a box of condoms. "We can protect you," he said.

'My response was as icy as I could make it. "That was considerate. In the future, however, do not assume I haven't already provided for every contingency. If I wish you to perform a service, I will request it."

'He hung his head, but a quiver of excitement ran through his torso. "Yes, mistress," he said.

'It was the first time, apart from my fantasies, that anyone had called me that. It sounded very sweet to my ears. It was, however, what the general called my mother. I wished an honorific of my own. "You may call me Ms Mueller," I said. I liked the idea of making an older person refer to me the way I had to refer to my teachers. "Ms Mueller," said the young man. I knew the title was just right. It rang through my cunt as if a tuning fork had been set to the individual frequency of my lust.

'My body humming with pleasure, I directed them to my bedroom. I pulled down the shades and ordered them to undress. The air smelled of my baby powder and their sweat. The redhead was wearing Old Spice cologne, the scent of which makes me wet to this day. They folded their clothes as they progressed: shoes, socks, khaki T-shirts and camouflage trousers. I loved the respect inherent in that neatness. The army had prepared them for me in many ways, a fact that became apparent as soon as their clothes were gone. They were hard beneath those simple uniforms, hard of muscle and hard of cock, two beautiful male specimens in their prime.

'I'd never seen completely naked men before. My sense of discovery was keen. I circled them, the way a drill sergeant will, but I circled them in silence. They remained eyes and face front, as they'd been trained, and they broke out in goose-flesh under my gaze. When I'd finished my survey, I removed my school clothes. That startled them, until they saw I had my own uniform. Beneath my T-shirt and jeans I wore a black merry widow. You know, the racy undergarment with the push-up cups and lace around the edges? It was satin and snugged at the waist by an arrangement of eyelets and leather laces, like an old-fashioned corset or a boot. I looked much as I do now, full-figured but strong. The redhead moaned. Then I slipped into a pair of five-inch patent-leather heels.

'"Oh, God," said the black-haired one, overcome by the sight.

'I slapped him sharply across his cock. "Don't speak unless you're spoken to," I said, then turned and slapped the redhead for good measure. "Equal punishment, boys. What one suffers, so shall the other."

'"Yes, Ms Mueller," they said, their cocks throbbing even more forcefully from my blows. A thread of pre-ejaculate stretched downward from the dark one's helmet, glistening in the soft golden light. His fingers twitched as if he wanted to wipe it free. Catching the movement from the corner of his eye, his partner shivered in sympathy. Neither man moved.

'My heart melted and my pussy. They were so lovely, so good. But if I softened now, it would be no kindness. I reached beneath the mattress and removed the general's belt, the same belt I had stolen from my mother's room, the companion to countless frenzied orgasms. I pressed it beneath the redhead's nose. His nostrils flared, smelling the leather, smelling me. He made a sound, small and mournful, but he did not speak.

'"Good," I said and bent forward to nip the pebbled tip of his breast. "Very good."

'I repeated the favour with my black-haired angel, then shoved him until he half-fell across my bed. Before he could regain his feet, I began whipping his buttocks with the doubled belt. He had dark olive skin and his bottom was firm. He could withstand a great deal of force, but I didn't want to leave marks that would not fade within the hour. I didn't want him to get caught. Because of this, I spread the blows over his buttocks, the sides of his waist, the back of his thighs. He could not bear the excitement this caused. His hips lurched forward. He rubbed his cock against the side of my box-spring.

'"No," I said, harsh and low. I wedged the pointy toe of my shoe between him and the bed to pull him back. "I say when you take your pleasure, not you."

'He begged my forgiveness and I slapped him with the belt again, lightly this time. I caught him beneath the balls, though, so the blow genuinely stung.

'"Turn around," I ordered. "Put your hands behind your head and watch."

'His cock was so hard now it strafed his belly. The head was wet, the veins ropy and dark. Pink stripes marked the sides of his waist. The sight of them made my pussy quiver. I wanted to draw the marks across his stomach as well, but the other waited, my other, untouched servant.

'"Kneel as he was kneeling," I said.

'The redhead complied without hesitation. He stretched his arms across the mattress and gripped the covers in his fists. He had a beautiful back, broad in the shoulder, cleanly muscled under satiny skin. The crease of his buttocks was shadowed with a lick of bright-red hair. I set about bringing his skin into harmony with it.

'The other began to cry as he watched, silently,

shuddering in an ecstasy of envy. His misery enchanted me. This one has earnt a special reward, I thought. This one will take me first.

'He was ready by the time I finished marking his friend, more than ready. His balls were drawn up against his body, plump as a Georgia peach, ripe as a hothouse tomato. A steady flow of fluid drooled from his cock; there simply wasn't another word for it, the stream was so copious.

'He seemed to feel this required an apology. "I'm sorry," he said, nodding red-faced at his dripping member. "I can't help it. This makes me so horny. I haven't let myself come since the last time we wrestled." His voice dropped till I could barely hear it. "I've been wearing a special ring at night so I'll wake up if I'm about to have a wet dream."

'His confession sent chills of excitement down my neck, but I knew better than to let on. I took the flange of his cock between my fingers and pinched until his slit gaped wide and a bubble of pre-come rolled out. He made a choking noise, caught between pain and ecstasy. I put my face right up to his, drinking it in. "I didn't say you could speak, did I?" He shook his head, his cheeks gone blotchy with embarrassment. Jealous tears shone on his skin. I couldn't resist him. I pressed my lips to his trembling mouth. He didn't dare kiss me, but I knew he wanted to.

' "You may kiss me," I whispered, "and you may take me. But if you come before I do, this will never, and I mean never, happen again."

'His breath rushed from him in hot, anguished longing. "I want to, Ms Mueller," he said. "But I'm afraid the first stroke would make me come. The first touch."

'This confession pleased me as much as the other. Unable to hide a smile, I lowered myself to the floor

137

before him, my thighs spread, my elbows supporting my upper body. The merry widow fastened between my legs with a single snap. My new slave licked his lips at the dampness of the cloth. I undid the snap and peeled the satin away, baring my secrets to his gaze. He blinked rapidly and one last tear rolled down his cheek. With two careful fingers, I pinched my clit out for him to see.

' "I said you could kiss me," I reminded him. "Or don't you know how?"

'He answered with a groan, already falling towards me. "Yes, Ms Mueller, yes."

'He did know how. He knew how very well. He spread me with his fingers and worshipped me with his mouth. He lingered over the spots that made me moan the loudest, but he did not neglect the rest.

' "May I help?" pleaded the other. Before I could answer he claimed my breasts, suckling the hard, hurting tips against his teeth. I pinched him for his insolence on the well-warmed skin of his bottom. Naturally, he wriggled with pleasure and moaned for more. Laughing, I obliged him, feeling freer and more joyous than I had in all my life. Sensations overwhelmed me: the mouth at my breasts, the tongue at my clit, the overwhelming champagne fizz of power. For all my confidence, I had never been touched so intimately. I came in a series of sharp, deep beats, my whole body clenching, my whole body pleased.

' "Now," I said, stroking the hair of the dark-haired one. "You may take me."

'He rose between my legs, his body hot and slim. He rolled on the condom with a flair I shall never forget, like a magician with a deck of cards. One second the latex was housed within the packet; the next it sheathed his cock. His hands came down beside my shoulders, supporting his weight for entry. He did not guide himself, but let his cock find its own slippery way between my lips and to my gate. I held my breath and bit my lip. I think that was when he realised how inexperienced I was, because he smiled reassuringly.

'Even so, he was surprised to find me a virgin, surprised and touched. "Oh," he said, halting at the thin barrier. "Oh, Julia."

' "Do it," I said, but it was as much plea as order. I slid my hands down his back and stroked his burning buttocks. "Do it, slave."

'He thrust hard, taking me in a single stroke. His cock seemed enormous. My insides were on fire, but pleasantly so. A brief sting was all I'd suffered for the loss of my virginity. Already my sheath was beginning to undulate around the intruder, hungry for more stimulation. My lover shuddered and held fast, his head dropping towards mine until our temples brushed. His was sweaty, mine throbbing. "All right," he said. "Don't move. I think I can hold on. I think I can make you come while I'm inside you."

'I let him do as he asked, but even lying motionless I tortured him. His every thrust inspired a groan, my every sigh a tremor. The redhead knelt on the floor to watch us, his breath mirroring ours, his eyes hot. After a minute, he pressed the belt into my hand. If he couldn't do, he wanted to watch, and he wanted to watch more of what had brought us to this point. I could not scold him, because I wanted the same. I looped the belt behind my lover's back, first just tugging his waist, then pressing the stripes that flamed across his rolling bottom.

'The touch was enough to arouse him beyond control. He screwed his eyes shut and began to pant, hard, as if he were engaged in a gruelling race. His pace increased and I pushed up to meet him, my cunt swimming at the thought of what he must be feeling: the sting and burn of his ass, the wet, squirming clasp of my sex, the hard edge of the leather. My excitement rose and with it the first ache of orgasm fluttered through me. I snapped the belt against his skin, as sharp as a spank. He cried out. He thrust faster. I came once, deeply, and immediately rose again. My need to climax was immense. I caught his mouth with mine and kissed him wildly. I slapped him again. Our tongues battled, trembled, and then we both shuddered together. This time the spasm seemed endless. I swallowed his moan; I drank in his sigh. He thrust once more, to the very depth of my sheath. I felt a final pulse, his cock spitting the last of its pleasure. Then he pulled carefully out. "Thank you," he said. "Thank you very much."

'And thus began my career as a dominatrix.'

The room was silent except for the crackle of the fire. Marty rubbed his stubbled face. Ben shifted against her knee and Zach was entirely still, his hands steepled before his mouth, his eyes wide. Julia told herself she was glad she had shocked him, glad she'd shocked them all.

'Jesus,' said Carolyn, the first to regain her powers of speech. 'I had no idea. We made jokes about you cracking the whip, but I had no idea.' She rubbed her hands down the front of her thighs and Julia realised she was aroused. The story might have shocked her, but it hadn't turned her off. 'You did see those men again. I know you did.'

'Yes, I did,' Julia admitted, her voice sounding distant even to herself. 'And I do. Every year on our anniversary, they visit me. I count them among my oldest friends.'

'Wow,' said Carolyn.

'Wow,' Ben agreed. He seemed shocked in a different way, more stunned than titillated.

Marty broke the tension by chuckling. 'I don't know about the rest of you guys, but if I don't get lucky tonight, I may need medical attention.'

'Amen,' said Carolyn and, with a musical giggle, she dragged an unresisting Zach from the room.

He didn't know what to think of Julia's story; didn't want to know what to think. He held his judgment back like a wild mustang he'd roped and hobbled. He didn't want to come down on one side or the other. He didn't want to judge.

The more he learnt about Julia, the more she fascinated him. What was this world she lived in, this Tibet of sexuality, this erotic Timbuktu? As she'd spoken, he could picture himself with the belt, could almost feel it in his hand: he, who refused to wear spurs in competition, who never slapped a horse except with the flat of his palm. Stranger still, he could also picture himself kneeling before her. She exerted such a pull on him. His heart was so full. She'd had a mother who didn't know how to be soft, and a father who'd died before she was born. This control she loved: it was herself she was trying to master, her own inadmissible hurt she was trying to whip behind its barrier. He could see that as clear as the nose on his face.

But he didn't want her any the less for it. He would have kissed her feet himself if he'd thought it would ease her pain. The impulse to go on to his knees for her was so strong, so foreign, it frightened him. So he held back his judgment on that as well. When Carolyn took his hand and pulled him away, his brain was too rattled to stop her.

* * *

141

Julia sat for a long time staring at the dying fire, trying to be glad for the bridge she'd burnt, trying to pull the walls of privacy back around her soul. Her psyche felt raw. She didn't notice when Ben drifted away, though he must have said something in parting. She came aware again when Marty knelt before her and placed a hand on each of her knees.

'I want you to show me,' he said with unaccustomed seriousness. 'I want to taste what it's like.'

'Oh, Marty.' She felt as old as the hills and as sad. Despite which, part of her unfurled at the thought of a new challenge.

He took her hand and kissed its palm. 'Do you think it's wrong for me to want that? You, of all people?'

'I'm not always kind,' she warned.

'But you'll be kind to me, and at least you know kindness should rule it. Didn't you hear your own story? You're still friends with those men. They still love you.'

'They love what I do to them.'

He shook his head. 'You know, Julia, for a smart woman, you can be pretty stupid. You've got a heart the size of Texas.'

'I don't.'

'You do.' He squeezed her hand. 'I've known that since you campaigned for Rich to hire Ben. Since two years ago. Do you think I want to fuck you just because you're a goddess? I admit that's a good reason, but I want to fuck you because I like you. And I want you to give me a taste of the whip because I trust you to do it right.'

She looked at him. He seemed so sure of himself – confident, excited, curious – exactly what a sub should be.

'Very well,' she said. 'If you're going to do it, you may as well do it with me.'

She led him to her room. She pulled the steamer trunk out from under the bed and unlocked the second compartment. Her toys lay neatly inside. Whips and paddles nestled beside cock rings and nipple clamps. The costumes sat folded to the right. The scent of leather rose from most, but there was silk as well, and lace. The power of classic femininity received its due.

Marty craned around her shoulder. He touched a cock-and-ball harness, thick fingers stroking the sturdy leather. Julia filed the reaction away. 'Jeez, Julia, you brought all this stuff on a business trip?'

'My last business trip.'

He stopped breathing for a moment. 'You're not going back to DMI?'

'I'm burning my bridges, Marty.'

To her surprise, his eyes filled. He hugged her. 'I understand. Rich is a Class-A Bastard. I'm amazed you lasted as long as you did. But, damn, I'm going to miss you.'

Julia patted his back, more awkward with this embrace than with an intimate one. When he pushed away from her, teary and tender, she could barely meet his eyes. She'd just lifted her hand to cup his cheek when the door slammed open. Carolyn stood on the threshold, mascara running down her cheeks, fists clenched in anger.

'Teach me what you know,' she said. 'Teach me how to master them.'

Julia realised Zach must have rebuffed her. For a moment she was happier than she had any right to be. Then she remembered. Carolyn must have fucked him seven times by now. Zach hadn't sent her away out of concern for Julia. He'd sent her away because she'd exceeded his quota.

'What are you talking about?' she asked, stalling for time. This was the chance she'd been angling for ever since Carolyn had told her to get her own man. But now she had the means for payback, she wasn't sure she wanted it.

Carolyn stepped into the room and shoved Julia's chest. 'I want them on their knees to me. They're never going to break my heart again.'

After a two-day romance, Julia doubted her broken heart was serious. 'You mean men?'

'Of course I mean men. I want you to teach me to be a dom. I'll pay whatever you want.'

At a loss, Julia turned to Marty. He lifted his hands and backed away. 'Oh, no. I said I wanted a taste of the whip, but not if Nelly Neurotic here is wielding it.'

In spite of herself, Julia laughed. 'Don't be silly. I can't teach Carolyn to be a dom. She doesn't have it in her.' She turned back to his nemesis, the way suddenly clear to her. She would teach Carolyn a lesson all right, but a lesson she could use. 'If you want, I'll teach you to be a better sub.'

'What?' Carolyn's eyes went round. 'You want to teach me to be a better doormat?'

She did indeed have a lot to learn. Julia rubbed her arm. 'You're a naturally giving person, Carolyn, not a doormat.'

'Then why do I always lose them?' Her voice broke under a renewed threat of tears. She pressed her fist beneath her nose. Julia knew better than to offer sympathy.

'You can't lose what you've never had,' she said. 'Those men never belonged to anyone but themselves.'

'That makes me feel a hell of a lot better.'

144

'Don't fight your nature. There's as much power in submission as there is in dominance. You simply need to learn to surrender power by choice.'

Carolyn shook her arm free. 'I'm supposed to believe all those men who beg to lick your boots are powerful? What a load of crap. You don't know anything.'

'Then why are you here?'

'Because I'm an idiot.' She wiped her cheeks with her hands and stepped back towards the door. 'Never mind. I'll toughen up without you, Mueller. You wait and see.'

Julia did not protest when she left, though she knew Carolyn would fail. This was the same tone she took after every lost-another-boyfriend crying jag. 'Never again, never again,' she'd say . . . until the next time. She never learnt. She never changed. 'Men are bastards' was all the wisdom she'd managed to garner. Wearily, Julia covered her face and shook her head.

Marty squeezed her shoulders from behind. 'I suppose the mood is ruined now?'

'Yes, I'm sorry. I just can't tonight.'

He eased closer and wrapped his arms around her waist. 'It's still as cold as a witch's tit in here.'

She smiled. 'Are you asking to stay?'

'Would you kick me in the balls if I were? Oh, right, you're not in the mood.'

She turned in his hold and ruffled his curls, weariness fading in the face of amusement. 'You're welcome to stay, Marty. I could use the company.'

Zach's hand froze in the act of rapping on her door. He heard the soft, wet moans of people kissing inside. He backed to the opposite wall and closed his eyes. He'd let her do it. He'd let Julia scare him off and now he'd lost precious ground he might never regain.

He knew better. The wildest horses always tested their handlers. Half the time their wildness was fear. They'd been mistreated, or sometimes just misunderstood. Horses had quirks, like people did. You had to work to understand them. You had to be patient, and persistent, and you couldn't let them scare you off. Julia wanted him. He could feel it, and it was more than a wanting of the body. She might not care to admit it; it might frighten her, but she yearned for him the same way he yearned for her.

But now he might never have her. Time was short. This blizzard couldn't last for ever.

Chapter Eight

Sunday morning

*S*he woke before dawn. Marty lay beside her in the double bed. She'd assumed he'd snore, but he slept as peacefully as a child. What was that like, she wondered: to see what you wanted and feel justified in taking it, to harbour no regrets, no second thoughts?

She eased out from under the covers and pulled on a robe. The room was warm. The power must have come on again. She padded to the window. The snow still fell, but gently now. In the pre-dawn light she saw drifts reaching past the sill. No way in hell would they make their scheduled noon flight.

I'm glad, she thought, facing the weakness. So much remained unsettled: Zach, Carolyn, the DMI traitor, her life. She knew she wanted to part ways with Durbin, but what about her life as a dominatrix? Did she, as Marty claimed, believe those games were wrong? And if she did, was she capable of leaving them behind? Even now, a corner of her mind was juggling the possibilities, intrigued by the thought of initiating Marty and Carolyn together. Those two had an interesting dynamic. She was sure she could use it to advantage, if she chose to.

'What do you want?' she whispered, a hiss as soft as the falling snow. 'Who do you want to be?'

That was the heart of it. Who did she want to be? One thing was clear. She couldn't be who she'd been with Durbin. That door had closed. But which would open? Was the answer taking a new sub, one she liked and respected, one she could be tender with? Tender. She cast her eyes to heaven. Did she even know how?

She thought of Zach's beloved horse, the one that snapped at her every time she went near it. The mare seemed to know hers was not a gentle spirit. On the other hand, the animal's rejection had hurt her. Surely she couldn't be hurt if she didn't have a heart, and if she had a heart, she could learn to be tender.

She clasped her hands at her waist. She could learn, and she would. What's more, she would begin today.

Zach walked in around the dozenth time that the horse nipped her hand. She spun around, then spun back again, her eyes brimming with tears of frustration. 'I'm sorry. I thought she'd get used to me. I didn't mean to upset her.'

Zach chuckled and emptied his bucket into Starlight's manger. The mare immediately fell to it. 'A full stomach might improve her disposition,' he said, seeing to the colt as well, 'but it wouldn't hurt to learn how horses think.'

'Obviously, they don't think much of me.' Her voice was too sharp. She blinked hard, her vision swimming.

'Hey, hey.' Zach set his bucket down and wrapped his arm around her shoulder. The embrace felt good, too good, but she couldn't bring herself to move away. 'Horses sometimes dislike a person for no good reason. They don't fancy their perfume or their voice, and they get jealous, too. Starlight here considers me her personal property. Perhaps she's realised she's got a rival.'

'I don't know how she could tell,' Julia muttered. Zach went still. Good Lord, why had she said that? She sounded like a sulky teenager pouting for attention. If this was what Zach brought out in her, she'd do well to keep him at arm's length.

Recovering from his surprise, Zach rubbed the back of his neck. 'Ah,' he said. 'Is that how your wind's blowing? Well, let me tell you, Miss Julia, you haven't given much indication you wanted to be a rival.'

'I don't.' She pinched the bridge of her nose, willing the lie to be true. 'Not really. I'm just being childish.'

'It isn't childish to want an animal to love you,' he said. 'That's something God put into us humans so we wouldn't be a bunch of bastards, at least not all the time.'

Julia pinched her nose harder and pressed her lips together. She'd be damned if she'd cry in front of him. 'Can you show me?' she asked, her voice as firm as she could make it. 'Can you teach me how to make her accept me?'

'Sure can.' He led her to a hay bale to sit down. 'Nothing easier. Only we'll wait till she's finished her breakfast.' He patted her thigh. 'You need a hankie, Julia?'

'No,' she snapped, then held out her hand for it.

Once she'd blown her nose, they sat in silence. A few times she thought Zach was about to speak, but in the end he held his peace. Smart man, she thought, though part of her was disappointed. Most men would have jumped on her admission that she and Starlight were rivals for his affection.

When the horses had finished eating, Zach led them into the paddock that adjoined the barn. As soon as he released their halters they took off for the opposite fence. The colt seemed delighted with the snow. He danced through the drifts with his tail held high, nickering at his mother as if to say, 'Look, Mummy, look!' While his show was entertaining, Julia didn't see how she was going to make friends with his mother from over here.

Zach's voice came inches from her ear. 'Horses are flight animals,' he explained. 'She'll feel less cornered if you give her room to run.' He put his arm around her back again and led her slowly into the paddock. 'What you want to do is talk to her, kind of sing-song, so she gets used to the sound of you. Tell her she's a pretty horse, a good horse. She's got a swollen head, Starlight has, and she falls for that sort of thing.'

'Does she?' Julia's smile was sceptical.

He released her and gave her a little push. 'Try it for yourself. Don't look at her eyes, though. She's apt to take that as a threat and hare off. Keep your head down and walk slowly. If you get behind her, she'll run forward. If you move towards her head, she'll go back. So aim for her belly. That's her neutral point. And don't forget to sweet-talk her.'

Julia felt foolish, but she told Starlight she was a pretty horse, a good horse. The mare flicked one ear at her.

'That's good,' said Zach, plodding through the snow a short distance behind her. 'She's listening to you. Keep it up.'

She looked bored to Julia, but Julia kept it up. 'Beautiful Starlight,' she said. 'Good Starlight. Nice

150

Starlight. I'll give you a carrot when this is over. In fact, I'll peel you a whole bag.'

One horse-length from success, Julia made the mistake of meeting Starlight's eye. The horse snorted, shook her hide and raced off to the opposite side.

Julia stomped her boot in the knee-high snow. 'Hell.'

'No, no, no,' said Zach. 'That was pretty good for a first try. When I'm breaking a new horse, we can go on this way for hours.'

'Hours!' Julia moaned.

He grinned. 'You can give up if you want. But I wouldn't advise it. With horses it's best to set a small goal and stick with it. Otherwise, they learn they can get the better of you. Besides, today's a good day to do this. The snow will tire her out pretty soon.'

'It'll tire me out, too,' Julia grumbled, but she began the slow trudge back. 'Good Starlight. Beautiful Starlight.'

She heard Zach laughing softly behind her.

On the fifth try, she got within touching distance. The horse turned one ear towards her, but other than that she didn't acknowledge that Julia was there.

'Oh, God,' she whispered. 'What now?'

'Now, reach out, nice and easy. You want to put your fingers together and pretend your hand is a horse's nose. You're gonna touch her side with the tips of your fingers and rub it in a circle, as if you're nuzzling her.'

'Nice Starlight,' Julia said, her hand creeping out, her voice shaking. 'Nice horse. Pretty horse.' Her fingers touched the horse's side. Starlight's hide shivered and she shifted her weight, but she didn't move forward. Julia drew a little circle with her hand. 'Oh, oh, Zach, her fur is so thick. It's so soft.'

'That's right,' said Zach, behind her shoulder now.

'She's got her pretty winter coat. Don't you, girl?' Starlight whuffled at him in answer. 'What you're doing, that's what mothers do to reassure their colts. It's basic horse talk. It says, you're all right. There's nothing to be scared of.'

'No,' Julia crooned. 'There's nothing to be scared of.'

'That's good. She's standing nice and calm. You can put your whole hand on her. Just stroke her nice and slow. Work up around her neck there. That's it. She likes that. Now step up close so that she can feel your whole body next to her.'

Julia moved closer and inhaled the mare's wonderful horsy smell. She was warm and solid. Her neck came around and she snuffled at Julia's coat, but there was nothing of fear in the sound, nothing of anger. Julia buried her face in her thick black mane. 'Beautiful Starlight,' she said, her throat tight with love for this big wild creature who'd given her a second chance. 'Beautiful Starlight.'

Suddenly tears were running down her cheeks. She didn't try to hold them back. This was what she'd been searching for, this sweet emotion, as strong in its way as her love of power. Waves of tenderness flowed through her as she stroked the mare's muscular neck. Something bumped her from behind. She thought it was Zach, but when she turned, the gangly colt was there. He butted her chest as if he wanted attention, too. 'Oh, you're beautiful, too,' she said, sliding her hand over his velvety muzzle.

Like any adolescent, he wouldn't stand much fussing. Soon he was dancing off again, kicking up snow with his sharp black hooves. He bounded through the drifts as if his legs were made of springs. She watched him for a moment, then turned to Zach. He was smiling, but his eyes were as full as hers. She couldn't help wondering – hoping – that his expression held more than a teacher's pride.

'Thank you,' she said from the bottom of her heart. 'That was wonderful.'

His moustache twitched up on one side. 'Wasn't my doing,' he said. 'Anybody would love you if you gave them a chance.'

She pressed her fingers over her mouth, afraid she was going to break down, then sure she was. He opened his arms. 'Oh,' she said, 'oh', and stepped into them.

He held her tightly, rocking her back and forth and kissing the cold curve of her ear. 'You are something, Miss Julia. You got me all turned upside down.'

'I didn't mean to,' she said, even as she hugged him back and nuzzled the warm skin hidden beneath his collar.

'Doesn't matter. You did it anyway.' He turned his head and their mouths found each other.

The kiss was tentative. Tongues stroked lightly; lips brushed softly. Their breath rose in clouds between their glancing faces. For once in her life, she welcomed tenderness and offered tenderness. Like Starlight, Zach was one of God's darlings. Julia felt more gratitude than she could express. She wove her hands through his short, silky hair, caressing the bare spots at his temples, the strong line of vertebrae behind his neck. Zach's hands flowed over the back of her coat, pushing the leather closer, pushing their bodies closer.

Hunger rose like the thumping approach of a steam engine. She clasped his cheeks even as he cinched her back. Their mouths closed together, greedy and impatient. They reached deep and sucked hard until Zach broke free with a ragged gasp. 'We keep this up, we're gonna make Starlight jealous again. Come on.'

153

He nodded towards the stable. 'I've got a bale of hay with your name on it.'

She followed him eagerly, laughing as he tugged her through the drifting snow. He slid the barn door shut behind him and smiled at her. 'Oh, darlin', have I been looking forward to this. You have no idea.'

'I might have some idea,' she said, returning his smile. What was the point in lying now, either to herself or to him? Happiness bubbled inside her. She felt as fresh and clean as the snowy world outside.

Something in her expression brought a flush to his rugged face. He pointed towards the ladder to the loft. 'You'd better climb up there before I throw you up.' With a swiftness that conveyed his desire to waste no time, he gathered an armload of blankets and followed her up the ladder. He spread them haphazardly over a loose pile of hay. 'Wouldn't want you to get prickled to death,' he said in his most humorous twang, but his voice was rusty and his cock a thick ridge at the front of his jeans.

He undid three buttons of his shirt and wrenched it over his head, cursing when the cuffs caught on his hands. Julia dropped her coat over a bale of hay and sat to remove her shoes. The top of his thermal underwear flew in the same direction as his shirt. She rolled her leggings to her ankles, her eyes on the show. She'd been wrong to deny herself the pleasure of seeing him naked. He had a good chest: well muscled, broad in the shoulder, firm at the waist. Tiny rose-brown nipples peeped through his light chest hair, their centres sharply erect. Reluctant to lose the sight even for an instant, she peeled off her sweater and tossed it into the growing pile of clothes. Zach's hands were fumbling over his jeans front. He stopped when he saw her sweater fly. He turned his head to her. His eyes widened.

Her brassière and panties had been custom-made in Paris. The silk was a pale, icy pink, the lace a mellow cream. Julia smoothed her hands over the front of the bra cups. He rewarded her with a sharp intake of breath.

'Lord, that underwear is pretty,' he said. 'If I didn't want you naked so bad, I'd let you keep it on.'

'Let me, like hell.' She unsnapped the front catch and shrugged the lacy bra off her shoulders. Her breasts spilt free, full and tipped with fire.

Zach's pupils dilated. He took one step forward as if he meant to grab her, then shook his head. 'Naked,' he said. 'I want both of us naked.' He slid one hand down his half-open jeans, covering his erection, then yanked the zip down. With his thumbs he gathered both long johns and denim together. He pushed them down his legs in a single sweep.

Julia couldn't help sighing in admiration. His body was sturdy, but lean; strong, but graceful. His cock was as beautiful as she'd remembered, as hard as she could have wanted. It angled up towards his rippling belly, the shaft curving slightly, the tip swollen to a ripe, seeping mouthful. She licked her lips. Zach didn't miss the instinctive reaction.

'Take your panties off,' he said, his voice even hoarser than before.

She wriggled them over her hips, then stood with her arms at her sides, her skin pulsing with awareness as she let him look his fill. His cock jerked and a tiny spurt of clear fluid jumped from the deep-red slit at its top. Oh, he was too tempting, too responsive. She stepped up to him. She clasped his neck with one hand and his cock with the other. It leapt in her hand and

155

spurted again. She rubbed its agitated glans around her navel.

He groaned as if the world were ending. His mouth caught hers in a greedy kiss, his hands roving her curves and swells. His fingertips played over the crease at the top of her thighs, then tightened on her bottom. He lifted her off her feet. His hips jerked back, pulling his cock free of her grasp. He hitched her higher and shifted his hold. His fingers wrapped her thighs in bands of steel. She hadn't expected him to use such force, but she honestly didn't care. She wanted him inside her now, immediately. The head of his cock probed her swollen lips. She gasped at its slippery heat.

'Now I've got you,' he growled against her mouth. 'Now you're in my arms.' He didn't wait for her to lift her legs around his waist. He pressed into the narrowed entrance. The fat bulb slipped inside, then an inch of throbbing shaft. She moaned and felt herself tipping backward on to the blanket-covered hay. Suddenly it was too much, too out of her control.

She heaved upward, digging her heels in, but that only pressed him deeper. He still had her thighs trapped between his and the feeling of being filled to bursting made her head spin. He grunted and shoved further. Her sheath let down a warm gush of cream. His tongue quivered inside her mouth, then withdrew.

'All right,' he panted, his hands sliding up her torso, over her heaving breasts. 'All right, I'll slow down. Promise.' He kissed her cheek. 'You're where I need you now. I'll slow down. Oh, darlin', you don't know how good it is to have you in my arms. You don't know how hard it's been to wait.'

'Let me –' she began, then lost what she'd meant to say as he began to thrust, slowly, gently into her constricted passage. He couldn't thrust far in this position but it hardly mattered. Her nerves were squeezed so sweetly to his hardened flesh that she could almost forget he'd taken control. The easy rock and pull of his cock lulled her, enchanted her. The hay rustled beneath them, its summery scent as provocative as leather, as horse. His hands slid along her arms until they reached her wrists. He cuffed them with warm, hard fingers and dragged them over her head. She thought of stopping him, but he seemed so gentle now, so safe. Soon it was too late. Her arms were held taut, her body stretched. Strange feelings swirled within her, dark ink curling through murky water. She couldn't say if it was fear or excitement. Then her sex released another flood of moisture. A shadow of panic prickled across her scalp. She shouldn't be reacting this way. She'd never liked being overpowered.

'No,' she said, but her cunt said yes, jerking upward and tightening around those lazy thrusts.

'You're not enjoying this?' he whispered, his expression stricken. She couldn't answer, not in word or deed. His thrusts stopped for a moment, then began again, more shallowly, as if he knew he ought to stop, but couldn't quite bring himself to. His hands loosened on her wrists, then tightened. Julia moaned, wanting more, fearing more. He bent to kiss the tip of her breasts, playing his tongue over the sharpened nipple. 'Tell me what you want. Anything. I'll do my best to give it to you.'

'Suck my tit,' she said, trying – and failing – to make it an order.

Plea or order, the words broke his hold on himself. He shuddered. His mouth opened and drew her in. She cried out at the strength with which he pulled, swells of delicious pain-pleasure washing through her flesh. The edge of his teeth scored her breast. His tongue rasped like sandpaper. She could feel how much he wanted her; could hear it. He whimpered with hunger, low puppyish sounds that called up an involuntary echo from her own throat. The ache of wanting him literally hurt. This slow slide and draw was not enough to soothe it. She wrenched one hand free of his hold. She had to come; couldn't bear to wait. But he anticipated her, increasing the speed of his thrusts before she could. In a move too quick to counter, he whipped one leg between hers and pressed her thigh outward, trapping it beneath his bent knee.

She clutched his thigh, meaning to push it away but instead found her hand sliding up the labouring, hair-covered muscle. Sweat rolled down the crease of his buttocks. His sac spanked her fingers as he thrust. He muttered something against her breast, then released it.

'I've got you,' he said, catching up her stray hand. He dragged it over her head again. 'Don't worry, I'll take care of you.'

This time she couldn't twist loose. He held her too tightly. He'd trapped her. He hadn't even slowed his thrusts to do it. She quivered deep inside, her sex clenching and weeping with excitement. She didn't want this to stop. She was loving it. His words spiralled in her head: I'll take care of you. I'll take care of you. They stabbed her pussy with knives of heat. Oh, God, what was happening to her?

'Deeper,' he said, gasping for air. 'Got to get deeper.'

She struggled beneath him as he humped her faster, harder. She could not get free. She could only thrash from side to side. She could only dig in with her one free leg and thrust at him and wail at him, while pleasure sang through her at every pound of his cock.

Her reactions careered out of control, immense, unstoppable. She came with a low groan. He sank his teeth into her shoulder and she came again. Her whole body shook with the strength of it.

'Julia,' he cried, his hips beating white lightning through her sex. 'Julia. Jesus. I'm going to come. Hold me. God, hold me.'

Suddenly, her hands were free. They fell to his back and clutched his sweaty muscles. She held him, tightly, desperately. He shifted his second leg between hers and yanked her thighs up and wide, pinning them under his forearms while he thrust ever deeper. Now she could move even less than before. His cock seemed to pummel her womb. The muscles at her groin stretched and, oh, Lord, another orgasm rose, this one building ache upon bone-deep ache. She could not draw it nearer. She could not push it away. Her pleasure was all in his power, in his frantic, heavy drive.

Please, she mouthed, though no sound emerged. Please, Zach.

'Julia,' he gasped, his face a mask of torment. He wasn't going to take for ever to come this time. His cock swelled inside her. He drew back and slammed forward, grunting with effort. He held fast, his pubis grinding over hers, the root of his cock mashing her clit. Their hair rasped like silk. She tensed, dying for release. His head dropped back, throat bared, veins pulsing. He came. The first spasm rolled down his cock. He grunted, relief in it and awe. Then her climax broke. She'd never felt the like. She wailed as her back arched off the ground, as hot arcs of pleasure made the world disappear. Her awareness shrank to her own shudders of ecstasy and to him: his hard, shooting cock, the bite of his hands on her thighs, his hiss of pleasure when her sheath sucked him deep, and then his weight sagging, his sigh, the satiny brush of his lips when he settled against her, cuddling, nuzzling. Tingles of warmth spread through her limbs, a numbing lassitude. She knew she couldn't have stood to save her life.

'Oh, darlin',' he said, his cheek hot and wet against hers. 'A man could get used to this.'

The words slapped her back to sanity. She lay beneath him as if a hurricane had blown her over. What the hell was wrong with her? She'd behaved like a sub with a fetish for constraint. Her breath panted in and out, as much from shock as fatigue. No, it was just a fluke. It had to be. But it was over now. All done. She shoved at Zach's weight and squirmed free. He mumbled but didn't rise, no doubt too exhausted to move.

She stumbled when she stood, her knees barely strong enough to hold her. Jesus, he'd done her in. She looked down at him, at his big, beautiful naked body. Her chest tightened. She'd left scratches on his back – long bloody rakes. Not on purpose, either. She hadn't even realised she'd done it until she saw them. The marks disturbed her more than any deliberate injury ever had.

She'd lost control. She'd given up control. Worst of all, she'd enjoyed it.

With an effort, she shook herself and turned away. Accept it and move on, she thought. But she had a feeling it wasn't going to be that easy.

Zach lifted his muzzy head. Julia was gone.

'Fuck,' he said. He sat up and scrubbed at his hair, willing his wits back into his brain. He couldn't have dozed off for more than a minute. A renewed pounding at his groin told him he was hard again. 'Fuck.'

Obviously he'd done something wrong, but damned if he knew what. She'd been fire in his arms. When she came, she'd clutched him so tightly he'd thought she'd yank it off. At that moment, she would have been welcome to. He'd have handed her his cock on a platter and said: It's all yours, sweetheart. Keep it as long as you want. God Almighty, he'd never felt anything so right as fucking her. Maybe he'd gone a little overboard in the enthusiasm department, but she'd liked it. A man would have to be deaf, blind and numb to think otherwise. She'd wailed like a calf getting branded. Her cream was still wet on his cock!

He dug the heels of his hands into his eyes. If he had to go through another song and dance to get between her legs again, he'd –

Oh, you'll what? He cut himself off. You'll do whatever it takes and you know it. That gal got under your skin. One or two or, for all you know, a hundred rolls in the hay won't cure you. He sighed and reached for his clothes. This heartsick puppy business was a pain in his hind parts. Come to think of it, Gracie had more dignity than he did. She didn't whine when Julia patted her head and went on her way.

Muttering to himself, he carried the blankets to the tack room. He found Carolyn waiting there, the last person on earth he wanted to see right then. Like a lost waif, she sat hunched on his decrepit office chair. Her nose and eyes were red and she'd clasped her thin little hands between her knees. She didn't look up as he entered, just twisted back and forth on that creaky chair.

He didn't need to be told she'd heard them making love.

161

He opened his mouth, but his mind chose that moment to seize up. He couldn't think of a solitary thing to say, not even a stupid thing. They'd never had the ghost of a tie between them, unless you counted pity. Surely even she'd scorn that. Maybe not, though. She'd posed herself before him just as pitifully as she could.

He set his mouth on a different kind of silence and walked past her with the blankets. Damned if he'd apologise for making love to the woman he should have waited for in the first place. He'd explained how it was last night when Carolyn tried to squirm into his room. If she chose to shadow him around in spite of that, that was her problem.

Unfortunately, when push came to shove, he couldn't quite walk out cold. He stopped beside the old chair and laid his hand on her shoulder, letting her feel its simple, human warmth.

She sniffed hard. 'I heard you,' she said. The words wobbled like a newborn foal, despite the accusation in them.

'Carolyn.' He touched her short, feathery hair. 'Don't do this to yourself.'

'You love her, don't you?' Her eyes were hard. 'You love that fat bitch.'

He pulled his hand back. He might have said a lot of things to that, but it wasn't his way to kick a woman when she was down. 'You're getting yourself into a taking for nothing. You know there never was anything between you and me.'

'There could have been,' she said, high and wild. 'You never gave me a chance.'

He spoke gently. 'I'm not a stranger to my feelings, Carolyn. I know when there's a chance and when there isn't.'

She covered her face and began to sob. He didn't comfort her a second time.

Marty sat on the edge of Julia's bed, dressed except for his socks, which he was sleepily pulling on. In her current state of mind, Julia had no desire to face him. Pride, however, was sufficient to keep her from turning back at the door.

'Good morning,' she said.

He grunted, then got down on his hands and knees to fish his shoes out from under the bed. Julia had to turn away. His position was too suggestive. Her palm tingled like a drunk's mouth watering at a whiff of bourbon. The shift from worrying about unsuspected submissive tendencies to fearing she might never escape being a dom made her dizzy. She stared at her open trunk of toys. Yes, the sight of the leather still made her pussy quiver. But so did the memory of Zach pinning her on those rough wool blankets. Her buttocks were hot. She suspected her skin was abraded from the vigour of his thrusts. The sensation shouldn't have made her want him again, but it did. Damn him. Why did he have to be the one to call this urge to grovel from her? She wanted to wrap herself around him, kiss him, lick him, fuck him until they both were raw.

No. She slammed the lid of the trunk down, then jumped when Marty's hands began kneading her neck.

'You up for a rematch tonight, Mueller?'

Julia rolled her head and tried to enjoy his ministrations. 'We might not have enough time to do a good job. The snow is slowing down. They'll dig us out soon enough.'

Before Marty could respond, Carolyn burst through the door. Her cheeks were mottled, her nose red, but the look in her eyes was steely. 'I'm ready,' she said, not sparing Marty a glance. 'Whatever you want to teach me, I'm ready to learn. If I'm going to be a doormat, I'm going to be the best damn doormat around: the toughest, the hardest. No one's going to break my heart again.'

'You know,' Marty said, 'you might knock.'

'Fuck you,' she snarled. Julia began to think she might have a little top in her, after all. She had no intention of saying so, however, or explaining that sensitivity was more prized in a bottom than toughness.

'Carolyn,' she said in a cool, clear voice. 'Apologise to your fellow trainee.'

Carolyn set her jaw and narrowed her eyes. 'I'm sorry,' she said with very ill grace.

Julia pointed at the floor. 'On your knees and kiss his feet.' Carolyn gaped. Marty laughed. Julia snapped her fingers in his face, close enough to make him flinch. 'Either you accept this gesture with dignity and respect or I'll have *you* kiss *her* feet.'

Marty's jaw tightened at that, but he nodded. He stood unmoving, unsmiling while Carolyn performed the obeisance. Arousal was not yet part of their reactions. That would come later. Just thinking about it, anticipation thickened the tender folds of her sex. Julia hadn't trained two at once since her rangers. The challenge would be heady – just the distraction she needed.

Carolyn rose to her feet and awaited further orders. Her expression was sullen, her cheeks pink. Marty rubbed his bushy eyebrow.

'That is all,' Julia said to both of them. 'If you wish to continue your training, return to my room after dinner.'

'Together?' Marty sounded reluctant.

Julia tossed her head. 'Together or not at all.'

When they were gone, she tapped her lips and smiled. She might not be thinking clearly right now, but, wise or not, she was going to enjoy this.

Chapter Nine

Sunday evening

Nothing could put Marty off his feed, but Carolyn picked at her dinner, despite Zach having served a lean roast chicken for once, instead of the eternal beef. Though Julia understood the woman's nervousness, she could not allow this behaviour to stand. If Carolyn did not begin showing more respect for her body, she would make a very poor slave indeed. At the very least, undernourishment put a deplorable strain on the hormones. No one wanted a bottom whose libido might give out at any moment.

She handed Carolyn a plate as soon as she entered her room. She pointed to the bed.

'Sit,' she said, 'and eat.' Carolyn began to argue but Julia silenced her with a sharply raised hand. 'You claim you want to be strong. You can start by cleaning that plate.'

The dish contained chicken and steamed vegetables, a modest portion of each. There was, after all, no point

166

in asking more of Carolyn than she could give. Once Julia saw she was eating – somewhat mechanically, but eating – she turned to Marty.

He smiled, a combination of mischief and approval. 'Are you going to give us safe words now?'

'No,' she said so coolly his smile faltered. 'I don't use them. I require my trainees to place their complete trust in me. If you do not feel that level of trust, I advise you in the strongest possible terms to leave immediately.'

'No, no,' he said, palms outward. 'I trust you.'

'Good. Now remove your clothes and don't speak again unless I address you directly.'

Carolyn's head came up at the coldly worded order. Marty looked at her, then at Julia. A flush crept over his stubbled cheeks. His hands moved to the collar of his pale-yellow shirt. He pushed the first button through its hole, then the next. He had a barrel chest, not fat, but bear-like. A thick mat of hair led down his belly, circling his navel and diving into his casual trousers. His nipples were larger than most men's. They pouted now through his dark curls, beginning to erect in earnest. Carolyn's mouth fell open as she stared.

'You may watch,' Julia said to her, 'so long as you continue to eat.'

While Marty disrobed for his wide-eyed audience, Julia opened her chest of toys. She removed a spanking paddle, the cock-and-ball harness that had fascinated Marty the night before, and a purple bustier. The lingerie was for Carolyn. During this session, Julia would remain in her oversized sweatshirt and leggings. She preferred not to dress up when breaking in new trainees. If topping them required too many

167

props, she had no business trying. The force of her personality must sway them on its own.

The clank of a belt buckle hitting the floor signalled Marty's progress. Julia turned and found him naked. His cock was half-hard and rising. She saw that Carolyn had finished her meal. The plate sat unheeded on her lap while she gaped at Marty's steadily engorging prick. Her cheeks were pink, her breathing shallow.

Julia was pleased. Carolyn's unwilling attraction to Marty would make her job easier. She retrieved the empty plate and set it aside. Carolyn was too busy checking out Marty to notice. Suppressing a smile, Julia pulled the room's single chair away from the window. All the guest rooms had these royal-blue armchairs. Their backs were fan-shaped with curving arcs of stuffing: old-fashioned comfort furniture. Julia would have laid money on Zach's grandmother having chosen them. In any case, they were appropriately throne-like.

Julia sat and crossed her legs, their firmness revealed by the skin-tight cotton of her leggings. Both Marty and Carolyn eyed her calves. Good. She had their attention. She nodded at Carolyn. 'You. Remove your clothes. Slowly, if you please, and with a bit of flair. By the time you finish I want Marty's cock hard enough to pound nails.'

As she'd expected, Carolyn balked. 'Fuck that,' she said.

Like a cobra striking a mouse, Julia reached out, grabbed Carolyn and turned her over her lap. The VP didn't even have time to shriek before the paddle fell with a resounding smack, striking her bottom cheeks in quick succession.

'Ow,' she protested. Julia covered her mouth and spanked her again, spreading the blows until the beating's heat radiated through her expensive cashmere trousers. Carolyn hiccupped her shock into Julia's palm, close to crying but not yet there. Julia laid down the paddle, her arm buzzing pleasantly from the brief exertion. She slid her hand over Carolyn's bottom and between her legs, then pressed the soft ivory cloth between the lips of her vulva. Carolyn moaned. She was very wet, wetter even than Julia had hoped. Her humiliation had to be intense. Not only had Julia subjected her to the ignominy of a spanking, but she'd aroused her with it. Far from besting Julia in a battle of the cunts, now her cunt belonged to Julia. Revenge was indeed sweet.

She pushed Carolyn's trouser seam into her dainty, cream-drenched folds. Her mons didn't have much flesh but it was nicely arched. Julia's hand was large enough to swallow it whole. The disparity in their sizes seemed to strike Carolyn at the same time. A wash of pink crept up her cheek. She trembled.

'You see,' Julia said, 'you can't fight your nature.' She worked her cloth-draped finger closer to Carolyn's clit, teasing the accretion of nerves. Carolyn squirmed, but not precisely away. 'You like being disciplined. You need it.'

Marty choked on a sound, drawing both the women's attention. Apparently, he'd enjoyed watching the spanking as much as Carolyn had enjoyed receiving it. He was fully hard now, his skin as stretched and red as a prime New York salami.

'Hm, it looks as if you've got a head start on your goal.' Julia helped a shaky Carolyn to her feet. 'But that doesn't mean you can skimp on the show. I want to see how a good slave strips off.'

This time, Carolyn's technique improved. Marty pressed his hand to his heart as, piece by piece, she slithered out of her clothes. When the last scrap of silk had fallen, she crossed her arms over her stomach and shivered. She was thin, painfully so, but even that could not obscure her fundamental loveliness. Her skin was translucently pink, her breasts delicate and high. A ballerina would not have scorned such graceful limbs. Twenty pounds more, Julia thought, and men would fall to their knees before her. As it was, her beauty tugged at the heart. A breath of wind might blow it away.

Julia stepped up to her, her eyes stinging against her will. It hurt her that any woman would do this to herself, and out of what: some perverse sense of what was fashionable? Carolyn would not look at her or Marty, only at her slender bare feet.

'Very pretty,' Julia said, more gently than was her wont. 'Now uncross your arms. I have something for you to wear.'

Carolyn's tension increased, then eased as Julia wrapped her in the mulberry-coloured basque. She kept her motions slow and soothing, her caresses maternal. She doubted if Carolyn had taken female lovers, but she did not flinch when Julia cupped her breasts to settle them into the lacy cups. In fact, their soft, apricot peaks budded under her palms. Promising, Julia thought, a tingle warming the tips of her own breasts. Carolyn sighed as she tightened the laces. It was a happy sigh, perhaps the sign of a latent bondage fetish. Julia filed the knowledge away for possible future use.

She stood back to study the results. The shiny satin basque stopped at the swell of Carolyn's hips and bared her narrow mound. The effect was a fraction short of tartish, an effective transformation. Gone was the successful businesswoman with million-dollar portfolios in her care; this Carolyn was a creature made for pleasure – seductive, soft and pliant. Julia circled her new possession. Apparently, she maintained the grooming habits of her youth. Her trimmed brown hair covered her pubis like smoke, the strands no more than a quarter-inch long. The peak of her clitoris peeped between her nearly nude labia. Its hood was peachy pink and glistened with fluid.

'Very pretty,' Julia repeated, giving the tiny erection a flick with her finger.

Carolyn squeaked and went up on her toes, but Julia had already moved on. She took Carolyn's shoulders and turned her to face the other way. Now Marty could watch Carolyn's bottom receive its share of caresses. Its flesh was too soft for the sort of discipline Julia liked to administer, but it did have a lovely high curve. Moreover, the pink glow that the spanking had left improved it considerably. Julia slipped her fingers down its deep, curving cleft. She reached a gathering of down, then the crisper hairs that circled her anus. Carolyn bit her lower lip and clenched her hands, seemingly determined not to react again.

Her determination would not serve. Julia knew she'd invaded a territory even more private than Carolyn's sex. Gently, she stroked the tight circle of folds. From the way they twitched at the tickling caress, it seemed no hand had ventured here before. The omission did not surprise her. Carolyn would not have chosen her many lovers for their imagination. Now, shocked by Julia's boldness, but probably too proud to complain, she could not restrain a tremor of excitement, or stop a tiny drop of cream from rolling down her inner thigh.

'This is a very nice bottom,' Julia said, careful to hide her knowledge of Carolyn's distress. 'Especially now that it's pink and warm. By far your best feature. Wouldn't you agree, Marty?'

Marty coughed. 'Uh, yes.' His voice was so thick it sounded strangled. Did he suspect the depth of Carolyn's inexperience? Julia thought he might. Carolyn's woman-of-the-world pose was flimsy to everyone but Carolyn.

She leant closer to her ear. 'Do you hear his voice?' she murmured. 'Everything I do to you excites him. Your helplessness excites him. Your passivity. Your embarrassment. You can see I spoke truly when I said a slave wields power.'

Carolyn shuddered but did not answer. Her control was too steady. Obviously, it was time to challenge her again.

'Turn around,' Julia said. 'I want you to dress your fellow slave.'

She handed her the cock-and-ball ring. The change in tactics startled Carolyn. She squinted at the intricate leather contraption, then at Marty. The harness was designed to fit snugly around the base of his shaft and to lift and separate each testicle, creating – so Julia had heard – a pleasant stretching sensation. When tightened, it would restrict the flow of blood from Marty's penis. He would be harder and bigger for longer; a useful effect, since the last thing Julia wanted was a premature end to this game. Carolyn fiddled with the fasteners, then nodded her head. Julia had been prepared to instruct her, but apparently the VP's intelligence included a certain amount of mechanical savvy. Her only problem seemed to be how to put the harness on without touching Marty's prick. If it hadn't been a breach of authority, Julia would have laughed. Marty wasn't making things easier for Carolyn. Each time her

172

fingers brushed him, his cock wriggled like an anxious puppy.

Finally Carolyn muttered something under her breath, grabbed the base of his shaft with one hand and stuffed him into the harness with the other. Annoyance drove her to cinch the strap tight. Marty swallowed back a whimper, then looked down at himself and flushed with pride. Julia didn't wonder at that. He was gorgeous: a short, hairy gladiator with a cock of steel. The shaft stood out thick and proud, its veins gnarled and strong, its head immense. She was sure he'd never seen himself look quite so imposing.

But there was no way Miss Priss was going to lick those hairy balls. Julia knew that as well as she knew her own name. She pulled a small jar from a hidden corner of the trunk, her private stash of custom-made depilatory. Only her best slaves received this treatment, but this was a special occasion. With an evil grin, she spread the cream over Marty's uplifted testicles. His eyes began to tear almost immediately. To his credit, he didn't utter a word.

Julia pressed her lips to his ear. 'Burns a bit, doesn't it?' He nodded and jigged on his feet. 'I had the cosmetologist put a dash of pepper in it. Otherwise it's very mild. It will leave you as smooth as a baby. I think Carolyn will enjoy that, don't you?'

His gaze snapped to hers, sharp with interest. Obviously, he liked the idea of Carolyn's attentions on his balls. Julia told him no more, merely wiped off the fast-acting cream with a soft, damp cloth. Once she'd removed the last speck of depilatory, his scrotum was as smooth as she had promised. Its surface was inflamed by the pepper, now the colour of a sweetheart rose. He would find the skin sensitive, deliciously so.

Despite her satisfaction, Julia pretended to tut at the

fit of the harness. 'This looks a bit snug.' She touched the uppermost strap and revelled in Marty's squirm. In truth, the fit was perfect. Julia had spent three months apprenticed to a Japanese bondage expert, and six picking the brains of one of New York's finest paramedics. No student would be injured on her watch. She'd learnt in the past, however, that her powers of persuasion were strong. She straightened and looked Marty in the eye. 'I think it's going to be very difficult for you to come while you're wearing this. Perhaps impossible.' Marty winced. Julia smiled. 'Ah, well, I suppose we'll have to hope for the best.'

She snapped for Carolyn to kneel before him. 'Start with the balls, slave.' Carolyn jerked at being called this for the first time, but she did grab his knees and bend forward. She gave his clean pink testicles a tiny lap, a kitten testing a titbit she wasn't sure of. Marty shivered. Carolyn lapped harder, using the full flat of her tongue and dragging it from the bottom of the constricted sphere to the top.

'That's it,' Julia praised. 'Give him a good washing. He's going to need a distraction from the pain.'

The pain was her province. She retrieved the paddle and shook her arm muscles loose. She drew back and swung. Marty hissed through his teeth as the first blow hit the meat of his buttock. Julia wasn't worried. She knew what he could take. His skin was thicker than Carolyn's, less likely to bruise. She basted his right cheek, then his left. Marty grunted, but Carolyn's whimpers were louder than his. She quivered with excitement at each slap. Her pelvis humped the air. Inflamed, Marty shoved his balls at her mouth. Her tongue lapped more energetically. All was as Julia wished. The mingling of pain and pleasure would be very close. Soon they wouldn't know the difference.

Her veins thrummed with energy. These two were her puppets, her creatures. She made their pleasure possible; she polished it; she sharpened it. Without her, they would never glimpse this knife-edge ecstasy. Her senses sharpened. She felt goddess-tall, goddess-strong. She knew she could not make a wrong move. She had found the smooth, slick groove of power, where instinct and intuition hold hands.

'Suck his dick,' she ordered, and Carolyn immediately obeyed. Marty cursed with pleasure. 'Silence, slave. And put your arms behind your back. You are not to touch her. Ever.'

Both Marty and Carolyn moaned.

Her arm was tireless, her aim sure. But there was a boundary here, one she must not cross. A minute later, she halted the spanking. The sudden silence was filled with the harsh, excited breathing of her two new slaves. Carolyn still sucked Marty's dick but Marty hadn't come. Julia knew he would have by now if she hadn't planted the suggestion that he couldn't. Now his subconscious would keep him from it, even though Carolyn was focusing her efforts almost entirely on the head of his cock: Marty's personal ultra-hot spot. His skin shivered as twinges of feeling flashed through his nerves; not just the skin of his groin, but his shoulders, his calves, even the muscles of his cheeks flickered with overstimulation. His face was swarthy and tight, a mask of tortured lust. He was in for a treat, she thought. When she finally released him, he was going to blast off like the space shuttle.

She betrayed none of this knowledge as she knelt down behind his fellator. Her greater height dwarfed the smaller woman. Carolyn stiffened, but did not stop what she was doing.

'Hm,' Julia said, so close her breath ruffled the thick

175

black hair at Marty's groin. 'You have not made as much progress as I'd hoped. Perhaps you need instruction in the fine art of oral sex.'

'Like hell I do,' Carolyn gasped.

Julia punished her with a slow, mocking smile. She knew they were both thinking of Zach, and of Zach's ultimate choice in partners. Carolyn subsided with a sullen grimace. 'Good. Now if you're ready to listen, I will instruct you. First of all, you need to use more force. Marty here isn't made of glass. Second, if you can't get all of him in your mouth, there's no law that says you can't use your hands.' By way of demonstration, she lifted Carolyn's right hand and wrapped it around the base of his cock. She cupped the left around his balls and gave it a light squeeze. 'Here you can be gentle.' She nudged both her thumb and Carolyn's over the rosy swollen curve. Marty's skin twitched. 'See how sensitive he is here? You want to pay close attention to his reactions, and adjust your technique accordingly.'

She dropped her hands so that Carolyn could try again. 'Yes, that's the idea, but get him wetter. Spit is a crucial component of a good blow job.'

Carolyn shuddered. Julia took her jaw in her hand and pulled her free. 'Does my suggestion disgust you?'

'No,' said Carolyn, but she didn't sound sure.

'Oral sex is not a coin you offer to get something in return.' She pinned Carolyn's eyes, refusing to let her look away. 'There's no substitute for loving this, for loving a man's silk-covered heat in your mouth, his textures and smells, his taste. You will have few opportunities to give a man more pleasure, or to have him more completely in your power. Whatever prejudice is standing in your way, I advise you to get rid of it.

176

Technique will never be more important than enthusiasm.'

She stroked Carolyn's cheek, her voice deceptively gentle. 'You said it was love at first touch between you and a man's cock. Here's your chance to enjoy.'

'*My* chance to enjoy!' Carolyn burst out. 'Try his.'

Julia drew her forefinger across Carolyn's trembling lower lip. 'Do you begrudge him his enjoyment? Do you begrudge all men their enjoyment?'

'If they don't return the favour, I do.'

Julia smiled for her honesty and kissed her, a gentle moulding together of closed lips. It was not a sexual kiss, but not quite a platonic one, either. It seemed to shock Carolyn more than the spanking had. Her body jerked as if electrified, but her mouth remained soft and accepting. When Julia released her, her eyes did not immediately refocus.

'If you want to do this well,' Julia said, 'you need to give freely and expect nothing in return. Let the act be its own reward. Your gift, Carolyn, is to take pleasure in giving pleasure. When you fight your nature or choose partners who do not appreciate it, that gift is wasted.'

Carolyn's gaze turned to Marty. Julia could feel her weighing his potential for appreciation. The line between giving freely and acting the fool was fine, but Julia knew it existed. For the moment Carolyn would have to take it on faith.

'I understand,' Carolyn said more staunchly.

'Good,' said Julia. 'Now stop swallowing and get the man wet.'

Carolyn's squeamishness was still in evidence as she slathered Marty up and down, but he obviously appreciated the change. His heightened responses soon struck sparks in his partner. Her rhythm steadied. Her sucking grew louder. Her body moved as if they were making love. Now, Julia thought. Time for the *coup de grâce*.

Still kneeling behind Carolyn, she began to stroke her, her fingertips trailing from knee to hipbone. The touch was intended to be pleasant, but not obviously sexual. Only gradually did she shift to the more sensitive skin of her inner thighs. Carolyn seemed oblivious to the change. Marty's rather galvanic reaction to her new technique had distracted her. Instead, Julia's actions crept subtly, insidiously into her awareness. First they relaxed her, then aroused her, and then – when her arousal became too strong to ignore – they unnerved her. But it was too late to deny her pleasure. By the time Julia's hands closed, one over her breast and one over her delicate mound, Carolyn had been roused too well to turn the touch away. Julia took her earlobe between her teeth, slid one finger between her labia and massaged the weeping furrow.

Carolyn's breath hissed inward. She slapped her hand over Julia's. For a second it seemed she would try to pull it away. In the end she pressed it tighter.

'Oh, God,' said Marty, quivering at the sight.

Firmly, mercilessly, Julia returned Carolyn's hand to Marty's shaft. She slipped her own under the lacy cup of Carolyn's basque and pinched the pointy nipple she found within. Carolyn cried out. Julia pinched her again and a gush of cream dampened the palm that wrapped her sex. 'Don't presume to instruct your teacher,' she said in a low, velvety tone. 'Ms Mueller knows what pleases you. More importantly, she knows what you deserve. In the future your hands will remain where I place them.'

She resumed her slow exploration of Carolyn's cunt, spreading her juices through its twists and turns, pinching her clit, dipping briefly, teasingly into the squirming heat of her sheath. Carolyn began to groan around Marty's cock. Her hips rocked back and forth under Julia's hand. She was close to coming, very close.

'Now,' Julia purred, taking her clitoral hood between finger and thumb. Too lightly to make her climax, she used the soft skin to massage the slippery pearl inside. Her own heart pounded. Her own cunt swam. This was the moment when all was won or lost, when she pushed her slave past what the slave believed she would ever do. 'Answer me a question, slave.' Carolyn whimpered as she strained for the orgasm Julia held just out of reach. 'Tell me who is the boss here?'

Marty's cock slipped from her mouth with a rude popping noise. 'Fuck,' she said, fighting this final surrender.

Julia slid her last two fingers into Carolyn's sheath and tapped them, gently, but firmly, against Carolyn's G-spot, just hard enough to tease her with the promise of release. 'Tell me, slave, and I'll let you come. Who is the boss?'

'Oh, fuck. Shit. You are, damn it. You are.'

'I am what, slave?'

Carolyn groaned. Her forehead sank to Marty's hip and rolled from side to side. 'You're the boss, Ms Mueller. You're the boss of me.'

Immediately Julia brought her to a hard, jerking climax. The ripples clutched her pumping fingers, drenching them in warm, musky fluid.

'Ah,' Carolyn cried as Julia drew the spasm out. 'Ah, ah, ah.'

She collapsed back against her when it ended. Julia held her for a moment, stroking her damp hair, then lifted her off and propped her on the bed. She was pleased with Carolyn's surrender, but more objectives remained to win.

She rose to face her second slave. Marty took an instinctive step back. His gaze slid to her fingers, shiny now with Carolyn's juice. How delightful he was, how predictable. Smiling, she wiped them on his bushy chest hair. His pectoral muscles jumped, but he did not break form. His arms remained clasped behind his back, his sturdy legs spread.

'What do you think, slave? Wasn't that the sort of show any red-blooded male would enjoy: two lusty women taking pleasure in each other?' She stuck her pinky in her mouth and sucked it clean. Marty blinked sweat from his eyes. 'You may speak, slave. I wish to know what you think.'

'I think –' His voice was so gravelly he had to clear his throat. 'I think I'd appreciate your taking off this fucking harness so I could come . . . Ms Mueller.'

'But it looks so pretty,' Julia said. She drew one finger up his raphe. The ridge was hard as bone. His veins pulsed madly under the light touch. 'I really think I could make it come. It just needs extra –' she swiped her thumb over the bulging head '– special treatment.'

'Please.' An edge of panic entered his voice. 'I really can't stand any more. Please, take it off.'

She kissed his rough cheek. 'Don't you trust your teacher? Don't you know how good a hard come is?'

He couldn't answer. He moaned behind tightly clenched teeth. He seemed to have forgotten his hands were free. He could have loosened the harness himself, if he chose. This was enough of a surrender for Julia. She slid her hands down the sides of his body as she knelt, caressing the slight love handles at his waist, the heavy muscles of his thighs and calves. Behind her,

180

Carolyn gasped in surprise. The lesson hadn't sunk in yet. But she would learn that no act was inherently subservient. The server could rule and the ruler could serve. Julia licked her lips. Marty's cock vibrated with excitement as her mouth approached. She rubbed her cheek up its side and kissed its dripping crest.

'Tell me, slave. Is the other slave watching us?'

In a low, trembling voice, Marty verified that Carolyn was.

'Good. Tell her to touch herself.'

'What?'

'Tell her to touch herself.' Julia kneaded the inside of his thighs and rubbed her face down the other side of his shaft. 'You have my permission. I want you to give her explicit instructions.'

She continued stroking Marty's thighs while he told Carolyn to touch her breasts, to pull her nipples out and let them snap back, to stroke her belly and comb her fingers through her thatch, to part her thighs and expose herself to him. His instructions were half-panted, half-groaned. Julia did not need to turn to know Carolyn obeyed. Pre-ejaculate ran down his shaft in oily streams. Stretched taut by the harness, his skin was a hot, angry red. Even his balls seemed to stand erect. When he told Carolyn to part her labia and stroke her clit, Julia swallowed his cock-head.

His knees wobbled and for one disobedient instant his hand cupped the back of her head. Ignoring the infraction, Julia began a steady push and pull on his shaft.

'Oh, yeah,' he said, recovering. 'Yeah, pull back the skin so I can see your clit. Now use your other hand and put your – oh, God – put your finger in your –' He huffed to speechlessness as Julia fluttered her tongue beneath his glans. 'Put your finger in your pussy and get it wet. Yeah, that's good. Now two fingers. That's right. Push them in and out. Faster. That's it. Jesus. I'm dying, Julia. I can't stand it.' His knees jerked back and forth. 'Oh, God. I need to come. I can't fucking come.'

'Shh,' she soothed against the head of his cock. 'You're almost there.'

'No. The harness is too tight. I can't fucking come. I can't.'

'You can.' She pressed her thumbs behind his lifted balls, pushing their pads into the firm swell of his perineum, where the root of his cock extended inside his body. Such a sweet, neglected erogenous zone. She worked her thumbs in slow circles, digging them in and then vibrating them quickly in opposite directions so that ripples of feeling could pass deep, deep into his flesh, through his cock and into his swollen prostate.

Marty gasped something unintelligible. His hands jerked forward, then snapped back to their designated position.

'It's all right,' she said, and swirled her tongue around the flare. 'I want you to hold my head. I want you to fuck my mouth. It's the only way you'll come.'

'Yes, teacher,' he said, his tone dazed and reverent. He pressed her ears between an iron grip. Thus braced, his hips rolled strongly forward. His cock was just long enough to breach her throat, but she was ready. When he saw she could take him, he went wild. He jerked in and out, his thrusts frantic, out of control. He moaned each time she tightened the suction of her lips. 'Yes,' he cried. 'Yes.' His thigh muscles knotted. He gulped for air. 'Please. God.' He thrust. His cock quivered in her mouth and swelled, and shot hot bursts of come. He growled with the spasms, his hip marking time as if he were hammering tacks. The pulses slowed. He sighed. His hands relaxed and stroked her hair. He thrust slowly, drawing fully in and out, milking the sweetness until finally he slipped from her mouth, wet and sleepy-limp.

Julia wiped her face on the back of her sleeve and smiled at him.

He shook his head as if he couldn't believe what she'd done. Then he dropped to his knees and kissed her, deep and sloppy, rocking her from side to side in a rib-creaking hug.

'Enough,' she said, laughing as she wrestled free. 'Your teacher needs to breathe.' She used his sweaty shoulder to push herself to her feet. Carolyn was lying flat on the bed, her legs still splayed, her hands curled over her thighs. Her eyes were closed. Julia suspected she'd brought herself to as spectacular a finish as Marty. Satisfied that all was well, she headed for the door. 'I'll leave you two to pull yourselves together.'

'Wait,' said Marty. 'What about you?'

Julia winked at him over her shoulder. 'Trust me, Marty. I had my reward.'

She had, too. He'd reminded her how much fun domination could be. Her body sang with arousal, but her climax would keep. She assured herself she wasn't saving it for anyone special. That would have been foolish. Besides, she had other uses for that energy.

A soft sound caught her attention as she advanced down the hall, a sound like footsteps moving quickly away. When she reached the great room, however, no one was about. She wondered if someone had been watching them from Carolyn's room. She'd drawn the blind down on her side of the wall, but there could have been a crack. Her brows pinched together. Zach might have an interest in what she was doing, but she couldn't imagine him with his nose to the window and his ear to the wall, even if he were curious. No, the noise was probably nothing. Maybe Gracie the cow-dog had snuck into the house and didn't want to get caught.

Nonetheless, she couldn't quite shake her unease as she headed down the stairs to the gym.

Sublimation could be productive, she decided as she turned under the hot, pounding spray. Between her lingering arousal and Zach's free weights, she'd worked up a good endorphin rush. She felt tired now, but utterly relaxed. The lack of interruptions had been nice: just her muscles, the weights, and pumping towards the burn. Life definitely had its moments.

She braced her hands on the acrylic-sealed brick and let the shower pummel the muscles at the back of her neck. The ranch had been designed to support the needs of at least a dozen guests. Zach had incredible hot-water pressure. Julia sighed with pleasure. A woman could get used to this.

The sound of the door creaking open brought her head around. A halogen lamp with a conical shade hung from the room's central arch. The illumination it provided was bright, but Julia's marathon shower had filled the room with steam, great rolling clouds of it. Whoever had opened the door was only a tall, dark shadow. She turned to face it, interested but not alarmed. From what she could tell, the shadow was naked. It touched the control panel by the door and four more shower heads sprang to life, roaring like Niagara Falls. Whatever the intruder intended, no one would hear it but her.

She didn't ask who it was. That would have given the shadow too much advantage. She stood, calmly, and waited for it to come to her.

Halfway across the room, the shape resolved itself

as Ben Isaacs. So. He'd grown impatient. He stalked her cautiously through the steam, as if he expected her to run. He looked angry. When he finally grabbed her hands and slammed them into the wall on either side of her head, he felt angry, too. Julia knew then that he'd been the eavesdropper in Carolyn's room. The cock he pressed into the curve of her belly was hot and long and wrapped in filmy latex. He felt good naked. His satiny skin draped lean, hard muscle. He tightened his hold on her wrists. Unlike Zach's display of aggression, however, Ben's did nothing for her.

Well, she thought, half-disgusted, half-relieved. At least that narrowed the problem down. She didn't bother to fight his hold or the press of his body which, admittedly, was not unpleasant. She knew he'd state his business soon enough.

He brought his face close to hers, his nostrils flaring, his toast-brown skin glittering with spray. When he spoke, his voice was as hard as his cock. 'Tell me, Julia. Why is it you'll screw everyone on this ranch but me? Marty and the cowboy I could understand, but Carolyn?' He snorted. 'She's hardly worth your time.'

'Ben.' She searched for words that would not hurt him. 'Forgive me if I'm wrong, but you can't really want to pretend you're my slave.'

This took him aback. His grip on her wrists loosened. 'That's all you're about? Playing those sick little games?' He shook water from his eyes. 'I don't believe it. There's more to you than that.'

Julia opened her mouth to explain. Sick wasn't a particular act; sick was an attitude. Sick was a lack of respect for yourself or your partner. But what was the point? To Ben, what she'd done with Marty and Carolyn was sick. Why try to convince him otherwise? What good could it do him? She didn't think he'd enjoy S&M, even if she could convince him to try it.

'It's what I like,' she said instead. 'It's what I'm good at.'

The smudged charcoal arch of his brows drew together. 'Maybe you've never had the right lover.'

Julia laughed softly at his naïveté. 'I've had more lovers than you can count. I enjoy vanilla sex, but that's all it is to me: vanilla. And I'm a caramel ripple, choco-chunk kind of woman. That's what I like.'

'I don't believe it.' He kissed her for the first time, a hard press of lips against her cheekbone, a wilful kiss, a denying kiss. 'You've got a big heart, Julia. I've seen it.'

She sighed and wrapped her arms around his back, more as comfort than embrace. 'I think you've got a saviour complex, Isaacs. Or maybe you think you need an excuse to fuck another white woman.'

'Don't.' He turned his mouth over hers. 'Don't be ugly. This isn't like that.'

He kissed her. Julia did not stop him. He was a beautiful, potent creature. She had neither the energy to reject him nor the will. With lazy pleasure, she caressed his strong back. They had left the centre of the spray. Its edges prickled like Perrier over her arms. She remembered the story he'd told by the fire. Was he watching his dark hands explore her water-dappled paleness? Was he ashamed of himself for being aroused by the contrast? Did all his fantasies have to be routed into tracks he could approve of?

She smiled. If she'd let that stop her, she'd never have had sex in the first place.

Ben felt the smile but not the thoughts behind it. He drew her closer. He must have believed she was giving him a chance to prove his point. His hands slid over her buttocks, gently moulding and parting. His height matched hers precisely. The blunt crown of his cock probed her lips, sliding through water and cream, through curls and flesh. He broke the kiss and she knew, despite his guilt, that he couldn't resist watching it go in. Julia looked down herself. His cock was darker than the rest of him, like newly turned earth. Her curls gleamed gold against its brown, a provocative sight, even for her. He began to tremble as he pushed, slowly, slowly, prolonging the entry. His cock had a lovely upward curve, as if it had been designed to fit a woman's body. He would press her G-spot as he thrust, without even trying. Julia shivered. She stroked the tight, wet curls of his skull, the bowed arch of his neck. He was still no more than halfway in.

He panted against her upper chest but didn't say a word. Perhaps he didn't dare. So many forbidden thoughts must be racing through his mind. She curled her hands behind his shoulders and hiked her legs off the floor. She wrapped them around his waist, her heels digging into the high round muscles of his buttocks. With that for encouragement, he pushed her into the wall and hilted. He made a low, tortured sound. His erection throbbed strongly inside her, as if he'd gone a long time without coming. Perhaps he didn't approve of jerking off. Julia melted at the thought. That would certainly explain why he'd charged in here tonight. If he'd been watching people pair up all weekend, while taking no relief for himself, he must be quite frustrated.

He shifted his hips and pressed a fraction deeper. 'There,' he said.

Julia wasn't sure what to make of the satisfaction in his voice. She stared at him. He seemed untroubled by her watchfulness. He stroked her hair back from her

187

face. He licked a drop of heated water from the corner of her mouth. Both were tender gestures, both sweet. A devil whispered in her ear. Instinct told her to heed it.

'Are you going to save me now?' she teased.

'Damn you,' he said, but his cock remained insistent.

She let her amusement show. 'Don't fuck the woman you want me to be. Fuck the woman I am.'

She thought he'd pull out then, but after a moment of stunned silence, he gripped her tight and started pounding.

'You're more,' he said, underscoring the claim with a heavy, ploughing thrust. 'You're not just a dominatrix. You're more.'

He spread his feet wider, their soles slapping the wet tile. His balance sure now, he pushed harder, grunting with pleasure when she crossed her heels a little higher on his back. His energy was impressive. She'd have been more impressed, though, if he hadn't come so quickly. Three minutes passed at most before he screwed his eyes shut and spasmed. She was sure he hadn't meant to. His groan of dismay spoke eloquently enough, even if he hadn't immediately gone to his knees to mouth her to her finish. He was skilled enough at that. She couldn't help wondering, though, as he drew her closer to climax, whether he liked her pretty blonde thatch as much as Marty had. He wove his fingers through it as he worked, combing through the wet strands. Though his fascination intrigued her, she had no desire to draw this out. She came almost as swiftly as he had.

It was a perfectly ordinary orgasm, physically satisfying, emotionally neutral. It meant no more to her than a swallow of water when her mouth was dry.

When it was over, Ben rose and touched her face.

Before he could make another argument in defence of vanilla sex, she covered his mouth with her fingers. She felt dangerously close to tears and suspected he'd respond to them in a way she didn't want. He'd taught her something today, though probably not what he'd hoped. She knew now that her sexuality wasn't as flexible as her encounters with Zach had led her to believe. She also knew she wasn't as ashamed of being a dom as she'd led herself to believe.

She didn't want to be saved, certainly not by Ben and maybe not by anybody. Redemption was too big a responsibility to put in anyone's hands but her own.

Which still begged the important question: who did Julia Mueller want to be?

Chapter Ten

Sunday night

After her shower, Julia wrapped herself in a thick terry-cloth robe with TAYLOR RANCH embroidered on the back. It seemed silly to wear any more when everyone in the place had seen her naked.

Ben, of course, remained in the cellar to dress. She didn't wait for him. Their encounter had left her more restless than satisfied. She wandered into the kitchen and realised she was starving. A peek in the big refrigerator revealed, among other goodies, a bowl of leftover scalloped potatoes and half a bunch of seedless red grapes. The promise of a solid dose of carbo-hydrates had her mouth watering. She zapped the potatoes in the microwave and set them on a tray with the grapes to take to her room.

The sound of Marty comforting someone stopped her outside the great room. She assumed it was Caro-lyn and that she was struggling to assimilate what had happened during their first training session. Julia didn't want to interrupt this slave–slave bonding, or be drawn into participating. Unfortunately, there was no way to reach her room without passing through this one.

When she entered, though, she saw only Marty. He was hunched over one of the phones in the adjoining office alcove. The receiver was wedged between his shoulder and ear and he was squeezing his temples. 'No, sweetheart,' he was saying. 'You don't want to do that.'

He waved Julia over as soon as he saw her. The smell of food must have caught his attention because he grabbed the bowl of potatoes and dug in. Standing next to him, she could hear a plaintive female on the other end of the line. If Marty had looked any less worried, she'd have abandoned him and her late-night snack. Instead, she sat on the arm of his chair and rubbed the broad expanse of his back. He slipped his arm around her waist.

'Didi,' he said into a brief pause, his voice patient and firm. 'Didi, call your sponsor. Call Harriet. No, I can't wire you any money.' He winced at another burst of sound. 'Whether I have it or not isn't the point. You know you can't go to Atlantic City. I don't care if the Long Island ladies are only going to see the shows, you can't afford to go near a casino. It's only been six months since your last slip. Do you want to have to start from the beginning again?'

A fusillade of promises shot through the line. Marty closed his eyes. 'Didn't you promise the last time, too? Don't you always promise? And don't you remember how bad you felt when you couldn't keep your promise? Please, Didi, call Harriet. You can go to a meeting together. It'll be – no, don't ask Miriam Rafferty to float you a loan. Didi? Fuck.' He let the phone slip from between his ear and shoulder. 'She hung up.' He stared at the receiver, then gathered himself. 'I'm not supposed to do this, but to hell with it.'

He punched in a number that was obviously familiar. 'Hi, Harriet? It's Marty Fine. Look, I know Didi is supposed to call, not me, but I'm out of town and she's having a little crisis. She wants to go to Atlantic City to see a show. Yeah. Tom Fucking Jones, only he just happens to have lemons for eyes and a long silver arm. Do you think you could go over there and talk to her? I know. No promises. But you're supposed to be better at telling her she's full of shit than the near and dear.' He laughed at something Harriet said, a rough, strained sound. 'I'll take that as a compliment. God bless you, Harriet. I'll send you a mink for Christmas. Oh, right, you'd only hock it and blow the money on lottery tickets. Bye then, sweetie. You know I won't blame you if it doesn't work.'

He hung up with a sigh and sagged back into the calfskin chair. His arm still hugged Julia's waist. He pulled her into his side. 'That was Didi's sponsor at Gamblers Anonymous. Great lady. They assign veteran members to look out for the "newly recovering". They reckon the old dogs have tried every trick themselves and won't be taken in.' He rubbed his hand over his face, pulling its tired lines towards his jowls. 'Didi gets like this when I leave town. Says it makes her nervous. But I can't stand guard over her all the time, and I can't let her make me responsible if she fucks up.'

'No, you can't,' Julia said.

The eyes Marty turned to her glistened with tears. 'So why do I feel like such a skunk?'

Julia didn't hesitate. She slid into his lap and held him. He buried his face in her neck, his tears spilling on to the collar of her robe. 'Oh, God,' he said with a snorting laugh. 'I am a skunk, a philandering skunk who doesn't deserve anyone's pity, much less yours.'

'I'm no saint,' Julia said.

He snuffled, calming, but still holding tight. 'I'll bet you never lied to a lover.'

'Does Didi always tell the truth?'

'Ha. We lie to each other. It's our strongest bond.' He sighed, a little-boy sigh from a big, boisterous man. 'Letting go today was good, Mueller. Letting someone else be responsible; it was really great.'

She rested her cheek against his curly hair. 'I suspect you wouldn't want to do it all the time.'

'Nah. Probably not.' He sat back from her and wiped his face. He grinned. 'I got a maternal streak you wouldn't believe. I always gotta be taking care of somebody.'

'Then you and Didi are a match made in heaven.'

He rolled his eyes. 'That, or someplace warmer.'

Despite Julia's fatigue, sleep eluded her. Pictures turned through her head: Starlight in the paddock, Zach in the loft, Marty and Carolyn, Ben. She seemed no closer to answering the questions that plagued her, except for one: the identity of Durbin's traitor. With a compulsive gambler for a wife, Marty certainly had financial cause to sell out DMI.

But would he? Whatever his faults as a husband, Marty was obviously supporting Didi through thick and thin. Was that the behaviour of a traitor? But if not Marty, then who? Ben was too much the straight arrow and she was beginning to doubt Carolyn had the nerve, unless jealousy had driven her to it. She had resented Marty's promotion.

Julia turned on to her stomach and punched her pillow. She wished she'd never agreed to spy for

193

Durbin. This was one mystery she doubted she wanted to solve.

Zach should have been asleep. Days started early out here. Unfortunately, memories of Julia slipping away after they had made love in the loft kept him wired. For the hundredth time, he relived the moment when he woke and found her gone. How did a man like him get through to a woman like her, especially when he had so little time? He knew once she returned to New York, she'd forget him. She'd force herself to. For whatever reason, he made her too skittish to respond any other way. He reached overhead and flicked on the wall lamp, wishing he could banish his inner gloom as easily. She'd barely said 'boo' during dinner, and afterwards all his guests had disappeared. It was enough to make any man toss and turn.

He needed time to court her, to understand her. He hadn't finished making sense of the story she'd told by the fire yet, or the feelings it stirred. Julia was a dominatrix. She whipped her lovers for pleasure, theirs and hers, and she'd been doing it since she was a teenager. Zach didn't doubt there were one or two like-minded females in Montana, but the fact was he'd never met them; had never even watched those talk shows where they trotted such people out like two-headed calves.

Why did people do these things and what did it say about him that he wasn't horrified, that he was, truth be told, halfway down the road to titillated? Was Julia a dangerous character? He couldn't imagine it. She seemed a paragon of responsibility. But was she sick? For that matter, was he? Most of all, where in hell was he going to get the information he needed to reason this through?

Then he remembered his grandmother's secret library. She'd shared this suite of rooms with his grandfather. There was a length of panelling, near the head of the bed, that slid aside to reveal a hidden stack of shelves. It held Grandpa's favourite issues of *Playboy*, dirty books various guests had left, and a few educational tomes that Zach suspected Grandma had bought for herself. She'd always had a curious mind. Grandpa liked to say she'd read anything that wasn't nailed down. Consequently, Zach was pleased, but not surprised, to discover a volume on dominance and submission.

Its presence eased some of the tightness from his shoulders. If Grandma thought the topic worth studying, how bad could it be? He opened the cover and began to read. To his surprise the essays inside were not by psychiatrists, but by people who actually practised 'the lifestyle', as they put it. The frankness of the accounts fascinated him. Many shocked him more than Julia's had, but some he could sort of understand. Taming a submissive wasn't so different from taming a horse. The point wasn't to break their spirits, but to form a partnership that offered each more pleasure than they could find alone. To Zach's way of thinking, any trainer who didn't want a happy horse wasn't worthy of the name.

Still, he couldn't deny some of this stuff sounded silly. A chapter on erotic enemas had him wrinkling his nose. Could that really be pleasant? A tap on the door jerked him upright. His face sizzling with embarrassment, he slammed the book shut and shoved it under the bed.

'Zach,' said the voice at the door to the sitting room. 'It's Julia.'

He moved so fast his socks skidded across the floorboards. She looked startled when he opened the door, and a bit shy, as if she wasn't sure of her welcome. Her gaze drifted down his bare chest to the front of his thermal underwear. Zach's crotch felt heavy from speculating on the things in that book, but he didn't think he was hard.

Of course, he might get that way quick if she kept staring at him.

'Come in,' he said, and stepped aside to let her.

She smoothed the front of her grey velvet robe. 'I don't want to intrude.'

'Nothing to intrude on,' he said, disinclined to tell her what he'd been doing.

She turned in a circle, taking in the sitting room: his computer and desk tucked in the corner, the wingback chairs and fussy mahogany tables left over from his grandmother's day. The bookshelves held volumes on every topic under the sun, most of them hers, but some of them his. Julia's expression was calm as she scanned the titles, but he knew thoughts ticked like calculator keys inside that elegant head. He tried not to hold his breath.

She opened the lid of a carved cedar box and found his boyhood collection of river rocks. Though she couldn't have known which was his favourite, she lifted the palm-sized, butter-smooth rose quartz and rubbed it absently over her lips. His cock thickened at the unconsciously sensual gesture. She was nicely oral, his Julia, nicely tactile. The trait inspired all sorts of depraved ideas.

'This is a nice room,' she said, still tapping the clear rock against her lip. 'Very cosy.'

The stubborn part of him dared her to disapprove. 'It's pretty much the way Grandma left it. I wanted to keep that last bit of her around. We were close.'

'I got that impression,' she said, her grey-green eyes warming with amusement.

She looked different when she smiled, less perfect, but more appealing. The smile was crooked, a little wry, but there was understanding in it. She might laugh, but she wouldn't judge. He realised how lonely he'd been for that since Grandma passed away. His heart turned over with a funny lurch, then beat so hard he felt the pulse in his throat. Lord, he thought, I am in love with her.

The question spilt out before he could stop it. 'Did I do something wrong this afternoon?'

She didn't pretend not to understand. She stepped closer and twined her hands behind his neck. That one point of contact sent a shiver of heat down his spine. Her smile was gone, but her face remained soft. 'You made me nervous,' she said.

Nervous, he repeated silently. That didn't sound good. He forced himself to breathe. 'I didn't mean to come on so strong.'

Her fingers stroked his nape. 'I didn't say I didn't enjoy it. I said it made me nervous. I thought –' A faint flush crept up her sculpted cheeks. 'I thought we might try again, so I could see if I'd imagined how good it was.'

He blinked. The hair on the back of his neck stood up. She wanted to try again? She thought she might have imagined how good it was? He knew she wasn't telling the whole story, but at that moment he didn't care. She was inviting him to do what he longed for most in all the world. Not needing to be asked twice, he untied the belt of her robe and slipped his arms inside, circling her naked waist. He loved how tall she was. When he pulled her closer, her breasts nestled against his chest and her hips snugged his groin. He hadn't known such comfort existed short of heaven.

'I'll be gentle this time,' he promised, stroking the long, warm curve of her back. 'You'll have no cause for nervousness tonight.'

Julia didn't know how to tell him her nerves were exactly what she wanted him to test. She needed to know whether her response to his roughness had been a fluke, as her lacklustre experience with Ben might suggest. If the effect was repeatable, she'd know more about her future options. On the other hand, what he was doing now felt very pleasant.

He nibbled his way down the side of her neck, tender, teasing kisses that left soft bursts of warmth in their wake. He parted the lapels of her robe, smoothing it back over her breasts and shoulders until it dropped to the floor. She almost tripped over it when he nudged her backward, but he caught her before she could fall and lifted her off her feet. Warnings of hernias sprung to her lips, but he kissed her into silence, kissed her with lips and tongue and teeth, with an intensity of attention that robbed her of breath, let alone words.

She couldn't get over how good he tasted. The effect wasn't toothpaste or mouthwash: it was him. Her head tipped back under the invasion, a hum of pleasure warming her vulnerable throat. He answered it, delved deeper, then broke free.

'I've got a bed right back there,' he said, moving towards it. 'A nice wide bed with a prickle-free mattress.'

She tucked her head into his shoulder and clung to him. For one singular moment, she knew what it meant to be small and delicate, to be a woman that a man could sweep off her feet. It wasn't bad, not when Zach was doing the sweeping. He laid her gently across the bed and stood back, his eyes admiring her curves, while his thumbs slid in a restless arc beneath the waistband of his thermal underwear. Such a plain, homely garment. Hard to believe what that loose, porridge-coloured knit did for him, and for her. There was something so old-fashioned about it. It inspired fantasies of seducing old-fashioned men, overcoming old-fashioned inhibitions. She pressed her fingers to the pulsing hollow at the base of her throat. Oh, what his erection did to that stretchy front placket! She could see a slice of its arch between the two flaps, a hint of blood-bronzed skin and gorgeous branching vein.

'Shall I take them off?' he asked, demonstrating a surprising awareness of her fascination.

She nodded and he pushed the undergarment down his legs. Creases marked his lean stomach as he bent. When he straightened, his cock rose in a thick, smooth arrow from the dark cloud of hair at his groin.

Once again, she marvelled at its beauty. Someone should make a mould of him, she thought, and put him in a temple, twenty feet tall and wrapped in beaten gold. The village maidens would kiss him for luck on their wedding nights, and the village men would quail before his strength.

'What are you grinning at?' he said, climbing on to the mattress and hanging over her. His bed was big and heavy and simple. A soft rumpled blanket covered it, stereotypically masculine in bold red and black checks. His rodeo buckles glinted above the crackling fireplace, the cowboy version of counting coup on vanquished enemies: vanquished bulls, in this case. Zach might be gentle; he might leave his beloved grandmother's furnishings intact, but here in this bedroom she could see he was all man. Her grin broadened.

'What?' he said. 'Tell me what's so funny.'

She smoothed her hand up the centre of his chest. 'Just a fantasy.'

'I like fantasies. Want to share?'

'Actually, I'd rather you told me yours.'

Her words caught him halfway towards suckling her nipple. He backed up. 'Don't know that I have any.'

'You must. Everybody does.' She ringed the base of his cock between her finger and thumb. Zach's pupils dilated. Pleased, she pulled lightly until the head slipped free of her hold, then repeated the caress with her second hand. 'There must be some image that goes through your head when you get yourself off. Something you always wanted to do but never got the chance.'

Zach wriggled under her third teasing stroke. She knew he had something in mind from the way his eyes evaded hers. 'Maybe there is something,' he said. 'But I don't know that it qualifies as a fantasy.'

'Tell me.' She reached for him again.

He caught her hand and carried it to his lips. One by one he kissed the tips of her fingers. She shivered at the brush of his moustache.

'Well,' he drawled. 'Seems I never get to make love as slow as I'd like. Just once, I want to take my time without the woman wondering whether there's something wrong with me.'

'I see,' she said. This was not what she had expected. Given what she'd seen of him, as slow as he'd like could be very slow indeed. 'You wouldn't want the woman to wait to come until you did, would you?'

'Of course not,' he said, but a sheepish wince gave him away.

She laughed and shoved his shoulders. 'You would!'

He hung his head. 'Well, in my fantasy she waits, though I can see that might be inconsiderate in real life.'

'No, no, Zach. You've put me on my mettle now. I feel obliged to put my self-control to the test.'

Test it, he did. He began with a leisurely kissing tour of her body, one that searched out all her tender spots and culminated between her legs.

'I think this is cheating,' she gasped as his fingers slid over her plumping folds.

He kissed the cushion of her mound. 'No such thing. A woman needs to be wet for the sort of ride I have in mind. Anyway, you won't be able to come from what I intend to do to you.'

That promise did not reassure her. He opened her slowly, petal by petal, lick by lick. Rather than trying to fuck her with his tongue, he rimmed the entrance of her sheath, staying where the nerves were thickest, never penetrating more than an inch. His moustache grew as slick as his mouth. Then he turned his head to suck either side of her gate between his lips and tongue, deepening the feeling. Through all this, he did not touch her clitoris. Nothing distracted her from the subtle ebb and flow of pleasurable sensation. Her body alternated between relaxing and tensing, between wanting it to end and wanting it to go on for ever. All her strength of will was required to refrain from pulling him closer.

'Now.' He shifted up her body in a smooth, brushing glide. 'I think these trains are ready to couple.'

'I don't get to tease you?' Her voice was gaspingly weak.

He shook his head with laughing eyes. 'This is my fantasy and in my fantasy –' he reached between them to align his cock with her body '– I'm the only tease around.'

She had agreed to this, if only by implication. She could not back out now. Indeed, she forgot she wanted to the moment he entered her, a slow gliding pressure that didn't stop until his pubis nestled flush to hers. The heat of him warmed her from the inside. She counted pulse beats. Hers? His? His head lowered. He rubbed their cheeks together, then their lips, dry silk rasping.

'You feel like home,' he whispered, shy and serious.

A strange, tingling rush moved through her at his declaration. She found she could not hold his gaze. This man is brave, she thought. Braver than I am.

He fucked her slowly, dreamily. He spread her hair across his pillow. He kissed her. He stroked her. The way his body rocked hers reminded her of a lazy massage, one that was supposed to arouse, one she could moan at as loudly as she wished. His cock slid to and fro inside her cunt, mesmerising, memorising probes, as if he were reading her through his thinnest, most sensitive skin. Though she'd expected him to try to make her come before him, he did not. The pleasure he inspired was diffuse, like molten toffee spreading out across a pan. Like toffee, its level rose millimetre by millimetre until it seemed a breath would make her come.

She stretched beneath him, hands and legs roving his work-hard limbs, revelling in the deepening tension, needing to throw it off.

'Almost there,' he whispered, his eyelids heavy, his mouth soft.

She closed her eyes and stopped thrusting, just feeling the soft in-and-out glide, the damp warmth of his skin, the gentleness of his callused hands. She had to breathe deeply to keep her climax off. The pulsations of his cock within her sheath, and of her sheath around his cock, were almost enough to push her over. She could not control the twitching of her inner walls. Her sex had taken on a life of its own.

'Look at me,' he said.

She looked at him. Her face tingled, and her hands, and the front of her body, as if warm, liquid electricity were running over her skin. The tingle reached her pussy. He shivered.

'Do you feel that?' he said. 'Your cunt is magic.'

But it wasn't her. It was him, the soft, blue heat in his eyes, the animal knowing in his hands. An ache began to gather deep inside her. 'I can't stop it,' she said. 'I'm going to come.'

He smiled, eyes crinkling, moustache lifting. 'Count to three, darlin'.' He drew back even more slowly than before, then pushed. Her muscles tightened around his re-entry, naturally, without strain or effort. One, she thought, and sighed when he withdrew. She slid her hand down his spine and around his buttocks, cradling his sac from behind as he pressed forward again. His balls were tight and hard inside. She compressed them gently. His hips juddered in reaction. Two, she thought, thrilled by the tiny quake. As he pulled back one last time, she felt him thicken and heat. Her orgasm teetered on its edge.

'Three,' she said, and came with his push. Her contractions were slow and deep, an intense but dreamy climax. He joined her before the second wave of sensation faded. Swimming in his own pleasure, he moaned, a rich, drawn-out baritone. Her body softened at the sound, melting even as it throbbed. When they'd both gone limp, he withdrew and sank to her side.

'Nice,' he said, hugging her loosely. 'That was real nice.'

Without warning, tears stung her eyes. She pressed her palm to the centre of her forehead, trying to force them back. Lord, what a leaky tap she'd been lately. She couldn't help it, though. He could have mastered her again, easily; could have forced her to come twenty times before he'd finished. Instead, he'd shown her the sweetest, most egalitarian lovemaking she'd ever known. It wasn't 'nice'. It was earth-shattering.

She hadn't thought once of the general or his belt. In fact, she hadn't visited that fantasy with Marty and Carolyn, or with Ben. Her hand fell to her side. She hadn't thought of the general since Zach made love to her in the loft. By that single act, he seemed to have exorcised a lifelong obsession.

But how could that be? How could any of this be? And what if Zach were the only man who had this effect on her?

As if he sensed her worries, he shifted closer and nuzzled the hollow between her neck and shoulder. 'Don't let me sleep all night,' he said. 'Now that I've got you in my bed, I don't want to waste a minute.'

A chill gripped Julia's heart. She remembered his nickname, and the reason for it. Oh, God, she thought. Two down and five to go.

Twice more that night he made love to her. The first was hard and fast. He woke her with stinging kisses and drove his cock inside before she was ready. Her dryness shocked him.

'Oh, darlin'.' He clasped her face and closed her eyes with penitent kisses. 'I'm sorry. I'm sorry.'

But it didn't matter. His very roughness had woken her sex; had drawn the smooth, rich fluid from its scarlet walls. Too sleepy to worry about her reaction and too aroused to deny it, she wrapped her heels behind his neck and drew him deep, deep inside. He coughed, no doubt surprised to find her so flexible. She laughed. 'Fuck me like you mean it, cowboy.'

'Oh, I mean it,' he assured her, beginning to pump. 'Christ, do I mean it.'

His broncs couldn't have bucked harder than she did. She wanted it rougher; wanted everything he had. He gritted his teeth and gave her his all. The box-spring squealed. The headboard thumped against the wall. Every breath he took had a sound: a gasp, a grunt, a tortured groan. He worked one arm under her hips to steady her.

'Easy,' he said. 'Easy.' But neither of them could slow. Their bodies collided within a clinch of arms and legs, drawing back just far enough to gather momentum for another thump, another pump, another bone-bruising grind. He gripped her hair hard and pulled her head back, his mouth clamping on the exposed skin.

He'd mark her again, but she didn't care. She dug her nails into his buttocks, thrilling to his flinch, then drove her longest finger into his anus with as little preparation as he'd driven his cock into her cunt. He froze. He released her throat and panted in her ear. 'What . . . are you doing?'

Had no one touched him here before? Such a childish thrill, that she should be the first. She could not shake it off; could not resist it. She'd always enjoyed breaking virgin ground. She pushed her finger in an inch, enough for a neophyte. His sphincter twitched; tightened in protest. She stroked the sensitive flesh just inside his entrance. His cock jumped.

'I guess –' he began, his voice frayed. His hips

205

wagged, intensifying the pressure her finger exerted. 'I guess there is something to be said for playing around back there.'

The laugh burbled out of her. She licked his crimsoned earlobe. 'Yes, there is, and it's just as much fun when you're the one doing the playing.'

His eyes widened. He made a leap she didn't expect. 'You'd let me do that? You'd let me take you the way Marty took that pool-boy?'

'That way and plenty more.'

His pupils glittered, as if all the ways he might take her were flashing through his mind. Then the reins snapped. He drove his cock downward into her sheath, deep and quick, pumping the head and ridge tight to the back wall. It was a selfish stroke, one that ignored the placement of her most sensitive nerves, one she doubted he indulged in very often. She loved it. She loved that she'd made him forget himself. She loved that he was out of control, that he was racing towards climax in a way he never had before. She let herself come before she normally would because she didn't want to miss a second of his crash and burn.

'Yes,' she hissed, gyrating her finger inside his rim. 'Come, Zach, come.'

He thrust so hard the back of her skull hit the headboard. 'Fuck,' he said. 'Julia!'

He came with the low, kick-in-the gut bellow she'd heard Carolyn draw from him that first night. Her sense of victory was as sweet as it was unexpected. She hadn't known she wanted that proof until she heard it. He sank on to her with a groan of contrition.

'Julia.' He rubbed the bump on the back of her head. 'Julia. My God.'

A second later he was dead to the world. She held him as he slept, rubbing his back with his cock spent but nestled inside her. Unlike Marty, he did snore – softly, but he did. Julia didn't care. The way his moustache fluttered against her neck made her smile.

He hardened before he woke. She lay there, laughing to herself, waiting for him to register his own condition. She had more than enough time to reach in his bedside table for an assortment of condoms. Three decorated her cleavage by the time his brain caught up to his cock. 'Mph,' he said, choosing one with bleary eyes and fumbling fingers. She put the others aside, but she didn't help. She loved watching him handle himself, especially since he wasn't all business. He seemed to enjoy touching himself as he smoothed the latex down, as he circled the crest with one lazy finger, as he squeezed the base with his fist.

Still half-asleep, he turned her on to her belly. Immediately, Julia knew what was coming. She'd given him permission and now he couldn't wait to play. He kissed her bottom and pushed her thighs gently outward. He parted her cheeks. He dipped into her sheath with his cock, swirling it around a few times before shifting back to that other, darker mouth. She'd grown wet as he slept inside her, and adding this to the condom's lubrication allowed his cock to slide easily past her sphincter.

'Oh,' he said in revelation at the warm, satiny passage. Then all she heard was the concentrated rhythm of his breathing as he worked deeper and deeper and finally began to thrust. He curled his hand under her mons, supporting her for his strokes. The broad flare of his glans was heaven against her outer reaches. He seem to know it, for he drew fully in and out each time.

'Shh,' he said when she tried to move. He seemed to require nothing beyond acquiescence. She could have gone back to sleep if she'd wanted, but she didn't. This was too lovely, too luxurious, feeling his slow rise towards orgasm, his hums, his sighs. Her very own intrepid explorer. He came before she did, then palmed her to climax, remaining inside her to the end. Her own finish was a gentle burst of pleasure, a knot of tension falling open. When it was over, Zach turned her to face him and cuddled her close as if she were a much smaller woman.

'I've been curious about something,' he said, the words slurred by satiation. Lulled, Julia hummed her willingness to talk. 'Is your mother still alive?'

She lifted her head. Of all the questions he might have asked, she hadn't seen this one coming. Her hands pressed the hard curve of his upper chest, opening an inch of space between them. 'Why do you ask?'

He shrugged. 'Just wondered. You seem kind of detached from the usual ties.'

Was that what an orphan was: detached? Or was that what Julia had been since the day she was born?

'She died when I was eighteen,' she said. 'A drunk driver hit her on her way to my high-school graduation.' She blew the air out of her lungs; blew away Zach's murmur of sympathy. 'I didn't want to go. I barely knew my classmates. But Mother assumed we would, even acted – in her stiff Swiss way – as if she was looking forward to it. She'd bought a new camera. When the paramedics cut her from the wreckage, it lay on the seat next to her. Didn't have a scratch on it.'

Julia shook her head, remembering the discovery. Her mother never took pictures of anything, but she'd wanted to take pictures of Julia's graduation. Her mother had loved her more than she'd realised. She'd just never known how to show it.

'And after that you were alone,' Zach said.

Julia closed her eyes. She hadn't been alone, not entirely. 'After that, I went straight to secretarial school. I wanted to be out in the world supporting myself.'

'You didn't want to work for the army?'

'No.' Her neck was stiff. Zach's hands crept under her hair and kneaded the cramped muscles. Apparently, he read her body as easily as he read his horses'.

'I don't suppose the general had anything to do with your wanting to leave.'

Julia could not deny his guess. The general had everything to do with her hasty departure from the base. He'd been crazed with despair; too crazed not to turn to the one person who knew his secret, who had it within her means to offer the only kind of comfort he craved.

'I almost stayed,' she said, not sure why she was answering. 'Part of me wanted to.'

'I see,' he said. 'I guess you needed to stretch your own wings, not your mother's.'

'Yes.' His tone was so tolerant she thought he must not understand what she'd meant. Her chest hurt. He begged me to whip him, she wanted to say. He cried and clung to my knees. I wanted to do it. I almost did. Even now, she wasn't sure what stopped her.

'He was a father to you,' he said, his perception uncanny, at once terrifying and welcome. 'He should have treated you like a daughter.'

'Yes,' she said. She could admit that hurt now, that betrayal. She hadn't always viewed him as a daughter should, but at that time, fair or not, she'd wanted him to offer a father's unconditional, undemanding support. Instead, he'd tried to make her over in her

209

mother's image. Her hand curled into a fist over Zach's heart.

He lifted it and kissed its knuckles, one by one. 'I'm glad you're here,' he said.

Her throat tightened. Why did this man's kindness mean so much to her? Why did his presence comfort her when they couldn't have been more different?

'I'm glad I'm here, too,' she said. Her voice shook. He had lightened the pain and it frightened her. Did he guess that, too? She looked at him. His gaze mild, he kissed her brow.

'Sleep,' he said, and she did.

He woke her at sunrise. This time, he rolled her on top of him, letting her take him at her own pace.

'Won't the horses be hungry?' she asked.

He smiled and smoothed her tousled hair down the rise of her breasts. She tried to remember the last time anyone had seen her so mussed. 'The horses will wait this once,' he said. 'You look beautiful like this. I wish we could stay in bed all day.'

So did she, but she knew it couldn't be.

Chapter Eleven

Monday morning

Julia entered the dining room just as Zach set one last steaming platter on the table. His smile was warm but cautious. She should have known he would not flaunt his conquest. He was a private man himself, a private man with private limits. Her answering smile felt like a grimace. She took the seat that had become hers, opposite Marty and Ben.

Marty said something that made Ben laugh. Julia didn't have the faintest idea what. She spread a film of butter across a slice of chewy home-made bread. Her skin prickled. Without looking, she knew Zach was staring at her. This had happened now and then with a new submissive. A bond formed, almost preternatural. She would know when she had their complete attention; could guess what they wanted before they did.

What did Zach want? She turned and their eyes connected. He smiled over the rim of his coffee mug.

She remembered how his moustache tickled when he put his mouth on her sex. Her pulse quickened. Her concentration slipped. It was hopeless. She could not interpret the thoughts behind his grin. Zach was too guarded for her, too patient. Too alien, she added, though for all she knew he'd been visiting the same memory. Vaguely irritated, she turned back to the rest of the table.

Carolyn, she noticed, was quiet this morning. His maternal streak showing, Marty filled her plate and made sure she ate what was on it. Her head was down, her slender neck bowed. But it wouldn't have mattered if she'd lifted it; her gaze was turned inward today.

Julia had seen this before. Carolyn was absorbing her first submissive experience, examining it, savouring it. She stroked her silverware as if the world had, overnight, become a more sensual place. Julia knew the VP was feeling more alive than she ever had. She could not, however, decide what she felt about Carolyn's transformation. Triumph? Satisfaction? Unease? She could admit to all three. But her emotions had no focus. They were muddled and shifting.

She sipped her orange juice, the cool liquid slipping down her throat. She could not ground herself. She felt disjointed. She knew Zach was the reason why.

'Where the hell are you?' Durbin demanded, his voice bullish. 'It's nearly noon. We've got that client lunch today.'

Julia swivelled her chair to face the windows. She sat in the office alcove next to the great room. Outside, snow drifted like drunken feathers to the ground, little more than a flurry. Beautiful as it was, the dwindling fall depressed her. 'Haven't you heard?' she said. 'We're snowed in.'

212

'Snowed in? As in no planes taking off?'

'That's right.'

'Oh.' She heard his blunt fingers drum the desktop, thwarted anger searching for a target. 'Well, when do you think you'll get back?'

'I'm not a weatherman.' Her answer was purposefully cold. His breathing shifted and she knew she'd inadvertently aroused him. He inhaled as if to say something, but she cut him off. 'Take Jody Lundeen with you to lunch. The union men like her and she knows those tax-free municipals inside out.'

'I thought I'd take Charlie. He's been golfing with them.'

'You can't take Charlie if they're serving alcohol. He gets too loud. Anyway, Jody knows their portfolio better.'

Durbin sighed. 'I hate it when you're right. I also hate it when you're gone.' His chair creaked. She pictured him bending closer to the phone. 'You have no idea how much I look forward to Monday. All weekend I dream about you sailing into the office in those snug grey suits. I love hearing you snap out orders to the rest of the staff. I always think maybe that night or the next, you'll be snapping out orders to me.' The words came from low in his chest, gravelled with lust. The evidence of her power over him made her pussy swell. Peeved with herself, she uncrossed her legs and straightened her spine.

'I told you,' she said. 'I'm ending our relationship.'

'Never,' he growled. 'You know you're lying. What we've got is too hot to give up. Shit, we've been on the line two minutes and I'm hard as a rock. I've got my hand in my pocket, Jules. I'm rubbing my big, hot prick. I'm almost coming from knowing you're listening on the other end; from knowing you're sitting

213

there, creaming those French silk panties you like. I'll have to pull my zip down pretty soon or I'll leave a big wet spot on my fly. You know I'm not wearing underwear. You know I wouldn't dare disobey you. But maybe you want me to make a mess. Maybe you want to order me to do it.'

He was breathing roughly, probably as close to coming as he'd threatened. Was he crazy enough to shoot off inside his trousers minutes before a client meeting? Julia didn't know the answer any more. She didn't want to play along, but she didn't know how else to stop him from making a fool of himself.

'I didn't give you permission to touch yourself,' she said in her sharpest, most domineering voice. He moaned and she knew she had seconds to act. 'Open your zip. Now!' She heard the rasp of the metal teeth; heard his whimper of pre-orgasmic panic. 'Roll your chair under your desk. Grab a tissue.'

Wheels squeaked. Something fell to the floor. Durbin cursed, then groaned. She knew it was too late. She knew he was coming. She waited.

'My hand,' he gasped when he could speak again. 'I couldn't get the tissue in time, Ms Mueller. It's dripping all over my hand.'

No doubt he expected her to punish him for that. Julia closed her eyes and prayed for patience. 'Fine,' she said. 'Just tidy up and put your cock away.'

'All right,' he said. Obviously disappointed, he didn't forget his manners entirely. 'Thanks, Jules. That was great.'

Julia didn't tell him he was welcome. 'Is there anything else?'

'What? Oh, yeah. Have you made any progress finding our leak?'

'No,' she said, more emphatic than truthful.

'No?' He made a throat-clearing noise. She knew this was not the answer he'd expected. 'Well, keep at it. I'm sure you'll dig up something.'

'Right.' She pinched the bridge of her nose. 'Do you have any more questions?'

'No-o,' he said unsurely. She wasn't usually so brusque when discussing business. 'Just get back here as soon as you can and, you know, call me. I miss you.'

'I'll see if I have time.' She hung up before he could complain. 'Fuck,' she said to the silent phone. Durbin was in worse shape than she'd known. Maybe she should have told him she'd slept with Marty. Frankly, though, she wasn't sure the knowledge that she'd seduced his entire management team would be enough to disenchant him. He'd think she'd done it for him, to torture him. He thought everything centred on him.

She twisted the chair away from the window and found Zach standing in the middle of the great room, her long leather coat draped over his arm. A flush darkened his rugged face. His brow puckered with what could have been worry or disapproval.

He must have heard her conversation with Durbin. An unwelcome heat suffused her cheeks. Part of her, a disturbingly large part, wished she could have hidden the exchange from him. Hearing a story about her sexual practices was hardly the same as seeing them in action. But screw that, she thought. She had nothing to be ashamed of. Her relationship with Durbin was consensual and intended to give pleasure on both sides. The problem lay not in what they did, but in Durbin's inability to keep it in perspective, a problem she fully intended to address. None of which was any of Zach's business.

'I, uh –' He lifted her coat in silent explanation. 'I

215

wondered if you wanted to help me with the horses today.'

Julia folded her hands in her lap and tried to forget this was the man who'd made love to her all night long. Six times now. Six times he'd turned her inside out and showed her she didn't know herself at all. 'I have plans,' she said.

His flush deepened at the chill in her voice and, damn it, so did hers. For a second she thought he'd leave, but he dropped her coat and walked towards her. He cupped her face, his eyes wrinkling with concern, his thumb stroking soft as goose-down over her cheek. 'Are you all right?'

Meeting his laser-blue gaze required an effort of will. 'Don't imagine I'm a victim here. My boss hasn't forced me into anything. Our relationship is entirely consensual and it continues only so long as I want it to.'

He nodded and swallowed, then turned his face to the frost-rimed window. 'It's none of my business.'

'Exactly,' she agreed, though she wasn't sure either of them meant it.

His eyes returned to hers. His hand fell from her cheek. Immediately, she missed its rough warmth.

'Do you really have plans today?'

She nodded. Again, it seemed as if he'd leave but at the last moment he turned back and kissed her. His tongue played at the seam of her lips before pressing gently inward. She gripped the arms of her chair, wishing she could fight even as she opened to him, even as her spine sagged with pleasure. The motions of his tongue were as delicate as butterfly wings. Where had this big man learnt such tenderness, and why did he offer it to her? She lifted one arm and cupped the back of his silky head. His breath sighed against her cheek. He changed the slant of his mouth.

The kiss gentled even more, a lullaby of lips and tongue. When he finally drew away, her body was as loose and warm as if she'd been lying in the sun.

He trailed one finger down the side of her face. 'Save some time for me, darlin'. Life is short and feelings like this don't come along every day.'

Then he did leave. She almost called him back. What feelings was he talking about? Did he love her? Could he? In spite of everything he knew?

She slammed her hands on the arms of her chair. 'Could he love me?' Her lips made a silent simper of the words. She was behaving like a schoolgirl, the sort she'd never been and never hoped to be. One more fuck, she told herself. One more and it was over for her and 'Sev'.

She ignored the way this made her stomach clench. She rose to prepare for her slaves.

This time she dressed: full regalia, her blood simmering with a defiance she hadn't felt since her mother died. She knew her behaviour was childish. She couldn't reclaim her shaken identity by playing dressing-up.

But she could remind herself how good it felt to don the trappings of power.

She pulled the black deerskin boots up her legs and nodded with satisfaction. Criss-crossed laces extended from their steel-tipped toes to their thigh-high hem. She snugged them, loop by loop, and tied them at the top. The tall heels tightened her buttocks and calves, the tilt making her aware of her height, her power, her femininity.

A leather corset, also black, topped the boots. This leather was thick and brutal. She cinched it just tight enough to enhance the natural curve of her waist, but not tight enough to restrict her breathing. The corset's bra was a warrior queen's breastplate. Two brass nipples studded each circular cup. Inside their hollowed centres, her own nipples lay, tightened by cold and arousal. A pair of black opera-length gloves completed the ensemble, their fingers cut out so as not to hamper the administration of discipline.

Her slaves entered at precisely the appointed time. They wore the white cotton robes she'd given them earlier. Carolyn resembled a tiny karate student in hers, Marty a jolly monk. When Carolyn caught sight of Julia in full gear, her lower lip quivered.

'Ms Mueller,' she whispered, and dropped to her knees to kiss Julia's boots.

Marty's eyes widened as if to say: I hope you don't expect me to do that. Julia shook her head and eased back from Carolyn.

'I will tell you when I wish you to perform obeisance,' she said.

Carolyn bowed her head, her body vibrating with excitement. 'Yes, Ms Mueller.'

The intensity of her response disturbed Julia. A slave needed a certain amount of resistance, both to protect herself and to give her master something to work against. Carolyn seemed to be surrendering all after a single session.

'Take off your robe,' she said, setting her qualms aside for the moment.

Carolyn obeyed without hesitation, then resumed her kneeling position. Julia circled her, thinking, planning. With the snow melting, she might not get another chance to discover the truth. She needed to break the VP now, today. Carolyn dried her palms on her naked thighs. Her pink-tipped breasts trembled with the beating of her heart. She shifted on her heels, her knees easing further apart. Julia spied a sheen of moisture on her mouse-brown curls. Her sex gave a little jump, the old pleasure twining round her core like a soft black cat. Whatever the drawbacks, a wholehearted surrender had its charms.

When she judged Carolyn's tension had reached a sufficient pitch, she lifted a willow-ware bowl from her bedside table and handed it to Marty. 'Open the window,' she said, 'and fill it with snow.'

Carolyn shivered. Obviously, she had some idea of what was coming. When Marty returned with the heaped dish of snow, Julia toed Carolyn's lily-white thighs apart and ordered her to lace her hands behind her neck. The position lifted her delicate breasts, which shimmied with agitation, their nipples drawn into hard pink buds.

Marty stood at Julia's shoulder in the pose of an obedient acolyte, eyes lowered, both hands holding the bowl before his chest. His erection pushed his robe out before him, the tip nudging through the flaps. Good. She had his attention, too.

'We're going to play a game,' she said, scooping up a handful of snow. 'It's called "Truth is its Own Reward".' She trailed the snow up the underside of Carolyn's raised arm. Carolyn bit her lip but did not make a sound. Julia smiled to herself. Just wait, she thought. Just wait. She watched a trickle of ice-water roll down Carolyn's ribs before continuing. 'In this game, I ask a question and if you tell me the truth, you get a reward. Are you ready?'

'Yes, Ms Mueller.'

'Very well. Here is the first question. Do you think DMI pays you what you deserve?'

Carolyn's head snapped up. Obviously this topic caught her by surprise. Her mouth gaped for a moment before any sound came out. 'No,' she said with a hint of her old spirit. 'I think I deserve to be paid more.'

'Very good,' said Julia. 'And here is your reward.' She bent over Carolyn from behind. The position offered Marty a fine view of her corset-plumped breasts. She didn't want him wondering why she'd chosen this line of inquiry. Happily, his eyes homed in on her cleavage, then followed the approach of her snow-filled glove to Carolyn's breast.

Carolyn's breath hissed between her teeth as the snow touched her nipple. Its distension immediately increased and its colour deepened to a fine, plummy red. Julia circled the areola, then cupped it, trapping the snow between Carolyn's breast and her palm. Carolyn struggled not to jerk away.

'Cold, isn't it?' Julia said. 'It excites even as it numbs. Makes you feel all warm and tingly inside.' Carolyn's tongue crept out to moisten her upper lip. 'I'd bet you'd like me to do the other nipple, too, wouldn't you?'

'Yes,' Carolyn whispered. She moaned when Julia drew her hand away.

'For shame,' she said. 'You can't have a reward until you've earnt it. Here's your second question: does Marty Fine turn you on?'

'God, no,' Carolyn said, then flinched at Julia's mocking laugh.

'Liar. I guess I'll have to give Marty your reward.'

'No!' Carolyn cried, but Julia refused to respond. Instead, she pushed Marty's robe open, grabbed another handful of snow and cupped it over his balls.

Marty yelped, almost dropping the bowl in shock. His erection sagged over Julia's hand.

'Poor thing.' Julia tutted in crocodile dismay. She went to her knees and drew his waning shaft into the hot wet comfort of her mouth. At once it rallied, despite her continuing to press snow over his shrinking sac. He widened his stance to keep his balance, which gave her more access. As she sucked, she rubbed the melting snow over his perineum and on to the tight wrinkled star of his anus. Marty went up on his toes. His cock swelled in her mouth, harder than it had been before she shocked it. She let go and backed away.

Marty panted once and set his jaw against whatever protest he'd wanted to make.

'Now.' Julia dipped into the bowl and turned to Carolyn. The woman's hands were fisted on her thighs. 'Let's try this again.' She held her icy handful above Carolyn's breast and let it drip. 'Are you jealous of Marty Fine?'

Carolyn's gaze darted towards Marty but did not rise. 'Yes.'

Julia shifted the snow so that it dripped directly on to her nipple. 'Were you annoyed when he was promoted and you weren't?'

'Yes,' she gasped, straining upward towards the taunting hand.

'I bet you'd have done a great deal to get even.'

'Yes,' she said. 'Yes!' Her face was red, her breathing quick and light. Julia lowered her dripping hand. Carolyn twisted, trying to reach it without leaving the position she'd been ordered to assume. She was Julia's creature now. She'd answer any question, admit to any crime, even a crime whose exposure could end her career. All Julia had to do was ask: did you betray DMI to Santorini?

Without warning, Julia's stomach turned over. She felt queasy, her enjoyment gone. For a moment, she could not imagine why this should be so. But then she knew. It was not her awareness of Carolyn's fragility that had ruined the game, or her niggling fear that Zach would discover what she'd done and disapprove. No. The problem was that *she* disapproved. She had broken her own rule, and the most sacred at that: that this should always be done with the intent to heighten pleasure. Not to steal a secret. Not to find a traitor for a man who, Julia knew, had done little to earn anyone's loyalty.

This was a travesty of all she believed in. It must stop.

Her arm fell to her side. Her fingers opened. The snow splashed to the toe of her boot. She didn't care. She didn't care.

'No,' Carolyn wailed, clutching her knees. 'I'll be good. I'll answer anything you want. You're the boss of me, please. You're the boss of me.'

Julia closed her eyes. She had put those words in Carolyn's mouth; she and no one else. What had she done to this vulnerable young woman? She prayed she could undo it. Gathering her strength, she clasped Carolyn's face and lifted it, one glove warm, one glove cold. 'I lied to you,' she said, putting all her persuasion into her gaze. 'I'm not the boss of you. You are. You always were. You always will be. Any power I had over you, you gave me.'

'No.' Carolyn was sobbing in earnest now, hiding her face between Julia's knees. 'You can't leave me like this. You can't take me this far and leave me.'

'Julia.' The voice was Marty's. She looked at him, feeling as lost as Carolyn sounded. His expression was strange. Did he know what she'd been trying to get Carolyn to admit? Did he know because he was guilty? She shook her head, throwing off the question. To hell with that. It didn't matter.

'Julia,' Marty said again. He opened his arms. 'Give

her to me. I'll take care of her.' Carolyn clung and cried but he managed to prise her free. Then she clung to him. He stroked her bony back. The sharpness of her shoulder blades made Julia's breath catch. 'It's all right,' Marty said to both of them. 'I'll take care of her. Just go.'

But Julia couldn't just go. She met his eyes, taking his measure. Did he realise Carolyn wasn't the responsibility of a night or a week; that she was perhaps a responsibility he could not handle without professional help – and not Julia's sort of professional help? He already had his wife to take care of. Did he really want to add Carolyn to the mix?

'I can handle it,' he said.

'And if you can't?'

'Then I'll find someone who can.'

She saw that he meant it; that the challenge had energised him. He had the potential to be an excellent switch, dominant or submissive as the situation required. Perhaps that was what Carolyn needed: someone who could feed her submissive tendencies while also inspiring her aggressive ones. Perhaps together they would find a happy balance.

Grabbing the first clothes that came to hand, she nodded at Marty and withdrew. The last thing she heard as she headed to the bathroom to change was the sound of a brisk spanking. For the space of a heartbeat, she wondered who was administering it.

She went to the stables; searching for Zach, she admitted, though the horses were a lure as well. If they rejected her, she would know she'd slipped beyond redemption. If they accepted her, she didn't know what she'd do. Hope, she supposed. But for what, and from whom?

The question turned out to be moot. The horses were absent and so was Zach. She wandered into the tack room feeling wobbly and strange. A broken bridle lay across his desk, the same one she'd seen there before. They'd been keeping him busy, or perhaps his chores were always more than he could keep up with. She knew he wasn't lazy. His work ethic was one characteristic they shared. A melancholy sigh escaped her iron grip. When had the stupid cowboy become a man she admired?

Pushing the question away, she sat in his beat-up desk chair. The impression of his buttocks had shaped the seat. The hollows clasped her, taunted her. She ran her hands along the edge of the tan metal desk. Her fingertips took inventory of the scratches and dents, the coffee stains and sticky spots. Which had Zach made, and which his grandfather? The number for the vet was taped to the bottom of an old rotary phone. Oh, how awful if the horses got sick, she thought. How lost Zach would be. She touched the receiver. Scores of fingerprints dulled its black plastic shine. No one had cleaned this for a long, long time.

The multi-generational mess should have horrified her. Instead, for no reason she could fathom, she burst into tears.

Once they started, they fell in torrents, as if every hurt she'd refrained from crying about must be cried about now. She cried for her father and her mother, married but not in love. She cried for the general and the dog she hadn't been allowed to buy. She cried for Carolyn and Marty, and for Marty's poor compulsive gambling wife. Mostly, though, she cried for herself. What was the matter with her? How had she become this ridiculous drippy mess? If this was what it meant to have a heart, the vanilla world could keep it.

'Hey, what's wrong?' said a soft, masculine voice. A hand settled between her shoulder blades. It wasn't Zach's. It was Ben's. She grabbed a dusty rag. It looked like an old T-shirt. The cotton smelled of Zach, in other words: wonderful. She cried harder.

'Hey.' Ben crouched down beside her and pulled her close. 'Tell me what's wrong. I'm sure it's not as bad as you think.'

She blew her nose into the rag and blinked at him through blurry eyes. What a confessor he would make: sure to disapprove, unlikely to understand. But maybe she needed someone to agree with her own estimation of her sins. Maybe that would snap her out of this idiocy.

'Are you sure you want to know?' she said. 'It isn't a pretty story.'

He shook his head and smiled. 'If I can help, I want to know.'

She didn't tell him about Zach. She didn't share her crisis over being a dom. She did tell him about training Marty and Carolyn. As she'd expected, that was enough to shock him. When she explained what she'd almost forced Carolyn to admit, however, she saw something she'd never expected to see in his handsome face: she saw guilt.

'Julia.' He rubbed his smooth lean jaw, his eyes looking everywhere but into hers. 'There's something I need to tell you.'

No, she thought. 'No,' she said. She rolled the battered chair back from him, but retreat was useless. The pieces fell together against her will. She remembered his description of the first white woman he'd slept with, the woman he'd said he met at an office party. The whispery voice, the big doe-like eyes. They could only belong to one person: Sheila Fassbinder, the wife of Go-Tech's chairman, the company whose account had been stolen from DMI. She didn't understand the connection between that and Ben's betrayal, but she knew there was one. 'You?' she said. 'You leaked our proposal to Santorini?'

He seemed relieved not to have to initiate the confession. Still crouched on the balls of his feet, he picked at the peeling arm of her chair. 'You know the woman I told the story about? She was Nate Fassbinder's wife. I slept with her a few times. She liked to talk about her husband after we, you know. She told me he was using Go-Tech's accounts to launder drug money. She didn't have proof, but I didn't want DMI to win their business and end up getting tarred with the same brush.'

'And you couldn't tell Durbin not to bid without telling him where you'd heard the rumour.'

Ben spread his hands, his eyes begging her to understand. 'I couldn't betray Sheila's trust. She didn't want to leave her husband. I feel bad enough that I sent an anonymous tip to the Securities and Exchange Commission. I don't know what will happen if they investigate.'

'Oh, Ben.' Julia covered her face. She didn't want to be hearing this, not when she'd finally decided the traitor's identity didn't matter.

'I'll tell Durbin everything,' he said, 'as soon as we get back.'

'But he'll ruin you.' She took his hands and squeezed them. 'He won't care that you were trying to protect him. He'll make sure you never work on Wall Street again.'

Ben's expression assumed a stubborn cast. 'I can't keep it a secret now I know he's suspecting the others. It wouldn't be fair.'

'Fuck fair,' Julia said. His eyebrows rose. She pushed

herself to her feet and paced the tiny room. 'I know there's a way out of this. I just need to think.' A spark of an idea shimmered through her mind. She stopped. She pressed her hands over her mouth and smiled. Oh, it was too delicious.

'What?' asked Ben.

She faced him. He was standing now, his long frame propped back on the cluttered desk. 'I've thought of a huge favour you can do me.'

'Name it.'

Her glee rose. She tossed her head and laughed. 'You can tell Durbin I'm the traitor. I know just how to prove it, too.'

'I can't do that,' he said.

'Oh, yes, you can,' she answered. 'Because it's the only way I'll get clear of him.'

He took some convincing, but she talked him round in the end. At last, she'd found a sin Durbin would not forgive: a threat to his bottom line. When he heard about this, he'd demand she never see him again. Even Ben could see the value of that.

'But what if he tries to get even?' he said.

'That's the beauty of me taking the fall. Durbin wouldn't dare expose me because I'd expose him. Believe me, I've got the evidence to do it.'

Ben waved his hands in front of his face. 'I don't want to know.'

That's when she knew she had him. Otherwise, plausible deniability would have been irrelevant.

Considering the morning that preceded it, lunch was not pleasant. Carolyn was subdued, Ben jittery and Zach as stone-faced as the carvings on Mount Rushmore. Asking people if they wanted seconds appeared to require a major effort. Was he angry at her for

227

refusing his invitation to help with the horses? Or at himself for suggesting he wanted her to? Whatever the reason, he was making up for his earlier openness. Of the five of them, only Marty seemed calm, and he was too caught up in his thoughts to contribute his usual witty repartee.

As soon as they'd cleared the dishes, Julia headed for the well-appointed office Zach kept for his guests. She refused to waste time smoothing ruffled feathers. She had work to do and futures to safeguard, her own included.

She used Zach's modem to connect to the network in New York. After that, planting the evidence of her 'crime' was simple. Julia knew DMI's system intimately, having been involved in testing it prior to purchase. She inserted a few incriminating files into her personal computer, pre-dated them, then deleted them, but not so completely they wouldn't leave a trace. Then she hacked into the main server, a task made easy by possession of access codes usually reserved for designers. Once in the main server, she copied the incriminating files to the company's back-up system which, unbeknownst to most employees, recorded their every keystroke. Luckily, the back-up wasn't due to be removed for off-site storage for another week. Finally, she terminated the connection and hacked into the network. Careful to leave a mess behind her, she faked an attempt to delete the back-up files she'd just introduced. Now it looked as though Julia had modemed the Go-Tech proposal to Santorini, become afraid she'd got caught, then tried – unsuccessfully – to delete the evidence. DMI's overworked computer geeks might take a while to notice the break-in, but once Ben returned with his tale of treachery, they'd be certain to look for confirmation.

Satisfied they'd find it, she leant back in the swivel chair and stretched her arms. It had taken three hours to dot her 'i's and cross her 't's, but she was reasonably certain her deception would stand up under scrutiny. Durbin wouldn't want to believe she'd sold him out, but he'd be forced to when he saw this.

Her gaze swept the woods outside the house. The snow had ceased. She'd burnt her last bridge. A tension that was part excitement, part dread tightened in her chest. From this day forward, her old life was history.

She was rehearsing how she'd coach Ben to deliver the revelation, when Marty strolled in and pulled up a second chair. He patted her hand. 'You done working for the day?'

'Yes.'

'Good. I've been meaning to talk to you. You looked a bit red-eyed at lunch. I wanted to make sure you were OK.'

Her hand flew to her face. Her weeping fit came rushing back. She cried so seldom she'd forgotten what it did to a person's looks. Had Zach noticed? But, no, he wouldn't have been so ill-tempered if he had. 'I'm fine,' she said to Marty. 'I was upset but I'm over it.'

'She's all right, you know. Carolyn likes to be dramatic. Always gives a hundred and ten per cent to everything, including misery. But she'll bounce back.' He wagged his bushy brows. 'She might even decide she doesn't need my masterful help.'

Julia rolled her eyes. 'That might be the best thing. Carolyn could turn out to be a handful.'

'Nonsense.' He winked. 'I enjoy a new project. It makes me feel needed.'

She did not ignore the opening. 'If you really want to feel needed . . .'

'Yes?' he said.

'You could keep an eye out for Ben when you get back.'

He frowned. 'For Ben?'

'He might find himself in over his head.'

'In what over his head?'

'Trust me. You're better off not knowing.'

Marty's frown deepened, but after a brief stare he shrugged. 'All right. Keep your secrets. I'll look out for him. To tell you the truth –' he bumped chair wheels with her '– I've been thinking of starting my own operation. Investment advice for individual investors, preferably rich ones. I was hoping I could lure Ben with me. Those blue-haired biddies love that man's manners.'

'That might be a good idea.'

He scratched his stubbled cheek. 'Actually, I was hoping I could lure you away from Durbin, too.'

The prospect did not appeal as much as it might have. Marty would never give her as much responsibility as Durbin had. He wouldn't need to. Marty was capable of staying on top of things himself. She smoothed her skirt over her knees. 'It's kind of you to think of me.'

'Yeah, well, too bad the Big Apple won't be seeing you for a while.'

She stared at him. 'I never said I wasn't going back to New York, just not to DMI.'

'No?' He brushed a piece of lint from his shoulder. 'I must have been mistaken.'

'You were.'

Was that a smirk he was hiding? If it was, when he looked up it was gone. 'Maybe I'll give you a call then, when I'm set up.'

'Fine,' she said, still annoyed and hardly aware what she was agreeing to. How ludicrous. Why wouldn't

230

she return to New York? Surely he couldn't imagine there was anything to hold her here.

Zach couldn't keep to his rooms. His bed was too empty and the sound of icicles dripping from the eaves was driving him nuts. The wind had changed. A thaw was setting in. The time that remained to break down Julia's wall was getting shorter by the minute.

He found her in the great room, sitting in the dark staring at the fire. Shadows leapt around the room, bathing the andirons, the ceiling beams, her regal silhouette.

'Are you all right?' he asked.

She started in surprise. A smile curled her lips. 'I'm fine,' she said. 'I took steps towards leaving my employer today.'

'Oh.' He rubbed his moustache. 'That's good.'

'Yes,' she said. 'It is.'

He wondered what, if anything, he ought to make of this. Would she be taking up with Marty now? Something was going on between those two, though he couldn't figure out what. Too distracted to consider whether his company was welcome, he plunked down beside her on the couch, half a cushion stretching like a gulf between them.

They sat in silence. Julia stared at the rodeo picture above the fire, the one his grandma had dusted clean every Sunday morning, last thing before she went to church. Its glass was a shifting river of gold and black. Zach wished he could think of something – anything – entertaining to say. After five of the longest minutes of his life, she turned towards him with a soft, crunching squeak of leather. Her knee brushed his thigh and a wash of heat flooded his groin. Unfortunately, she wasn't making a pass. 'When did your grandmother die?' she asked.

231

It was the first personal question he could recall her asking. She'd gone to the heart of him with it, as if she'd read his mind. He pressed his palms into his thighs, willing his arousal to recede, willing his brain to work. 'Last year. Right around this time.'

'You miss her.' It wasn't a question.

He nodded. 'I loved Grandpa, but she was my best friend in the world. The guests adored her. She always knew how to make people feel at home. I sure as hell wish I did.'

Julia touched his cheek with the back of her fingers. His heart literally skipped a beat. 'You do all right.'

The touch broke his patience. He faced her. 'Hell, Julia. We made love and it was really special. It kills me that I don't know what to say to you that won't scare you off.'

Not that, apparently. Her hand withdrew, leaving a patch of cold behind. 'You don't mean that. You don't even know me.'

'Then tell me what I don't know!' His voice cracked in frustration. 'I'll listen to all of it. Every heartbeat. Every hope. You name it, Julia, I'll open my ears and try to understand.'

She jumped off the couch, her eyes huge in the firelight, her hands clutched together before her breastbone. She looked wilder than he'd ever seen her, panicked. 'It's only a weekend,' she said, backing away. 'You don't even know me.'

I know enough, he thought as her footsteps receded towards her room. He knew his heart was set on her and nothing would shock him out of it, more fool he. He rose to damp the fire. The thought of what he was willing to do to keep her happy didn't scare him half as much as the thought of losing her.

Chapter Twelve

Monday night

Once inside her room, Julia smacked her thighs with her fists. She was a fool, a rabbit bolting for her hole. What was she thinking, telling him he didn't know her? In one weekend, he'd learnt more than most people who'd known her for years. The stories she'd told weren't the only reason, either. The cowboy had instincts. He knew things about her he probably didn't know he knew. Why he hadn't run screaming she couldn't say, but she knew why she was scared. Because it *was* only a weekend. As Carolyn's experience proved, those ladies in Taylorsville didn't call him 'Sev' for nothing.

She stripped off her clothes and threw them into a corner, pausing only when a plane rumbled overhead. She stared at the pine-panelled ceiling. A plane. That meant the airport was open. As soon as they cleared a path down this mountain they could leave. Fine, she thought. The sooner the better. But she balled up her panties and tossed them angrily away. Pulling on her favourite silk chemise, she crawled into bed and curled up around the pillow. She gritted her teeth against an urge to cry. Once a day was plenty.

The knock took her by surprise. Heart pounding, she sat up. Zach entered without waiting for a response, his tall frame backlit by the light from the hall. He wore the long underwear that had given her such a creaming fit the night before, except this pair was red. The sudden hum in her groin told her she was developing a new fetish. The red cotton hung from the solid points of his hipbones, draping the hefty basket that dangled between his legs. Immune to the cautions of her brain, Julia's body softened in welcome. Zach elbowed the door shut and pulled a chair to the side of her bed.

'I can't let things go on like this,' he said.

She almost asked what he meant, but she hadn't grown as dishonest as that. Instead, she smoothed the covers over her waist. Zach heaved a weary sigh. Every cell in her body yearned to soothe him. Was this love, this helpless tenderness? Had she found what she'd been seeking even as she ran from it? Flo from the Coffee Stop had misled her. This was the man those women wanted to marry; not the indefatigable love machine, but this shy, earnest hunk. God help her. Julia wasn't any more sensible than they were.

When he took her hand in his, his palm was cold. 'Do you want to hear about my first lover, the story I wouldn't share that night by the fire?'

She couldn't make out his expression, but his eyes glittered in the dark. She knew this offer meant something to him; it had set his pulse racing. 'Yes,' she said, without letting herself wonder why he wanted to tell her, without letting herself hope. He shifted in the old-fashioned chair.

'Her name was Constance,' he began. 'She was my father's lover.'

Her spine straightened in surprise. She knew other people's families weren't perfect, but she hadn't expected Zach's to engage in adultery. 'Your father's?' she said.

He shrugged, a hint of defensiveness in it. 'He wasn't a womaniser. Constance was his only affair. If my mother knew, she pretended not to. Too old-school, I guess. Anyway, Constance and my father were habitually on-again, off-again. The way they fought you'd have thought they were married. My brother and I knew about her, but not my sisters. Tom and I made sure of that.'

Zach turned her hand and smoothed the cup of her palm. Julia couldn't take her eyes from his shadowed profile. She assumed Tom was his brother. He'd mentioned sisters, plural. Were there more than two? Her brain shifted, trying to fit this into her picture of him. The rodeo was there already, and the lovesick women of Taylorsville. The man who'd fucked her into submission in the loft was part of it, and the one who'd loved her to exhaustion in his bed. And who could forget the hedonist who'd let Carolyn blow him in broad daylight, or the saint who'd taught her to pet a skittish horse? Now to all this she could add a family: one with a philandering father and at least a pair of sheltered sisters. She bet Zach was the eldest. Were you? she wanted to ask, but she was afraid to break his storyteller's nerve.

His thumb traced the soft pads of flesh at the base of her fingers. 'My father and I didn't get on. We had different ideas about how stock should be treated and

235

my rapport with the horses made him nervous. Dad believed in breaking horses, in whipping them into submission. Whenever I showed him that my way worked and, what's more, worked better than his, he'd act as if I'd slapped him. So we never did get on and Constance knew it.

'On my seventeenth birthday, he and Constance had a big fight. Like most ranchers, my dad is careful with money, sometimes too careful. As I recall, he wouldn't lend her a couple of hundred to repair her car. They were hollering about it in front of the feed shop. I thought someone would hear and get word back to Mom, so I offered to loan Constance what she needed. I had some rodeo prizes stashed and nothing in particular I wanted to spend them on. I wasn't trying to make Dad look bad. I was just trying to shut Constance up. But he was so angry he got in to the car and drove off without me. He stranded me twenty miles from home in the dead of winter.

'Constance couldn't drive me since her car was shot, so she told me I could stay with her. I guess I was pretty naïve because I didn't think anything of it. She was a lot younger than my dad but, to me, I was a kid and she was a grown-up. I learnt differently when she crawled into my bed that night. I'm not sure I can describe what her hands did to me. Up till then, I'd never had a girl do more than kiss me. Now, this voluptuous older woman was touching me in places that had never felt any hand but mine, plus a few that hadn't felt that. She'd come to me naked. Her breasts were softer than anything I'd known. I hardly dared touch them, but her hands were all over me, waking my nerves like firecrackers, and suddenly I realised I was supposed to touch her. That was what was fair.' Zach's moustache slanted with his smile. 'I nearly fainted when I felt her nipples bud up under my palms. I couldn't have been more stunned if I'd woken one morning knowing how to pluck rabbits out of hats. My skin was on fire; my cock so hard it stung. I was so excited I could hardly breathe.

'Lord, I was a mess. Constance had to pull me on top of her or I would have spent all night going over her like a blind man. I jumped halfway to the ceiling when she wrapped her fingers around my cock. Then she put me inside her.

'I thought I'd died and gone to heaven. She was warm and slippery and her sex moved around me like a cat on heat. I was shaking worse than a newborn calf. I knew I was supposed to move, but I couldn't figure out how to balance and thrust at the same time. Finally, she rolled me under her and straddled me. She was a beautiful woman and, boy, did she love to rock and roll. I remember watching her come and thinking this must be how people who found Jesus felt. Sex was that amazing to me: a revelation.

'As things progressed, though, I started to wonder if something was wrong with me. Everything felt incredible, but I hadn't come yet. My friends who'd done it said it only took a few minutes, a few seconds the first time.

'When I apologised for taking so long, Constance laughed. "You take as long as you want, Little Zach." I could tell she was enjoying herself, so I relaxed and let her explain a few things about the female body that my buddies had never mentioned. "What a dear!" she said when I did what she'd showed me to her clit. I did it some more and pretty soon she came again, even harder than the first time. When she caught her breath, she told me I'd earnt a reward. By then, I was ready for one. I thought I'd bust if I didn't come. Constance pulled off me and took my cock into her mouth. Then I really thought I'd gone to heaven. I blasted off in about two seconds. The orgasm was better than anything I'd ever done for myself, deeper and harder. I thought for sure she'd wrung me dry, but a minute later, I was raring to go again. Just thinking about what we'd done got me all steamed up. We went at it until we were both too tired to move. Constance could be a bitch, but she was pure fun between the sheets. I was enjoying myself so much, I never stopped to wonder how my father would feel about being kicked out of his mistress's bed by his own son. Or how I'd feel if he didn't forgive me. I was too damn randy to use my brain.

'That first night led to a second, then to a week, then two. Constance called in sick at work and we screwed morning, noon and night. In the end, Grandpa came down from the mountain to give me a talking to.'

Zach's laugh was a rush of air. 'Grandpa never raised his voice, but he had a knack for making a person see the error of his ways. Before long I felt lower than a snake's belly. I said goodbye to Constance, thanked her for being such a good teacher and dragged myself back home. Unfortunately, my dad wouldn't let me in the house. My grandpa had come with me, expecting there'd be trouble, but even he couldn't convince my dad to forgive me. Grandpa took me home with him and, apart from holidays and birthdays, I've spent every night since under this roof.'

'You and your dad still don't talk?'

'We say "howdy" and shake hands, but we never talked much to start with. We disagree about most everything. It's easier for everybody if we keep our distance.' He patted her hand as if to comfort her. His was shaking, a token of how seldom he bared his soul.

She squeezed his fingers. 'Why did you tell me this?'

'I want you to know me,' he said.

It was a simple answer: no promises, no declarations, just 'I want you to know me'.

Julia stared at their joined hands. She supposed she'd wanted a declaration of love. But maybe this was better. He wanted her to know him. Even if the knowing didn't outlive another dawn, for a private man like Zach that offer was rare. Didn't she have the courage to accept it, regardless of the cost to her heart? She fought a sigh. She couldn't deny any longer that her heart was at risk. Whatever love was, this turmoil he stirred in her must be a cousin to it. But she'd taken too long to respond.

'Julia?' he said. She lifted her head, glad of the darkness that hid her brimming eyes. He carried her hand to his chest and pressed her palm over his heart. When he spoke, his voice was hushed. 'Tell me what you want from me. Do I need to bend to you? Do you want to use your belt on me?'

'No,' she said, shaken by his offer.

'I'm not sure I'd mind. I suspect I'd find you irresistible even if you painted me blue and chained me to the bedpost.'

'No.' Her free hand reached for his face. 'That's not what I want from you.'

'Then what do you want?'

She stroked his cheek from temple to jaw. 'I want to make love again. I want to show you how tender I can be.'

His smile brought a crease to his beard-shaded cheek. 'I'd like that very much.'

She tugged him on to the bed and pushed him gently down, knowing it was the last time but feeling as if it were the first. Her hands tingled with awareness. A

239

small brass reading lamp extended from the wall above the bed. She flicked it on. Zach lay quietly, watching as she stripped off her rose-pink chemise and draped it over the shade. The light dimmed and warmed. Zach shifted his hips. His erection formed a thick arch behind the red cotton drawers, but he did not reach for her. Slowly, giving herself time to enjoy the unveiling, she peeled the long underwear down his legs. When she reached his feet, she bent to kiss his toes. He had crooked, battered toes, but they were as sensitive as the rest of him. They curled strongly at the touch of her tongue. Sucking one into her mouth, she scratched his soles with her nails. His knees wavered up and down. He truly was a pleasure to tease. She would miss that most of all.

'Come here,' he growled, but he lay as passively as if she'd bound him.

He probably thought he was being a gentleman, letting a lady take the lead. To a woman of her bent, however, any subservience carried a special cachet. A peculiar thrill quivered up her spine, peculiar because it felt so fresh, as if she had never mastered anyone before. She knew her control over Zach was fragile. He might overturn it at any moment. That was thrilling, too, perhaps because she knew she'd let him.

She crawled up his body and straddled his hips. He clasped her waist but presumed no further. She sat back until her bottom rested on warm, hairy thighs. His hands slid up her ribs. She caught them before he could fondle her breasts.

'Let me,' she said, her voice unrecognisably soft. 'Let me pleasure you. Let me go as slowly as I want.'

Surrender and anticipation mingled in his sigh. He nodded.

With a sigh of her own, she traced his receding

hairline with her fingertips, lingering on the smooth, sensitive skin at his temples. His golden-brown hair was clipped so short it bristled like a Marine's. His quadriceps tightened when she tickled the rims of his ears. He closed his eyes when she scratched back over his skull.

'I'm going to touch your forgotten places,' she said, stroking her thumbs together towards his chin. 'I'm going to love them all.'

'Julia,' he whispered.

She caressed the winter-chapped fullness of his lower lip. She smoothed his eyebrows, then his nose, then the silky brush of his moustache. With his eyes shut, she could study him as she wished. She loved the seams that Montana's weather had left in his skin. More than laugh lines; these were character lines. They spoke of hard work and sunshine and strength. They spoke of patience and pain and a big capacity for love. His face would age well, she thought. Sadness spread through her chest in a hot, heavy wave. She would never see him age. She would never find another man who called so strongly to the different sides of her soul. She would never fall in love.

Unless she had already.

But what if she had? What use was denying it, or crying over it? The world was full of people who'd lived through broken hearts. She would, too. She was Julia Mueller, the terror of DMI. She wouldn't let love make a coward of her. With a wistful smile, she bent forward to lick the corded tendons of his neck. His cock lurched under her belly. His hands tightened on her waist.

'Shh,' she said, and his grip loosened. She bent to suckle his tiny, sharp nipples. His fingers spread over her bottom.

241

'Julia,' he said, stroking her curves. 'That feels so good.'

She kissed his nipples until his back arched with pleasure. Then she coaxed him on to his belly. He relaxed into the full-body rubdown as ecstatically as his horse. She smiled to herself, half expecting to see his ears flop down. Maybe he'd had the right idea about how to tame a lover. She licked the salty crease between his buttocks and legs, then spread his cheeks. Lubrication was as close as the warm, weeping slit of her sex. When she pressed her slippery fingers to his tightly pinched anus, his head came around on the pillow, alert but not alarmed. Despite all he knew of her, he trusted her. Her gratification was immense. This man, neither slave nor submissive, trusted her. Excitement gushed from the heart of her sex. Tonight she'd take him all the way.

'I'm going to go further this time,' she said. 'Tell me if anything hurts. Because it shouldn't. It should only feel good.'

To her relief, he relaxed instinctively. Her two longest fingers slid easily into the flickering passage. As she progressed, he hummed like a man considering a new wine. The hum deepened abruptly when she found the small, hard swell of his prostate. She stroked gently, relishing his twists and squirms, the expressions of pleasure that twitched the muscles of his face. Then she pressed.

'Ah,' he said, jerking. 'Do that again.'

She did it again, and again, and bent to knead his buttocks with her other hand. She bit their muscled curves: lover's bites, a tender mingling of pain and pleasure. He thrust at her, fucking himself on her fingers. The mattress creaked. The sheets rustled. A fevered glow washed over her at the sight of the sweat that bathed his muscled back. Her juices trickled down her inner thighs. Unable to bear the wait, she rubbed herself against the bulge of his calf. She licked the skin next to her working fingers. He moaned, low and anguished in his throat. He didn't come, though. For long, panting minutes he took what would have sent most men over the edge twice over. His tension wound tighter. His moans grew louder.

'Enough,' he gasped. 'It's too good. I can't take any more.'

She pulled free and wiped her hand. He turned over between her legs. The skin of his cock bore sheet marks from being pressed so tightly to the bed. She saw veins she'd never noticed before, bulging blue and thick around the shaft. Sweat matted the hair at the base. She combed it outward with her fingers, then ran her hands up his chest.

'Fuck me,' he said, his blue eyes burning, his ribs moving quickly in and out. 'Fuck me hard.'

'Soft,' she said, with a teasing smile. 'Soft and slow.'

He moaned when she positioned him for entry, parting her lips with the hot red silk of his glans. They sighed together as she sank on to him. It was good to be filled, good to have something to work that deep, wet ache against.

'Julia,' he crooned.

'Zach,' she responded, a laugh in it.

She kissed him and he clasped her face. Their mouths tangled, and their desires. His cock pulsed inside her. He pushed deeper. They broke free from the kiss to drag air into their lungs.

'Now,' he said, smiling, flushed. 'Please.'

She pushed back on her arms and began to rock, as slowly as she'd threatened. He did not oppose her. He followed her pace and force, and nothing in him seemed to resent it. He held her gaze with his and every so often he'd grin and say her name, as if pleasure were bubbling up inside him and that was the only way to release it. Julia slowed her breathing. Without being told, he matched that, too, until their ribs expanded in unison. An eerie energy sprung up between them, flowing between and around their bodies. It felt like water, or a light breeze. She'd experienced something like it that night in his room, but this was even stronger. The current had a slow rhythmic beat. Julia knew it must be her heart and yet it seemed as if it were the mountain's heart, as if the earth beneath them had joined their play. She had never felt so close to another human being. She wanted to ask Zach if he felt it, too, but she was afraid to hear he did. What did it mean? Her throat hurt. Her pussy tightened. When she came, she came alone.

Zach nursed the spasms with his thumbs. 'That was real nice,' he said, once she'd settled. 'I felt that down to my toes.'

Julia shook off her melancholy and grinned. 'I'll show you nice.'

She eased off his rigid cock and took it in her mouth.

'Oh, God,' he said, hips arching. 'Julia.'

She sucked him deep, well aware that she was fulfilling his seventeen-year-old definition of heaven. His penis was smooth and hot and tasted of her and him. With her tongue she learnt its swells and folds, its sweet spots, its ticklish patches. He was every bit as responsive as she'd hoped and, for the first time since she'd met him, she sensed him trying to hold back orgasm, rather than strive for it. He didn't want to go over. He wanted to savour this.

She slowed her rise and fall; gentled her suction. He sighed with heartfelt gratitude and spread her hair across his groin, petting it in a rhythm she was wise enough to follow.

'Julia,' he murmured. 'Darlin'. Sweet. Heart.'

She held his hips to steady him, to quiet his compulsive thrusts. His hands fisted in her hair. He groaned. She rose to his glans, swirled her tongue around the flare, then plucked the rosy plum with a soft, smacking kiss. She released him and watched his flesh shudder. The slit at the tip of his cock fluttered, pushing out a thick drop of pre-ejaculate.

'I'm going to finish you now,' she whispered, the words a breeze across that lust-tautened skin. 'I want you to breathe deeply and bear down.'

With her palm she gathered his scrotum, plump now and high with arousal. The tips of her fingers rubbed his perineum. Its ridge shifted as he bore down internally. She swallowed his shaft. His body tightened: thighs, arms, belly. For a moment he forgot to breathe and then she heard him remember, first with a short, hitching breath and then a deep one. She rubbed and squeezed and sucked to the pattern of his inhalation. A groan rattled in his chest. He clutched her head. He thrust. Then he let go. His shaft stiffening, he pulsed hard against the verge of her throat. Every throb was sweet, every gasp.

She released him with reluctance and kissed him goodbye.

After that, she lacked the will to move. He bent over her and pulled her up the length of his body. Before she realised what he intended, he'd positioned her leg over his hip and worked his softening penis into her sex. He curled his hands over her buttocks and snugged her safely close. The feel of his soft, wet length was strangely comforting. She tightened her calf behind his thighs.

'Now this,' he said, 'is heaven.'

Julia's head fell to his shoulder as if it had been meant to fit there. It was over. She'd expected to fight tears, but she was drained of emotion. She told herself she had nothing to regret. She'd done what she'd meant to do. She'd proven that when her heart was engaged, the softest lovemaking could be as rewarding as the hardest. Now all she had to do was find a man who called to her as Zach did, a man who set no numerical limit on his relations.

Bitterness escaped by way of a muffled snort. That shouldn't take more than a lifetime.

Zach stroked her hair, the motion languid. 'What's wrong?'

She kissed his jaw. 'Nothing.'

'Would that be an "I don't want to tell you" nothing or a "please keep asking until I do"?'

Julia couldn't think of a single snappy answer. She hugged him tighter.

Zach yawned. 'If you give me half an hour, I might get a second wind.'

'Mm,' said Julia, then realised what he'd said. She pushed back from his chest. Zach grabbed her waist before she could de-couple them. 'What about your limit?' she demanded.

'My what?'

'Your seven-fuck limit, the one you set to keep the women round these parts from dragging you to the altar.'

He blushed to the arch of his hairline. 'Oh, that limit. Shit. Who told you about that?'

'The kindly waitress at the Coffee Stop.'

He scratched the back of his head. 'I didn't mean for you to know. Anyway, I wasn't keeping count.'

'Well, I was and that was seven.'

He rolled her beneath him before she could escape, his weight pinning her to the mattress. His cock hardened with a swiftness that shocked her. Apparently, anger was an aphrodisiac for him. 'I don't want to count with you. I want to keep going.'

But Julia wasn't putting herself through this again. She'd prepared herself for seven fucks. She'd made her peace with it. She pushed his shoulders. He didn't budge. 'Come on, Zach. What if I'm like those other women? What if I decide I want to marry you?'

His jaw ticked with anger. His cock stretched. He shoved it deeper. 'I guess I'd thank my lucky stars.'

That shut her up. At least for a moment. 'No.' She shook her head. 'You don't mean that.'

His expression softened, though it didn't grow any less stubborn. 'I know this isn't the way to tell a woman you want her to stick around, but the airport's open and I don't exactly have time to be romantic.'

'You want me to stick around,' she said, deciding she must have misheard him before. 'Stick around' made sense. 'Marry me' was crazy.

Zach stroked the side of her face and took a deep breath. 'I've been thinking I could use someone like you to manage my properties while I get my horse-training business started. I need someone who can stand up to those smarmy Californians who want to turn this state into a theme park for rich people. It strikes me you know a lot about finance, and you did say you and your boss are parting ways.'

She narrowed her eyes. 'Let me get this straight. You want me to work for you.'

'Not just that.' He pinched his moustache and let the words out in a rush. 'Shoot, Julia. I fell in love with you pretty much the first time I heard your voice. I know it's crazy, but I can't help that. Nothing I've

learnt about you since has made me feel any differently. If anything, I'm twice as hooked as I was before.
I never met a woman who turned me inside out the
way you do. I feel as if I never knew myself. I want
things I never knew I could want. Not necessarily to
get down on my knees and kiss your boots, but I
guess –' his brow furrowed '– I guess if you really
wanted that I'd give it a try.'

'I don't want that,' she said. ' Not from you.' She
touched his cheek, needing to reassure herself she
wasn't dreaming. Hearing him echo her own thoughts,
that she made him feel as if he never knew himself,
brought a threat of tears. She blinked them back and
asked the one question that couldn't wait. 'You fell in
love with me?'

He shifted on his elbows. 'I couldn't help it. Look, I
know you don't love me, but it seems to me there's a
chance you might some day. We get on pretty good
when we put our minds to it. I'm not the sort of man
to hobble a creature he loves and shut it in a box. I'd
give you plenty of running room. All I ask is a chance
for us to get to know each other, to build something
that will last.'

'Oh!' she said, the word a cry just short of tears. It
was a pathetic sound: a girlish sound. Julia didn't give
a damn. She pressed her hands together in front of her
trembling lips, then flung her arms around his back
and hugged him with all her might.

Zach grunted, half-startled, half-pleased. His cock
gave a funny leap inside her, as if it were wriggling with
happiness. His mind caught up a second later. 'Does this
mean you don't mind my being in love with you?'

'No,' she said, finally spilling over. 'I don't mind at
all.'

* * *

248

She tried to break the news to Marty early the next morning, while Zach did his chores. Marty had chores of his own, however. She found the senior VP occupied with Carolyn's continuing education. While Carolyn was obviously annoyed by the interruption, she seemed to have put her misery behind her. Julia smiled to herself and shut the door on their bare-bottomed tableau. She'd talk to Marty later.

Ben turned up at the kitchen table, hunched over his first cup of coffee. He sighed when she told him she'd be staying on with Zach. 'Well, he is an improvement over Durbin.'

'It's not a reflection on you.'

He rubbed his handsome, sleepy face. 'Of course it is. But so what? I should have known I couldn't handle you.'

She squeezed his hand and felt a wisp of the old attraction. He was a lovely man. Nonetheless, she was more relieved than sorry to be parting.

'You'll be happy,' he said. 'He's a good man. And it will be easier to serve you up as the sacrificial lamb knowing someone is taking care of you here.'

'I've asked Marty to look out for you if you get into trouble with Durbin.'

Ben rolled his eyes. 'God help me if I need Marty's help.'

'Don't make a face. When it comes down to it, Marty is stronger than Durbin. Not more powerful, not yet, but more reliable. You won't go wrong if you stick with him.'

Ben leant across the table and kissed her on the lips. 'I'll remember,' he said, 'and thank you for worrying.'

Marty caught up to her as she typed their last notes into one of Zach's computers. Durbin might or might not end up reading this report, but if he did he'd find no fault with his three portfolio managers' work.

Marty pulled a second chair next to hers. His curls were wet from a recent shower. 'Did you hear the snow plough go by?'

She nodded. He sighed.

'Ben tells me you're staying with Zach. Please tell me you're not giving up being a dominatrix. You can't. You're Michael-fucking-Angelo. A real artist. And what if I need more training? Mastering Carolyn won't be easy.'

Julia pinched his doleful cheek. 'Mastering Carolyn might be impossible. In fact, if both of you are going to be happy, you might have to learn to switch hit.'

'All the more reason to continue my training.' He bent over his knees and clasped his hands together. 'Can't I come and visit now and then? Get a refresher course?'

The idea intrigued her, but she wasn't sure how Zach would respond. How odd that was: taking someone else's moral preference into account. But it wasn't altogether unpleasant. If their positions were reversed, she'd want Zach to consider hers. 'Maybe,' she said. 'And in the meantime, you can certainly call for advice.'

'You'll miss New York,' he predicted.

Julia shrugged. 'Zach has an adventurous streak. He might enjoy the occasional trip to Sodom and Gomorrah.'

Marty surrendered with a grin. He hugged her. 'Be happy, Mueller.'

'I suspect I will,' she said.

Later, but not much, she stood alone on the back veranda. The portfolio managers were packing. Zach was shovelling the driveway. Perhaps she would go and help soon, but it was good to have a moment to herself, to let her decision sink in. Patches of blue had appeared between the clouds. Water dripped from the icicles with a cheery plinkety-plink, melting as surely as her heart. The Ice Queen was dead. Long live Julia Mueller.

She stared through the curtain of drops at the next mountain over, and the next and the next, until the range faded into an iron-grey mist. The breeze was warm; a chinook, Zach called it. He'd promised to take her out Going-to-the-Sun Road once the thaw was sure. He wanted to show her Glacier National Park. 'The best Montana,' he'd said, button-bursting proud. 'The dazzling Montana.' She'd been dazzled from the start, but she supposed her heart could take it. 'And skiing,' he said. 'You'll love Big Mountain.' He was so pleased to discover she liked to ski, she might have given him the Nobel Prize. Her cowboy certainly was cute. She hugged the corner post and grinned, even though their plans scared her witless.

They'd made a deal, a one-year agreement to cohabit and work together. After the year, they'd reassess. 'Not that I'll need to,' Zach said with a confidence she could barely comprehend. His sureness made her fear for him. She didn't want to hurt him, and she couldn't guarantee she wouldn't.

That's life, she reminded herself. That's what it means to live by your heart. Despite which, her grin didn't fade. This love business was pristine territory for her, a new adventure, perhaps her biggest adventure yet.

She leant back from the post and swung like a truant schoolgirl. Maybe she would miss her whips; and maybe she and Zach would find a way to play that pleased them both. He certainly hadn't ruled it out and, with or without whips, there would be games. When men and women came together, there always were. One of the things she liked best about being a dominatrix was bringing those games into the open.

Still ... She watched a hawk ride an up-draught towards a stony outcropping. It wasn't uninteresting to let the struggle for power slip underground; to play the game without props or calculation. Nor was it uninteresting to explore the precarious edge where top and bottom met, where no one was in charge. Zach offered her the opportunity to walk both these roads. Maybe someday she would tire of them but, at the moment, she couldn't imagine when.

Zach watched her from the kitchen. She was swinging on the rail in her sloppy sweatshirt and leggings. She seemed achingly young, even innocent in her joy. He was looking forward to coaxing her into a pair of well-worn jeans, maybe with one of his old flannel shirts to top it off. You might as well brand her, he teased himself, but his pride in even partial possession was irrepressible. How had this gorgeous blonde Amazonian princess ended up in love with him? She hadn't said it yet, but he knew she was, same as he knew Starlight loved him. It was in the eyes; in the way she leant into his touch and sighed his name. She loved him and some day, by God, she'd tell him so.

He grinned. Grandma must have put a good word in with the angels. Stubborn as Julia was, he couldn't believe he'd convinced her to stay a year. He'd have been grateful for another week, not that he'd tell her that.

Her head turned as soon as the screen door creaked open before him. He handed her the steaming mug of coffee that was his excuse for interrupting her reverie. She took a sip, hummed at the real cream and sugar, then handed it back to share. They leant shoulder to shoulder over the railing. Zach thought he'd never been so happy.

'Second thoughts?' he said for the pleasure of hearing her deny it.

She didn't disappoint him. 'No. I think I've never been so happy.'

His grin threatened to crack his face. Grandma and Grandpa used to share words that way. God willing, he and Julia would be together as long as they had. 'Did you tell the others you'll be staying on?'

Julia slanted a look of amusement from under her brows. 'Yes. Ben was relieved. He thinks you're going to save me from my wicked ways. Marty says *mazel tov*, and Carolyn was too busy moaning "harder, Marty, harder" to say much of anything.'

'Ah,' Zach said, surprised by this last bit of news. But who was he to say it wouldn't work out? Cats and dogs had been known to do more than fight. Then it occurred to him that 'harder' might not mean what he'd assumed. He'd heard some odd sounds as he'd been walking through the house earlier. 'Julia, was he spanking her?'

She bumped his shoulder and winked. 'Can't pull any wool over your eyes.'

Obviously, some people could. He turned sideways to face her. 'Was that what you were doing when you disappeared the other day: playing dom for them?'

Her eyes twinkled, but her gaze was sharp. 'Shocked?'

'No,' he said slowly, and he wasn't. Interest heated his groin, the blood pooling and pulsing so strongly each beat drummed fire through his cock and balls.

Julia eyed his crotch, marking his erection's speedy rise. Her beautiful lips curled in a smile. She reached out and cupped him from beneath. Her fingers rippled over his sac, sending a spine-tingling wave of sensation through his groin. He had to swallow a moan.

'Want me to tell you about it?' she offered, Scheherazade's timeless lure.

'Maybe later,' he said, and pushed himself into her hand.

Epilogue

Julia stood naked before the bedroom window, her hair spilling cool and long down her back. She gazed into the darkness towards the barn where three new mares and a two-year-old colt had joined Starlight and Buck. A heady bouquet of smells wafted around her: alpine flowers, spring grass, hay, horses and, best of all, the soapy-musky scent that her lover left tangled among the sheets.

Seven months had passed since they'd formulated their agreement. Overseeing Zach's business interests didn't take much time once she established a routine. Consequently, she'd been helping him with his little herd. Zach was teaching her to work the new horses on the lunge line. The going was slow; she'd had to learn a whole new language of control. Amazingly, Gracie the cow-dog was her biggest help. She'd nip those horses' heels if she thought they weren't showing 'her' Julia enough respect. Bit by bit, though, she and the horses were developing a rapport.

She loved every minute of the work, even the hard

minutes, and she had calluses to prove it. Zach teased her about acting like a teenage girl, more horse-crazy than boy-crazy. He claimed she'd rather spend the night in the stable than with him.

That, at least, wasn't true.

She looked back at the king-sized bed they shared, admiring the sturdy pine frame Zach had built and finished himself. Julia hadn't wanted him to change his granny's old rooms, so they'd knocked together four of the former guest rooms to make one large bedroom that was all their own. She'd never seen a man work so hard, or so enjoyed soothing his aches and pains. Sometimes she hardly recognised the woman she'd become.

Except this morning, in honour of her birthday, he'd given her a pair of handcuffs. 'For your use or mine,' he'd said. 'Whichever you prefer. Whenever you're ready.'

His gift lay now on the bolster of the turned-down bed, gleaming in the light of a dozen beeswax candles. She'd already decided she'd let him lock her up.

Smiling, she swept one hand down the slope of her breast until her palm covered the softly erected peak. There she let it rest, feeling the hardness increase. The prospect of turning herself over to him inspired a tremulous pulse of excitement, one coloured neither by fear nor regret. Time and again he had proven himself worthy of her trust. She was far more hesitant about exerting mastery over him.

She had a feeling, however, that Zach was going to put an end to her hesitance soon. He'd been goading her lately, wrestling with her until she couldn't resist wrestling back, or assuming subtly submissive postures during lovemaking. He knew his behaviour aroused her, and she knew he wouldn't let her abandon half her nature.

Or half his own, she thought with a delicious shiver.

As if on cue, his reflection appeared in the window pane, tall and smiling, wrapped in a rumpled flannel bathrobe. How her cowboy made such homely apparel seem sexy she'd never know.

She turned and beamed at him.

'I have a surprise for you,' he said, his grin creasing his face. He undid the tie and dropped the robe.

Julia covered her mouth with her hands. He wore his old fringed rodeo chaps . . . and not a stitch more. He pirouetted slowly, like a runway model, showing off the wide, floppy leather. She supposed the chaps were designed to protect his inner thighs, because they didn't cover much else. His hard, muscular butt was bare, and most of his outer legs, and all of his family jewels. His cock thrust thick and high towards the belt that secured the chaps at his waist. The crown looked terribly pert, as if it were sniffing around for something good. The laugh she'd been holding back bubbled free.

'Oh,' she gasped, both arms wrapped over her belly. 'Oh, I'm sorry. It's just –' She dissolved again. 'It's just that outfit doesn't hide any good parts, does it?'

Zach crossed to her and hugged her close. He chuckled into her hair. 'I thought this would get you.'

She tilted her head to look at him. 'You wanted me to laugh?'

'Well,' he said, his drawl as comical as his get-up. 'At first I wanted to you to laugh. Then I reckoned you'd realise how handy this outfit is and we'd get down to business. These chaps are leather, you know.'

Julia sighed and wiped her eyes. 'I've had men make fools of themselves for me, but never just to hear me laugh.'

'Your laugh is my favourite music,' he said.

Her eyes filled again, and not with laughter.

'I love you,' she said.

'I know,' he said, his moustache twitching with mischief.

They smiled at each other, supremely pleased with themselves, their lives precisely as they desired.

Stand and Deliver

Helena Ravenscroft

Chapter One

*L*ydia paused as she approached the front steps of the house, her senses suddenly alert as the gravel of the walkway crunched behind her. She turned around and fixed her gaze on the highly polished black riding-boots; she knew who wore them without having to raise her eyes to his face.

She watched his striding approach, carefully disguising her hostility with a neutral smile; Valerian Hawkesworth was cruel and only someone distinctly lacking a sense of self-preservation would deliberately provoke him. His arrogant nature showed in the imperious tilt of his head and the way he stared down his aristocratic nose with cold, dark, almost black eyes which seemed to slash straight through her long petticoats and trace the curves of her body beneath.

He had his late father's height and lean dark looks. Although he was the younger of Lord William's two sons, he exuded a natural air of command and had quickly assumed the role of lord of the manor, riding rough-shod over his dying father's last wishes and imprinting his malign influence as soon as the burial vault was sealed.

He stopped in front of her, so close that her nostrils flared as she caught the citrus tang of the pomade that slicked his ebony hair back from his wide brow and tamed it in the satin ribbon at his nape. She kept silent and he raised one dark eyebrow.

'Cousin.'

His drawl was lazily measured, low and thick as treacle. If he weren't so unpleasant he would be very attractive, she thought, as she tried to anticipate his next move. Living with Valerian was like being involved in a perpetual game of chess, except that her pieces weren't marked and the board kept tilting out of reach.

Glancing swiftly over his shoulder as if to check that they were not being watched, he stepped forward and suddenly grasped one of her breasts with one hand, his other snaking around her waist to pull her to him.

'What an unexpected pleasure.' His finely chiselled lips curled in a malevolent smile and, through the tight lacing of her bodice, he massaged her nipple with a rough thumb and forefinger. Lydia slapped his hand away and spat her words into his face.

'Pray don't touch me, Valerian. You may have set yourself up as lord of the manor, but you are not master of all you survey!'

'Oh, but cousin, I am. Much as I hate to contradict you, I must remind you of the situation.' His fingers tightened on her and she felt a sharp stab of pain as he squeezed her breast. 'My father shuffled off his mortal coil without leaving a will, and therefore you are unprovided for. You remain in this household on my sufferance. Perhaps you should be a little more gracious if you expect me to provide a roof over your head and a bed for you to sleep in.' His malignant tone lingered on the word 'bed' and Lydia felt her cheeks flame.

'But you are not the sole heir.' She controlled her breathing with as much calm as she could muster, willing herself to ignore the insistent thumb pressing at her nipple. 'Drummond will be found soon and as the elder son he will inherit the estate.'

'Forget Drummond! My esteemed elder brother is dead. Naval recruits are notorious for becoming cannon fodder, and the recent battles with the Spanish have been vicious. Oh no, my sweet cousin, he won't save you this time.'

He sprang forward suddenly, grasping her waist and jerking her into the unyielding circle of his arms. His hard mouth crushed down on hers as she opened it to scream, his hot tongue probing while one hand swiftly lifted a handful of her petticoats to grasp at the bare flesh beneath. He stabbed shockingly between her thighs and Lydia struggled, horrified at her own responsiveness. She stiffened against him and tried to wrench herself free, but he held her tighter, imprisoning her arms and insinuating the tip of one forefinger into her.

'So, my little cousin. You are virgo intacta.' He laughed softly, his black eyes filled with spite. 'I often wondered whether Drummond had plundered the treasure during your walks together in the forest. I am thrilled to discover that he left that pleasure to me. And it will be a very great pleasure, Lydia, to deflower you and mould you to my desires.'

Hot dry lips grazed her face and he gripped her sex, pinching and twisting the swelling flesh. Lydia arched against the rigidity of his muscular body and closed her eyelids, feigning surrender. As if encouraged, he raked his hands around her, grasping her smooth buttocks and wrenching her closer, trying to mould her body to his as he curved her backward like a flexed bow. The potency of his hard cock strained against her thigh with painful insistence. Lydia struggled one arm free. Bracing herself against him, she swung her hand back and slapped his face with the full force of her anger.

'Bitch!' he hissed.

She almost fell as he dropped her to clutch his cheek, but seeing an escape route open up before her, she staggered on to the lawn, turned quickly, and ran into the main house, her footsteps echoing eerily on the stone-tiled floor of the great hall.

She heard him shout after her: 'I'll allow you to

escape, this time! It excites me to see you run. There's no hurry, I'll have you yet.'

His derisive laughter echoed on the latticed windows. Lydia tried to ignore it as she ran up the sweeping staircase two steps at a time, bunching her skirts in one hand. Pausing as she went along the dark gallery, she glanced briefly over the balustrade to see if he had followed.

He had not.

Up on the next floor, she hurried to her room and swung the heavy door closed behind her, resting against the polished oak to steady her legs. Hatred for Valerian – and something darker, something nameless – wrenched at her gut, and she glowered around the room, stepping forward to search for something to break. A tiny statuette wobbled on a spindly table as she brushed past and she grabbed it, raised her arm to throw, and then paused, remembering that it was one of the few mementoes of her own family. She set it carefully back down and sniffed hard.

The four-poster bed with its vast snowy coverlet beckoned and she threw herself headlong on to the quilt. Face down in the bolster, she burrowed into the depths of the mattress and exhaled hard into the pillows, enjoying the hot return of her own breath.

She hated Valerian, had loathed and detested him since the day of her arrival at Hawkesworth Manor as an orphaned child. The fire which had engulfed her home and parents had spared her, allowing fate to sweep her from one impatient neighbour to the next. Finally someone had seen fit to contact her late father's brother, and had deposited little Lydia Hawkesworth and her solitary trunk of belongings on a stagecoach bound for the West Country.

Valerian's wicked, mocking face floated before her closed eyelids. Loathing tempered with fascination welled up in her; he was as familiar as a brother, and she had watched him grow from a vicious little boy into an unpredictable man, yet every time she was in his

264

presence she was spellbound. She twisted her head and clamped her teeth on the linen of the bolster, feeling her body tense at the memory of his brutal touch.

Slowly, in an action which mirrored his, she slid her hands under the layers of her petticoats. Her fingers slid over her sex, still moist from Valerian's ministrations. She rolled over on the bed, kicking at the pillows and spreading her legs, tentatively rubbing a finger over herself. Languid waves rippled through her relaxed body and she tipped her head back over the edge of the bed.

A sudden movement across the room caught her attention and her heart leapt for a brief moment, until she realised that it was her own reflection.

She stared at the image in the gilded cheval-glass. The scene was sensual: an odalisque reclined upon pale scattered pillows, one leg hooked about the vertical column of the bedpost, her head tilted back so that long ebony curls spilled over the side of the mattress almost to the floor.

Aroused by the sight of herself, she repeated her hand movements until she felt herself slick and wet; then, mimicking Valerian, she plunged a finger into the tightness that ached so delectably. She imagined that it was Valerian who touched her – a gentle and tender Valerian – and she found herself arching her back and gasping his name.

Looking into the mirror made Lydia quiver and her skin prickle. She concentrated on her reflection as slow rhythmic waves began to ripple through her and a delicious feeling of coolness brushed across her skin, while inside she was burning and drowning in a pool of searing golden sensation. She tightened on to her own finger, her mind conjuring images of Valerian with his stern jaw and hypnotic, jet-black eyes. She tried to grasp the sensation, but it slipped away, elusive and desperately sweet.

Ultimately unsatisfied, she fell into a drifting, disturbed sleep, peopled with men who ground their hips on hers and whose faces were versions of Valerian's. Then came Drummond. He walked into her dream like a dark shadow, and his half-remembered mouth bore down on hers. He became passionate, ardent, pulling her legs quickly up and around his muscular back, burning kisses on to her eyelids, her cheeks, and her straining breasts. She could feel his hands stroke her thighs, and he ran a tingling finger from hip to ankle and back up again.

A light breeze from the open window disturbed her sleep, and Lydia shifted as the coolness fanned across her hot skin. She sank deeper into the vivid, achingly sweet dream. Beneath her questing lips the salty tang of the sea mingled with the masculine muskiness on Drummond's firm skin. He pushed her back on to the quilted counterpane and parted her legs with strong fingers, dipping his head and flicking his tongue over her.

Lydia opened her eyes to gaze unblinking at the canopy of the four-poster. She was awake, the dream rapidly receding from memory. But the deliciously warm, probing tongue remained. Lifting her head, Lydia gazed down over her own stomach to see a blonde head buried between her thighs. As if sensing her wakefulness, the owner of the sleekly combed saffron hair looked up and smiled.

'Oh, Miss Lydia. You looked so inviting lying there in your undress. I simply couldn't stop myself.' Angel, the diminutive upstairs maid, smiled and parted her pink lips slightly; Lydia could see the fascinating pearliness of her teeth. 'I can sense you don't object.'

She slowly dipped her head, locking Lydia's eyes with her own, and lapped tantalisingly with the tip of her long tongue. Surrendering, too languorous to protest, Lydia closed her eyes and let her breathing gradually slow to shallow gasps, tentatively winding her fingers into the abundant golden hair and loosening its restraints.

As if feeling Lydia's enjoyment, Angel pressed with

her tongue, making tiny movements until Lydia felt that she would expire from pure, delicious sensation. Then she felt Angel probe with her hands and suddenly, deeply, insert her warm tongue and one finger.

Lydia sighed and arched her back, tilting her hips and bracing one foot against the bedpost. The pulsing rhythm of Angel's hand and mouth radiated through her body and she cried out as the elusive sensation she had so desperately chased earlier finally gripped her and she was bathed in pleasure, bittersweet and as hot as a blacksmith's forge, with swirls of ecstasy echoing inside her head, and searing, bubbling, racing, all the way down to her toes.

She lay still, rawness constricting her throat, while her whole body felt exuberant and tinglingly alive. The other girl raised her slender form and rested her weight lightly on Lydia's sated body, smiling down and tracing a finger across the velvet cushion of her partly open mouth.

Drummond Hawkesworth, muscular legs firmly braced, stood on the rough wooden deck of the ship and revelled in the brisk salt wind as it ruffled his already tousled brown hair. Shielding his eyes with one bronzed hand, he directed his gaze towards the thin strip of land which curved, barely visible, on the distant horizon.

The shores of England at last.

His heart swelled at the thought of home, a tantalising prize at the end of an uncomfortable sea voyage. The unvarying diet of biscuits and salt beef had begun to pall by the second week, and Drummond was desperately in need of a hearty meal. He had travelled far since receiving the belated, much forwarded letter from Lavendale's Solicitors. The marked and torn yellow parchment with its barely intact wax seal had taken months to reach him, and when he had finally read its melancholy contents, his father had long since been sealed in the family crypt.

His ever-restless mind wondered how Lydia was

faring at Hawkesworth. In his absence, Valerian would undoubtedly have seized control of the manor and all who lived under its gabled roof. Lydia was a young woman of twenty-one now; she would have changed in the five years of his self-imposed exile, and he smiled at the incongruous thought of the chubby girl with untameable hair and wild ways growing up to be a woman of poise and dignity.

Drummond stared down into the stormy sea, casting his mind back to when he had seen her last. The morning of his departure, he had crept along the dawn dark corridors into the womb of the house, and had gently pushed at the barrier of Lydia's room door. She had been sleeping, as he had expected, but he could not leave without bidding his own farewell.

Drummond had dropped a feather-light kiss on her lips and stroked a vibrant curl as it sprang from her brow to tangle temptingly across the white pillow. The hot June night had been too sultry for bed linen, and Lydia had kicked away the coverings in her sleep, leaving a pale expanse of delectable calf to glow in the soft bloom of the dawn.

Drummond had gazed, entranced, at his childhood friend, and saw no longer a tomboy hoyden intent on climbing trees and making sling-shots, but a ripening, fragrant fruit, the swell of her breasts tempting and succulent beneath her virginal Dutch linen nightgown.

His hand had stolen across the bed, almost of its own volition, and he had felt as if he were watching someone else, voyeuristically enthralled as the hand lifted the hem of her chemise. He had swallowed, his mind reeling with possibilities hitherto undreamed of.

She had stirred slightly and rolled on to her front, pressing her hips down on to his hand so that it was trapped beneath her. He had savoured her warmth for a moment, feeling the heat of her sleeping body and the pressure of her thighs on the back of his hand. Then, desperate not to wake her, he had eased his hand free and tiptoed backward across the room.

Now, almost five years later, he was finally on his way home, and he wondered how that promising fruit had ripened. Aware that the memories had stimulated a hardening in his tight breeches, Drummond pulled the wide skirts of his travelling coat more closely around him and leant forward on to the blistered rail of the ship.

In the candle-lit darkness she arched her body above him, tipping her head languorously back to reveal her snowy throat, and pushing the full silken orbs of her glorious breasts forward. Her hair tumbled, unbound, behind her, and he could feel its satin weight stroke across his thighs and balls, causing him to contract and push his cock deeper into her.

He gripped a handful of the silken skeins and gently eased her head further back, admiring the tilt of her chin and the velvet pout of her lips which had so recently been clamped caressingly around his rigid member. A tiny groan escaped from her and he smiled, moving beneath her body with deliberate intent.

Stroking his strong hands around her hips and gently up to her tiny waist, he eased her willing body up and down the long length of his cock. Her full breasts invited him to cup them and he lightly massaged their heaviness, feeling her deep arousal as her nipples sprang to life beneath his thumbs and forefingers. Her pale hands began to mirror his, and the bronze discs of his own nipples puckered into erectness as she squeezed them. She was gorgeous, and his eyes gloried at the sight of her soft, milky-white skin contrasting with his own burnished copper musculature.

He lifted her, gently gripping the sides of her hips to raise her to her knees. Kissing the curve of her belly, he began to trail his tongue to the hollow at the top of her thigh. He could feel her skin tingle beneath his touch, could almost sense where she wanted him to kiss, and his lips burnt with the knowledge of her pleasure.

She moved forward, lifting a knee over his broad

269

shoulder to position herself directly above his face. Tonguing gently, he explored her sex with his lips, breathing her scent. He spread his hands wide on her behind and gently pushed her forward until she repositioned her other knee beside his face, gorgeously imprisoning his dark head between her thighs as he lapped at her, as with the thirst of a man who had spent years in the desert.

He kneaded the twin ovals of her buttocks with his hands and suddenly pushed his tongue deep into her, making her cry out and arch above him as the dark stubble surrounding his mouth grazed her.

'You're so wet: you taste like honey,' he murmured, his thumbs stroking and smoothing. She seemed unable to speak, trembling above him and pushing down on him for more.

Sliding further under her, he nibbled gently at the curve of her buttocks, taking gulps of her smooth flesh, caressing with his searching, searing tongue. Easing out and round behind her, he twisted agilely and came up to press his muscular chest into her smooth back. Biting softly at her neck, he lifted heavy handfuls of her hair so he could suck and nibble her shoulders and nape.

She leant her weight back against him and he held her imprisoned for a moment, the length of her straining body stretched against his; then he snaked one forearm around her waist while the other leant weight on her shoulders, arcing her forward until she buried her face into the welcoming softness of the pillow.

'Please! Please!' Her hands kneaded across the bolster to grip the brass rails of the bedstead.

Stimulated almost beyond control by the sight of her tiny waist above the beautiful flare of her hips, he held her close with his hands. His fingers slid to her tight anus and he circled it with the tip of his thumb, his short square nail rubbing and making it pucker tightly. He felt her tremble, and he moistened his middle finger with his own saliva, holding her buttocks wide and gentling her.

'Oh God, no,' she murmured. 'It'll hurt me, won't it?'

'Let me try,' he whispered, almost unable to stop as his finger slipped and twisted at the barrier to what he knew would be a smooth, tight haven.

She nodded, her reply muffled by the pillow under her face, and he moved before she could change her mind, pressing inside, passing the constricted sphincter into the warmth beyond. He heard her gasp and he smiled as she pushed herself back towards him, opening her bottom and almost sucking his finger in.

He reached underneath and caught his own tight balls in one hand, holding and squeezing for a moment, then running his fist along the length of his straining cock. When he judged she was ready, he pressed into her sex, his eyes fixed on the tumbled hair which spread wide on the sheets, obscuring her face.

She could be anybody.

The thought of taking an anonymous woman almost pushed him over the brink as he felt her velvety warmth envelop him. He was able to slide his finger deeply into her anus now, she was so ready and aroused, and he could feel the steely glide of his own cock through the paper-thin membrane that separated her inside.

His free hand raked around her, and gripped one of her breasts so tightly that she groaned. He rode her, staring down at the glisten of her juices, his mind clouded with the sweetness of each inward stroke. He had a sudden desire to see her come, to watch her face contort as she submitted to him.

'Turn over. You feel so good, but I want to see your face – I want to watch you come – I want to see you cry out.'

He released her and then quickly twisted her on to her back. She encircled him with her thighs as he pulled her on to him. The silken wetness of her sex shimmered as he rocked his hips, slowly pulling himself back and forth within her.

Gradually building his speed and rhythm, he gained momentum, feeling an exquisite sensation as the satin

271

skin of his foreskin was stretched by her firm grip. He could feel himself spiralling inside her, twisting and ramming with increasing speed, a fine sweat beginning to sheen across his shoulders and chest. He pressed her with one thumb, seeking and finding the exact spot he knew would tip her over the edge, and he ground his knuckle against her.

She cried out as her deep orgasm engulfed her, sending pulsing waves through her and on to his slickly encased shaft. He smiled, enjoying the sight of her as she tensed on the bed beneath him, her hands clawing sideways to grasp handfuls of the creased sheets and pull them up to her chest.

At last Drummond began to pant, gasping and thrusting deep into her as he felt a curious sensation of constraint and release. His climax burst over him like a broiling tide of pleasure and he cried out: 'Lydia!'

He was aware of a rush of displaced air the instant before her balled fist struck him hard across the side of his face.

'Who the hell's Lydia?' spat the innkeeper's daughter, her face flushed and angry. Raising his hands to protect himself against the slaps which rained upon his face and chest, Drummond felt his mind spin with confusion and disbelief at his own outburst. He caught at her, but she fought him wildly, and he needed all his strength to grasp her hands and still them. Gripping her wrists, he pushed the girl down into the softness of the mattress and silenced her with a hard kiss.

'Hush, Bess. You know that a man must have more than one lover in a lifetime. How else would I have learnt to satisfy you so well?'

He nibbled her lower lip caressingly and she frowned up at him, searching his brown eyes. He thought for a moment that he would have to say more to convince her, but abruptly, like a summer storm, her temper was gone and her cheeks dimpled.

'Oh, sire.' She caught and held his head between her hands. 'I don't rightly care how many you've had. 'Tis

272

a rare treat for me to tumble with a gentleman like you. My usual bedfellows are bald of pate and thick of waist.'

She pulled him down and kissed him deeply, her mouth opening beneath his and her tongue moving to test the tender nerves in his lips. She began to move suggestively beneath him, wrapping her arms and legs around him, binding him to her and scratching her nails softly down his back.

'Remind me again what you've learnt from your other lovers.'

She giggled as he rose above her again in the crumpled bed, his cock jerking obediently against his navel.

Once on the road, astride the black mare that he had purchased that morning in the harbour town, Drummond reflected on his unguarded cry of his cousin's name the previous night. For weeks she had flickered around the deeper recesses of his mind like a ghost, her spectral image growing stronger as he came closer to home.

The mare bridled suddenly under his breech-clad thighs as muffled cries came unexpectedly through the dappling tree branches. The copse was small and lonely, but the road below him looked well-travelled, and he knew that the route was popular with cross-country travellers. Spurring the mare on, he rounded the curve of the wooded path to see that the road forked ahead of him. Two horsemen, slung low in their saddles, sprinted away at a gallop down one lane, while on the other, shadowed by trees, he could make out a distressed band of travellers and a stationary carriage.

As he drew closer he could see that there were at least four men on the roadway, all on foot. One was bound with rope; another two staggered on the wayside with cloaks tightly wrapped around their heads and faces. The coachman struggled in his attempt to loosen the rough bands which looped around his barrel chest, a blend of rage and fear washing across his ruddy features as he perceived the lone horseman approaching from the darkened archway of the forest.

Drummond dropped nimbly from his saddle and strode to the quailing group, holding his open palms up to show his lack of weapons. His stout boots sank into the mud which swamped the rough track.

'Are you stuck in this damned mire, sirs?' He glanced curiously at their various bindings, trying to decide which to help first.

'A mire it is, but not of mud!' spluttered a white-coiffured man of apoplectic complexion. 'A mire of rogues and thieves! Footpads and vagabonds! No road is safe for travellers!'

The coachman, having rid himself of his hempen cords, jumped down from the stagecoach and began to untie his beleaguered passengers. Drummond helped him, pulling the cloth from the head of the man nearest to him.

'Do you mean that you've been robbed?' He was surprised that the thieves had struck in broad daylight.

'Aye, it was the tobymen. Two of them, the blighters,' replied another whose black garb and high white collar marked him out as a parson. 'They've plagued this highway for months. They should be caught and strung from the gibbet, like that good-for-nothing Dick Turpin.'

Drummond helped the party back into the coach as he listened to their tale, wondering whether he should have given chase to the two men he had seen fleeing on the other road. Thoughtfully, he watched the mud-spattered coach as it wound its way towards the dark tunnel of trees, then patted his ebony mount.

Swinging his long leg over her back and settling into the saddle, he decided that when he reached the next town he would invest in a pistol or two. He hitched his warm circular travelling cloak closer around his power-ful shoulders and urged the mare forward, anxious to finish the long journey home.

* * *

Four days in the saddle had rendered Drummond weary and travel-stained. But the sight of the familiar town which nestled in the sunlit valley below cheered him, and he pulled the horse up so that he could gaze at the land. It rolled away like a verdant carpet, stretching and arcing in the sunlight. A far-flung prize hid just out of view over the brow of a distant hill: Hawkesworth Manor. His home was clear in his mind's eye as he dropped from the saddle and led the horse down into the valley.

When he reached the town, Drummond mounted again, shortening the reins and trotting the obedient horse through the edges of the busy market, carefully avoiding the pedlars with their laden barrows. The dry summer had made the roads dusty, and he watched the clouds of brown chalk puff underfoot and grime the hooves and legs of his mount.

A ragged group of filthy beggars held out grimy palms as he approached. The familiar gap-toothed smile of one caught his attention, and he reined in before them, searching in his pouch for coins. As he dropped a few shillings into the scarred and blackened hand, the beggar dropped a curtsy.

'Thank you, sir.' Her voice stirred his memory, and Drummond leant forward, frowning into her lined, defeated face.

'You are a Hawkesworth servant, woman. Why are you begging in the streets?'

She stepped away from him slightly, squinting up and twisting her hands in her grimy shawl.

'I'm no longer at the manor. The new master prefers his own staff.'

Valerian. So this was his brother's doing: purging the household of their father's faithful retainers and replacing them, no doubt, with hand-picked mercenaries.

'But why are you begging? Surely your references are good enough to secure you another post? And your severance pay, what have you done with it?'

The woman barked a laugh, bitter and mirthless.

'References? Severance pay? I don't know where you hail from, sir, but the old master is dead. There's a new liege at the big house now. He don't waste time with nonsense like that.' With a wracking hawk, she spat on to the ground at his feet. Before Drummond could sufficiently recover his wits to speak, she had gone, dragging her pale, wraith-like children behind her.

'Wait!' he cried, but she ignored his call, turning abruptly at the corner and disappearing down a dark, stinking alleyway.

He had intended to go straight to the house and announce his return, but he found himself loath to do that now. Heaven alone knew how his unpredictable brother would react at the loss of his assumed power. Drummond needed more information before he could declare himself.

Rubbing the coarseness of his unshaven chin with one hand, he thought of Jim Handfast, a retired gamekeeper and his father's oldest retainer. Jim was the only one he could trust to keep the secret of his return, and he would probably know enough to update Drummond on events at the manor. Turning the horse, he took the road out of town and began the short journey to the dilapidated cottage on the outer reaches of the Hawkesworth Estate.

'Lad, it's good to see you. Those at the big house have given you up for dead, but I knew you'd return someday.'

The old man clasped Drummond's firm hand in his gnarled grasp and shook it, his lined face full of pleasure.

'Master Valerian has been asserting himself and now most of the servants fend for themselves. He's replaced a lot of them with his own henchmen and cheap untrained labour. The poachers take a lot of the deer, now.'

He thrust a mug of sour ale on to the rough surface of the wooden table and looked at Drummond, concern in his pale, rheumy eyes. They sat silently for a few minutes, then the old man coughed before he spoke again.

'I know why you left, lad. Valerian hasn't changed one whit. A man of injustice and cruelty whose actions helped send your poor father to his early grave, God rest his soul. A sniff of your return and that young whippersnapper will be on your tail again, and this time he won't fail, unless you've gotten faster than him with the sword.'

He nodded at the pale scar which marked Drummond's left cheek, a constant reminder of the events which had led to his dawn departure. Rather than carry tales to their sick father, Drummond had left home and taken the King's shilling. Life on the sea had been exciting, and he had revelled in the roving life style which suited him far better than his old life of pampered ease. He had seen most of the world, won a few battles, and conquered his own demons. There was no way that he could let his brother take the one thing he wanted more than anything else: his birthright.

Drummond banged a clenched fist on the table-top.

'I'll challenge him!' he declared. 'I've learnt to wield a sword better than any man I know.'

'Aye, but desperation will sharpen his point. He has more to lose now,' Jim reminded him. 'No, Master Drummond, you must bide your time. It's the eldest surviving son who inherits when a man dies intestate. And, as far as everyone knows, you're dead. The will is missing and it's you who has to find it. Master Valerian is hardly going to help you: methinks he'd rather be branded a murderer than hand the inheritance to you. Where do you think your father would have put it? Can you remember the whereabouts of his strong-box?'

They talked late into the night, and when Jim finally pulled a straw palliasse from under the truckle-bed, Drummond found he was past tiredness. Through the small hours he tossed fitfully on the prickly mattress, his mind twisting and turning, picking at his dilemma as if it were an itching scab. He was determined to regain his inheritance and desperate to help the servants who had been deprived of homes and livelihoods.

As an early pink dawn stole over the thoughtful planes of his face, an idea germinated and slowly flourished. Remembering the travellers that he had helped on the road, the victims of two fearless highwaymen, he rolled over and folded his arms under his head. He would find the will, but in the meantime he had conceived a plan – daring and dangerous, but entirely necessary – to redress the balance and put Hawkesworth money back into the pockets of those wronged workers.

He would haunt the roads, and each time he encountered his brother's carriage, he would hold him up and take the equivalent of one servant's wages in gold or jewels: no more, no less. It was a fair, albeit temporary, way to settle it.

As he drifted to sleep, a smile curved across his mouth: the image of himself in a black mask and a hat pulled low over his brow had a certain romantic appeal, and he was impatient for the first confrontation.

Chapter Two

'Stand and deliver!'

The command rang clearly through the crisp air, and the coachman pulled the horses up, his eyes rolling with shock and fear. The highwayman, darkly masked and cloaked, dismounted and gestured with his pistol at the man's chest.

'Your weapons, man. Give me the arms you bear.'

After stripping the coachman of his only protection, he swiftly bound him to his seat and tied the cloth of his long coat over his head, rendering him helpless. The man continued to struggle and cry out, yelling loudly for help. The highwayman hesitated, his body taut with indecision. Then he swung his pistol round and brought the heavy handle down across the coachman's neck.

There was silence.

As he approached the carriage, Drummond glanced at his own family coat of arms so familiarly displayed upon the highly polished timber of the door. He took a deep breath, bracing himself. What had seemed so easy in his thoughts, in the dead of night, was much harder in the cold light of day.

He ducked his head and looked through the open window to see a velvet-cloaked woman shrink into the shadowy recesses. There were no other occupants and

Drummond was disappointed at his brother's absence. A mere woman: one of Valerian's mistresses, no doubt. Maybe her jewellery would be worthwhile.

He glanced into the carriage and sighed. This was not quite as simple as he had anticipated.

'Come, madam. I will not harm you. Give me your money and your jewels and I'll be away.'

He extended a leather-gloved hand and was relieved when a kid pouch of jingling coins was placed on his outstretched palm. There was a long pause.

'And your jewels, madam,' he urged.

'I can't. They are precious to me. A gift. Please don't ask me for them.'

Her voice, although taut with fear, was soft and low, the words caressing him like swansdown as they curved towards him from the shadows. His head swam and he shook it to loosen the hypnosis.

'Your jewels or your life.' The words sounded harsh even to his own ears.

There was a long silence, then a small hand reluctantly placed two pearl eardrops and a slender circlet of gold into his grasp. Recognition lanced through his body in a shocking wave: the bangle was his own birthday gift to Lydia when she had turned twelve, and he had never seen her without it. Grasping the still-extended wrist with a vice-like grip, he jerked her forward into the light.

Wide eyes met his, thick lashes shading the fear in the emerald depths. Her beauty took him by surprise, and he gazed, spellbound, drinking in the opalescent skin of her face and neck, and the carefully tamed black ringlets which clustered around her cheeks under the dainty tricorne hat.

Shock made him speechless, and he could only hold fast to her arm, his breathing rapid and his thoughts confused, as he waited for her to recognise him.

Lydia, who had heard whispered tales of fearless highwaymen, stared back. She held her breath as he drew

280

her fingertips to his chiselled lips and kissed each finger lightly, caressingly, before relinquishing her hand. His eyes glinted through the slits in his black mask and he nodded, a smile quirking the corner of his generous mouth.

'A fairer jewel than any other is seated in the carriage before me. With your permission, madam, I will step inside.'

'No. You can't. I'm alone. I – I have no chaperone.' Lydia tried to quell her nervousness by twisting her hands into the soothing velvet of her cloak. His eyes narrowed. Ignoring her words, he pulled the door open and stepped up into the carriage.

'Without your permission, then.'

Lydia's heart hammered as she shrank into the far-thest corner, putting as much space as she could between them. When he sat on the seat beside her, his long muscular legs stretched the tight seams of his knee-breeches and she felt her throat tighten and constrict at the evidence of his physical strength. There was a tang of danger in the close air of the carriage as he stripped off one leather glove and placed a strong hand under her chin, tilting her head back to gaze searchingly into her face.

He raised one eyebrow.

'No chaperone? What a tragedy. Your mother should know better.'

'I – I have no mother.' She froze as she felt his hand caress her face, his thumb travelling lightly across her lips and down under her chin, lighting a fire under the passage of his touch. She reached up to push his hand away, but he grasped her wrist in his iron grip and forced her hand down to his thigh; she jerked it away as if he had burnt her.

She squeezed her eyes shut as he left her chin to travel down to the fastening of her cloak, and she felt the fabric part as he undid the clasp. The heavy velvet slithered from her shoulders and she suppressed a shudder. She clutched at the mantle, trying to pull it back up but he casually knocked her hand aside and pressed her into the corner until her back arched painfully against the hard timber behind her.

With sudden vigour he crushed her to him, pulling her bodily into his arms to kiss her hungrily. Lydia twisted her head to escape him, but he held her fast and she felt the first stirrings of fear laced with an uncontrollable arousal at his kiss. As she fought against the iron hardness of his chest, he jerked the hat from her head, and with one hand fumbled at the pins and ribbons which held her hair until it tumbled, unfettered, down her back.

He became fierce, ardent, shocking her as his tongue probed between her teeth, and she struggled harder, sensing a rapacious hunger which was barely under control as he forced her further back into the corner of the coach. She tried to cry out, but his lips sealed hers with the effectiveness of a gag, and she could only twist her hands against his unyielding body and bite him, sinking her teeth into the fleshy pad of his lip.

'You little vixen.' He drew back, wiping his mouth with the back of his gloved hand. There was a streak of crimson blood on the black leather and a corresponding bead on his lower lip. He stared at her, his eyes, cinnamon lit with gold, devouring hers with frightening intensity. Lydia was the first to drop her gaze.

She was unprepared for what followed.

One strong hand slid to the back of her neck, his mouth descending on hers as his knee forced between her legs and his hard leather boot knocked her feet apart. He grabbed her wrists and forced them behind her back, pulling one of the remaining ribbons from her hair and winding it tightly around to secure her hands. She struggled, but he was much stronger than she was; he jerked her shoulders back, making her sit upright, and she was aware of her breasts straining against the lacing of her bodice. She could almost see herself through his eyes, helpless but glowing, her eyes bright and her skin feverish, her breast rising and falling with rapid panting breaths. She knew that he wanted what he saw, and that she would have to fight hard to prevent him taking it.

As she glanced at the swollen bite-marks on his lower lip, a tiny voice in her head seemed to ask her if she really wanted to stop him. He was so handsome, uncompromising, and virile. Surely there were worse fates to befall a girl?

'Please,' she said, trying to speak calmly. 'If it's money you want, then I have plenty at home. I'll fetch it for you. I could bring it back here. Please let me go.'

'The only thing you'd bring back is a magistrate, and a length of rope to hoist me to the gibbet. I don't want your money. I want you.'

His hands went to the neckline of her gown and he plucked the lacing open with the speed and expertise of someone well versed in the intricacies of women's clothing. The chemise below was fine muslin, and, placing a finger at the top of the delicate fabric, he tore it from breastbone to navel in one fluid movement. Lydia gasped and flinched, her shock mingled with admiration for the determination which hardened his handsome face. He gripped the two edges of her bodice and jerked them back and round, trapping her arms more firmly and effectively than any ribbon.

She was his captive.

'Sweet Jesus, you're beautiful.'

Before she could take a breath he had leant forward and opened his greedy mouth to her breast, using his hands to shape the rounded form, his lips questing over the sensitive flesh and fastening on one nipple, which tightened beneath his teeth. He circled it with his tongue, then drew it into his mouth, licking and sucking until it gleamed and lengthened, and Lydia felt hot needles dart from her breast to her thighs.

She arched her back slightly, pushing herself out to his mouth and drowning in exquisite sensation; her body ached as it had when Angel had touched her, but everything was somehow hotter, her skin more alert, her mind more clouded. She breathed shallowly and softly, afraid to disturb his caress, but her nose was still full of the smell of him: the masculine scent that emanated from his hair and clothes as he moved across her lap, a half-familiar soapy muskiness, tinged with wood-smoke, that she had smelt before but could not place.

'Look at me! Kiss me!' It was a command, not a request.

She shook her head, her eyes tightly shut. He gripped her jaw, squeezing her cheeks until they hurt and turning her face up to his.

'I said, kiss me. Kiss me now.'

She opened her eyes and risked looking at him. His tousled hair had tiny sunlit streaks, and it was tamed and flattened at the sides by the coal-black mask he wore. The breadth of his shoulders almost blocked the light from the window, and the carriage seemed small and very dark. She could feel the heat of his breath on her face where his mouth was close, so very close to hers.

It would be so easy, she thought. And there was a part of her that desperately wanted to feel his mouth with her own.

She took a deep breath and leant forward, tentatively touching. He did not kiss her back at first, staying very still as her lips flickered across his with a butterfly touch. When he did respond, the kiss was long and deep, his mouth hard yet soft against hers, and she was left gasping and disappointed when he pulled away from her. He stood up, so tall that his head brushed the roof of the carriage.

Watching her, as if assessing her reaction, he pulled at the buttons which joined his shirt-front and impatiently jerked the shirt-tails out from the waistband of his breeches. Lydia stared at his bare skin, at the satiny, sun-kissed bronze of his chest and the line of crisp, golden hairs which snaked between the muscular curves of his pectorals down to the bulge that pressed insistently against the fastening of his breeches. She felt a sharp, jolting kick in her stomach as an almost unidentifiable feeling – excitement mingled with fear – flooded through her body. He popped the first button of his breeches and her eyes shot to his face: she saw that there was never going to be a chance of escape.

He took her bound and half-naked body in his arms and lay her back until she felt the cool firmness of the leather seat beneath her skin. One hand ran lightly from her neck, down over her breast, to the flatness of her stomach; then he pulled her skirts up, his fingers probing between her thighs and sliding over her with practised ease. Lydia tried to press her knees together.

'Please – oh, please!' She was unsure whether she was pleading with him to stop, or carry on. His mouth became stern as he firmly prised her legs apart again and curved a possessive hand over her. She shut her eyes, her body trembling as his weight pressed down on her and burning kisses rained across her face, her neck, her breasts.

'You're beautiful, so beautiful. I won't hurt you. Let me stroke you, you're gorgeous. You smell so fresh.' His lips were soft and questing as they moved to her eyelids, kissing and pressing the delicate skin as he slid his hands over her trembling body.

He was insistent but gentle, and she felt herself respond. A primitive throb swelled somewhere deep inside herself, and she tried to push it away, to deny it, but it grew stronger and thicker. The unwilling stirrings of desire swelled and grew as he stroked her tingling flesh, lingering on the smoothness of her thighs and then moving inward to her sex, touching the tight opening, gentling her.

She lay still, shaking and afraid but warmed by his embrace, concentrating on the sensation of the tips of his fingers: she felt that she was swollen and open, and so soft under his touch.

He held his weight above her body with one sinewy arm while unbuttoning and releasing his cock, rigid and taut as it sprang eagerly from the constraints of his clothing. Lydia glanced down, and then quickly away, unable to believe that a man could be so different from herself. She held her breath as he curved his hand over her sex, parting her. When she felt the throbbing heat of him, her self-possession deserted her and she felt her bound hands trembling under the small of her back, her fingers tingling and fluttering inside their bindings.

As he entered her she struggled: too late. They were both beyond the point of no return, and Lydia let her head fall back on the cushion of her discarded cloak, her eyes fixed on his.

He stopped abruptly at the unexpected barrier, his pupils constricted to pin-points.

'Have you – ? Are you – ? Oh, Christ!' He paused, panting, as if teetering on the brink of an enormous precipice. Then, as she instinctively lifted her ankles and wrapped herself around him, he closed his eyes and pressed firmly through.

Deep into her.

Lydia was lanced by sharp pain, and tiny hot tears smarted at the corners of her eyes. The highwayman whispered in her ear, words of endearment that she could barely hear or understand. She thought he said her name, but sensation clouded her senses and she stopped listening, aware only of the feel of silken lips soothing her face and neck, satin hands sliding over her hips as he moved.

He was almost impossibly gentle, shifting slowly above her and cradling her in his arms. She felt the harsh rawness gradually superseded by a sweet pleasure as he drew his length back and then drove luxuriously into her again, his strokes developing into a voluptuous rhythm as she gradually relaxed beneath him and began to rock her hips against him, her mind centred on the exquisite torture of his touch.

She arched her back against the red leather seat, her heart beating faster, with feverish waves radiating out-ward over her whole body and raising the myriad downy hairs on her skin. She could feel a tingling which started in her toes and fingered up her spine to pulse across her scalp, and soon she was foundering, sinking, drowning. Senseless, totally hypnotised by dark sensation, she gripped his waist with her knees, almost unaware of the sudden low groan that the highwayman gave as he climaxed, shuddering into her with muscular thrusts of his taut pelvis.

She felt his cock resonate and jerk, and gave herself up to the sweetness of her own sensation, fluttering and rippling beneath the weight of his body. A curious relief seemed to free her, and she wished that her hands were not bound so that she could reach around him and anchor herself firmly to him before she floated away.

They lay spent, and she inhaled the seashell scent of their embrace. Drummond raised himself above Lydia, resting on one elbow, his smooth biceps bulging against the taut cotton of his shirt.

He bent his head to hers and kissed her swollen lips tenderly, almost lovingly, his eyes bright with some emotion that Lydia could not decipher. She would not, could not, kiss him back; her mind was too full. She lay still beneath him.

'I must be away. I have stayed too long.' His voice was low, intimate, and sweet to her ears. She shifted beneath him, conscious of a cramping in her bound hands.

He lifted her, pulling her torn chemise and the unlaced bodice forward. When her hands were free, Lydia tidied and re-pinned her hair in silence, conscious of his inscrutable gaze tracking her every move.

When they had dressed, she glanced at him, a small frown creasing her brow.

'There is something I must do,' she said, standing up and turning to face him.

There was a pause, then Lydia raised her hand and brought it down with the full weight of her body, landing a slap on his cheek which cracked as it hit him. He recoiled with shock, but in the depth of his eyes was a silent understanding; he did not touch the livid finger

287

marks which flushed on his jaw, but simply reached out and fingered a tiny lock of hair which coiled across her temple. He opened his mouth, drawing breath as if to speak, but suddenly turned away and jumped down from the carriage.

He turned to look at her through the open door, then reached forward and grasped the hand that had struck him, pressing his lips into the palm.

'Good day to you, madam. A safe passage.'

Abruptly, he was gone, running light-footed to his ebony steed. He was up and away at a gallop before she could cry out. Leaning her head and shoulders out of the carriage window, she watched him as he crested the hill, his silhouette dark in the morning sun. Then he disappeared from sight.

Liberty, thought Lydia, that's what it is. She smoothed the fashionable dark green stocking up over her knee and paused to check her reflection in the mirror. Her leg was as sleek and shapely as it had been yesterday morning, but somehow everything about her body looked different. Everything was different, everything had changed. Now she knew. Now she was no longer – what was it that Valerian had called her? – virgo intacta.

She dropped the petticoats over her stockinged legs and ran her palms across her skirt, her eyes still fixed to the glowing reflection in the mirror. If she leant forward she could see that even the colour of her eyes was different: lighter, brighter, a glinting emerald with tiny pin-point pupils, constricted by the morning sun which lit the surface of everything around her.

She wondered what he was doing, where he was.

The ruthlessness of the masked highwayman had given her first full sexual encounter an added zest, and his anonymity made her memories all the more heady.

Who was he?

She rubbed one finger over the fullness of her lower lip, imagining the swollen wound, the bite mark, which would mark his mouth for several days.

Would she ever see him again?

Her body, melting and honey-soft at the core, hoped that she would, and soon. Now that she had found sex – had not even had to seek it – she was filled with an unquenchable desire to experience more of its pleasures.

She gave one more pouting glance to her reflection, then went down to breakfast, wondering whether anyone would notice how different she looked and ask themselves why.

Leaving the overnight guests to fortify themselves with breakfast before the hunt commenced, Lydia stepped out on to the stone steps. Ghostly tendrils of morning mist fingered lightly around the sturdy oaks in the panoramic gardens. The cold dampness of early autumn caused several of her stray curls to coil around her face, and she tucked them impatiently into the hat which tipped low over one eyebrow.

Flexing her supple crop between leather-clad hands, she strode purposefully around the gable end of the house, the full green skirts of her riding habit swirling around her legs. She could hear the hounds in the yard, baying as they milled around the shining legs of the mounts.

As she rounded the corner she saw Valerian, resplendent in close-fitting breeches, his pale satanic beauty enhanced by the scarlet coat which stretched across the breadth of his shoulders. His right arm suddenly flung up and back, as he brought his whip down on the cringing shoulders of a young stable-hand.

'Damn you,' he snarled, raising his arm to strike again. 'When I say polish it, I mean polish. Look at it, boy, look at it! I will not be seen in public with such a filth-encrusted bridle.' He drew himself up to his full height. 'Clean it again or I'll thrash you to within an inch of your life.'

'But, sire, I –'

'Don't be impertinent: I am your master!' Valerian shrieked, fury and petulance stiffening his body as he raised his whip to lash again. The young groom cried out as the stinging tip caught his outstretched hand, and Lydia ran forward to pull Valerian's arm down with both of her own, dropping her crop to the ground.

'Valerian! No! Don't beat him. Please!' She pulled at him, willing him to face her. The groom scrambled to his feet, hesitated, and then fled as Valerian swung his enraged body round, his narrow lips forming a gash across his face, the deep pools of his black eyes glazed and bloodshot.

'Valerian,' urged Lydia. 'Please, cousin, look at me.'

She had seen his rages, knew that he would become unrecognisable, unaware of his surroundings, focussing totally on the violence that raged within him.

Suddenly his stormy eyes snapped on hers, and he curled his lips venomously as one strong hand flipped quickly up and grasped the frills of her shirt-front. He jerked her roughly towards him, and as she felt his foetid breath fan her face she flinched, fear worming in her belly. He shook her by the neck like a drowned kitten, then abruptly threw her away from him so that she landed heavily on the stone floor of the yard, skirts flung up around her knees.

Valerian raised his leather whip before awareness dawned in her, and he brought it down, missing her by a hair's breadth. Panting with disbelief at his violence, Lydia screamed and cast wildly around, hoping someone would help her.

There was no one. The guests were still breakfasting, and even the hounds were cowering, away at the end of the yard, as far from their master as they could get.

Lydia was suddenly aware of a highly polished boot kicking her legs apart. Firm hands grasped the edges of her skirts, paused, then tore their length from hem to waist, revealing the green stockings which encased her legs, all the way up to where an inch of pale, smooth flesh was vulnerably visible.

Seeing the intent deep in Valerian's coal-black eyes and the rigid rod of his cock bulging in his breeches, she scrabbled furiously away. Grazing her hands on the ground as she moved crab-like from under him, Lydia turned, half crawling, and pushed herself to her feet. Panic began to swell in her breast as she heard his muttered expletive and felt the talons of his fingers swipe at her hair.

Then suddenly the gate was before her and she was over it, her torn skirts flinging wide as she swung her legs. She glanced back to see Valerian's smooth boot bottoms skeetering over the cobbles as he tried to regain purchase.

'Stop!' he shouted, the frustration audible in his throat. 'Come back here or I'll set the hounds on you!'

Without pausing, Lydia jumped from the top of the five-barred wooden gate, twisting her ankle slightly on her heavy landing. Trying to regain a footing on the dewy grass, she slipped a little and, holding her ruined skirts up, raced headlong, dodging through the sparse trees of the estate grounds. At last, out of breath, she reached the edge of Hawkesworth Forest, where dark sanctuary waited.

Lydia paused in her flight, rubbing her fingers along her ribs where a burning stitch tore at her side. She felt as though she had been running for hours, although it must have been only twenty minutes. She had skirted the edge of the shadowy woods at first, afraid of the silent interior, but when she heard the hounds give tongue as they were loosed from the yard, she had pushed her superstitious fear to the back of her mind and plunged into the dark green heart of the forest.

As she ran through the undergrowth, brambles and thorns scratched at the flesh of her calves until tiny droplets of crimson blood beaded the surface of her skin; the autumn-bare branches snatched at her hair, tangling into its already tousled fronds as she impatiently pulled herself free. The ground before her sloped down, its loamy surface covered with a carpet of crisp leaves: russet, gold, and brown.

Lydia slipped and slid, sideways and downward, the forest growing darker around her as she progressed down into what appeared to be a ravine with a tiny gurgling brook in the bottom. The morning sunlight hardly penetrated the gloom: just a few dusty fingers filtered through the lofty branches as the trees curved protectively overhead.

She reached the brook and stood, breathing heavily, leaning on a tree-trunk to steady herself.

There was silence. The deep, ominous quiet in the cathedral-like clearing was broken only by the sound of the brook, and the creak and scrape of brittle branches. A dead leaf floated down and lightly brushed her arm, making her jump and glance round. Behind her the slope was steep and the tracks of her descent clearly visible; Valerian would have little difficulty following and finding her, and she was certainly no match for his dogs.

As if on cue, the distant hounds gave tongue again, picking up her scent on the edges of the forest. Fear made her heart beat thunderously and the blood swished in her ears. She picked up her torn skirts and stepped determinedly into the stream. The icy water made her gasp and smarted the tiny scratches on her legs, but she pushed on, knowing that if she could follow the water for long enough then the dogs might lose her trail.

She splashed over stones and fallen branches, staying in the centre of the brook and travelling against the current. She wondered where the spring originated, hoping that it would bring her round and behind the hounds. She could then double back to the manor, to warmth and safety.

The thought of home was so inviting that, losing her concentration, she stumbled, tripping over a boulder and falling to her knees in the freezing water. Her hands went forward to break her fall and her palms scraped across the rough edges of the huge rock. She could hear the dogs gaining ground behind her, crashing through the ferny undergrowth and sliding – some yelping as their paws caught on sharp stones – down the ravine towards her. She scrambled upright and forged ahead, heedless of the pain in her twisted ankle and the heavy sodden fabric of her skirts.

Veering to the left, she splashed out of the water and up on to the bracken-covered slope where she ran more freely, casting a terrified glance over her shoulder. The leader of the pack was gaining ground, frothing saliva drooling from its yellowed fangs as it sensed the despair of its quarry.

Lydia screamed, long and piercing.

'Halt!' commanded a rough foreign voice. Turning, she collided with a solid expanse of muscular chest, and two powerful arms held her, almost lifting her off her feet.

'Help me! Oh, please, help me!' she gasped, briefly grateful, thinking she was safe until she looked up into the hard, uncompromising face of Conrad, Valerian's Nordic manservant.

He surveyed her calmly, then without a word he swept her up and threw her over one of his broad shoulders, kicking at the lead hound as it launched itself at her. Drooping over his shoulder, her long hair stream-ing almost to the ground behind him, Lydia shouted and beat her fists against the rigidity of his back as he turned and splashed across the brook, his powerful legs making short work of the journey back up the ravine.

Valerian waited, astride his huge chestnut stallion, a second manservant patiently standing at his side.

'Run to earth then, dear cousin?' he asked, a mocking lilt to his calm voice. 'Thank you, Conrad. A job well done. I shall reward you appropriately.' He reached into his scarlet jacket, drew out a pouch of sovereigns and tossed it. The tall Norwegian, hardly breaking his loping stride, caught it easily with one huge hand.

'Put her up behind me,' commanded Valerian. The servant deposited the struggling Lydia on to the stallion, where she instinctively held on to Valerian, gripping the waist of his crimson coat.

'Bring the pack home.' He nodded at the henchmen, then spurred his horse, turning and heading through the forest. Lydia clung to him, her despair turning to relief as she saw that they were heading home.

Chapter Three

The trees thinned and they trotted across the open parkland of the estate. The chimneys of the house were just visible, a welcoming drift of smoke curling out of the tops. As they approached, Lydia saw Anderson, the butler, waiting at the gate by the stable-yard.

'My Lord,' he said, clearing his throat tactfully. 'The guests are wondering about the hunt.'

'Send them home,' replied Valerian curtly. 'Inform them that my cousin has a minor indisposition and that she requires rest and quiet. Here, Sam!' He beckoned the groom whom earlier he had so cruelly chastised. 'Take my horse.'

The youth touched his calloused hand to his forelock and hastened to do his master's bidding. Dismounting, Valerian pulled Lydia into his arms and bore her indoors, through the great hall and up the sweeping staircase. Lydia struggled slightly as they passed her room door without stopping. She searched the hard planes of his face but did not speak, a tiny flame of excitement flickering within her as he kicked open the studded door of his own room. Lydia had not been inside since childhood, and glanced around with interest, half expecting it to be littered still with the trappings of boyhood.

Heavy scarlet drapes were pulled across the wide windows and the room was in partial darkness, lit only by the embers of a dying fire in the grate. The ebony floor was devoid of any coverings save one large tiger-skin stretched before the grand, black marble fireplace. An upright wooden chair, throne-like, stood at the side of the rug, with brass studs securing the raven leather of the seat and armrests, and lengths of soft cord looped around the front legs and each armrest. Beside the throne a bound casket rested on a footstool.

Across the room Valerian's huge bed dominated the space; it was at least seven feet across and raised, altar-like, on a dais, black and red silken drapes concealing the softness of the mattress. Ebony wood legs held it aloft, and yards of drifting crimson voile formed a canopy, suspended from a perfectly circular cast-iron loop set into the beamed ceiling. The starkness of the room and the scarlet and jet hues of the fabrics stimulated Lydia's sensuality. She found it hard to imagine Valerian sleeping here: it was a room designed not for restful repose but for some other, far more disturbing, activity.

Glancing up into Valerian's eyes she saw, with fascination, a look of abject hunger and lust which she felt mirrored deep inside herself. A tingling heat thrilled across the surface of her skin, and she felt her breath catch in her throat as he gazed at her with unsmiling intensity.

'You cannot escape me, Lydia,' he purred. 'You can run. Indeed, you excite me with your running, and I shall always give chase. But I will also catch you. Every time.'

He sat her down, almost tenderly, in the throne-like chair, placing her hands on the armrests so that she instinctively gripped the carved globes at the ends. Looping the silken cords around her wrists, he tightened them securely before moving down to do the same to her ankles.

Lydia watched him, unsure whether to struggle or cry

out, wondering what he planned to do. The chair was broad and her legs were parted under her gown, her ankles tied firm and wide; she felt exposed and open despite the coverings of her heavy wet skirts.

Valerian knelt before her, surveying his handiwork with satisfaction, apparently pleased with the enforced uprightness of her position and the rigidity of her spine which thrust her breasts towards him. He reached down and eased her sodden shoes from her feet, tossing them abruptly aside. Lydia tried to remain impassive, her feelings confused at his intimate behaviour, as he unfastened the hooks at the side of her skirt and pulled it down over her hips.

'Lift.' It was a command that would tolerate no disobedience.

Lydia lifted, bracing her hands and raising her buttocks from the seat. He slid the skirt and petticoats off as one piece, briefly unlooping her ankles from their bindings to free the garments before they joined the shoes, forming a wet, torn, untidy pile across the room.

He stared at her, feasting on the nakedness of her lower body, clad only in dark stockings. She could feel the bare skin of her buttocks sticking slightly to the leather seat, a slick juicy patch slowly forming where she rested on the firm surface.

She watched Valerian as he opened her coat and blouse, then unlaced her corsets to free her breasts; he did not touch her, content to caress her with his eyes alone. She sat quite still, naked to his inscrutable gaze, a liquid stream of hot desire coursing through her as she longed for the feel of his hands, for him to touch her, take her, do something.

Still he did not. Instead, he peeled the stockings from her scratched legs with great care before rising to his feet to walk to the far end of the room. She watched him as he lifted the ewer and poured water into a china bowl. Kneeling before her once again, he gently washed her wounds with the cool water, his fingers hardly touching her feverish skin which jumped and goose-bumped under his tender ministrations.

Finished, he pushed the china bowl of rose-hued water to one side and grasped her ankles with his firm hands. Holding one cleansed foot, he surveyed its pale length, softly stroking the underside with the pad of his thumb before suddenly engulfing her toes with the melting velvet of his lips, sucking and drawing.

Lydia stiffened, finding the exquisite sensation almost too much to bear, and she dropped her head back on to the high curve of the chair back. She could feel his lips following the arch of her instep to her ankle where his tongue rasped her pale flesh, and her fingers tightened on the wooden globes beneath her hands.

She abandoned herself to the delectable pleasure his mouth induced, as he supped, moving his mouth gradually and inexorably upward, the salty tang of his saliva stinging her bramble scratches. She winced and he smiled secretly, enjoying the tiny evidence of her pain. Continuing up her leg, he moved his face to the soft pad of her inner thigh where he inhaled deeply, savouring the scent of her excitement.

'You smell like a bitch in heat.'

Shocked by his sudden crudity after apparent tenderness, she snapped her head forward, glaring at him through narrowed lids.

'I thought you kept mangy curs away from your bitches!' she retorted.

With unexpected power he suddenly grasped her hips and jerked her pelvis forward to the edge of the chair, exposing her to his close scrutiny.

'Only the best stud dogs take them,' he muttered.

She could feel his hot breath upon her as he dipped his head, and she wriggled back, remembering belatedly that this was Valerian and she disliked him intensely, considered him the enemy. He had been the mortal foe in their game of cat and mouse in the forest.

He regarded her with a dark, brooding intensity, his sloe eyes half closed and glittering with sudden fury.

Coldly, deliberately, he grasped her again and pulled her firmly to the edge of the chair once more, then freed one hand and encircled her neck with a vice-like grip. Lydia stared at him, fear mingling with desire at his authority. He bent forward and took her mouth with his, crushing her lips against her teeth.

'You're hurting me,' she hissed, twisting her head to one side. He grasped her face and jerked it back until her eyes met his.

'If I want to hurt you, then I will,' he said. 'You don't seem to have realised, yet, that I can do what I like to you. You belong to me.'

Maintaining his collar-like grasp, he bent his head to her thighs, plunging, penetrating, and thrusting his insistent tongue into her burning flesh. Her senses swirled and she arched her back, tipping herself forward and on to his face, desperate to feel more, trying to grind herself on to him. He sucked and licked and teased, until the familiar waves trembled at the edges of her awareness; as if sensing her impending climax, he withdrew.

'Oh, no! Please!'

She surveyed him through half-closed lids, her lashes casting a shadow over her flushed cheeks. He curved his thin, hard mouth in a semblance of a smile, patently revelling in his control over her. One hand slid lightly up her inner thigh, and suddenly he thrust two fingers deep into her. She arched her back against the hardness of the throne and cried out, jerking her pelvis and clenching on to him in a vain attempt to retain his fingers, but they were gone, leaving her empty and incomplete.

All thoughts of her hatred for him gone, Lydia swallowed her pride and whimpered, imploring him wordlessly to release her from her exquisite frustration. He raised himself up before her, leant close and whispered in her ear.

'You'll have to beg, dear cousin. I want to hear you beg.'

She shook her head vehemently.

'Never!' She twisted her wrists in their bonds, but the tight cord burnt weals into her flesh and seemed to grow even tighter. Valerian knelt between her legs, his eyes fixed on her face, studying her reactions with the scrutiny of an alchemist experimenting with the philosopher's stone.

She stared back, tracing the line of his straight nose, the curve of his upper lip, the shadow that stubbled his jaw despite the fact that he must have shaved only a few hours ago. She saw the cleft in his strong chin deepen under her gaze and felt an overwhelming desire to lean forward and put her mouth there, to bury her tongue in the fissure and lick his chin. Holding her breath, she resisted the urge, knowing full well that he would not tolerate such a gesture of tenderness.

Smiling, a malicious pleasure washing over his face, Valerian walked across the room and stood by the raised crimson dais, apparently deep in thought. Suddenly he snapped his fingers and came stalking back across the bare floor, his boots ringing on the varnished surface. He threw open the lid of the casket and reached in. As he withdrew his hand, she saw something small and metallic glinting in his closed fist.

Before she could protest, Lydia saw him fix her erect nipples with tiny beaten silver stars. They clamped tightly around the puckered peaks, thrilling her with delicate, almost unbearably painful pleasure. Gasping, she thrust her hips forward in an involuntarily wanton gesture, and Valerian laughed cruelly, leant over, and engulfed her ready mouth with a hard and possessive kiss, plunging his rigid tongue deep into her throat until she almost gagged, sick with desire and penetration.

He stood back, admiring his handiwork before reaching again into the casket and withdrawing a small corked crystal decanter. He grasped the stopper with his teeth, jerked it free, and spat it into the fire where it smouldered briefly and then burst into licking orange flames. He tipped the bottle, and an amber liquid

300

dripped, almost sinuously, over her breasts, inflaming her nipples before drizzling down to the scoop of her navel; it collected there briefly, a shimmering copper pool, before pouring down to wet her dark curls. The liquid burned her already incandescent flesh and she squirmed, gasping at the pleasure which bordered on pain.

Valerian leant his muscular body forward, leaning dominantly over her and dipping his lascivious mouth to the rivulets of brandy, sucking her imprisoned nipples into steel peaks before following the stream of cognac downward, inserting his tongue roughly into the conduit of her umbilicus, drinking the nectar from her belly. His mouth burnt, accentuating the scald of the amber liquid as he drew the tiny dark curls of her pubic hair between his teeth, tugging them with a ruthless ferocity before unleashing his tongue on her. He licked and sucked, plunging his muscular thumb into her before suddenly withdrawing moments before she came.

Wild with the need for sexual release, Lydia bit her lips, desperate not to submit. She closed her eyes to force back tears of frustration, willing her sensual need to dissipate. She hoped silently that he would not be able to hold himself back, that he would need to spend his passion upon her; but, glancing through the slits of her almost closed eyelids, she observed his control and restraint as he stood before her, his hooded stare vigilant and watchful.

Raising one dark, winging eyebrow, he half smiled, enquiringly, but Lydia shook her head, refusing to capitulate. An impatience washed across his features, and he bent forward to briskly tighten the leashes which bound her wrists and ankles. She pulled fiercely against them.

'This hurts, Valerian!'

With a satisfied nod he tilted her chin and ground her mouth with a bruising kiss, before squeezing her left breast with rough brutality. He raised his arm and

301

struck her forcibly across the face with the flat of his palm and, hardly pausing, ripped open the fine cotton of his white shirt to reveal the pale-skinned masculinity of his hairless chest.

The sight of him exposed excited her already taut nerve endings and she feasted her gaze on his musculature, the smooth pink discs of his aroused nipples, and the line of dark hair that tapered from his navel down into the taut sleekness of his riding breeches. His arousal was evident in the bulge that pushed at the finely woven fabric; she imagined his rampant cock exposed and almost fainted with desire and unsatisfied lust, wanting only for him to possess her, to invade her flesh. She moaned slightly as he slowly unbuttoned himself. His cock was glorious and swollen, the statuesque length rearing from his trousers as he advanced towards her desperate lips.

'Suck me,' he commanded.

Opening her mouth to encase him, Lydia abandoned herself, revelling in the salty taste of him as she strained her neck forward to take as much of him in as she could. She opened her mouth and throat, drawing him in and sucking his strength, imagining that she could leach his power and enslave him to her own desires. His hands steadied her head, and she felt his thumbs caress her ears and then her temples as he gave a sighing exhalation above her.

He was giving in. Submission trembled in his fingertips: she could sense it as clearly as if he had spoken. His hands became gentle, tenderly moving over the satin of her hair and smoothing the shape of her head. She could feel his thumbs making tiny circular motions on her crown, and she deepened her hold on his cock, lapping her way to the root and pressing her nose against his belly.

He jerked back without warning, leaving her mouth suddenly bereft, one hand pushed against her shoulder as if to subdue her into the chair. Recovering himself, Valerian stared down at her.

'No,' he said, laying a long forefinger on her cheek. 'That's my game, not yours. I am the master. Now beg, just say it. Say "I want you". Say "Give it to me, Valerian". Ask me, damn you!'

He suddenly became angry, a scowl marring his features. He reached into the casket again and withdrew a thin silver thread the length of his longest finger. First looping it so that it formed a ring, he then bent, and Lydia flinched as she felt his fingers harden on to her clitoris. He tied it, encircling the hard little bud with the loop and pulling it tight. She felt as if every sensation had been forced into that tiny part of her: lances of hot pleasure darted around her sex and she cried out when he touched the very tip of her with his long fingernail.

'Ready to beg, cousin of mine?'

Seeing her quick shake of refusal, he took her clitoris between the nails of finger and thumb. Scratching, flicking, and squeezing, he stared into her eyes and she felt her own fill with tears of frustration. Hatred and longing swelled her breast and she thought she would burst as she felt him tighten the silver thread. Her mind raced.

'Damn you. Come on, just say it.' He grasped her shoulder and shook her roughly. Through the haze of pain and desire, she heard the last word that he said: 'Please!'

She knew then that her submission was also his.

'Fuck me, Valerian. I beg you.' It was a honey-clad whisper of defeat and victory.

With a cry of savage triumph he fell upon her, biting her full lips with possessive fervour, gripping her thighs and pulling them wide before sinking to his knees to plunge the full length of his hard cock into her. He ruthlessly plundered her, gaining speed and rhythm until she thought she could bear it no longer and she bucked her hips against him, matching his boundless energy.

Once she gasped at him, begging him to stop, and obediently he paused, long enough for her to sob, 'No, don't stop!' Then he slammed into her again, pulling her forward, crushing her against his chest until they both climaxed, quaking on to each other for what seemed like hours before subsiding limply, damp foreheads leaning together in harmonious fatigue.

Presently Valerian withdrew and tilted her chin for a tender, graceful kiss.

'Well, cousin. You are a fine lay, but no longer a virgin, I discover. Pray explain your lack of maidenhead.' His dark eyes probed hers and Lydia was the first to drop her gaze.

'Temptation surrounds me,' she murmured submissively.

'It should have been me!' he cried. 'You belong to me, Lydia!'

Angrily he untied her with rough hands and, picking her up, bore her to the crimson bed, pushing her willing body face down on to the softness of the coverlet.

'I regret, cousin, that I must punish you.'

He grasped her wrists, pulling them up and above her, winding a length of the crimson voile around and between her fists before jerking her up to her knees. He passed the voile through the wrought-iron loop and pulled on it until she was suspended from the low, beamed ceiling, her body limp and exhausted, her knees barely skimming the slippery satin of the bed.

'Now, you little slut. You will take your punishment.'

'What are you going to do to me?'

'Watch me.'

She felt him reach for something just outside her field of vision, then jumped as the lash of a long whip stung her. He whipped her repeatedly, punctuating his flagellation with hard scratching of his nails down the length of her back, and she sighed, overcome with the exquisite pain as the tip of the whip burnt her skin. It was like a lashing tongue that caught her just below the buttocks, in the tender crease which sloped to her thigh, and she felt it pushing her into paroxysms of pleasure.

She felt Valerian take her hair and wind it around his wrist, pulling her head back and down. The whip seemed now like stinging kisses, tiny puckering embraces that printed fiery weals across her body. She was caught by a thrust of desire that pulled at her, and she hung by her wrists, sobbing and writhing until she heard herself beg him to take her again.

This time he entered her from behind, filling her with his engorged length, taking her roughly until she was almost there, then suddenly, unexpectedly, pushing the knotted handle of the whip into her anus. And she came instantly, utterly filled and shocked to the core.

When Lydia awoke, she had no idea of the time, for the room was in silent darkness which stretched infinitely outward. Her whole body ached with unaccustomed use and she gave a secret self-satisfied smile which lent a feline slant to her eyes.

Stretching her arms outward across the rumpled linen, she found the bed empty and sat up, straining her ears against the inky blackness. There was a scratching metallic sound, and then a light flared as Valerian lit the candelabra next to the bed. He moved about the room, lighting candles of all sizes which had been set on every available surface as well as in banks across the floor. He came to stand by the bed, towering over her, the tapers flickering and casting eerie shadows on his face; his mouth curved in a smile which hardly reached his eyes.

'Awake at last? I trust that you are rested.'

'Yes, but I'm thirsty.'

He moved across the room, lighting the last few candles which stood in tall black iron stands at the end of the dais. In the golden glow she watched him as he moved with the muscular grace of a leopard; he uncorked a bottle of ruby liquid and poured four goblets, turning slowly to place one in her outstretched hand. Lydia drank deeply, the alcoholic fire burning her mouth and throat as she swallowed. Valerian urged her to drain the goblet, then he refilled it.

She sipped the second glassful more slowly. A warm glow seeped through her and she relished the lightheadedness she felt. Recklessly, she tossed back the contents of the glass and gestured for more. Valerian smiled, poured, then watched as she drained the goblet. 'You were thirsty,' he murmured. 'You've almost emptied the bottle. I shall have to send for more.' He strode to the door of the room, threw it open, and beckoned to someone outside. Conrad, tall and serious, entered the candle-lit chamber, and Lydia pulled the silken sheets up around her.

'Come, don't be shy.' Valerian grasped the sheets and pulled them away. 'Conrad will be seeing much more of you than that soon enough.'

Lydia looked up at him, confusion clearing as her gaze slid sideways to the two spare goblets on the table. Conrad lifted one of them and it was instantly dwarfed by his huge hand. He raised it to her in a silent toast and drank deeply and appreciatively, his blue eyes remaining fixed on hers.

She stared back challengingly, the wine lending her extra bravado. So Valerian wanted his manservant to witness his prowess; well, she was not averse to that. In fact, she thought, squeezing her bare thighs together and enjoying the pressure, it might prove very interesting.

What transpired was more interesting than she could have imagined in her wildest dreams. She allowed Valerian and Conrad to spread her arms and legs wide, then bind each ankle and wrist to the four corners of the bed so that she lay like a starfish, open and vulnerable on the sliding black sheets. She closed her eyes, breathing shallowly and curving her head back to savour the moment before Valerian came into her.

She felt his weight dipping the mattress as he knelt between her spread legs, and her flesh tingled as his fingers rested briefly on her narrow waist before trailing a line of fire down over her stomach. He gently spread her, and she felt herself grow moist and full as he inserted a finger, then two, twisting them inside and sliding out before repeating the action.

She tilted her hips up, pushing towards the source of pleasure. He pressed deep within her twice more, then slowly withdrew the fingers to replace them with the hard, hot tip of his cock. The creamy fingers slid a trail up over her belly to anoint her hard nipples and then dip over her chin to her mouth. At first she was repulsed, imagining the taste of herself to be unpleasant, but the fresh muskiness made her open her lips. One slick finger was pushed inside her mouth and she caught it with her tongue, fascinated and allured as she tasted herself.

She kept her eyes shut, visualising Valerian as he arched above her, with his manservant watching from the far end of the room, aroused but impotent. Ostentatiously, she tossed her head from side to side, moaning with genuine delight and straining her hands against the leashes to tease the watching Viking further.

Suddenly she was filled with a man who stretched her impossibly wide and she cried out, widening her eyes in shock to see that it was not Valerian between her open thighs but Conrad himself, huge and muscular, his mane of red-gold hair framing his strong features as he stared down at her.

He paused a moment, as if relishing the rigidity of her suddenly contracted sex and the look of horror upon her face, then he moved with long, generous strokes. She held herself firm, refusing to capitulate to the sensuality of his movements, forcing herself to deny the slow build of pleasure that he created.

She felt his big hand stroke her waist and then slide over her hip. He teased and caressed her satin skin, making her feel deliciously small and extremely relaxed. The gentle thrusts of his hips, combined with the soothing strokes of his huge hands, made her sigh and slowly melt, surrendering herself to blissful sensation. He rode smoothly above her, moving gradually faster with practised ease and athletic stamina until she was gasping, drowning in pleasure, then he withdrew abruptly upon Valerian's softly spoken command.

'Please, let him finish.' Her eyes sought Valerian's, but he ignored her and strode once again to the door. This time he drew his second manservant into the room.

Joseph, short, squat, and powerfully built, paused inside the door. At a word from Valerian he shrugged out of his clothes and Lydia watched him advance across the room, fascinated by the way the candles burnished his oiled black skin, lending it the lustre of ebony wood. She was filled with a mixture of fear and arousal by the sight of his burly form as he approached the bed, deftly lifted her hips with one hand, and pushed a scarlet cushion under her. She felt utterly exposed and open, and tried to pull her legs together a little, but the bonds which held her were firm.

As if to ensure that she would not escape, Conrad and Valerian each took one ankle and firmly pinned her into the soft down of the mattress, while Joseph positioned himself and then entered her, long and hard, until she was full, then pushing in a little more. She realised that he was so large that she could not accommodate him. The gratifying sense of fullness intensified almost to the border of pain, and she arched her back, trying to curve on to him to take him further in. He fucked her gently, almost lovingly, and she came sweetly, biting her lips to keep her climax a triumphant secret from Valerian.

Quickly, before she had recovered her senses, she felt the many hands of the three men untie her. She was held upright by Joseph, his bulging biceps easily supporting her weight beneath her arms. Valerian grasped her legs, almost roughly, and jerked them round his waist as he entered her from a standing position, sliding effortlessly in, so wet was she from her own and Joseph's juices.

He plunged the heat of his cock repeatedly into her, and she was captured by the easy glide of him as he achieved a steady rhythm, delicate pearls of sweat beading his brow. She felt herself impaled by his eyes, narrow and dark as they stared, their expression unreadable.

Then he thrust hard into her and stayed still, his shoulders drooping and his cock twitching inside her. She was unsure whether she could come again so quickly, but the sight of him so near to her, his eyes closed with the force of his climax, and the other two men breathing heavily on to her shoulders and belly in the candlelight, made her tremble and find the spot in her mind where ecstacy hid.

Valerian lowered her legs down. She knew that they were too tremulous to support her weight, so she hung, grateful for Joseph's strength as he held her, her mind blank and her body sore, her sex chafed. Conrad poured more wine into one goblet and all four drank deeply from it. Just before she drained hers, Valerian dipped his thumb into the dregs and smeared it across her forehead, almost as if he were baptising her.

'You're mine now. Always,' he whispered.

When the bottle was empty, Conrad lay down on the bed, his proud cock rigid and standing erect from the circlet of red-gold curls which covered his loins and upper thighs. He beckoned Lydia, and Valerian pushed her towards the bed, his hand cool in the small of her back. She walked to the bed, obediently straddling the Nordic giant.

She poised momentarily over him, then slowly lowered herself, feeling her plump and slightly sore lips unfurl over him. She raised herself and lowered again, enjoying the raw sensation of her flesh sliding over and gradually encasing him, almost sucking him in. She felt a hand grip the back of her neck and push her down until she was lying full-length along Conrad's body, her face pressed on to the hardness of his golden-haired chest, her toes resting halfway along his wide calves.

She felt a weight press upon her from behind, and Joseph mounted the bed, parting her buttocks with his firm black hands. She tensed as she felt him probe the entrance to her secret, most private place, holding her

309

breath and anticipating the exquisite pain as he pushed firmly and unhesitatingly between her buttocks.

'Please, no,' she murmured, part of her not wishing for him to hear her, or heed her request.

There was a long pause before he breached her, and she tensed, almost sobbing with fear and lust as she made herself open for him. Then he pushed and she was slowly filled and stretched, Joseph easing her tightness wide with care.

She began to move of her own accord, tentatively at first, and then felt herself voraciously plundered as the two men began to move inside her, their contrasting skin colours illuminated by the lustrous glow from the candles which filled the room. She let them take her, her exhausted body grateful for the pleasure, her mind giving up responsibility and need so that she was simply a resonant vessel, full of pure pleasure with no thoughts to hinder her.

Turning her head, she could see Valerian. He had drawn the leather throne close and sat in it, half reclining with one leg hooked over the armrest, his left hand stroking the slender length of his rigid cock, while the other cupped and squeezed his own balls. Mesmerised by his hand movements, Lydia watched, the hot rise of her climax harmonious with his.

She felt Conrad jerk his powerful hips upward and Joseph push inexorably downward and abruptly she lost all reason as the rhythmic waves surged through her lower body. She trembled, black shadows flickering at the corners of her senses, almost fainting with the violent force of the sensation that flooded like boiling cream through her body.

Time extended infinitely, then Valerian stood and drew a scarlet robe around his pale nakedness. He looked silently down at the tableau on the bed before him, then curled his top lip upward in distaste.

'So, my dear. Who do you think is lord of all he surveys now?'

Shocked by the sudden change in him, Lydia stared

up and then remembered her own words to him a few days previously. Her face flushed and she struggled free of the muscular tangle of the henchmen's arms and legs.

'You'll never have power over me. Never.'

With as much dignity as her nakedness would allow, she stalked from the room, pausing briefly to scoop up her torn clothes from their sorry pile.

Valerian laughed cruelly and, as she slammed the door, he muttered softly: 'Oh, but I have had, cousin. And will do again.'

Chapter Four

As the autumn sunlight filtered through the dia-
mond-paned windows, Lydia rested her head on
her hand and watched the swirling motes of dust dancing in the warm air. She had been sitting in the low
fireside chair for most of the morning, refusing Valerian's imperious and repeated summonses to come
downstairs.

An embroidery ring lay upside down on the red rug
where she had tossed it, the stitches knotted and poorly
worked. She kicked it, and watched as it flipped up into
the fire, caught behind the fender and slowly burnt at
the edge of the coals. An acrid scent filled the air and
was fanned by a cold draught as the door to her
bedchamber was pushed open.

Angel tapped on the wood panel of the door, bobbed
a curtsy, and then frowned, sniffing the air.

'Why, I can smell – something's burning!' She dashed
forward and twisted the blackened stitchery out of the
fire. She stamped on it with one foot, holding her dark
skirts above her ankles. 'Miss Lydia, your embroidery!
It's ruined!'

'Oh, leave it, Angel. I don't care: I hate stitching. It's
so boring.'

'If you're bored, perhaps you would care to join the

master for dinner now. He's sent me to bring you down: a final request. He says that there is a guest coming.' Angel looked down at Lydia, her fine blonde eyebrows slightly raised. Lydia met her eyes and then looked away, slumping her chin on her hand again.

'Well, the master, as you insist on calling him, will have to greet the guest alone. Tell him I am not coming down.'

'That won't please him. He threw a dish at the wall when you refused earlier.'

'If he chooses to ruin a whole dinner service, the answer will still be the same.' Lydia pursed her lips and stared into the fire, a deep crease between her dark brows.

' 'Tis an important guest, I believe. I've been asked to air the Blue Room.'

'I don't care! Just go away and leave me alone.'

'Very well.' Tight-lipped, Angel turned to the door.

'Wait!' commanded Lydia, jumping up from her chair and grasping the maid's elbow. 'Give him a message from me. Tell him he has no power to force me to come downstairs for any meal at which I am expected to share the table with him.' Angel reluctantly nodded and made for the door again. 'And Angel, when you have done that, please be so kind as to bring me some cold meats from the kitchen.'

'Certainly, miss. Whatever you say.' There was a trace of sarcasm in the words that made Lydia feel slightly guilty for her sourness. She curled her feet up under her in the chair and hugged her knees, feeling miserable and frustrated.

She stared into the fire for a few moments, then leant forward to grab the poker and give the dying embers a vicious poke. It really needed more fuel, but she knew that she couldn't ask Angel to go and fetch some. The maid would probably refuse after the rudeness she had been subjected to. She bit her lip and decided to be particularly nice to Angel when she came back from the kitchens; she liked the girl and enjoyed her company.

Without warning, the heavy oak door flew open behind her and crashed against the wall, making the mirror rattle in its gilt frame. Lydia jumped, dropping the poker; it fell with a heavy clang and rolled across the rug to lie by the fender.

'What is the meaning of this?' roared Valerian, advancing into the room with long, angry strides. He stood at the other end of the fireplace, a towering monolith radiating fury and impatience, his black hair unruly and his wide mouth set in a hard line. Lydia gazed up at him, swallowing her sudden fear and trying to quell the flicker of excitement which licked her insides. She took a deep breath, stood up, and walked across the crimson rug to stand directly in front of him. She spoke calmly.

'There is no meaning, Valerian, other than that which you surely comprehend. I do not wish to share your table.' She tilted her chin mutinously upward and forced herself to meet his eyes. He stared back at her, spite and lust smouldering in the ebony depths of his anger, as he drew his brows down and narrowed his eyes to impenetrable dark slits. He remained silent for a moment, a muscle flickering in his taut jaw as he sought to maintain control.

'My dear Lydia, your truculence is unbecoming.' He ground the words out through clenched teeth, his voice hard and low. 'You will do as I say. I require your presence at the dinner table immediately. I have a guest arriving and should like you to act as hostess. Accompany me down the stairs this instant!'

'No.'

'What did you say?'

'I said no. I don't want to. You think you have power over me, but you haven't, I do not –.' Her words were swiftly curtailed on a gasp as Valerian slapped her face with the back of his hand. The colour leapt to her cheeks as she raised her hand to cup the burning flesh.

'How dare you!'

'How dare I? Oh, quite easily. Like this!' Her head

snapped back as he repeated the slap, this time to her other cheek.

Incensed, she aimed her clawed fingers at his face, but he caught her wrist with ease, laughing malevolently. Then, without warning, he scooped her up and expertly turned her round. He pushed her forward over the nearby chair, throwing her petticoats over her head to reveal the twin ovals of her buttocks.

Lydia shouted, struggling, but it was no help: his iron grip rendered her helpless beneath the heaped skirts which fastened her arms as firmly to her sides as if he had bound her with rope. He applied ten smacks in quick succession to her bare flesh, and her hips jerked with each slap, her anger and indignation gradually replaced by a smarting pleasure.

Furious with Valerian, and angry with herself for succumbing to his treatment of her, she cried out in feigned distress and struggled again as if to free herself. He smacked her buttocks twice more and then firmly stroked the heel of his hand over her exposed sex, causing an involuntary shudder which Lydia sought to conceal by grinding her pelvis forward into the hard chair and pressing her thighs together.

'Since my father's death, you have consistently failed to understand the way things are here. I shall have to punish you for your wilfulness.'

Another resounding slap stung her, and then she felt Valerian's booted foot as he insinuated it between her feet and kicked her legs roughly apart. Biting her lips and pushing her face firmly into the cushions of the chair, Lydia hardly dared to breathe as his fingers harshly kneaded the tender flesh of her inner thigh and then abruptly entered her from below, the knuckles of his two forefingers grazing her as he pushed in. He withdrew slightly and rubbed her fullness with his thumb, then pushed into her and pressed his forefinger against the firm bud which stood slightly proud of her swollen sex.

Lydia moaned and eased herself back against him as

he withdrew, relishing the feel of his fingers as they forced abruptly back in, opening the pliable folds of flesh and delving deeper into her. Stimulation coursed like a fever through her veins; she could see nothing, but sense everything. And what she sensed was pure sexual exhilaration.

As if he could feel her enjoyment, Valerian began to thrust his hand into her more severely, withdrawing and brutally plunging into her again with gradually increasing speed with one hand, while the other continued to apply vicious smacks to her buttocks.

'How dare you disobey me!' His voice resonated with the knowledge of his own power. 'You will do as I say. No more, no less. If I tell you to come downstairs, then you come. Do you hear me?'

'No!' she gasped. 'You don't own me.'

'Oh, but I do. You have nothing, nothing! Everything you eat, everything you wear, comes from me. You belong to me, body and soul.' His mouth was suddenly close to her ear and she could feel the hard length of his body pressing her into the chair, squeezing the breath out of her lungs and almost suffocating her. 'If you don't do as I tell you, then I'll punish you. Do you need to be shown who is master here? Do you?'

'There is no master. Not until Drummond comes home.'

Lydia realised she had hit a raw nerve as she felt fury stiffen his already taut body.

'Why, you little –!' He jerked her upright and held her hair, yanking on it and using it to pull her round, turning her face until she could see his. Her neck was twisted painfully, and her eyes stretched at the corners by the strength of his grip on her hair. She cried out, real fear mingling with her arousal. He was so unpredictable that she was unsure whether he was under control. She tried to break free, but he pushed her roughly back down into the chair. As her chin hit the damask cushion, her cheek caught between her teeth and she could taste the sudden salt of her own hot

316

blood in her mouth. She struggled beneath the heavy folds of her skirts.

'Let me go! Help! No!' She squirmed as he swiftly withdrew his rigid fingers, spanked the bare cheeks of her bottom again, harder this time, with his slickly juiced hand, and then rammed it back between her thighs, introducing a third finger which deliciously stretched her and stilled her struggles. The blood in her mouth tasted foreign, metallic, and she sucked and swallowed, finding the taste of it bittersweet and subtly arousing.

She felt his other hand grasp the back of her gown, and he hauled her into an almost upright position, pushing the layers of petticoats to one side and groping at the tiny fabric-covered buttons at the back of her bodice. Impatiently, he pulled at the fastening, plucking and fumbling until she felt a button give, popping from its mooring to spin across the floor. Unable to master the rest of them with his trembling fingers, he roughly grasped the neckline at the back and, with a single movement, tore the fabric from shoulder to waist, revealing the snowy skin of her back. Encircling her with one arm, he imprisoned her hands at her sides and jerked her backward again until Lydia felt his hot breath on the damp curls at the nape of her neck.

'I will show you who is master here,' he whispered.

Without pause, he sank his teeth into her shoulder and sucked at the pad of flesh there, his sharp teeth contrasting provocatively with the melting heat of his lips.

Lydia moaned and sank back against him, her knees weak and her mind clouded, as he raked his teeth across the sweet skin of her back towards the undulation of her spine. His fingers moved savagely within her: once, twice, and then withdrew to fumble with the fastening of his breeches.

Wondering if this was still part of his punishment, Lydia felt heat emanating from him as the burning head of his unconfined shaft rested briefly between her but-

317

tocks. He seized her hips with both hands, and lifted and positioned her with a sudden brutal jerk. Lydia panted, then held her breath as she savoured the hiatus, the waiting, as she was suspended with his hot, silken cock pressing, momentarily denied entry, between the engorged folds of her sex.

Abruptly, his fingers biting into her skin, he moved her hips and his own, sinking deep inside her. He paused for a moment as if to recover from the suddenness of his entry. Lydia tilted her head back so that she could feel the hard muscle of his shoulder beneath her neck, and succumbed to the sensations that built within her. Her scalp tingled and she could feel the down on her forearms lift with arousal and her nipples harden as she relaxed her body against Valerian's thrusting.

He moved inside her with sharp lunges and a barely controlled ferocity, holding her waist tightly in a way which almost impeded her panting breaths. She could feel a febrile sheen beading across her brow, and the edges of her senses tingled. He reached around her and viciously pinched and rubbed her exposed clitoris, sending a shudder quaking through her body.

She could hear his breathing, feel the ragged exhalations as he mouthed her ears and neck, murmuring crudities which inexplicably heightened her own stimulation. As she heard him call her a disobedient slut, she climaxed shudderingly on to him, feeling the echo as his cock jerked in reply. He moved quickly, pumping his hips as he emptied himself into her, and Lydia sagged against him, unable to support her own weight.

She closed her eyes and slowed her breathing as he relinquished his grip on her and lowered her forward until she rested against the chair. She sensed him slip out of her and felt suddenly empty, swollen, and lacking, her desire for him satisfied for the present but not wholly spent.

She wondered if it would ever be wholly spent.

'Tidy yourself, my dear.' His words were flat and coolly spoken, no element of emotion warming his tone.

Lydia turned her head warily to observe him from the slanting corners of her half-closed eyes. 'You're due to play hostess in less than an hour. I will receive my guest in the great hall.'

'And if I refuse?' she enquired.

'I think we both know that you won't do that.'

He buttoned the smooth front of his immaculate breeches and gave her a mocking glance before turning on his heel. His polished boots beat a tattoo upon the uncarpeted expanse of wooden floor as he stalked to the door. Pausing, he hitched his thumbs into the pockets of his long waistcoat and turned to face her once more.

'Oh, and cousin? I have a fancy to see you in red. Wear the scarlet gown that was made for you for the Wilkinson's Ball last winter.' He smiled, his lips hovering between mirth and contempt. 'A scarlet gown for a scarlet woman, how amusing!' With a last insolent stare he left, allowing the heavy door to crash closed behind him.

Lydia remained motionless for a long time, staring with unconcealed hostility at the space where he had stood; then she reached down, picked up the poker from where it had fallen on the hearth-rug and threw it.

The resulting gouge in the door gave her great satisfaction, and she spent the time while she dressed imagining that it had been Valerian's head that the fire-iron had hit.

The commotion in the hall was apparent from the upper floor where Lydia had paused, one hand resting on the dark balustrade, to watch with detached interest as the servants ran this way and that at Valerian's bidding. The huge front doors were wide open, allowing a frosty draught to lick up the stairs towards her. The butler, Anderson, was standing with ramrod erectness just inside, and Lydia could see the smoky huff of his exasperation as his orders were instantly counter-manded by his master's.

Two footmen ran across the hall and went through

the door at a trot; they came to a standstill just outside, positioned like a pair of matching guard-dogs on the top step of the entrance, while Valerian snapped peevishly at a servant who was applying bellows without obvious success to the cavernous fireplace on the west wall of the great hall.

If she leant out, Lydia could see the vast dining-table laden with food, gold cutlery, and the best dinner service: a sumptuous array which she had not seen since a long time before Lord William's death. She wondered who the guest was that Valerian held in such obvious high esteem. He had no close friends beyond the hunting members of the local aristocracy and his London club associates, so she could not imagine who he had seen fit to welcome in such an ostentatious manner.

Smoothing the crimson brocade of her full-skirted gown, she glanced down to check her *décolletage*. The low-cut affair had been one that she had insisted on having for last year's ball, after she had seen pictures of ladies of fashion in London wearing wide overdresses which hung loose from the shoulders and fastened in the front with ribbons. Under it she wore a contrasting linen petticoat with the new quilting which kept her legs deliciously warm as the weather grew cooler. Last year, the gown had been a great success, and she had hardly sat out a dance at the Wilkinson's.

Valerian gave a final barking order to Anderson and then stalked to the foot of the stairway to stand with feet firmly apart on the magenta carpet, watching her descend. Unusually for him, he wore a full wig over his own hair and had powdered and patched his face like a town dandy. Azure silk stretched across his wide shoulders and the buckles on his shoes gleamed.

He swept an insolent gaze from her toes up to her face. His dark eyes paused for a long, lascivious moment at the soft skin which swelled enticingly like succulent, forbidden fruit at her neckline, then he extended a pale hand to her and assisted her descent of the last two steps.

'Thank you,' she murmured demurely, the thick lashes of her downcast eyes creating dusky shadows on her cheeks. She found herself unable to meet his sardonic black gaze as memories of their frenzied quarrel and his punishment rose unbidden to the front of her mind.

'Thank *you*,' he replied, apparently enjoying her slight discomfort. 'My memory served me well: that is a marvellous gown. I am sure you will impress our guest.'

'Who is coming, Valerian?'

'A very great friend of mine from London, Madame de Chaillot. She is always very accommodating to me when I stay there, and I wish to return her kindness by offering hospitality here at Hawkesworth. She is newly widowed and desirous of quiet and solitude.' His head turned slightly, listening to the crunching sound of a carriage drawing at a steady pace across the gravel driveway. 'This must be her now.'

There was an unmistakable leap of excitement in his eyes and voice, and Lydia was curious as she watched him stride energetically towards the entrance. He had never been enthusiastic about his father's guests, preferring usually to feign languor and disinterest, and retreat to a corner of the room to scowl. He must be very fond of the old widow: perhaps she had become a mother figure to him during his time in the city. Lydia felt her own interest stir and walked out to see for herself how the dowager had fared on the long journey.

A dark coach drawn by four white horses completed its manoeuvre around the sweeping curve of the drive. It came to rest at the bottom of the golden stone steps just as Lydia stepped out into the weak afternoon sun. The wheels were mud-spattered and filthy, the leather roof pelmet soiled. The timber of the lower part of the coach was painted a beautiful vermilion which could just be seen beneath the grime of the road. Even the brass studs were dirty and dull.

A periwigged coachman reined in the horses and the Hawkesworth footmen dashed forward, one to steady the lead horse's head, the other to swing open the carriage door and position the steps which would help the elderly widow to alight. Two of Madame's own liveried servants hopped down from the back of the coach and came forward to assist.

A hand clad in ivory satin extended from the interior and a footman took it to assist the lady. Lydia glanced at Valerian, who seemed almost to be holding his breath, and when she looked back again, the widow had descended from the coach and was standing at the foot of the steps, looking up at Valerian with coolly smiling hauteur.

Lydia stifled a gasp.

This was no elderly mentor: Madame de Chaillot looked hardly a day over thirty-five. Her face was as pale and smooth as alabaster and her powdered hair swept up and back from her unlined forehead in the most fashionable style; her milky colouring was contrasted beautifully by the lush darkness of a hooded sable pelisse which swept the ground as she advanced. The thinly pencilled arches of her brows raised slightly as she turned to Lydia, who felt instantly gauche in her rustic finery.

Madame de Chaillot narrowed frosty eyes and surveyed her with barely concealed disdain, then extended her hand to be kissed. Lydia dipped her knees briefly and touched the cold satin with her lips, unable to speak.

'Madame. I trust you had a safe and uneventful journey?' Valerian stepped forward, bending his lithe body in a deep bow.

'Thank you, Valerian. We did.' Her voice was low and throbbed with some nameless emotion that Lydia could only guess at. Valerian took Madame by the elbow and led her up into the house, his low words of welcome and his familiar gestures revealing the intimate terms on which they were acquainted.

Lydia glanced towards the coach. A powdered and plump lady's-maid emerged, pulling her luxurious mantle around her ample bosom against the chill of the autumn afternoon. She took the footman's proffered hand, treating him to a lascivious look from beneath her lowered lashes before stepping on to the gravel. Her hand lingered in his a little longer than was necessary, and he flushed, a deep staining red which rose from his immaculate white stock, up over his powdered features to disappear under his wig. Turning, the woman glared at Lydia with open hostility.

'I am Maxine Laurent, Madame de Chaillot's personal maid and companion. Pray arrange to have our baggage sent to our rooms. And I hope the beds are aired!' She shuddered and looked peevishly at her surroundings. 'Clancy, come at once!'

From the interior of the coach sprang a child of maybe six years old, wearing an Eastern-style suit and a turban with an enormous ostrich feather pinned to it. His chubby black face split into a grin and he leapt agilely down from the carriage, ignoring the steps, to land neatly at Lydia's feet and bend into a sweeping, flourishing bow.

'Good afternoon, your ladyship,' he said, carefully enunciating each syllable. He straightened and beamed up at Lydia. 'May I present myself to the lady of the house? I am Clancy: I fetch and carry and tie shoelaces!'

Lydia laughed; he was so sweet and charming, and obviously had a great sense of his own importance. She felt slightly cheered by his presence and took his tiny hand in hers.

'Pleased to make your acquaintance, Clancy. I am Lydia Hawkesworth,' she said with mock seriousness. Clancy bobbed and chuckled before her for a few moments before being summoned away by the frowning Maxine. He sprang up the steps with enormous vitality and disappeared into the candle-lit interior of the manor house.

Lydia gave a huge sigh and picked up her skirts. A ray of weak sunlight streamed down from the cloudy sky to warm her shoulders briefly before she stepped inside the door to the great hall. The air indoors, despite the huge fire and numerous candelabra, seemed cold, gloomy, and very unwelcoming.

The afternoon passed slowly, with Valerian and Madame laughing and talking together in low, intimate voices at one end of the dining-table, while Lydia hunched at the other end, miserable and sick with something she refused to acknowledge as jealousy, picking at the slices of goose which congealed upon her plate.

Finally she excused herself and went upstairs, sure that the other two had hardly even noticed her departure. Valerian had been engrossed in sliding frosted grapes between Madame's thin, rouged lips, and Madame herself had spared Lydia only a cursory glance before returning her attention to the young man beside her.

In her room, Lydia watched the dark evening draw in: tendrils of mist formed a halo around the crescent moon and icy beads of moisture clung to the window-panes. Chilled, she undressed hastily by the crackling fire and buried herself beneath the down-filled quilt to fall into a deep and troubled sleep.

Unsure of what had awoken her, Lydia lay for a moment in the dark, straining her ears to catch any sound. The house was silent. Relaxing, she snuggled again into her bed and closed her eyes, but sleep would not come. She turned over, turned back, punched her pillows, and then finally gave up trying to sleep.

Sliding from the bed, she pulled a heavy robe around herself, pushed her feet into thick tapestry slippers and curled herself into the window-seat to watch the stars. Her warm breath melted the crispness of the tiny glass panes and she rubbed with her cuff to clear a circular peephole.

The darkness of the estate was relieved only by the silvery gleam of the crescent moon. Inky shadows cast by trees and bushes lay long on the dark grass, and Lydia thought that it must be somewhere near midnight. A rabbit loped into view just beyond the steep slope which led down to the grassy ride, and she watched as it hopped about and then suddenly took fright at something. It dashed away, its tail a sudden streak of white in the darkness.

A prickle ran suddenly up her neck to her hairline, and Lydia sat up sharply as a dark shape detached itself from one of the trees and moved stealthily across the lawn to a tree nearer the house. Squinting her eyes, she could just about make out a long cloak and a tricorne hat; whoever it was had even masked their face with a dark kerchief over the nose and mouth. She could not see any evidence of a weapon, so he could not be a poacher; besides, they usually came in pairs with sacks and traps dangling from the belts of their short coats.

She waited, curious, for a moment longer, watching the figure in the garden. Then she grabbed her own hat from on top of the wardrobe, wound a velvet stole around her neck, and sped through the dark house to the door which led out into the kitchen-garden. The coolness of the night air closed around her like an icy glove as she pocketed the huge metal key and crept noiselessly around to the front of the house.

Skirting the rose beds, she avoided the noisy gravel and padded across the damp grass to a cluster of elms, careful to keep in the shadow of the big bushes that dotted the informal sweep of lawn. Crouching behind a trunk, ignoring the dampness of the nightgown that clung to her legs, Lydia narrowed her eyes and searched for the cloaked figure. For a moment she thought she had lost him, or alerted him to her presence in some way. Then she spotted a movement as a cloud raced across the moon and she fixed her eyes on his stooped position by the laurels.

Whoever it was seemed to be observing the house, moving gradually closer and watching the windows continuously. She felt a shiver of fear as she wondered whether he was a housebreaker: but then surely he would have an accomplice. Frowning, she decided to creep a little closer and try to identify his face.

As she moved, so did he, and any sound she made was masked by his own movements and the rustle of his heavy cloak. He stepped around the laurels, and Lydia quickly raced to the cover they provided, slipped, lost her footing on the cold, damp grass and skidded into the solid wall of the intruder's back.

Grasping at his cloak to save herself as her feet went out from under her, she stifled a cry and he swept around to grip her wrists, glaring into her eyes.

'You little idiot, what are you doing out here?' he hissed, his eyes filled with anger and impatience above the darkness of the kerchief around his lower face. Lydia twisted her wrists in a vain attempt to free them as she glared at him in silent recognition.

It was the highwayman.

'What are you doing here yourself? I shall raise the alarm this instant!' She opened her mouth wide to scream, but a hard leather-gloved hand instantly gagged her and he pulled her roughly towards him, crushing her arms into her ribs. Momentarily unnerved, Lydia inhaled the masculine scent of him and stared at the face so close to her own.

Her memory was curiously full of him: his smell, the feel of him in her carriage on that day, the strength of his muscled chest as he held her tightly against him. Unable to speak but desperate to communicate, she slid her tongue out between her lips and pressed the tip against the cold leather of his gloves, silently relishing the musty taste. He looked down at her with incomprehension in his eyes, then slowly loosened his grip on her.

'If I take my hand away, will you promise not to scream?'

Lydia nodded. He held her gaze, his eyes searching and a deep frown creasing his brow. The glove slid gently down over her chin, but his eyes remained fixed on hers with searing intensity. As if unable to help himself, he lowered his covered mouth and kissed her through the cloth with a tenderness that almost brought tears to her eyes.

Lydia did not move, her breath tight in her chest and the hardness of her cold nipples pressing into the coarse texture of his cloak. Almost crushing her ribs with a fierce hug, he reached beneath her knees and swept her up into his arms with effortless strength to carry her across the lawns away from the house. She knew his strength and did not struggle, aware that it would do no good. She watched the dark house recede over his shoulder.

'Where are we going?' Lydia breathed, as they ducked beneath a low branch and entered the darkness of the forest edge.

'The folly,' he said simply.

The stone tower had been built as the Hawkesworth hunting-lodge many years ago. It was deep in the heart of the forest, set by the lake which shimmered mysteriously on the edge of the estate: a two-storey folly with a crenellated miniature battlement and a spiral stone staircase. She had often played there as a child, setting up house and clearing away cobwebs, only to cry bitterly when Valerian burst in and spitefully kicked her efforts to pieces before her eyes.

Once, Drummond had challenged him to a fist-fight on her behalf. The two boys had stripped to their breeches and pummelled each other until Valerian had fallen knee-deep into the lake and capitulated with bad grace, scowling his forced apology to her as she hid behind the twelve-year-old Drummond. He had been five years older than she, and her hero from that day forward.

Sighing, she pushed her thoughts away and looked up at her captor's masked face. He gently set her on her feet and untied the horse which was standing patiently by a slender sapling.

They reached the folly within minutes, the horse

trotting sure-footed through the woods, almost as if it knew the route. The highwayman lifted Lydia down, and, holding her hand, bent his head to enter the low doorway set in the side of the little tower. The old wooden door hung on rusty, broken hinges, and the inside of the folly was dark and cold. Worn stone stairs twisted away up to the next floor, and as they climbed several bats took flight, flapping noisily around the ceiling before swooping out of the tiny aperture which served as a window.

The highwayman knelt in front of the fireplace and swept cobwebs away with one gloved hand. He pushed dry twigs into a pile and used his tinderbox. A flicker of orange flame swiftly consumed the pile, and Lydia hurried to gather dry leaves and other pieces of wood from the floor. They knelt together before the little fire until it was truly alight, then the highwayman spread his cloak for them to sit on and turned to Lydia, a serious expression in his eyes.

'There's something I must say to you,' he began, but she silenced him with two fingers laid across his covered mouth. She shook her head.

'You don't have to say anything. What happened that day: I've thought about it. You were very bad to do that, but things have happened since then, things that have changed me. And now, well, I'm glad it happened, and I want it to happen again,' she said softly, caressing him with her eyes as she felt desire quicken in her body. He returned her gaze with equal intensity.

'I wanted to see you again,' he said. 'I want to return this: I can't bear to keep it.' He slid something out of his pocket. The glow from the fire turned it into a golden serpent which lay coiled and still on his outstretched palm. It was her bangle. Lydia felt a rush of pleasure as she quickly took it and slid it on to her arm.

'Oh! Thank you. I've missed this so much. I used to wear it every day, and it feels strange not to have its heavy clank whenever I move or knock it on something.'

'I know you love it,' he said. Pausing imperceptibly,

he continued: 'I remember the day I gave it to you. You kissed both my cheeks and danced around the library.'

Her eyes flew to his face and widened, filled with alarm and disbelief. Before he could stop her, or do it himself, she had reached up and ripped the brown kerchief from his face. As she knelt before him, staring, her heart thudded and her throat became constricted with an emotion that felt like fear, but was something else. She searched his eyes, then placed one finger on his jaw to turn his head from side to side, studying him intently in the firelight.

'It's you,' she murmured, her expression changing gradually from disbelief to incomprehension. 'It really is you. You've changed so!' She could not think what to say, how to speak. Her eyes smarted with unshed tears, but then she felt rage fizz through her veins. 'Why haven't you come to the house? Don't you know that Valerian is ruining things, gambling away all your father's money while you're out here playing highwaymen?'

She leapt to her feet and stood, quivering with fury and cold, staring down at him with unconcealed anger.

'Drummond, what do you think you're doing?' She was suddenly unable to contain herself and slapped at him as hard as she could, her hands stinging as her palms caught repeatedly on the rough fabric of his cloak and on his ears, his cheeks, his neck. Catching sight of his bemused face, she burst into tears and fell on him, holding his broad shoulders and raining kisses on to the parts she had smacked.

'You're back. You're back. Oh, Drummond, everyone said you were dead! Oh, my love, my love.' She wound her arms around his neck and he laughed, holding her away from him momentarily before returning her kisses.

'I'm back, and what a welcome. I thought that you hated me for a moment there. There's so much I have to tell you. Oh, Lydia.' He pulled her face to his and kissed her with a hunger that quickly turned to passion.

Lydia felt him lower her on to the coarseness of his

cloak, tenderly spreading her long hair and holding handfuls of it up to his face to inhale the glorious smell of her. He cupped her face in his bronzed hand and sank his mouth to hers again, his firm lips mobile and questing, his tongue gently probing until Lydia opened her mouth to him. She sucked gently, tasting his salty warmth and feeling her body melt beneath his sure touch.

A roughened palm brushed her nipple, which instantly sprang to granite hardness, and she arched up to meet him, pulling him down until his weight was heavy on her and she could revel in her own breathlessness and feeling of vulnerability.

They kissed for a long time. Finally, as if he could bear it no longer, Drummond lifted himself up from her and pulled the nightgown over her head with one movement. Lydia sucked her breath in as the cool air dimpled her skin. She pressed her knees together and felt the juice of her own arousal damp on her thighs as she anticipated his touch.

As if reading her thoughts, he trailed a hand down her bare body, pausing at the curve of her breast to outline its rounded shape with his fingers, before descending to the dark curls which shadowed the pale skin between her legs.

'Move your leg,' he murmured. The infinitesimal pressure of his warm hand separated her thighs, and he slid his fingers between, entwining his forefinger in the velvet mound as Lydia tilted her pelvis and raised her hips towards his hand. He slid his fingers into her moistness, and Lydia gave a mew of pleasure, drooping her eyelids like a cat that had found a sunny spot. She sighed and curved her body up towards his hands.

Drummond moved between her legs, bending his head and placing his mouth on her, inhaling the lingering scent of her muskiness and tentatively pushing his tongue on to the swollen bud which pressed out at him, the width and colour of his little fingertip. He licked, gently at first, then with increasing fervour. Her slick juice rimed his lips, nose, and chin, lubricating his face as he pushed deliciously at her tenderest parts. Lydia twisted her fingers in his unruly brown hair and gasped, pushing herself up to meet him, widening her legs and pulling his head and face into her as if she would devour him with her sex.

Slowly, he moved up her body to kiss her long and deep on the mouth, his tongue probing the very depths of her throat and his body pressing urgently on top of hers. She could feel his cock like a steel ridge in his breeches and yearned to feel it, to see it, and hold its length in her hands.

'Let me undo you,' she whispered. He smiled and she moved her fingers to the buttons of his flat-fronted breeches. Together they unbuttoned and slid off his clothes until he was as naked as she was.

Lydia knelt beside him, gazing down at his out-stretched body and feasting her eyes on the muscular limbs and chest. He was sun-kissed and athletic, the distribution of his colouring indicating the long hours he had worked, stripped to the waist, on a ship's deck; his broad shoulders tapered to narrow hips and long legs with well-developed thighs.

Lydia thought how differently his body had developed to that of his brother, who rarely exercised and whose pale skin indicated his preference for indoor pursuits. Drummond's body was a glorious celebration of manhood, lightly sprinkled with glowing, golden-brown hairs which gave him an earthy, masculine, hungry look; Valerian, by contrast, was lightly muscled but with a predatory strength and a mean streak which Lydia, against her better nature, found electrifying.

'You're so big.' She shivered as she spoke. 'Hold me. Tell me this is real.'

'It is real. You can't imagine how often I've dreamt of this.' Drummond opened his eyes and gazed at her for a few seconds, then, smiling, pulled her down to lie along his body. The warmth of him permeated her skin

331

and she felt a feverish shudder which began at her toes and rippled upward to engulf her completely.

She slid her hands across the silken skin of his shoulders, up across his throat to his jaw, sensing the roughness of his unshaven chin beneath her fingers. Aroused by this evidence of his masculinity, she dropped her mouth to his and devoured his lips with her own, holding his chin with one hand while the other delved into the tumbled mass of his hair and gripped him, controlled him, moved his head to her rhythm. Biting his lips with a sudden fervour, she groaned and moved her face, rubbing her soft cheek against the sandy texture of his beard and simultaneously sliding her legs apart, curving her back until she was sitting upright and astride. She pressed herself insistently on his hardness.

Drummond seemed driven almost to a frenzy by her movements, by the rocking motion of her hips, and she felt him reach around her waist to grip her and raise her above him. Their kiss fragmented and broke as she was lifted, and Lydia pressed her hands flat against the muscle of his chest to help him.

They paused a moment, surveying each other in the coppery glow from the fire, before moving in harmony: Lydia sank her weight down on to him as Drummond eased himself up and guided the hot, straining head of his cock into her.

Both paused, then exhaled as one and Lydia rode down, down on to the hard shaft which thrust into her so deliciously, filling her, pushing into every crevice and corner of her being until she thought she would scream with the fullness of it.

She raised and then lowered herself, feeling herself unfurl as his width and length pressed her and then withdrew, almost to the shining hot tip, before she engulfed him again, and again, and again. Repeatedly, without conscious thought, they enjoyed each other and the blissful sensations, until Lydia began to tire and move more slowly. Her thighs ached from the burden

332

of her own weight and the chill of the night air that settled around her shoulders.

'Here, let me: come down here by me. Does that feel nice?' Drummond drew her face down and kissed her mouth, pressing his soft, warm tongue between her lips and imbuing her with his own strength.

He slowly rolled them both until they lay side by side on his cloak, noses touching and lips brushing. He cradled her leg with his arm and raised it around his hip, almost at the level of his elbow, and continued to plunge into her, grinding himself against her and sucking her tongue with a delirious intensity.

Lydia felt a tightening which began somewhere beneath her eyelids and tingled through her body, pushing her awareness to an almost dream-like pitch. She jerked her mouth from his and cried out, unable to maintain any sort of control as her climax slipped over her, wavering and silky. She stiffened, her back arched and her body rigid, digging her nails into the firm flesh of Drummond's back.

He gasped, crying her name and burying his face into the tangled damp hair which wound around her neck, breathing heavily and crushing her against him. He thrust into her until she felt him come, hot and hard, and she bit into the muscle of his shoulder.

They lay motionless. Lydia felt that her limbs were too heavy to move, and Drummond seemed exhausted and unwilling to surrender his hold on the body that, for so long, had been no more than a drowsing fantasy.

The fire, now barely more than a few smouldering sticks, flared and then subsided, leaving an inky darkness and a chill which began to permeate the air around them. Lydia, half dozing, turned her head and watched the tiny amber glow in the old hearth. The smell of Drummond's skin, and her drowsy recall of their lovemaking made her loath to move, but the cool night was beginning to chill the side of her which was furthest from the fire. She could feel, by stroking her hand lazily down Drummond's flank, that he was growing cold too.

'We should get dressed,' she whispered, moving her lips tenderly against his ear. He lifted his head and smiled at her, his pleasure in their shared climax bright in his eyes.

In silence they felt about the floor, bumping heads and hands in the dark, their touches reluctantly parting and then rejoining as if their bodies would not let them separate for more than a few moments. Finally, fully clothed, they leant together and kissed, Lydia straining her breasts against the thick leather of Drummond's brown jerkin as he reached around her to fasten his cloak under her chin.

'There, that'll keep the dawn mists out.' He smiled and kissed the cold tip of her nose.

'Drummond, when will you come home?' she asked, scanning his shadowed face. 'Valerian has taken control of everything at Hawkesworth. We need you.'

Drummond kissed her forehead and then rested his chin on her head, inhaling the perfume of her hair and holding her tightly against him.

'My love. My dearest Lydia. You know that I want to do that more than anything in the world. I haven't spent months travelling home just to skulk in the woods like an outlaw; but if I declare myself now, there's a risk that Valerian will make another attempt on my life, just as he did before I left. I'd be poisoned, or something similar, and my death passed off as the result of some tropical disease. I have to come back legitimately, with my father's will, and discredit my brother, enough to force him to leave and make a life for himself elsewhere. It has to be done properly.'

Drummond held her away from him, looking into her eyes and searching their clear depths. 'Will you tell no one of our meeting? No one at all? Please, trust me and wait for me. It's all that I ask of you at present.'

Reluctantly, Lydia nodded. She held tightly to him as they rode back through the forest, thinking of all the ways she could help him, trying to remember long-forgotten conversations with her uncle and recalling significant visits from his solicitor, Mr Lavendale.

When they reached the edge of the wide sweep of lawns, she slipped from the back of the horse and wordlessly they kissed, their lips lingering and hands clasped. Then Lydia turned and ran quickly away, her slippers leaving tiny dark marks on the silvery grass as she sprinted, silent and fleet of foot, to the house.

Chapter Five

*L*ydia closed the heavy kitchen door and returned the key to the hook behind the pantry door. The cold of the marble shelves chilled her fingers as she broke a piece of bread from a loaf that lay on a wooden board and twinned it with some crumbly cheese made in the Hawkesworth dairy. It tasted delicious and she swallowed it quickly before foraging for more.

A low sound from the kitchen made her start guiltily, and she slid the carving knife back on to the breadboard as quietly as she could. Thinking that Cook was making a very early start, Lydia wiped the crumbs from her mouth with the back of her hand before going to the open door of the pantry.

What she saw made her stop abruptly and pull back into the shadows of the little whitewashed room. Maxine Laurent sashayed into the kitchens wearing little more than her petticoat and corset, her ample breasts spilling over the top of the tightly laced garment like over-ripe gourds. Behind her, his face reddened and coarse with ale, lurched one of the footmen, obviously very drunk. Lydia recognised him as the one to whom Maxine had given that lascivious flutter of eyelashes on arrival that afternoon. Lydia could see that they had been together for some time by the familiar way they laughed together, and the manner in which Maxine drew him into the kitchen by grasping his breech-clad loins.

'Oh, Harry, come and play with me,' wheedled Maxine, her accent growing more pronounced as she became newly aroused. 'Come: you have seen what I like. Give me more, *mon cheri*.'

Harry grasped her left breast and squeezed it roughly with his hand, then fell upon it, gorging with his mouth as if he had not eaten for a week. Maxine leant her hips against the wooden table in the centre of the kitchen, and Lydia watched with fascination as Madame's maid tipped her auburn head back and groaned with pleasure, her hands cupping her own bosom and proffering it to Harry, who sucked with greed upon her large, brown nipple.

His hands gripped her waist and lifted her up so that she sat on the table. He hitched up her petticoats and then took her knees, clad in slightly wrinkled stockings, and spread them suddenly wide. Fumbling a little, he unbuttoned himself and pulled his cock free of its constraints, pausing to stroke its glistening, veined length.

Lydia swallowed, feeling herself begin to moisten at the sight of it. Bigger, possibly, than Valerian's or Drummond's, it was thick and crude, like a tool, but with a shiny texture to its reddened skin. Lydia reached involuntarily down to the soft, crumpled linen of her nightgown and pressed through the fabric on to her own throbbing sex, fingering herself lightly at first but with increasing pressure and pleasure as she watched through the half-open door.

Maxine lowered herself back on to the table until she lay full-length upon the rough, scrubbed surface, her buttocks poised at the edge. She spread her legs impossibly wide and carefully placed her stockinged feet to grip the edge of the surface. Harry reached between her thighs, scooped a generous fingerful of her juices and liberally doused himself with it, stroking and coaxing his own flesh to even more rigidity. When he placed the gleaming head on to her, Maxine quivered in anticipation, opening around him like a rose about to bloom, and Lydia could see the glistening pink of her sex as she spread herself with her fingers.

Harry reached forward and roughly massaged her breasts, his cock lying ramrod stiff across her sex, then he took his prick in one hand and sharply slapped her, making her gasp with the unexpected pleasure. Lydia firmly pressed her own finger up under her nightgown and into herself, her eyes fixed on the actions of the footman. She clenched herself on to her own deeply probing finger as Harry continued to smack himself against Maxine. He laughed and muttered, manipulating his cock with one hand and kneading her breast firmly with the other.

Maxine arched her back, offering herself up to him, her arms splaying wide and grasping at the surface of the table as she cast around for something to hold on to. Her face was pink in the glow from the range, and her eyes closed, her mouth loose and open: the picture of sensual abandon. Harry also watched her for a time, then ceased his slapping and placed his thumbs at either side of her entrance, holding her pink folds wide like wings before plunging suddenly and ramming himself into her with a guttural cry.

He gripped her fleshy thighs with firm hands, moving her on to his cock while simultaneously working his buttocks back and forth. Lydia watched, enthralled, as his muscular arse, liberally sprinkled with coarse black hairs, contracted and thrust, like one of the stable-yard stallions covering a mare at full speed.

Unable to support her own weight with her trembling knees, Lydia leant against the door jamb and held her chemise high with one hand, working at her sex with the other. Her long fingers rode firmly over herself, alternately pressing and stroking, occasionally plunging in to bury themselves knuckle-deep inside. A liberal flow of cream wet her hand and the silken skin at the tops of her thighs. Glancing down, she could see the silvery trail and smell the gorgeous dark scent of her own arousal.

Maxine cried out in the full flush of her climax and Harry shuddered, groaned, and fell on to her, panting and burying his face in the tumbled mass of her Titian curls, his hips suddenly still.

Harry recovered first and murmured into Maxine's ear. Despite straining her ears, Lydia could not hear his words and had to content herself with leaning close to the open door, pressing her eye to the crack to see what the footman did as he moved about the kitchen. For one heart-stopping moment she thought he would enter the pantry, for he seemed to be gathering items for a meal, but he simply wandered about the main kitchen, lifting lids and peering into stone jars, removing vegetables from the basket by the door and cream from the cooler.

Maxine, meanwhile, arranged herself decoratively upon the table, one leg hooked up and over the horizontal pole intended for bunches of drying herbs. Harry set his ingredients on the wooden surface beside her, and together they perused the items. Maxine delved a long forefinger into the cream and licked the thick curds from her hands, with a suggestiveness that made Lydia tingle with anticipation. It also seemed to communicate an idea to Harry, for he took the bowl and stood over the prostrate Maxine, frowning with lecherous intent.

After tearing her own clothing from her body, Maxine massaged her breasts and giggled her approval as Harry began to spread the cream over her ample form. Unable to contain himself, he began to lick and suck at every inch of her body, beginning with her breasts, but moving swiftly to her shoulders, back to her breasts, down her arms, lingering in the warm crease of her armpit. He trailed his broad tongue down between her bosoms and lapped at the swelling curve of her belly, before thrusting his nose between her thighs.

Lydia watched Maxine wriggling beneath his face and mirrored his actions with her own hands; her fingers

339

traced a light pattern over her nipples, arms, and belly, and she shuddered, feeling her blood begin a heated throbbing. Harry continued his feast down thighs which were lathered with the heavy cream, nibbling at the backs of Maxine's knees until she begged him to stop.

Finally he turned her over and anointed the ivory cheeks of her behind, before falling carnivorously upon them as if he would actually devour her flesh. She squirmed and squealed beneath him, the skin of her buttocks quivering and rippling as she thrust herself out to him, her movements becoming quickly more frenzied as he applied a handful of the buttery curds to the neat puckered rose of her anus. He rubbed around it, circling with his thumb and forefinger, and then dipping his head to rim her with his stiffened tongue.

'Oh, Harry, *c'est bon,*' muttered Maxine, her hands extending and gripping the opposite edge of the table. Harry straightened and rubbed the heel of his hand up her spine, watching her arch under his hard caress.

He reached towards the pile of food that he had gathered earlier, and Lydia watched with increasing excitement and disbelief as he selected a thin, under-ripe baby marrow and gently worked it into the opening flower of Maxine's rear, to the accompaniment of groans of pleasure and encouragement gasped in her native tongue.

He was leisurely, and spent a long time inching it in and then easing it out again, waiting to hear her tiny gasps, then pressing further in until most of the six inches had disappeared between her pink buttocks. Next, he chose a long, thick carrot and pushed it slowly into her swollen sex, twisting and pulling it back before pressing it in to its full, hard length.

Lydia stared through the narrow crack of the pantry door and concentrated on Maxine's reaction to this double plundering with the hard vegetables. She could just see the side of the maid's face, partly obscured by the tumble of her dark coppery hair, Maxine's eyes were closed, and her cheeks flushed with a sexual glow; her lips were parted and her neck arched back to reveal her snowy throat and the pulse which beat just below her jaw-line.

Behind her, Harry ravished her with a gradually increasing and insistent rhythm, until she cried out and he reached around to silence her with one strong hand to stop her alerting the household of their nocturnal activities. His hand disappeared from Lydia's view, but there was silence; then he leant back, groaning, the tendons on his thick neck standing out in coarse relief as he pumped his cock with one fist and jerked his thick come across Maxine's naked back.

Lydia trembled in the pantry: her sex felt thick and heavy to her own fingers, and she bit her lips with frustration, unable to achieve her own orgasm for fear that the suddenly silent couple would hear her.

Removing the carrot slowly from Maxine's swollen sex, Harry casually bit the end off and crunched it with big square teeth.

'Same time tomorrow?' he enquired. Maxine reached up and gripped his semi-erect penis, squeezing it gently.

'*Mon cher*, I will expect you in my room soon after midnight. I think that being stuck here in the country may have its benefits after all.' She slid her arm around his neck and drew his mouth down to hers, and, as Lydia watched, their tongues twisted and entwined while Maxine massaged Harry's balls with her cupped hand.

The maid and the footman left the kitchen, abandoning the food for Cook to imagine what she wished in the morning. Lydia counted silently to one hundred before stealing along the darkened passageway into the main house, avoiding floorboards she knew to be creaky. The clock on the half-landing chimed four as she passed it, making her jump and hurry up the last few stairs to the warmly carpeted gallery that led to the sanctuary of her own room.

The softness under her bare feet felt warm and com-

341

forting after the chilly stone of the pantry, and Lydia paused for a moment, one hand placed flat on the wall, as she savoured the sensuous luxury beneath her toes. She pressed her tender soles downward into the close-textured cushioning, and momentarily closed her eyes in the inky darkness.

When she opened them again, she could see that a golden glow of light had appeared which lit the darkness a little further along the corridor. Someone had opened a door. Not wishing to be discovered prowling through the house at dawn, Lydia shrank back against the dark wall and held her breath.

The door swung wider, and she could see into the room, where a huge, blue-draped four-poster bed could be seen in disarray: the bolster tossed to the floor, the sheets crumpled and pushed into ruched humps as if the occupant of the bed had writhed in a feverish convulsion. The Blue Room was part of a suite that Valerian had allocated to Madame de Chaillot for the duration of her visit, so Lydia, thinking that Madame must be ill or in need of assistance, started forward to go to her aid.

Almost instantly, Lydia jumped back and pressed herself against the wall behind her. A dark shape had appeared in the lighted doorway, too tall to be the diminutive Madame. As she watched, the figure turned and the glow from a taper in the room fell upon the smooth planes of Valerian's face as he leant forward to kiss the naked woman who stood just inside the room.

Lydia caught her breath and her eyes widened as Madame, serpent-like, slid her pale, slender arms around his neck, and drew his head down to receive her returning kiss. Their tongues were visible as their lips drew slightly apart and Lydia watched as Madame sank her sharp teeth into Valerian's fleshy bottom lip.

Expecting him to be angered by this, Lydia was surprised to hear the low rumble of laughter and his tender whisper as he slipped his mouth along Madame's cheek to the slender stem of her neck. He raked his teeth across the smooth porcelain of her skin there and bit down hard on to the curve of her shoulder. Madame groaned and arched herself against him, like a cat luxuriating and rubbing itself on its master's leg. Her nipples hardened and lengthened, cork-like and ruby red, and Lydia watched with fascination mixed with revulsion as the woman reached down to the growing bulge at the front of Valerian's loose white shirt. He laughed and stayed her hand, and, reluctantly it seemed, they parted.

As the door closed gently, Valerian stepped away into the dawn shadows.

Lydia darted forward.

'How dare you?' she hissed. 'You're disgusting. How can you stoop so low as to bring your – your – whore into this house?'

He swore, then there was a flare and she saw him light the candle in the wall sconce above her head. In the soft light she saw him raise an eyebrow, and his mouth widened in a sardonic smile. He seemed completely at ease, and not at all surprised to see her.

'Good morning, cousin Lydia. What brings you here at this hour?'

Momentarily caught off guard, Lydia hesitated before replying.

'I was hungry; I went down to the kitchens for some food.'

'Indeed. Have you given your maid the night off? Really, Lydia, you must utilise the servants, or they will become redundant and I shall get rid of them.' He casually examined his nails in the dim light. 'Staff are a needless expense if you persist in doing their work yourself.'

'I didn't wish to wake Angel for such a simple task,' she whispered.

'Your generosity is commendable, dear coz. Perhaps you will extend the same consideration towards my so-called whore and refer to her by name. Either that or refrain from meddling in affairs which do not concern you.' Valerian moved closer, and Lydia could smell the feral scent of his masculine sweat mingled with a darker, mysterious odour which caught at her senses.

She stepped back carefully and he advanced again, as if they were performing some slow and ritualistic dance movement. As he moved forward, Lydia felt the cool pressure of the wall behind her, the stone chilling her shoulders through the fabric of her nightgown. Curiously, it did not make her feel cold, but merely intensified the warmth which stole through her body at his proximity, a feverish heat which tingled along her taut limbs and caused her to inhale a little more deeply, as if out of breath from a sudden exertion.

'Affair is just the word, Valerian. And, as you say, it certainly is not my affair but quite patently yours. I don't care what relations you enjoy with this French woman, but I do care that you sully our name by conducting yourself so shamelessly.' She glared up at him through angrily narrowed eyes, just able to make out the darkened curve of his jaw in the shadow of the candlelight. Valerian gave a low, malevolent laugh.

'I do believe you're jealous,' he whispered, stepping even closer so that their bodies almost touched, and Lydia could feel the warmth which emanated from beneath his loose white shirt. A burning flush rushed to her cheeks and she shook her head in denial, hardly trusting herself to speak. Valerian's eyes fixed on hers in the dim light, his hooded gaze intense and probing; Lydia dropped her eyelids, afraid of betraying herself.

She prepared to push him away, fight him if need be, and was surprised when his hand moved tenderly up her forearm to her elbow, where his thumb stroked her skin before moving downward in a sensuous trail to her wrist. His fingers interlaced with her own, gripping her. He lifted her hand firmly, sliding up the cold smoothness of the wall until she was stretching upward, lifted almost on tiptoe, her arm extended high above her head and her breast thrust up and out. She gasped, just in time, as his pliant mouth found hers, and he

344

kissed her with a breathtaking intensity, his lips soft yet hard, his tongue tip just touching hers before he withdrew to bury his face in the mass of shining hair which tumbled freely over one shoulder.

'Aah, Lydia, so fragrant and fresh. You smell of the crisp dawn breezes which drift through the gardens. I could swear that you have been outside.'

He inhaled again, and then kissed the softness of her cheek and the curve of her jaw before mouthing gently at the sensitive lobe of her ear. Lydia felt herself melt beneath the unexpected restraint and passivity of his caresses, and she tipped her head back to reveal the innocent arc of her neck. Valerian kissed her there, lingering at the pulsing beat which thrummed through the taut skin. He placed the tip of his tongue on the camber of her throat, and drew a line slowly upward to the pointed tip of her chin, teasing her with light bites from his gentle teeth before claiming her lips once more.

As his mouth skilfully seduced her, so his hands tempted and toyed. His fingers played idly at her waist for several moments, then stole up to weigh the firmness of one breast in the palm of his hand. His thumb brushed lightly over her already firm nipple, and Lydia felt herself tighten as he rolled it between his first two fingers, pulling lazily, squashing and kneading her in his large and powerful grasp. His thigh pressed insistently on to hers, and Lydia shifted her leg a little to allow his to press between her trembling knees. She could feel the masculine rigidity of his cock pressing against the bony curve of her hip, and the pressure of its potent strength excited her almost beyond control.

She raised her hands to his face, and drew him down so that his mouth grazed hers as she pushed him towards her breast. His hands grasped the linen of her nightgown, pulling downward and sideways to reveal the rosiness of her flesh. When he fastened his lips at last to her nipple, she pushed desperately against him, feeling him suck and draw with his lips, tonguing at the puckered flesh which rose to a peak beneath his mouth.

One of his hands cupped her proffered breast, while the other slid firmly down the line of her belly to the soft down at the top of her thighs. The springy curls pushed at him through the cotton fabric as she tilted her sex towards him, and he groaned, stepped back away from her and stared at her from beneath lowered brows.

'God, Lydia, I swear –!'

Without finishing, he pulled her to him once more, and Lydia pulled at the nightgown with him, lifting the hem high around her waist. She reached for the loose folds of his own oversized shirt, and pulled at it, eager to see and feel him against her again, revelling in the gradual exposure of his lean hips and the rampant stiffness which reared out towards her from the tangle of black hair.

Valerian grasped her waist, lifted her, and turned, propping her buttocks on to the polished timber of the balustrade. Lydia sensed the steep drop behind her, but the slight frisson of fear was quickly overtaken by another, far more urgent, sensation, as he spread her with one hand. She caught her breath and closed her eyes as he slid his cock, ramrod stiff, into her creamed and ready sex. She arched her head back, her inky black hair tumbling behind in waves as it merged with the darkness of the stairwell behind her.

Suspended in time and space for an eternal moment, Lydia was roughly pulled back to earth as Valerian jerked out of her and grasped her neck with his hand.

'Why, you're as wet as a tuppenny whore after a whole troop of soldiers!' he hissed, thrusting his fingers deep into her moistness. He withdrew and lifted his hand to his face, widening his nostrils as he inhaled the scent which clung to his forefinger.

'You slut! You stink like a bitch in heat! Who else have you had?' He shook her by the neck until she thought that she would fall backward over the banister and be cast to certain death on the stone flags far below. 'Tell me, you strumpet. Where have you been? You've been fucked as surely as Madame has, but it's not my seed that perfumes your inner parts, by God!'

Lydia pressed her lips together. Meeting his penetrating gaze, she shook her head and twisted her neck beneath his firm grasp.

'I'll be damned if I tell you. If you have to be angry then I am your target.'

'Angry? Angry? Livid is the word. I am livid that my cousin sees fit to squander her most precious commodity and sneaks around in the dead of night to do so. You cheap little trollop, did you think I would never find out? To think that for one moment I thought – I really felt as if – as if there was something more between us than kinship.' He shook her again and she wriggled forward, trying to slide off the banister and on to the safety of the landing, but he held her fast with an iron fist. 'I'll find who you've been with if I have to torture all the men in this household to do so! I am the master here. I will be obeyed and respected! By deceiving me, you have lost all claim on being treated as one of the family. Henceforth, you will be locked in your room without privileges unless I feel inclined to bestow them.'

He took her hair in his steely grip and yanked her harshly down from the banister. As she fell, Lydia tried to stand, but he quickly jerked her head downward so that she could do little but crawl behind him, holding her own hair slightly above his hand to ease the pain in her scalp, as he used it like a leash to drag her along the hallway. Her knees grazed the carpet, which felt no longer like velvet, but coarse hemp beneath her, and she struggled along behind him, her eyes smarting at the pain of her tender head.

As they neared Madame's doorway, Lydia held her breath for fear that the occupant would hear the scuffling in the corridor and emerge to investigate, but everything remained dark, and Valerian continued to drag her along until they reached her own bedchamber.

'You will remain in here until I decree that you may be released,' he muttered, tightening the cords with which he had leashed her wrists to the bedpost. 'Don't imagine that struggling will loosen your bonds. I'll also tie this around your mouth: I don't wish the household to be disturbed by your calling or crying.'

Lydia jerked her head to one side, but Valerian caught her expertly and fastened a leather belt across her mouth, buckling it firmly at the back of her neck so that she could feel the bite of the hard leather around the soft skin of her face. He stood back to admire his own handiwork: Lydia's slender body was upright against the carved wooden post with her arms lashed behind her, another wide leather belt encircled her waist and held her tight to the bedpost, while a third bound her bare thighs. Her hair tangled over her shoulders and covered her breasts like a dark mantle, while her eyes above the gag were wide and full of fear.

Valerian narrowed his eyes, and then leant forward, his lips curved in a malevolent smile as he roughly tore her thin cotton nightgown from her body and kicked it to one side. She wilted, but found herself held fast by her bonds, and he raked his eyes over the exposed ivory skin and tender curves.

'My, what a pretty sight,' he murmured. 'If another had not had you so recently, I think I would indulge myself by spreading your legs wide and taking you there. To have you bound and delivered up to my mercy is an appealing temptation.' He stepped closer and slid his hand down her hip, his mouth so close to her ear that she could feel the humidity of his breath on her cheek.

'You may demur, but I think you enjoy my touch more than you care to admit. Perhaps your nakedness in this chill morning will cause your appetites to cool and your head to clear. Pray, do tell your maid if you decide to advise me of your lover's name.'

Then he was gone, the door closing softly behind him, and Lydia was left alone to shiver in the gloom. She closed her eyes and rested her head on the smooth wooden curve of the bedpost behind her, swallowing angry, frustrated tears as she prepared to wait for Angel's first visit.

Angel started slightly at the harsh sound of the summoning bell. Glancing at the board, she saw that she was required in the study. That will be Master Valerian then, she thought grimly, smoothing her muslin apron and tucking an escaped wisp of gold into the plaited coil at her nape. She hurried up the three flights of stairs from the basement, and knocked gently on the oak panelling of the study door.

'Come!' The demand was compelling, and she felt her legs carry her into the room as if they had a will of their own.

Dropping a deep curtsy, she studied the edge of the vast Aubusson rug, not daring to raise her eyes to her master.

Eventually, the silence was such that she began to imagine that she had entered the wrong room by mistake, and flicked her eyes upward, quickly, to see Lord Hawkesworth lounging on the other side of a wide, beautifully varnished desk. One polished black shoe was propped on the gleaming surface where he rested his leg; the muscles of his shapely calf stretched the taut fabric of his leaf-green hose, and the underside of his knee was clearly reflected in the mirror-like gleam of the timber. Angel felt her pulse begin to race as her gaze followed the line of his leg relentlessly upward. The master was obviously at ease with himself and with the world: a careless insouciance seemed to emanate from the soft fabric of his olive-green coat and the gentle folds of pure white cotton which frilled beneath his smooth cravat.

Angel's eyes continued their ascent, observing with deepening interest the swarthiness of his cheek, the dark shadow which cast a masculine pall across his finely chiselled jaw, the long straight nose, the sweep of raven lashes. Her heart leapt to her mouth and she tucked her head down swiftly. The penetrating look in those hooded eyes was intense and searing; Angel swallowed her sudden irrational fear and willed herself to meet his commanding face. His top lip raised contemptuously as if he sensed her fear and despised her for it, and Angel tipped her head up proudly, pulling her shoulders back and throwing him a challenging stare.

'Did you require something, milord, or did I mishear the bell?'

'You heard correctly, Angel. I wish to discuss your mistress and the punishment I have deemed fit for her to endure.'

'Punishment?' Angel stared at him, her faintly drawn eyebrows raised. 'Why is Miss Lydia to be punished?'

'Her crime is not your concern. Her care is. I have decided that she will be locked in her room for a period of – oh – four days,' he announced arbitrarily. 'During that time she is to receive no visitors, her meals are to consist of bread and water, and she is allowed no fire in her room. Do I make myself clear?'

'But, milord, it grows so chill at this time of year. If Miss Lydia is not allowed a fire, her room will be uncomfortably cold.'

'Do I make myself clear?' Valerian wrenched his leg from the desktop and sat suddenly upright, banging his clenched fist on the timber as he did so.

Angel jumped and nodded, determining then and there that her mistress would have the choicest morsels from the kitchen smuggled to her room, whatever her crime. She watched Valerian rise to his formidable height and rest his knuckles on the desk, leaning forward as if to create an air of greater authority. Boldly, she met his eyes and flinched a little, but did not drop her gaze. She bobbed a small curtsy, deep enough to acknowledge his superiority, but shallow enough to suggest a distinct lack of servility.

'Yes, milord. It's very clear. Will that be all?'

'Get out.' His lips curled in a sneer and he waved an imperious hand.

She backed away across the rug, and turned as her

soft pumps sensed the edge of the rug. Instantly she froze. There, just to one side of the study door, and until now hidden from view, sat Madame de Chaillot. Her slender form was perched on a gilded salon chair, her blue silk gown arranged artfully around her shapely legs, so that the fabric appeared at once to reveal and yet conceal. Her back was ramrod stiff and her thin hands were folded neatly in her lap.

Angel thought for a moment that she was relaxed and careless, hardly listening, but the whiteness of her knuckles showed her tension, and as the maid glanced up she saw the woman's cold eyes fixed on her with a pale intensity. Angel interpreted the look as anger, but as she moved towards the door and came close to Madame de Chaillot, she saw that the other woman appeared consumed with a predatory hunger as her gaze remained fixed on Angel's waist. Feeling the flush which warmly stained her own cheeks, Angel paused slightly as she reached the door.

Madame remained motionless, her body rigid, but her eyes mobile and devouring as they roamed over the younger woman's body, as if memorising the details of her curving hips and the small, pointed breasts which pushed at the fabric of her dress.

Angel composed her features into a mask of distaste. Slanting her gaze sideways, she gave Madame an insolent stare before she left the room, leaning briefly against the door to steady herself as she closed it behind her.

Chapter Six

*L*ydia had been imprisoned for three days. Cold and hunger had not bothered her as much as Valerian had planned, for Angel had visited at intervals bringing hard bread and jugs of water, but with her apron pockets covertly filled with pieces of capon or goose. Warm bricks wrapped in flannel had kept the bed aired, and frequent nips of cognac from a bottle Angel smuggled into her room kept dismal spirits at bay.

At first Lydia had thought that boredom would defeat her, and had sat in the window for long hours gazing out at the colours of autumn. Slowly the leaves on the trees changed from darkest green to curling browns and reds. Angel's visits gradually took on a significance of their own, and the tiniest sound at the door would send a flicker of excitement coursing through Lydia's veins, and set butterflies fluttering in the pit of her stomach.

When she first attended her mistress, Angel had been shocked, and gently ministered to her by untying her bindings, washing and soothing her body, dabbing cologne at her temples, and helping her to dress. They did not speak of Valerian or his cruelty.

On the second evening, Angel's hands had softened as she unlaced Lydia's stays, and a smooth finger had crept inside the stiff fabric to lie on the flushed skin around Lydia's ribs. Lydia had become very still and held her breath as the fingers began stroking the flesh beneath her breasts, while the other girl's tiny exhalation warmed her shoulder. Finally, Lydia had shuddered with desire and the spell had been broken, the hands removed, and Angel had reached for the linen nightgown before helping Lydia into bed. When the covers were pulled up, Lydia watched Angel's face, hoping to meet her eye and give her a sign of encouragement; but the maid had kept her lashes modestly downcast, and bid Lydia goodnight in a low voice before leaving.

On the third day, Lydia laid in bed until she heard the grandfather clock strike midday deep in the interior of the house. Angel usually woke her with breakfast, but she had failed to arrive that morning. Lydia rolled on to her stomach and tried to ignore the hunger pangs which rumbled around her insides. Where was Angel? She was just beginning to feel bad-tempered when there came the familiar sound of a key scratching in the lock and she sat up, composing her features into an expression of deliberate petulance.

'Where have you been? It's noon, and you've usually been to see me by this time!' As she spoke, Lydia realised the strange dependency she had come to feel on seeing her maid, her absolute reliance on this contact, and it made her feel even more fractious. 'Have you brought me anything to eat? I'm ravenous.'

'Here. It's baking day and I've brought you some fresh bread. It's still warm.' Angel smiled and perched on the edge of the bed, as she broke the loaf and passed fragrant handfuls to her mistress. 'I couldn't come up earlier. The master has had me running around all over the house preparing for the ball. It's like a madhouse downstairs!'

'A ball?' queried Lydia, between mouthfuls. 'Is there to be a ball?'

'Only a small affair. He decided yesterday, and I think Madame had a lot to do with it. He wants her to be hostess, would you believe! Lord William must be turning in his grave to see his son's whore parading around Hawkesworth as if she were the lady of the manor.'

'Tell me about the ball.'

'Well, invitations have gone out to ten local families: the usual county set, I believe, and two or three of Master Valerian's friends from his club in London. The great hall is being decorated today. Oh, I wish you could see it,' she added, laughing. 'Anderson is directing them, and the footmen are all up on ladders with sprigs of –'

'Am I to be released?' demanded Lydia. Angel paused, glancing sideways at Lydia, then shook her head.

'The master says you're to stay here for another day.'

'I will not! Angel, give me that key!'

'I can't, you know how much trouble I'd be in if –'

'And you know how much trouble you'd be in if Valerian found out that you'd been feeding me. Now give me that key!'

'You wouldn't tell him!'

'I would! And I will unless you give me that key.' She changed her tone to a wheedle, sensing Angel's reluctance to be bullied. 'I won't use it until later, when the ball is in full swing. Please, Angel. I'll go mad if I have to stay in here while people dance and be merry without me. I'll only watch: no one will see me.'

'I can't let you. He'll know that I gave it to you. I'll be in terrible trouble, and you know what he's like if he gets angry.'

'He shall not know. If he does find out then I'll tell him that I stole it from you while you were dusting or something. Please, Angel.'

Lydia sensed that the other girl was weakening, and she reached out and stroked her fingertip lightly down Angel's forearm, raising the fine golden hairs which downed her skin. The other girl shivered and sighed, a frown creasing her brow. She raised her eyes and looked into Lydia's face, one hand clamping suddenly on to Lydia's forefinger and trapping it against her own arm.

'All right, but you'd better not get me into trouble,' she whispered.

'Thank you.' Lydia found that her own voice had sunk to a whisper too.

With her free hand she reached up and tucked a stray strand of Angel's flaxen hair behind her ear, stroking the silken skein until it joined the coiled plait at the nape of Angel's neck. The other girl remained motionless, but somehow taut, expectant, and Lydia moistened her own lips with her tongue, hesitant and wondering.

As if she sensed Lydia's indecision, Angel turned her face and leant forward a little to kiss Lydia on the lips. Her mouth was mobile and gentle and oh, so soft: Lydia thought that her own mouth would explode just from the touch of the girl's lips. Her experience of kissing had, until now, been limited to men. Their lips were so male: hard, hungry, and devouring, leaving her breathless and incandescent with excitement and arousal at the predatory masculinity of their searching mouths. She had never considered another girl's lips, or felt them, apart from that time when Angel's mouth had given her an unrepeated pleasure. The memory of that stolen afternoon made her feel languorous and trembling with a weakness which began somewhere behind her knees and stole up the trembling muscle of her thighs, to create a hot and feverish anticipation in her belly and below. She reached up and held Angel's face between her hands, returning her kiss now, tasting the salty rose-petal of her tongue and feeling the tiny, sharp teeth just behind.

Angel took Lydia's hand and pressed it firmly to her own breast; Lydia squeezed gently, feeling the button-hard nipples which pressed against the thin fabric. She sensed, rather than consciously felt, Angel's fingers find the puckered tips of her own and pushed herself forward against the girl's hand. Gradually, she lowered Angel to the bed until the girl lay full-length on the slippery violet satin of the coverlet; then she lay her own body over her, their mouths still conjoined, their lips still gently questing.

Lydia felt an arousal as strong as any she had felt with the men she had recently experienced, and the discovery of her own limitless capacity for sexual pleasure made her groan and thrust her tongue deep into Angel's throat, sucking and biting with a sudden frenzy of sensual need. She pulled at the other girl's skirts until her stockinged legs were revealed to the hip, and then she knelt between them, gazing down and feasting her eyes on the exposed thighs and her pearly moistness.

Angel bent her knees up either side of Lydia, and tilted her pelvis upward as if inviting Lydia to do more than look.

Lydia, at once fearful but desperate to indulge her own desires, placed her two pale hands on the skin of Angel's thighs; they were already damp with a milky viscidity, and Lydia slid her thumbs over the slippery curve of flesh and tentatively pressed. Angel drew in a sharp breath, and Lydia watched her as she drooped her eyelids and seemed to disappear into herself, her cheeks flushed and her face soft and relaxed. Her mouth fell slightly open, and the fleshy pink pad of her generous bottom lip reminded Lydia of the swollen flesh beneath her thumbs. She pressed slowly, sliding across the ruched flesh, noting the tiny shell up near the tips of her thumbnails, which seemed to beg for her attention. She lightly ran the pad of her forefinger over it and saw that it was as responsive as her own.

She applied a little pressure. It enlarged. She applied a little more. It swelled. Rubbing repeatedly, she watched with fascination as Angel became wetter and wetter, and the tiny shell-like bud became longer and more engorged, like a delicious barley-sugar that begged to be sucked. Lydia bent her head and licked. Angel tasted sweet: darker and more delectable than any marchpane Lydia had ever eaten. She rubbed with the rough surface of her tongue, while Angel arched her back above her and made delicate sounds of pleasure. Suddenly, she grasped Lydia's head with her hands and pulled Lydia on to her. Lydia thought momentarily she would suffocate, but then her tongue entered Angel and she felt the girl come on to her mouth, jerking and shaking and wetting Lydia's lips with the cream of her arousal.

Afterward, she lay her head on Angel's milky thigh and savoured the musky scent which emanated from the other girl's wet, springy curls, lazily stroking and curling a lock around her forefinger.

'I suppose you'll be wanting that key now, then?' Angel raised herself and propped her head on one hand, looking down at Lydia's flushed face, her expression of interest tinged with cynicism. Lydia stared up at her indignantly.

'Do you really think that, well, that I only did that just to obtain the key? Angel, I didn't.' She reached up and grasped the maid's fingers tightly between her own.

'It doesn't matter, I'll give it to you either way. I just wanted to be sure that you meant it.'

'I meant it.' Lydia stood and leant over Angel, holding her little pointed chin in the cup of her hand. Angel tilted her head back and closed her eyes as Lydia gently kissed her mouth before releasing her and taking the proffered key.

'Maxine, pass me the little box of velvet patches.'

Madame de Chaillot turned her head first to one side and then to the other as she examined her reflection in the gilt mirror. A gloating smile lifted the corners of her carefully painted lips, as she leant closer to correct a smudge of the black powder that elongated her eyes. Taking the lacquered box from her maid, she sighed and picked over the contents with a slender forefinger.

'Which shape were they wearing in town?' she asked.

'I think the moons, Madame.'

She checked her reflection again before selecting a

tiny heart-shaped velvet patch which she placed high on her cheekbone, then a crescent moon was added just to the left of her scarlet mouth.

'You look wonderful, Madame.' The maid's voice was low and full of admiration. 'That blue gown is like a waterfall. Master Valerian will not be able to resist you.'

'He never can.' Madame stuck a last pearl bodkin into her coiffure, and smoothed her beautifully piled-up curls. The silvery powder that shimmered over her hair complemented her translucent complexion, accentuating her porcelain skin and setting off the cold blue of her eyes.

She rose from the low stool and strolled across the velvet carpet to the full-length looking-glass, stroking her hands over her waist and stomach. Her body was taut, narrow like a boy's, and her gown hung perfectly straight, almost undisturbed by breasts or hips. The front of the bodice clung to her narrow form with slippery ease, while the back – cascading loose from her shoulders to the floor – was almost like a negligee. It was fastened from breastbone to hem with tiny jet ribbons, and beneath it she wore a sheer black petticoat through which careful observers would see that she was naked but for stockings and sumptuously jewelled garters.

Placing her feet into high-heeled black mules, she watched herself as she stroked her hands over her breasts, pinching her already taut nipples and pulling them to prominence. Now her small breasts looked as though they would pierce through the diaphanous fabric, her areolas darkened circlets beneath the midnight colours. Madame shivered: sexual arousal was never far away, but tonight she anticipated something very special from the repressed local aristocracy.

She reached for her bottle of perfume, and then paused. As she lifted her gown, she rubbed a finger lightly over her sex, which swelled a little, warm and inviting. She was ready now, but there would not be time for even the quickest satisfaction. First wetting her finger with her own cassolette, she then touched the fragrant cream to her pulse points: each wrist, behind her ears, and finally into the shallow scoop of her cleavage.

'Resistance would be futile,' she murmured. Maxine smiled and held out an ornate feathered fan.

A thrill of feverish anticipation rushed through Madame's veins as she paused at the top of the staircase, one hand on the smooth banister. Her excitement was mirrored on several of the upturned faces, and she recognised some of the young libertines who, with Valerian, frequented the Avernus Gentlemen's Club in Piccadilly. Later, when the older and more staid members of the county set had made their way home in their horse-drawn coaches and carriages, Madame would preside over a private gathering of these men and a select group of the younger, more promising local inhabitants.

Anticipation was a fine aphrodisiac, she thought, as she felt the quicksilver pull of arousal and the throb of the hot blood which raced through her veins. The libertines were well known to her; they were handsome young men, fit and muscular with the stamina of youth, but the dissolute experience of older men.

She caught the eye of one of her favourites, Andreas. He smiled up at her, and she saw the gleam of his pure white teeth, saw him slide his hand slowly over the front of his tight breeches in a discreet but clear gesture of sexual promise. Madame coolly ignored him, composing her features into the customary, expressionless mask as she descended the stairs. Valerian materialised at her side and swept his dark eyes over her body with silent appreciation. She met his look with an imperious tilt of one thinly pencilled eyebrow, and together they stepped into the great hall.

The wainscoting had been polished to a sheen which reflected the glow of hundreds of lighted tapers; the chinaware that usually rested in the recesses had been replaced with huge candelabra and vases of fragrant greenery. Against one wall, a long table bowed under the weight of platters of sweetmeats, roast swan, jellied fruits, and a centrepiece of suckling pig, while a well-stoked fire roared beneath the ornate mantelpiece.

The warm smell of food and fifty perfumed bodies assailed her, and Madame flared her nostrils as she took a glass of syllabub from a passing footman. Valerian held his own glass to his lips and surveyed the hall.

'What do you think?' he enquired.

'So many people at such short notice,' murmured Madame, fluttering her fan in front of her chin. 'A sign of acceptance of your place in society. Would you agree?'

'Indeed.' Valerian smiled and bowed at an elderly gentleman who passed by. 'The only obstacle now is to have my departed brother declared legally dead.'

'Have you spoken to Lavendale recently?'

'The man urges caution. He insists that Drummond must be missing for seven years.' His cheeks flushed with irritation. 'Then, Claudine my love, I can take my rightful place, but for now I am merely the unofficial Lord Hawkesworth. Everyone knows he must be dead. All attempts to trace him have failed, and between you and I, my dear, if by some miracle he sent word of his continued existence I'd burn any letter before it became public.'

'What if he should come in person?'

'Then God help him. I'd rather see him at the bottom of the deepest lake on the estate than renounce my claim!' Valerian felt the cool pressure of Madame's warning fingers on his arm.

'Let's begin the dancing,' she suggested, smiling up at him. He held out his hand and they moved into the centre of the hall.

As she moved among the throng, Madame silently appraised the younger guests, and tried to memorise the faces of those who showed most promise: romping nearby was the energetic Lord Irving, a young aristocrat whose muscular thighs and broad shoulders made her heart jump. Then she passed a sweet-faced girl of maybe

360

seventeen years, who looked incorruptible and therefore truly challenging. Later she offered a dish of comfits to a blushing priest, whose habit of wearing his long, pale hair bound with a scarlet ribbon belied his air of humble seriousness. As it neared midnight, she exchanged smiles with a pretty matron whose smooth bosom swelled longingly out of her tightly laced busk.

Finally, she noticed a flash of chartreuse velvet which moved at intervals in the minstrel's gallery far above: Lydia. She pretended to ignore the partly hidden figure who knelt behind the balustrade. Smiling across the crowded room at Valerian, she savoured thoughts of a suitable punishment for his cousin, and quivered with amusement at the thought of the innocent girl's shock when she witnessed the spectacle that Madame planned for later.

'I think the evening has been a success, *mon petit*,' Madame murmured to Valerian. A cool night breeze lifted several loose strands of her hair as the couple stood in the main doorway bidding farewell to the last of the gentry. Valerian turned with an enigmatic smile and steered her indoors.

'The evening, my dear, is still young, and I anticipate even greater success. As I am sure you do.'

'Indeed. I thought you did particularly well persuading Squire Matthews that his wife would be escorted safely home. Thank you.'

'My pleasure. What do you plan for her?'

'Aaah, you must anticipate a little longer.'

She strode ahead of Valerian, back to the hall. The food lay ransacked on the table and the tapers had burnt low, throwing long shadows across the floor. Near the imposing fireplace, the young men of Valerian's acquaintance filled their goblets with claret and ensured that the remaining guests were equally replenished.

Madame glanced around, wondering where to start. Excitement stirred her, and she felt a fluttering in her breast as she wavered between the blond priest who sipped his claret, and Lord Irving, who stood alone and remote on the far side of the room.

Making a sudden choice, she approached the priest and spoke softly. He smelled pleasantly of soap and beeswax, and she moved closer, relishing the look of surprise that widened his deep grey eyes. He blushed as her hand slid teasingly down his black garb to linger at his groin. Pleased with what she felt there, Madame rose on to tiptoes and kissed him fully on the mouth, pressing her thin lips to his and insinuating her serpent-like tongue between his teeth. He stepped back, but she leant closer, massaging him with an insistent hand until she heard his low groan of defeat.

Behind her, she heard Squire Matthew's young wife, Sophie, gasp as one of the libertines mirrored Madame's performance with his own kiss and caress. Initially, Sophie seemed reluctant, but the wine she had con-sumed – and the inattention of her overweight husband since their marriage – made her respond with growing passion to the young man's overture. Another young man joined the first, and soon any observer would have found it hard to distinguish between the three bodies and their exploring hands and mouths.

Madame watched as Sophie savoured the ecstasy of having one man suck on the swell of her bosom while another nibbled at her exposed and extended neck. She had obviously never experienced such ecstatic sen-sations, and appeared almost to swoon from sheer erotic pleasure.

One of the young men encircled her with muscular arms and lowered her back on to the scarlet couch behind her. At once she was surrounded by Valerian's entourage who tended her feet, hands, and legs. One cherub-faced boy with wildly curling ringlets slipped her satin shoes from her feet and sensuously rubbed her toes with the fleshy pads of his thumbs; another slid her bracelets from her arms and fastened his questing mouth to the tender inner curve of her elbow. A blond

Adonis began the task of unlacing her bodice to free her bosom and waist, while Andreas, a youth with the colouring and fierceness of a Romany, lifted her petticoats and began to knead the pale softness of her thighs.

As she continued to entwine herself around the increasingly ardent priest, Madame noticed Lord Irving standing in a shadowed recess near the fireplace. He was watching Sophie Matthews intently, and had unbuttoned his breeches to stroke himself, but his attention seemed caught by something else, for his eyes widened, sliding along the length of their prostrate bodies and lifting to a higher level.

Madame twisted a little to follow his gaze, loosening her hold on the priest's cock and watching Valerian approach the cherubic youth from behind. He unbuttoned himself with practised ease, spread the young man's plump buttocks, and spat on his own fingers before moistening the youth with saliva. With a swift contraction of his lean hips, Valerian entered the boy and rode smoothly back and forth, sensual enjoyment playing across his face as he closed his eyes. The cherub gave a moan of pleasure and bent forward to accommodate his friend, pressing his arse back and arching himself keenly. His face brushed against the side of Sophie's foot, and he turned slightly to slip his mouth over her largest toe, engulfing it with his pink lips.

Madame stared in fascination as the lad's rounded cheeks curved inward with the strength of his sucking. She heard Sophie gasp at the intensity of the sensation, but the sound was swiftly silenced as another man bent to kiss her with bruising passion, before straightening and holding his swollen cock to her mouth. At first she seemed to hesitate, her eyes round and wondering, but then she opened her lips to the straining shaft and began to pull with a vigorous thirst.

Madame glanced back at Irving: his muscular body was taut and expectant, his eyes closed. She abandoned the priest and darted to him, soundlessly reaching out to grip his cock tightly between her thumb and forefinger. His eyes flicked open in surprise as he found his climax abruptly halted.

She held the forefinger of her other hand to her lips in a silencing gesture, before running that same oval-tipped digit down over the ivory flatness of her chest to the first ribbon which fastened her gown. She pulled smoothly and slipped it free before placing it between her lips. Holding one end, she slid the ribbon across her tongue, and Irving stared as if hypnotised as the narrow sliver of black satin was finely coated with saliva. Her other hand sought his swollen balls and freed them from his breeches, then she wound the wet ribbon tightly around him until he was firmly trussed.

He was completely harnessed, unable either to subside or ejaculate.

Madame's eyes remained fastened upon his as she slowly bent forward and wrapped her lips around him. She sucked once and withdrew, sucked again, then delved the point of her tongue into the little slit that opened the top. Irving groaned above her, and she smiled before sliding her tongue under the cuff of his foreskin and riding around it. She played like that for a few moments before she gave him a final hard suck, then straightened up with a flick of her tongue over rouged lips.

Taking his hand, she led him into the centre of the candle-lit room and pushed him into a straight-backed chair, before striding away and stepping up on to the dais at the far end of the room. Lord Irving gave her a beseeching look, which she cruelly ignored as she took her seat on a carved throne. She could feel the skirt of her gown dampen beneath her, treacle-thick and warm, as she looked at the bodies below her.

Joseph and Conrad, Valerian's faithful henchmen, stepped forward to help her remove the diaphanous garments which clung to her slender form, and she sat erect, naked but for her stockings and jewelled garters, her feet tipped on her impossibly high black mules. She stayed very still, imperiously surveying the tableau.

Below her, Sophie, surrounded with libertines and plundered by their probing tongues and cocks, came shudderingly as her various attendants climaxed almost simultaneously into her mouth and hands. The cherub bit down hard on her toe, as Valerian stiffened and spasmed behind him, and Sophie quickly jerked her foot away from the sharp teeth. Almost immediately, she was lifted upright by a team of muscular arms and shepherded to a chair beside Lord Irving. Others grouped around, the cherub leaning over the back of Sophie's chair, with his hand lazily squeezing one of her breasts.

There was a silent expectancy in the hall.

'My friends.' Madame stood and stretched herself to her full height, her nakedness glowing in the soft light cast by the flames from the fire. She paused for a long time before speaking again, ensuring that she had undivided attention, aware of the many eyes that devoured her body. 'You are all here tonight by your own free will. Each of you has, by now, deduced the manner of our revelry, and if any should wish to leave, then I suggest that you do so at this moment.'

There was a long silence. No one moved, and finally she smiled, inclining her head slightly as if to acknowledge their choice. 'Then let us feast.'

She stepped back and sat in the throne once more, her legs crossed and her back ramrod straight. Her posture thrust her ribs forward and her small breasts stood proud. Admiring her own body, she stroked her hands over herself, pinching her ruby-red nipples, pulling them out to hard lengths which she rolled between her fingers. When she was satisfied with their shape and position, she stretched her slender arms elegantly out, and Joseph and Conrad moved towards her. She grasped their naked cocks, one in each fist, and gripped them tightly.

Her predatory gaze circled the room, until she lit upon the priest who sat, still fully clothed, on one end of the semicircle of acolytes.

'Father Clarence, please rise. You appear flushed. Could it be that you are warm? Undress yourself, I pray.' As the priest fumbled to obey, she continued: 'But wait: leave your clerical collar on. I wish to see you wear it as you break your vow of celibacy.' Her hands continued to work at Joseph and Conrad as she surveyed the others present. 'Little Miss Madeleine.' She smiled benignly at the young maiden who was perched, hands demurely folded, on a low footstool at Valerian's feet. 'Your education should be started by a man of the cloth, I think.' The girl dipped her eyes virtuously, her sweet face blushing and her bottom lip trembling. 'Come, my dear, these gentlemen shall make you a bed with their bodies, and we will see how the priest excels with his tongue.'

At her words, three of the libertines moved forward from the shadows and lay side by side upon the woven carpet. Madeleine remained where she was, her knuckles showing white on her folded hands. Valerian, behind her, raised his eyebrows and smiled with satisfaction as if he enjoyed her reticence. Madame sighed.

'Oh dear. Little Madeleine has become shy. Valerian, my love, persuade her.'

She watched, holding her breath, as Valerian reached down and grasped the girl's chin. He twisted her face upward and Madame swallowed as he bent to crush Madeleine's lips with his own. As he feasted on her mouth, one hand slid into her bodice, and Madame could see the outline of his fingers as he squeezed the girl's breast, rubbing his thumb firmly over her nipple. Madeleine struggled, but at a signal from Madame, the cherub and the Adonis grabbed her arms and twisted them behind her back, holding her captive. Valerian finished his kiss and stood up straight, his eyes catching Madame's and a cruel smile twisting his lips.

'Bring her,' commanded Madame.

The two libertines dragged the now vigorously struggling girl to where the bed of men lay. She stood between them, her chin tilted defiantly up, and Madame

366

felt her heart skip a beat: the fighters were always so much more thrilling, she thought. Madeleine's dark eyes burnt into hers, and then, as if the girl could read her mind and knew how to win, she slumped between the two men, her body soft and passive, the fight gone from her limbs. Madame ground her teeth, her lips pursed and angry. She glared at the girl through eyes which became two narrow slits of glittering fury.

'Get on to the bed!' she spat.

Madeleine slowly advanced until she stood by the head of the nearest prostrate man. Unsure of how to proceed, she paused to throw Madame an appealing glance.

'Mistress Sophie, please help her undress.' Madame squeezed the cocks in her hands as she spoke, but neither Joseph nor Conrad showed any reaction. Sophie Matthews went to Madeleine's assistance and removed her silky garments until Madeleine's perfect young body was bare.

Several of those watching inhaled audibly, for the girl was a veritable Venus, with high, creamy breasts and an auburn thatch which curled shyly between her shapely legs. The thought that she was also as yet untouched caused Lord Irving to shift in his chair and finger the ribbon which laced his swollen genitals.

Sophie took both Madeleine's hands in hers and gently eased her back until the girl lay upon the bed of men. The one upon whose chest her head rested reached up and gripped one of her wrists in his fist; the other arm he pinned to the ground with his strong thigh so that she was displayed like a butterfly, her wings outstretched and imprisoned for all to see and feast upon.

Under Madame's instruction, the priest advanced and knelt between her raised knees.

'Kiss her, Father.'

He feasted his eyes momentarily on the exposed body before him, drinking in the sight of her. His cock leapt and jerked, straining outward as if it would go to her even if its master wished otherwise, which he obviously did not. He leant forward, pressing his tongue between her parted thighs, and Madeleine squirmed beneath his mouth and cried out, trying to close her legs and deny him entry. His hands were heavy on her thighs as he prised them apart again, his thumbs leaving a white imprint on her flesh, and she sobbed a little but then seemed to relax under the pressure of his tongue. Father Clarence spread her knees further and buried his face in her scented flesh, lapping thirstily.

Madame watched with intense interest, leaning forward slightly and pausing in her masturbation of the henchmen. She called to one of the libertines.

'Andreas, come to me.'

He broke away from the group in the shadows and stepped lithely up on to the dais. He seemed to know what she wanted without having to hear her words, for he dropped to his knees before the throne and placed his hands on Madame's rigid thighs. Delving with firm thumbs, he held open the swelling of her sex to reveal a thick golden loop: a ring which entered the skin at one side and disappeared deep into her labia before glittering in the light where it protruded. Andreas licked it once and then leant forward to place his stiffly held tongue on the finger-like protrusion of her unusually large clitoris.

Madame closed her eyes momentarily, savouring the sensation as he licked and sucked, her hands closed tightly on the rigid cocks she clasped. Joseph, the more well-endowed of the two, gasped and shuddered, the muscles of his ebony belly contracting in spasms as he tried to control himself.

Madame's ice-blue eyes snapped open, and she stared fixedly at Mistress Matthews.

'Sophie, I wish you to lie upon Madeleine. Lie on your back atop her, and allow her to reach around you and squeeze your breasts. She will oblige or she will know the consequences. Father Clarence will enter you, and Madeleine will receive every sensation of being fucked, but without the loss of her maidenhead. That's

368

right: now, Father – that's it. Tup her well, Father, and allow young Madeleine to feel every thrust that you make. Every plunge of your sword, every slap of your balls, will thrill her parts until she imagines that it is she, not Mistress Matthews, who feels the divinity of your cock. Oh, Father, I would that you could see yourself, fulfilling the aims of God's creation and teaching a maiden the ways of heavenly pleasure.'

Madame became still as Andreas plunged two rigid fingers deep inside her, and she was thrust into an engulfing climax that seemed to burn and tear at her flesh. She gasped and her long eyelids fluttered, casting deep shadows over her cheeks as her hands tightened on their twin handles.

Joseph and Conrad quivered and groaned deeply as they climaxed on to the pale skin of her shoulders and neck. Father Clarence drove into Sophie Matthews with a final ferocity while Madeleine moaned beneath them on her bed of men; there was a strangulated cry as Lord Irving tore the ribbon from himself, and cradled his aching cock in his palm as he spurted viscous seed on to the timber floor. Then he slumped, sobbing, in his chair.

There was a silent pause as all lay spent.

Madame, rubbing her sticky neck with a leisurely hand, stood and pushed her three attendants aside. She stepped down from the platform and strode to the tightly woven bodies on the scarlet carpet. The exhausted priest had buried his face into Sophie's abundant hair, and Madame bent to stroke his head with an almost maternal tenderness.

Kneeling, she slipped her hand between his muscular thighs to stroke her forefinger over Madeleine's dewy parts. Lifting her hand to her nose, she inhaled the delicate virgin scent before gliding that same finger into Sophie's soft mouth. The sensation of the other woman unexpectedly sucking the juices from her moist digit caused a welcome thrill of sensuality and power to flood feverishly through her, and she stood to survey them all for a long moment.

'Who would like the virgin?' Her gaze swept the men present, and she met Valerian's eye with a slight upward twist of her thin lips. 'I give her to you. But it must not show. Leave her maidenhead intact.'

Madeleine struggled as Madame grasped her wrist and jerked her to a sitting position. Her face was pale and her eyes wide, entreating the merciless Madame.

'No, please. Don't hurt me,' she pleaded.

'You have no choice,' murmured Madame, bending so that her lips were almost touching the girl's ear. 'I know you want to. I saw the look in your eyes when you felt the priest take Mistress Sophie. I saw envy! Now turn over.'

'No.'

'Turn over, or I'll have them make you.'

Madeleine glanced around at the faces that surrounded her in the candlelight. Her eyes were still wide, but the hint of fear that had shadowed them before had been replaced by interest as she studied Valerian. She pouted.

'No.' She seemed almost to be challenging them. Madame felt a thrill of desire as she stared at the girl and wondered whether it was too late to change the plan and have her to herself; then she remembered Lydia upstairs and smiled, her pulse skipping as she anticipated possessing her. She took a step back and gestured to Valerian.

'Turn her over.' Her voice was taut and the libertines obeyed immediately. They grasped Madeleine's arms and legs and twisted her, expertly flipping her so that she lay face down on the floor. One of them reached for a padded footstool and slid his hand under her waist, lifting her and positioning her over it so that her face was pressed into the carpet and her plump little bottom was raised and open.

She struggled, tiny whimpers coming out from under the cloud of auburn hair, and they all bent over her, stroking her back and limbs while Valerian knelt behind her and smoothed her buttocks with his soft palms.

'Madeleine, I shan't hurt you,' he murmured. 'And I shall not disturb your maidenhead. That will be left for your husband, whoever he may be. Enjoy this now, feel it, savour it, for it is certain that any husband your father provides you with will never have the imagination to repeat the experience for you.'

Her body relaxed under the caresses, her tight muscles softening as she listened. The cherub lifted up her curtain of hair and bent to kiss her cheeks and then her lips.

'She is smiling, my lord,' he said softly. Valerian nodded, then bent to examine her sex. He gestured to the others and several of them clustered around him, their eyes intent, their breeches bulging as they observed his long fingers sweeping across the folds of tender skin. She was very aroused, and a slick of warm cream came away on Valerian's forefinger; she seemed to press herself out towards them, encouraging them. In turn, they each slid their fingers over her, lightly touching but not entering. When he judged that she was ready, Valerian steadied her with one hand, his fingers long and pale across the pinkness of her bottom, then he slid his forefinger into her anus.

She bucked in surprise, then held herself still, rigid, as she waited for his next move. He eased his finger in, pushing as far into her as he could so that his knuckle was pressed up against the flesh of her behind. The room was silent: no one moved, or breathed. Valerian slipped his finger out and bent to press his tongue to her, moistening her.

'Madeleine, you will feel me enter you.' He spoke softly, his hand stroking the length of her spine. 'Ready yourself, make yourself open for me, and it will hurt less.'

The others watched as he pressed forward, the cherub kissing her face and several others gripping her when she struggled suddenly as he broached the virgin

371

entrance. Her initial cry of alarm was silenced by a deep kiss from the cherub, his tongue sliding easily into the mouth she had opened to scream, and others grasped her breasts from below and massaged them firmly until her struggles subsided and she submitted to Valerian.

He took a long time, his movements very slow and leisurely. Madame came to kneel near Madeleine's head, her eyes holding his, and when he moved gradually faster, he stared almost unseeing into the glass-pale depths.

'She likes it,' murmured one of the libertines. 'By God, she's lubricating him.'

Madame leant forward and smiled as she saw that Valerian's plunging cock had been anointed with a mysterious cream from deep within Madeleine's body. She heard him groan and she leant up to kiss him deeply as he gave a final thrust and became still, his thighs taut and rigid as he came.

'Who shall be next?' Her voice was low and amused as the libertines moved forward, each vying with the other to be the one to fill Valerian's place. She heard Madeleine sigh, and felt a swell of heat deep inside her own body. She held out her hand.

'Valerian. I need you now, my love. Let us retire to my chamber, alone.'

Arm in arm, Valerian and Madame left the debauchery, their bodies taut with the anticipation of private revels still to come. Halfway up the curving sweep of stair they paused, and Valerian kissed his mistress with the depth and passion of a man possessed. Impatiently he bent and swept her slight form into his arms and ran up the remaining steps. There came the sudden, echoing thud of the bedchamber door as it slammed shut behind them.

Then silence.

Chapter Seven

The darkness was complete. Velvety and thick, it was like a cloak around her as she raised her head from her arms and blinked to dispel the sleep. The only sound was the low and constant ticking of the great clock on the landing. Lydia moved slightly, easing her cramped legs and listening for other movement. Nothing stirred.

Below her she could just make out the distant glow from the dying embers of the fire, but the light was only enough to give a gilded hue to the fender and slate hearth, and the solitary, unidentifiable body which curled, sleeping, on the hearth-rug.

Wondering how long she had been asleep, and what had caused her to wake, Lydia sat up and stretched her arms wide to ease the life back into their numbness. At once her heart was in her mouth and she gasped, dread filling her limbs as her fingers felt the hard flesh of another.

'Who's that?' She patted the shape beneath her hands and wondered at its smooth hairlessness. 'Angel?'

'You'd like that, wouldn't you?' The low reply had a slightly mocking lilt, and Lydia recognised the hardness of Madame de Chaillot's lightly accented voice. 'But it is I. My dear, I cannot sleep and wish for company: pray come to my room.' Her fingers grasped Lydia's wrist in a bony circlet, and Lydia found herself being pulled to her feet with a strength that belied Madame's delicate frame. Reluctantly, she stepped after Madame and walked the short distance from the minstrel's gallery to the guest suite.

The salon was lit by numerous creamy church candles set in black and silver candelabra. The dark oak wood of an enormous four-poster bed glowed softly, and the blue sheen of the hangings invited the fingers to stroke and the hand to caress. As Lydia advanced, guided by the coolness of Madame's hand in the small of her back, she felt an almost overwhelming urge to sink into the cerulean sea of the quilt which covered the bed.

She had all but obeyed her impulse, when she saw that the tumbled sheets already possessed an occupant. Black hair lay in stark contrast to the snowiness of the white pillow. His face relaxed in sleep, Valerian gave the tiniest of snores as he dreamt. Lydia stopped, turned almost to stone. Glancing at Madame, she saw the other woman quickly veil her triumph with a look of tender concern.

'But my dear Lydia, I was certain that you knew: Valerian and I have been lovers for years.'

'Of course. You've left no room for doubt.'

'There can be no doubt.' As she spoke, her fingers caressed the curve of Lydia's elbow. 'We first met in London when Valerian was just a boy of sixteen. He was fresh from the country, sent up by his father for tutorials with the Jesuits; but one of those irrepressible fathers took him to the Avernus Club, gathering place of rakes and libertines, and from then on he needed very little guidance. His hell-raising quickly became legendary in certain circles, and I engineered a meeting between us. I was a full ten years older than him, but it soon became apparent that we were two of a kind, two faces of the same coin, and we have been inseparable in town ever since. You have no idea how boring this provincial little place has become for him; he needs every diversion he can obtain while he is here.'

Lydia's cheeks burnt as she inferred that she, and indeed everything at Hawkesworth, was little more than a 'diversion' for a bored philanderer. Her chin went up in defiance and her eyes flashed at Madame.

'You may think that he is in need of every diversion, Madame, but I assure you that Valerian is always very well provided for here. He lacks for nothing. You forget that before your arrival my cousin was nobility and you were nothing but a common *putain*.'

'*Touché*, my dear. I had no idea you were conversant with my native tongue. However, I must correct you. A *putain* fucks for money; I fuck for the gratification of my own desires. But, when you have tasted all that I have, the palate becomes somewhat jaded and is enlivened only by the most piquant of dishes. Valerian and I explore the full menu together. Perhaps in time you will understand: at present I understand that you are still a virgin.'

'Well, you understand incorrectly.'

Too late, Lydia saw that she had been led into a trap, teased and gently reeled in like a small fish on the end of a very dangerous line. Madame's eyes burnt with a near zealous fanaticism as she moved towards Lydia. A slender hand pushed between her legs, pressing through the velvet of Lydia's gown.

'Indeed.' The hiss was sibilant, hypnotic. 'What a bad girl you are. I think that you're lying.'

Lydia stepped back, aroused in spite of herself by the firm pressure of the older woman's fingers against the heaviness of her skirts. A primitive thrill fizzled through her as the pressure increased, and she found herself almost unconsciously pushing herself forward. Madame arched one thinly plucked eyebrow and curved her lips in a predatory smile.

'Despite my earlier feast,' she murmured, 'I find that I am still hungry. Would you care to sup with us, Lydia?' Her eyes penetrated Lydia. 'I see that you would, in spite of yourself.'

She placed her hand flat against Lydia's chest and

pushed her back until the buttoned leather edge of a couch pressed behind her knees. Lydia, finding her legs were weak and tremulous beneath her, sat down abruptly and allowed Madame to twist her into a reclining position. Madame's fingers moved across the fastenings of the chartreuse velvet gown, and Lydia's breath came more quickly as she was made naked. Madame delved suddenly, viciously, between the tenderness of Lydia's rounded thighs.

'So, you did not lie. How interesting. The little virgin is actually as much of a *putain* as any common little streetwalker! Oh, no! Don't try to get up! If you are going to be difficult I will have to bind you.' She raised one eyebrow. 'I see in your eyes that the idea does not revolt you. Come, give me your wrists. And, I think your ankles: no, not your ankles. I want your legs free for the moment. We may wish to have access to you when we are done with each other.'

Lydia made little struggles, more for show than with any real desire to escape. Madame swiftly tied her wrists, and slid her cool hands smoothly down Lydia's naked arms to the warm curves of her armpits, then inexorably to her breasts. As she watched, the painted fingernails raked the camber of her tender skin which puckered and goosebumped. When Madame bent her head and flicked the rosy nipples with her narrow tongue, Lydia cried out, arching her back and closing her eyes. She was incredibly aroused: the thought of Valerian sleeping only feet away, and the memory of the sights on which she had spied earlier, made her feel wanton and shameless. She pressed the warmth of her shoulder-blades on to the cool leather of the couch, surrendering to sensation.

Suddenly her eyes snapped open.

Valerian towered over them, his face stern. 'Claudine, you infernal slut. What are you doing?'

'What, my darling, do you think?' Madame stood and pressed herself against him, wrapping her arms around his neck. 'She claims not to be a virgin, and I wanted to verify her words. It is in your interests, Valerian. You do realise that you'll have to give her a larger dowry if she has lost her maidenhead?'

'An ample dowry was set aside by my father. I know she's not intact: some dog has sniffed around her skirts once too often, but she refuses to tell me who.'

'Well, for now, my sweet, we have nothing to lose by sharing in his good fortune! Wouldn't you like her as a dessert?' Madame's pale blue eyes bored into Valerian's, and her hunger was reflected in his face. A cruel smile curled the corner of his mouth, and he glanced over his mistress's shoulder, feasting his eyes on Lydia's bound nakedness. Lydia writhed and widened her eyes as he pushed Madame aside and strode to where she lay.

'Dessert. Oh, indeed, but she should not be able to call for help.'

He lifted one of Lydia's own discarded stockings from the floor and tied the emerald-coloured silk swiftly around her lower face, gagging her with the diaphanous fabric before she could protest. Lydia could feel the warmth between her legs become a searing heat as he towered above her, vulpine and predatory. She waited for him to touch her, her sex pouting and anticipating the pressure of his long fingers, but he abruptly turned on the bare pad of his heel and strode to Madame.

Lydia watched, surprised, as he bent in supplication to kiss her tiny feet. He applied his tongue to the arch of her foot, licking and polishing her feet and ankles with his mouth.

'You worthless creature,' Madame snarled. 'You cannot even protect the innocence of a girl placed in your care. You shall be punished for that.'

Lydia was astounded at the way Valerian, usually so dominant, bowed his head and humbly stroked Madame's calves. She could just see the tiny smile that played around his handsome mouth, and the shiver of pleasurable anticipation which rippled his skin. At first she felt repulsed that her omnipotent cousin should display such submissiveness, but gradually, as she observed the exchange between Valerian and Madame, she realised that their game had the delicate intricacy of a complicated dance with a long-established routine.

Madame was fully in control.

'What happens to people who need to be punished?'

'Madame, I know not.'

'I think you do.'

'Please. No.'

'Oh yes, milord. Approach the bed.'

'Madame! No!' Valerian cried out, but his eyes told a story of tormented desire as Madame opened the carved chest at the foot of her bed. From it she extracted a long and beautifully plaited horsewhip. She gently caressed the shining leather, her hand gliding over the chestnut sheen while a ruthless smile curved the corners of her lips.

'Assume the position, milord.'

Valerian moved to the bed and stood near the side of it, his feet half-hidden in the pool of azure silk which drifted down the side of the mattress. Madame buckled his wrists with thick leather manacles. Lydia saw that the cuffs were lined with a soft padding of amethyst-coloured fur, and she noticed that Valerian shuddered as his arms were imprisoned and pulled wide before Madame fastened him to the bedposts. His pale body hung between the two uprights, the muscles taut under his ivory skin, and Lydia felt her breath come in ragged gasps as she stared at him. He was so beautiful, suspended there like a crucified man, awaiting his punishment.

The first lash licked his flesh with lightning speed, and Lydia leapt simultaneously with Valerian. Fascinated, she watched as a cruel red weal snaked across his back. Madame, impassive, flayed him again. This time he yelped, and a second crimson mark glowed parallel to the first.

Lydia watched the chastisement, her own arousal becoming ever stronger as the marks on Valerian's body gradually crept lower towards the hard crescent of his buttocks. She was desperate to touch him, to kiss the scarlet lines and lick his pained flesh, but her own bindings held firm, and she could only observe in a storm of desire and wonder as he received his castigation.

'Have you been very bad?' Madame's hiss cut through Lydia's dream-like state, and she glanced at the woman who stood only two paces away. Madame's eyes were narrowed to thin slits and the light which shone from under her lashes gleamed with pure savagery. Her small breasts rose and fell with the effort of her exertions, and through the light fabric of her negligee Lydia could see her arousal in the hard nipples which pressed out through the fabric like jewelled bottle-stops. As she moved, her gown parted and revealed the pearly skin of her thighs, showing the tiny dewdrops which had glazed the smooth flesh there.

Lydia felt the blood in her veins rage and swirl, leaving her faint as if she were in a state of fever; her own sex became suffused and almost liquid as she drank in the other woman's power. She tried to cry out, to attract Madame's attention to herself, but the murmur which sounded from behind the gag served only to irritate Madame, who, without looking round, savagely flicked the whip in Lydia's direction. The tip caught the girl's tight nipple and a shock of exquisite pain licked her senses.

'Answer me! Have you protected this girl's virginity?'

'I have not,' came the gasping reply. A further application of the whip was greeted by a tortured groan, and Valerian sagged, kept upright only by his cuffed wrists.

Madame threw the horsewhip to the ground and stood directly behind Valerian, leaning forward so that her small body moulded to his and her chest was pressed to the wounds she had just inflicted. He flinched away at the contact, but she gripped his hips and jerked him on to her so that his weals were covered by her belly and breasts.

'Oh, you naughty, naughty boy. I think I have just the thing for you.'

Her fingers sinuously slid on to the polished surface of the bedside table and grasped the string of polished topaz beads which lay coiled there. She weighed them in her hand, a sly smile curving her mouth, then she scooped the handful to her lips and toyed with them, the tip of her pointed tongue lapping at the pearlescent droplets and the silken string between. She slid downward, knelt behind Valerian and smoothed her hand up the hairiness of his leg to reach under and cup the crepey sac of his balls. His buttocks convulsed at her touch, and she gripped his scrotum, twisting slightly until he moaned. Her nose was level with the underside of his left buttock, and she rubbed against the skin there, inhaling and savouring his scent, tickling him with her exhaled breath.

Her tongue, red and moist, flicked out and licked the crease which ran from his thigh up to the hollow at the base of his long spine. Placing both her hands on the twin curves of Valerian's arse, she pulled the cheeks apart to reveal the tender pucker which nestled there. Her tongue shot out and rimmed it suddenly, completing a full circle before pushing inside.

The man above her sighed and pressed out towards her as she withdrew her tongue, circled the place once more, then again pressed back in. When she was satisfied that he was lubricated, she lifted the handful of topaz beads to her mouth and drew them slowly in, until her mouth was crammed full of them and only one on the silken string remained outside. Then she pressed her nose into the crease of his buttocks and worked the necklace into him with her tongue and fingers.

At last she stood back to admire her handiwork. All the beads had been pushed in except for a tiny length, just enough for her to grasp with her fingers. Valerian, obviously stimulated beyond control, rocked his pelvis back and forth as if begging her for release. She walked around the bed and stood on the opposite side from him, staring into his eyes before dropping her negligee to the floor and mounting the bed.

When she was in front of him, almost touching, she took his swollen cock in her hand and stroked him, watching him grow to greater length and thickness, while she caressed herself with a stiffened forefinger. She held his stare as she lay across the bed and hooked her legs around his hips and waist. With a sudden jerk, she impaled herself upon him and Valerian cried out, perspiration beading his body in a glistening sheen as her agile body moved on his.

He thrust with her, until, with a trembling in his legs and a sudden stillness of his clenched thighs, he came to his peak. Madame, continuing to work her hips on him, reached around him and jerked her wrist to quickly withdraw the topaz beads from his anus. He cried out, almost as if in pain, as he climaxed into the depths of her demanding body.

Lydia lay stunned. She wanted nothing more than for Valerian to turn and take her too. Now. Here on the dark hide of the couch while Madame watched. She pressed her thighs together and bent her knees up to her chest, aware that the bindings and gag she wore made her an appealing sight. The flower of her sex, engorged and full, swelled between her enfolded thighs like a juicy fig, dark and moist with a luscious, edible centre.

Madame, involved in unbuckling Valerian's manacles, noticed nothing, but Valerian had twisted around to gaze at the effect their hedonism had had on his untameable cousin. Seeing her sex framed by the paleness of her milky thighs, his softened cock leapt in response and he jerked impatiently at his cuffs.

'Wait. You shall have her in good time.' Madame took him by the hand and led him to a gilded chair set near Lydia's feet.

'Sit,' she commanded. 'You may observe as I ready her for your delectation.'

She stalked the room, lighting more candles, gathering armfuls of fluffy blue towels and pouring water from the ewer into a large porcelain bowl. When everything had been arranged to her satisfaction, she knelt on the rug next to where Lydia lay and smiled at the girl.

'My dear. You are superb, but I wish to make you exquisite.'

Soapy fingers trailed down over Lydia's belly and delved into the soft curls at the join of her thighs. She lathered and rubbed, while Lydia tried to lie as still as possible. She watched curiously as Madame lifted a small brown leather case and opened it.

Then the woman withdrew the cut-throat gleam of a long razor.

Lydia gasped beneath her silken gag and struggled, pulling at her wrist bindings, thrashing her legs and bucking her foam-soaked hips. She could feel the fear fizzing through her veins, and perspiration sprang to her forehead as she begged for mercy with her widened eyes.

Madame, observing her with interest, gave a slow, thin smile which failed to extend as far as her eyes. She deliberately ran her fingertip along the silver blade until it beaded with crimson blood, then slipped it between her lips. There was a long pause while she sucked.

'Are you afraid, my dear? There is really no need. You see, I have no intention of holding this implement to your beautiful throat as you seem to imagine. No. Watch. And be still. Do not even flinch, for you have seen how sharp I keep this. When I say I wish to make you exquisite, that is precisely what I mean. Hairless. Sensitive. Exquisite.' Her smile broadened and she leant forward so that her lips almost touched Lydia's, and the girl could smell the delicate scent of her breath. 'So much more hygienic, don't you think?'

She glided down Lydia's body, and her face became a pale mask of concentration as she trimmed the dark curls which covered Lydia's mound. Fluffy clouds gradually gathered in vibrant clusters on the floor and in scattered wisps on Lydia's widely spread thighs. Lydia raised her head and watched, absorbed in the glittering flash as she was pared to the bare skin. She was fascinated by the movement of Madame's fingers over her undulations and the change in her own appearance as the crisp hairs were scythed from her body.

Soon she was smooth and denuded, the skin cool and bare. Madame lifted a small crystal bottle and poured a sweet-smelling unguent on to Lydia, who quivered as tiny rivulets ran from her belly down into her creases. Madame's fingers kneaded her flesh, massaging the sticky oil into the shaven folds, dwelling on the grooves between the naked lips. When she was satisfied with the results of her labours, she arranged the blushing flesh to her satisfaction and sat back on her heels, admiring the newly depilated aperture.

Lydia felt strange. The hairlessness made her feel exposed and very vulnerable, but she was titillated by the sensation of her own flesh sliding over other parts of herself without the dulling of a layer of hair. The moistness of the perfumed oil, combined with the cream of her own arousal, made everything feel slick: somehow larger, more important. She opened her legs wide until her knees touched the surface of the couch either side and looked up at Valerian, clear invitation in the depths of her liquid green eyes.

He remained motionless but somehow taut, expectant almost, while Madame moved her hands once more to the little case. She drew out a long length of black cord, knotted at equal intervals, which she held in one hand. With a firm pressure, she pushed Lydia's legs together and wound the cord around her thighs, midway between her knees and her hips. It was tight and the knots cut into her flesh. Madame smiled and urged her legs upward, so that her knees rested on her breasts and Lydia could feel her oiled shaven sex protruding between her thighs. Valerian's eyes were fixed intently upon Madame's hands.

The cord was wound twice around her ankles, and then a length taken around and slipped between her legs so that a large knot pressed on to her clitoris. The rope snaked over her sex and down to cut between her buttocks. Finally, Madame passed the end around Lydia's waist and tied it firmly to itself, ensuring that there was a good tension on the rope and that it held Lydia in position. The knots were hard against her flesh, making it feel sore but stimulated. She knew that her sex, creamy and plump, was swelling either side of the thick black knot that pressed there.

Madame bent to the case again. She took out a phallus-shaped object made from glossy, dark leather. It was some seven inches in length, and its thickness was that of a well-endowed man. Madame caressed it lovingly, a secret smile curving her lips. Then she lifted it and slid it into her mouth, moving it in and out until the supple leather gleamed with her saliva.

Wordlessly, she placed it on to Lydia's neck and stroked her with it, dragging it slowly over her breast-bone and then to one nipple, which contracted tightly. The other nipple also puckered in response as the dildo was slid over it, and Madame smiled, guiding the firm leather baton down and around until it rested on the plumpness of her shaven sex. Lydia waited, hardly daring to breathe, marvelling at the toy. She could feel herself melting and unfurling in anticipation, while the hardness rested purposefully between her legs.

Then Madame, with a leisurely action, held the pink folds apart with the fingers of one hand, easing the thick rope aside. She pushed the dildo and Lydia felt it glide sleekly in. It was surprisingly hard. And cool. And quite unlike her experience of men.

'Does that feel good?' Madame moved it firmly, easing it out and smiling at the slick sound of Lydia's wetness. Then she plunged it back in, a little further this time, and Lydia could feel the firm nose opening her deepest recesses. Her knees were almost up to her chin, and she could feel the dildo probing her body more deeply than anything had ever penetrated before. She gasped and let her head drop back, arching herself and focussing totally on the long strokes of Madame's device within her, concentrating on the heat and liquid between her legs and the pleasure that was released there. Her body turned to pulp and she could feel a beat throbbing in her temples, while a thousand tiny bubbles seemed to fizz inside her head as the first waves of orgasm trembled through her.

The promised release was sublime but short-lived.

Madame withdrew the dildo and waited. When she was sure that the crisis was passed, she gently pushed it back and slowly pulsed and twisted it until Lydia once more found herself teetering on the brink of delicious rapture.

Again it was removed.

Lydia, unable to move her hands or speak for her bindings, made a mute appeal with her eyes, but Madame simply waited and gazed back at her. When this happened for the third time, Lydia felt helpless and began to cry, tiny salt tears trickling across her cheeks.

Madame seemed pleased by this and stood up, gesturing to Valerian to take her place. His satanic features were suffused with lust as he knelt beside the couch and filled her emptiness with two long fingers, his thumb giving extra pressure to the knot that crushed her clitoris. She clenched herself on to him and silently begged him to finish her orgasm, but he also withdrew, although more reluctantly than Madame.

Lydia watched as Valerian moved along the couch and raised himself up on his knees beside her. The animal smell of his proffered cock served as an added stimulus. It swayed above her face and she inhaled the scent of sex, musky and feral, while Valerian untied the stocking which gagged her. She twisted her head and took him between her lips, momentarily surprised by the taste of Madame which silvered the hard flesh. He moved closer and slid easily to the back of her throat as she opened her mouth wide to accommodate as much of him as possible.

She was vaguely aware of the emptiness between her

legs being filled once more and she curved her buttocks upward in response. She felt herself being swept up and carried along on a tide of ecstasy, as her long-denied orgasm built within her. Glancing down the length of her shins, she marvelled at the sight of Madame nestling at the end of the couch, moving the leather cock not with her hands as before, but with her mouth. Her lips were stretched wide around the end of it, her teeth gripping the black leather, and she slid it back and forth while spreading her hands wide on the softness of Lydia's thighs, her forefingers dipping ever closer to the slightly open pucker of her anus.

When she felt Madame's fingers enter her bottom and stretch her as wide as the dildo was stretching her sex, Lydia was instantly tipped over the brink and into glorious orgasm, the culmination of everything she had seen and experienced that night erupting and burning through her folded body until she gave an almighty shudder and screamed her release against Valerian. Madame gave the dildo one final push, pressing it far into her silky depths as Valerian jerked himself free, pumping his hot, gushing climax on to Lydia's hair and eyelids.

Later, as she drowsed in the aftermath, Lydia was aware of unhurried fingers releasing her bindings, and then the soft weight of a sable cloak covering her nakedness. She saw Madame and Valerian sink into the ocean of the vast blue bed with their limbs intertwined, then there was welcome blackness as she surrendered to the opiate heaviness of sleep.

Chapter Eight

The Chequers Inn was almost full. Situated on the northbound road, it caught most of the passing trade on market-day; farmers and traders clustered at the rough wooden bar, lifting tankards to thirsty mouths, while the staff threaded through the heaving mass bearing platters of capon and enormous flagons of ale.

The inn was dark, the only light being a flicker of orange from the crackling grate and a few guttering tallow candles, but the man who stood alone at the bar could see well enough. His hooded gaze was fixed on a table near the chimney breast where a small man of skinny build sat nursing his third tankard of ale. His greasy hair was combed thinly over a pale head and his long nose had the bruised ruddiness of a long-term drinker.

Drummond had heard that this man, the notary Silas Peake, could be found at the Chequers most nights, and his informer had added that Silas's unguarded tongue could easily be loosened with the local brew. Swallowing the last of his own ale, Drummond banged his tankard on the counter.

'Fill this up, would you? And I'll have one of whatever he drinks.' He jerked his head to indicate the notary. He wound his way through the throng and sat opposite Silas Peake. The other man glanced with interest at the tumblers in front of Drummond.

'You thirsty?'

'Are you?'

'A man is always thirsty after an honest day's work.'

'What line of work would that be?'

Silas Peake squinted up through tiny dark eyes. He swayed slightly and then sniggered.

'You'd be a stranger to these parts, but I'm thinking that I know your face.'

The tallow on the table flickered and Drummond wondered whether he could shift it unobtrusively to prevent Peake from recognising him. On the pretext of moving his own drink, he pushed his forearm against the candle-holder and slid it to the edge of the table where it could not light his face so effectively.

'No, my friend, you wouldn't know me. I'm a traveller, passing through. If you're thirsty, take this second tankard. My own thirst is not so sharp now that I've started on this one.'

Peake needed no further encouragement. He tossed back the dregs of his own and started eagerly on the fresh one. Halfway down the tumbler he paused for breath, smearing the foam from his lips with the back of his hand before nodding thanks to Drummond.

'So you're a notary?'

'Did I say that?' Peake frowned, confused for a moment, then his brow cleared. 'Aye, we were talking about the thirsty work. Oh yes. That's me.'

'I suppose you handle all the work for the family up at the big house, then.'

'Sometimes, sometimes.' He nodded sagely, swallowing his ale. 'Mostly Mr Lavendale deals with them, but I am his personal clerk. Oh yes. The Hawkesworths need people they can trust.'

'Well, you certainly look like a man they could trust. I imagine you're privy to all of old Lord Hawkesworth's documents.' Drummond tipped his weight back casually, the image of a man in careless conversation. He

388

surveyed the crowd at the bar: the smell of roast meat made his stomach growl.

'I was. Oh yes. Mind you, stranger, old Lord William is no more. No, he's been dead more than a six-month, now.'

'Indeed? My sympathies for the family. Would you care for a refill?' Drummond indicated the near-empty cup. As a girl passed nearby with a pewter flagon in each hand he nodded at her, and she hastened to refill their tankards. Drummond, admiring her tiny waist and sumptuous hips, smiled lazily into her eyes and she blushed, bending lower to their table to afford him an improved view of her firmly buttressed cleavage.

'What's your name, lass?'

'Molly, sir.' She smiled broadly and, having poured, she rested one of the flagons on the curve of her hip.

'Molly, what's the food like in this inn?'

'Very good, sir. Plenty of juicy meat and fresh vegetables on market-day, and very attentive maid-servants.' Her honey-soft eyes promised far more than her words, and Drummond found himself smiling at her forwardness.

'Well, then. I think I shall dine here later; perhaps you could reserve a private room for me.'

'Certainly, sir. Will you be requiring a maid to serve you, then?'

Drummond considered her for a long moment, then nodded. Molly arched one dark eyebrow and told him that she would see to it personally, then turned with an exaggerated sway of her hips and returned to the bar.

Drummond turned back to Peake, and caught a look of naked lechery in the weaselly little man's eyes as he watched her retreating bottom.

'Oh, yes. You have a way with the wenches, stranger. Perhaps you'd care to leave me your pickings when you've done?' His narrow tongue flickered out to touch the crusty corners of his mouth. Drummond fought an overwhelming urge to push him off his chair.

'Perhaps, friend. But first, finish what you were telling me about Lord William's will.'

'The will? Ha. I copied it myself, earlier this year. Oh, yes. I had it for some weeks and then Lord William gave it –'

His chin suddenly dropped to his chest, then he gave a start and tried to focus on Drummond's face. 'What's that, stranger? Oh, I remember not. I care not.' He waved his hand and leant forward to rest his head on the table-top. Drummond heard him belch and then snort. Staring in disbelief, he realised that Peake had fallen into a drunken stupor from which he would not easily be roused. He shook the other man's bony shoulder.

'What? Oh, let me be. Tired – I'm tired, stranger.'

'What did Lord William do with the will?' Drummond hissed at him, impatience fermenting in his limbs. To come so close, to be so successful in getting the man drunk, only to be thwarted at the last moment by the demon sleep! He shook Peake again, this time more roughly.

'He took it to . . .'

The words dissolved into a long snore, and Drummond threw himself back in his chair with barely controlled anger. Damn the man! Getting the notary to talk had been his best plan. He couldn't stroll into Lavendale's plush office and ask the same questions without alerting Valerian to his presence in the town. He couldn't go up to the house; he couldn't claim his rightful place. He could do nothing without the will. Draining his ale, he reached for the half-full tankard that Peake had left and gulped that down too. The warm glow in his gullet and belly comforted him, and he stood, thinking he would return to the bar.

'Whoa there, young fellow! The Chequers ale is stronger than you think!' A plump, ruddy-faced farmer eased Drummond back to standing, and he realised that he must have fallen.

390

'Sweet Jesus, what do they do, lace it with gin?' he asked.

'Nay, but it's famous in these parts. I see old Silas has wound up early tonight!' The farmer had a hearty laugh and a friendly face, and Drummond decided to risk a query.

'Yes. He was just telling me an interesting story about the old Lord and his will. Shame he didn't get to the end. Now I shall never know how the story goes.'

'That old tale. There b'ain't no ending to it, son. Lord William died without naming an heir. The elder son is missing and the younger is waiting to take his place. Far as anyone knows, the will be lost. But between you and me, I think young Master Valerian destroyed it himself.' His huge hand, like an enormous piece of ham, almost felled Drummond as he clapped him on the shoulder and gave a loud guffaw. 'But it don't matter, do it? Because he's the only surviving son anyway.'

'Not if I have anything to do with it,' muttered Drummond, lurching away and wondering whether he should go outside to be sick. As he headed for the door, he caught sight of a pretty face smiling at him from behind the bar, and all at once remembered why the drink had gone to his head, and legs, so quickly: food. He needed food. And Molly was going to serve it to him. His heart swelled and he made his way over to her, trying to appear sober and dignified.

'My!' She giggled, two dimples puckering her cheeks. 'You've obviously not tried our ale before. Come and soak it up with some rabbit and roast potatoes. I've laid up a room just above the bar. Come through here.'

She lifted a hinged section of the wooden bar and led him along a narrow, dim corridor which stank of warm beer and sweet wine, the dregs of which he could feel underfoot as he walked. He followed Molly's swaying curves up a staircase which opened out into a wide landing with several doors leading off.

The room she gestured for him to enter was simply furnished with a clean table and chairs, a cushioned

391

window-seat, and a welcoming fire which crackled and popped in the small grate. Drummond sank into the comfortable haven in the window and peered out through the smoke-stained lattice. Below him, outside, it was dark and quiet: a few horses snickered in the ostler's yard, and the revelry in the tavern echoed unevenly against the walls of the stone outhouses. The cool panes soothed his hot head, and Drummond felt sobriety stealing slowly back into his limbs.

'Would you like to eat straight away? I can ask the kitchen maid to come and help me serve when she has finished in the next room.'

'You seem busy here tonight.' Drummond was hungry, but his desire for company made him reluctant to send her below stairs immediately.

'Market-day is always like this: most people do their business in the town and then come here to slake their thirst. It gets quite rowdy, sometimes.' She stepped a little nearer. 'You aren't from round here, are you?'

Drummond turned from the window, relishing the chill of the damp night-dark panes through the cotton of his shirt. 'Not exactly,' he replied, smiling. 'But I know my way around. Are you local?'

'Yes, I am. My Pa farms some land here. I've got plans for a better life, though. If I work here for long enough, maybe a gentleman will pass through and fall madly in love with me and carry me off!'

'Well, make sure he puts a ring on your finger first. These gentlemen can be quite ungentlemanly at times.' Drummond gave a wry grin. Molly's eyes widened with mock innocence.

'Well, I'm not sure I know what you mean, sir. Perhaps you'll have to show me this ungentlemanly behaviour so's I can watch out for it in future.'

'I'd be happy to show you.' Drummond's mouth widened with good humour and a stirring of lust as he reached for her. The girl moved forward into his arms, and he propped her on his knee as he explored the laces at the neckline of her simple white chemise. Her head dropped comfortably on to his shoulder, and their fingers entwined slightly as she reached up to help him.

Beneath her top, Drummond was excited to find that Molly was wearing a beautifully boned red and black corset, which nipped her already tiny waist into handspan proportions. Above it, her breasts were pushed upward and spilled over the top like ripe fruit tumbling from an overfull basket. He grasped one strawberry nipple between thumb and forefinger, and rolled it, savouring the pertness and the increasing rigidity of the muscular button beneath his hand. His mouth quickly followed his fingers. He sucked thirstily at her breast, and heard her gasp as his teeth gently grazed her erect flesh.

Her fingers delved into the unruly tow of his hair, and she cradled his head to her bosom, breathing heavily and pushing her ribs outward to offer his mouth the maximum amount of her peachy skin. Beneath her soft thighs, Drummond could feel his cock stirring and pushing in his breeches, a bulging rod with an independent spirit which pushed at his fly and insinuated itself against the cushion of her skirts. He shifted his position a little, and Molly pulled away slightly to stare into his eyes, her own soft chestnut depths framed by the sooty smudge of dark lashes. An unspoken question hung in the air between them for a long moment, then she stood and stepped back a little.

'Wait.' Drummond reached for her again, but she evaded him with a sway of her sumptuous hips, a smile curling the corners of her full lips.

'No. You wait,' she said simply.

Obediently, he waited and watched, his tension growing as the girl loosened the chemise from where it had fallen around her waist. She lifted it over her head, and Drummond watched in fascination as her breasts rose, lifted by the movement of her arms as she slid the cotton top up over her face and dropped it on to the floor beside her. Next, she unbuttoned her skirt and let it fall in a pool of blue serge at her feet, where the creamy drift of her petticoats soon joined it.

Drummond held his breath, afraid to move, for the aching in his groin had now become a merciless burn. Molly stroked one hand over her breasts and met his eyes. She looked beautiful: tall and curvaceous, her pale skin gilded by the glow from the fire behind her. The scarlet and black corset hugged her body and moulded it into a perfect hourglass shape, and the long, opaque stockings which skimmed her legs to just above the knee gave her an elegance more suited to a French courtesan than a country barmaid.

Smiling, Molly began to unbraid her honey-toned hair, and said, 'I can see you wondering. This corset was a present from another ungentlemanly gentleman.' Her cheeks dimpled and her fingers moved rapidly over her lustrous tresses, parting and spreading them over her shoulders where they lay gleaming, burnished by the light from the single candle on the table. She delicately sidestepped her discarded garments. 'So if you are one of those who suffer from guilt, please don't. Guilt-free loving is my speciality.' With that, she came towards him and Drummond forgot everything, immersed in sensation.

She released him from the prison of his breeches with expert hands, her fingers finding and gripping the shaft of his firm cock before she moved her mouth on to his hot flesh. Exquisite ripples of pleasure quaked through him as the plump satin of her lips fastened on to him. She found the slit at the top, which opened beneath the pressure of her pointed tongue, and he leant back against the cold window, his mind spiralling into the abyss of pleasure as she alternately sucked and probed, fucking him with the tip of her tongue, while her hands kneaded his balls and he felt his sap rise unexpectedly quickly within him.

His climax came suddenly, erupting with great force, like molten lava flowing through his loins and along his cock, and shooting into the back of her throat as she swallowed around him, arching her long neck to accommodate his heady pulsing. Drummond groaned as she licked his manhood, sucking the sticky residue from every inch of his silken length, and polishing his swollen glans to a varnished sheen with her lips.

Amused, he lifted her chin and smiled into her satisfied face.

'You're like a little cat, lapping a bowl of cream. I don't think I've ever seen a girl enjoy the taste of a man so much.' His forefinger stroked a pearl from the corner of her mouth, and he slid it between her pouting lips. The feel of her mouth as she sucked his finger created a tingling arousal in him once more, and he knew then that he would be ready again before very much longer.

Bending, he kissed her salty lips, and was surprised to find that the taste of himself upon her was not as unpleasant as he had supposed. Probing with his tongue, he searched the depths of her mouth, plumbing the moist recesses and running across the hard ivory of her teeth. She fastened on to him, sucking and drawing on his tongue, pulling it into her until he felt a tautness at its root and he pulled back slightly, his hands roaming from her waist to the fleshy roundness of her bare buttocks as he pulled her astride his lap. She settled on to him, stretching her legs wide either side of his hips, until he felt the soft pliability of her sex resting over the renewed hardness of his prick.

Drummond's hands caressed the taut curves of her figure, gradually moving forward and down until his thumbs lightly stroked the triangle of hair which nestled plushly at the base of her corsetted stomach. She shuddered beneath his grazing fingers and pressed herself on to his thighs, her mouth still fastened to his, her hips rocking as she wordlessly urged him to continue.

Drummond could feel the heat that rose from her, the humidity of sweet arousal, and he delved further, parting her moistness with his thumbs and burrowing into her folds. The knuckle of his right hand brushed the protruding bead of her clitoris, and she bucked above him, her mouth momentarily breaking contact with his as she reached down to push his finger firmly on to the stiff jewel. Drummond obediently curved his hand under her, fitting it to her and rubbing her quickly until she squealed for mercy, biting at his neck and pressing against him.

'Do it now,' she whispered. 'I want to feel you all the way up inside me.'

He lifted her with both hands firm on her waist until she was poised above him, and stared into the depths of her eyes, seeing his own flushed reflection in the pools of her dilated pupils. Then he thrust into her, plunging himself upward with a strong jerk of his lean hips as he brought her firmly down on to his hardness. Crying aloud, they moved together with abandoned sensuality, she arching and falling while he moved his rhythm beneath her, the sinews on his bronzed forearms standing up with his exertion as he pumped in and out of her.

'Oh! Sweet Jesus! You feel so good!' he cried.

When they came it was a simultaneous crescendo, intoxicating and exhausting. They collapsed on to each other, and Drummond leant back against the window; the heat of their ardour seemed to melt the ice on the panes, and a coolness trickled down Drummond's back, soaking his shirt and mingling with the sweat of his animal passion.

'Molly, you're gorgeous.' He cupped her face in his hands, kissing her lightly. 'I'm so hungry now. I bet you do this to make us poor fools spend more on feasting!'

'Indeed!' She frowned up at him, pretending to take offence. 'Well, you'd better not disappoint me by refusing your food, now.'

'I could eat a horse,' he confessed, as she moved away to pick up her abandoned clothing from the floor. The sight of the twin crescents of her luscious behind stirred him again, and Drummond stood, reaching for her and pulling her backward into the curve of his waist.

'But I could eat you, too.' He nuzzled her ear, nibbling

396

and sucking at the plump lobe through the scented cloud of her hair. Laughing, she pushed back against him, pressing herself into his belly and causing his cock to stir against her naked flesh. He slid a finger into her from behind, revelling in her warm readiness and the clinging velvet of her sex as she tensed on to his probing hand.

'I believe you'd do it again, if I let you,' he murmured.

'Let me? I doubt if you'd be able to quite so quickly.'

'Try me.'

He turned her quickly and sat her up on the table. Her face registered her surprise when she saw the ramrod stiffness of him as he moved towards her. Jerking her legs apart, he entered her with a sudden thrust of his hips, gripping her thighs with his strong hands until white marks paled around his fingertips. He plunged deep into her and she gasped at his sudden ferocity, sinking back on to the table and hooking her legs tightly around his waist.

'Oh! Oh, yes. Do it hard. Do it harder!' She bucked and writhed beneath him as he ruthlessly rammed her with every stroke of his throbbing cock until he felt the waves of her orgasm shudder on to him. Her taut body undulated, and she gave a loud cry, arching her neck and tipping her chin up towards the ceiling. The sight and feel of her pleasure tipped him over the edge and he too came in a torrent. Hot flames licked through him and he collapsed, panting, on to her prone body.

'Well, not many of my gentlemen would be ready again so quickly,' she murmured, her mouth soft against his ear. 'You're a regular stallion. Will you be staying long in the town?'

'Long enough.' Drummond raised himself from her and smiled down at her curvaceous form spread on the table beneath him. She was gorgeous and vital, but he was reluctant to encourage her hopes. Commitment was something he had never been enthusiastic for, although the prospect of repeat visits held a certain appeal.

He ran a long forefinger down her body and buried his hand in the soft down between her thighs.

'But don't get any ideas about rings from me. You keep looking out for a real gentleman. One will come along soon enough.'

Molly pouted and looked vaguely offended. She slid off the table and picked up her clothes.

'That wasn't quite what I meant,' she said firmly. 'I know you're not for me: but there's no harm in us getting together sometimes, is there? Guilt-free I said, and that's what I meant.'

'Here, let me help you.' Drummond turned her and began buttoning her skirts from behind. 'If I'm ever in need of company, I assure you that this is one of the first places I'll come. Now, where's that rabbit and potatoes? A man needs food as well as love.' He gave her padded bottom a resounding smack as she headed for the door.

The food she served was excellent, and Drummond ate slowly, washing his meal down with a sweeter and less potent ale than that which he had taken at the bar. He sat in the window-seat for a long time after, gazing out at the darkness, but absorbed in his own thoughts.

When he took his horse from the ostler's lad, he gave him a coin and turned to lead the mare out. A sleek horse in the next stall, a sixteen-hand stallion with perfect palomino colouring, caught his eye and he stopped to give the velvety muzzle a gentle stroke.

'You're a beauty; what's your name?'

The horse's breath warmed his hand, and Drummond smiled in the half-dark, glancing at the saddle which adorned the animal's back. The Spanish leather surface was polished and well cared for, and the initials of his owner were tooled neatly into the flap near the stirrup length: V OH.

Valerian Olivier Hawkesworth.

It could be no other. The thought that his brother was at the inn made his blood chill, and he suppressed a shudder. Had he been seen? It was almost impossible to tell. He gave a low whistle and waited.

'Jake. Did you see the owner of this horse arrive?' The ostler's son, a relation of Jim Handfast, was a lad he had come to know well since his homecoming.

'Yes. He came here almost an hour since. He always takes a meal with Molly, one of the serving wenches, and then tries his luck at cards or dice with one of the other gentlemen.'

Drummond nodded. He was wryly amused that his brother's taste in wenches could be so similar to his own, and wondered whether he was the gentlemanly donor of the red and black corset.

'Jake, do you remember we discussed you helping me sometimes? Well, if you have a need for a sovereign or two, then I can give you a job to earn it.'

The man and the youth spoke quietly for several minutes, then Drummond mounted his horse and trotted swiftly away into the darkness of the night.

Valerian leant back in his chair, drew on his cheroot and surveyed the other man across the card table. The private gaming room of the Chequers Inn was small and lit by guttering tapers which added to the dark smokiness of the atmosphere. The pile of gold and silver pieces before him glittered; not an hour since, he had been losing badly, and Madame's words about the dowry he would have to pay out for Lydia played repeatedly through his mind. His quick exchange of the dice-box for a specially painted false box had enabled him to throw winning numbers on the three ivory dice and reclaim much of what he had lost.

'You have the devil's luck tonight, Hawkesworth.' The opponent, Squire Aldridge, slumped dejectedly in his chair. 'I can't let you take all my gold, so I think I'll retire gracefully. Until the next time, what?'

'It's your decision.' Valerian nodded graciously, and stabbed his cheroot into a plate of half-eaten food. He scooped the coins from the table-top and tipped them, clinking, into a large hide pouch which he slipped into his breast pocket. The weight was reassuring against his chest, and he leant forward to shake hands with Aldridge.

'Until next time, as you say.' His hand moved rapidly over the baize surface as, with a sleight of hand worthy of a magician, he replaced the false dice-box with the true one before standing and draining his tankard.

When he reached the darkened stables, there was no sign of the ostler's lad and no one to help him mount; he muttered with displeasure as he swung his polished black boot over the stallion's hindquarters. The route was dark, and the path which wound out of town towards Hawkesworth land had few other travellers. When he reached the wooded copse which signified the eastern reaches of the estate, a fine drizzling rain began to fall, and he shrugged his cloak higher around his cheeks, muffling his ears. The horse beneath him shied a little, ears flickering.

'Come on,' snarled Valerian. 'Let's get home before an infernal storm sets in.'

The stallion took a few reluctant steps forward and then halted. The swirling clouds had partially blocked the waxing moon, and the darkness around man and horse was almost complete. A dry stick cracked somewhere to Valerian's left, and he urged his mount onward with a jab of his spurs. The steed flared its nostrils and bridled sideways, shaking its huge head and prancing in the middle of the path.

'Come on, damn you!' Valerian was impatient now, and pulled the reins in tightly to give him greater control, but the horse continued to pull sideways, both eyes rolling and shining white in the darkness. Valerian felt the first flicker of unease and squinted, straining to see the road ahead.

It was empty and silent. There was nothing to fear. He dug his heels in and the stallion reared, almost unseating him. He swore viciously. At that moment the ragged clouds parted and the scene was brilliantly lit with silver moonlight.

Where the road had been empty, there stood a large ebony horse with a solitary rider, motionless, some ten yards ahead, blackly silhouetted against the pewter shingle of the hill behind. Valerian saw with a quickening of his heart that the rider held a cocked pistol, and, beneath his tricorne hat, a mask occluded his features.

'Get out of my way!' The brave words sounded hollow even to himself, and he could feel a nervous twitch start in the muscle of his jaw. The highwayman remained motionless. 'Get out of my way, damn you! I am Lord Hawkesworth, and if you dare to touch me I'll have you strung up from the nearest gibbet by sundown tomorrow!'

There was still no movement or reply, and he felt fear turn his bowels to water as the shingle on the path behind him crunched loudly. Twisting in his saddle, he saw the dimly lit shadow of another horseman blocking his retreat. Slowly the dark figures advanced until they were only feet from him, fencing him in fore and aft. But still they did not speak. The rider in front leant forward and grasped Valerian's bridle, jerking it out of his hands and pulling the nervous stallion in close.

'My dear Lord Hawkesworth.' The formal address was spoken with withering sarcasm, and Valerian flinched as the other man brought his pistol up and held it against his throbbing temple. 'I believe you have been possessed of good fortune at the gaming table tonight. There are people who need that money more desperately than you, and I intend to give it to them. So, my dear sir, it's your money, or your life.'

Valerian, frozen with fear, had no thought other than to save his own skin. He lifted his hands in a gesture of surrender, and the pistol was moved fractionally away from him.

'I have money: here, take it. There is near on a hundred gold pieces in this pouch. Will that satisfy you?' He thrust the jingling pouch at the highwayman, and saw a brief gleam of white teeth as the other smiled.

'Indeed it does. I am very satisfied. For now.' The pouch disappeared beneath the thick, dark cloak that the highwayman wore. 'It's a shame that you choose to give us no sport by putting up a fight. But of course your vanity will have you tell everyone at the manor that you bravely fought your assailants, so we'd better give you proof of your valour.'

Swiftly, before Valerian had even absorbed the significance of his words, the man had drawn a thin blade and flashed it across Valerian's cheek. The wound was shallow and only an inch in length, but the pain and shock made Valerian wince and hold his hand up to his face. His ivory kid glove slowly stained with crimson blood, and he gave a choking sob and fumbled for his silk kerchief.

The highwayman gave a roar of mirth which echoed against the trees, and Valerian's head shot up. There had been something familiar in that laughter. He mopped at his wounded cheek, and the two men released his horse.

'Good night! And thank you, *Lord* Hawkesworth!'

And they were gone, their shadows flitting into the blackness of the night and dissolving into the trees at the side of the path.

He was alone.

The rain came in earnest then, lashing out of the clouded sky with needlepoint sharpness. Valerian steered his skittish horse for home, a slow rage smouldering in the pit of his belly.

Chapter Nine

*T*he morning sun streamed in through the window-panes, warming the corners of the library and making the newly made fire in the grate almost unnecessary.

Lydia was curled in the corner of a well-padded sofa, a copy of *Roxana* propped on her lap. She had devoured the salacious *Moll Flanders* during her imprisonment, and found Mr Defoe's vivid narrative entertaining as well as educational. She nibbled her thumb as she read, totally absorbed in the story which unfolded on the coarsely cut parchment pages.

There was a sudden distant pounding from the hall-way of the main house which startled her. Slipping an embroidered marker into her book, she set it aside, rose, and tiptoed towards the door. The library lay off the west corridor leading from the great hall, and she could hear one of the footmen welcome a visitor. Gently, and as silently as possible, she eased open the library door and pressed her eye against the gap.

She almost expired with shock as Valerian, not two feet away, strode into her field of vision, and she shrank back, catching her breath and trying to steady her hammering pulse, silently praying that he had not seen her. But Valerian continued along the corridor and shouted a command to the visitor.

'Enter, my good sir! We will discuss the matter in my study.'

Lydia was consumed with curiosity, but she knew that the route to Valerian's study would take them both right past the library door. She pushed it closed and leant back against the carved wood surface, straining her ears for every footfall.

As soon as she heard them pass, she opened the door wide and recklessly stuck her head out, craning round the jamb to see Valerian, followed by the taller, but slightly stooped, figure of Mr Lavendale, the lawyer. She moved back inside the room and softly closed the door.

She wondered what purpose Valerian could have in asking Mr Lavendale to the house. It must have something to do with the inheritance, but she could not imagine why he had called a meeting with the lawyer. She had not seen her cousin all day, although she knew that he had returned late the previous night and stormed straight up to Madame's room, shouting about brigands and slamming all the doors in his wake. She thought of Drummond, out in the forest somewhere, unable to come home, and her heart ached for him. She decided to waylay Lavendale on his way out and try to extract information which could be of some use.

A floorboard creaked and a door banged somewhere in the depths of the house. Lydia jumped up out of the sofa. Delving into her work bag, she rummaged amongst the knotted threads and jumbled wool until she found a small bottle of eau de Cologne. She dabbed some on her temples and throat, smoothed her hair and, as an afterthought, lifted her skirts and applied a smear of the scent to her thighs. Throwing the little bottle back, she pinched her cheeks and bit her lips to make them attractively red before hurrying to the door. If she timed it just right, she could swing the door wide and innocently step out right into Mr Lavendale's path.

She pressed her ear to the door. There was silence.

Her heart thudded in her chest as she waited impatiently for the solicitor to pass. No one approached. To pass the time she checked her *décolletage*, pulling the lace-edged neckline lower and plumping her breasts up a little. At once, she heard a shuffle and footsteps outside the door, took a deep breath, and pulled the door wide.

'Why, Mr Lavendale! How lovely to see you. If I had known that we had guests, I would have arranged for a tray of tea.'

'Good morning, Miss Lydia. How kind.' The lawyer was nearing sixty, with silky white hair and a hawk-like nose. His penetrating grey eyes fixed on her cleavage, and Lydia felt almost embarrassed. Steeling herself, she gave a coquettish smile and folded her hands demurely before her.

'I trust that my cousin has looked after you. Have you taken refreshment?'

'No, Miss Lydia. He offered some brandy, but I fear that it is too early in the day for me.'

'Perhaps you would care to join me for tea? I was just about to ring for some. Please stay awhile. I am often starved of company.' She smiled, dipping her chin and looking up at him from the corners of her wide eyes. He seemed to hesitate, and then nodded.

'Very well: it would be my pleasure. It isn't often that an old man like me can take tea with a pretty young thing like yourself.' His eyes ran boldly down her body.

Lydia pretended to simper at his compliment, holding the door wide and gesturing for him to enter.

'Oh, Mr Lavendale. You're hardly an old man! You look remarkably strong and vital.'

Having summoned a servant for a tray of tea, Lydia sat on a low stool at Lavendale's feet, a position in which she hoped to give an effective view of her cleavage. Folding her hands around her knees, she smiled at his air of distraction.

'Would you like milk and sugar?' she asked.

405

'What? Oh – ah, yes. I mean no – no, thank you. Just tea.'

As they sipped, Lydia filled the silence with inconsequential chatter about the weather, the view from the library window, the fashion for taking tea with lemon, and anything else she could think of. Lavendale grew progressively more uncomfortable as she warmed to her task. He loosened his cravat twice; he fidgeted with his watch-chain; he rubbed the edge of his nose. Finally he knocked his half-empty cup from the saucer and spilt tea on the pale blue fabric of his hose.

'Oh, Mr Lavendale! Let me help you: it will stain. Here, let me rub it with the lemon. Oh, your poor leg!' Lydia could hardly believe her luck as she rubbed back and forth on the solicitor's calf: she could feel him leaning closer and closer down to her. She decided to catch him off guard.

'Mr Lavendale, do you know what happened to my uncle's will?'

'Heavens, my dear, what a strange thought to enter your head. Master Valerian was just discussing the exact same subject. Although that is confidential, you understand.'

'Of course. I know he is anxious lest it disturb his claim.'

'Well.' Mr Lavendale patted her hand, obviously mistaking her concern. 'Have no fears on that score. He will be declared Lord in good time. Perhaps you will marry then? I know it was Lord William's fondest wish to see you safely settled.'

'Really?' Lydia lowered her eyelids thoughtfully. 'So, do you have any idea what Uncle William would have done with such a precious document?'

'Put it in a safe place and forgotten all about it, I expect.' Mr Lavendale moistened his lips and moved to the edge of his seat. 'But it is of no concern. With only one surviving son, there is no cause to worry.'

'So you don't have it?'

'My dear young lady! What are you suggesting?'

'Nothing at all. Forgive me, I'm being fanciful.' Lydia smiled and stood up, moving away to stand near the desk. 'Thank you for taking tea with me. Shall I call for your horse?'

'There is no hurry. I would rather venture abroad when my hose is drier.'

Standing, Lavendale smoothed his waistcoat over his chest and stomach, appearing to admire his reflection in the mirror above the fireplace. Lydia watched him, wondering about his wife, a notorious nag. He was really quite a fine figure of a man, despite a slight tendency to stoop, but she supposed that was due to his extraordinary height. She tried to imagine him achieving conjugal relations with his nagging wife, but decided it was simply too awful to contemplate.

Lydia saw that the book she had been reading earlier was caught under a cushion, its pages creased, and she leant over to retrieve it, smoothing the pages with one hand. She slid open a desk drawer and stowed *Roxana* inside, only half aware of Lavendale moving soundlessly across the room to hover at her elbow.

'Aaah, Defoe. You are familiar with such literature? I am surprised your reading habits are not kept under tighter rein.' Lavendale seemed visibly to adjust his opinion of her, and stared into her face, one silky white brow raised.

'I have always had free rein in the library.'

'Disgusting. Improper.' He leant close and inhaled as if to draw in the odour of decadence. 'If Lord William were alive, he would have had such books thrown from the house.'

'Indeed?' Lydia studied the flaring of his nostrils with distaste. 'I think you would have found that Lord William was very enlightened in such matters. It was he, after all, who allowed me to attend lessons with the boys and gain an education.'

'To what end, Miss Lydia? A lady has no need of any knowledge other than sewing and instructing servants.

If one wishes to make conversation, then one seeks the company of gentlemen over port.'

'How dull.'

'Give a woman an education and see civilisation on the road to corruption.'

'Really, Mr Lavendale, that seems a little excessive. What can you mean?'

'Sin, my dear.' He took a step closer to her, and she could smell the scented powder on his hair and periwig. 'There are women in this world who, having read the works you have, would seek to avail themselves of the same experiences as, say, Moll Flanders. Soon you, too, may seek to taste the pleasures of the flesh. Disgusting though they may be.'

'If they are so disgusting, why are they called the pleasures of the flesh?' Lydia found her hip pressed against the edge of the desk, as the lawyer advanced inch by inch and she correspondingly eased herself backward. She was not sure that she liked the way the conversation was progressing. Their talk seemed to have wandered from the location of the will and uncomfortably close to a lecture on carnal knowledge. She stared up into his face, and noticed the gleam in his eyes as well as the tiny hairs which protruded from his flaring nostrils.

She was taken by surprise when he sprang forward, imprisoning her against the desk, and grasping one of her breasts in his large, bony hand. Her sudden instinctive struggle seemed to inflame him further, for he leant his body weight on to her, bending her backward, while his free hand reached up to grasp her ringletted hair and twist it up to his face. He gave a groaning exhalation.

'You wanton temptress. Do you think I don't know why you invited me in here? I know your sort, you educated women: you seek to tempt and tease a man with trickery learned from vile books. You know very well why they are called the pleasures of the flesh. I can imagine you, writhing on that sofa with your hand under your petticoats, expecting a man to stay sane and pass the time of day.'

Lydia strained her hands against the embroidery of his waistcoat. With a strength that belied his years, Lavendale swept her up and deftly laid her on the polished surface of the desk, simultaneously catching the hem of her skirts and pushing them up to expose her pale thighs. Like a man possessed, he fell upon her in a frenzy, feverishly pulling at her and parting her legs until she could feel the steeliness of his fingers on her sex.

She gasped and struggled to sit up, but he abruptly twisted and the weight of his body came down across her, pinning her helplessly, his head diving suddenly between her thighs, until, before she could draw breath to cry out, his mouth was fastened on to her.

'Stop it!' she gasped. 'Mr Lavendale, stop it this instant. I shall call for help.'

He did not reply, but simply pressed his long hard tongue into her moistness with a skill that surprised her and made her hesitate. She gave a last feeble wriggle as he probed and licked, sending the first flickers of sensual pleasure through her body. His tongue was long and hard, and he used it with consummate skill. Lydia let her body soften under his caress, and wondered whether she could use this encounter to her own advantage. With his knowledge of the workings of the law he could be a useful ally, and the enthusiastic application of his tongue excited and inflamed her.

'Wait! Please wait one moment, kind sir. We may be disturbed. If we are to proceed, let me at least lock the door.'

He hesitated momentarily, then stood to watch her slide off the desk and hurry to the door. When she rejoined him, he seemed to hesitate, his features flushed and his eyes uncertain.

'I beg your pardon,' he murmured, his usually resonant voice quiet. 'Miss Lydia, I have behaved abominably. Will you excuse me and forget that this happened?

409

I mean you no harm, it is simply that your beauty, and your knowing eyes, led me astray.'

Lydia watched him straighten his silk coat and prepare to leave. She was surprised at his humility and sudden change of heart; she felt a little worm of displeased vanity stir inside her.

'Mr Lavendale, do not be so hasty. I admit that I was at first shocked by your advances, but on calm reflection I think I would like you to continue. Your touch is not repulsive to me, and you leave me wanting more. Come now, the door is locked. We shall not be disturbed.'

She perched on the edge of the desk again, this time lifting her skirts herself and revealing the pouting, newly depilated sex which swelled and throbbed under his intense scrutiny. The lawyer seemed to fight, and lose, an inner battle, for he breathed heavily and tried to drag his gaze away, but the sight of her partial nudity proved irresistible, as Lydia had hoped it would, and he advanced slowly to place his hands on her spread thighs.

Lydia watched in fascination as he tentatively pushed his tongue on to her, stiffened it and applied pressure. She gasped and leant back on one hand as an exquisite warmth engulfed her senses and she allowed her eyelids to droop, her head reeling and sending images of other seductions to her mind's eye. The solicitor's expert mouth became Drummond's, and she remembered the night in the folly and could feel trembling waves shiver at the edges of her senses.

Sliding her hand down to grip Lavendale's soft white hair, she recalled the first time that Angel had played her, using her tongue like a musical instrument, then Valerian with his unique brand of ferocity and devouring barbarity. Suddenly the sensuous images came quickly, one hardly finishing before being superseded by another, each more erotic than the last, until her voluptuous mind was reeling and swooning from the blissful pleasure of the lawyer's tongue and her own delectable imaginings.

She could feel his hand easing along the yielding skin of her thigh, and sensed the firmness of his finger as he entered her. The pressure he applied drove her over the edge, and she moved her hips in a rhythmic impulse, silently demanding that he fulfil her need. She felt his lips close around the sweetness of her sex, and moaned as he pressed another finger in, then another until it seemed that his whole hand would ease into her. He plunged inward, stretching her and filling her rapacious body as she climaxed suddenly and sweetly, feeling the waves break over her as he sucked and plumbed her depths. She felt the pulsing of her sex and the shivering ripples of her skin as she came, and heard him groan as he became still. She realised that he had been rubbing himself with one hand, and had achieved his own satisfaction along with her.

'Do you still desire the company of gentlemen, with their port and cigars?' A smile curved her lips as she surveyed him from the lofty height of the desk. He fell to his knees, cradling his groin in one hand as a slowly spreading stain darkened the pale fabric of his knee-breeches.

'Miss Lydia, I am completely in your thrall. Your company has infinitely more appeal.' His hands, slightly trembling, helped her to rearrange her garments. 'If I can ever be of service to you, you have only to ask.'

'Thank you.' Lydia demurely slid down from the desk. 'I shall bear that in mind.'

Outside, she watched him mount his grey mare and carefully arrange his full-skirted coat about his lap. He saluted her and rode away. Musing on his potential uses as an ally, as well as on his surprising sexual prowess, she wandered slowly back up the steps and into the house.

In the library, she ran her fingers over the smooth surface of the desk and smiled, her body still humming and warm. She wondered where Drummond could be; she felt a strong desire to see him again. If he were looking for help or a place to hide, then she imagined that Jim Handfast's bothy would be the first place he would go.

As the trees ahead of her thinned out, Lydia could see the ramshackle cottage set in a clearing. The glow of the low sun touched the walls with a golden hue which made the little building seem more appealing than it actually was. As she drew nearer, she saw that several slates had dropped from the sloping roof, and the wooden lintel was rotten and split.

She found them at the rear of the cottage. Jim was perched on a felled tree stump sucking on a foul-smelling pipe, while Drummond – stripped to the waist and gleaming with fresh sweat – rested on the handle of a long axe. A pile of chopped logs lay near his booted feet.

Lydia paused, unobserved, a shiver running through her as she stood motionless in the shadow of the eaves and admired his wiry masculinity. His bare skin shone cinnamon-brown in the late afternoon sun, and the bulging muscles beneath stood in burnished relief around his long bones, his biceps corded and pumped up with his recent labours.

Lydia breathed gently, afraid to disturb him and wanting to revel for a moment in his semi-nakedness. She felt aroused and allured by the delicious thrill which pulled at her and caused a fiery juice to swell and moisten her sex. Pressing her thighs together to prolong the silky pressure, she wondered how she could get him alone.

Her mind played tricks as she imagined what she would do to him, and he to her, when they were together in some lonely part of the forest. She could almost feel that burnished skin puckering under her tongue, as she slid her mouth in a perfect arc over the flatness of his belly to his navel, there to dip and lap until he grasped the back of her head and pushed her further down to nestle her nose and mouth against the straining buttons of his breeches.

412

As if he could sense her presence and the force of her thoughts, Drummond raised his head and looked straight at her, his eyes burning into hers and a slow smile curving his mouth.

'Lydia. How did you find me?'

'Oh, I followed my nose and it led me here.' She stepped forward, out of the shadows, and strolled across the clearing, leaves crackling under her feet. Jim stood up and gave a small bow.

'Evening, Miss Lydia.' He glanced at Drummond. 'I'll go inside and put that soup on the stove.'

They watched him go, and then Lydia turned back, gazing up at Drummond.

'Do you mind me coming? I had to see you and this was the obvious place to find you.'

'If it was obvious to you, then it will be obvious to others if they become suspicious.' His shoulders heaved as he swung the axe, embedding it deep into a convenient log, and stepped forward. His proximity and the musky smell of his hot body made her tremble inside and feel helplessly sensual as well as ravenous for him. She fixed her eyes on his nipples, seeing the coppery smoothness of the outer edge and the rigid peak which rose from the centre. Her own seemed to tighten under her stiff bodice as if in response, and she felt a coolness flush across her scalp in spite of the warmth of the evening.

'Are you certain no one followed you?'

She shook her head, unable to drag her gaze away from the curves of his chest.

'Did you tell anyone that you were going out?' Impatiently, his hand came under her chin and tilted her face up to his, forcing her to meet his questing eyes.

'No, I let myself out of the kitchen door and cut behind the stables. I'm sure nobody saw me and they won't miss me for hours, now.'

'How can you be sure?'

'Valerian and Madame have gone to the Spa. They won't be back until tomorrow.' She was unable to stop herself as her fingers stole to the smoothness of his chest, and she stroked the satin skin, her nails curving under the crisp golden hair. 'Listen, Drummond, I spoke to Mr Lavendale earlier. He seemed to think that you were on the verge of being declared legally dead, and that – that Uncle William wanted me to marry Valerian.'

To her surprise, Drummond threw back his head and laughed. Arching one eyebrow, she stared up at him.

'But that's not funny, it's horrible! I can't possibly marry him. He's disgusting, and so cruel.'

'Don't fret. You don't have to marry anyone that you don't want to. Father planned a decent dowry for you, and you'll have your pick of the best suitors for miles around.' For some reason, this did not reassure her. She was left wondering, as he grabbed her hand and led her towards the cottage, whether he included himself in the list of eligible bachelors.

Jim had scrubbed the wooden table and propped a sliver of wood under one leg to stop it rocking. The floor had been hastily swept and three earthenware bowls set to warm on the stove. Lydia curled her legs up as she sat in the only chair, her hunger sharpening at the smell of thick broth and the sight of the game pie which had been set on a chopping board.

'I take it you'll eat with us, miss?' Jim lifted the iron cauldron from the stove and set it on the table. Lydia nodded, leaning forward to sniff appreciatively as he removed the blackened lid.

'It smells delicious. I'd love some.'

Jim ladled the stew and carved chunks of game pie. When they had eaten, Lydia snuggled further into the depths of the chair, resting her chin on her hand as she watched the men smoke and drink small cups of dark liquor. She felt deliciously full, warm and relaxed. Her eyelids drooped sleepily.

'I'd better walk you home.' Drummond's voice cut across her drowsing thoughts and she sat up, smiling at him.

'I can find my own way back.'

'No, you can't: it'll be dark in less than an hour. I'm coming with you.' His tone brooked no refusal, so she thanked Jim Handfast and wound her cloak around her shoulders before following Drummond to the door. He lifted a dark, full-skirted coat from a hook and shrugged himself into it, leaving the brassy buttons open over his linen shirt.

'I'll see you later, Jim. Don't wait up.'

They walked in companionable silence at first, Lydia trying to match her steps to his long-legged, rangy strides. Glancing sideways at her, he grinned and slowed down, catching her hand and tucking it into the crook of his elbow.

'I'm glad you came to find me,' he said. 'It was the best surprise I've had for a long time, to turn and see you standing there.'

'Good.'

'When you spoke to Lavendale, did you think he was honest?'

'Honest? Well, I suppose so.' She thought for a moment. 'Do you think he may not be?'

'Well, you know what my brother's like. He can sniff out the corrupt at twenty paces. If he thought he could turn a situation to his advantage, he'd have no hesitation in blackmailing someone to work for him.'

Lydia walked in silence for a few minutes, holding tightly to Drummond's sleeve and thinking of her encounter with Lavendale. Was he corrupt? Was Valerian bribing him? It was possible, she supposed. But surely he would have more to lose – his reputation and profession – if he were found out. Or maybe he had done something to compromise those things; perhaps Valerian knew and had threatened to reveal it. The memory of the lawyer's practised tongue made her shiver, and she considered the possibility that he made a habit of employing it on others. If he did, and Valerian knew, then blackmail was a strong probability.

'I really don't know,' she said. 'It's possible. Do you think he has the will, but is pretending that it's lost?'

'I don't know. I don't trust anyone at the moment, except you, of course. And Jim. I think I should come to the house. If I show myself, even if there is no will, then I inherit. I am the eldest: it's simple.' He stopped, as if suddenly struck by a new thought. 'Unless Valerian tries to say that I'm an impostor. It's been five years since anyone saw me, so he could throw doubt on my identity quite easily.'

'No! I would stand up for you. Nobody would believe him!'

'They would if Lavendale concurred with him and not you. You're only a woman.'

Troubled, and slightly angry with his dismissal of her, she stared up at him, thinking how handsome he was despite the narrow white scar which marred his cheek. Reaching up, she slid her hand to the back of his neck, where a thin leather thong secured his unruly hair, and pulled his face down to hers.

The first light touch of his lips reawakened slumbering urges. An image of his flat stomach sprang unbidden to her mind, and she quivered inside at the memory of the line of crisp hair that passed between his nipples down into his waistband. Her mouth opened and a flame of pure pleasure shot through her at his touch; his lips were so firm on hers, his tongue so delicate as it rubbed against the ivory hardness of her teeth.

She let him be gentle at first, revelling in the softness of his touch, kissing him with small movements, entwining her fingers in his hair, enjoying the smell of his skin and the feel of the light stubble that roughened her cheek as he rubbed against her. Gradually, she felt her pulse quicken with need and she pushed against him, seeking the resistance of his belly and hips as she rose on to tiptoes and arched against him. She wanted to feel the promise of his arousal, needed to have the granite hardness of his cock pressed against her.

Responding eagerly, he took her waist in his hands and crushed her tightly on to him, tilting his pelvis and grinding into her. His tongue sought and found hers, his kiss so urgent and forceful that her lips tingled and she gasped against his mouth.

'Please, take me here. I need to feel you. I want you inside me.'

'I'm going to fuck you so hard you'll beg me to stop.'

'No, I won't. You'll beg *me* to stop.'

Her hands grasped the lapels of the thick black coat and jerked him closer, her mouth grinding on his and her knee forcing between his thighs. Taken by surprise by her forthrightness, he paused, then held her elbows and thrust her roughly backward.

She felt the roughness of tree bark behind her as he pushed. The breath slammed out of her lungs as she hit the trunk, and the bones of her spine protested. Catching her breath raggedly as he lifted her, she instinctively raised one leg and wrapped it around his waist, her fingers sliding down his shirt-front to grapple with the buttons of his breeches.

He did not speak, merely stared into her eyes as his fingers stole between their straining bodies and pulled at the ribbon-fastening of her skirts, jerking her clothing free. A coolness chilled her bare legs and hips, complementing the lush heat between her thighs, and she felt herself tremble as sexual need exploded through her body. Her hands fumbled at his waistband.

'Here, let me.' His fingers joined hers and unbuttoned the front panel of his breeches until her thumbs could part the fabric. She sensed the energy which emanated from him, could feel his hardness as she slid her hands inside.

Suddenly impatient, she grasped the waistband and thrust it down, catching and gripping him in her fist, pulling him to her. He was rock-hard and dark with lust, his cock rearing from the pale fabric almost to his navel. She stroked his length, briefly savouring the satin glide of skin over solid muscle before guiding him towards her, silently demanding fulfilment.

'Lydia,' Drummond murmured, his face buried in her hair. Kissing his way round her neck, he licked her throat with tiny sensual movements of his tongue as if tasting her; then his lips widened and he sucked hard, pulling her skin into his mouth and biting, as if he would devour her. This rough caress intensified the sensations which curled around her hairline to the nape of her neck and tingled down her spine, making her shiver and search for his mouth with her own.

Holding her buttocks in his hands, Drummond lifted her a little further and she felt the rasping bark against her naked hips. Curling her other leg up and around him as he supported her weight, she moved her hips, searching for him. They moved together, and she felt the luxuriant parting of her swollen sex as his hard length pressed against her, then pushed in: only a little at first, but then more, further in, until she was full of him and her breathing came in ragged gasps as she clung to his broad shoulders.

He held her so that she was hard against the tree with her buttocks stretched wide beneath his fingers. She moved slightly against him and he drew imperceptibly out of her before ramming himself home, once, twice, then faster and harder, until Lydia closed her eyes, her head tipping back and her fingers clutching at the thick lapels of his long coat. She absorbed his rhythm, pulling him fiercely into her.

His thrusting became more urgent, and violence replaced tenderness. Her back slammed against the mossy bark and her hair suddenly loosened, tumbling over one shoulder. Drummond caught her neck with one large hand, and jerked free the narrow ribbon which secured her hair. As he grasped handfuls of her curling locks, he twisted them up to his face, inhaling her scent before winding a thick hank of it around the back of his own neck so that their faces were pulled tightly together and she could no longer move of her own volition. All her movements were his now, every gasp smothered by the tense curve of his neck, every vigorous thrust he made echoed through her taut body.

She clung to him, her legs scratched by the rough

texture of his heavy coat, her arms tight around his shoulders. Her skin felt tinglingly alive, and tiny shivers oscillated along the length of her spine and around her ribs until she thought she would be unable to catch her breath. The smell of his neck, just by her nose, and the feel of his muscular buttocks clenching repeatedly beneath her entwined ankles made her lose herself and she came suddenly and violently, shuddering against him.

He paused momentarily, as if surprised by her quick response, and then pumped his lean hips into her ever faster until he reached his own climax as hers subsided. As she felt the tautness of him, sensed the abrupt stillness of his body and heard his harsh groan, Lydia felt a second wave of ecstasy thicken inside her and throb on to him. She squeezed her legs tightly around his back to prolong the blissful sensations and the delicious heat which curled inside her.

She clung there, limpet-like, breathing heavily and listening to the sound of his heart hammering against hers.

'Let me put my legs down,' she murmured, her arms still wound tightly around his strong neck.

'I'm sorry, did I hurt you?' Breathing hard, he eased her away from the tree and smoothed his hands over her bare legs. Reaching up, she kissed him softly on the mouth, her hand sliding around his hard jaw and up to his forehead, wiping the beaded perspiration there. The look on his face touched her, and she felt a swell of love for him.

'You don't ever hurt me. I like what you did. I like what we did together.'

His mouth descended on to hers. His kiss was gentle and soft as he pulled her to him and cradled her. His voice was low and caressing.

'I wanted you so much. Every time I see you I get hard, and I have to have you. The tree seemed a good place.'

'It was a good place. Although the foliage in my hair

419

may raise my maid's eyebrows.' She smiled, retrieving her ribbon and swiftly bunching her hair into it. She knelt before Drummond, pushing his breeches up. Just before covering him, she gave his softened cock a long lick from root to head. It jerked in response and he laughed, tilting her chin up so that her eyes met his.

'Not just yet,' he said. 'Let's walk on a while first.'

Chapter Ten

They broke away from the path to circle the lake, which was just visible through the last line of trees.

'It'll be dark soon. The days are getting short now and I suppose winter will be upon us before long.' He narrowed his eyes against the glare that set the glittering black water of the lake to flame. The sun had just dropped below the trees, and the sky above them was beginning to change to the enveloping blue of night.

'At least it's still warm. When the cold weather comes it won't be a good time for you to be camping out at Jim's and holding up carriages on the road. You'd better decide what you want to do before very much longer.'

He walked on a little further, the toes of his boots scuffing the dry leaves on the path. Lydia thought for a moment that he had not heard her. When he finally spoke, his voice was low and tense.

'I don't know. I really don't know. If I knew Lavendale was honest then I'd go straight to his chambers, but – oh, damn! I wish there was someone to tell me what to do! If my father was alive –'

Lydia suddenly felt irritated.

'Well, he's not!' she cried.

Drummond, even during his absence, had been someone she had always felt she could depend on, the one

421

person who could sort out the mess at Hawkesworth. Her anger at the delay since he had come home suddenly got the better of her, and she quickened her pace, swinging round to face him and slapping her hands against the lapels of his coat. Her temper flushed her cheeks and made her eyes sparkle dangerously.

'He's dead and there's no one to tell you what to do! It's up to you now. You're the head of the family, Drummond, so act like it. Make a decision and stand by it.' She softened her tone a little as she caught the look of surprise and hurt on his face. 'Look. I'll do all I can to help you and so will many others, but we can't wait forever while you make up your mind.' As he returned her stare, she saw the confusion and doubt edged away by something steely and resolute: his eyes held a focus and strength which had not been there before.

Grasping her wrists, he held her still.

'You're right.' He stared over her head as if he could see something in the far distance. 'You're right. There's only me now.'

He dropped her arms, twisted on his heel and strode ahead, leaving Lydia to run after him as he dodged between the thinning trees. He skirted the shore of the dark lake, his stride determined and his face closed and thoughtful.

'Wait! Wait for me,' she called, almost losing sight of his broad, retreating back. His pace did not lessen and she was soon left alone. Exasperated, she kicked at a stone on the path. It hit a tree and rebounded, cracking painfully against her ankle, and she winced, kicked it again, and then trudged on along the path.

Out from the cover of the trees the darkness seemed less dense. The sky was a warm pinky-blue low over the lake, deepening to twilight overhead. There was a sprinkle of tiny silver stars, and the reflection of the moon glittered on the lake. In the distance she could see the stone folly casting a long shadow, and under it, hunched on a large rock at the water's edge, sat Drummond.

As she approached, he looked up and held out a hand. She came close, standing at his side, then placed her hand in his. He sighed.

'We used to come here so often as children. I wonder if Valerian ever remembers those times, when he's gambling the family fortune away?'

'I doubt it,' said Lydia. 'He seems to have no memory of times past. Or if he has, he never says.'

Drummond interlaced his fingers with hers and she looked down at his hand, stirred by the sight of his long fingers squeezed between her pale ones, her arousal pricked by the tiny golden hairs which roughened the back of his hand and disappeared under the stark white of his linen cuff. Her thumb stole up and round to rub the pad of it over his wrist: she enjoyed the calm throb of his pulse which she felt quicken slightly at her touch.

'Do you remember swimming here? Valerian threw me in once and you dived from this rock to save me.' She chuckled. 'You didn't know that old Starchy had been teaching me to swim. Your face was a picture when I calmly struck out for the opposite shore!'

Laughing, he caught her waist and pulled her to him.

'Yes. Explain to me just how that old witch got you down here and swimming without anyone knowing.'

'It was no secret. We would finish conjugating verbs and then she'd suggest a walk, while you two were still struggling over the multiplication she'd set you the previous day.' As she spoke, Lydia kicked off her shoes and tucked her long hair up on to the top of her head. 'We'd run down here and strip, like this –' she let her skirt drift in a soft pile to her ankles and began to unbutton the fastenings at the front of her bodice '– and then my swimming lesson would begin.'

She stretched before him, enjoying the look of dark lust on his features as he took in the length of her bare legs, the nip of her waist, and the upturned curve of her full breasts. He slid off the rock and reached for her, but she was too quick, evading his grasping hand as she skipped to the water's edge.

'Catch me if you can!' She sprinted into the shallows, steeling herself for the inevitable chill on her warm skin. The touch of ice bristled and she could feel her whole body shudder and tingle with the autumn freshness of the lake. Looking down, she saw her pale feet tinged green with the cool water which lapped at her knees. Her hand stroked up over her waist and she lightly touched one hard nipple, watching the tip tighten further with her cold fingers. She scooped water in her cupped hands and trickled it over herself, shivering as the rivulets ran like icy fingers over her breasts and belly.

Turning, she scooped both hands together and sloshed water back at Drummond, who hopped on one foot on the shore, struggling to pull off his heavy boots.

'Damn, that's cold!' he cried. 'I hope you don't want me to come in there and get you.'

'Of course not!' she mocked him. 'You mustn't get your poor self wet and cold.'

She panted a few times, steeling her nerves for the plunge, then threw herself forward into the water, diving under and coming up gasping and spluttering. The top few inches had been warmed by the day's sun, but under that the water was glacial; her scalp felt as if it had shrunk on to her head, and her nipples were as hard as acorns. Desperate to get her blood moving, she struck out vigorously for the centre of the lake, her feet kicking through the weed in the shallows until she reached clearer water.

'Don't go too deep! You might get cramp and then I'd have to save you!' Drummond yelled.

Lydia turned on to her back to float and watched him between her toes. He had flung all his clothes on to the shingle beach and climbed up on to the rock, his rangy form poised at the overhanging edge as he prepared to dive. His body hit the water and sliced it with knife-like precision, then he disappeared with a sharp kick of his legs. Lydia waited for him to surface. He stayed under for a long time, then burst up a few feet away from where she floated, snorting and shouting at the freezing temperature.

He stood chest-deep and swiped his hair back from his eyes, blinking and grinning at Lydia. She thought how little he had changed since boyhood: his exuberance was undimmed, despite the difficulties he faced with his brother.

'This is the coldest water I've been in since I swam in a lake in Acadia,' he gasped, sinking into the water and swimming over to where Lydia calmly floated with her toes wriggling above the surface.

'Where's Acadia?' she asked.

'In the Americas,' he replied. 'It's the New World. Everything is so big over there: the trees here would look like knee-high stumps in comparison.'

Lydia glanced at the tall trees which shaded the lake and smiled with disbelief. Then she dipped her head back and gazed up at the rapidly darkening sky. She could feel the lapping of tiny wavelets as Drummond swam closer, then the warmth of his breath on her ear as he moved behind her. His legs came up beneath hers and he slid one arm around her, under her breasts, and moulded his body to hers in the cold of the lake.

They floated like that for some time, then Drummond shifted under her and she could feel the hardness of his cock pressing against the curve of her buttock. It felt smaller in the water, kept thin by the cold, and she wriggled against it, letting the solid head bounce against the crease of her buttocks.

'The water's too deep here: let's swim into the shallows,' he whispered.

When they were in only a few inches of water, he lay back on the sandiest part of the beach and pulled Lydia on to him so that she lay nose to nose with him, her legs slightly apart and her toes resting in the water. Their lips bumped and then joined, and she felt herself being pulled into his warm embrace, her chilled body gently heated by his vitality and her own anticipation. She raised herself slightly and reached for his cock, but his firm hand stilled her.

'Wait,' he said. 'We can do something better.'

He whispered in her ear and Lydia giggled.

'That won't work.'

'Believe me, it does.'

'Stay still, then.' She raised herself above him and used the shallow water as a lubricant to smooth her passage as she swept her body up and down him, the plumpness of her sex brushing his muscular lower abdomen and rubbing the underside of his cock as it hardened towards his navel. She moved faster, the water easing her movements, and she felt him jerk to rock-hard proportions under the sweeping glide of her body. The gradual pressure of his rigid length on her mons aroused her in a very subtle way, and she moved faster and harder, grinding herself down on him, watching the changing expressions on his face below her. The sight of his pleasure increased her own, and when she felt him jerk between the compression of their bellies, she cried out triumphantly. He gripped the back of her neck, pulling her down for an open-mouthed kiss, their bellies sliding slightly on the hot pool of come.

'Where did you learn how to do that?' she asked, sitting up and easing her legs astride.

He smiled and shook his head, then rolled her over until she was underneath him, her body shadowed by his and her back pressed into the wet sand. He scooped handfuls of water and trickled it over her, making her arch up as she felt her skin prickle and her nipples extend with the cold. He then picked up a handful of smooth round pebbles and began to arrange them on her body: one on each of her nipples, one in her navel, a line between her breasts which snaked down to her bare sex. He trailed a stone lightly over her there.

'Where's your hair?' he asked. Lydia felt herself blush; her whole body became hot and embarrassed as her mind considered various explanations. Glancing up at him, she saw enquiry and amusement in equal measures in the depths of his golden-brown eyes. She thought of the question she had just asked him, then mimicked his reaction by smiling and shaking her head.

He laughed, then bent his head to her mouth and plunged his seeking tongue between her lips. She sucked him in, and, when she felt his hand press her thighs, she let her legs fall open. She felt a cold, hard pressure as he placed a stone there, and she froze for a moment, but pleasure soon overcame her reluctance and she let her limbs fall heavy and loose, allowing him do as he would.

He filled her with smooth stones, each one the size and shape of an egg. Then he made her tighten herself on to the stones repeatedly, while he flicked the roughened edge of his thumb over her clitoris until it swelled and she could feel her whole body begging for release. She relaxed under his hands and he played with her, smoothing her sex then squeezing the flesh until it pouted, glossy and engorged. He coaxed, cajoled, and finally put his mouth to her, until she capitulated and shuddered on to him, calling his name and gasping with the intensity of her climax and the muscles that oscillated on the cold hard stones inside.

'What are you doing sitting there in the dark? You made me jump.' Lydia leant against the cool timber of the door and held her hand to her throat, her heart thumping and forehead prickling with fear. Angel rose from the low stool by the fire and advanced across the darkened room.

'I was waiting for you,' she said. 'You've been gone for hours.'

'Since when has it been any concern of yours? I'll go where I want, when I want. I get enough of this from Valerian, so don't you start telling me what to do.' Her voice was harder than she meant it to be. Part of her mind had told her that the dark shadow awaiting her was Valerian, back early, and it was only when Angel had lit a candle that the relief had flooded through her.

'I was just worried, that's all.' Angel's voice was now low and soothing: she stood close to Lydia and laid one hand on her arm. 'You're freezing, and your hair is wet! What's happened to you? Are you hurt?' Her firm hand drew Lydia into the room and closer to the warmth of the glowing grate. 'There are thieves in this region, did you know? The master was set upon late the other night: that's why he has that cut on his cheek. And two masked men were seen at the gates yesterday. I've heard that they only steal to give money to the poor, but they wouldn't hesitate to do something worse to you. It would be too tempting. Miss Lydia, have you been set upon?'

Although her words were gentle and sympathetic, Lydia could detect the frisson of excitement and vicarious pleasure in Angel's voice. She caught the girl's hand and pushed her back down on to the stool.

'Oh, it was terrible! They chased me through the woods and –'

Angel's hands flew to her mouth, her eyes wide and bright above them.

'How many?' she gasped.

'Three,' said Lydia, beginning to enjoy herself. 'They all wore dark masks so that I couldn't see their faces, and cloaks with golden clasps and hats pulled down low over their fierce eyes! As they chased me, their cloaks swirled behind them, catching the wind and rippling in the night air. I reached the lake and there was no escape, so I turned to face them. They were so close that I could see their terrible eyes shining like wolves as they circled me and surrounded me. One of them had a golden earring which glinted in the moonlight. Another had a knife: a long silver blade that he held between his teeth as he advanced.'

Angel sat motionless, simultaneously horrified and enthralled, and Lydia could see her knuckles whiten as she squeezed her hands together in her lap. Encouraged, she licked her lips, her mind racing as she dropped to her knees in front of the other girl.

428

'The one with the earring caught my wrist and jerked me towards him. I struggled, twisting my arm and trying to shake him off, but his grip was so strong, like a thick rope. He dragged me up the shingle and threw me into the arms of the third man, who waited at the edge of the beach. They laughed and spoke in a strange tongue, or two of them did, for the one with the blade in his mouth was silent throughout. The third man had a strange mark around his neck, a painting of many colours, and when he came close to me I could see that it was the likeness of a serpent that coiled around him, its tail disappearing into his shirt. Its huge striped head was painted across his throat, so that when he swallowed the fangs seemed to move and bite.'

Lydia warmed to her theme, holding Angel's hands in her own and squeezing her fingers, feeling the other girl wriggle a little on the stool and seeing her breath begin to come a little faster, her eyes dewy with partly concealed excitement.

'The serpent-man held me from behind, pulling me by the wrists so that I was stretched up and had to curve my arms around the back of his head, knocking his hat off. That made him angry: he thrust his knee into the back of my legs and grunted something in my ear. His partner, the one with the earring, slapped my face and told me in broken English to be careful, that they didn't want me to be able to recognise them again. Then he leant forward and bit my neck, while sliding his hand down the whole length of my body, pausing just long enough at my breast to squeeze and pinch my nipples. After that he moved lower, lifting up my skirts and showing the Blade my naked thighs.

'The Blade bent over too, and they both inspected me closely; I could feel myself growing hot, blushing beneath their scrutiny, and I twisted, trying to hide from their piercing eyes. The Serpent hissed in my ear, something cruel that frightened me, and I held on to the back of his neck, desperate not to let go and fall to the ground lest the other two pounce on me. The Serpent felt strong and I clung to him. His hands wound round me from behind and grasped my waist, pushing my hips out with a flick of his wrists and tilting me towards the Blade.

'The Blade stood up and stared into my eyes: his were cold and blue, the palest blue that you ever saw, like chips of bone. He stared for a long time, then took the knife out of his mouth and placed it on my breastbone. The point was sharp and I knew that if he applied the slightest pressure it would pierce my skin, slide into me, enter my breast, breach my heart. I was terrified, but then he did something even more horrible.'

She paused, her gaze fixed on Angel's face, aroused by the trembling of the girl's plump bottom lip and the feverish sheen which pearled her pale skin. She gave tiny panting breaths and her eyes were glazed and wide. Lydia knew that she was almost insensible to her surroundings, that she could touch the girl anywhere and the other would think that it was one of the three brigands, for she was totally immersed in the tale.

'He opened his mouth and tried to lick his lips. But he couldn't. Because at some time his blade had worked its cold magic on him. He had only the shortest stump of tongue, thick and hard, and he curled his lips up and leered at me. I knew that although he could not speak, he could use that tongue to terrible effect, so I tried to look unafraid, but inside my body was trembling and petrified. I felt everything turn to water and my limbs became useless as the Blade and the Earring snarled at the Serpent and he laid me down. I could feel the shingle under my back, sand broken with tiny hard stones. I tried to protest, to move, but they filled my mouth with some vile and oily rags; then they turned me on to my stomach and stretched my arms and legs out, driving thick stumps into the ground to tie me to. I struggled and kicked, but they were so strong: the Earring's hand felt like a huge weight that had been dropped on to my left ankle. Strangely, he was also the most gentle, for his other hand crept up my inner thigh

430

like velvet, softly, smoothly, until he reached the crease of my buttock and fingered the bare flesh there. He was like fleece against my tortured skin and I closed my eyes to savour such tenderness.

'Suddenly I felt the point of a knife at my neck and I gasped, almost choking on the oily rags. The Blade sliced my clothes from neck to hem and tore them open, so that I felt the chill of the night air on my back and legs. There was no pause to savour the sight, as before. Almost instantly, I felt cruel fingers prise my buttocks apart and the sharp sound of someone spitting. I felt his saliva hit my bottom, warm and wet, and tried to close myself against him, but I was powerless. The Blade knelt between my thighs and pressed his mouth down, his short tongue pushing against me, the hard stump opening and probing as his teeth grazed the rosebud flesh there. At the same time I felt something hard against my sex, something unyielding and terrible. I thought at first that it was his cock. But no, it was the hilt of his dagger. He pressed it up into me, fucking me with it, plundering me with the dirty plaited leather handle, and while my mind said "No, please, no!", my body betrayed me utterly and I felt myself melt against the rough thing that stretched my tender parts and rubbed me until I bucked my hips. When they saw that, the men became excited, the Serpent and the Earring speaking at once, and one of them pulling the Blade away. He fought them at first, his huge fists flailing while his deformed tongue and the hilt of his weapon did their deed; but they were two against one and he succumbed to their superior strength.

'I thought I was saved and that they would let me go. I felt a blessed relief, but also a strange burning disappointment that flared in me and died the minute the Earring knelt between my outstretched legs. His fingers were gentle, easier to bear than the other's tongue and hilt. He stroked me, opening me softly, and I could feel my bottom flare under his tutelage as he coaxed me. He

431

spent a long time there, easing me open, until I longed for him to do something more.

'I felt his breath on the back of my shoulder as he curved his body to mine, felt the bristle of his spiky chin and smelled the fresh sweat which clung to his body, tempered by the dark odour of his leather coat. He was heavy and I felt crushed beneath him, small and frail but very alive, as his cock pushed neatly between my gaping buttocks and he breached the tight muscle there. Slowly. So slowly.

'He filled me.

'We were both still, and I could hear the slick sound of hand on flesh and turned my head to see that the Serpent had knelt before my face, his wet cock in his hand. He slid his fist up and down the engorged length, and I felt my arousal grow to fever pitch as he pulled the oily gag away and plunged the fingers of one hand into my mouth. He coated himself with my saliva. His fingers tasted bitter, strange, and I knew that I could cause him great pain if I bit down. He knew this too, for he watched me. His eyes became the colour of melting chocolate as his gaze held mine, and I noticed the thick lashes which fringed his eyes: they were so silky and long, and his eyes so soft and pleading, that I did not bite, but simply ran my tongue along the groove between those fingers and wet them as much as I could. He used this to lubricate the passage of his hand along his shaft, and I watched as he stroked himself to full hardness next to my face.

'By the time that he pressed his glans to my lips, I was ready to beg.

'I lay there, pegged to the little stakes, my body a starfish that had been washed up on the shingle of the beach, my mouth full of hard cock and the taste of the sea, while my flesh was stretched and filled from behind by a nameless man who kissed my bare shoulder with lips of fire. I reached with my bound hand and the Blade knelt, fitting himself to my palm, and I pleasured

432

them while they pleasured me, in the dark, by the lake in the silver gleam of the full moon.'

'What happened? Did they – well – you know – did they –?'

'Yes, Angel. They did. But not until I had achieved mine. I felt myself lifted: not bodily, but in my mind. The tingling that began at the top of my spine released my head to float and soar above the scene, and as I felt the first trembling waves deep inside me I could see myself, and the three men, through a blurring haze of sensation as I rippled and tightened on the sand while my mind was set loose and free. They felt it too. The Serpent was the first to come: my tongue was too sweet for him to bear, and I swallowed his lust as he pumped his hips and gripped my head tight with his hard hands. The Earring gasped a string of foreign words and I felt him tense, then release himself. He was hot: hot as the poker when you leave it in the fire, and I felt him scald me inside and clenched myself to keep him in.

'The Blade saved himself for the last victory. His face contorted, and I could see the stump of his tongue as he tried to speak his pleasure, but no words came. His cock jumped in my fist and he reached down to grasp his own balls, pulling and twisting them to milk out the last drop, as it fell on my arm and creamed the nakedness of my shoulder.'

Angel slowly let out the breath she had been holding. She closed her eyes briefly, and when she opened them she fixed them on Lydia's face. Her hands were warm as they slid up to cup her chin and she bent quickly, before Lydia could move, and devoured the other girl's mouth with her own.

They went to the floor in a tumbling embrace. Angel pulled at the laces of Lydia's bodice until her breasts were bare and golden in the dying firelight. Lydia let her stroke and unclothe her, then she closed her eyes as Angel reached between her trembling thighs and pressed a finger into her in mimicry of the Earring. She filled her with fingers, plundering and stretching her tight little sphincter before testing the juiciness of her sex with her thumb.

Lydia arched and cried out, her arousal strengthened by the story she had told. She gasped as Angel used both hands to pleasure her, and then felt her teasing and licking with the very tip of her pink tongue.

When her climax had subsided, she pushed Angel roughly over the stool so that her knees were firm to the floor and her buttocks pushed out behind her. She swept up the petticoats and bunched them on the girl's back with one hand, while the other moved to the slickness between her peachy thighs.

'My name is the Serpent,' she growled, her voice foreign and hard. 'You will feel pleasure and pain in equal measures.'

Her fingers moved to the pucker between the twin crescents of Angel's pale buttocks. She placed the tip of her forefinger there and rubbed gently, teasingly, until the little mouth opened as if to kiss her: then she rammed the finger in as hard and as fast as she could, pushing and probing and revelling in the smoothness that soothed her fingertip and the muscle that gripped repeatedly at her knuckle as if it could swallow.

Leaving the petticoats to tumble to one side, Lydia stroked her other hand across Angel's hip, slipped her fingers under, and then slid them into the creaminess of her sex. She could feel the pleasure, sense the movement that was needed, and she moved accordingly: sometimes gentle, sometimes hard. Slow. Fast. Then still. Angel's soft inner flesh gripped and undulated on her fingers, and she dropped a kiss on the warm curve at the base of her spine, the little hollow that dimpled her beautiful back. She curved her body over Angel's, and they stayed still for a long time, kneeling and watching the light in the grate as the last embers died.

Chapter Eleven

'Where's Lydia?' demanded Madame, peevishly. 'We were supposed to leave at one and the clock has just struck half past.'

She tapped one foot on the slate hearth, her fingers plucking at the ribbon on the front of her sable cloak. She had been pacing the floor for some time, and now she could feel that her impatience was beginning to get the better of her.

'Clancy! Come here this minute,' she snapped. The little page came at a trot, his chubby face split from ear to ear with his usual happy grin.

'Yes, missus.'

'Run upstairs and find out what's happening with Miss Lydia. Tell her that if she tarries any longer I shall go to the Jefferson-Handley's without her.' She sat down heavily on a nearby chair, poked around in her reticule until she found her jewelled snuffbox, and helped herself to a generous pinch.

'I am here now, Madame.' Lydia came lightly down the stairs, pausing to give Clancy an affection tap on the shoulder with her fan. 'Is the carriage at the front?'

'Yes, it is. And it has been for quite some time.' Madame's mouth twisted unattractively as she looked Lydia up and down. Every time she saw the girl, she had to push away an irrational surge of jealousy. Valerian had enjoyed her far more than Claudine had expected. The pearly smoothness of her young skin, coupled with the growing air of confidence and sensuality which seemed to cling about her like an invisible perfume, served to make Claudine feel her own years acutely. She shivered, suddenly cold, as the air cut through to her thin bones. She pulled the thick sable collar closer about her shoulders.

'Come along, we'll be late. They are expecting us for dinner at two.' Turning to Clancy, she sniffed and narrowed her lips to a thin line. 'Make sure you have those red slippers cleaned by the time I get back. I wish to wear them tonight.'

Angel stood at the window near the top of the stairs, a soft cloth in one hand and a three-branch candelabra in the other. She watched the carriage bear Madame and Miss Lydia away from the house, then craned her neck against the latticed glass to watch it disappear from sight.

'They've gone, Angel.' The hair prickled on the back of her neck. 'We're alone now.'

Turning, her pulse skipping feverishly, Angel held the candelabra before her like a talisman to ward off an evil spirit.

'I'm working, milord. See, I've nearly finished this one.'

'Well, finish it then. I have a fancy to see your fingers polish and stroke the brass shafts.'

Angel hesitated.

'Proceed.' Valerian folded his arms across the blue brocade of his long waistcoat and leant back against the wall, his dark eyes fixed on Angel's slender hands. 'Proceed, my dear. Don't make me angry.'

Angel carefully placed the candelabra on the wide window-seat and applied the cloth. She had already given it a reasonable shine, and it was the work of moments to make it gleam. Her slender fingers pushed the cloth up from the base to the curling lip of one of the branches. The thick creamy candle at the top shuddered. Holding her breath, she slid the cloth down again, her hand curving over the cylindrical shaft; her actions made her feel languor instead of her usual quiet rebelliousness.

She moved to the middle section and rubbed the dull brass to a high sheen. Her own face was reflected there, slightly bowed out of shape, moon-like, and she saw that her cheeks had flushed and her bottom lip looked swollen and full as if she had been kissed. Her heart began to beat a little faster, and heat prickled beneath her arms and behind her neck. She knew Lord Hawkesworth was watching, studying her every move, and the knowledge made her rub harder and more diligently as the silence lengthened between them.

She sensed rather than heard him move behind her, his stealth that of a nocturnal animal stalking prey. Angel stood motionless, her nose full of his smell: that slightly acid citrus tang with which he dressed his hair, accompanied by the musky perfume of his clothing as it warmed with his body heat. By contrast, his hand under her chin was cool, his fingertips almost icy, and as she turned she saw that his eyes were glacial as he swept his gaze from the top of her head to the toes of the wooden shoes which peeped out from beneath the hem of her apron.

'On your knees.' His voice was so low that at first she thought she had not heard him correctly. She hesitated, and he gripped her chin, twisting the soft flesh there, forcing her face round to one side. His head thrust suddenly forward and she thought that he was going to kiss her, but his mouth barely grazed her cheek and she felt the heat of his breath on her ear lobe.

'On your knees, Angel.' The sibilance of his hiss tickled at the downy hair that curled at the nape of her neck. She shivered as she heard him laugh, a horrible low sound that reminded her of a metal spoon being

437

scraped around the inside of a saucepan; she gritted her teeth.

'Are you afraid of me?' he asked, bringing both hands up to imprison her face and pull her upward, closer to him. She had to stand on tiptoe to ease the pain in her stretched neck.

She shook her head.

'No.'

'Wrong answer!' The shout was deafening, and Angel stared into his face, her mind rapidly working out all the possible replies.

'Yes, master. I am very afraid of you.'

The grip on her face was released and she dropped back on to the soles of her feet. She bowed her head and waited for him to speak again.

'Very good.' He gently stroked one finger from the hollow under her chin up to her mouth, following the curve of her face until his fingertip dipped between her lips and Angel could taste the bitterness that clung to his nails. She had sampled something similar before, but her head was so full of fear, and a subtle arousal, that she could not recall where. She stood still, her mouth slack around his fingers. He raised an eyebrow.

'You are supposed to be on your knees.'

The words had barely left his lips when his hands descended like weights on to her shoulders. Felled by the pressure, she dropped abruptly to the magenta carpet with a dull thud, her head bowing with shame as she realised what he intended. His left hand cupped her neck and he urged her forward with a light but definite pressure. The tip of her nose touched the immaculate cream fabric of his breeches, and she could detect the masculine smell of him behind the smooth frontage. She closed her eyes.

'Now, my dear Angel. There is something you can do for me. Something you can do for your lord and master. If you do it well then I shall reward you. If not . . . well, I would hardly like to say.'

She kept her eyes tightly closed and swallowed, dropping her chin almost to her chest. He seemed pleased by this gesture of humility, for his hand stroked the back of her neck and he bent to place a kiss on the parting of her pale hair. His mouth, unlike his fingers, was hot and seemed to burn her skin through the smooth layer of her sleekly combed hair.

'Mmm.' He moved his lips against her. 'Like silk. Everything is silk: your hair, your lashes, your eyebrows.' His lips traced the features as he named them, and she could feel the skin beneath his touch tingle and then throb. She swayed slightly on her knees, stimulated by the hot glide of his mouth over her face.

Abruptly, he seized one of her wrists.

'But not your hands, eh, Angel? No, your hands show how far beneath me you really are. Despite the care you take with your toilette, despite your aping of your mistress, you'll never be anything but my servant. A maid. What would you do if I turned you out? Nothing. You'd be on the streets.' His mouth was by her ear now, and she gave a quick little inhalation as he sank his sharp teeth into the fleshy part of her tender lobe. 'So better make it good, Angel.'

She nodded dumbly, unable to speak, determined that he would gain no satisfaction from hearing how near she was to crying.

She sensed him pull away from her and straighten up, his shirt-sleeves whispering over the satin brocade of his waistcoat. Her spine crinkled at the sound of his hands sliding on the sheer material, over his hips to the fastenings of his breeches. The top button gave under the firm pressure of his thumb, and she shuddered, unable to move away although she knew that she ought to. Her every instinct told her to jump to her feet and flee down the stairs, away from him, but her treacherous body would not obey. It made her stay. Still. With the smell of him in her nose and the sound of buttons popping through fabric as he undid himself. Her treacherous body lied to her – or was it her mind lying to her body? – as a gush of cream slicked the curves at the top of her thigh.

She felt the feverish heat of his cock as it bounced against her cheek and then stood by her ear. Without opening her eyes, she could sense the nearness and the readiness of him. She moved her head slightly, just a tilt, and her nose touched him. He was as hard as rock and as hot as a furnace, and her eyes flew open as he gripped the back of her head and levered her round.

'Suck me. Slowly,' he said, positioning her so that her lips were poised at the very end of him, and she had an uninterrupted view down his long, slender length. He smelt divine, so aroused, so ready. There was a tiny glistening drop just within reach, and she flicked her tongue out and over him, taking up the seashell tear-drop and pressing it up to the roof of her mouth, where it mixed with her own saliva and dissolved. She opened her lips and encircled him. He breathed out heavily, his eyes fixed on hers.

'Careful,' he said. He watched her intently as she kneaded the muscles of his thighs, which tightened and then relaxed under her hands. Her thumbs worked up and underneath him, cradling him and then sliding under, moving towards the tip until she could feel the pout of her own lower lip. She lightly stroked the smooth upper surface and then gripped him firmly, between thumb and forefinger, as she had seen the pipers do their flutes in the market-place. She slid her lips a little way down his engorged shaft and gave a tiny suck.

He quivered and rotated his hips. Glancing up, she saw that his head had tipped back a little and his eyes were closed. She could feel the palms of his hands, hot now, against the back of her head as he pulled her on to him with little bobbing motions and his cock slid towards the back of her throat.

Her hands slid under the warm fabric of his breeches, and she hitched them down so that they rested tight just above his knees. Her fingers walked up the back of his legs and nestled under his buttocks, her nails stroking the curve there until she felt his skin pucker and he shivered. Her hands traced the curve of his hips and dragged slightly over his flat belly before meeting over the swollen skin of his cock, which jerked against her palm as she gripped it.

Slipping her fingers gently back and forth, she revelled in the smoothness of velvet over honed steel. Then she softly lapped at the underside, her tongue flat and hard against the musky taste, as she gradually worked her way down his length until her nose ruffled the crisp hairs which collared him. Her fingers slid under and she cupped his balls, cradling them in the palm of her hand and wrapping them in her fingers. He gave a low groan of appreciation, and she felt the hairs on the back of her neck rise in anticipation.

She glided back up to the swollen glans and circled it with the pointed tip of her tongue, searching beneath the soft collar and stroking, licking, sucking lightly, feeling it straining against her. Above her she heard a hoarse moan and a laboured exhalation as he closed his lips and flared his nostrils. She took him in deeply, warming him with the soft insides of her mouth, then slid down and began to move more definitely against him: more pressure, tongue curved, lips tighter as she felt him swell and grow to greater hardness. Her fingers gripped his hard buttocks, preventing any escape, and she felt his hands flutter over her hair, loosening it.

There was a tiny sound as one of her pins fell to the carpet and bounced, coming to rest on the polished timber at the edge of the stair, under the banister. Then silence, as the thick skeins of hair were gathered and bunched around her ears, muffling and shutting out the sound of the world until she felt as if they were the only people in it, the only two people alive. And pleasure the ultimate reward. Her own arousal was hot and thick, and she felt her sex swell, the lips there as pouting and wet as the ones that fellated him.

He came, with sudden white-hot spurts and a heady

441

pulsating of his cock against her tongue. He gave a sharp cry and thrust his pelvis forward, knocking his glans to the back of her throat, and Angel swallowed around him, her mind on fire and her own juice trickling down her leg as if what she absorbed had gushed through a hollow vessel and pooled on the magenta carpet below. She felt him gradually relax and bend over her slightly, both of his hands stroking her jaw and cheeks. When she looked up, she saw that his dark eyes gleamed as he buttoned his breeches.

'Thank you,' he said. The words sounded unfamiliar on his lips, as if he rarely said them and was not quite sure of their meaning.

'Oh, no, milord. Thank you.'

He raised an eyebrow and then frowned, his hands sliding into the pockets of his breeches and pulling the fabric taut over his subsided cock. Angel dragged her gaze away and looked up to meet his eyes.

A secretive smile curved her lips. She took a step forward until she stood very close to him, the top of her head just level with his chin. Placing her hands on the smooth brocade that stretched across his wide shoulders, she rose on to tiptoes and paused momentarily before kissing him full on the lips. She felt his mouth open a fraction under hers with his surprise, and she felt the tingling contact as she flicked her tongue out, just once, to lightly touch his. Then she turned away from him to pick up the candelabra and cloth.

She hummed a little tune as she began polishing, and was aware that he did not move for a long time: his curious eyes seemed to burn into the skin of her back. Then he was gone, as silently as he had approached, and she was alone again.

She slid the thick creamy candle out of the holder and caressed the rounded end lightly before slipping it into her apron pocket. Kneeling, she rubbed the cloth over the silvery, crystalline patch which caught the light on the dark carpet; it took a few moments, but soon it was gone, Angel sat back on her heels, wondering how long

442

she would have in the privacy of her attic bedroom to slake her own arousal.

'Thank you so much for dinner,' Lydia murmured, her eyes downcast as she tried to avoid the lecherous gaze of Oswald Jefferson-Handley. His grip on her hand, warm and slightly slimy with excessive perspiration, did not lessen, and she thought for one horrible moment that she would have to publicly shake him off. He was a huge barrel of a man, almost as wide as he was tall, but his flesh did not have the jocund ruddiness of many country squires: Oswald was pale and mealy with skin the colour and consistency of cold porridge. A vague odour of urine clung to his clothes, and Lydia privately wondered whether it was his own, or that of the skinny dogs who shadowed his every move.

She gave her hand a little tug; he squeezed her fingers with his own, the pressure turning the nails an ugly yellowish-white. He smiled at her, his pale eyes glassy and his mouth working as if he sought to rid his gums of some remnant of stale food.

'Come now, Ossie!' His wife Rosamunde, the former Honourable Lady Rosamunde Bentley and an old London friend of Madame's, tapped his arm with an ornate fan. 'Leave the girl alone.' She turned to Madame and her mouth curled in a conspiratorial smile. 'Claudine, darling, I shall see you in town very soon. I'm so grateful for your visit: you've quite cheered me up by bringing this delightful young lady to see me. She really is very easy on the eye.'

The two women stood side by side and pushed the odious Oswald behind them, almost out of sight. Lydia felt herself blush to the roots of her hair as their appraising eyes swept the curves of her body.

'Maybe you'll bring her to town?' murmured Rosamunde, her full red lips pursed assessingly. Claudine frowned a little, as if thinking.

'Yes,' she said. 'I think she will do very well there, don't you? With a little training.'

'Yes. A little training would go a long way.' Rosamunde reached a hand up to smooth the light layer of powder on her rich auburn hair. '*Au revoir*, then, my darling. And good day to you, Miss Hawkesworth. Ossie will hand you into the carriage.'

Lydia endeavoured to climb the three steps without assistance, but Oswald was there with a speed which belied his bulk. His hand trailed across her ankle; she aimed a quick little kick sideways and felt it connect with his knuckles. Satisfied, she settled into the corner of the carriage and sulked out of the window, disgusted with Oswald for being so familiar, and furious with Madame for showing her off like a possession.

As the cultivated lawns of the parkland gave way to the tangled hedgerows of the local countryside, Madame sighed and picked at an imaginary piece of fluff on the flawless satin of her full-skirted gown.

'I don't know why you have to be so objectionable, Lydia.'

'I was not objectionable. I was perfectly polite to your horrible friend and her disgusting husband. You have no cause to complain.'

'If you deem it polite to mope over the soup and cast a sour eye over the syllabub, then you English have even worse manners than I have previously credited you with. And as for kicking dear Ossie. It was most unnecessary.' She glanced out of the window and then sneaked a look at Lydia. 'But I have to confess to wishing that I had done it first. You realise that she only married him for his money, don't you? We're all waiting for black-edged funeral invitations and then we can all relax again. Rosamunde will be back on the scene, thrilling all and sundry once more.'

'Was she one of Valerian's lovers, too?' Lydia wished that she had not asked; a sick feeling almost overwhelmed her and she found that she did not want to hear the answer. The snort of laughter that greeted her question served only to deepen her misery.

'*Mon dieu*, no! Rosamunde's wonderful breasts are far

too – too – womanly for a man like him. No, Valerian prefers his girls to be like boys.' She straightened in her seat as if to accentuate her own narrow chest and hips. 'That's why you'll never be anything more than a passing fancy, a diversion, as I've said before – why are we stopping?' She tapped her fan on the communicating panel and raised her voice. 'Why are we stopping, coachman?'

There was no reply. Only an ominous silence. Dappling shadows from a roadside tree rippled across the polished interior of the motionless carriage, and Lydia held her breath. She suddenly knew why they had stopped, and she waited to hear the familiar cry of 'Stand and deliver'.

None came.

'This is ridiculous!' Madame gathered her skirts in one hand and leant forward to look out of the window. 'Grief, the man's running away. Come back here: come back here at once!'

A shadow fell across the doorway, and Lydia stifled a giggle. The look of shock on Madame's face was mirrored in Drummond's astonished eyes as he quickly pushed his mask back in place. That he had expected Lydia to be alone was obvious, and for a moment she enjoyed his discomfort at the tangle his audacity had thrown him into. Leaning forward, she grasped Madame's sleeve and shook it.

'Oh, Madame,' she gasped, her voice high and full of feigned alarm. ''Tis an evil highwayman. He'll rob us blind and steal our virtue. What can we do?'

Madame glanced at Lydia with impatiently pursed lips, and then stared back at the highwayman. Her blue eyes travelled the length of his body, and Lydia could see her lecherous thoughts as plainly as if she had spoken them. Her gaze lingered on the muscular thighs which were just visible beneath his short, stout coat, and then drifted up to inspect the width of his shoulders and the bronzed jaw which twitched slightly under her scrutiny.

'Well, well, well,' she murmured, lifting her hand to the neckline of her gown as if to protect her modesty. 'A highwayman! And a handsome one at that, I judge. We mustn't disappoint him: come Lydia, your money.'

'I have none,' protested Lydia. 'Give him yours.'

Madame laughed, her hand patting her reticule which rested on the seat beside her.

'Monsieur Highwayman, it seems we are at your mercy. My friend has no money, and I confess that I too have travelled without any.' Her eyes searched his face, a look of blatant challenge making her blue eyes gleam brightly.

Lydia watched as Drummond coughed into his glove, and she wondered how he would extricate himself without causing suspicion. He stepped nearer to the window and took Madame's hand in his. It lay on the rough surface of his dark glove like a slender flower, pale and delicate and trembling slightly. He regarded the hand for some moments, deep in thought, and then smiled up at its owner.

'My dear lady, it would be rude of me to steal from so gracious and beautiful a traveller. I shall be on my way with nothing more than a kiss to your tender hand.' He bent his head, and Madame remained motionless as he pressed his lips to her bare skin, lingering over her hand. Lydia saw a look of secret hunger stiffen Madame's face: it was as if a mask had fallen over her features, turning her to porcelain. Only her eyes seemed alive, burning as they moved assessingly over the breadth of the man's shoulders. Lydia glanced from one to the other, waiting to see how each would react.

'A gentleman thief,' said Madame, her voice slightly breathless as if the tight lacing of her bodice suddenly constricted her movements. 'Forgive me, sir, but you'll make a poor footpad if all you are going to steal are kisses. I imagine that you will hold fast to the maxim of "your money or your life"? I shall be sorely disappointed if you will not trade.'

Drummond straightened, Madame's small hand still

446

captive in his own. He looked at her, his eyes roving over her face, neck, and breasts, then travelling down over her gown to her tiny feet, clad in damask slippers, which rested on the dusty floor of the carriage. Lydia then met his gaze as it travelled across the floor and up over her body to her eyes. His stare seemed to sear into her, questioning, enquiring, seeking permission of a kind. She curved one corner of her lips upward in a minute gesture of complicity, unseen by Madame.

'Ladies,' he murmured. 'I shall not take your lives, for that would see me branded a murderer, but we could trade. I change my maxim, for today only, and make it "your money or your virtue". Would that be a fair exchange?'

'Yes!' Madame and Lydia both spoke at once, then glanced at each other. Drummond leant into the carriage and grasped Lydia's hand, pulling both women towards him.

'But do I have your word that neither of you will try to run? I am outnumbered two to one, as you see.'

'Oh, come, now.' Madame's voice had an edge of impatience to it. 'A man such as you should be able to keep us both so busy that neither would have energy or chance even to consider escaping. But speed is of the essence, or that damned coachman will have a search party organised and we will be discovered *in flagrante*.' She gave the door a little kick, and Drummond handed her down from the carriage.

Lydia watched him take Madame's wrist and lead her to the shadow of a large oak tree girded by leafy bushes, where he unribboned her sable cloak and spread it, fur side up, before sitting her down. He returned to the carriage and lifted Lydia bodily from the step, pulling her easily into his strong arms and bearing her to the makeshift bed.

He laid her next to Madame and stood above them, his legs astride their feet and his heavy boots firmly planted on the leafy ground. He placed his leather-clad fists on his hips and stared down, as if considering the

447

treasure he had captured. Lydia felt her heart swell with desire for him, and a sensual hunger to see his body twinned with Madame's. Her thoughts weakened her limbs and stirred a trembling lust, which began behind her knees and licked up the soft flesh of her inner thigh to heat the inside of her. She looked sideways at Madame, whose fingers picked at the lacing of her gown and whose legs were revealed up to the knee where she had begun to lift her own skirts, and her arousal deepened as the pale curves of Madame's little breasts were bared. She tentatively reached out and slid the tip of her forefinger over the ruby nipple, which hardened at her touch. She heard Drummond draw breath, and was aware of his sudden movement as he shrugged his short coat off and knelt beside them, his hands joining hers to cup and stroke the soft flesh. Two hands caressed the perfectly shaped breast: one large and leather-clad, one small and milky-pale.

Lydia pulled at the lacing and freed Madame to the waist, her eyes devouring the small bare breasts and flat stomach. Keeping her gaze fixed on Drummond's hands as they massaged and smoothed the other woman's breasts, Lydia unhooked and unlaced herself, sensing other hands – feminine hands – at her back and at the fastening of her skirts. Both women were gradually bared almost to the stockings, Madame retaining her smooth-boned stomacher and Lydia the black velvet-and-pearl cuff which braced her slender neck.

Lydia lay back on the shimmering sable cloak and shivered at the curious, sensual hunger that the fur gave as it slipped and slid under her bare limbs.

Drummond, faced with the two delectable bodies which writhed and tangled before him, wondered how best to satisfy both without neglecting either of them. He feasted his eyes on Lydia's creamy curves, partly covered by Madame's draping thigh, and on the languid softness of her violet-tinged eyelids. He gazed at the deep shadow cast by her lowered lashes, and at the puffy redness of her recently kissed lips. Madame's fingers splayed across the curve of her belly, and Lydia's hips pushed upward as if seeking the pleasure of that hand.

Feeling his cock jerk against the taut fabric of his breeches and the heat which gathered in his loins, Drummond saw in Lydia's wanton thrusting the way to satisfy them all at once: he could give Madame the fuck that she so desired, and have her give Lydia sublime pleasure and hold her there until he could have her himself. He stripped off his gloves, throwing them impatiently aside, then pulled his soft cotton shirt over his head without bothering to unbutton it. The warmth of the sun which danced between the oak branches stippled his skin and lit the curves of his muscular body with gold. He reached for Madame, his hands sliding over Lydia's legs and dwelling on the tender skin of her knees. He parted her thighs with one hand, his other sliding around Madame's hips to lift and position her.

'Kneel for me,' he said, turning her so that she was able to gaze down at Lydia's outstretched body, and he could press his chest against the length of her slender back. Her bare flesh was broken only by the satin corset which clung to her, boning her waist and keeping it tiny. He spread his hand on her thin spine between the sharp fins of her shoulder blades, and then pulled on the laces until the corset was unnaturally tight. Madame gave a tiny moan as her breath was squeezed out.

Drummond leant away slightly to consider her shape and smiled to himself with satisfaction. Her figure was beautifully shaped now, her shoulders and hips flaring above and below a tightly constricted waist. She looked feminine, curving, and wholly desirable. He bent her forward to take her but his cock betrayed him and he came before he was ready.

'Lick her. Lick the girl,' he muttered, his hand spread on her hair as he guided her head. She took no second urging; her body curved forward and she sank into Lydia, her hands spread wide on the tender pads of flesh on Lydia's inner thigh, while her tongue sought and found the hardened bud to which she fastened her lips and tongue. Beneath her, Lydia's eyes suddenly widened and she stared up at Drummond, her gaze a deep emerald which reflected the forest canopy above them, her pupils wide and black as she fixed them on his, and he felt himself drowning, sucked in and under, swirling in the vortex of her desire as she relaxed under Madame's expert tongue.

Unable to contain his own lust, Drummond stroked his hands from the deliciously corsetted waist down over the pale crescents of Madame's buttocks. Her sex was framed by the curve of her white thighs, dark and mysterious and creamed with her arousal. He played a thumb lightly over her, and she shuddered, swelling and opening to him as a fresh gush of liquid heat pouted the already puffy lips.

His nail caught on something smooth and hard and he glanced down, surprised and aroused to see that her labia had been pierced and threaded with a thick gold loop, similar to an earring. It had been positioned towards the rear of her sex and slightly restricted access to her, as well as promising a subtle friction to the entrant.

His need was suddenly urgent. He did not stop to part her or make it easy for her to receive him: he held his straining cock in one hand, rested the burning head against her, and entered, almost savagely, giving a sharp cry as she opened and then gripped him, pushing his tender skin tightly back as he plunged into her. He jerked his pelvis, impaling her in one thrust which hilted him, and he could feel her tight against his balls, the ring hard against his shaft.

He reached up and encircled her tiny waist with his hands, his fingers almost meeting around the satin corset. Using this as an anchor, he pulled out and then drove himself into her again, relishing the softness inside her which unfurled and parted over the steel of his cock. He heard her gasp and felt her legs shift, widening a little to give him better access, and he pushed his own knees forward, deep inside her now, the front of his thighs welded to hers and the sticky heat of her sex splayed against the hairs which covered his belly and groin.

Beneath them both he could see Lydia, her head tipped back and her ebony hair loosened to spill and mix with the dark sable of the pelisse on which she lay. Her eyes were closed, her cheeks flushed, and her slender arms thrown up to frame her head. One of Madame's hands cupped and squeezed her left breast, rhythmically moulding and releasing, while the other was buried deep between Lydia's thighs, and Drummond could only imagine what sensual pleasure her fingers gave as they worked in time with her tongue.

Madame seemed to sense that his attention had wandered from her, for she reached behind her and grasped his hand, roughly pulling it down to grind it over the milky folds that clamped around his cock, forcing his fingers to press and circle the hard, protruding little nub. She worked him with her hand, guiding his fingers until they were coated with her juice and slid helplessly against her. Her sudden seizing of control, her silent demand for fulfilment, made him feel lust and anger in equal measures, and he determined to tame her.

He lifted his other hand to his mouth, moistened his forefinger, and circled it into her anus, waiting for the telltale buck as his knuckle stretched her wide. He pressed down, feeling the slippery glide of his own cock through the smooth membrane separating her two sheaths, and began to move his hand in time with his hips. He felt her tighten on to him, both apertures grasping him, almost sucking at him as she shuddered with the build-up of her orgasm.

He slowed a little, cruising against her, his thrusts shorter and more paced, then he felt her senses spill over and he thrust quickly, rapidly, until she raised her head from Lydia's dark wet sex and cried out – shouted hoarsely – as her vagina gripped and spasmed, and

Drummond felt his own heated climax throb and rush through him, searing his loins and scorching his balls with red-hot sensation.

He jerked out of her and held his surging cock in one fist, crimson needles burning the inside of his eyes, as he watched the hot spurt of his come spray on to the pale skin of Madame's back and darken the crimson satin of her corset.

He fell against her, covering her body with his and pressing into the slick come which branded her. He could smell the dark perfume she had dabbed on her pulses earlier that day, could almost taste it as his lips opened around her ear and he kissed her, sucking the pearlescent lobe and drawing it between his teeth. She rubbed her head against his, and as she shifted, he saw that her hands were buried between Lydia's legs and two fingers were knuckle-deep inside.

'Don't stop now. Oh, help me.' Lydia urged her hips up towards them both, her eyes open now, wide and dark and filled with sensual need. Her hands grasped Madame's and she pulled the woman's fingers deeper into her.

With a hoarse cry, Drummond thrust Madame to one side and scooped Lydia bodily into his arms, beating hard little kisses on to her flushed face and kneading her belly, squeezing her breasts, pressing his chest to hers and seeking her tongue with his own. He could feel Madame's small hands fluttering over his buttocks, pressing his hips and legs; as he sensed what she intended, his body did her bidding, rolling over so that he lay prone and ready.

He lifted Lydia and sat her astride him, feeling the luscious wetness of her sex spreading on the hard muscle of his lower body and his ardour returned in a rush, his body primed and his cock swinging up to hook against the curve of her hip. He saw that her face was almost obscured by her long hair, thick masses of jet-black silk which tumbled to his chest and stroked his nipples. Glossy tendrils of it had caught across her cheeks, and she reached up with an impatient hand to sweep them aside as she flexed her thighs over him.

There was an extra weight on him, and Madame's legs squeezed his as she slid up behind Lydia, her hands gripping the girl's hips and easing her up until the tip of Drummond's straining shaft was poised at her plump lips and he could feel the prickle of her partly regrown pubic hair. He felt the welcoming relief of her juicy flesh engulf him as she sank down on to his body, her thighs framing his waist.

Madame stood, and moved around him on the slipping fur cloak to cup his head between her knees. Her face was upside down above him, with her curious pale blue eyes slanting at him and her rouged lips curving in a smile.

'A gentleman thief. Mmm. How well you ply your trade.' She leant forward, and he felt the butterfly caress of her lips on his for a brief moment before she reached for Lydia, catching her under the chin and pulling her forward for a full-mouth embrace. Her lips were wide on the puffy rose of Lydia's lower lip, her tongue darting and sliding over her small white teeth. Drummond could see their hands entwined in each other's hair; he could feel the tightness of Lydia's sex as she slid down over his cock; if he reached up he could touch the rosehip tautness of two pairs of nipples above him. He sighed with pleasure, and drove himself up into the gripping sheath of one woman, while cupping the hips of the other and urging her over his waiting face.

Madame shifted a little and he caught a drift of her scent, the muskiness of the sexual pleasure he had given her, and as she lowered her sex to his mouth his cock jerked to its full length, almost painfully, and he felt Lydia arch against him. He drove into her, repeatedly battering as if he would gain entry to the very depths of her soul, while his tongue plunged and thrust at the fragrant folds of Madame, drinking her, devouring her, his mouth wide and greedy as he worked her into a frenzy of grinding and writhing above him.

Lydia came first: her frustration from being so aroused and yet unfulfilled as Drummond had pleasured Madame from behind, was suddenly, gloriously, tipped over into a pulsing vortex. Her tongue thrust into the mouth that sucked at her lips, while her pelvis crushed down, grinding sensitive female flesh on to the hard resistance of the man below her. She gasped, climaxing, her head jerking suddenly back and her throat pale and arched in the shaded sunlight. Drummond felt her soften over him, her body suddenly lax and her dark head drooping towards Madame's shoulder, and his hand left the thin woman's hips to probe between her thighs and seek the golden ring that slid alternately over his nose and teeth. Looping his forefinger through it, he gave a slight, almost imperceptible, pull and hardened his tongue against the rigid clitoris which quivered in response.

When Madame came, it was silent, her body suddenly still and stiff, the only sound that of a sudden breeze rustling the leaves above them. He felt her fingers seek his nipples, and he gasped at the sudden intense pain as she pinched them hard, cruelly twisting. As her sex undulated over his mouth, a fresh gush of cream flooding his tongue, he felt his own white-hot response and emptied himself with muscular jerks of his lean hips. He heard Lydia sigh, and felt the oscillation of her muscles as she gripped him with her sex and sucked him upward, lengthening his pleasure almost unbearably.

'You'll have to help me.' Lydia went to step up on to the coachman's seat, her hands gathering the leather reins. Madame was standing beside her on the rutted path, her reticule open, tucked under her arm, and her fingers smoothly applying her customary cochineal potion to redden her lips. She glanced at Lydia, dropping the little pot back into the satin-lined bag.

'I'm not going to help you. I would have thought that you, countrified as you are, could manage to drive a

454

carriage without help from me. Besides, it'll ruin my hands to hold those smelly, dirty reins. I think we should wait here for help.'

She turned away, but Lydia grabbed at her, catching her shoulder.

'Help might not come. That man probably hasn't been paid for weeks: I should think he's cut his losses and gone home. Get up there and help me with these horses.'

'Take your hands off me this minute.' As Madame jerked herself away, her bag dropped to the ground. The button fastening popped open and the contents spilled out at their feet: the jewelled snuffbox, a tiny violet handkerchief, the pot of lip colour, and a velvet pouch which clinked as it hit the hard-packed mud of the road. The neck of it gaped loosely and a handful of glittering gold coins spilled out. Lydia stared at them, then nudged the nearest with the toe of her shoe.

'Why, you had money all the time. There must be thirty sovereigns there! Why didn't you give it to him?'

Madame knocked Lydia's hand off her shoulder, one thinly pencilled brow raised enquiringly as her eyes traced the girl's nose and mouth.

'Would you really have preferred it if I had? And if you say yes, then I shall call you a liar. Now drive the coach.'

Chapter Twelve

'Tell me again,' urged Valerian, his voice thick with lust.

Madame was in front of him, her skin naked and softly lit by the dozen or more candles that lined the walls of Valerian's study. She sat on a dark wooden chair, the seat of which had been carved out to leave just a wide rim; the occupant could make themselves comfortable, but also allow access from below. Heavy drapes were drawn across the window to shut out the night, and a low fire glowed in the grate. Valerian knelt on a soft rug, fully clothed, but with a look of naked lechery etched across his handsome features.

'Again?' she asked.

'Yes, tell me again. I want to hear it again.' His hand worked at the crotch of his breeches briefly, but Madame kicked it aside.

'I said that you were not to touch yourself!'

'Oh, please!' he begged, bending at the waist as if in pain. 'Please, if I mustn't, then you do it. I need it.'

'Well, you'll have to need it a little more than that, if you are to satisfy me.' Her long nails played over the flat plain of her stomach and then upward to count each rib that jutted through the translucent ivory skin of her chest. Her gleaming eyes never left his, and her mouth

456

was set in a stern line, rouged this time with a dark shade that matched the amethyst rug on which Valerian kneeled. Her nails reached her breasts and she toyed with them, leading his eyes inexorably to the taut nipples that pushed out to her own touch, the ruby centres proud and stiff as they reared from the flattened discs of her dark areolae. She pulled them, leaning forward slightly as if she would offer them to his mouth, but when he leant forward she lifted one foot and placed it flat against his chest. She raised her eyebrows at his groan of agonised disappointment.

'Exactly which part do you wish to hear again? Would it be the secret dalliance I had with Rosamunde today while the others innocently ate their dinner around us?' Her fingers dropped to her thighs and she stroked them gently, her thumbs easing slowly inward in ever-decreasing circles. 'It was so easy to slip off my damask slippers and do this with my toes. You know how brilliant my toes can be. Altogether more brilliant than my fingers at times. Look: this is what I did to Rosamunde, and not a soul saw, except perhaps the footman, and Rosamunde has him under strict control.'

Her forefingers, in a mime of what her toes had done, slid over the plumpness of her sex and eased back the hood of her clitoris. One thumb, covered with a thimble-like ring, rubbed lightly over the surface. The ring was covered with a series of bumps and grooves, giving it the appearance of a minute bunch of grapes. As she toyed with this, Madame closed her eyes and concentrated on the sensation, her breathing rapid and her legs trembling. To give herself better access, she hooked one leg up over the arm of the chair, knowing that the sight of her – open and vulnerable – would push Valerian to the limits of his endurance.

'Or perhaps you would prefer to hear about this afternoon in the woods, when the masked man bent me forward and pushed my face into your delicious cousin. He opened me from behind and took me savagely, his cock wide and splendid as it stretched me, before thrusting his finger into my arsehole and twisting it until I cried out. I swear, Valerian, he was almost as good as you.'

She pouted her thin, purple-stained lips and leant forward, interested to gauge his reaction. As she could have predicted, his face flushed a dark angry red and the veins in his neck stood proud, bulging lividly above the soft white collar of his shirt.

'No one is as good as me,' he snarled.

'I said almost, my love. Almost.' Her voice was soothing now, soft and maternal; she beckoned him to her. He fell forward on to her lap, and she cradled his head against her breast, her fingers stroking his hair.

'No one could ever be as good as you, Valerian,' she whispered. 'Unless, of course, you had a brother.'

'My brother is dead!' He jerked out of her arms, his eyes black and malicious as he stared at her. 'Don't you ever forget that. He'll never be better than me again and I'll prove it!'

'Show me,' hissed Madame, her eyes glittering, her breasts jutting out and her sex suddenly full and heavy. She loved Valerian when he was roused with fury. His rages were always the most potent aphrodisiac, and she rarely missed an opportunity to provoke him. The ancient rivalry between Valerian and his late brother was a newly discovered vice, and she decided to use it to push his prowess to the limits. 'Show me how much better you can be. Would he do this? Or this?' Her hands moved swiftly from her breasts to her sex, and she used her fingers as if they were a man's penis, hard and stiff against her swelling skin.

Valerian gave a low, throaty groan, the sound of an animal that had been teased beyond all tolerance. He lunged forward, gripping her knees and pushing her back so that her spine hit the chair with a crack. She laughed mirthlessly, her eyes goading him, and her hands fending him off as he struggled to grasp her wrists and pin them forcefully down on the armrests.

'Oh, he'd be stronger than that,' she taunted him.

458

'He'd overpower me quickly and pin me down to take me: rough and totally in control. He wouldn't care for my pleasure, only his own.'

Valerian stood up, resting his booted foot between her legs at the front of the chair. His mouth curled with distaste, and his hand shot out and grasped a handful of her hair at the top of her head, pulling her upright and curving her body forward so that her sex was jammed painfully against the hard toe of his shiny leather boot. He shook her by the hair, his eyes black and burning, and she felt herself sucked into their bottomless depths as she stared back at him. His mouth came down hard on hers and he ground her lips with his own, his teeth bruising and tearing as if he would devour her mouth. She thrilled at his savagery, her heart pumping and the blood swishing in her ears as she eagerly kissed him back.

Gasping, he jerked his mouth from hers and wiped it with the back of his hand before tearing at the fine lawn of his shirt. The front gave with a loud rending sound which seemed to split the air around them, and he used the pieces to bind her wrists and pull her arms taut above her head, standing on the chair between her legs to tie the ends tightly to a hook set in the beam above them. He dropped back down and stood still for a moment, his upper lip curved in a leering smile.

'Is this the best you can do?' asked Madame, her sex swelling into the hole carved in the seat of the chair, her arms stretched painfully up above her head. 'If your brother were alive, he would have had me by now. I'd be screaming for more and he'd know how to give it to me. You're just a pale shadow of him, that's all you've ever been: that's why –'

'Shut up! Shut up, or I'll make you.' Valerian's hand cracked across her face. His signet ring caught her jaw and she winced, pain sending fresh waves of arousal shooting through her taut body. The look of tortured suffering which clouded his face made a secret frisson of pleasure spiral up her legs, and she curled her toes in anticipation, widening her knees and thrusting her sex forward to show him how ready she was. She could feel the slickness between her thighs, smell the spiciness of her own vibrant scent, and she felt suddenly desperate for his touch – any touch – any satisfaction – as long as it was hard and fast.

Valerian turned and strode away from her, and she mewed with frustration, thinking for a moment that he intended to abandon her. He reached the door and turned the key in the lock, then jerked it out and carried it back to where she sat. His fingers caressed the forged iron key momentarily, then he reached down and prised her sex open before pressing the cold key to her clitoris. She bucked under the pressure and he laughed, a low and malevolent sound, then took one of the torn remnants of his shirt from the floor and bound her, winding the fabric strip around her sex and strapping the icy metal to her. She writhed a little as the narrow, cold key pressed unbearably against her, then she whimpered as he kissed her again, hard and demanding, his tongue probing her mouth and throat until she gagged.

He tore his lips from hers, and dropped to the floor out of her line of vision; she half-closed her eyes, tilted her head back, and waited for the next barrage of cruel sensation to hit her. She could see his long black boots stretched out on the amethyst rug, his toes pointing upward as was the huge bulge in his breeches. She longed to lean forward and grasp him there, to squeeze and knead. But her hands, bound to the beam above, kept her still and in position.

She waited, then jumped as if she had been burnt. Something warm, wet, and soft probed her from below, through the hole in the seat. She squirmed with pleasure, part of her wanting to evade, and part of her needing to press herself down on the circling wetness.

It was his tongue. Long and rigid, he pressed it around her from below, easing it between the engorged folds of her sex, then giving long deliberate strokes to the fleshy grooves. She felt his forefinger penetrate her, and she sighed, tightening herself on to the length of his probing finger; he introduced a second finger, then a third, while his tongue played with the golden ring that pierced her. The combination of soft and hard, stroking and penetrating, cold key and warm breath, made her quiver, and she thought that she would die if he did not fill her. A slick of her musky juice eased his passage, and she sensed a fourth finger stretch her; she moaned, and exhorted him in a low voice to take care. He ignored her, pushing further in, the ring taut now against her full flesh, and she heard him speak through a haze of painful pleasure.

'I'm using my whole hand. He wouldn't do that to you; he wouldn't fill you. I know what you like. Only I know what you desire. Say it. Say you love only me. Say that no other can satisfy you as I can. Tell me the truth: that I'm the best.'

'No,' she gasped, unbearable ecstasy filling her body and tightening her swollen sex on to his hand. 'No. He would do better. You have no imagination. I am nowhere near my climax.'

'God's blood, I'll make you say it!' His other hand reached up, and she felt the sting of his palm as he slapped the cheeks of her arse. His fingers continued to work inside her, filling her to the brim with pleasure, but then a new, teasing sensation opened her, and she felt his tongue prepare the way for his other hand.

She was as full as she could be, her sex wide open and her clitoris throbbing beneath the key, when she felt his thumb ease and twist into her anus. She tried to close against it, sure that she could not accommodate more, but he pushed beyond the tightness of her sphincter, aiming upward and inward until she could feel his fingers rubbing his thumb through the membrane that separated her there. He moved his hands separately, one going inward as the other eased outward, and she felt herself relinquish control and let go, her body turned to water, to cream, to burning oil as she came, hard, on to his hands. He was instantly still, just pressing up, while she rocked and quaked on the chair, a guttural cry wrenched from the depths of her body.

Almost before she had finished, he slid his hands out of her and came up between her legs, his face flushed and his breathing rapid. He knelt before her, then stood to release the bindings that stretched her up. Her arms felt useless, cramped, but he did not appear to know or care; he picked her up like a rag-doll and held her to him, his cock painfully hard against her pubis.

'You'd never come like that with anyone else but me, and you know it.' His lips tore at hers again, biting, licking, covering her mouth with his. He half-carried, half-dragged her to his desk and pushed her over it, face down. She laid a cheek on the cool surface, gently inhaling the waxy aroma of the polish, and thought of the flaxen-haired maid who polished the wood. She imagined her leaning over the desk, duster in hand, wearing her ever so slightly too-small dress, the fabric of which clung so closely to her breasts that the darkness of her nipples could almost been seen through the worn cotton. Madame closed her eyes and shuddered, her thoughts making her insides quiver with longing and loosening a fresh wash of sexual juice to slick her already creamy thighs.

'Oh yes, he would,' she ventured, when she had regained her equilibrium a little. 'No brother of yours would have stopped there. He would have fucked me senseless. Your brother would have fucked me until I hurt, until I begged him to stop, and even then he would have carried on. His stamina was probably greater than yours.'

She yelped as his hand slapped against the cheek of her vulnerable buttock, and she could feel the reddening imprint as he reached for an abandoned riding-crop which lay against a pile of leather-bound books. The plaited leather made a taut 'thwack' as it made contact with her skin, and she gripped the opposite edge of the desk, pain and arousal coursing through her veins like hot treacle. She ground her hips against the timber underneath her, sighing and rubbing her mouth on the desk, kissing the waxy polished sheen and dampening it with her hot breath.

'Come on, little brother. Give it your best shot,' she goaded him.

She heard him grind his teeth near her ear, and felt the weight of his body as he moulded himself to her. The scent of fresh sweat caught in her nostrils, and she could feel the slickness of his chest, the perspiration that beaded him as he pushed against her with unsuppressed rage. She expected him to take her conventionally, for his hot cock to slide in front of the ring that pierced her labia; so, when the burning head of his shaft probed between her buttocks, she felt the thrilling shock of his unpredictability.

One of his hands spread her cheeks wide, the other she could feel below, and she winced as the tip of his finger caught at the gold loop and pulled it downward, dragging and pulling her anus into a vertical oval. He rotated his hips, easing himself into her with the familiar screwing motion she had seen him employ on the countless young men of his acquaintance.

Excited and hurting all at once, she jutted herself back out at him, her hands leaving the slippery table-top to come behind and grip his thighs. She held her breath momentarily, then jerked herself backward as she pulled him into her.

'Little brother, little brother,' she taunted him, through gritted teeth. 'Show me who is the best of all. Oh, *nom de dieu*. Valerian. Fuck me hard. Do it harder than your brother could ever dream of!'

Their bodies heaved and writhed; she could feel the slap of his tight balls on the back of her thighs as he drove into her, his movements frenzied and irregular. He felt huge, stretching her almost unbearably, and she wished that he had filled her sex instead. Reaching down, she used her own fingers to fill herself, pushing into her wet, aching body and squeezing her eyes shut, her forehead bumping on the desk and her breasts pressed flat on the cool wood.

She felt him stiffen and strain against her, then the familiar lambent heat as his cock resonated and jerked with muscular little tugs deep inside her. She gave one last, desperate thrust with her fingers and felt herself teeter on the brink, her senses flailing in the infinite second before she fell, gasping, into orgasm, her body gripping his with invincible, rhythmic strength. She clutched at the desk with her free hand, her head twisting round and her lips seeking his.

He gripped her neck and pulled her to him, his mouth hard against the corner of her mouth, and his breath hot as it cut across hers.

'Is it me?' he whispered.

'It's always you,' she replied, her lips stroking his and her throat constricting at the sight of his flushed and beautiful profile.

'Sam? Sam, are you in there?' Lydia tapped on the wooden panel of the stable door. Shafts of afternoon sunlight cut diagonally through the open door and caught the motes of straw dust that danced in the warm air of the stable. Dandy Beau, the old mount who had belonged to William Hawkesworth, and whom Valerian was determined to send to the slaughterhouse, whickered, and Lydia gently stroked his velvety nose.

'Still here, old boy?' she murmured, nuzzling him with the tip of her nose. He smelt of hay and saddle polish, and she felt a sudden wave of nostalgia for the days when her Uncle William had ridden him every morning, and she and the boys had followed on their ponies.

Glancing around, she wondered where the groom was. She had a letter that she wanted him to deliver, and Sam was one of the few people that she trusted not to gossip. Fingering the wax seal, she studied the curving black ink that spelled the name of the solicitor, Mr Lavendale. He had promised help if she ever needed it, and she had decided to call in the favour and appeal to him on Drummond's behalf.

Shuffling and a barely audible moan sounded through the boards just above her head.

'Sam, are you up there?'

She moved away from the stalls and stood at the bottom of the ladder that led up to the hayloft. There was silence. Dandy Beau, behind her, shifted his huge hooves on the straw, and for a moment she thought that her ears had deceived her and that his movement was what she had heard.

There was another moan, this time accompanied by a long inhalation, and she was convinced that there was someone up in the loft. She tucked the letter into her pocket, kicked off her scarlet-heeled shoes, and began to climb the sturdy wooden ladder. At the top she paused for a moment to accustom her eyes to the gloom and pick a piece of straw from her hair.

At the far end of the wide loft, a half-open door let the sunlight in from a window beyond. The corner of a low pallet was just visible, and sitting on it was the groom, his shoulders hunched and his head bowed nearly to his knees. A loose shirt hung from his body in tatters, the yellow linen stained with the slowly spreading crimson of fresh blood; as she tiptoed nearer, Lydia could see that the wide muscular back was criss-crossed with inch-wide weals.

'Sam.' She spoke softly, partly because she did not want to startle him and partly because of the thick lump that had risen to her throat. He glanced up as she reached the door, and she rested her hand on the frame to steady herself. His deep brown eyes fixed on hers, and she read in them a combination of fear and helplessness mixed with an angry dash of vengeance. He did not move or speak, and Lydia pushed the door wider before sinking to her knees in front of him. As she took his huge calloused hands in hers, she was aware of the stable odour that clung to him: the leather and hay mingled with honest male sweat and the piquant tang of tobacco from the open pouch that lay on the blanket next to him.

'Did Valerian – Lord Hawkesworth, I mean – did he do this to you?'

'Aye,' murmured the groom, his auburn head dipped as if in shame. His shoulders heaved, and Lydia frowned, reaching up so that her hands lightly touched his powerful shoulders.

'Sam, look at me,' she said gently. 'Please. I am so sorry. My cousin is an animal with no respect for people or things. I apologise for his behaviour, and I will do my best to ensure that this never happens again.'

Her fingers slid under his chin and she tilted his face up. His eyes glowed like bronze coals, and his thick brown lashes shone with unshed tears. The pallor of his skin made the sprinkle of freckles prominent on the bent curve of his nose, and a muscle worked in his jaw as he met her gaze.

'Miss Lydia, you don't have to apologise. It weren't your fault. Everyone knows what the master's like, but it don't mean that we think any less of you. We only stay because of you, and the hope that Master Drummond might one day come home. Everything will be all right then.'

'Oh, Sam. If only that could be soon.' Remembering the letter, she thrust it into his hands. 'Take this into the town for me, would you? You would be helping me more than you know.' As he rose and turned away, she stood and touched his flailed skin lightly with one finger. 'Wait. Let me wash the blood from your back: those marks look sore, and they'll heal better if they're clean.'

When she returned with freshly drawn water, she saw that he had gone to stand near the open window; a twisting spiral of golden smoke rose from the pipe in his hand and was drawn by the current of air from the casement. On a low table beside him was a mug and a leather-bound bottle which Lydia uncorked. Sniffing it, she wrinkled her nose, and then slopped a generous amount of amber liquid into the mug.

'Here. Have some of this. It might help.'

He did not take the mug from her, merely stood very still and stared down at her. She was aware of how close to him she was standing, of the proximity of his bare torso and the scent of him that clung in her nostrils. She wondered whether she should step back, move away, but found that her legs would not do her bidding. He frowned, his brow creasing with a deep vertical cleft which mirrored that which divided his stubborn chin.

'I'm no coward,' he said.

'I know you're not. But it will hurt. Drink some.'

As he took the mug, the hard tips of his fingers grazed the back of her wrist and she jerked away, clasping one hand with the other as if it had been burnt. The sensation that flashed through her body at his touch was amazing, almost as if a closed fist had punched into her belly, and she stepped back as he moved, shocked by the strength of her own desire.

Sam, his strong face set and the frown still clouding his brow, sat heavily on the edge of the nearest mattress and slugged back the brandy. Lydia stirred herself from her contemplation of the way his thighs strained at the fabric of his rust-coloured breeches. She began to tear up one of the sheets, then refilled his cup. She took a mouthful herself before dipping the corner of one of the calico cloths into the bucket of cold water.

Drawing a lantern nearer, she inspected the groom's back and winced, almost able to feel the smarting of his skin. Valerian had given him a thorough beating: the pale, freckled skin was bright red and criss-crossed with countless lash marks beaded with blood.

His body recoiled as she touched the cold cloth to his back, his muscles flickering under the skin. He hunched forward, shoulders rounded and russet head dipped so that all she could see were the rugged cords of his neck and the clean stubble of his hairline. As her fingers moved tenderly over him, she became aware of a curious stillness in the warm, scented air of the hayloft, and she slowed down, wanting the moment to last as she cossetted the fragile skin of the youth on the bed beside her.

'Does that hurt?' she asked, deliberately pressing a hard seam into one of the raw wounds. Sam shuddered and jerked forward a little, then straightened himself and leant back, shaking his head. The straw mattress rustled underneath him, and Lydia leant forward, her fingers playing over the skin of his back from his shoulders down the tapering line of his ribs to his waist.

She could feel him shuddering, trembling under her touch, and she knew then that he had felt it too: that flash of tense desire when their hands had met accidentally. She knew that he wanted her, that he was hungry for her, that his trembling was as much that of lust as of pain from his wounds. It also came to her that he would not do anything about it, that he would not move first, for he was a servant, and she the lady of the house.

Her forefinger reached the firm waistband of his breeches and she let it rest there, dwelling on the rough texture of the fabric, as she tried to imagine the hard flesh beneath. Her heart was pumping quickly, her breathing a little more rapid than normal, and she tried to slow it down, to control herself. But it was no good: she was beyond control, and she knew it.

Placing both hands squarely on his shoulders, she raised herself to her knees on the mattress behind him, her silk-skirted gown whispering against the rough blankets. She placed her mouth very close to his ear and felt him tense his muscular frame beneath her, his body bent forward slightly under the firm pressure of her breasts, like a supple bow being drawn ready for the arrow. When her nose was almost touching his hair, she breathed softly into his ear and spoke.

'Sam,' she murmured. 'Sam, are you obedient to your master?'

'Yes, miss.'

'Are you obedient to your mistress?'

He did not reply, but she could feel the labouring of his breath as he steadied himself and absorbed the import of her words. He moved his head in a tiny dipping movement that she took to be affirmative.

'Look at me,' she whispered, her nose so close to his cheek that she could feel the scratch of the short bristles that stubbled his jaw and she closed her eyes, filling her senses with his animal smell and the warmth that emanated from his half-naked body.

She felt him shift on the mattress, his body twisting, and she kept her eyes closed as his hands gripped her waist and raised her up and over; over until she lay across his now supine body and their combined weight settled into the bed. His hands were tight on her hips now, and she could feel the rigidity of his thighs beneath hers and the smooth, hard flesh of his chest under the silky fabric of her bodice.

'I would never disobey you. I am your humble servant, and I would give my life for you, Miss Lydia.' His voice was hoarse, and she opened her eyes to look at him, to study the ruddy planes of his young face and trace the mobile curve of his bottom lip.

'I'm not asking for death, Sam. Only pleasure.' She dropped her mouth to his and felt a sense of glorious relief as his lips opened and she felt the warm touch of his tongue on hers. He tasted of liquor and tobacco, and she drank in his flavour as she kissed him, her lips questing his and her tongue seeking more as she felt his arms encircle her and his hands close over her.

They kissed for a long time, the mattress rustling under every tiny movement. The gentle breeze from the window gradually fanned Lydia's hair into tangled skeins which coiled and twisted like ebony serpents across the calico sheet. There were no words, only touch, and she felt her arousal like a hard shell in the pit of her stomach that abruptly cracked, falling open to reveal a molten gold yolk that trickled through her veins until it reached the farthest corners of her being.

She felt feverishly hot, then shiveringly cold; the tiny

hairs on the back of her neck lifted under the light touch of his fingers as he pulled her hair aside. She waited for him to unhook the fastenings at the back of her gown, to open it, to peel it back, to stroke her pale bare skin with the coarse tips of his workman's fingers. But he did nothing. Merely kissed her again and shifted beneath her.

She waited for him, silently begging him to undress her, but he did not move. His eyes were closed, and she raised herself on one elbow to study the shadow that his lashes cast across his cheeks. She was struck by his youth: he was younger than she was – eighteen, nineteen at the most. A sudden thought came to her in a rushing revelation.

'Sam, you have been with a woman before, haven't you?'

His eyes flickered open, deepest brown with wide black pupils that almost drowned her as she gazed into them. He blushed and frowned, his eyes dipping and a look of intense shyness colouring his face.

'No, I haven't, miss. I never have.'

Lydia was touched by his bashfulness; she stroked his hair and rested her forehead on his, forcing him to look up into her eyes.

'I'm surprised, I really am. I thought that stable-lads had the run of every wench in town. Why not you?'

'Well, there aren't many willing ones out here at Hawkesworth. The maids in the house don't care for us on the outside, so that only leaves ancient Tessie in the dairy, and I don't quite . . .'

'No, I can imagine,' agreed Lydia, smiling. Her hands slid between their conjoined bodies until she felt the hard curve of his cock beneath the buckskin front of his breeches.

'So, no girl has ever done this to you?' She arched one eyebrow enquiringly. He shook his head, a dark flush creeping up his neck accompanied by a sharp intake of breath. His eyes anchored hers, and she felt herself

470

tremble a little as the thought of untouched flesh finally sank home.

Pushing herself away from him, she sat astride, arranging her petticoats high around her legs so that he could see the pearliness of both thighs above the opaque blue of her stockings. Her knees were tight on his ribs, and beneath the curve of her buttocks she could feel his ramrod stiffness as his cock shifted inside his trousers.

'Oh, Sam. You're in for a treat,' she breathed, her fingers smoothing over the satin of his chest to dwell on the hardening discs of his brown nipples. His hands twisted out from beneath the drifting silk of her skirts and he gripped her wrists, stilling her and pulling her forward slightly.

'This isn't right,' he said. 'You shouldn't do this. Not with me.'

'Oh yes, I should. I want to. Just relax and it will be all right.'

'But, miss —'

'No buts, Sam. I know you want this as much as I do. Don't you? Or are you trying to tell me that you don't like me? Aren't I beautiful enough? Perhaps you wanted someone better for your first time?'

'Someone better?' He snorted derisively. 'You're the most beautiful lady I've ever set eyes on, but a lady is what you are, miss, and —'

'And a man is what you are, Sam. So let's stop talking and find out just what kind of a man you can be.'

Her lips were hard on his this time, partly to silence him and partly because she could wait no longer. The feel of his muscular body underneath her was almost unbearably sweet. She pulled his tongue into her mouth as she ground herself on to him. His cock jerked in reply, the hardness of his erection straining at the fabric that separated them; Lydia twisted her hands downward and wrestled with his buttons until she felt the warmth of his exposed skin. Easing her body back, she pulled her mouth from his and sat up to look at him.

He was big: long and hard with gorgeous twisting

veins and two tight balls that seemed to want to fight with each other for proximity to the base of his cock. He curved up and out of his fly with the strength and vigour of a young tree, and it was all Lydia could do to stop herself from falling on to him and taking him in her mouth then and there, but the agonised expression on his face told her how near the edge he was. Having a girl so close, and having her put her hand on him and pull his cock out of his breeches was the nearest to sexual ecstasy that the lad had ever been; Lydia decided to tread carefully for fear of having him come too soon. She wanted pleasure, too.

'Help me,' she said, sitting back and arcing her leg over and away.

She unlaced her stays, guiding his fingers to the places that needed his touch and smiling at the waves of awed wonder that broke across his face at the baring of each new piece of female flesh. The pads of his thumbs were coarse on her skin, and the callouses teased her breasts as she closed her hands around his and made him cup her, coaxing his thumbs up and over her nipples.

His touch was tentative at first, his eyes timid and his handling of her wary, but as he saw her pleasure and felt the puckering of her skin under his touch, he became more sure. Lydia found his movements inexperienced but sweet, his fingers careful but delicious as they moved down to loosen her skirts.

'Here, let me.' She stood up to let the cascade of silk and linen drop to the floor, and she saw him draw a deep breath, his hand going involuntarily to his cock. He stroked himself, and as she watched his movements, Lydia felt a welcoming rush of syrupy juice slick her insides and impatience to possess him seized her.

She moved to the edge of the bed, the late afternoon sun gilding the glossy new hairs that curled around her sex. She could feel the warmth on her naked back and relished the last moment before she conquered the youth on the bed. Then she raised one leg and swung it over his hips.

'Wait, miss. I don't think this is right. We shouldn't.' She heard his voice as if it came from a far-off place, and she frowned down at him. She could feel the heat rising from his body, the febrile warmth of his straining cock. She placed the flat of her hand against his chest and pushed him into the straw mattress.

'Shut up, Sam.'

She crested him, her warm sex unfurling as she hovered, butterfly-like, over his straining helmet. She watched him through half-closed eyes, a hint of emerald glinting between her thick lashes as she drank in the sight of the vanquished stable-boy. He lay flat against the calico sheeting, his big hands thrown wide and his head tilting, so that his strong chin jutted up as if he would kiss the lath ceiling. His Adam's apple bobbed with each swallow of the air that he gulped, and Lydia could feel by the tense stillness of his hips that he would come if she moved so much as a muscle.

'How does that feel?' she crooned, her fingers drifting lightly over his taut stomach.

He groaned and shook his head, unable to speak, but she could feel him under her, could feel the contraction of his lean buttocks as he eased himself up into her with tiny jerks, quick, slow, gasping and gritting his teeth. Leaning forward until the tips of her pointed nipples brushed lusciously against the satin of his hairless young chest, she placed her mouth close to his ear.

'Let it go. Let it go, Sam. We can do it again later.'

With a groan of long suppressed ardour, he swung his hands round to grasp her hips and hold her still while he thrust himself upward. She felt her sex anoint his shaft as she sank on to him, felt her lips wrap tightly around his length until the hard grind of his balls pressed against the gentle curve of her buttocks. With him deep inside her, she held her breath, her sex fluttering on to him and then losing him as he withdrew slightly.

He was clumsy, his fingers knotted first into her hair and then white-knuckling as he slipped down to grip her thighs with iron hardness. His movements seemed unpredictable: one thrust, then two, then a long pause as he grunted and mouthed her earlobe. Then fast, fast, fast, in a quick succession of feverish, frantic jerks that culminated in a long, hot leap of his cock as he pushed hard into her, almost hurting her as he buried himself deeply, practically punching himself into her womb. Surprised, Lydia felt a shimmering release strum along her spine and open over her hips in thick, rippling waves which resonated on to his suddenly still cock.

He tilted her chin and gazed into her face, wonder and uncertainty lightening the brown of his eyes to an amber clarity.

'Was that the same for you? Did you feel that too?' He wound his burly arms around her body and crushed her to him, his mouth bruising hers with a desperate, hungry kiss. When he was still, she let her tongue coast over his face with a myriad of tiny licks before tucking her head under his chin and resting her cheek on his chest.

She felt a contented warmth steal through her limbs and smiled, her fingers sliding around and beneath him to wedge tightly in the fold of his neat buttocks. She felt sensual and languid, satisfied and free, yet hungry for more, and she ground her sex on to the crisp slickness of his pubis in a promise of further pleasure.

As she dozed, the reason that had sent her to seek Sam in the first place shot unbidden to the forefront of her mind. She sat up and prodded the sleeping figure below her.

'The letter,' she said. 'Sam, will you take the letter now? It must reach Mr Lavendale before he closes his business for the day. Will you go? I'll come back here later, but please go now.'

Chapter Thirteen

When she tiptoed through the yard in the dark of night, Lydia thought that she would find Sam alone, and that he would have found a pretext to send his fellow groom away. She was surprised to find, when she pushed open the door to the stable, that two young men awaited her. One lounged on a pile of soft, fragrant hay, his familiar body and auburn hair lit by the soft glow of a lamp. The other, tall and dark with the slender coltishness of youth, sat on a bale, tentatively chewing his thumb. He started when she entered and glanced sidelong at his friend, who had the grace to look slightly abashed.

'Evening, Sam. Evening, Jemmy.' She leant against the closed door and tucked her hands behind her in the curve of her back. She watched them covertly from the shade of her lashes for a few moments. Sam was the first to rise: he dropped nimbly from the bale of straw and approached her slowly, caution making his steps hesitant.

'Miss Lydia,' he began, stopping just in front of Jemmy, so that the light was interrupted and the other boy was cast into darkness. 'I thought that we could show Jem what we did. He's never done it either, and if you could just show him, he'd be very happy and grateful.'

'Are you mad?' Lydia's imperious voice cut across the young man's speech, sounding like her cousin even to her own ears. She drew herself up to her full height, very aware that even on tiptoes she was a full head shorter than Sam; if he chose to, he could force her to submit, although she imagined that he wouldn't have the courage or brains to do that. 'If you imagine for one moment that I have come here to give myself to you in full view of another stable-hand, then you are very much mistaken. Jemmy, leave us, please.'

She stepped forward into the circle of light thrown by the lantern and placed both hands on her hips. One foot tapped impatiently on the lightly strawed wooden floor, and she tipped her chin upward to give herself an authoritative air. Sam frowned and thrust his big hands deep into the pockets of his breeches; his face was red and his russet head drooped a little as he studied the floor.

Behind him Jemmy stood up, uncurling his long slim body from the pile of loose hay on which he had been lounging. Lydia could not see his face clearly because of the shock of silky brown hair that flopped over one eye, but she could see that he was deeply embarrassed and, if it was possible, even redder in the cheeks than Sam. He glanced towards her, one long brown hand sweeping his hair back over his head, and Lydia was struck by the innocent disappointment that lurked in the depths of his deep blue eyes. He gave her a mischievous half-grin and shrugged before turning to go.

Lydia watched him walk away, fascinated by the movement of his long legs as he stepped over the obstacles that littered the floor of the stable. She took a step forward and brushed against Sam, suddenly acutely aware of the warmth of his body and the evocative smell of saddle polish and tobacco that reminded her so forcibly of events that afternoon.

She felt a constriction in her throat and a sudden pull at her sex which belied her previous words of indignation and hauteur. Making a sudden decision, she

476

reached out to take Sam's hand, enjoying the rough feel of his palm against her own skin, and then she called to Jemmy as he disappeared into the darkness at the back of the stable.

'Jemmy! Wait! I was too hasty. If you can find some way of barring this door so that we are not disturbed, then I would like you to stay.'

The sudden tightening of Sam's hand on hers was small but telling, and as Jemmy bounded back into the circle of light, looking for all the world like a delighted and energetic puppy, Lydia found herself laughing with excitement and anticipation. Jemmy laughed too, his eyes crinkling at the corners, as he grasped her other hand, and between them the two stable-lads drew her towards the fragrant mound of piled hay.

'I think I shall bind you, my sweet.' Madame pressed her nose to Valerian's, her mouth a wide smile, her eyes hard and calculating. 'And blindfold you, I believe. Then you will have only your ears and your imagination to give you clues.'

Her mouth crushed his in a hungry kiss and Valerian moaned against her lips, his fingers fumbling feverishly at the fastening of her long robe. She slapped his hand away and encircled his wrist with her own, leading him to the bed. Pushing and pulling at his limbs, she arranged him in the widely spread position she desired. He lay on the slippery sheets, his skin luminous and pale against the harsh black and scarlet satin.

She had stretched his arms far above his head and manacled his wrists to the bedposts, while his legs had been pulled wide apart, his ankles and feet encased in yards of soft black leather ribbon which she had wound around the legs of the bed at the foot.

'I want to see you,' he protested, as she advanced with a trailing length of silk in one hand.

'Well, I don't want you to see me,' she replied. 'Look now, then. One last glimpse to fuel your appetite, and then I shall blind you.'

She opened her robe and raised one eyebrow. He gazed at her, his eyes devouring her from neck to toe, and she was gratified to see the sudden twitch of his erection as it strained towards his belly. When she had blindfolded him, she ran her hands down the length of his body, feeling the shiver of his muscles and the tension through his legs. Then she stood above his feet, dipped her head, and fastened her lips around his toe, sucking and rubbing the underside with her tongue. He groaned, his head dropping to one side and his fingers cramping into tight fists.

'That was pleasure,' murmured Madame. 'Now feel pain.'

She reached into her pocket and placed two heavy golden clamps on his thighs. She slid them slowly across his skin until she saw his balls tighten at the approach of the cold metal. He cried aloud as she fastened the clamps to his sac, the weight of the gold dragging and pulling at the tender skin, but his cock seemed to grow and swell while his hips thrust upward as if seeking more.

'Patience, *cheri*,' she whispered. 'This is only the beginning.'

The bracket of the piping grated ominously against stone, and Drummond paused in his climb. Below him shadows fell away, the depth of four or five men, to the level of the rose beds, and he knew that if he fell that far he would be injured or even killed.

Cussing softly under his breath, he eased himself up a little farther until Lydia's window-ledge was within reach. He was fairly certain that the room was empty, although it was past midnight, because he had stood on the path below for what seemed like an age, tossing pebbles up against the glass, but she had not come to the window.

'Either she's not there, or she's a very heavy sleeper,' he murmured to himself, grunting slightly as he used the sill to heave himself up to a sitting position. His legs dangled over the side and the ledge was precariously narrow, but he could see in by a combination of twisting and leaning sideways. The leather of his gloves creaked in the cool night air as he reached up and rubbed at the panes with the flat of his hand.

The room was dark: only a slight glow from the grate lit the hearth-rug and a chair nearby. On the far wall he could just make out the big bed, partly curtained against the chill of the night, and the long pale bolster that had fallen to the floor beside the night-stand. He adjusted the black velvet mask he wore, pressed his nose to the glass and tried to see whether the humped shape just visible was Lydia, or merely blankets and linen heaped up. He knocked gingerly on the panes and waited, but there was no movement, no shift in the shape on the bed.

He debated whether to slide back down the piping and trudge through the forest to his warm mattress. As he wiped his face with the back of his gloved hand, he could feel the bristles of his unshaven chin even through the tough leather; he needed a shave, and a bath. The initial excitement of living in the woods was beginning to pall. He made his decision: Lydia, and hot water.

Twisting lithely, he then held his scarf against the window and, with his fist bunched, brought the heel of his big hand hard against the leaded glass. There was a tinkle as the broken bits scattered on the timbered floor below, then silence.

The room was warm and fragrant as he strode to the fireplace to light a taper. He set it on the nearby table and covered the room with two strides, one hand reaching out and tearing back the damask curtain to reveal a rumpled but very empty bed. A chemise lay across the pillow, and he scooped it up, holding the soft fabric to his face to inhale the lingering scent of Lydia's body: jasmine and rose-petals simmered in his nostrils and he felt his chest tighten as a sensuous heat spread across his lower belly.

Where was she?

* * *

479

The candles were burning low, some guttering in the iron sconces, but neither Madame or Valerian noticed. Valerian, still blindfolded and bound, was in the throes of orgasm, his cock twitching against his belly while Madame milked him with one hand. She had encased his hard length in a spiral of pearls, her own beads, and was using this to rub and manipulate him to his climax.

When he was spent, she leant over his face, her rouged lips almost close enough to kiss his cheek.

'I think you deserve a reward, my love,' she whispered. 'I shall go and awaken your delectable cousin. Would you like that?'

The lantern flickered, and Lydia stared down into the luminous brown eyes of the youth who knelt before her. His auburn head was tilted back, but the tip of his tongue, and his nose, were buried in the scented folds of her sex. She inhaled deeply, heat flickering through her veins and the beginnings of true pleasure building and growing towards the devouring abandon that she knew was within her grasp. Sam's large hands gripped her naked hips, and she could see in the lamplight the difference between his sun-toughened flesh and the pale, lustrous sheen of her own skin.

She tipped her head back until she felt the sweep of her long hair brush lightly across the curve of her buttocks. When she felt it grasped by another hand, she knew that Jem had taken a silken hank and was winding it around his slender wrist, tighter and tighter until she could no longer raise her head, and she was captive. Caught between two young men whose only desire seemed to be to give her blissful, delicious pleasure.

She felt Jemmy's other hand slide up her back, his fingertips soft and sensual as they stroked and kneaded along her spine to the nape of her neck and back down to the crescent of her bottom. His fingers drifted, feather-light and barely touching, to the neat little parting between her buttocks, and followed the line down and under. She pressed herself back out towards the seeking hand, arching her back and sighing deeply. Sam, momentarily denied the honey that bathed his lips, pulled her forward again and pushed his tongue more firmly across her swollen flesh, until she felt a sob well up from the depths of her being.

'Jemmy . . . push your finger into me. Put your hand under me and find where Sam is . . . please!'

Two long and slender fingers trembled between her legs, Jem's inexperience making him hesitate against the warm, wet folds, unsure of his ground, uncertain of Lydia's intent. She murmured, begging him, and felt utter, blissful relief as Sam's hands parted her thighs a little and cupped Jem's hands, guiding them, teaching them, much as she had shown him earlier that day.

Jemmy's fingers were long, filling her completely, and she could feel the fascinating combination of his slippery, petal-soft hands working into her, aided by the coarse hardness of the callouses on Sam's thumbs. She could feel the one urging the other, giving motion to Jem's nervous stillness, and she sighed again as she felt the two pairs of fingers work together, sliding inward, out, and then in again, moving together in a gliding rhythm to the accompanying sound of her own juicy arousal.

She reached sideways until she felt the hard beam of one of the stalls beneath her hands, and she gripped it, steadying herself as she felt the rising sweep of languor course through her body. A fire seemed to light up her fingertips, burn her scalp, and she moaned out loud, perspiration sheening her body like dawn dew, as the motion of the two stable-hands brought her to the brink of release. The smell of her own body, mingled with the soft, fragrant hay and the scent of the two healthy young men whose muscular bodies glistened below her, tipped her, spiralling, into a glorious, gasping, full-bodied shudder.

The door creaked a little as it swung open, and Drummond leapt back and behind it, flattening himself

481

against the wall. A small dark shape, satin robe glistening in the dim light from the single taper, stepped into the room.

'Lydia! Thank God!' Drummond caught her and pulled her into his arms, his masked face dipping to bury his nose in the unbound hair that covered her shoulders.

'What a pleasant surprise.' The voice was foreign, as was the scent that clung to the hair which clouded around his face. Drummond jumped back, dropping the woman and spinning her round. The shoulders beneath his strong hands were thin, narrow blades of bone that seemed to cut through the rich fabric of the negligee. Raising his eyes to her face, he saw beautiful porcelain skin and glass-pale eyes that seemed to burn with excitement and intensity.

It was Madame de Chaillot.

'Why! It's the gentleman thief,' she purred, stepping forward so that the toes of her slippers touched the tips of his postilion boots. 'Are you here to rob us, or have you come seeking intimate knowledge of Miss Lydia's bedchamber?'

'Where is she?' demanded Drummond, easing back to escape her heady scent. He felt the wall, cold and firm, against the back of his coat as he stared down at her, frowning at the determination which hardened the planes of her oval face. She smiled, a cat-like curving of her lips which hardly reached her cool eyes.

'Where is who?' she sighed, one hand reaching up to lie flat against the coarse linen of his shirt-front. Drummond was disturbed by her nearness: the smell of her reminded him of their previous, memorably sensual, encounter in the woods, and he felt himself harden, blood rushing through his veins to concentrate in his groin and thighs.

'You know who,' he said, trapping her hand beneath his glove, for it had begun to wander towards the bare skin of his chest which showed through the unbuttoned portion of his shirt.

'I have no idea where she is. I heard the sound of glass breaking and came to see if she needed my assistance. Instead I found you, the masked marauder.'

Madame leant close to him, her face upturned and her eyes narrowed. He could feel the sleek front of her robe as she pressed her body against him, her free hand sliding up around his neck and pulling his face down to hers. He tried to resist, but his nostrils were full of her smell and he could feel her pulse beating rapidly against his gloved thumb. When her lips touched his, he groaned and crushed her body against his chest, sinking his mouth to hers and devouring her with big, hungry movements.

He felt her hands flutter against him, pushing back his thick coat and letting it drop to the floor before tearing at the leather front of his waistcoat. He pulled his arms free and tossed the garment aside, pausing only to grasp her wrists and pull her to him once more. She seemed to thrill under the hurried roughness of his caresses, her body quivering against him and her mouth trembling with half-suppressed excitement as he bent her backward and fastened his lips to her neck.

His eye was caught by a flash of white on the floorboards near the bed: the drifting linen of Lydia's discarded nightgown. It was as if a cold douche had been thrown over his head, icy trickles running down his neck under his loose shirt. He thrust Madame from him, cursing as he untangled himself from her fingers. She did not open her eyes, merely clung to him, her head extended and her throat pulsing as she waited for more kisses. He shook her lightly until her eyes snapped open.

'Where's Lydia?' he said, his jaw hardening and his fingers biting into her upper arms. She did not reply at first, the surprise in her face slowly replaced by a spiteful narrowing of lips and eyes.

'I don't know, and what's more, I don't care!' she spat, reaching out to grasp his shirt-front and jerk him towards her. Her other hand went to his breeches and she outlined his cock with her palm. 'I want this, gentleman thief. You liked it last time, in the woods, and so did I. Give me that pleasure again. Now. Come here.' Her tone became almost wheedling and she snuggled against his chest, her face softening again. He paused, torn, as she dipped her head and rubbed her soft hair against the bristle of his chin. 'You want to, *cheri*. You know you do. And Lydia, the poor fool, will never know.'

Hearing her speak Lydia's name so carelessly made Drummond feel an intense anger. He thrust her away from him again, his face flushing. He heard her swear in her native tongue and watched her bristle, hands on hips, as she faced him and he saw how cold her eyes seemed, how thin and mean her lips were. All his desire for her fled, drained away, replaced by a slow-burning fury.

'I want to see Lydia,' he said, trying to stay calm and reasonable.

'I want! I want? What about what I want?' demanded Madame. 'I want you to fuck me, you idiot. Look! How can you refuse? No one ever refuses me!'

She ripped the ribbons which closed the front of her dark negligee and dropped it to the floor. In spite of himself, Drummond felt a pull at his guts. She was beautiful: a small, pale frond that glowed in the soft light, her body cinched by a leather corset with impossibly tight lacing, which pinched her waist to a handspan size and swelled above and below to encase her narrow hips and cup the buds of her breasts. Her nipples were huge and stuck out from her body like succulent fruit. As if she knew that these were one of her best assets, Madame raised her hand and toyed with one, pulling and squeezing, teasing it until it was red and hard and as long as her thumb. Drummond swallowed.

'Where is she?' he repeated hoarsely.

Madame's hand left her breast and slid down, over the lacing and leather that honed her figure to hourglass perfection, towards the creamy flesh at the tops of her

484

thighs. Her legs were encased in dark stockings which glimmered slightly, and she ran her fingers lightly over the woven tops, sliding one finger inside to rest momentarily between the silken fabric and her skin, before pressing upward so that both hands met at her sex.

She cupped herself, framing her glossy curls with her flower-like hands and squeezing inward so that her sex puckered up, juicy and inviting.

Drummond caught a tang of her musky scent and shook his head as if to clear it.

'I want to see Lydia,' he said, repeating it like a mantra to protect him against the temptation that was being offered so lasciviously in front of him. Madame raised one eyebrow, her lips curling contemptuously.

'Your sweet Lydia is probably out fucking. Perhaps being tupped by one of her cousin's lusty henchmen. I forget which is her favourite now. Is it the Norseman? Or is it the Negro? Perhaps she told you?'

Drummond gave a roar and pushed her aside, blundering forward to sweep up the nightgown from the floor. He brandished it at Madame.

'You lying whore!' he shouted. 'Where is she? What have you done with her?'

'Oh, she's the whore.' Madame smiled sweetly. 'But I think they're so much more exciting that way, aren't they? Now are you going to have me or not?'

Drummond gazed at her: he felt revolted now by the sight that had previously seemed so deliciously inviting. He saw her fingers delve quickly inside herself and watched as she withdrew them, her eyelids flickering closed with pleasure, before she sank them knuckle-deep again.

'Get out,' he said, with quiet loathing.

Her eyes opened and she met his look with one of pure venom.

'You'll regret this, gentleman thief.'

She picked up her robe and slammed the door behind her.

* * *

Lydia slid her lips along the length of the hard cock, her mouth rounded and her tongue flat. He tasted wonderful, like a delicious meal that she could eat over and over again until she was sated, blown with her own gluttony. His hands slipped around the crown of her head and pulled her into him a little more, his slender fingers looping into the loose strands of ebony silk and winding them between his knuckles, playing with her. Above her, she could see the curve of his jaw, the shadow of his young beard, and as he smiled she caught a sparkle of his white teeth between full, pink lips.

'Oh, that's good,' he sighed. 'Your mouth feels so . . . you're so warm, so nice.'

She had slipped all the way to the tip, and then moved to lap her tongue along the underside. He tasted different there, salty, and she savoured him, giving him long licks until she reached the tightness of his balls. She drew them into her mouth until they both lay, warm and slightly fuzzy, against her palate, then she closed her lips and gave a small suck. He gasped, jerking his hips with the intensity of the sensation.

'Christ, woman. Be careful, I might – well, you know.'

'He means that sometimes, when he thinks I'm asleep and the blankets move fast over his hand, he spurts some spunk and that it might not be polite to do it near you.' Sam chuckled, his breath warm on Lydia's back as he nestled up behind her.

'All right, all right,' protested Jem, blushing to the roots of his hair. 'You do it too: I've heard you in the dark, batting against the sheets.'

Lydia sat back, smiling and curving her fingers around Jem's swollen, straining length.

'Do you ever do it together?' she asked. 'At the same time, I mean. I think if I heard someone doing that in the bed next to me, I'd be tempted to go along with it and enjoy myself too.'

The silence that followed, and the sheepish way that Jem glanced at Sam, suggested to her that they had. The thought excited her, and she leant forward to take the swollen head of Jemmy's cock between her lips again. As she sucked, she heard a rustle in the hay and stopped to watch as Sam lifted up her corset and petticoats and gestured to Jem.

She sat back, stroking the soft underside of her thighs as Sam laced Jem into the corset, fumbling a little and concentrating hard on the eyelets as he threaded the lacing and pulled it tight. Next he set the silken drift of white petticoat around Jem's lean hips and fastened it, propping the split open around the rearing cock which brushed against his hand.

Lydia watched, fascinated, hardly daring to breathe, as Sam hesitated, then caught the swinging rod in his fist and stroked it with clumsy reverence. He was shorter than Jem, his auburn head grazing Jem's ear, but it was only a moment before he turned his face up and caught Jem's soft pink lips with his own. Lydia moaned softly, her heart swelling as if it would burst, and a beating, rushing sound echoed in her ears. She stood up and fumbled in the pocket of her discarded skirt for a moment, before pressing herself against the two hard bodies.

Their arms entwined around her, drawing her into their charmed circle, and she felt Sam's lips press against her temple and Jem's hand slide up the curve of her back. She opened the tiny pot of cochineal that she had retrieved from her pocket, and, with a trembling finger, applied a slick of crimson to Jemmy's mouth. He smiled at her, looking for all the world like a beautiful painted doll, and she rose up on to the tips of her toes to kiss him, thrilling at the taste of the crimson salve and the unaccustomed sensation of a hard male mouth made slippery with a woman's make-up.

Sam had watched her with interest and unconcealed excitement. When she drew back from kissing Jem, he replaced her mouth with his own, his lips firm and open. Lydia, only inches away, could see Jemmy's scarlet pout soften and his tongue catch at Sam's. She was almost overcome with lust, and leant forward again to join her own mouth to theirs, feeling them welcome her with tiny licks and sucks, and she knew she was drowning in sensual pleasure, sinking into delirium as their strong arms clasped her in a muscular embrace.

She felt herself being moved by Sam's big hands. He pushed her to her knees and coaxed her head forward until she took Jem into her hot mouth again, her hands clasping the softness of the petticoats that covered his strong thighs. She felt her hips being eased back, her body arched until she was open and ready; then she heard Jem groan as he watched Sam sink down behind her. His knees eased hers apart and she felt his fingers on her buttocks, firmly prising her open. She stuck her bottom out farther to welcome him in. At first he eased her with long languorous strokes of his fingers until she was wet and creamy, a trail of juice slicking her thighs and his palm. She was so aroused that she felt like screaming, crying out, but her mouth was so full of the seashell taste of Jem that she could not – would not – because she did not want to leave this feast of cock. Instead, she stayed still, shivering under Sam's suddenly expert handling of her body.

He had come a long way from the tentative virgin boy of that afternoon, she decided, as his hand slid around her belly and his fingers delved into the softness of her sex to seek and stroke the tight little bud that protruded there. She arched her back further, pleasure flooding through her and filling her from toes to scalp with tingling, bubbling bliss.

When she had coated his fingers, and her pleasure had been elevated to an almost unbearable level, she felt Sam change his position behind her. He rested the burning head of his shaft against her and she felt herself tighten under the sudden hot contact.

'Please, sweet love. Please let me in.' His voice was soft and humble, his tone filled with suppressed lust. She felt her sex soften and pushed herself out against him.

'Thank you. Oh, that feels so good. You're beautiful, you feel so tight and creamy on me.'

He gave a moan as he pushed in, easing his width into her, and she was motionless for a moment. Waiting. Afraid to close her mouth on to Jemmy for the moment. When she felt him all the way in, his cock stretching her impossibly wide, she took Jem in her hand and eased him back between her lips, feeling totally at home, utterly fulfilled, as Sam began to move behind her and Jemmy's hips contracted and pushed his hardness to the back of her throat.

She could not keep still, could not wait passively for Sam to get his rhythm and take her. She moved herself, easing back and forth on to him in short, compact strokes; she squeezed him, milking him with her muscular sex while he gasped and grunted and held her hips, one hand still framing her sex from the front. The sensations were hot and hard, gripping at her insides and making her breath hard and fast, her nostrils flaring as she strove to maintain the clamp of her lips on Jemmy. She ground herself against him, harder and faster until it almost hurt and she felt him shudder, his cock stiffening deep inside the smoothness of her body. Aware that he was about to come and that she had neglected Jem, she let Sam take over and relaxed beneath his tempo as he found the pace she had set.

Both her hands cupped Jem, one catching his balls and pulling down, squeezing and coaxing, while the other curled around the upper reaches of his shaft, hard against the crisp hairs at his root, while her mouth worked – hard and soft, wet as a butter churn – around his helmet. She felt a flash that tore through her body as Sam came, his guttural cry like music to her ears, and she redoubled her efforts with her lips. The pumping of the huge cock inside her made her cream against his fingers, and she felt him press and rub until she came too, arching herself and trembling at the spasm of pure, hot, molten treacle that flooded her veins.

Jem opened his eyes as he ground his hips into her

face, and she watched him, their eyes locked, as he muttered and swore, his lips still smeared with rouge. When he came it was hot, sticky and searing, as she felt him pulse at the back of her mouth and she swallowed in a reflex action, gulping him and gripping his lean hips to pull him farther in. Sam's body curved over her, warm and protective, and she could feel his breath on her shoulder as he bent to kiss her cheek. Leaning back, one hand still on Jem's spent shaft, she turned to kiss him and felt him lick the tiny salt droplets from the corner of her mouth.

Chapter Fourteen

Drummond stepped out into the hallway. Madame had disappeared into the inky shadows, leaving behind her a trail of heady perfume and angry spite. The big house was dark, a warm velvety blackness, and he could smell the once-comforting aromas that he thought he had forgotten: polish and flowers, musty wall-hangings and ancient carpets scented with the dust of generations. The smell of home, although in some strange way it no longer seemed like home. It had changed. It seemed like a stranger's house now; his absence had been too long.

He turned left outside Lydia's room, his feet taking him almost without conscious thought to his own bedroom door. Inside, he could see the shadows of unfamiliar furniture and smell Madame's perfume. On the floor by his foot lay a drift of diaphanous fabric and a casually discarded piece of jewellery. Everything that he had once called his own had disappeared. Hastily, he pulled the door closed. It was no longer his room: it had been changed and given to another, used as a guest room, all trace of his presence erased. His heart felt heavy and his steps faltered as he went towards the room that had once been, and maybe still was, his brother's.

Outside, he paused momentarily, undecided. His heart skipped with a sudden nervousness and he wondered what he would do if Valerian was inside. On the stone wall near to his head an ornamental sword hung in a metal bracket, and he lifted it down, testing its weight in his hand, rubbing the blade lightly with the calloused pad of his thumb. His brother was unpredictable, he knew. It would be as well to have some means of defence.

The door opened smoothly on well-oiled hinges and Drummond was surprised to see that the room was partially lit. Candles of varying sizes and colours stood around the room, lighting the shadowed corners with ghostly flickering. On the huge bed at the far end of the room, a man's pale body lay spread like a heathen sacrifice on a crimson and ebony altar, the eyes blindfolded, the hands and feet bound to the four corners.

As he drew closer, Drummond saw that Valerian was relaxed, possibly sleeping, and that he had partaken in some bizarre sexual game. The evidence of his previous arousal was silvery on the skin of his belly, slowly hardening and crisping the curling hairs around his navel.

Drummond was almost unable to absorb the scene. His overwhelming desire was to laugh, to shake with mirth at the sight of his notorious brother bound up by a woman and inadvertently delivered to his, Drummond's, avenging hands. He walked quietly across the room, his boots stealthy on the soft tiger-skin rug. At the side of the bed he paused, noticing the sudden alertness of the body in front of him, the raised hairs on the forearms, the tension in the muscles.

'Claudine?' whispered Valerian.

In reply, Drummond raised the sword in his hand and gently rested the tip at his brother's waist. The point created a small dip in the even surface of the smooth skin, but did not pierce it.

'Claudine, what are you planning now? Your head is full of evil, wonderful games. Prick me again.'

492

Drummond obliged, his mouth widening into a grin. This was marvellous, so much better a confrontation than he had anticipated. He slid the sword along Valerian's flank until it rested on the side of his thigh. A tiny red scratch appeared in its wake. Valerian inhaled audibly, his chest rising and then falling. The sword slipped around, skirting his loins.

Drummond paused. Emasculating his brother had appeal, but he swiftly discounted such barbarity and moved around the bed until the point of the weapon pressed into Valerian's ribs. He saw with amusement that his brother's erection was beginning to stir, and decided to end the game before he was forced to see it fully aroused.

Dragging the tip of the sword up to Valerian's throat, he bent over him and placed his lips so close to his ear that he could almost taste him.

'No, dear brother. It is I.'

There was a momentary pause.

Then the figure on the bed convulsed, hips rising off the bed, claw-like hands clutching at the air, while his wide mouth twisted into a frenzied snarl.

'Untie me! Untie me, you bastard!' Valerian raged, the tendons in his arms buckling and twisting into knotted cords.

'Careful,' warned Drummond. 'Be still, or I shall accidentally run you through.'

Valerian, the tip of the sword still pressed to his throat, slumped back, his body flaccid and the only movement the rapid rise and fall of his chest.

'You coward. Won't you even untie me and fight me like a man?' he goaded him.

The point was pressed closer to his throat, the skin around it blanching.

'A man? Is that what you call yourself? You didn't exactly fight like a man when you gave me this scar I bear,' hissed Drummond, his amusement gone and replaced by a hard determination which left his face pale and his eyes narrowed to golden slits. 'Never fear,

I am not going to kill you. Merely enjoy the sight of you trussed up like a chicken ready for the broiler. Look at you! If Father could see you now, he'd turn in his grave.'

'Father can roast in hell. And you, too. Now untie me or I'll have you horsewhipped before I have you killed.'

Drummond threw back his head and laughed. The sound echoed coldly from the walls.

'Have me killed?' he mocked. 'You just don't see, do you? Oh, I forgot. You can't see, can you? Your lovely mistress has blindfolded you. Dearest brother, let me uncover your eyes and perhaps you will see the seriousness of your predicament.' Drummond moved the sword and, with a quick flick of his wrist, sliced the side of the blindfold and the strip of black fell, catching at the side of Valerian's head and resting on the scarlet pillow. 'You don't have the power to have anyone horsewhipped or killed. Least of all me.'

He slid the tip of the sword downward until it rested centrally on Valerian's chest, the point digging in a little, the blade rising and falling under the harshly beating thud of Valerian's heart.

'Where is the will?' demanded Drummond, his face hard and uncompromising.

'I don't have it,' sneered Valerian. 'And even if I did, you wouldn't want it. It'll do you no good.'

'I'll ask you again. Where is Father's will?'

There was the sound of a sharply inhaled breath behind him, and Drummond half-turned to see Madame rushing across the room, her arms outstretched and her red robe flying behind her like a cascade of blood. Her face was a white mask of hatred, and her teeth were bared as she launched herself at Drummond, flinging the full weight of her small body against him. He threw up an arm to fend her off, but she leapt on to his back, her nails clawing at his face and her teeth snapping at his neck like a vulture preparing to tear its food apart.

'Leave him alone!' she screamed.

There was a cry from beneath him as Drummond felt

494

her weight bend his body forward and his chest pressed on to the hilt of the sword. He experienced a momentary stillness and then he felt the ornamental sword yield beneath him. Thinking that it had broken, snapped beneath their combined weights, he twisted his head and saw in horror that the blade had pierced his brother's chest, and a dark wash of crimson was slowly spreading over Valerian's milky skin. Finding his strength, he pushed at the harpy who tore at his hair, sending her crashing to the floor.

'Valerian!' he cried, his hands trembling as he cupped his brother's face. Valerian's dark, tortured eyes fixed on his, and Drummond saw unremitting hatred deep in the dilated pupils.

'You'll hang for this.' A bubble of scarlet, air laced with blood, slowly formed at the edge of his lips and he gasped, his eyelids closing slowly as if he were deeply tired.

Drummond gripped his brother's shoulder.

'Oh, Christ. Oh, God. Quickly, send for a surgeon. A surgeon, woman!'

He span around, almost falling in his haste. Madame stood behind him, her pale eyes wide and ringed with dark shadows. As he moved towards her, she threw her hands up before her as if to ward him off. Then she began to scream.

The room was bright with light as Lydia pushed open the door. The scene was frozen for an instant as she took in the significance of the sword and the reed-like body of Madame who stood, as motionless as Lot's wife, at the foot of the bed. The air was rent with the sound of her screams.

Hardly pausing, Lydia turned and ran down the stairs, back to the stables, her heart frozen and her body numb.

'Quickly! Sam, take one of the horses: go to the surgeon and bid him come. Hurry! My cousin may be dying. Get Mr Lavendale, Jem. Waste no time!' As she spoke, she began to drag open the low stalls and pull at Dandy Beau's saddle. The stable-lads, kicked into action by the urgency in her voice, swung up and were away almost before she had buckled the last strap. Hardly pausing to watch them disappear into the blackness of the yard, she raced back to the house and took the stairs two at a time.

Madame turned and caught at her as she ran past, long nails raking across Lydia's forearm. She shook herself free and rushed towards the bed, but stopped as she heard Valerian emit a choking, guttural sound. Frozen, unable to move, she saw that Drummond had cut the bindings and removed the sword; he was staunching the flow of blood with the sheets. Valerian's face was creased and pale, his breathing shallow and rapid.

The screaming stopped as suddenly as it had begun and the room was blissfully silent. There was a whisper of movement as Madame went to the other side of the bed, her hair tumbling across Valerian's face and chest as she bent over him to take his hand in hers.

'Oh, my love. *Mon pauvre petit.* Speak to me, *mon amour.* Valerian, speak.'

'Is he dead?' Lydia dropped to her knees in front of Drummond, her hands fluttering over Valerian's face. His eyes opened, met hers briefly, and then left to search for Madame's face.

'Take me away, Claudine. Take me away from these ... people,' he muttered, his voice shadowed with pain. 'Tend me, Claudine.'

'The surgeon, thank God!' Lydia rushed to the door and drew the portly little man into the hall. 'Quickly, there is a man upstairs who is wounded. Come now! Bring your bag.'

When she had shown the doctor to Valerian's room, Lydia hurried down the stairs. Drummond was sitting on the bottom step, his knees curled up and his head drooping forward. Lydia gently laid one hand across the back of his neck, filled with tenderness and concern.

'Drummond, what happened?' she murmured. 'How did that sword come to be in him?'

'It was an accident. An accident. Not that anyone will believe me. If he dies, I'll be swinging from a gibbet before sundown tomorrow.' He lifted his head and she saw that his bronzed skin was pale and his face haggard. She drew him to her and rocked him, like a baby, in her arms.

'Sssh,' she whispered. 'You won't hang. They won't hang you: you're Lord Hawkesworth, now.'

'Never,' he said, dragging himself upward and away from her. 'There's nothing for me here, now. This house has forgotten me. It's not my home any more.'

'What do you mean? It has always been your home. It always will be.'

'No.' He shook his head, biting at his lower lip thoughtfully. 'I can never live here, not now. I'm going back to sea. That's where I'm truly happy.'

'Drummond, please. Don't be so hasty. We need you here. You can't let this . . . this . . . *accident* ruin all that.'

'*Accident*. You see, even you aren't sure. Even if the surgeon saves him, I can't live here with everyone glancing sidelong at me and whispering "Fratricide" whenever I pass. I'm leaving. My brother is welcome to the house and the title.'

'Don't go.' Lydia stared uncomprehendingly as he stood and moved away from her. 'Drummond, this is a mistake. Everyone knows the threats he made against you: they will understand that you killed him in self-defence.'

He turned towards her, his eyes tired but gentle, and a tiny smile lifting the corner of his mouth.

'My love, I wish that were true,' he said. 'I must leave now, before the lawyer comes. I could have been happy with you, but I cannot stay and let them hang me. Be careful.' His arms enfolded her and she felt his lips bruise hers as he kissed her, fiercely, on the mouth. Then he was gone, the huge studded door banging behind him.

The surgeon materialised at Lydia's elbow. He sighed impatiently.

'Madam, I can be of no service here. I am a doctor, not an undertaker. The gentleman upstairs is dead.'

'The will has always been in my possession, Miss Lydia. It is my regret to inform you that I acted under the instructions of Valerian Hawkesworth – er, the late Valerian Hawkesworth, I should say.' Mr Lavendale stood in front of the fireplace in the library, his coat raised slightly to allow the fire to warm his legs. Lydia, her hand paused over the brandy decanter, looked up at him with some surprise.

'Do I take it that Valerian gave you financial remuneration for this deviousness? I should not have to remind you that he was not the true Lord Hawkesworth.'

'Indeed, madam. You are more correct than you know. There is no Lord Hawkesworth. There has been no male incumbent since your uncle's death.'

'What can you mean?'

'Oh, dear, Miss Lydia. This is so very difficult.' Lavendale sighed and rubbed his chin, a deep frown creasing his wide brow. 'Your cousin Drummond, he . . . well . . . he incurred the wrath of Lord William when he left. It was seen by his father as a defection, a betrayal, you understand. And as time progressed, it was clear to Lord William that Valerian had neither the inclination nor the sanity to manage an estate of this size and wealth. He changed his will some four months before his death and cut both of his sons right out. They were to receive nothing under the terms of the new will.' He sighed again. 'That is why Master Valerian chose to act as he did. He felt that Hawkesworth was rightfully his. He did not want the new beneficiary to inherit. At all.'

'And you colluded in this?' Lydia stared at him and he fidgeted uncomfortably.

'I did. I agreed with him that he was more able than the selected beneficiary. I was wrong.'

'And who is this beneficiary that you all deemed so incapable?' Lydia lifted a glass from the tray.

'Yourself.'

The glass fell to the floor and smashed at her feet. She stared at it dazedly, thinking irrelevantly how pretty the shards of crystal were as they caught the light and formed clusters of tiny rainbows on the polished floor.

'Me?'

'You, Miss Lydia. Indeed it is a tangled web. However, I hope that you will see beyond my temporary lapse of professionalism and maintain me as your advisor? Your dear uncle would have wanted it so.'

'We shall see, Mr Lavendale. We shall see.' Lydia selected another glass and slowly poured a generous measure of brandy. Without offering him any, she drained the glass.

Lady Lydia of Hawkesworth Manor, she thought. It really sounded very satisfactory.

Sitting back in the winged chair, she slowly crossed one stockinged leg over the other and folded her hands in her lap. She took a deep, calming breath and met Lavendale's heavy-lidded gaze.

'Exactly how much did you say the estate is worth?'

One Year Later

As the bow of the enormous ship hit a wave, a spray of ocean spume washed up and over the rail to darken the planking of the deck. Lydia waited a moment until the swell had eased, one hand on an adjacent pile of ropes to steady herself. She tipped her face towards the morning sun and inhaled the fresh saltiness of the open sea, letting her hood fall back on to her shoulders and the brisk wind tease her hair into long ebony skeins. A sense of enormous happiness and well-being swelled in her chest, and she moved forward and up the steps to stand by the rangy figure whose weathered brown hand loosely guided the wheel of the ship.

They had been at sea for almost a month, and were halfway to the Americas. Lydia had sold her inheritance, and a vast fortune in gold now swelled the securely padlocked coffers that were stowed in the ship's hold. She had left England with a vague feeling of regret, tempered with anticipation to see the New World that Drummond had once described to her. She was extremely wealthy, she had her health, and above all she had her youth and beauty to guide her through whatever awaited her on the other side of the vast ocean.

She took her hands out of the mink muff that had warmed her fingers, toying for a moment with the sparkling ring that adorned her left hand: a wide band of gold set with rubies and emeralds that fitted snugly to her finger and emphasised the narrow paleness of her hands. The man at her side glanced down, his blue eyes warm and interested, his vigorous white-blond hair escaping from under his scarlet bandanna with each successive tug of the wind. He was taller than she was, and broad; his shoulders stretched the seams of his leather jerkin while the bare V of his chest showing at the neckline of his open shirt gleamed like beaten copper in the sun.

'Thinking of your late husband, Mistress Hammond?' he enquired. Lydia glanced up at him, then her brow cleared as she remembered her assumed role of a grieving widow bound for the Americas to seek out her late husband's family.

'It gets a little easier each day, Captain Jefferies,' she replied, smiling and tucking her hands back into the muff. She paused to admire his lean hands, watching with fascination the easy way they commanded the ship through the polished timber wheel. Capable hands, strong hands. She found herself imagining how they would look set against the whiteness of her thighs, then roused herself to enquire nonchalantly: 'How much longer before we have sight of land?'

Towards dinner-time, Lydia returned to her cabin. It was on the seaward side and had been newly decorated with velvet to befit lady passengers. Having closed the door behind her, she leant one hand against the timbered wall.

'When will I get my sea legs?' she sighed.

'Probably when we disembark,' came the wry reply. Angel, beautifully attired in black mourning taffeta, smiled and patted the place on the settle beside her. 'Come here. I do believe he's smiling. The wet-nurse says that it's the wind, but look! Look at that!'

501

The baby on her lap gurgled and cooed, then his chubby face split into a toothless grin. His shock of unruly brown hair stuck straight up from his round head, and his golden eyes crinkled with jollity.

'Oh, Angel. He's so beautiful. And that is definitely a smile, I don't care what Gertrude says.' Lydia stroked the baby's round cheek with her forefinger, her heart swelling with love for her little boy. At that moment, from the carved wooden crib beside them, a strident wail cut the air.

'Oh, Lord,' cried Angel. 'Here, miss. Take him. His majesty has woken, and about time too. I thought he was going to sleep all day.'

She carefully settled the smiling child on to Lydia's lap, and reached into the crib to lift out an identical baby boy. The only differences between the twins were in their eyes and hair: the newly awoken cherub had jet-black hair and dark sloe eyes that stared imperiously at the world.

Lydia gestured for Angel to hand him to her, and settled back into the soft cushions with her sons. She nuzzled their delicately scented hair and closed her eyes, conjuring up images which tried to remain hidden in the back of her mind: Drummond striding through the woods of Hawkesworth with his cloak billowing and his unruly hair ruffled by the wind; Valerian in his tall leather boots and immaculate white stock, sitting astride his magnificent stallion.

Would she ever know which of these strong but flawed men had fathered her children, she wondered. As the babies snuggled happily against the silk of her bodice, she let the images fade and sighed contentedly, deciding that she did not really care: perhaps it had been both.

Taking Liberties

Susie Raymond

Chapter One

Beth stood up and glided across the office, her movements slow and deliberate. Behind her, through the open doorway into her boss's office, she could sense Simon watching her again. He had done a lot of that lately. In fact, it was a wonder that he ever got anything done at all; his mind clearly wasn't on his work when she was around. She grinned slyly to herself.

As she stooped over the drawer of her filing cabinet, Beth could feel his eyes burning into the back of her thighs. She straightened slowly and began to amble back to her desk. Out the corner of her eye, she surreptitiously examined him in return, admiring his well-proportioned physique and dark good looks.

Being brunette herself, Beth was usually more attracted to fair-haired men, but there was something about brown eyes that always drew her like a magnet. Simon had the deepest, darkest coffee-brown eyes she had ever seen. When he watched her, as he was doing now, it was almost as if she were being sucked helplessly into them, powerless to resist. Soon, she promised herself. Very soon now.

Once she was back out of sight behind her desk she allowed herself another quick grin and reached for the next document in her in-tray. As she resumed working her way steadily through the mound of accounts awaiting her attention, she hummed contentedly to herself. She had always been good at maths and she took quiet satisfaction at the way the neat columns of figures flowed from her pen and bowed to her will. It was all so easy, so logical. She had been away from the financial world for far too long and it was good to be back.

Taking a short break, Beth sipped her already cold coffee and glanced happily round her domain. It was a pleasant room, if a bit on the small side. The dark wooden desk and leather chair pleased her, even though they weren't anywhere near as plush or expensive as those in Simon's office. It was a warm day and she wriggled slightly in her seat, enjoying the feel of the cold leather on the bare skin of her thighs.

She slipped her feet out of her shoes and smiled as she rubbed her toes gently along the carpet, luxuriating in its velvety softness. If she did that in Simon's office, her toes would disappear in the thick pile. She had trouble simply walking on it in her high heels. Of course, nothing was too good or too expensive for Simon Henderson. Even the visitor's couch would put most luxury beds to shame. She smiled again, then put her empty mug back down and returned to her work. Images of Simon's liquorice eyes and wide, sensuous lips danced tantalisingly in her mind, full of promise.

Five minutes later Beth finished bringing the Simpson account up to date. She leant back and glanced thoughtfully out of the window. Being Saturday, the high street was busier than usual and from five stories up she had a good view. As she watched the weekend shoppers scurrying frantically to and fro like ants with their whinging children in tow, she sighed softly. Despite the apparent bustle, you couldn't help noticing how run down and neglected the area had become in recent years. Small towns like this, with their tiny family businesses, were part of a dying era. They just couldn't compete with the

506

huge, modern shopping malls springing up everywhere. No wonder Simon was planning to move to a brand-new business park further out from the London area. There was nothing to keep businesses here any more.

Thoughts of Simon reminded her that it was time to provide him with a little further distraction. As she reached out to gather up the stack of financial projections and investment options she had just been working on, her mind filled with the pleasures soon to come and her skin began to tingle.

'Since you are going to be away all next week, we really need to get the Simpson account put to bed before you go.' His words from the previous day ran through her mind. His choice of expression had not gone unnoticed. Nor had his hands, which had wandered on to her thigh before she had twisted out of his reach.

'I know it's a bit much to ask,' he had added, 'but perhaps you wouldn't mind if we both came in tomorrow morning, just to finish up?'

He must have known how flimsy the excuse had sounded. The money in the Simpson account was already securely invested and would be perfectly all right for the week she was due to be away on her training course. Besides, if it had really been all that important, he could quite easily have returned to the office the previous afternoon after his lunchtime appointment with a client.

Of course, he must also have known that there would be hardly anyone else in the building on a Saturday and no clients would be knocking on their door. Whatever Simon wanted her in the office for this morning, Beth was certain that it had little to do with customer care. It would seem that her teasing over the past weeks was finally about to bear fruit. This was the moment she had been waiting for.

Beth slipped her feet back into her high heels and stood up. She smoothed down her short skirt and carefully checked her appearance. Satisfied, she walked leisurely into his office, her hips swinging from side to side.

As soon as he spotted her, Simon reached for a client file. He opened it quickly and pretended to be concentrating avidly on its contents. His face looked slightly flushed and Beth hid her smile at the thought of what he may have been up to with his hands under the desk. Her eyes twinkled mischievously.

'Here's the Simpson account. I've completed the financial projection up to the end of the month. I think you'll find everything in order.'

As she spoke, Beth examined his hard, athletic body and perfectly proportioned features, trying to assess his thoughts. His dark hair, normally so immaculate, looked slightly tousled, as if he had been running his fingers through it. Her own fingers itched to smooth it back in place.

'Thank you, Beth.' His slight smile was full of hidden possibilities and his liquorice eyes glittered in a way that made her whole body tingle with longing.

He watched her closely as she reached across the desk to place the documents on the far side in the only available space. It would have been much easier to reach from the other side, but less easy for him to reach her. As she leant over, she kept her legs straight so that her skirt lifted slightly to reveal a brief glimpse of lacy stocking top.

She took her time, pretending to tidy up a few pens and pencils and put them back into his pen holder. Finally, she stood upright again and ran her hands down her sides so that her blouse pulled tight over her nipples. Simon's eyes narrowed and his whole body seemed to tense as he stared at her breasts. She heard him sigh gently as she turned to walk back to her own office. There was a soft rustle of clothing as he stood up.

'What's your hurry?' he questioned. 'We haven't finished yet.'

Even though she was expecting it, Beth pretended to jump in mock surprise as Simon made a sudden grab for her from behind. She allowed him to put his hands round her waist and run them up towards her breasts until the tips of his fingers were just touching the outer curves. Although his hands were large and firm, his fingers were surprisingly long and slim, lightly tanned and silky smooth. She twisted away and turned back to face him.

'Don't do that.' She forced anger into her voice. 'What would anyone think if they walked in?' As she turned away again, Beth reached out and brushed a pile of papers with her hand. With a soft thud, the whole heap landed on the floor.

'Damn,' she cursed under her breath. Bending deliberately from the waist, she started to gather them up. She took her time, certain that he would be enjoying the view. Suddenly, she heard the sharp click of the office door locking. How in the world had he got over there so quickly and quietly? Although surprised, she pretended not to notice and continued to gather the scattered documents.

Finished, Beth stood up slowly and put the papers back on his desk. As she smoothed her skirt down over her hips again, she could sense Simon hovering just behind her. Without warning, he put his hands around her so that her arms were effectively pinned to her sides as he began to caress the swell of her breasts. Beth could feel the outline of his erection thrusting urgently into her buttocks. She resisted the urge to push herself hard against it and began to struggle feebly in an effort to escape his grasp.

'Simon! Stop it. What if somebody comes in?' It was just possible, albeit unlikely, that a cleaner or someone from one of the other companies with whom Henderson Finance shared the six-storey office block might come by.

'They can't. I've locked the door.' His voice was thick with desire. His hands began to move inwards towards her already hardening nipples.

'Oh!' Beth gasped. She prayed that he would think her cry was caused by her shock and not because of the exquisite tingling sensation that was running down her spine at the feel of his fingers on her nipples. She increased her half-hearted efforts to escape.

Clearly excited by her struggles, Simon grabbed a handful of her blouse. Beth gripped his hand in hers, as if trying to pry his fingers loose, and pulled hard. The buttons immediately began to pop out of the carefully enlarged buttonholes. Beth squealed and twisted away so that the pressure on the buttons increased. The cotton snapped on the final button and the garment gaped open.

Beth faked another squeal and placed her hands across her chest as if trying to protect her tiny white bra. Simon made another grab for her and Beth automatically put her arms out in front of her to push him away. His fingers hooked over the front catch of her bra.

'Stop it.' Beth twirled and tried to duck under his arm. The bra lifted up and one of her breasts popped out. 'Oh!'

Simon's eyes widened at the sight of her naked breast. He tugged harder and the carefully doctored stitching on the catch gave way. The bra snapped open and her other breast bounced into view.

Beth quickly covered her breasts with both hands. In the struggle, her skirt had ridden up over her stocking tops and she suspected that he might even be able to see the bottom of her silk thong. She had chosen it carefully; the elastic wasn't very strong and she was sure that he wouldn't have any trouble pulling it off.

Keeping her arms up in front of her, Beth took a small step backwards. Simon grabbed for her again. As she pulled away, she gave her shoulders a quick shrug so that her blouse slipped off into his fingers and her bra straps began to slide down her arms. Pretending to lose her balance, Beth stumbled back over the cushioned settee.

Her skirt rode up even more. Beth pushed herself along the cushion until her hem was up around her buttocks and the soft elephant cord was gently caressing the tops of her thighs. She pretended not to notice her skirt and concentrated on her naked breasts, fondling her swollen nipples as she tried to cover them with her hands.

Simon's eyes were fixed on the small triangle of white silk covering her mound. She could feel her breasts heaving with excitement as she stood back up, exposing even more thigh. Casually, she shook the bra off her arms. It fell to the floor beside her feet.

Simon seemed to be staring at her as if in shock. Her tattered blouse was still clutched between his shaking fingers and his face was deathly pale. For one awful moment, Beth was afraid he was about to lose his nerve and start apologising. She gazed down ruefully at herself and made a feeble attempt to straighten her skirt. Her breasts danced and bobbed tantalisingly in front of her.

She pouted seductively. 'Now look what you've done. That really was very naughty of you.' Her voice automatically adopted the tone one might use when scolding a naughty child. She noticed with satisfaction that his eyes were moving restlessly back and forth between her breasts and crotch. She leant down casually and picked up her bra.

'You've broken the catch. I won't be able to wear this again.' She dropped it in the waste-paper bin and then quickly covered her breasts with her hands again, as though she had suddenly remembered her exposure.

'You are going to give me my blouse back, aren't you?' she queried, as she held out one arm towards him and tried, in vain, to conceal her breasts with her other hand.

Simon stared blankly at the blouse still clutched between his fingers, then raised his arm as if he were about to give it back to her. Obviously, he needed another little prod in the right direction.

'Or are you going to make me work topless?' she continued. She lifted her hands and glanced down at her puckered nipples. 'It would be a bit hard to concentrate while I'm trying to cover these up,' she added.

It worked. Simon immediately pulled his hand back.

Beth gazed up into his eyes. His face was flushed and his breath was coming in short little pants.

'Not for what I've got in mind,' he whispered hungrily.

Beth could hear the longing in his voice. She didn't have to glance down to know how his penis was straining against his flies. She was convinced that all he needed was one more little push and he would lose his final inhibitions. She shivered with a combination of fear and excitement. She had been anticipating this moment for weeks.

Beth reached out for her blouse. She hesitated in apparent confusion, then quickly tried to cover herself again. As she stood shivering in front of Simon, she did her best to look nervous and indecisive. Almost absent-mindedly, her fingers began to tease her nipples again.

Simon glanced down at her skirt and Beth followed his gaze. The top button had popped undone during their brief struggle so that he could see a glimpse of her panties. Beth noticed his whole body was quivering. Another surge of desire threatened to engulf her when she saw the almost desperate expression on his face.

'You don't need that, either.' He dropped her blouse to the floor and reached out to grasp the corner of her skirt. He pulled hard and the skirt opened. He let it fall to the ground beside her blouse, leaving Beth standing in just her panties and stockings. She stepped back.

Immediately, Simon made another lunge for her. Beth dodged, squealing indignantly. As she bent forward, she placed one hand across her breasts and turned her head away to hide the look of satisfaction on her face. Her other hand slipped down between her thighs and, in her excitement, her fingers began to squeeze her mound as if to try to stem her own growing passion. If anything, it made things worse.

Simon pushed his fingers under the elastic of her thong and began to peel it down over her buttocks.

'Or these,' he added softly.

'No. Stop it,' she protested weakly as she twisted away

from him again. With both her hands crossed over her breasts, Beth began to dance nimbly around the chairs and desk. Simon lumbered after her, his hands everywhere.

As soon as she reached the visitor's couch again Beth deliberately lost her footing and fell forward. Simon pounced. As he pushed his finger under the elastic of her panties, Beth wriggled back, so that they began to slip down towards her knees. Simon immediately let go of her and stood up. Without taking his eyes off her exposed mound, he raised his hand and started to undo his belt.

Beth stared up at him, mesmerised, her eyes unblinking. Yes, she thought excitedly. That's it. Tie me up with your belt. Strap my hands behind me so that I can't defend myself and run your fingers all over me until I beg for mercy. She felt another surge of longing race through her.

Simon released the catch on his trousers and slowly undid his zip. She noticed the shiny wrapper of a condom in the palm of his hand and almost sighed with relief at his forethought. She watched silently as Simon slid his pants down over his erection and his stiff cock sprang free. She wasn't disappointed.

When he saw the direction of her gaze, he smiled and ripped the condom wrapper open with his teeth. Wordlessly, he smoothed the sheath down his rigid penis. Beth shivered again as he grasped himself in his hand and moved his fingers slowly down himself, checking the fit. She had always known that it would be fun, pushing him like this. She hadn't anticipated the powerful extent of her own arousal.

As Simon grabbed her panties to finish tugging them off, Beth squirmed back away from him, still feigning resistance. She rolled off the settee and landed on her stomach on the floor. Simon bent over her and continued to pull at her underwear. Beth squeezed her legs together to try to stop him. She didn't want him to think it was

513

too easy. Her own excitement was building urgently. Her thighs were already damp and her nipples were aching to be sucked.

Simon gave another sharp tug on her undies and suddenly they were down at her ankles. Changing tactics, Beth opened her legs as wide as she could to make it difficult for him to get them over her feet. In doing so, she totally exposed her sex lips to his burning gaze. She heard him groan and felt a rush of moisture flowing from her.

As Simon grabbed one of her legs and tugged her underwear off, Beth whimpered in mock fear and tried to wriggle across the floor. He was too quick for her. As he grabbed both her legs to pull her back, he crossed her ankles and forced her to turn over. She gazed up at him, doing her best to look helpless.

'Please don't,' she whispered.

Simon ran his eyes hungrily down her naked body while his hand continued to fondle his erection.

'You don't mean that.' Slowly, he leant back over her and began to tug at her stockings. As soon as he had pulled one off, he tied it to the arm of the settee and looped the other end round her right wrist. Beth immediately tried to free herself, but Simon grabbed her again and whipped the other stocking off. He knelt over her chest so that his erection was only inches away from her mouth.

She twisted and bucked under him until she felt his crotch resting on her breasts. She continued to squirm, kicking with her feet and trying to wriggle out from under him. Swiftly, he tied the other stocking to her left wrist and attached it to the desk leg. His cock was so close to her face that it was all she could do to resist sucking him into her mouth.

'That should keep you where I want you,' he whispered.

Trapped, Beth began to wriggle her bottom up and down in an attempt to escape. Please don't let him see how much I want this, she breathed silently as he moved back so that he could examine her whole body.

As she continued to roll her hips from side to side, Beth made a futile effort to cross her legs to protect her mound from his burning gaze. Another whimper of desire burst from her lips and she could only hope that he would think it was one of fear. She rolled on to her side away from him, and started to tug against the restraints holding her wrists.

'Behave yourself.' Simon raised his hand and smacked her buttocks. Beth jumped at the force of the blow and her eyes began to water at the unexpected sting.

'Ow!' she cried. She gritted her teeth as he smacked her again. 'Stop it. Let me go.'

Simon ignored her. He ran his fingers slowly up the back of her legs and rested them on her buttocks. Beth squirmed and rolled on to her back again to try to trap his hand underneath her.

Simon grinned and grabbed her right breast. Beth gasped and tried to free her arms from their restraints to protect herself. She lifted her leg as high as she could to push him away. She could hear his breathing growing heavier and more laboured as she continued her half-hearted struggle. Clearly, he was enjoying it as much as she was.

'Stop it. Untie me,' she demanded in the sternest voice she could manage. 'Look. I'll pretend nothing has happened if you just untie me now.'

'Nothing has happened, yet.' Simon moved closer and pushed his fingers between her legs. 'But we'll soon change that.'

Beth clamped her thighs together as tightly as she could. 'Let me go,' she repeated in a deadly whisper. She did her best to ignore the tingling sensation his touch was causing.

Simon gave her a small smile and moved down towards her feet. She noticed that one of his hands was busy fondling his cock again and the sight of his bursting

515

erection throbbing between his fingers caused her to gasp aloud. He pulled her ankles apart roughly and knelt between her feet. Slowly, he began to work his way back up her legs, forcing them wider and wider apart. She felt the fingertips of his free hand caressing her thighs softly.

Beth shuddered from tip to toe. He was so big and so hard. She lifted her head up off the floor as far as possible so that she could watch his prick throbbing and twitching in his hand. She couldn't remember ever being this excited before. Not even with Jonathan and his two friends. Her breath was coming in short little pants and she had to bite her tongue to stop herself moaning with anticipation. She waited impatiently while he ripped open his shirt and pulled it over his head without bothering to undo all the buttons.

'Don't you dare,' Beth hissed as he took his cock back in his hand and guided it towards his target. She made another supreme effort to wiggle free, but he pushed her down easily and squeezed her right breast painfully.

'Lie still.'

Beth fixed him with a cold stare, as if daring him to go the whole way. As she felt the tip of his manhood begin to penetrate her, her whole body trembled with another spasm of excitement.

'No!' She uttered what she hoped would sound like a cry of total despair.

Simon ignored her pleas and squeezed her breast even harder. 'Keep still,' he commanded hoarsely.

Keep still! Jesus. She knew she mustn't let him realise how much she was enjoying it, but how could she keep still when his cock was teasing her like that? She tried, without success, to suppress another shiver of longing.

Slowly, ever so slowly, Simon pushed himself into her. Beth wanted to shout aloud for the sheer pleasure and success of it. She gritted her teeth so that all that came out was a subdued moan.

Simon reached under her and grabbed her buttock with his free hand. As he leant forward over her and began to kiss her, he squeezed her bum with his fingers and forced his full weight down on to her. Beth gasped as he began to pump slowly in and out. His body pressed down on her and his mouth covered hers so that there was nothing she could do but let him have his way. Gradually, he began to thrust harder and faster.

'Oh, Christ,' he moaned. 'I've wanted you for so long.' She sensed him slowing and changing the rhythm as he tried to prolong his pleasure. Instinctively, she tightened her legs around him and thrust her pelvis up to meet his strokes, squeezing him with her muscles. He groaned again and a feeling of triumph shot through her as he stiffened and came.

Just the thought of his climax was enough to push Beth over the top to her own release. She was sobbing helplessly. He must have known that she had enjoyed it as much as he had. Just so long as he didn't realise that she had deliberately planned the whole thing.

Simon slid himself out and lifted his weight off her. Without saying a word he stood up, pulled his pants up and walked across the room towards the little kitchen area.

Beth closed her eyes and lay completely still, gloating over her success. She made no attempt to cover herself or to stifle her little sobs of pleasure as her mind savoured every moment of the experience. After a few minutes, she heard the sound of the kitchen bin closing and then his footsteps returning. She opened her eyes.

Simon had picked up his shirt and tie and was pulling them back on over his head.

Realising that he was just going to leave her there, Beth slipped her wrists from the ineffective restraints of her stockings and stood up slowly. She was surprised at how shaky her legs still were from the intensity of their lovemaking. She couldn't remember when it had last been quite that good, if ever.

Beth picked up her skirt and wrapped it round her. Only one button remained intact and her thigh was completely exposed. Her blouse wasn't in much better condition. The whole outfit was good for nothing but the rubbish bin. Perhaps she could claim for new clothes on company expenses!

Despite her earlier plans for him, Beth knew that she was too weary to even try to turn him on again. Without saying a word, she headed out into her own office. Through the open door, she could see that Simon had finished dressing and returned to his own desk. She wondered what was going through his mind.

What would he do now? Was he wondering what to say to her or what she might say to him? Would he try to pretend that he hadn't meant it to happen, that he had just lost control? Would he dare try it again? Could he do it again? Despite her weariness, her clit tingled.

It was just over a month now since the interview that had led to this job. The advert had sounded perfect. Just exactly the opportunity she was looking for. Her brief but intense fling with Alec had come to a natural end and Beth was ready for something new in her life.

Her job in the newsagents seemed completely dull once young Jonathan was no longer there and she had resigned within a couple of weeks of him moving away.

Beth couldn't believe how much she still missed Jonathan. They had had so much fun together – even if she had lived in constant fear of what would happen if anyone had ever discovered that she was having an affair with a sixteen-year-old schoolboy! Not that there had been anything dirty or sordid about it. At the time, she had been lonely and insecure after her marriage breakup and Jonathan had been, well, Jonathan had been sweet and young and very innocent, and totally consumed by his insatiable passion for her. While it lasted, what they had enjoyed together had been both very special and very beautiful. It was a memory that she would always treasure.

The real motivation for her change of career, though, was her ex-husband, Tony. Ever since he had discovered how much she had changed in recent months, he had been finding one feeble excuse after another to visit her. He had even gone so far as to let himself in with the spare key one day while she had been in the shower.

Just because he still paid her maintenance, it didn't mean he had any rights. She regretted the way she had led him on when she had first discovered how much he now wanted her. If she were ever to be free of him, she needed to find a way to make herself financially independent and there was little chance of that while she was working in a newsagent.

It had been her best friend Ann who had come up with the idea of her returning to the financial world.

'After all, you used to earn good money once,' Ann had reminded her. 'And you've never lost your interest in financial matters. If you hadn't married Tony, you might have really got on as a career woman.'

A quick refresher course in office skills had soon brought her CV up to scratch, and then it was just a matter of finding the right company. She had hardly been able to believe her luck when she had seen Simon's advert for a personal assistant in the local paper.

Although his name had sounded vaguely familiar, it had only been when she had attended the interview and come face to face with him that she had remembered Simon Henderson.

Beth had known straight away that he did not remember her. Why should he? They hadn't seen each other for years. Not since she had married Tony and left work to become a housewife. She had been a bit on the plump side in those days and not an obvious choice for someone like him.

Simon had been the office heartthrob and all the girls had yearned after him. For a while, before Tony, Beth had been hopelessly infatuated with him. Apart from taking advantage of her to run his errands and do all his dirty work, as he took advantage of everyone, Simon hadn't even known that she existed.

She wasn't really surprised to discover that he had done so well for himself. He had an unpleasant talent for sucking up to those in power and advancing his own career at everyone else's expense. She could still remember how he had once outmanoeuvred Tony for a promotion he most certainly didn't deserve. And now, here he was, the director of his own financial advisory company. How typical of the man.

Right from the start, her interview had gone well. It was obvious that Simon was interested in more than just her experience and qualifications. He had hardly been able to take his eyes off her breasts from the moment she had walked in the door, and his pointed comments about 'needing someone who would give everything to the job' had not escaped her notice. Well, as her friend Gerri always said: if you've got it, flaunt it. She had relished how avidly he had watched her body while they chatted.

Her initial reaction, once she had recognised him, had been to leave. He had always been an arrogant bastard; he certainly wasn't her ideal choice for a boss. It irritated her that he so obviously did not remember her at all. He must have noticed from her CV that they had once worked for the same company. Even though she had only been a junior member of the team, she would have thought that he might have shown some spark of recognition.

It was such a good job, though. Just what she was looking for. Jobs like this were few and far between. It was only after she had actually received his job offer that Beth began to realise just what an opportunity she had for a bit of extra fun. As she sealed the envelope with her acceptance letter inside, Beth made herself a promise. He might not remember her now but, by the time she had finished with him, Simon Henderson would certainly never forget her again.

Thirty minutes later, Beth had finished the last of the outstanding work in her tray. She gathered up everything that required Simon's immediate attention and headed back into his office. While she waited for instructions, she stood well within range of his hands and began to fiddle awkwardly with her gaping clothes, deliberately drawing attention to her semi-nakedness.

Simon pointed to one of the letters. She was pleased to see that his finger was shaking.

'What have you done about this?' he demanded, obviously doing his best to ignore the state of her clothing. His voice was shaking even more than his finger.

Beth leant over the desk and let her skirt open wide. Simon's eyes homed in on her thighs. She leant over further and her left breast partially flopped out of her blouse.

'I sent confirmation yesterday,' she replied, then jumped with surprise as his hand began to slide gently up her leg. She made no attempt to pull away.

Simon spun his swivel chair round to face her and put his knees either side of her legs. One hand started to caress her thighs while the other played with her pubes. Beth pursed her lips and struggled not to react. Although she could clearly feel the muscles of her bottom tightening and relaxing at his touch, she doubted that he would notice. She gasped with shock and pleasure as he pushed his finger on to the bud of her clit. She was afraid even to look at his groin in case her face gave her true thoughts away.

'It was entirely your own fault earlier,' he told her, as he continued to explore her.

Beth closed her eyes and prayed that he wouldn't stop. She said nothing.

'You've got such a fabulous body. I get a hard-on just thinking about you.' He lifted the hem of her skirt, pulled her down on to his lap and began to kiss her neck.

Beth could feel his erection rising up urgently underneath her. One of his hands was fondling her sex, the other her breast. The goosebumps were springing up all over her skin at the feel of his lips. It was almost impossible not to show him how much she was enjoying herself. God, he had wonderful fingers.

'You didn't really mind, did you?' he whispered.

Beth found she was having trouble breathing again. She tried not to so much as move against his fingers, lest she involuntarily gave him the answer he wanted.

'I'm sorry, Beth.' He removed his fingers. Beth almost collapsed with a mixture of relief and frustration; she had been so close. She melted into his lap. Before she could say anything, he put his hand under her arms and lifted her up off him.

Beth tried to stand but Simon twisted her round and continued to push her forward so that she fell across the desk. Instinctively she stuck out her hands, pushing everything on to the floor. Passively, she allowed him to manoeuvre her into position.

'I have to have you again.' Simon pulled the hem of her skirt up and tucked it into her waistband, then put his hand under her crotch to lift her up. Beth lay across the desk with her buttocks twitching. He slid his hands down over her hips and pushed her legs apart.

Beth obediently opened them and stood on her toes to give him the best possible access. She knew she was already damp with desire. He must realise how ready and willing she was. Had he been apologising for what he had done, or for what he was about to do? Beth felt a tinge of apprehension mingling with her desire.

'Please, not again,' she whispered softly, determined to play her role to the end.

Simon stood back, staring at her apparent surrender. Beth stifled a small whimper as her climax began to build up inside her again. She was sure that, if he so much as touched her there, she would come. She wouldn't be able to help herself. She whimpered softly again, pleased that she seemed to have mastered the art of turning her groans of pleasure into sobs and whimpers of surrender.

'You do understand, don't you?' She heard his zip

open and his trousers fall to the ground. 'Tell me you don't mind.'

Her whole body was shaking with her desperate need. Just get on with it, she begged him silently. She could barely breathe. Every muscle was trembling and twitching. She couldn't hold off any longer.

He started to fondle her buttocks again and Beth felt the tears welling up in her eyes.

'You've got a gorgeous bum, Beth.' As Simon bent forward and ran his tongue over her buttock, she felt both his hands still stroking her. He kissed the other cheek, then bit it gently. It was the final straw. With a deep, low-throated moan, Beth climaxed. Exhausted, she collapsed down over the desk, her legs almost too weak to support her.

Seemingly oblivious to what he had done, Simon pushed her further on to the desk and guided his cock into her. Beth was so numb she hardly felt him penetrate her. She was so wet that there was no resistance as he slipped effortlessly in and out of her with his thighs slapping rhythmically against her.

He pushed her against the desk with his hands, groaning and pumping faster and faster. Startled, she found herself responding yet again.

'Please,' she sobbed. 'Oh God.' For the first time, a feeling of panic swept through her. Surely she couldn't survive another orgasm so soon? She was afraid that, if she came again, she might actually pass out from the pleasure. Tears were running down her cheeks as she tried to wriggle out of his embrace. There was no escape and that knowledge increased the intensity of the experience.

'Please!' she panted as another climax tore through her.

Simon continued to pump harder and harder, his breathing ragged. His fingers were everywhere, squeezing and pinching her exposed flesh. One hand fondled her bottom and breasts alternately; the other held her hip, pulling her hard on to him. His thighs slapped loudly against her buttocks and he grunted loudly at every stroke.

As his climax approached, he began to groan urgently in time with his thrusting, increasing the pace as he slammed in and out of her. Finally, he gasped and rammed himself into her as deep as he could. Another gasp and it was all over. He slumped over her, totally spent.

Beth wasn't sure how long it had lasted. It had seemed like hours. She was so weary that she didn't even notice him withdraw. She was still lying there with her skirt up over her bottom when she heard him say goodbye. She fell asleep over the desk.

A police siren woke her. It took a few seconds for her even to remember where she was, then a rush of elation swept through her at the extent of her success. She could hardly believe what had happened, or how much she had enjoyed what he had done to her.

She groaned as she stood up and tried to ease the aches from her cramped muscles. She was so stiff she could hardly walk. Gingerly, she made her way over to the kitchen area and gratefully gulped down a glass of cold water. She began trying to rearrange her tattered clothing. It was a futile effort.

Had he any idea how much she had enjoyed herself? She almost writhed in shame as she remembered the way she had responded to his caresses. That wasn't quite what she had planned.

It was bad enough knowing what a conceited, arrogant bastard he was. She might not have seen him for years, but she could still remember all the office gossip of his many conquests. Even in the few weeks since she had started working for him, she had already seen how he behaved with some of his female clients and how they fussed and preened themselves for his benefit. She certainly hadn't expected to discover that he had anything to be conceited or arrogant about!

524

As she finished dressing, Beth was already contemplating her revenge. She knew she was being somewhat unreasonable, since it had been she who had led him on, but, somehow, when she got back from her training course, she was going to find a way to teach Simon Henderson a lesson he would not soon forget.

Simon took his time driving home. His thoughts were in utter turmoil.

He had known from the first time he had seen Beth that he had to add her to his list of conquests. He had always had a bit of a thing for brunettes. Beth's long, dark hair was complemented perfectly by her golden-toned complexion and those deceptively innocent hazel eyes. It was strange that he didn't really remember her from when they had worked together before. Why hadn't he had her years ago?

God, she had a fabulous body. Tall, slim and firm in all the right places. If he hadn't known that she was 38, he would have guessed her to be in her late twenties, early thirties. Next to her, his fair-haired wife seemed dull and mousy.

He remembered the way she had whimpered and struggled helplessly against him, pretending that she didn't want him to, when all the time ... The memory inflamed him. Beth had been every bit as good as he had anticipated, maybe even better. He had loved that innocent little-girl act she had put on for him; loved the feeling of power and control it had given him.

As he felt himself hardening, he wondered if he should go back and take her again. She had probably already left by now. His wife would have to do. Maybe he would rip Marie's clothes off and take her into the garden; she hated doing it outside. The very thought of it made his cock throb urgently.

525

Chapter Two

Fortunately, since she was due to be away from the office all the following week, there was no need for Beth to make any immediate decisions about Simon.

The course itself, in advanced financial-management software, was probably the most popular in their profession and held at one of the best training centres in the country. It was a brilliant opportunity to improve her CV and Beth knew how lucky she was to be given a place so quickly. Simon must have pulled a few strings to get her in. She felt no qualms about allowing him to pay for a course that would allow her to move on, as soon as possible, to better things. He had always been a master at using other people for his own ends. Now it was her turn.

The following Monday morning, as she packed her bag and prepared for the journey up to York, she couldn't help wondering how Simon would expect her to show her gratitude. Having had his way with her once he would, no doubt, believe he was entitled to enjoy her body as and when he pleased. It seemed ironical that such a bastard should also be such a fabulous lay. Her knees felt weak at the thought of what he had done to her.

* * *

Since she was unfamiliar with York, Beth took a taxi from the station. She was so preoccupied with her thoughts and plans that she scarcely noticed the admiring glances the taxi driver gave her in the mirror as he skilfully negotiated the rush-hour traffic. Her ex-husband had been pestering her again over the weekend and her determination to make herself financially independent of him was stronger than ever. She really needed to make the most of this course.

The training centre turned out to be quite near the heart of the city. It was a plain, modern brick building of indeterminate architecture and it stuck out like a sore thumb against some of York's more beautiful buildings. Beth noticed that the tiny car park at the back was already full and she was relieved that she had chosen to come by train. She had always hated driving in unfamiliar places.

As soon as she had checked in at the main desk and received her identity badge from a plain-faced, bespectacled woman who seemed to have forgotten how to smile, Beth nervously sought out her assigned classroom.

Several of the other trainees, all male, had already arrived and they stood around smiling sheepishly at each other and sipping foul-tasting coffee from flimsy polystyrene cups. Gradually, as ten o'clock approached, the classroom filled.

Beth chose a desk near the back of the room on the left so that she would be able to see out of the window. She settled herself as comfortably as she could on the hard, wooden chair and took out her notebook and pens. Giving up on the coffee, she allowed her eyes to roam around the room, eyeing up the men.

Most of them seemed slightly younger than her, but she noticed a few appreciative glances here and there and she gave an encouraging smile to those that looked the most interesting. She was not really surprised to discover that there was only one other woman. The financial world still tended to be somewhat male dominated.

One of the men who had been watching her ever since she had arrived walked over to her desk and bent forward to examine the name badge pinned over her left breast.

'Oh, Beth.'

Beth stood up politely and examined his badge in return.

'John, is it?' she responded with a friendly smile. 'Nice to meet you.' They shook hands as she appraised him openly.

At first glance, he was not really her type. Perhaps 30 to 35, he was tall and rather thickset with short, light-brown hair and hazel eyes similar in colour to her own. He had an attractive face with a square jawline and an enigmatic smile that hinted at a deep and thoughtful personality. She had the feeling that he was a man who knew just how to get what he wanted out of life. She also sensed that his interest in her was more than just casual politeness.

Another of the men spotted the opportunity to meet her and ambled over to join them.

'And who is this lovely creature, then?' Beth felt his hand brush her arm as she turned to face him.

Even taller than John, he was of much slimmer build with collar-length blond hair and pale blue eyes that were magnified by his tear-drop-shaped glasses. He was dressed casually in dark trousers and a soft leather jacket and his face had the tanned, weathered appearance of someone who spent a lot of time out of doors. Beth guessed him to be about the same age as John, maybe slightly younger. The man raised his hand to her name badge so that his little finger was resting lightly on her breast.

'Beth. That's a nice name.' A second finger made fleeting contact with her breast.

Beth smiled innocently and stepped back out of reach.

'Why, thank you –' she checked his badge '– Steve.'

Just then, the door opened and the instructor walked

in. To Beth's surprise and delight, she was female; a pretty blonde, probably in her mid-to-late twenties. She was very slim and had a rather boyish figure, emphasised by the mannish suit she was wearing. At least Beth would have more than one other ally against the men, although the other female trainee didn't look like she would create much of a diversion – but she wouldn't provide any real competition, either.

As they began to take their seats and settle down, Beth noticed that the men did not seem to be paying the instructor much attention. She wondered whether it was her masculine clothing that was putting them off, or if they just didn't like the idea of a female instructor.

'OK. Good morning, everybody. Welcome to Top Spot Training. My name is Lisa Williams and I will be taking most of the course this week.' She glanced round slowly, as if appraising the potential of the group.

'The primary aim of the course is to familiarise you with version 4.1 of Softtrend X. For anyone who doesn't already know, Softtrend X is fast becoming the *de facto* trends-analysis package in the financial sector. Since 4.1 has several major new features we've got rather a lot to get through so I will be moving at a fair old pace. Just call out if you don't follow anything. Also, there will be plenty of time to ask questions during the practical sessions. You'll notice that you've each been provided with a laptop for that.' She looked round again, her green eyes flashing. She seemed to have a slight trace of an accent that suggested she might be Swedish or Dutch.

'Now, before we get stuck in, I think it would help if you all quickly introduce yourselves. Maybe we can start here?' She pointed to the mousy woman who had seated herself in the front row.

As the introductions progressed, Beth began to doodle absent-mindedly in the margin of her notepad. Without realising what she was doing, she found herself scribbling down the names of those men who most interested her and including an odd and suggestive comment or two about them to help her remember who was who. She put a star beside Steve's name then, after a moment of hesitation, another star beside John. There was something about him that intrigued her. She had no intention of sitting alone in her hotel room every night.

When it was her own turn, she was pleased to notice that the room fell silent. She was fairly certain that more than one man was making a note of her own particulars, too. She kept her comments short and to the point and did her best to gloss over how short a time she had been back in the financial world.

As Beth sat back down, Lisa gave her a warm smile of thanks before she moved on to the next person. It was only after everyone had had their say that Beth realised she was the only one Lisa had smiled at. She noticed that one or two of the men were beginning to pay Lisa a bit more attention now that she had taken her jacket off and they could see her pert figure and the outline of her bra under her white blouse. Beth decided that it was likely to be an interesting week.

Lisa handed out a set of training notes and got stuck in to her first lecture. As she turned her back to write up a few pointers on the whiteboard, Beth let her eyes wander round the room again. She caught Steve staring at her and remembered the way he had allowed his finger to brush lightly over her breast while he had examined her badge. Cheeky sod. He reminded her of an older version of Jonathan with all that soft blond hair. Her pulse quickened.

She swivelled her head to look at John and caught him examining her again too. Did he and Steve already know each other? Even though John was a self-employed consultant while Steve worked for a large finance company, they hadn't acted as if they had only just met. Perhaps they had operated together before. Maybe they always worked as a team.

She noticed that Steve was talking quietly to another man and quickly consulted her notes. Brian. Well, Brian had been giving her more than the occasional appreciative glance. She rather liked the look of him. It was probably his gentle brown eyes and that friendly, carefree smile. He was dressed more formally than the other two, but he wore his dark business suit well. It was funny how some men looked good in a suit while others just looked like failed sales reps. She noticed a few silvery hairs at his temples and guessed him to be around her own age. She checked her notes again and saw that, like Steve, he worked for a big London finance house. Yes, she might enjoy whiling away a long evening with him.

Lisa finished writing up her notes and turned round to explain the first piece of practical work she wanted them to try. As she spoke, Beth glared apprehensively at the laptop on her desk, wishing that she could get over her instinctive dislike of computers and praying that she was not about to make a complete fool of herself.

To her great delight, however, she soon discovered that the work was easily within her capabilities. She had not realised how much she had already learnt from Simon. It was lucky that he was such a whiz with computers. As she typed away, she watched Lisa moving round the room, giving help here and there. Finally, she arrived at Beth's desk and crouched down to talk to her. She rested one hand on the back of Beth's chair and one on her desk, just inches from her knee.

'OK? Anything I can do to help?' She gave Beth another encouraging smile.

Beth could not resist. She had to find out, one way or the other. She turned to face Lisa and crossed her legs so that her knee was almost touching the instructor's leg.

'No. Nothing at the moment.' She leant forward so that she could whisper in her ear.

'Actually, I did quite a lot of studying before I came. It's very important for me to do well. The size of my pay rise depends on it.' Her nipple just brushed the back of Lisa's hand. She heard Lisa take a sharp breath and saw her give Beth's body a more than casual glance.

531

'Well, if there is anything I can do,' Lisa repeated, 'I'll be very happy to help. Anything at all.'

Beth smiled and Lisa patted her on the knee.

'I mean it. Any time, Beth.' Lisa gave her a conspiratorial look and her hand slipped a few inches up Beth's thigh.

Beth grinned. Despite her lack of familiarity with computers, she was fairly certain that she should be able to pass the course without any trouble and the pay rise was just a figment of her imagination. If she were being completely honest with herself, she could not resist the opportunity for teasing.

She had already learnt how much she enjoyed turning men on, but this was the first time she had ever tried to entice another woman. It thrilled her more than she could believe. Of course, a woman had to be harder for her to seduce than a man. Lisa's responses wouldn't be ruled by her prick, as a man's so often seemed to be. She smiled to herself.

At the morning break Lisa wheeled in a trolley of tea, coffee and biscuits from the corridor. Beth immediately found herself surrounded. She felt Steve brush his hip up against her and noticed that John's eyes were riveted on her cleavage. Brian wasn't exactly keeping his eyes to himself, either.

Although she was enjoying their attention, Beth couldn't help wondering whether she would be able to cope with all three men at lunchtime. Taking advantage of a brief lapse in their concentration, she excused herself politely and moved over to where Lisa was sipping her coffee – thankfully, this time, from a china cup. Out of the corner of her eye, Beth noticed looks of disappointment on the men's faces and she suppressed a grin.

After she and Lisa had chatted about the course work for a while, Beth asked where she could find a good place to eat for lunch.

'Oh, I usually go to a little place just around the

corner,' Lisa replied. She barely hesitated before adding, 'Why don't you join me?'

'Thank you. I'd love to.' Remembering the way Lisa had responded to her earlier, Beth felt a warm tingle of anticipation.

The rest of the morning seemed to drag, but finally one o'clock arrived and the class ended its morning session. As soon as they had left the building, Beth and Lisa headed up the main road towards the restaurant. Beth was still grinning at the look of disappointment on the men's faces when they realised that she would not be joining them. She liked the idea of them having to keep their hands to themselves over lunch. Or perhaps they would find another use for their roaming fingers. She started wondering who had got the most to offer and was soon fantasising about inspecting each of them in turn. In her mind's eye, she could see them wanking away for her while she made her selection.

'Is there something funny?' Lisa questioned, seeing her smile.

'No. Just a thought.' Beth quickly dismissed the image and forced her thoughts back to Lisa. Was she correct in her assumption that Lisa was interested in her? If so, how far was she prepared to let things go?

By the time they reached the restaurant, they were chatting away together as if they had known each other for years. Beth discovered that Lisa's mother was Dutch and that she had been brought up in Holland, which explained her slight accent.

Lisa confidently led her to a small booth in one corner. She stood aside to let Beth slide in first, then slipped herself in beside her. The waitress immediately came over with the menus. As Lisa leant over to point out the best items, she moved her hip right up next to Beth's. She was so close that Beth could feel the heat of her thigh and a small thrill of excitement ran through her.

Lisa half turned in her seat and pushed her leg up against Beth's. She patted her on the knee.

'Actually, I usually just have a cheese salad,' she said. 'They have a wonderful selection of cheeses here.' As she spoke, she moved her body again so that her hand was fully resting on Beth's thigh, just above her knee.

'Well, why don't you order for both of us?' Beth replied softly, doing her best to keep the tremor out of her voice at the unfamiliar touch of another woman.

Lisa gave her a beaming smile and turned to signal for the waitress. As she turned back, her hand slid, seemingly accidentally, halfway up Beth's thigh. As if suddenly realising what she was doing, she quickly apologised and slipped it back down before removing it.

Although she knew full well that it was no accident, Beth had decided to play along. Lisa had almost reached the top of Beth's stocking before she had stopped herself. Beth wasn't sure just how far she would have let her go. Her leg was still tingling and she was surprised to sense a slight dampness in her panties. She wasn't attracted to Lisa, exactly, but she was certainly excited by the forbidden aspect of it all. She realised that she really wanted to know what it would be like with another woman. She wanted to see if she could seduce Lisa or, better still given her own lack of experience, let Lisa seduce her.

She started to fantasise what it would be like. Would she dare? Could she do it? How would it make her feel? Excited, Beth placed her hand on her own leg and began to slide it gradually up towards her stocking top. Out the corner of her eye, she noticed that Lisa was watching her with a knowing smile. Another little tremor of desire rushed through her and her panties grew even damper.

The waitress returned with their order and Beth removed her hand to pick up her knife and fork.

'So, what are your plans for this evening?' Lisa asked her, as they began to tuck in. 'I'd be happy to show you around if you like. I've lived here quite a while so I know my way about.'

Beth thought quickly. She was more than tempted, but

decided that she needed time to think through the implications.

'Thanks for the offer,' she replied, 'but, to be honest, I'm completely shattered after the journey up here this morning. I think I'm just going to have a hot bath and get a good night's sleep.'

Lisa looked disappointed. 'Well, perhaps we could get together another evening?'

'Yes. Why not?' Beth was certainly not going to close the door on the possibility. 'I'd like that. When I am not feeling so drained.'

Lisa immediately appeared to cheer up and as they ate they chatted happily, their conversation ranging from topic to topic: music, food, holidays, everything except, surprisingly, men. Beth realised that it was the first time she had ever chatted for so long with another woman without the subject coming up.

As the meal progressed, Beth realised that she was taking quite a liking to her instructor. Lisa was very amusing outside the classroom. By the time they were on to the coffee, she had Beth in fits of laughter over some of the things various trainees had got up to in the past. Beth reached out and put her hand on Lisa's knee.

'I think I am really going to enjoy this week, Lisa. You are so much fun to be with.'

Lisa immediately covered Beth's hand with her own and pulled it up higher on her thigh. Beth's feelings of arousal increased and intensified. It was like when she was first touched by Jonathan: exciting and naughty.

'Well, I suppose I had better get back,' she joked breathlessly. 'The teacher is a bit strict. She might put me over her knee if I'm late.'

'Yes, she would enjoy that. She can be very demanding.' Lisa gave Beth's knee a final pat. 'I'll get the bill.'

'Oh no, really, I can't let you do that.' Beth reached for her shoulder bag.

'I insist.' Lisa snatched the bill and headed for the cash desk.

Beth watched her walk. She had a nice figure, she decided. Perhaps a bit boyish, but that was good. She wondered if Lisa always dressed in such a masculine manner. Would it be easier to make love to another woman if she dressed and acted more like a man, or would it be more fun to imagine herself in the masculine role, seducing the female? She imagined herself sliding her hand slowly up under Lisa's skirt the way Lisa had been doing to her earlier. She found the idea surprisingly stimulating.

On their way back to the training centre, Beth brought up the subject of women wearing trousersuits.

'I used to wear jeans all the time but now I find they make me feel a bit sexless,' she confessed, nonchalantly. 'I always wear skirts and stockings now because they make me feel so feminine.' Not wishing to sound too critical, she continued quickly, 'Mind you, if I had your job then I would probably wear trousers, too. With your figure, the men just wouldn't be able to concentrate otherwise.'

Beth hoped it was enough of a hint. She felt quite pleased with herself. It had been just the right thing to say about Lisa's figure. She could tell that Lisa was pleased with the compliment as well as a little thoughtful.

'I usually dress up in the evenings,' Lisa replied slowly. 'But not at work. To be honest, it's not really company policy.'

'I see.' Beth smiled. Contrary to what Lisa had just said, Beth had noticed several other female members of staff wearing dresses. She felt sure that Lisa had got her message.

They strolled the rest of the way back to the training school in silence, each seemingly lost in her own thoughts. By the time they reached the classroom, Beth had made her decision. She was going to go through with it.

'How about tomorrow night?' she suggested nervously. 'My treat.'

'Oh, I'm sorry. I can't. I have to see my mother.'

Beth looked disappointed.

'I can make Wednesday though,' Lisa added quickly.

Beth hesitated. She didn't like not being completely in control. Besides, now that she had made her decision she wanted to act on it. Perhaps she should have agreed to tonight? She really was exhausted.

'Wednesday is fine,' she said. 'Will you pick me up? I'm staying at the Hilton. I can let you have my room number tomorrow.'

'Yes, of course. Shall we say seven o'clock?' Lisa's face suddenly looked flushed and her green eyes were sparkling with excitement.

'Yes. That's great.' Beth wondered if it was really her mother Lisa was seeing. She was surprised at the twinge of jealousy.

Beth enjoyed the rest of the afternoon. Although it was far more comprehensive, the new software wasn't really all that different from the earlier version that Simon had on his office PC. Once she had got used to using the laptop, she had no trouble with the exercises Lisa set for them. To her, manipulating the stock market and predicting company trends had always seemed like some sort of a game. Although slightly sceptical of the real advantage of the some of the fancier software gimmicks, especially the AI relational database, she had no difficulty in creating fictitious companies and predicting the probable market trends.

During the tea break, she quickly found herself surrounded by John, Brian and Steve again. Although they kept the conversation strictly on financial matters, she was aware of the desire smouldering in their eyes as they cast appreciative glances over her body. The proximity of so much masculinity focused on her made her tingle all over.

To her surprise, Brian was the first to ask her out. For

some reason, she had expected Steve to be the first off the mark.

'Well, not tonight.' She turned him down gently. 'Perhaps tomorrow?'

Both Steve and John extended invitations of their own shortly afterwards.

'I know. Why don't we all go together?' Beth suggested brightly. She could tell that the men were not too happy with that idea. The possibilities from her point of view made Beth feel quite weak.

'It's either that or not at all,' she insisted. 'How can I possibly choose between you?'

Defeated, they laughed and agreed. Beth wondered what the evening would bring. She studied each groin again surreptitiously, trying to guess who had the most to offer. Unless he had any extra padding down there, she thought it was probably John.

Beth finished her work early and asked Lisa if she could go to her hotel. She was suddenly feeling extremely grubby and weary after the excitement of the day, and she couldn't wait to get into a hot tub. Lisa followed her out.

'Take the stairs, Beth, the lifts can be a bit slow.' She followed Beth into the stairwell. 'I'm really sorry I can't make tomorrow but I always see my mother on Tuesdays.'

Before Beth could reply, Lisa gave her a quick kiss on the lips. Although it took her by surprise, Beth didn't pull away. She smiled when she saw the flush on Lisa's face. She noticed that the other woman was panting slightly and studying Beth's reaction carefully. Beth did her best to keep her own face neutral. Her lips tingled as her leg had done earlier at the other woman's touch.

'I suppose I'd better get back to work.' Lisa's hand lingered momentarily on her arm.

Beth took a couple of steps towards the stairs and felt Lisa's hand slip reluctantly from her arm. She looked round over her shoulder. 'OK. I'll see you tomorrow then. Thanks again for lunch. Bye.'

The hotel was quite close to the training centre and it didn't take Beth long to find it. She checked in at reception and was given room 309 on the third floor.

'Turn left from the lift. It's the end, corner room,' the bored-looking receptionist told her. 'Do you want someone to carry your bag?'

'No. It's not heavy. Can I get a sandwich sent up?' Beth was suddenly too tired even to bother about dressing for dinner.

'Yes, madam. Here's the room service menu.' He handed her a small leather folder. 'Just ring down when you have decided.'

'Actually, I'd love a prawn sandwich,' Beth replied without looking at the menu. 'Brown bread, preferably.'

'Of course, madam. How many rounds?'

'Two, please. And some coffee.' She suppressed a grin when she saw his eyes linger over her breasts. He would be quite good-looking if he took that sour look off his face.

'I'll have it sent up in about ten minutes.' His eyes finished their journey down her body and she was gratified to notice that his expression was distinctly less bored than it had been a moment earlier. She could sense him still watching her as she walked over to the lift.

Beth made her way up to her room and looked around curiously. It had two wide beds, a television, a kettle and a few nicely decorated cupboards and drawers. There was a separate bathroom and the view out of the windows was terrific. She could practically see the whole of York spread out before her and, being on the corner, she could see in both directions. She pressed her nose to the glass and peered out.

To the east, she could see the castle wall and a glimpse of the river glistening in the late evening sunshine. She turned her head and gazed up the main street. It really was a beautiful town, full of character and with such diversity in the buildings. Beth had never seen such clean streets. They put London to shame. She was almost tempted to go out for a stroll, but couldn't quite summon up the energy after her long day. Besides, her food would be arriving shortly. Her tummy rumbled hungrily; she adored prawns. Especially when Simon was paying.

Beth bounced on both beds and chose the one nearest the window. She unpacked her bag quickly and put her blouses and skirts into the cupboard and her underwear in the drawers. By the time she was finished, there was a knock at the door and a young girl's voice called, 'Room service.'

Beth picked up her purse and opened the door. The girl brought the tray in and placed it on the table. Beth smiled gratefully and gave her a tip. The girl thanked her politely and left, closing the door quietly behind her.

Beth locked the door and then stripped off her top layer of clothes to avoid getting any prawn juice on them. She sat down on one of the beds. There was a full-length mirror on the far wall and, as she ate, Beth studied her figure.

Her breasts looked great in the crop top. It had been a good choice. A bra would have made Steve's attentions to her badge less interesting. The material of the crop top was so fine that she had been able to feel his touch as if she had not been wearing anything. Better, actually, because the silk was so smooth.

She had to admit that it had been a neat move of his with the ID badge, managing a surreptitious caress of her breasts. Of course, it was always awkward for women, not knowing where to pin a badge. Men just stuck it on the lapel of their jacket. Maybe there should be a new rule, making them wear it on their flies? Now, that would be more like it! She pictured herself bending down to inspect each name in turn while her fingertips lingered on each one, getting the measure of them ... She raised one hand and stroked her breasts lightly, enjoying the sight and feel of her nipples hardening as they moved under the soft silk. Her nipples were not as big as she would have liked, but big enough. Lisa had smaller breasts than her. What would it be like to touch another woman? She looked at her legs in their stockings and tried to imagine Lisa's hands caressing them. A small shiver ran down her spine.

Beth finished eating her sandwiches and then started to fondle her buttocks. She slid her finger inwards until she met the elastic at the top of her crease and wondered if all three men had been trying to figure out what she was wearing under her skirt.

The sudden thud of a door closing in the corridor outside broke her train of thought. Smiling at her outrageous fantasies, Beth finished her coffee and went into the bathroom to run the bath. She undressed deliberately, practising her striptease and imagining an audience of men watching her, their hands busy in their laps under the table.

God, she was feeling horny. She regretted not agreeing to go out with one of her invitations. Still, it had been a long journey that morning and, anyway, she liked to plan what she intended to happen before she went out.

Beth stepped into the bath and gradually submerged her whole body. She was glad she had thought to bring a sponge. She washed the dirt of the day off and soon felt clean and relaxed. Her thoughts drifted to her planned revenge on Simon Henderson. She was going to enjoy that. She started to go over the details in her mind then dismissed them, returning to the next day and her triple date. She began to plan what she intended to happen. Should she take the lead or let them think they were in control? What should she wear? She was fairly sure that she could expect a lot more flirting and accidental touching during the day. If she wore a tight skirt, it would have the advantage of showing the outline of her stockings and garters to encourage them.

Of course, whatever she wore, Lisa would see her, too. She had a date with Lisa on Wednesday. What did you

541

wear to excite another woman? She had never really considered it before. Well, that was Wednesday's problem. She returned to the following day: tight silk skirt, stockings and garters – perhaps the lacy top and no bra. Then again, the lacy top only came down to her midriff. Remembering Steve's brief caress earlier, she began to fantasise about him accidentally catching his finger in the top and pulling it up until she was totally exposed to everyone. Hmm, perhaps not. Maybe she had better wear something else.

She settled on a low-cut satin blouse and lacy half bra. That should keep them interested, yet not give too much away. Of course, she could stick close to Lisa all day. That would frustrate the men. She wanted to be sure that she teased them sufficiently to get them really excited for their date. What would she wear for them, then? She reviewed her limited wardrobe again in her mind.

How about her short, loose skirt? A quick twirl and it would fan out around her, showing everything! She could wear it with the bare-midriff top, and just a thong and stockings underneath. It was a good thing that the weather was so mild. She would suggest that they take her to the restaurant Lisa had told her about, one where they also had dancing. There would be plenty of opportunity for wandering hands on the dance floor. Then, back to her room, not one of theirs.

Beth lay back in the hot bath and pictured each of the three men in her mind. They were all quite handsome, although she thought she probably liked Steve's rugged good looks and silky blond hair best. There was something about that smile of John's, though. Instinct told her that John would be a very interesting man to get to know better. She really would have to decide whether to take control or let them. She thought about Simon and how good it had felt letting him think he was in charge. Would she be able to keep all three under control? She would need to be very strict.

She pictured them lined up in a row, waiting for her

to make her selection. Perhaps she could have a contest to see who had the most to offer. She could sit on the bed, her skirt up round her thighs, with Steve and Brian on each side of her and John in front, looking up her skirt. She let her imagination have free rein.

'OK. One at a time, drop them. You first, Brian. I want to inspect your credentials.'

She could clearly picture the smile on John's face. They both already knew he had nothing to worry about. She couldn't wait to see for herself.

She imagined the other two protesting, trying to make excuses. Perhaps she would be forced to give them a little more encouragement?

Beth pushed her hand down under the water and put it between her legs. She imagined the look on their faces if she started to play with herself in front of all of them. She would get them all hot and panting for it, then insist they obey her or leave.

She began to caress her clit with one finger. She pretended it was Brian touching her, while John and Steve looked on enviously. She would let him fondle her, even allow him take her hand and place it on his cock. She would squeeze his hardness and feel him growing in her hand. Beth shuddered and pulled her fingers away.

She could see them lined up, red faced and desperate. She conjured up a picture in her mind of each of them in turn beginning to unzip himself. If she was not very much mistaken, John especially was destined to be quite a handful. She remembered the more than obvious outline at his groin and suddenly felt almost dizzy with longing. The fantasy was so real.

She pushed the tips of her fingers into her vagina and imagined that John was thrusting his huge prick deeper and deeper inside her. There was a loud crashing noise and Beth slipped under the water in shock. She came up spluttering and opened her eyes. Her fantasy men disappeared. What the hell was that?

'Room service. Have you finished with your tray, madam?' Someone was knocking on the door.

Damn. Now she would have to wait until tomorrow to see if she had got it anywhere near correct. Why on earth had she turned them all down tonight? Ignoring the door, Beth moved her hand back down under the water and lay back contentedly. As John's erection magically reappeared in her mind, Beth sighed with anticipation and resumed fondling her tingling clit.

John, Brian and Steve met up that evening in the bar of the hotel in which they were staying. Brian ordered a round of drinks and they sat at a corner table to unwind after the long day.

It was not the first time the three of them had been on a training course together and, for a while, they chatted about their work and caught up on each other's news. Soon, they moved on to the day's course work and began speculating about Lisa.

'She's quite a looker, in her way,' Brian commented. 'But she seems a bit hard. Somehow, I don't fancy my chances.'

John nodded thoughtfully. 'Actually, I suspect Beth is more likely to appeal to her than you are,' he suggested. Brian's eyes widened at the implication.

'She's quite something, isn't she? Beth, I mean. How old do you reckon she is?' continued John.

Brian blew the froth off his beer and took a long, satisfying gulp. 'That's great. Just what I needed.'

Steve shrugged. 'Early thirties, maybe? She certainly is gorgeous. I still can't believe she's agreed to go out with us all tomorrow.'

Brian licked the beer off his upper lip and frowned. 'I just wish she'd agreed to go out with me alone. No offence, but I did ask her first and having you guys along will just cramp my style.'

'Maybe she's got a thing about having more than one man at a time,' Steve suggested hopefully. He sighed heavily at this somewhat optimistic fantasy. 'She certainly is one classy lady. Not only beautiful but intelligent too, by the look of it. Did you notice how fast she finished the practical work this afternoon? I was still only halfway through when she left.'

John watched them both thoughtfully. He, too, would have preferred to take Beth out on his own. He had the feeling that Beth was a woman who enjoyed playing games and he had more than a few games of his own in mind.

'I think you'll find that there is a lot more to Beth than meets the eye,' he told his companions softly. 'And, I don't think she is anywhere near as sweet and innocent as she pretends, either.'

No one with a body like hers could be that innocent. Those eyes of hers were enough to drive a man insane. She had been playing with them all, even Lisa. He raised his beer glass in a toast.

'Cheers.' He took a small sip and examined the other men over the rim of the glass.

'Something tells me that tomorrow night is going to be very special,' he added softly. 'Very special and very memorable.'

Chapter Three

Lisa kept them all hard at it the following morning, so that Beth found she had little time to dwell on her various dates to come. Determined to frustrate the advances of the men until later, she kept close to Lisa during the mid-morning break. Since it was such a lovely day, the two women took their coffee outside and sat on a low wall in front of the training centre. Beth took advantage of the opportunity to question Lisa more closely about the aims and goals of the rest of the course. If she could get any advantage out of her friendship, she was determined to make the most of it.

As if by mutual consent, neither of them mentioned their date for the following evening. Beth realised that she was growing increasingly nervous about the whole thing. Short of asking Lisa outright, she couldn't see any way of finding out just how experienced she already was with other women. Despite her erotic thoughts about fondling Lisa's legs, Beth could not really see herself in the dominant role. She wouldn't know where to begin.

No, for once, she was going to have to take the submissive role. She promised herself that she would do whatever Lisa did or told her to do. Possible scenarios immediately flooded her mind and Beth shuddered, partly in fear, partly in anticipation.

When they returned to the classroom, she found it difficult to concentrate on the lecture. Her thoughts kept returning to images of herself caressing Lisa's silky thighs. By lunchtime, she was so eager to get on with the experience that she was tempted to suggest to Lisa that they go to her hotel room right then. While Beth hovered indecisively, Lisa gathered her things together and hurried off without saying where she was going. Beth wondered if she had a date with someone else.

Resisting the temptation to follow her and see what she was up to, Beth sneaked away before any of the men could suggest lunch. After a quick sandwich, she whiled away the time window shopping in the nearby shopping mall. She went into several boutiques and was unable to resist trying on a gorgeous red silk blouse that would go perfectly with the skirt she intended wearing that evening. She examined the price label ruefully, knowing it was far too expensive for her budget. Then she shrugged. She would just have to find a way to lose it on her overall expenses. Simon owed her some new clothes, anyway.

That afternoon, the course continued to go well. To her delight, Beth was beginning to discover that she was well ahead of most of the group and was sure that she would not have any trouble gaining her certificate. Of course, her friendship with Lisa gave her a better insight into what was required. Still, it annoyed her that she wasn't really learning anything new, yet needed to complete the course just to get a piece of paper to say she had passed. It was all such a waste of time. However, the fact that it was also wasting Simon's money did much to pacify her. Besides, considering the other possibilities that were opening up to her, the compensations promised to more than make up for it.

She amused herself during the afternoon tea break teasing yet avoiding close contact with her three male admirers. It was time to forget Lisa for now and concentrate on the potential delights of the coming evening.

'So, which of you is going to pick me up tonight?' Beth questioned as they were packing up their belongings at the end of the day. She had decided to let them take control at first but she needed to retain the option to change her mind later. It would be easier if she could think of a way to get them back to her room, rather than going to one of their rooms at a different hotel. She could already feel herself growing excited wondering which of them would try to take her first. She wanted all three at the same time. Would they do that?

She thought about Simon again. She hadn't struggled that much with him. Tonight would be different. After they had got so far, then she would really put up a fight. Perhaps they would force her into submission or hold her down? Maybe two of them would hold her while the third took her? She tingled all over at the idea.

'We'll all meet up first, then come for you,' John told her.

Beth smiled to herself. Obviously, they didn't trust each other not to take advantage of being alone with her. She told them which room she was in so they could call up for her from reception. It was important that they knew her room number for later, too.

As soon as Lisa released them, Beth rushed back to the hotel to allow herself plenty of time to get ready. She had another long soak in the tub, improving further on her fantasies, then lingered over her dressing and make-up.

Everything went according to plan. A call came just before eight o'clock. By the time she had locked her door behind her, the three men were already on the landing waiting for her. Beth asked if one of them would hold her key, since she had nowhere to put it. This had the added advantage of drawing attention to her clothing. She saw them all scanning her, looking for pockets. As she had decided the day before, she was wearing a mid-length black button up skirt, long enough to cover her stocking tops unless she twirled. Her new blouse was cut low and a little too tight so that there were gaps between the buttons when she stretched. As she moved, the men could see quick flashes of her skimpy bra.

'I'll look after it.' Brian was not slow to take up the opportunity on offer.

Beth handed the key over and watched nervously as he dropped it into his top pocket. It was out of her control now.

Beth could smell the drink on their breath as they crowded in the lift. As he casually placed his arm round her waist, Brian tried to slip his fingers between the buttons of her blouse. She twisted out of reach and scolded him in a joking, friendly way.

Escaping Brian, however, meant that she had stumbled against John, who began to caress her thigh with his fingertips. By the time they had reached the ground floor, all three of them had taken the opportunity to fondle her. Laughing, she stepped out of the lift ahead of them.

'I can see that I have got my hands full tonight,' she complained cheerfully.

'Not yet,' Steve countered suggestively. Beth ignored him and tried not to look down at his crotch.

They were using Brian's car and John was quick to open the door for her. She rewarded him with a brief flash of stocking top as she climbed in. One should always encourage a gentleman.

Beth had already told them about the restaurant that Lisa had recommended to her. There had been no disagreements and she had had the feeling that it did not really matter to them where they went to eat. Perhaps their thoughts were already on the after-dinner entertainment? They were not alone in that. She was already tingling all over again.

Although there were lots of jokes and laughter in the car, the conversation was rather forced and unnatural. Beth found herself wondering if they had already made the decision that they were going to have her, no matter what. She thought they probably had.

She smiled to herself, slightly nervous of what was about to happen but also exhilarated. She remembered that Simon had taken her twice. Would they all want to have her more than once, too? Could she take it? She had felt so drained after Simon that she had just sprawled over the desk. Now, here she was, deliberately provoking three men. This was far more exciting and dangerous. If things got out of hand, she would stand no chance of stopping them

She thrilled at the idea. Although she hardly knew them, she instinctively felt sure that she could trust them not to harm her. She wanted all three at once. It made her feel weak just thinking about it. By the time they arrived at the restaurant, Beth had vividly imagined half a dozen ways they might take her and she was already damp with her arousal. She just hoped that they would not disappoint her.

As she was sitting in the front seat, there was not much opportunity for any of them to take advantage of her during the journey. Beth half-twisted round in her seat, so that she could talk to John and Steve in the back. Her skirt rode up a bit and she noticed Brian giving her little admiring glances from time to time.

She leant forward, allowing both the other men to get a good view down her top. She carefully avoided looking at their trousers. That would only show inexperience. Besides, it would also let them know that she was deliberately teasing and give the game away.

Steve dominated the conversation. He was really quite witty. Beth found that she enjoyed his dry sense of humour and laughed at his jokes. As she had guessed, he was a keen sportsman and sailor. He kept them all amused with his exaggerated tales of adventure on the high seas in his small yacht. She wondered what it might be like to spend a weekend sailing alone with him.

All the men kept eyeing her hungrily and she was

certain that they assumed she didn't realise how much she was revealing of herself. Considering the way their eyes were running all over her, she would have had to be totally stupid not to realise. It was always an advantage to be underestimated.

When they finally arrived at the restaurant car park, Steve leapt out of the back seat and held the door for her. She slid out of the seat, her skirt riding up so that he got more than a quick glimpse of panties as she stepped out.

Since he was holding her hands to help her out of the car, it was a few seconds before she could smooth her skirt down – long enough for the other two to hurry round to enjoy the spectacle. She couldn't have planned it better herself.

While Brian was locking the car, Steve and John quickly got either side of her. They took hold of her arms and pulled them round their waists.

'Your lucky day, with a man on each arm,' Brian joked when he saw what was going on. 'Not so lucky for the chauffeur,' he added ruefully, as they set off across the tarmac.

As they approached the door, Brian started talking with the *maître d'*. Beth was sure she saw some money exchanging hands. Certainly, the *maître d'* was all smiles as he asked them to follow him.

Even though the restaurant was relatively quiet, he led them to a secluded booth well away from the main dining area. Beth slid on to the bench seat with Brian and Steve on either side of her. John sat opposite and slightly on her left, presumably to make the most of her gaping blouse.

As the *maître d'* left, he signalled to the wine waiter.

'I don't really think I should drink anything,' Beth confessed quickly. 'I tend to get a bit silly after just one G and T.' She tried not to smile at the looks they were giving each other.

'Very silly after two and practically under the table at

three,' she added. 'Do you think I could just have an orange juice?' She knew that she was not meant to notice the little nod Brian gave John.

'I prefer to get them from the bar,' John announced as he stood up. 'That way I can see what they are doing.'

'I'm sorry?' Beth pretended to look confused.

'If you don't watch them, they pour you a short measure or give you one drink and charge you for another,' he explained. Steve and Brian nodded agreement.

'I see. Well, just an orange juice for me, then,' Beth smiled.

Brian and Steve both asked for lager and John went off to fetch the drinks, his face a picture of innocence. Beth could read his mind like a book. He had obviously done this before. He thought he could add alcohol to her drink without her realising. Was he in for a surprise! Not only could Beth actually drink with the best of them, but she had already had a milk shake and a quick sandwich to line her stomach before leaving the hotel. If they wanted to play games, let them. It would be even easier for her to take advantage of them if they thought she was drunk. Pretending to chat with the others, she watched John at the bar and saw the barman turn round to the bottles with a glass. So, she had guessed right.

John brought the drinks back, his face still expressionless.

'Everything OK?' Steve questioned.

'Yeah, no problem.' Beth pretended not to see the wink John gave the other two men.

'You mean they didn't try to fool you?' Beth queried innocently, knowing exactly what was meant. She did her best to look bemused when they all laughed at her comment.

She tasted the drink carefully and felt a slight warmth at the back of her throat. It was probably vodka.

'Thank you. That's very good.' She took another long gulp and put the glass down. 'I really needed that. I've been dry all day.' She quickly polished off the drink then pulled a face. 'It's a bit sharp.'

'Don't you like it?' Steve questioned anxiously.

'Oh yes. It's just a bit sharp, but very good. I wonder what brand it is? I'll have to remember to order it in future.'

All three men began laughing and Beth quickly joined in. 'Oh dear. I think I've got the giggles now,' she spluttered. 'It's not that funny.' This caused another paroxysm of mirth from the three men. Beth continued to look bemused.

Finally, they calmed down and settled down to order. Beth chose pâté with toast followed by a chicken salad. The others also ordered and sat back to enjoy their drinks. Music was playing softly in the background and one or two couples had gone out on to the dance floor.

'Would you like to dance, Beth?' Brian took her hand and pulled her from the booth before she had a chance to respond.

'As long as it's slow.' Beth accidentally missed her footing and made a grab for the side of the booth to steady herself, bending over to give them all a quick flash of stockings and panties. She had practised these sorts of manoeuvres at home for Simon's benefit and was certain she was so good that no one would ever guess she was doing it on purpose. Since they all thought she was a bit drunk, it gave her even more opportunity to be careless.

She half stumbled into Brian's arms. Instead of leading her to the dance floor, Brian started dancing with her in the small space behind the booth. He pulled her close and placed both hands on the small of her back.

Beth waited to feel his fingers over her buttocks and was surprised when instead he slid both hands down and pulled her even tighter against him. It was a neat move, effectively trapping her arms under his. She wriggled, trying to get free, but could not escape. Eventually, when she realised that her struggles were only adding to his enjoyment, she gave up and let him fondle her. As his fingers continued to caress her softly, he clasped her buttock tightly with one hand, pulling her close against his hardness and making it difficult for her to get away without making a scene. She allowed him his small victory. When he tried to slide a hand round on to her breast, however, it was Beth's turn to hold him tight so that he failed.

'Why don't we go on to a nightclub or something later, just the two of us,' Brian whispered. 'We don't need the others.' The feel of his breath in her ear made Beth shiver.

'It's hardly fair,' she replied. 'After all, I did agree to go out with all of you. Maybe another night,' she added.

The music ended and Brian held on to her, reluctant to release her. Beth was just about to slip out of his grasp when Steve appeared, cutting in. The music started again and, like Brian's, his hands were soon all over her. He started to lift her skirt and Beth was forced to twirl out of his grip, slapping the material back down and pretending not to notice that this had only caused the other side of the hem to lift.

'You mustn't do that, you naughty man,' she reprimanded him girlishly. 'Someone might see.'

Just then, the food arrived so they left their impromptu dance floor and went back to eat. As soon as Beth sat down, Steve and Brian moved close, thigh to thigh. She pretended to ignore them and concentrated on her pâté, which was delicious. She had been really enjoying the dancing and was sorry that it had had to end. Hugged up so close to them it had been impossible not to notice the obvious physical effect she was having on them. She was certainly getting them going, that was for sure.

She had noticed the little beads of perspiration on their faces, the intense expressions and the triumphant glitter in their eyes as she surrendered to them. She was also intensely aware of the animal scent of them; a scent not masked by their aftershaves. It was far more intoxicating than the doctored orange juice.

Apart from the insistent pressure of their thighs, the first course passed without any further incidents. Feeling cramped, she tried to move her legs, but it just seemed to encourage Steve to push even harder.

Beth had almost finished her second orange juice when John asked her to dance while they waited for the main course. As she stood up she used both hands on the table to push herself upright, giving him a great view down her blouse at the same time.

'Just so long as you promise to behave yourself.' She deliberately slurred her words slightly.

John grinned. 'It's a promise.'

She had to slip past Steve to get out. He wasted no time in taking the opportunity to push his hand up under her skirt to give her buttocks a quick pat. Beth squealed indignantly.

John pulled her tight against him as he steered her around the floor. She was intensely aware of his excitement pushed hard against her as his hands began to squeeze her nipples.

'John. Don't. Somebody might see.'

'Not unless you make a fuss,' he responded, giving her left nipple another tweak.

'Ow. I mean it. Stop it,' she repeated in a more demanding voice.

John reluctantly removed his hand. He pulled her even closer so that his lips were against her ear.

'Your little-girl act might be fooling the other two, but it isn't fooling me,' he whispered softly. 'You are no more drunk than I am and you know exactly what you're doing.'

Beth stiffened. 'I don't know what you mean,' she protested weakly.

'There you go again,' he responded as he continued to fondle her breast. 'Not that I mind,' he added, as his lips

555

gently caressed her neck. 'Your little games are very endearing. I promise I won't let on.'

Beth didn't reply. She made no further attempt to thwart him. Her pulse was racing as the implication of his words sunk in. She pushed herself hard against his hand as though to try and block anyone else from seeing what he was doing and pretended not to notice that he had undone her top button.

'That's it, Beth. Surrender to the inevitable.' She was infuriated by that smile of his.

When Beth and John finally joined the others, Brian quickly slipped his hand under her as she sat down, so that she found herself perched on his over-inquisitive fingers. She leapt to her feet again.

'Brian, stop it!' She took his hand and placed it firmly on the table. Brian and Steve roared with laughter. Beth continued to hold his hand while she sat down again.

'Now, stop it. It's not fair.'

By the time her bottom made contact with the seat again, Steve's hand was there. She grabbed it quickly, so that she was now holding both their hands. Of course, this meant that she could not smooth her skirt down. The plastic cushion of the seat was cold and hard against her bare thighs. She shivered with excitement.

Steve and Brian now had a great view of her legs and stocking tops.

'You're spoiling the evening,' Beth muttered petulantly. 'I don't mind a little fun, but you are going too far,' she scolded them all unconvincingly.

Despite what John had said, Beth was pleased with her performance. She could tell that Steve and Brian, at least, didn't know quite how to take her comments and behaviour, the drunken giggling and the girlish modesty. Her voice was saying one thing, her body language quite another. She was driving them both to distraction and loving every minute of it. How far did she dare push it?

The main course arrived and the men returned to

casual chatting and joking, their comments very much on the suggestive side.

'Would you like another drink?' John asked her as she emptied her glass.

'It's my round.' She was determined not to let John get the better of her. As she stood up to go and fetch the drinks, Steve grabbed her skirt, pulling it up. Beth instinctively sat down again. She discovered that there was no skirt under her at all. The hem was practically around her waist and she could feel a cold draught on her exposed buttocks.

'Be careful,' she protested. 'You almost ripped my skirt off.'

Brian winked at her. 'That was the general idea,' he admitted. 'John will get the drinks.'

Just then, the *maître d'* headed towards their table. Beth quickly rebuttoned the top of her blouse and attempted to straighten her skirt.

'Is everything all right?' the *maître d'* enquired.

Beth was tempted to tell him that things were coming along nicely but, instead, she smiled innocently and replied, 'Oh yes, delicious.'

'Do you want anything off the sweet trolley,' he questioned, 'or would you prefer just coffee?'

'We'll have three coffees,' Steve replied. 'The lady is just going to have another orange juice.'

Brian sniggered and Beth smiled, marvelling at how stupid they must think she was as they winked and nodded to each other over her supposed drunkenness.

She tried to pull her skirt down under her, but Brian stopped her. She sighed and reached for the drink John had now placed in front of her. John leant over the table and pretended to study her bracelet. He took both her hands in his.

'You've got lovely hands, Beth,' he told her.

She was just about to thank him when Brian and Steve put their hands on to her legs under the table. Beth tried to pull away but found that John was gripping her wrists tightly.

The two men slid their hands slowly up her legs and on to what were, by now, the wettest pair of panties she had ever had.

'Stop it,' she whispered urgently as realisation dawned.

'Stop what, Beth?' Brian questioned in mock innocence as he tried to force his hand between her clenched thighs.

Beth immediately crossed her legs but this only gave Steve a better attack. She felt his fingers trying to find their way underneath her panties and she immediately squeezed her legs tighter. All that did was to make her own arousal even more urgent. She shifted her buttocks from side to side and bit her bottom lip.

Steve had almost got his fingers on to her clit now. She crossed her legs in the other direction and felt Brian's fingers start to explore her again.

'Stop it. John, let go.' Her voice was not loud enough for anybody to hear except for the three men at the table.

'I like holding your hands, Beth,' John told her. 'In fact, I can't see ever letting you go.'

Beth shifted her buttocks again, wiggling all over the seat, her excitement tinged with fear at how far they might be willing to go. John was so strong that she could not move her hands at all. She knew she could still put an end to it if she really wanted to, however – but she didn't want to. The fear was real enough, though.

Brian had managed to get his fingers right down inside her panties. She tried to cross her legs again, but Steve was waiting for this. As she uncrossed them, he placed his left leg over her right leg. Brian had both hands under the table and was pulling her left leg wide apart. He put his own leg over it so that she found herself both trapped and totally exposed. She could feel their fingers caressing her flesh but could do nothing but squirm. She hoped that they would think she was trying to escape. In fact, she was just wriggling with pleasure. She glanced round nervously to make sure no one was paying any attention to them. It seemed incredible that she was practically being finger-fucked in the middle of a restaurant and no one seemed to be aware of what was happening. She felt Brian trying to pull her panties down.

Beth knew she needed to put a stop to that. She didn't want to be stripped in public, too! She slumped down in her seat as far as John would let her so that, although they had got her underwear half off, they couldn't get any further. She tugged her arms again.

'John, please let go. You don't realise what they are doing.'

'I've got a pretty good idea, Beth.'

Beth felt her heart starting to thud. She stared at him in shock.

'Pull her up, John, so that we can get her knickers off,' Steve whispered.

John began to pull on her arms and Beth felt her buttocks lifting off the seat. She tried to resist but there was little she could do. She clenched her buttocks as hard as she could but could not stop the waist elastic from slipping down around her thighs. She sank back down on to the seat, her legs like jelly. At least they couldn't get the knickers any further.

'I'll get the bill then we'll take her out to the car,' Brian muttered thickly. Beth recognised the look of lust blazing in his eyes. His words sent a cold shiver up her spine. She felt weak with excitement and fear at what they might be planning to do to her.

Had she gone too far? Maybe she could still get away. As Brian moved away, John slipped in and pushed her back on to the bench. Beth froze as he lifted her skirt. He ran his fingers over her newly shaved mound, then smiled wolfishly.

'Nice. I like a woman who remembers to shave.' He pushed his finger up inside her waiting dampness and Beth felt herself melting at his touch.

Steve stood up and, with a lingering glance at her breasts, headed off towards the loo, leaving the two of them alone. John smiled coldly and nodded his head towards the exit that led out to the car park.

'Once we go through that door, Beth, then you become our plaything for the night.'

Beth stared at him, without speaking.

'We are going to take you back to your hotel room and use you for our own gratification,' he added softly. His finger caressed the outline of her swollen nipple.

Beth swallowed. She realised that he was giving her a final chance to back out. She could call the waiter over and then just walk away. She wasn't even sure that she could walk, unaided.

'But then, you already know that, don't you? It's what you intended all along,' John continued as Beth digested his remarks. She felt his other hand slide on to her thighs. Before she realised what he was doing, he had pulled her panties down to her ankles. She gasped and locked her ankles together.

'Step out of them.'

Beth was horrified. 'No!' She exclaimed.

'You can't walk with them around your ankles,' he told her. He reached down and lifted one leg to get her started.

Without taking her eyes off him, Beth did as she was told. She bent down to pick them up, but John pushed her firmly against the seat.

'Leave them.' As he took her arm to guide her out from behind the table, Beth gulped.

'I can't just leave them.' She imagined the waiter or even the next customer finding her damp underwear in a heap on the floor. God. She could never come here again. Everyone would know what they had been doing to her.

John half-supported, half-carried her towards the exit. She was midway across the room before she remembered her skirt. John's hip was pressed against her and she sensed that most of her left buttock was exposed. Frantically she tugged the material back down.

Oh God, her knickers! She had not intended to let them do that to her. She had decided that they could take control, though, hadn't she? She swayed against him, feeling dizzy and light-headed. She needed some fresh air; she couldn't think straight. She should have put a stop to this before it was too late. She knew she couldn't back out now; she wanted it as much as they did. John continued to guide her confidently towards the exit. As they reached it, she felt Steve return and take hold of her other arm. The door closed behind them and Beth swallowed hard. She was totally committed now.

Chapter Four

Outside in the car park, John and Steve continued to steer her towards Brian's car. She hadn't noticed when they arrived that Brian had parked in such a secluded slot. The car park was empty except for a few cars in the far corner belonging to the other diners.

It had turned chilly. The wind had picked up and she could feel it tugging at her clothes. Cold air crept up under her skirt and caressed her naked flesh. Considering how small her thong had been, it was incredible that the lack of it should make such a difference. She knew she was being over-sensitive. She also knew she was with three men who were all well aware that she was no longer wearing any panties.

After a few paces, John stopped and pushed her up against the side wall of the restaurant. Brian, who had the car keys, was still paying the bill. When Beth saw the predatory look on John's face, she barely stopped herself from crying out. Jesus. Surely they weren't intending to take her here in the car park? Not that she would stop them – nor that she could stop them. Still, it hadn't been part of her plan. She started to panic. What if they were seen? She began to imagine everybody in the restaurant coming outside to watch. She pictured the men calling out encouragement while the women looked on with feigned disdain and barely suppressed envy.

'Take your bra off,' John commanded.

'I'm sorry?' His words confirmed her predicament.

'Take your bra off, now,' he repeated loudly.

Beth shook her head. 'You must be joking,' she whispered as she glanced round again just in case anyone was already watching. Steve and John were now either side of her, making it difficult for her to escape.

John reached for her blouse and wiggled his fingers through the gaps between the buttons so that his fingertips were just touching her breasts. Beth took a deep breath.

The look of shock on her face was quite real. It was no longer necessary for her to play-act. He had already given her a chance to back out. By saying nothing, she had as good as told him that it was OK for them to have her. Now, it seemed they were going to make her strip right here.

'No.' She grabbed his hand with hers. All she succeeded in doing was to push his fingers harder on to her breasts. She gasped. She was having trouble with her breathing again. She could hear each breath rasping in and out noisily; she was practically panting for it. She let go of him and John released her blouse. She looked round at Steve. His glasses had misted up in the cold air. As he removed them to wipe them dry, she stared into his eyes and shivered at his hungry, expectant look. She turned back towards John and saw the same expression echoed in his face.

Seeing her watching him, a slightly sardonic grin broke out across John's lips. He parted them, exposing his tongue. Slowly, he ran it over his dry lips. The gesture was deliberately crude, provocative. She heard Steve swallow noisily as she started to move her hands up towards her breasts.

Trying to stop her fingers shaking, Beth slipped them inside her blouse and opened the catch of her bra. The click as it came undone seemed almost deafening. She flinched as a cat jumped up on to a nearby wall and began to wail. She could almost sympathise with the desperation in its call. She couldn't believe how excited she was becoming.

Beth closed her eyes. The cat fell silent. She could hear Steve shuffling his feet impatiently beside her. In fact, the air was now so quiet that she could hear the sound of his fingers moving against the material of his trousers. She realised that he had put his hand down inside his flies to adjust himself. She could imagine his erection straining uncomfortably against his pants and almost feel his excitement as he touched himself with his fingers. She felt a ripple of longing between her thighs.

Beth undid the buttons on her sleeves. She heard a sharp intake of breath.

'She's going to do it.' Steve's words were so soft she could barely make them out. John didn't respond, but she heard his breathing quicken. She pushed her hand up inside a sleeve and grabbed the shoulder strap to her bra.

A car pulled up on the other side of the car park and Beth jumped as the doors opened, then slammed. She could hear voices talking and joking as a couple headed towards the restaurant. John moved in closer, until she could feel his warm breath on the side of her neck. She reached up her other sleeve for the second strap.

With a sharp tug, Beth whipped the bra down her left arm and out of the cuff of her sleeve, like a magician pulling a rabbit from a top hat. She kept her elbow into her side as she held the bra out for them without showing anything. John took it from her without a word and let it drop to the ground. At the rate they were going, she would be leaving a trail of discarded clothing all the way back to the hotel – a bit like an X-rated paper-chase.

Beth realised that her breathing had returned to normal. She was feeling much calmer and more in control again now. She had evaded their intentions so easily. She almost grinned as she heard John's disappointed snarl.

'Oh, very clever, Beth,' John congratulated her. 'But, I think we'll just undo these top buttons anyway, don't you?' As he spoke, he reached for the top button of her blouse.

'Will you do it, or shall I?' he asked her. 'I don't mind either way, but if I do it, I might just get carried away and undo all of them.'

She might have won the first round but, obviously, John was not going to let her enjoy her small victory for long. Beth moved her fingers slowly up over her stomach and under her breasts until she reached the top button. She took her time, knowing that, for the moment, she still held the power.

She heard Steve smacking his lips as the first button popped undone. As she moved her hands down, she could feel her breasts. Any second now, she would be exposed. She slipped the button open and hunched over, trying to keep the material together across her chest. The blouse was so small and tight that it wouldn't take much now for her breasts to slip right out.

'Make her undo the next one,' Steve whispered hoarsely to John. It confirmed her suspicions about who was in control: John.

The restaurant door crashed open, making them all jump. Beth only just managed to stop her left breast falling out. She clutched desperately at her blouse.

'There you are,' Brian called as he began walking towards them. 'I hope I haven't missed anything.'

Nobody said a word. John took Beth's hand away from her clutched blouse and opened it slowly. Beth found herself beginning to tremble as his fingers moved closer to her breasts. She shuddered at the first touch, suddenly desperate for him to fondle her.

John grinned and stepped away so that they could all admire his handiwork. Brian's low-pitched whistle immediately reminded Beth of why women think of men as wolves. Brian's whistle sounded like the call to feed.

'Beth decided that she didn't need her bra anymore,' John finally responded to Brian's question.

'So I see.' Brian said. 'This lady has a bit of a habit of dropping her clothes about the place, doesn't she? The poor waiter almost had a nasty accident just now when he tripped over her knickers. You should have seen his face when he picked them up and realised what they were.'

Beth opened her eyes and stared at Brian in horror as his words sank in. She could sense that they were all waiting for her reaction.

'Yeah, I can imagine,' said Steve, his excitement palpable. 'What did he do with them?'

'You mean after he had sniffed them and licked his lips?'

Beth could sense her cheeks burning. She knew Brian was being deliberately coarse just to upset her. It was working. She tried to turn her face away. Even though it was getting quite dark, there were several lights on outside the building and John had managed to place her right under one of them. She could not escape their knowing grins.

She glanced down at herself and was thankful to see that she was still more covered than revealed. Without the bra, though, her nipples were quite obvious, as was the gleam of perspiration in her cleavage. Damn John!

'He was in seventh heaven,' Brian continued. 'He rubbed them all over his face. He even started licking them. I hope you don't want them back, Beth. You would break his heart.'

She knew they were still watching for her reaction. She couldn't stop the horror showing on her face. Supposing the waiter came out before they left?

'Excuse me, madam. You seem to have dropped your knickers. Shall I help you put them back on?' She shuddered with embarrassment, both at her thoughts and at the smirk on John's face – on all their faces. She could sense that they were waiting for her to say something. Her lips were very dry and there was a lump in her throat that she couldn't seem to swallow.

She knew that she was twitching all over but could do nothing to control it. She felt like a fish caught on a hook. They were reeling her in, inch by inch, and she could do nothing but struggle helplessly on the end of their line. She had never been so aroused.

The three men were still chuckling, revelling in her discomfort.

'What did he do then?' Steve demanded.

'Well, for a second, I thought he was going to start jerking off there and then,' Brian continued crudely.

Despite herself, Beth felt her curiosity aroused. What would the waiter want with her damp underwear?

'He pushed them down the front of his trousers,' Brian continued. 'I expect he's going to keep them for later.'

Steve leant against the wall and stared at her. 'What do you think he's going to do with them later, Beth?' His words were very slow and deliberate. He reached out and ran one finger down her throat, across the front of her blouse and on to her right breast. 'Do you think he wrapped them round his dick?'

Steve pushed her blouse out of the way so that she was fully exposed. Slowly and deliberately, he began to rub the knuckle of his finger over her nipple. As he started to peel back the other side of her blouse, he repeated his question.

Beth found she couldn't speak. Her whole body was trembling. All she could think about was her panties nestled up against the waiter's cock. She didn't know whether to believe it or not. She tried to mouth a few words but only succeeded in spluttering.

'You know what I think?' John suggested. 'I think that, at the first opportunity he gets, he'll nip to the loo, pull his pants down and wank himself with your knickers.'

Beth jumped at his words and twisted her head round to face him, her eyes wide with disbelief.

'You'd like that, wouldn't you, Beth? Like to watch him wanking all over your undies?'

Beth stared at each of the men in turn, not knowing what to do or say. Should she admit to enjoying the idea? She knew that was what they wanted her to do.

She had a quick vision of the waiter slipping her panties on and pulling them up over his tight little bum. There wouldn't be enough material to cover him. That thought excited her, too.

Finally, she found her voice. 'Please can we go now?' She was suddenly desperate to get back to the safety of the hotel room. She wanted them to throw her on the bed and take her, one after another.

'Please. Before the waiter comes out. Take me to my hotel.' Before I lose all self-control and start ripping your clothes off, she added silently.

'Hmm. Not quite yet, Beth.' John was taking charge again. She knew he was toying with her. Knew he knew what she wanted. Was he trying to make her beg? She would, too. She knew she would. Right now, all she could think about was getting one of them to take her. Even here in the car park.

'I think we should have a little contest first,' he announced.

'Contest?' Beth questioned incredulously.

'Yeah. Let's see if you can guess who's got the biggest one and whose is the thickest.'

'Biggest? Thickest?' Her voice rose an octave on each word. 'What do you mean?'

'I think you know what I mean. Come on. Don't try to tell me you haven't been wondering who's got the most to offer?'

'No, I haven't,' Beth denied the accusation. Her face started to change colour again.

John raised his eyebrows. 'I don't believe you,' he told her. He moved closer and stood right in front of her.

'Nice nipples,' he commented.

Beth opened her mouth, then covered it with her fist. 'Oh.' She had completely forgotten how totally exposed she was. Her face flamed.

John placed his hands on her hips then slid them down her thighs. Crouching slightly, he reached the hem of her skirt and started to move inwards towards the buttons on the front. Beth instinctively drew her legs tighter together.

To her surprise he didn't try to put his hand up her skirt, just opened the bottom button. His fingers moved up to the next one.

'Admit it, Beth.' She felt another button slip undone. Still she said nothing. His hands began to move up again.

'Yes,' she spluttered.

'Yes, what?' He opened the third button. Then, no longer needing to crouch, he stood up and stared into her eyes.

Beth still hesitated. 'Yes. I have been wondering who has got the biggest one,' she whispered finally.

Her words were not fast enough to save another button from opening. John stepped back. The next one was just inches away from her mound. Her stocking tops would be clearly visible when she moved and, if her skirt rose even a fraction when she walked, nothing would be safe from their eyes.

'Well, now's your chance to find out. I want you to give each of us a good grope and tell us who wins.'

'No.' Beth feigned shock, praying he wouldn't open the next button.

John ignored her. 'If you're wrong, we will just have to spank you when we get back to the hotel,' he continued.

'I won't do it,' Beth insisted boldly, already shaking with excitement and anticipation. She stared defiantly at him.

'Yes, you will,' John insisted confidently. 'Because, if you don't, Steve and Brian are going to take an arm each and spread you across the bonnet of the car.' He paused to let that sink in.

Beth could see that Brian and Steve were delighted with the idea and were already moving forward to grab her.

'Then, I'm going to lift your skirt up and spank you until you do obey me.'

As he finished his threat, Steve and Brian grasped her arms. Beth struggled frantically, digging her heels in and pulling and pushing against them. It was hopeless. Within seconds, they had dragged her across the tarmac and spread her, face first, over the front of the car.

Her breasts had completely popped out of her blouse at the first tug and the metal of the car wing was cold and hard against her skin. The breeze rushed up between her parted legs, teasing her trembling flesh. She lashed out with her feet, but the two men easily sidestepped her. Using the same trick that they had pulled in the restaurant, Brian and Steve hooked a leg around each of hers, pinning her in place.

'I'm going to enjoy this,' John smirked. Beth heard him spit on his hand and rub his palms together.

She whimpered softly as he lifted her skirt very slowly, inching his way over her thighs and buttocks until the material was up round the small of her back. He patted her gently.

'Yes. I'm really going to enjoy this,' he repeated.

Beth surrendered. 'OK. I'll do it, if it means that much to you.' She tensed her buttocks, waiting for the sting of his hand. The anticipation was worse than the action. The wind continued to ripple over her buttocks and caress the soft flesh between her thighs with its invisible fingers. The dampness between her legs was cold as ice.

John patted her softly again. 'Well, never mind. I expect I shall get another chance later. You're not the most obedient woman I've ever met.'

Steve and Brian let go of her arms and released her legs. They watched her closely as she straightened up, tucked her breasts in to her blouse and smoothed her skirt down. She looked around uncertainly, not sure where to start. Steve was closest. She was determined to make John wait until last.

Beth moved forward and bent down to unzip him. She felt John's hand on her bum. She straightened up and twisted away.

'I won't do it if you keep molesting me,' she protested.

John smirked and stared meaningfully at the car. 'Yes, you will,' he contradicted her. 'You will do whatever we say or . . .' He flexed his fingers. 'Anyway, that's not why I stopped you. You have to do it by touch alone. No peeking.'

Beth gulped. That wasn't the way it had happened in her fantasy. She wasn't sure she had intended to let them be quite this much in control. The quiver of her bottom lip revealed her indecision. She drew a deep breath and almost lost her breasts out of her gaping blouse again.

'All right.' She moved over to Steve and gripped his waistband with her left hand. Gingerly, she plunged her fingers down inside the top of his trousers.

'Remember, Beth. If you get it wrong . . .' John left the threat dangling in mid-air.

She wondered if they had already compared themselves. Was this some sort of man-thing? The biggest gets to go first? She fumbled around in Steve's pants until she touched his naked cock. She jumped and pulled her hand away in shock. God knows why. What else had she expected to find down his trousers? Warily, she pushed her fingers back and ran them down to the base, trying to make some mental measurements as she squeezed and stroked his unseen penis. His hard flesh twitched and jerked between her fingers and she could hear his laboured breathing. She couldn't believe how exciting it was.

Reluctantly, she withdrew her hand and walked over to Brian. Her fingers moved more confidently this time, quickly gripping his hardness. She was fairly sure that his was thicker, but could not decide whose was longer.

571

She certainly couldn't tell which of them was throbbing the most. She made a mental effort not to allow herself to squeeze her own thighs together. She knew John was watching her. She noticed that the look on their faces had changed from hunger to dumb pleasure at her touch and she experienced a surge of elation at the effect she was having on them.

'This is impossible,' she exclaimed as her fingers began their journey down John's front. As she had expected, it wasn't difficult to guess who was the largest; she had always known it would be John. She wasn't going to admit it to him, though, just yet. Without removing her hand, Beth reached out with her other arm and grabbed Steve. Pushing her fingers back down his pants, she made a great show of comparing the men. It wasn't really fair, because they had both grown even stiffer in the last few minutes. Reluctantly, she released John and tested Brian again, just for fun. She was thoroughly enjoying herself again now, revelling in the looks on their faces. As she fondled him, John had that expression of intense concentration she so loved. When she released him, she heard the long sigh that told her he had been holding his breath. She could see the sweat breaking out on Brian and Steve's brows. She wondered if she could make any of them completely lose control. It was tempting, but her own need was also becoming more urgent. She had a better use for their passion.

'John is the biggest and Brian the thickest,' she declared. 'Steve is the hardest,' she added quickly. She didn't want him getting a complex. It might adversely affect his performance. She looked around, loving the lust blazing in their eyes, the heavy sighs, the foot shuffling. That had certainly got them all on the boil!

'Well, am I right?'

John shrugged. 'How would I know? We'll find out later, won't we?' He frowned. 'I hope you're wrong. I've still got a strong urge to smack that very sexy bum of yours.' He patted her again.

Beth made another futile effort to contain her breasts.

'Let's just get back to the hotel,' Steve rasped urgently. Beth noticed that he had pushed his hand into his trouser pocket and was fondling himself. She shivered with excitement at his desperation for her.

Brian took the keys out of his pocket and unlocked the car. John moved closer. 'Steve, you get in the other side. Beth can go in the middle.' He opened the back door for her as Steve and Brian walked round to climb in the other side.

As Beth moved to get in, John flicked her skirt up. Holding it, he slid in beside her. She jumped as her cheeks made contact with the cold leather and quickly put her hands in her lap, trying to pull as much of her skirt over her as she could. Her breasts flopped free again.

As Steve slipped in beside her, she found herself wondering what was in store for her during the journey. She knew that it would not take much to push her to orgasm and she didn't think they were much better off. She tried to keep her face as expressionless as possible. Looking neither right nor left, she stared regally out at the front windscreen and let her mind run free.

I bet it will be John first, she told herself. He was obviously the leader. Brian next, perhaps? Brian started the engine and pulled off.

Her desire was building back up swiftly. She had never been at this level of sexual tension for so long without climaxing. She gripped her skirt tightly over her mound and began squeezing her legs together in her enthusiasm. The tensing of her body alerted John. He pulled her hands from her lap and placed them on her knees.

'Not yet, Beth. Later, for all of us.'

Beth flushed, not only for the implied threat of what she was clearly expected to do for them, but also because he had noticed her loss of self-control.

'What was she doing, John? Trying to inspect your dick again?' Brian laughed excitedly.

'No. Something else.'

'I didn't see anything. What was she doing?' Steve demanded. His eyes looked huge behind his spectacles.

Beth began to shake. Please don't tell them, she begged John silently with her eyes.

'Tell them, Beth.'

She shook her head.

'Tell them.'

Beth dropped her head on to her chest. She was so humiliated that she could feel tears burning behind her eyes.

'Find a quiet spot and pull over,' John ordered. 'Beth needs a little persuading. That bus stop will do.'

Beth's head jerked up. There were plenty of other cars about and the street lighting was good. If they were to put her across the bonnet now, people would see. Jesus. It might even get into the newspaper. Public exposure was all right in a fantasy . . . She stared desperately into John's eyes.

'Tell them what you were doing or everybody is going to get an eyeful.'

Beth was horror struck. 'I wanted to go to the loo. I was squeezing my legs to hold it.' The excuse sounded lame even to her.

'Pull over,' John commanded.

Brian obeyed. As soon as the car had stopped, he turned round expectantly. All three men stared at her.

'Last chance, Beth.' John obviously had no intention of letting her off the hook. Beth gave in.

'I, I was masturbating,' she whispered miserably.

'I'm sorry? What was that? We didn't quite hear you.'

'I was masturbating.'

'Better. But, I still didn't catch the last word. Why don't you run it by us again.' John was clearly enjoying himself.

Beth gritted her teeth. The tears were running down

574

her cheeks. 'I was masturbating,' she repeated loudly. She buried her head in her hands.

'There, there, Beth,' John reassured her. 'That wasn't so bad, was it? You must admit these little urges of yours. Like wanting to take your clothes off or wondering who has got the biggest cock and how much you want us all.' He grinned.

'You've been wondering who is going first, too, haven't you?'

'Yes,' she admitted quickly, still terrified at the idea of being publicly spanked.

'You see? Confession is good for the soul,' John told her, his hazel eyes sparkling with mischief. 'Now, show Brian and Steve what you were doing.'

Beth had managed to stop sniffling. All she wanted to do was to get back to the hotel as soon as possible. She replaced both hands in her lap and squeezed herself a couple of times. For a moment, she thought John was going to make her move the covering hand, so they could see exactly what she was doing. John, however, just smirked.

'Here. Dry your eyes and blow your nose.' He handed her a hankie and Beth dutifully dabbed her eyes and cheeks and wiped her nose.

She felt the car pull off. She cursed her stupidity. John was doing it on purpose. He was deliberately looking for any excuse to delay them and she had played right into his hands. He wanted her to beg for it. No way. She wouldn't beg and she wouldn't give him any more excuses to delay them. She would let them do whatever they wanted with her, once they got back to the hotel room.

To her surprise, they didn't touch her again, although she was acutely aware of their eyes devouring her, of their knowing grins and of the longing smouldering in their eyes. The silence was even worse than their comments.

'Whoops, I almost forgot.' John's voice made her jump

again. 'Brian, perhaps you could pull over again. Beth needs a pee.'

'No,' she exclaimed quickly. 'I'm fine. I'll go when we get to the hotel.'

Brian had already started to slow down.

'Oh, all right then. If you're sure? Carry on, James. Drive slowly. We wouldn't want to shake Beth up too much, would we?' John glanced at her again. 'Now, you are quite sure? It's no trouble.'

If she hadn't wanted him so much, Beth would have cheerfully strangled John.

'No. Damn it! No! I'm fine. Just get me back to my room.' She leant forward. 'Put your bloody foot down, can't you? This is a BMW, not a sodding hearse.' Beth rarely swore. Only when she was really provoked or under severe stress. It had never seemed more appropriate. If they didn't get there soon, she really would have to go for a pee.

She felt the car pick up speed. She squeezed her thighs tightly together again. The movement caused John to give her a sideways glance. She sat perfectly still, legs clenched, not daring to relax them in case he decided to stop again.

'You know, I've never actually seen a woman masturbating.' Steve started the conversation again.

'I have. Well, on films, anyway,' Brian replied.

'Not the same.' John patted her knee.

'No, they are not really doing it there,' Steve commented.

'Yes, they are,' Brian argued. 'You can tell a fake.'

'You reckon?'

Their deliberately crude conversation about female masturbation continued the rest of the way to the hotel. Beth did her best to ignore it but could feel herself getting wet with anticipation.

'We'll soon see.' Brian pulled the car into an empty slot. 'Beth is going to give us a little show now, aren't you, Beth?'

Beth did not respond. The talk had given her time to settle. She was feeling much more in control of herself now; calmer than at any time since they had first pulled her panties down. Holding her head high, she put a martyred expression on her face and clenched her teeth together. She promised herself that, no matter what, she would not beg again.

Steve climbed out the car. Beth began to slide across to follow him.

'This side, Beth.' John held her arm. 'You wouldn't want to get out in front of the main door like that, would you?'

She hadn't noticed where Brian had parked. She glanced down at herself in dismay then looked up at his face. Again, she experienced the urge to throttle him. She was sure that he knew just how close she was to total surrender. She would not let him win.

As she started to follow him out, he blocked the door, delaying her again. 'Wait until Brian is round here, too.'

Beth fixed him with an icy stare. She had no intention of giving them another public peep show. Let them wait.

'Right, now come out backwards and don't touch your clothing at all.'

Beth hesitated, then, remembering her promise to herself not to cause further delay, she did as she was told, ignoring the ribald comments and lecherous grins.

John was still laughing as he slammed the car door and took her arm. He led her towards the main entrance. 'You two had better walk in front or our Beth will create a bit of a sensation. We don't want her arrested for flashing, do we? I've got an urge that needs satisfying first.'

Steve and Brian laughed coarsely as they took up position in front. They moved quickly. Beth could feel her breasts bouncing up and down and she put her arm across her chest to try to stop them. She knew she must be flashing everything as she scurried to keep up with them.

Once inside the hotel, they made straight for the lift. Beth closed up as much as possible to the men in front. She didn't dare look round to see if anyone was behind them. She knew that this was her last chance to change her mind. It wouldn't be all that difficult to break out of John's grip. Her nails were long and sharp and it was only a few paces to the women's toilets. But no; there was no backing out now.

The lift door opened and an elderly couple stepped out. Beth turned her head so she would not have to look at them. They crowded inside.

It's not far, Beth kept telling herself over and over again. Steve moved up beside them and took her other arm. As he pulled it down to her side, she felt her nipples slip into view again. Only a few more paces to go. The lift stopped and John and Steve guided her firmly along the corridor.

She was so keyed up, she could barely think straight as Brian rummaged in his pocket and produced her key. Finally he opened the door and they led her inside and placed her face down on the nearest bed.

Beth lay motionless. This was it. Who would be first? She waited to hear the tell-tale sound of a zip opening. She wanted to be held down by two of them while the third took her from behind. She was growing more excited by the second. What were they waiting for? She could hear nothing but their breathing.

'Well, who's first then? How about me? After all, I did pay the bill and do all the driving.'

'Yeah, and?'

'Take it easy.' It was John's voice, naturally, taking control. 'There's plenty of time. Beth will take care of all of us at least twice, won't you, Beth? Wiggle your bottom if you agree.'

Beth didn't move. She sensed the smack coming and tightened her buttocks. After the third stinging blow, she wiggled her hips feebly.

'Good girl. Right. Before we do anything else, Beth

578

needs to know if she guessed right about us. Strip off, gentlemen.'

She wasn't surprised that Steve and Brian did not seem too keen on that idea. She was more surprised that they had continued to let John take charge of everything for so long. She hoped that they weren't about to start fighting over her.

'You two have got no finesse, that's your trouble. Beth wants to know who's got the most to offer her.' Beth heard John drop his coat over the chair. A deep surge of longing rushed through her. Who cared which one had the most to offer? She just wanted someone to get on with it.

John carried on undressing. Finally, she sensed the other two giving in. She resisted the urge to turn over and watch them. She heard a click and then music started playing.

'Come and see if you were right, Beth.'

Beth slid off the bed. Another of her skirt buttons had come undone and her crotch was clearly visible. She had already surreptitiously opened the rest of her blouse buttons. If John was determined to make her tease them, so be it. She was good at that. Besides, she was sure that Steve and Brian were not going to play John's games for much longer.

When she saw John's body, she had to bite her tongue to stop herself gasping. She had thought he was a bit on the tubby side, but now she could see that he was all muscle. He looked as if he could break the other two men in half if he wanted. No wonder they were letting him take the lead. God, his chest was bigger than hers! She gulped, hardly daring to look any lower.

'Well, did you get it right?' John questioned.

Beth dropped her eyes and made a pretence of scanning all three men, before returning her gaze to John. She almost licked her lips in anticipation. She nodded silently.

'Good. Now let's get on with it,' Steve demanded

impatiently. 'You can go first. Then Brian, then me.' Beth noticed the sweat glistening on his naked skin.

'I'm not sure that's entirely fair, is it? I mean, just because I've been blessed with more muscle than most, why should I automatically go first?' John replied. He smiled at Beth, clearly aware of her discomfort and enjoying it to the full.

'I think we should play cards for her.'

'Cards?' Steve and Brian spoke together.

'Yes. The first one to win five hands gets her.'

Beth whimpered under her breath. Where did this man get his self-control from? He wasn't even fully aroused yet, as the other two were. Perhaps he was all mouth and muscle? She felt a small rush of disappointment.

'OK. Let's get on with it,' Brian reluctantly agreed.

'As we are playing for the pleasures of your body, Beth, it seems only fair you should show us the prize. Strip, woman, strip.'

Beth didn't even hesitate. Before John had said 'strip' the second time, she had ripped her blouse off and begun to drop her skirt. As she started to peel her stockings down, she remembered that, in her fantasy, she had done this slowly and reluctantly. She was far too desperate for that.

'Not very ladylike, Beth. Anybody would think you were in a hurry,' said John. Beth did her best to ignore his sarcasm. She just wanted them to get on with the card game before she lost control completely.

'Now then, Beth. Why don't you make yourself comfortable on the bed? Kneel here with your thighs apart and your ankles together.' He patted the duvet encouragingly. 'That's it. Now, bend over and touch the bed with your nipples.'

Beth turned her head and pushed her breasts down on to the duvet cover.

John smiled appreciatively. 'Well, lads. That's what we are playing for.' He slipped his hand underneath her and ran his finger gently over her clit. Beth shuddered and fought the climax that was threatening to engulf her.

'Yes. I think she is just about ready for the winner.'

Beth kept perfectly still as they dragged a table and some chairs over. She heard the noise of cards being shuffled and dealt, and then Steve's voice asking for more cards. She didn't dare look up at them.

Brian won the first hand. Then there was a delay because no one had any paper or pen to keep the score. While John was searching around, the other two inspected the prize, touching and tormenting Beth until she began whimpering again, writhing around the bed as she fought her approaching orgasm.

'Right. Brian, Steve, John.' John called their names out as he wrote them down. The game continued.

After the second hand, Steve had the bright idea that Beth should entertain them while they played.

John pursed his lips thoughtfully. 'No. She's already boiling now. Let her start and she won't need us, eh, Beth? That's right, isn't it?' Beth chose not to reply.

He was right, of course. All she needed was a few seconds. Steve's suggestion would have been a lifeline. Once she had taken care of herself, she would be able to take control of the situation again. Damn John! She had more than met her match this time. She bit her lip, then flushed when she saw he was still watching her. Her eyes dropped hungrily to his crotch.

'Tell you what, though,' John added. 'Beth, why don't you kneel in front of us?'

Beth pushed herself up into a kneeling position.

'No, facing us, Beth,' he told her in a slow, patient voice.

Beth turned around and put one arm across her front. Quickly, she placed her other hand over her mound. John smiled. Wordlessly, he leant across and parted her legs, then moved her hands on to her hips.

The game continued with the occasional break so that they could rearrange her body into other poses; each

581

man clearly trying to outdo his companions with the imaginative positions they placed her into. Beth said nothing, not daring to refuse, no matter how humiliating their demands became. When Brian finally won, she almost shouted aloud with relief.

'Have you got protection?' John asked.

'Yeah. I've got plenty.' As he spoke, Brian threw an open pack of condoms on the bed. They spilled out beside the box Steve had also produced. Beth realised that there must be nearly twenty condoms on the bed.

Suddenly, Brian grabbed her, pulled her up and penetrated her from behind. The shock of it caused her vaginal muscles to contract, gripping him like a vice. She felt him pushing deeper and deeper into her and she clamped her lips tightly together to stop herself from crying out with sheer pleasure and relief.

She could sense the other two men watching and imagine their own excitement building. Part of her wanted to prolong the show as long as possible, torturing them with anticipation; part of her was so desperate for her own release that she knew she couldn't hold out. She gritted her teeth and closed her eyes, willing herself to resist.

Brian groaned urgently and increased his stroke. His hands reached round and caressed her swollen nipples and a small whimper fell from her lips. It was no good. She couldn't help herself. With a loud moan, her powerful orgasm rippled through her shuddering body.

Her obvious pleasure was too much for Brian. His cock jerked and she heard his urgent sigh of release. Beth pushed her head down into the duvet to smother her gasps.

'There. I told you she was ready.' John patted her arm. 'Your turn, Steve. Just a quick one first. We can take our time later.'

Beth just lay there, passively, revealing in her enjoyment. To her surprise, Steve entered her gently, almost reverently. From some of his comments earlier, she had half expected him to be the least considerate. Almost immediately, she sensed that he was not going to be able to last long. His whole body was rigid with his urgent need for release. Memories of Jonathan rushed into her mind. She had never been able to get enough of his desperate lust for her.

Steve built up speed quickly, pumping in and out of her with an urgency that enflamed her. 'Oh Christ,' he whispered. 'You drive me crazy.' His fingers caressed her breasts and his teeth nibbled her neck, sending little shivers down her back.

When he came, his climax was so violent and his moans of delight so intense, she was afraid that they must have woken everyone in the hotel.

Then, it was John's turn. She wasn't surprised when he rolled her over on to her back. She knew he wanted to watch her reaction. As soon as he penetrated her, she felt her muscles contracting again with the shock of his size. John wasn't having any of that. He pushed harder, forcing himself deeper and deeper. Beth put her fist in her mouth and bit her knuckles to stop herself crying out with sheer delight.

He increased his thrusting, pushing harder and harder until they were both gasping for breath and their sweat was mingling on their hot, straining flesh. Considering how long he had waited for this, Beth was impressed by John's restraint. She fought to match him, tensing her muscles and writhing from side to side as the pressure built and built. Then, with one final thrust that seemed to fill her whole being, they both climaxed together.

As he withdrew, Beth fell back exhausted with her eyes closed.

Before she had had time to recover, Steve and Brian lifted her up and carried her into the bathroom. She noticed that Steve's erection was already beginning to swell again and a wave of panic swept through her at the idea of them all taking her again so soon.

Brian lifted her into the shower and pushed her down

on her knees. All three men squeezed in beside her and began to soap her all over, while Brian took charge of the shower attachment to spray her body down, aiming the jets teasingly between her thighs and over her swollen breasts. Beth sighed with pleasure as the hot water caressed her aching limbs and revived her body.

Brian picked up the bar of soap and handed it to her.

'Why don't you make yourself useful,' he demanded. Hesitantly, she began to wash his legs and genitals, while Steve soaped her breasts and John took advantage of her buttocks with his fingers.

As her energy and enthusiasm gradually returned, Beth began to take a more active role, running soapy fingers over any penis that came within reach. Before long all three were fully erect once more and thrusting urgently against her slippery skin.

John rinsed her down then lifted her up and wrapped her in a soft bath towel.

'There, doesn't that feel better?' He dried her gently from top to toe and Beth was amazed at how excited she was becoming by his tender caresses. He was such an enigma, this man. So masterful, yet so gentle. She could see his own excitement rebuilding as he worked over her and, again, she marvelled at how big and hard he was.

The three men dried themselves off quickly and led her back into the bedroom. John pushed her on to the bed. He picked up a pillow and threw it to Steve.

'Push that under her.' He reached down and grabbed her hand. Beth gasped as he placed it on to his penis. 'Don't let go.'

As John knelt down beside, her, Brian did the same the other side. She felt her other hand being lifted and placed round his erection. She automatically closed her fist and squeezed gently, her eyes still fixed on John's cock. She slid her fingers slowly up his rigid shaft, shivering as she felt him twitching at her touch.

Steve pulled Beth's legs apart and she felt his hand opening her outer lips. His full weight came down on her body as he penetrated her. She pushed up to meet him and he began moving slowly in and out.

Beth whimpered softly and squeezed the other men even harder, tightening and loosening her grip in time with Steve's thrusting. He increased his stroke and she whimpered again, louder this time. This was so much better than she had ever imagined; her fantasies had not even come close.

She had no idea how long Steve lasted. She barely noticed when Brian released her hand from his cock and took his place at the bottom of the bed. She heard Steve move across the room to the loo and she instinctively tightened her grip on John's cock as Brian pushed himself slowly into her. She closed her eyes and let herself go.

'The best last, eh, Beth?'

Hearing his words, Beth realised that Brian had gone and John was about to penetrate her again. She sighed with anticipation and reached out behind her to grab the headboard. John slid in, deeper and deeper, further than she would ever have thought possible. She pushed herself up to meet him, hanging on to the bed as if she were tied up. She bit her lips to stifle her moans. John began thrusting confidently.

Some time later, through the haze of her own pleasure, she felt John climax and withdraw. She didn't move, just lay there, sated and motionless, with her hands still gripping the headboard.

She could hear the men moving around and talking in low voices. With supreme effort, she turned her head and looked at her travel clock. They had only been back in the hotel for a little over an hour. It seemed more like a week.

Beth felt her head being lifted up and a cup was pressed to her lips. Coffee! Some sweet angel had made her a mug of coffee. Beth let go of the headboard, pushed herself up and gratefully grabbed the mug from John's outstretched hand.

'Thank you.' She took half the scalding liquid in one gulp. John watched silently. She stared openly at his penis curled up against his body. Even like that, it was still huge.

'Drink it all up, Beth. You need your strength.'

Beth looked up at him, her eyes huge. 'No more,' she begged.

John smiled. 'Sorry. We've got a little bet on to see who can take you the most and no one wants to lose.' He licked his lips. 'Besides, don't forget you promised to entertain us, too.'

Beth looked puzzled.

'What you were doing in the car, remember?'

Beth reddened and shook her head in disbelief. Not now. Not after all they had already done to her.

John looked round thoughtfully. 'The second bed will make a good place for us to watch from. When you're ready.'

The strength flowed back into her limbs as the coffee revived her. She finished the mug and placed it on the bedside table. She was sharply aware of the three men lined up in a row on the second bed with their eyes devouring her. Despite her fatigue, she experienced a small tremor of lust at the way they were watching her. Time to get a little of her own back.

Taking a deep breath, Beth lowered her hand and placed it between her legs, using her thumb to stroke her clit.

'Don't forget, we'll be able to tell if you fake it.'

Beth jumped at John's words and stopped.

'Don't stop.' Steve was sitting on the edge of the bed, leaning forward eagerly. His cock was thrust up in front of him like an additional spectator.

Beth turned to face them and then lay back, sprawled across the bed. She drew her legs up, revealing herself totally. OK. I'll give you a good show, if that's what you want, she promised them silently. I'll give you such a

586

good show that you will all be wanking helplessly before I'm done with you.

She started slowly, building up. Soon she was totally immersed in her own gratification. She could hear their laboured breathing, the occasional exhalation. She raised her knee and started to slide her finger over her clit. She could imagine them fondling themselves as they watched her and the images it conjured up sent waves of desire rushing through her. She increased the pressure, using her other hand to play with her nipples. She heard a loud gasp from one of the men.

She removed her hand from her sex lips, put it to her mouth and sucked her fingers. She heard another gasp. She put her hand back between her legs and pushed the tip of her damp finger inside her vagina, arching her back and thrusting against her hand as if fucking an invisible lover. Her senses were so keyed up that she thought she could hear the sounds of the men's fingers moving up and down their stiff cocks.

She removed her finger and pushed herself upright until she was kneeling in front of them with her legs together as she rubbed her mound. She had not been wrong. All three of them were moving their hands rapidly up and down their throbbing erections. Their faces were dark with lust, their breathing fast and shallow.

She felt rather than heard the tiny mewing noises she was making in her own enthusiasm. Watching them watching her, seeing what they were doing because of her, was almost more than she could bear. She was already burning with the need for release again. Beth parted her legs and pushed her fingers up urgently inside her moist sex.

All three men gasped and increased their own movements. Her own mewing sounds changed to a cross between a purr and a whimper. Falling back on her ankles, Beth cried out softly as she climaxed.

'Yeah. Oh yeah,' Brian sighed urgently.

587

What happened next became a jumble in her mind. Afterwards, all she could remember was a medley of hands and pricks; of being pushed and pulled this way and that as the three men used every part of her pliant body for their own enjoyment and release.

Long before they had finished with her, Beth had drifted away on a cloud of sated exhaustion.

She never even heard them leave.

Chapter Five

*B*eth had trouble waking up the next morning. The insistent jangling of her travelling alarm clock seemed to take forever to penetrate her consciousness. As she sat up and gazed groggily round the hotel room, confused memories of the previous evening flooded into her mind.

Beth groaned as she slipped her feet out from under the duvet and padded slowly into the bathroom to shower. She felt as if she had just taken part in a world cup final, playing the part of the ball.

After three cups of strong, black coffee and a pile of thickly buttered toast, she was feeling much more human again. Thank heavens for room service. What a night! Not even her wildest fantasies had come close to the reality of it. She polished off the last of the coffee and glanced at her watch. She would have to get a move on if she didn't want to be late.

She pictured the knowing grins on the men's faces if she failed to appear on time. They would be convinced that they had been too much for her to handle. No way was she going to give them that satisfaction. John had already humiliated her quite enough.

She had got her own back though, she reminded

herself smugly as she wiggled into a soft jersey dress and pulled up her stockings. The look on their faces when she had masturbated for them! Talk about desperate. Had any of them actually lost control, watching her? She couldn't remember. She couldn't remember anything much of what had happened after that.

By supreme effort, Beth managed to arrive at the training centre before any of them. It was a small victory, but it pleased her enormously. She was even more delighted when she saw the condition they were in. All three of them looked half-asleep. Steve and Brian looked as if they were suffering hangovers. Funny; she didn't remember any of them drinking all that much. They had been far too busy trying to get her drunk.

She forced herself to smile at each of them in a friendly, detached sort of way. Steve and Brian managed a feeble nod in return. John, of course, had that infuriating, knowing grin as soon as he saw her. She turned away quickly before her face reddened.

Lisa looked different. Prettier, somehow. It took Beth a few moments to realise that Lisa had put on more make-up than she usually wore. It made her eyes seem much larger and the eye shadow she had applied emphasised the green and gold flecks within them. When she slipped her jacket off, Beth could see that Lisa was wearing a semi-transparent cream blouse. The outline of her bra was just visible when she lifted her arm to point at the whiteboard.

Was it for her benefit, Beth wondered? She was going out with Lisa that evening. In her preoccupation with the previous night's events, she had almost forgotten about that completely. It didn't seem quite so appealing any-more, somehow. Perhaps she should try to find some excuse to beg off?

Would the three men ask her out again? Brian had already suggested it. He was quite sweet, but Steve had been, surprisingly, the more gentle lover. As for John – she still didn't know how to take him.

590

'I don't think you've been paying attention this morning, Beth. Is something bothering you?'

Beth jumped at the sound of the instructor's voice right beside her. Lisa was bending over her desk, her eyes running all over her body.

'I'm sorry. I was miles away.' Beth sensed herself colouring.

'You've hardly started the exercise.' Lisa was examining her laptop screen. 'Is there something you don't understand?'

'What? Oh, no. I'm just having trouble concentrating.' Beth forced herself to pay attention to her work as she began hitting the keys of the keyboard furiously.

Lisa patted her shoulder. 'I'm looking forward to tonight, too,' she whispered, her own cheeks glowing. Beth smiled sheepishly. It was a good job Lisa couldn't read everything that had been going through her mind!

She was surprised when Lisa disappeared during the coffee break. She had expected her to stick close. Despite her comment, perhaps she was having second thoughts, too?

Beth moved over to the window and gazed out, sightlessly. She sipped her coffee pensively and tried to pull her muddled thoughts together. Suddenly, she felt a hand run down her back and over her buttocks.

'Sleep well, Beth?'

She didn't have to turn around to know it was John. 'Yes, thank you.' She was slightly disappointed when he lifted his hand away. She struggled in vain to think of something else to say to him and was relieved when the door opened and Lisa came back in.

Lisa looked round then headed straight over to them and put her hand possessively on Beth's arm. 'I've just hunted out a few additional training notes I thought you might find useful,' she told her. 'Mostly to do with stock market flotations, plus a bit about company mergers. If I can find time later, I'll get them photocopied for you.'

Beth noticed John moving away and felt a twinge of

disappointment. Teasing Lisa was fun, but there was something about John. She had never met a man before who could truly and totally dominate her like he could. She would give anything for the chance to make him squirm and beg for her the way she had done so submissively for him.

'Thank you. Perhaps I could copy them myself if you show me where the photocopier is?'

'Oh well, yes. If you don't mind then that would be a great help. I've got to attend a staff meeting at lunchtime, so I won't have much opportunity.' Beth noticed that Lisa's fingers were still resting on her arm.

'The only problem is there's always such a queue in the main office during break times.' Lisa continued. She pursed her lips thoughtfully, then brightened. 'There's an old machine in one of the storerooms down the corridor that I sometimes use.' She moved across to her desk and opened the drawer.

'Here's the key to the storeroom. It's the last door on the left. You can't miss it.' Lisa smiled coyly. 'The machine is a bit slow, but it will still be quicker than queuing.'

Beth took the key and moved her hand away quickly before Lisa could see her fingers were trembling. 'Thank you.' She remembered her promise to let Lisa have her room number. 'I'm in room 309, by the way,' she added. 'Have you decided what we're going to do tonight, yet?'

Lisa's eyes sparkled. 'I thought dinner at a small restaurant I know, then, perhaps, a club?'

'A club?' Beth wondered just what kind of club Lisa had in mind. She had heard of lesbian-only clubs. She wasn't certain that she actually wanted to go to one. Being with Lisa was one thing; she wasn't sure she fancied facing a room full of lust-filled women all ogling her body.

'Or I could take you back and show you my flat if you prefer,' Lisa added softly, almost as if sensing her thoughts. 'Nice and cosy. Just the two of us.'

That sounded more like it. Beth smiled. 'Let's just see how we feel later, shall we?'

By lunchtime, Beth had managed to pull herself together and was beginning to grow quite excited about the coming evening. She had had a taste of what it was like to be dominated by a man. What would it be like to be dominated by a woman?

Despite Lisa's warning, Beth couldn't believe how antiquated the photocopier was. She hadn't seen one like it for years. No wonder it was stuck away in a locked storeroom; it would have been more at home in a museum.

Beth switched on the light and pushed the door to behind her. It was a small room and the only other things in it, apart from the copier, were an old wooden chair and a couple of boxes of paper. The walls were painted a lurid green that looked like mould and the air smelt damp and musty.

Beth brushed the dust off the chair and put Lisa's folder down. She opened it to take out the first page of notes and sighed when she saw how many sheets there were. Thanks to the primitive design of the ancient machine, she would have to copy each sheet individually. She lifted the lid covering the glass and placed the first sheet face down. As soon as she had closed it again, she pressed the copy button.

The antiquated machine juddered alarmingly and the front panel lit up like a Christmas tree. Beth cursed and thumped the button again; nothing happened. She looked round, then spied the paper tray sticking out of one end. It was empty. She opened the top box of paper, grabbed a handful of sheets and quickly loaded the tray. The warning lights went out. She pressed the copy button again and, with a groan of protest, the old machine finally whirred into action.

As she mindlessly repeated the action of placing each sheet in turn under the lid, Beth's thoughts drifted back to John. What a body he had. He must work out every day to keep himself in such good shape. She found herself wondering what he and the others were up to and if they had looked for her to join them for lunch.

It would be fun to get John on his own. Steve and Brian were both very nice but, well, she had never met a man quite like John. Would he be very different, away from the others? Had he been showing off last night for their benefit or was he always so forceful?

Just as she finished the last sheet, she heard voices outside in the corridor and realised it was them. She heard Steve make some comment and then all three men laughed. She wondered if they were talking about her and moved closer to the door to listen.

'I've just got to get my jacket.' John's voice came quite clearly through the thin wood. 'Why don't you go on and I'll catch you up.'

'Sure. If we find Beth we'll keep her warm for you, shall we?' Brian's voice.

She heard them all chuckling and experienced a rush of anger at their presumption. Then, as their footsteps moved away, her heart suddenly began to race. This could be just the opportunity she needed. She remembered her earlier thoughts about dominating John and, as she glanced down at the now silent photocopier, a daring and delightful plan began to take shape in her mind.

Beth quickly removed the paper tray and replaced the unused sheets in the box. Then she picked up her copying and opened the door. Before she could lose her nerve, she hurried down the corridor and peered into the classroom. John was standing by his chair with his jacket in his left hand. His muscles rippled and flowed under his tight shirt and Beth shivered at the memory of his touch.

He looked up as she entered and she saw an amused grin spring to his lips as he recognised her. 'Hello, Beth. Is there something I can do for you?'

'Yes, actually.' But not what you're thinking, she added silently. 'I'm trying to do some photocopying, but I'm having trouble with the old copier. I think it's out of paper but I'm not sure how to reload it. Do you know anything about photocopiers?'

John pulled a face. 'I'm no expert,' he began, then grinned. 'Still, I'd be more than happy to have a look,' he continued cheerfully as he placed his jacket back over the chair. 'Anything for a lady. Besides, two heads are better than one, aren't they?'

Her pulse racing, Beth began to lead the way along the corridor to the storeroom.

'I heard you offering to do teacher's copying earlier,' John commented softly as they reached the door. 'It's nice to see you two girls so getting on so well together,' he added. 'Very cosy.'

Beth felt herself flushing from top to toe. Oh God. He hadn't guessed about that, had he? Was that why none of them had made a move on Lisa? Could they sense that she wasn't interested in men? After last night, they couldn't think the same about her. Did John know she was seeing Lisa that night? She pushed the thought away hastily and entered the room. John followed.

'It's not exactly the latest model.' She waved her arm towards the copier while pushing the door closed behind them with her other hand. She had already noticed the bolt on the inside and she slid it quickly across.

'You're in luck, Beth. I've used one of these old things before.' John moved round to the other side of the machine and slid the paper tray out. He glanced round then, seeing the box of paper, bent down and took a handful.

As he filled the tray, Beth leant against the door and watched him. He moved surprisingly gracefully for such a big man, she decided. Efficiently, too. No wasted effort. She noticed the way his muscles were tightening under his shirt and felt a sharp pang of longing to run her fingers over his broad chest. She reached behind her and slid the bolt open again, then closed it deliberately with a loud click.

John spun his head round in surprise as Beth pushed herself away from the door, an enigmatic smile on her face. As her actions registered on him, his lips twisted into that infuriating grin he was so good at.

'So. There is something else I can do for you.' He looked around the room eagerly, as if searching for a convenient place to take her.

Beth walked towards him slowly with her heart in her mouth. She could hardly believe her own daring. 'Yes. As a matter of fact, there is.'

As she reached him, she lifted her hand and slowly undid his belt. John grabbed her by the shoulders and pulled her towards him. Beth let go of the belt and put her hands flat on to his chest, pushing him forcefully away. She took a step back, out of arm's reach.

'Last night I played your games,' she told him. 'Now, it's my turn.' She was delighted to hear her voice so firm and sure. She wanted him to be in no doubt that she meant exactly what she said.

John smirked. 'You enjoyed last night, Beth. Don't try to deny it.'

'Yes, I did,' she agreed, returning his grin. 'But, it was still your game. Now, it's mine. You can walk away now or you can become my plaything.' She mimicked his warning of last night and gave him a few seconds to think it over. John said nothing.

'The rules are, you can't touch me unless I tell you and then only where and how I tell you.' Beth continued, watching his face carefully. If anything, his grin grew even bigger.

'Sure, Beth.'

'Sure, Beth,' she mimicked him. 'That's not what I want to hear.'

'Yes, ma'am.' He could barely contain his laughter.

Beth couldn't help wondering if he had played this game before, too. She tried to stifle the sudden pang of jealousy. The knowing grin on his face was really starting to annoy her. He was the most arrogant sod she had ever met, she decided. Probably even worse than Simon.

'Yes, what?' She raised her hand as if to slap his face.

John stopped grinning. 'Yes, ma'am. I am your property to do with as you will. I am here for your pleasure, not mine.'

'That's much better,' Beth couldn't help smiling. He had definitely done this before!

'I will only touch you where you say and I will please you as well as I can,' he added obediently, as if really beginning to enter into the spirit of her game.

Beth nodded silently and a shiver of lust rushed down her backbone at the implication of his words. She stepped forward again and resumed undoing his belt. She thought she could see a trace of doubt creeping into his eyes but, as she moved her fingers down to his zip, she soon discovered that it had not dampened his desire. Slowly, so that he would feel every tooth parting, she began to open his fly. Remembering the ID badges and her fantasy, she allowed her little finger to run down his erection.

John drew a deep breath when she first touched him and only released it with a rush when she finished undoing the zip. As she moved her hands up to undo the button, Beth let her fingers slide inside the opening. She pretended to be having trouble with the button while her little finger gently stroked the tip of his swollen cock. John's whole body stiffened at her touch and she heard him gulp as he swallowed painfully.

Beth kept her eyes glued to his face the whole time. She could see the little twitches in his facial muscles as she teased his button and fondled his tip. His whole body was rigid with concentration and she had a feeling that it would be easy to push him over the top. She was almost overcome by her feelings of power and elation at the look on his face. It was time to move on.

Beth clasped the sides of his trousers firmly in her

fingers and started to lower them slowly down over his hips and buttocks. As she moved, she gradually crouched down. She was disappointed to see that his shirt had dropped down in front, covering him from her eager gaze.

Resisting the urge to reach up and pull it away, Beth continued her downward journey, allowing her hands to run softly over the outside of his legs as she moved. She was so close to him that she could see the little hairs standing up on his skin as his body shivered at her soft caresses. She took her time.

Finally, she stood up again and stared wordlessly into his face. Little drops of sweat had formed on his brow and upper lip and his tongue was running repeatedly across his lower lip. His Adam's apple bobbed up and down nervously.

'I'm going to enjoy this, slave.' Beth leered at him suggestively, trying to imitate the look he had put on his face each time he had threatened to spank her.

John smiled weakly. His heart didn't seem to be in it. Beth's eyes narrowed.

'Well, slave. What's wrong? Aren't you glad that your mistress is enjoying herself?'

'Yes, ma'am,' he responded softly. 'I'm happy to be a part of your pleasure.'

He was doing very well so far, she decided, remembering how humiliated she had felt when he had made her openly confess her thoughts and desires. She stepped back and put her hands on her hips as she strutted up and down the small room. His eyes followed her every step. Beth frowned. His shirt was still in the way. It should be her who was getting the best view, not him.

'Pull your shirt up under your arms,' she commanded.

As he obeyed her, Beth's eyes lighted on his muscle-bound chest. She couldn't resist moving in closer to push the material aside and expose his nipples. She leant forward and nipped first one and then the other nipple with her front teeth. John flinched but made no sound.

Could he feel his own nipples hardening through all that muscle? She lowered her head again and felt him flinch in anticipation of her teeth.

Smiling, she ran her tongue over each nipple in turn and then began to use her fingers to tease them even more. Oh God. They were even bigger than hers. Was he enjoying this, she wondered? Was he imagining how it would feel if he were doing it to her? She could sense her own nipples starting to rise.

With her knees bent, she ran her tongue down his chest, kissing and licking every inch of his skin all the way down to his navel. She smiled at the way his thighs were tensing every time she touched him, revelling in the sense of power it gave her. She reached round behind him and ran her fingers gently down his spine. It was like wrapping her arms around a giant oak tree. She noticed that several of the muscles in his left buttock were jumping nervously.

Beth pushed her fingers inside his pants and cupped the curves of his buttocks in her palms. She had to press herself up tight against his body just to reach round him, so that his cock was pushed hard into her stomach. As she bit one of his nipples again, she flattened her body against his muscular stomach. She could hear his heart thumping rapidly in his chest cavity and feel the spasms of his rigid penis as it twitched and shuddered against her.

Beth arched her back and drew her stomach in, then pulled herself back as far as she could so that John had to strain forward to continue to press against her. Every time his cock made contact with her body, she squeezed his buttocks. His flesh was so firm that her hands seemed to make little impression on them.

She was just about to change her tactics when John suddenly gave a small groan and thrust his hips forward so urgently that his upper body slammed against her. The force of the blow almost winded her and the shock of it made her sink her teeth into his nipple. John gasped in pain and pleasure and, for a moment, she thought he was about to come.

'I thought I told you not to touch me without permission.' She refused to show any compassion.

'Sorry, ma'am.' He backed away.

Beth glanced round the room and spotted a long metal rule leaning against the wall in the far corner. She removed her hands from his pants and moved across the room to pick it up. Although it was worn and dusty and broken off at one end, it was still long and wide enough to suit her purposes.

'Turn around, slave, and take your punishment like a man.'

John shuffled round awkwardly to face the photocopier, his legs hampered by his trousers rucked up around his ankles. Beth leant round him and placed the ruler on the top of the copier where he could see it, then slipped his underpants off his bottom and on to his thighs. She was tempted to bite the inviting cheeks but she wasn't certain that she would even be able to sink her teeth into his solid flesh.

After she had left him to stew for a few seconds she picked up the ruler again, raised her hand and slapped his right cheek soundly with the flat edge. Although he must have been expecting the blow, he jumped violently, his muscles twitching. She gave him six more slaps, each one harder than the last. His bottom began to turn bright pink.

'Turn around.'

She was surprised to see his face was as red as his buttocks. She looked down and almost laughed when she saw how his pants had tangled up in his erection, pulling it out in front of him.

'Look at the mess you are in,' she reprimanded him as she put the ruler down on the copier again.

'I'm sorry, ma'am. It won't happen again.' John reached down and tried to untangle his pants. Beth moved closer and slapped his hand away. She crouched between his legs, finished extracting his swollen prick and pulled his pants down to his ankles. Her eyes lingered on his hardness as if it were the first erection she had ever seen.

John's body trembled as he swayed towards her. She knew he wanted her to take him in her mouth. His prick was so stiff and swollen that she could see every vein standing out clearly. The tip was already damp and shiny with his lubrication. She stood up slowly and reached for him with both hands.

'I need a permanent reminder of this,' she told him as she ran her fingers slowly up and down his shaft. 'A sort of souvenir, you might say.' As she spoke, she stared up into his finely chiselled face, searching for a reaction. His features seemed frozen, apart from the slightest twitching of his jaw muscles.

'You would like me to have a reminder, wouldn't you?' She increased the speed of her caress and felt him shudder.

'Yes, ma'am.' His words came out in a breathless rush and Beth realised that he had been holding his breath again. She smiled victoriously.

'Good. Bend over the photocopier,' she commanded as she released him.

John hesitated, obviously puzzled about her intentions.

'Right up over the glass,' she added. She saw comprehension dawn. For a moment, she though he was going to refuse and she reached for the ruler again.

With a small sigh, John climbed up on to the copier and leant forward. Beth smiled and hit the copy button. The copier whirred and she saw the beam of light passing along the glass. There was a loud thud as the paper chugged through the system and popped out the far side.

Beth walked round and picked up the sheet. John's eyes followed her. Beth pursed her lips and sighed with disappointment. 'Not good enough.'

She picked up several spare sheets of paper and

covered the exposed areas of glass around his body, then pressed the copy button again.

'Much better,' she told him a few seconds later as she studied another copy. 'Now, lift yourself up higher so that you aren't squashing all the best bits.'

John smiled at her words and raised his buttocks so that his cock and balls were only just resting on the top of the glass. Beth took her time readjusting the papers around him to cut out any unnecessary light and, at the same time, admiring the view. Finally, when she saw his muscles tensing from the effort of holding himself in such an awkward position, she pushed the button again.

'Perfect.' She examined the latest copy closely. 'Although I'm not sure it is quite as enthusiastic as it could be.' She placed the copy on top of the others and slid her hand between his legs and up on to his penis. 'Definitely room for expansion.' As she pushed the button to take more copies, she started to wank him slowly with her fingers.

'That's more like it.' She squeezed him firmly and then pulled her hand away. 'Now, you wank.'

It was quite difficult for John to get himself into position and Beth had to rearrange the surrounding papers several times before she got it right. She took three or four more copies, then stood back to enjoy watching him. From where she was standing, she could just see his balls moving with each stroke. She felt her own arousal increasing rapidly.

'Don't stop, but don't come either,' she ordered huskily. She picked up the last copy and examined it carefully. There was no doubt about what it was, or any doubt about what he was doing. She was tempted to make him go all the way. What a picture that would make!

She dismissed the idea regretfully. Even with his cooperation, the chances of pressing the copy button at the exact moment to catch his eruption were very slim.

'OK, that's enough. Get off and stand in front of me.'

She smiled to see that he was still holding himself but that, unsure what was required of him, he had stopped moving his fingers. His cock looked about ready to burst and his face was swollen with lust.

'You've pleased me, slave,' she told him. 'So I've decided to reward you with your fantasy.' She shivered at the look of hungry anticipation in his eyes as her words sank in.

Slowly, Beth lifted the skirt of her dress to waist level. She looped her fingers through the elastic of her lace panties and was just about to pull them down when she had a much better idea.

'Slave, kneel in front of me and take down my panties. Slowly.' As he began to lower himself, she added, 'When you've done that, you may satisfy me with your tongue and play with me with your fingers.'

John needed no further encouragement to obey those commands. Beth's idea of slow and his definitely did not match. He practically ripped her panties off in his eagerness, while his hands squeezed her buttocks and pulled her tightly on to his waiting tongue. As soon as her panties were around her ankles, Beth stepped out of them and opened her legs to give him full access. She sighed as his tongue began to dart back and forth over her sex lips, then gasped as he sucked her swollen clit right up into his mouth. As his fingers prised her cheeks apart, he pulled her even harder on to his mouth.

Beth placed her hands on his shoulders to steady herself, whimpering as one of his hands began to slide over her buttocks and the other reached up under her crotch to finger her sex. As his thumb began to push against the tightness of her anus, she bit her lip with shock and pleasure and tasted the coppery tang of blood on her tongue.

She was still so keyed up from the previous night that it would take very little to bring her to climax. As if sensing the extent of her arousal, John sucked harder on her clit. His tongue flicked rapidly back and forth over the sensitive flesh, and Beth dug her fingers into his firm flesh and groaned with delight as the pleasure engulfed her.

Shakily, she pushed him away. 'That was very good, slave,' she whispered as she struggled to come back down to earth. 'You can stop now.'

John reluctantly let go and fell back on to his heels. His cock was jerking from side to side as if it were waving to her. His eyes burned with passion.

Still holding her dress up, Beth crouched down in front of him. She reached out and gently slid her finger down the length of his erection. John's whole body shuddered.

'We can't leave you in that state now, can we?' she whispered, squeezing him gently.

'No, ma'am.' John's voice was tight with need.

Smiling, she straightened up and stepped back out of reach. She hooked the toe of her shoe into her panties and flipped them up into the air towards him. They landed on his chest and dropped down on to his prick. John's face darkened as her intention dawned upon him.

'Well, get on with it.' Beth stood back further, her hands still holding her skirt up. 'If it's good enough for a waiter, it's certainly good enough for you.'

John took a long, deep breath. Letting it out slowly, he took hold of the skimpy lace panties and began to rub himself with them. To her astonishment, his face had turned crimson with embarrassment again.

'Faster,' she demanded heartlessly.

John closed his eyes and began to pump himself urgently.

'Don't you dare close your eyes,' she scolded. 'I want you to look at me while you wank yourself with my knickers.' To her surprise, Beth realised that the commands were coming very easily to her. She knew she was being a bit crude but it did not worry her. She was thoroughly enjoying herself. It was no more than he deserved.

John opened his eyes and did as he was told. She

noticed that his gaze kept flickering down away from her face, not to look at her body, but to hide his shame and humiliation. The knowledge of the power she had over him at that moment gave her nearly as much satisfaction as his tongue had just done.

She looked down at his cock again and noticed how his balls were already drawing up tight against his body. His breathing was laboured and his fingers were moving more and more rapidly. She realised that he was certain to come at any second. Too fast, much too fast. She would never tire of watching a man masturbating because of her.

'I think you were right,' she breathed. 'I would have enjoyed watching the waiter wanking with my knickers.'

As she spoke, Beth reached out to slow him down and prolong her teasing. She was too late. With a loud groan, John dropped the panties and let go. The first jet of hot spunk was rapidly followed by another, then another. He groaned again and his face contorted with the violence and pleasure of his orgasm.

Beth lowered her dress and smoothed the material down. Silently, she picked up her latest batch of photocopying and turned to leave. Unbolting the door, she stepped out into the corridor and headed back towards the classroom. She smiled as she heard the door slam shut behind her and the bolt slide back across.

Beth was pleased to see how subdued John seemed that afternoon. For the first hour or so he said practically nothing and kept his head averted from her gaze. She could barely suppress her grin of triumph. Perhaps he would think twice before he tried to get the better of her again. She pulled the photocopies she had taken of him out from under the rest of the copying she had done and examined them keenly. She would certainly never forget John.

Lisa began to wander round the room to check work and Beth quickly pushed the copies out of sight under a folder. Maybe she should do some more photocopying tomorrow, too? Perhaps she could persuade Steve or Brian to give her a hand. Would John tell them what she had done to him? Somehow, she doubted it.

Later, as she stood sipping her afternoon coffee at the open window, she sensed someone standing just behind her. Thinking it was Lisa she turned to smile at her.

'Mind you don't catch cold,' John cautioned her. 'You really shouldn't stand by an open window like that when you haven't got any knickers on. What would you do if the breeze lifted your skirt?'

Beth gulped. She glanced round quickly to make sure no one else had heard his words. Obviously, he wasn't as subdued by his experience as she had thought.

'Do you want them back, by the way?' John put his hand into his jacket pocket as if he was about to produce her undies. 'Only you ran off before I had a chance to return them. Of course, they are a bit sticky . . .'

'No! Stop it.' Beth saw several of the other trainees walking back into the room, including Brian and Steve, who were already heading towards them. 'Don't you dare get them out here,' she hissed.

'Yes ma'am. Whatever you say.' His grin stretched from ear to ear.

Chapter Six

The phone rang and rang. Simon waited impatiently for a few more minutes then slammed the receiver down angrily. Where the hell was she? His wife never seemed to be around when he wanted her, which was not often. He glared into the empty adjoining office. If only Beth wasn't away on that damned training course all week. Maybe he could find a way to take her with him to Rome instead of his wife. That way, not only would he have her all to himself for a whole weekend, he wouldn't need Marie to find someone to look after the damned dog while they were gone.

It was only Wednesday. Beth would not be back until the following Monday. It had been the longest week he could remember. Why had he ever let her go in the first place? She didn't need any extra qualifications to do what he wanted her for, business or pleasure. She had been so damned insistent about it. He began thinking about what had happened the previous Saturday. His memories of what he had done to her were so powerful that he could feel his cock beginning to push hard up against his underpants.

God, if she were here now, he would tear her clothes off her and put her across his knee. He would spank that sexy arse of hers until she begged him to ram himself up inside her. If there was ever a body designed for fucking, it was hers. He wanted her, desperately.

Simon lowered his hand and opened his zip. He slipped his fingers inside and took his already throbbing cock in his hand. He fondled the tip softly and groaned aloud with his urgent need.

The way she had writhed and sobbed when he had taken her across the desk like that. Had she really minded? She hadn't stopped him taking her a second time. She could have struggled harder. He remembered the soft gasps, the way she had opened her legs for him. His hand started to move slowly up and down his erection, his excitement building as he continued to fantasise about what he wanted to do to her.

He was so carried away by his thoughts and actions that he barely heard the knock on the door. It was only when it was repeated, louder and more insistently, that Simon opened his eyes with a start.

Shit. There was someone at the door. It must be his eleven o'clock appointment, Madeleine West. Mrs West was a rich, middle-aged widow with lots of money she wanted to invest in the stock market and not a clue how to go about it. Simon planned to help make her – and himself – even richer.

But not now. He glanced down at himself. His cock was throbbing almost painfully. He could already see the dampness of his lubrication glistening on the dark, swollen tip. Christ, a few more seconds and he would have been there. He couldn't stop now.

'Mr Henderson. Coo-ee. Are you there?' Simon heard the sound of the door handle turning. Shit. Why hadn't he thought to lock it? He stuffed himself back inside his trousers and forced the zip up. Normally, he would have hurried over to the door and taken her arm to help her to the leather visitor's chair. He didn't dare stand up. He grabbed the phone quickly.

'. . . Look, I've got an important visitor now so I'll have

to call you back . . .' Simon put his hand over the mouth-piece. 'Mrs West.' He waved his hand towards the chair opposite his desk. 'Please, do come in and take a seat. I'll be with you in a minute.' He returned to his imaginary conversation.

'Yes, I realise that there's a lot of money at stake, but I can't discuss it now. I'll talk to you later.'

Madeleine West closed the door behind her and waddled across the room. She flopped down heavily into the chair and stared at him expectantly. Simon replaced the receiver and put on his most winning smile.

'Sorry about that. Please forgive me for not getting up, but I've, um, hurt my back. Golf,' he invented quickly. 'It's so painful, I can barely walk.'

Madeleine's face changed from displeasure to sympathy. 'Oh, you poor love. My dear departed Charley used to suffer with his back. Would you like me to rub it for you?'

'No!' Simon flushed with horror at the thought. The last thing he wanted was for her to come round behind his desk while he was in this state. The way he was feeling at the moment, even the tubby Mrs West seemed less undesirable than usual. If he pulled the blinds down and closed his eyes, maybe . . .

The realisation of what he was contemplating was enough to steady him. He glanced at her pasty-looking skin and shuddered. His erection began to subside.

'So long as I sit still, I shall be fine. Just seeing my favourite client and knowing how much I shall enjoy helping her capitalise on her investments is more than enough to make me feel better,' he flattered her outrageously.

Mrs West preened herself at his words and sank down on the leather chair. 'I've decided to let you invest the whole two hundred thousand,' she told him as she rummaged around in her enormous handbag for her chequebook. 'After what you said last week, I'm sure I shall be in safe hands with you.'

Simon barely stopped himself shivering at the idea of

having her in his hands. Watching her begin writing the cheque, however, made him feel almost as good as screwing Beth had done. If there was one thing in life even better than good sex, it was large quantities of other people's money.

'I must say, that's a very pretty hat you're wearing.' He could afford to be generous. The money he made out of her would easily finance his whole trip to Rome. 'You must tell me where you got it. I'm sure my wife would like one just like it.'

Mrs West beamed with delight.

It was all so very easy, he thought contemptuously, as he returned her smile. Like taking candy from a baby.

After Madeleine West had finally gone and Simon had tucked her cheque securely away in his desk, he allowed his thoughts to drift back to Beth. Pictures of her delightful tits and taut rump flashed though his mind and his cock surged back to full size. Determined not to be caught out twice, Simon crossed the office and locked the door.

Even before he reached his desk, his cock was already between his fingers again. As he began moving his fist faster and faster, groaning with pleasure, he realised he could not remember when he had last been reduced to masturbating over anyone. Normally, when he felt the urge, he just called one of his many female acquaintances to take care of him.

Maybe that's what he should do now. No one sprang to mind. Besides, he couldn't wait. His thoughts of Beth were just too strong and demanding. He kneaded himself gently and caressed his balls. Jesus, he was about to lose it, he couldn't hold on any longer. He grabbed himself again, pumping frantically.

One thing for sure. He was going to have to make Beth pay for reducing him to this. His come began spurting into his fingers. Just you wait, Beth Bradley, he threatened. He could hardly wait for next week.

* * *

610

It seemed to take Beth forever to get ready that night. First, she couldn't decide what to wear. Nothing seemed quite right and she still had no real idea what Lisa would find attractive.

After three or four attempts, she finally settled on a short, mid-blue woollen dress with front zip. Under it, she would wear her front-fastening half-cup bra with matching white lace panties and, to finish the outfit, suspenders and stockings.

When she came to do her make-up, Beth found she was so nervous that her hand wouldn't stop shaking. She had soon managed to smear mascara everywhere except on her lashes. By the time she had cleaned up and started again, the hands on her travel clock were showing two minutes to seven.

The phone rang, making her jump.

'A Ms Williams is waiting for you in the lobby, madam.'

'Thank you. Please tell her I will be right down.' Beth brushed blusher on to her already glowing cheeks and gave herself a final quick scan in the mirror. Nervously, she picked up her shoulder bag and headed for the door. Yet another new experience beckoned. This was turning out to be quite a week.

Lisa was dressed in a knee-length flared black skirt and a green silk blouse. She had curled the ends of her blonde hair under and was wearing a gold-chain necklace that disappeared inside her cleavage. Her legs were clad in stockings and she had sling-back high heels on. She looked very pretty, very young and very desirable.

As Beth stepped out the lift and started towards her, she noticed the receptionist eyeing them both up. He certainly didn't look bored now. She swallowed hard and tried to calm her nerves. Stop being so silly, she chided herself. You've spent all day with this woman in the training centre. You've had lunch together, chatted about most things and discovered you have a lot in common. It's just like going out with Ann or one of the other girls.

It wasn't, of course. Beth had never even contemplated doing with any of her girlfriends what she was about to do with and to Lisa.

'Hi, Lisa.' Beth greeted her warmly. 'Right on time. You look very pretty this evening. A skirt suits you.' Beth could picture the gap of bare skin at the top of Lisa's thighs. She imagined herself undoing the suspenders and rolling the stockings slowly down Lisa's legs. Her own legs turned to rubber.

Lisa grinned. 'Thank you.' She had made an effort to dress as Beth had suggested and was pleased Beth had noticed. She ran her eyes slowly over Beth's trim figure. 'And you, of course, look as lovely as always. I've booked us a table for seven thirty. It's not far, so I thought we would walk since it's such a nice evening.'

Long before they had reached the restaurant they were talking and joking together again like old friends and Beth felt herself slowly relaxing.

The restaurant was small and cosy, with a dozen or so tables and a tiny bar. The waiter led them to a secluded table in the far corner, well away from the other diners. Beth had the feeling that Lisa had booked it deliberately. Was this, perhaps, where she brought all her women? It was a strange thought.

As they walked across the room, Beth noticed a couple of men sitting at the bar, eyeing them up. The taller one turned to his friend and whispered something. They both laughed and Beth flushed. Were they just discussing their chances of making a pick-up, or had they recognised Lisa and her as ... as what? Lesbians? The label made her shudder.

'What a lovely place,' she gushed, as they sat down. 'Do you come here often?' she added before she could stop herself.

Lisa shook her head. 'Not really. I've been here once

612

or twice with my mother. The food's good and it's very friendly and relaxed.'

It certainly wasn't the answer Beth had expected and she wasn't quite sure what to make of it. She took her time examining the menu, trying to calm her fluttering heartbeat.

In the end, they both chose the same. Melon to start, followed by steak and salad with a side helping of french fries. Lisa asked the waiter for a carafe of the house wine, which proved to be both full bodied and fruity.

They filled the awkward moments while they waited for the food to arrive with chit-chat about books and films they had both enjoyed. Beth took several deep gulps of the wine, feeling in need of something to help relax her again.

'So, are you getting everything you hoped for out of this week?' Lisa questioned as she poured oil and vinegar dressing on to her salad.

'Oh yes. It's even better than I had expected,' Beth responded enthusiastically, thinking more about her extracurricular activities than the course. 'I never expected to learn so much,' she added with a smile. The wine seemed to be working.

Lisa reached out and placed her hand over Beth's. It was the first deliberate touch of the evening and Beth felt a small tingle of anticipation prickling her skin.

'And, have you decided what you want to do after we've eaten? I'll leave it up to you.'

Beth paused. She was very tempted to agree to going on to the club Lisa had suggested. She was more than a little curious to see what such a place would be like. She thought about being alone with Lisa at her flat, undressing her, running her hands over Lisa's slim body.

'I'd very much like to see where you live,' she replied slowly. 'If that's all right with you, of course.'

Lisa licked her lips and fondled the back of Beth's hand with her fingertips. Her touch was feather-light. 'I'd like that, too,' she whispered.

Her voice sounded slightly husky. Beth looked up into her face and saw a tell-tale flush of colour on Lisa's cheeks. Her pupils were dilated and her lips slightly parted so that Beth could see the tip of her tongue. What would it be like to kiss another woman?

Lisa's home was on the edge of the city centre, less than ten minutes' walk from the restaurant. It was more like a mews town house or a maisonette than a flat, and Beth fell in love with it immediately.

'It's gorgeous,' she enthused as she wandered round the main living-room and examined Lisa's collection of expensive-looking porcelain figurines. 'How long have you lived here?'

'Oh, about three years. I had to wait for it to come on the market. These sorts of places are in great demand.'

'I can see why. I'd love something like this,' Beth replied as she continued to wander round, exploring. A slinky Siamese cat jumped down off the window-sill, purring loudly as it wrapped itself around Beth's legs. Beth automatically reached down to stroke its silky fur.

'That's Suki,' Lisa smiled. 'Don't let her take advantage of you. She can be very persistent when she likes someone.'

Beth continued to stroke the cat. She couldn't help smiling at the fact it was female. Didn't Lisa have any males in her life at all?

'Would you like a coffee, or something stronger?' Lisa questioned.

'I'd love a gin and tonic if you've got it,' Beth replied quickly. The effects of the wine were already wearing off. If she had ever needed a little extra courage, it was now.

'No problem. Just make yourself comfortable on the settee. I'll get the ice and lemon.' Lisa disappeared with Suki following her, meowing demandingly. Beth perched nervously on the end of the long, soft couch and gulped hard to try and steady her hammering pulse. She wondered which door led to the bedroom. She swallowed again and folded her hands on her lap to try to stop them trembling.

When Lisa returned, carrying their drinks, she placed them on the coffee-table and sat down beside Beth so that their thighs were touching. Beth tried not to flinch at the touch. She failed.

Lisa stared up into her face thoughtfully. 'You've never done anything like this before, have you, Beth?' she asked softly.

The question took Beth by surprise. She flushed and shook her head. Lisa smiled encouragingly and leant towards her. Beth had a feeling that her admission had boosted Lisa's own confidence. She felt a rush of relief. Somebody had to find the courage to make the first move. She was too tense to think straight.

'Just relax. It's not so very hard,' Lisa whispered as she placed her lips gently against Beth's.

Beth closed her eyes and returned the kiss. It didn't seem all that different from kissing a man. When she felt Lisa probing her lips with her tongue, she willingly opened them to allow her to slip the tip inside. A tingle of desire shot through her. Kissing always made her weak at the knees.

Lisa pulled Beth into her embrace. Beth jumped with shock as she felt Lisa's hands running over the outer curve of her breasts. Her body instinctively stiffened and she opened her eyes again.

Lisa immediately stopped kissing her and moved her hands away. Beth felt a tinge of regret. Was Lisa turned off by her lack of responsiveness? She hadn't meant to react like that. It wasn't unpleasant, just unusual. Gingerly, she lifted her own hand and placed it on Lisa's tiny breast. She moved closer and leant forward to kiss Lisa's lips tentatively.

'I'm sorry,' she whispered. 'It's just that I've never felt this way before. I'm not sure about anything except being here with you.' She brushed her lips softly across the other girl's mouth again.

Lisa smiled and seemed to relax at her words. Beth squeezed Lisa's breast gently and immediately sensed Lisa's whole body quiver. Encouraged, she moved her hand inwards, seeking the nipple. It felt hard and swollen, even through Lisa's clothing. She felt Lisa shivering again and was suddenly consumed with an overwhelming urge to fondle Lisa's naked breast. She raised her other hand and started to undo the buttons of Lisa's blouse.

Lisa moaned softly and moved her own hand up to help. The blouse fell open, exposing her bra. Beth pushed it up with her fingers so that Lisa's firm breasts popped into view. She ran her fingers tentatively over the nipples again and felt them grow even harder. She realised that Lisa was beginning to undo the zip on the front of her dress.

'Put your hand up my skirt,' Lisa whispered as Beth's zip came open, exposing her to Lisa's eager fingers. 'Yes, that's it,' she sighed as Beth started to slide her hand slowly up the silky stocking. As she spoke, Lisa undid the catch of Beth's bra and pulled it open. She lowered her head and ran her tongue lightly over Beth's left nipple.

Beth stopped moving her hand and gasped with pleasure. Lisa's touch was so soft, so gentle. Like the touch of a feather. Men could be so rough sometimes in their enthusiasm. As a woman, Beth guessed, Lisa would know exactly what felt good and what didn't. Suddenly she no longer had any fears about what she should, or shouldn't, be doing. All she needed to do was to caress Lisa the way she, herself, liked to be caressed.

She moved her fingers further up under Lisa's skirt, remembering how she had already fantasised about doing this. Her yearning deepened. The skin on Lisa's inner thigh was so soft and smooth. She could feel her excitement building as she moved slowly upwards. This must be what a man feels, she realised. The thought sent little tremors of desire rushing up and down her legs.

She ran her fingertips lightly over Lisa's mound. Lisa moaned again and lifted her buttocks off the couch, pushing herself up against Beth's touch. 'Oh, yes,' she whispered.

Beth felt a surge of desire pulsing through her, so strong that she almost climaxed. She could imagine exactly how what she was doing to Lisa felt. It was almost as if she was masturbating herself, only much, much better. She slipped her fingers under the lace edge of Lisa's panties and caressed her clit.

Lisa writhed from side to side and sucked one of Beth's nipples into her mouth, teasing it with her tongue. It was Beth's turn to groan with pleasure. Lisa lifted her head and sat back, so that Beth's fingers slid down on to her thigh. She smiled softly.

'Slowly, Beth,' Lisa whispered, seeing how excited she was becoming. 'There is no rush. We have all night. Let me get those things off you.'

Beth leant back on the couch and allowed Lisa to pull her dress over her head and slip her bra straps off her arms. Then, clad only in her panties and stockings, she sat back up and helped Lisa out of her own blouse and bra. Lisa stood up and undid her skirt. She dropped it to the floor, stepped out of it and held out her hands. Beth ran her eyes appreciatively over Lisa's suspenders and stockings. It was easy to see why the sight of them drove men wild.

'Come on. We will be more comfortable in the bed-room,' murmured Lisa.

Beth allowed herself to be led across the living-room and through the doorway. Lisa flicked a switch on the wall and they were immediately bathed in a soft, pinkish glow from the two wall lights.

The room was decorated in beiges and greens and dominated by a huge double bed covered with a lacy

617

spread. Lisa led her, unresisting, to the bed and pulled her down on to it. She ran her fingers over Beth's nipples again and smiled at the way Beth shuddered at her touch. She leant over her and kissed them gently.

Beth lay back and closed her eyes again. Lisa's tongue was as soft as cotton wool. She sighed with joy as she felt the tip of Lisa's tongue leave her breasts and begin to slip slowly down her stomach. Instinctively, she reached for Lisa's breasts. As she cupped them in her hands, she gently teased the rigid nipples with her fingertips.

Lisa pushed her tongue into Beth's navel, caressing it with slow, circular movements that made Beth arch her back eagerly. The tongue moved on down, and she felt Lisa's fingers peeling her panties down over her hips. She squeezed Lisa's breasts harder and heard the other woman's breathing quicken in response.

'Oh, you have shaved,' Lisa murmured. 'I like that.' Beth felt Lisa's tongue begin its slow journey across her naked mound. She clenched her teeth in expectation of what was to come.

Even so, nothing had prepared her for the shock of Lisa's tongue caressing the swollen bud of her clit. The sensation was so exquisite that she bit her tongue and twisted her body to one side in an effort to escape.

'Please,' she begged. 'That's too much.'

Lisa lifted her hand and caressed her cheek. 'Just relax, Beth,' she whispered. 'We have all night.'

Beth nodded, too excited to speak as her orgasm built up and threatened to engulf her completely. She knew that as soon as Lisa touched her clit again, she would not be able to stop herself. She gritted her teeth as Lisa lowered her head back down between her thighs.

Lisa ran her tongue down Beth's left thigh then back up the right thigh. Beth let out a sob as the tip of Lisa's tongue started to probe her outer lips and slide up over the bud of her clit again. Lisa began flicking her tongue back and forth, her touch as soft and light as the breeze. It was more than Beth could stand.

With another sob, Beth climaxed. Her whole body convulsed with the intensity of it. 'Oh yes,' she sighed breathlessly as her body writhed helplessly under Lisa's unrelenting tongue and pleasure engulfed her. She slumped down on to the bed and sighed contentedly.

She sensed Lisa lying back down beside her and felt the other woman's fingers begin to caress her nipples again. Beth raised herself up on her elbows and gazed down at Lisa's perfect body. She was lying back peacefully with a slight smile on her face. Beth recognised it as the satisfied smile she often wore after she had successfully brought a man to climax. She leant down and kissed her gently on the lips.

Lisa raised her own head and responded with some urgency. Beth could almost feel the need burning deep within Lisa's womb. She was overcome by a desperate desire to return the pleasure to this woman who had so quickly and easily brought her to fulfilment.

As if reading her thoughts, Lisa moved closer to her. She reached up to pull Beth back down on the bed and straightened her legs out as she snuggled against her. For the first time ever, Beth found herself lying breast to naked breast with another woman. Her nipples were pushed up hard against Lisa's swollen tips and she could feel the other woman's soft pubes caressing her own shaven mound. It was incredible.

Lisa increased the intensity of her kisses, moaning softly as she pushed her tongue enthusiastically into Beth's willing mouth. Beth lifted her leg and placed it over Lisa's thigh, pulling her body even tighter against her. Her clit was pushed hard against Lisa's sex and she felt Lisa shiver with passion and thrust herself urgently against her, rolling her hips to increase the pressure on her own swollen bud.

Beth felt the juices of her excitement flowing from her. She put her finger to her mouth and licked it then slipped it down between Lisa's thighs, forcing them apart. She smiled as she saw Lisa's face register delight and heard the urgent gasp of pleasure escape from her lips.

Beth ran her finger over Lisa's clit and on down to the opening of her vagina. The two women were so close together that the back of her hand was brushing against her own sex as she moved and she was masturbating both women at the same time. It was one of the most exciting and erotic moments of her life.

She became aware of the dampness of the other woman's passion on the tips of her fingers. Lisa was so wet; she might have just got out the bath. Barely hesitating, Beth pushed her thumb up inside her and caressed her G-spot.

Lisa whimpered urgently and pushed herself hard against Beth's hand, moving her hips up and down so that Beth's thumb was pumping in and out of her like a tiny penis. Beth could see Lisa fondling her own breasts with her hands and hear her desperate moaning.

She was very aware of the urgency gathering between her own legs again. Without withdrawing her thumb, Beth lowered her middle finger on to Lisa's clit and began to tease it softly. Her whole hand was now pushed against Lisa's mound, kneading her, caressing her. Beth slipped her other hand between her own thighs, using her own lubrication to rub herself.

She felt Lisa's vagina tighten as the spasm of her climax rushed through her body. The knowledge that Lisa was coming was so exciting, so stimulating, that Beth almost lost control again herself, just imagining how it had felt. She withdrew her hands almost reluctantly and sat up on her heels, her breathing ragged.

Eventually, Lisa sat up beside her and placed an arm around Beth's shoulders. She planted a gentle kiss on her cheeks. 'Thank you, Beth. That was very good. And now we can take the time to really enjoy ourselves.'

For a moment, Beth looked startled. She had expected it to be over now that they had both come. Nevertheless, she was still tingling from the thrill of seeing and feeling Lisa climax. She remembered that this was not the first time Lisa had suggested that one orgasm was only the beginning. She shivered with anticipation.

Lisa crawled across the bed and reached to open the drawer of the bedside table. Beth allowed her eyes to examine Lisa's tiny buttocks. She reached out and ran her hands over one cheek, smiling at the way Lisa's muscles tightened. She raised her hand and smacked Lisa gently. Lisa squirmed with delight.

'Lie back and open your legs,' Lisa instructed. As she turned round, Beth could see that she was holding a vibrator in her left hand. Her eyes widened. She did as she was told, then closed her eyes. She heard the urgent buzzing as Lisa flicked the switch, then jumped as the cold plastic made contact with her inner thigh. She moaned as the tip of the vibrator slipped up inside her vagina. Unable to help herself, she began to push against it, forcing it deeper and deeper inside her, entering at an angle she was not able to achieve when using a vibrator on her own.

She moaned and bit her lip as she felt the fingers of Lisa's other hand seek out her clitoris. The double sensation of stimulation in both places at once was unbelievable. She knew she could not take much more of it without coming.

As if sensing her thoughts, Lisa began to slide the vibrator slowly back out, at the same time reducing the pressure of her fingers to the softest of caresses. Beth rolled her hips and sobbed with frustration. She was desperate to come.

'Please,' she begged helplessly. 'Oh God, Lisa. Please don't tease.' She pushed herself up, trying to force the vibrator deeper inside her. 'I want . . .'

'Yes? What is it?' Lisa questioned. 'Don't be afraid to say what you want.'

'I want to feel your tongue there again,' Beth whispered, still rolling her hips.

621

Lisa smiled knowingly. She pushed the vibrator back up inside Beth's vagina and then leant over her and flicked her tongue across Beth's throbbing clit. Beth shuddered and clenched her muscles tightly around the vibrator. She turned her head and saw Lisa slip her hand down between her own thighs and begin squeezing her mound. Her face was flushed and her breathing was shallow. Beth sensed that Lisa was getting ready to climax as well and another tremor of ardour raced through her body.

Lisa pushed her head even lower and encased Beth's sex bud with her lips. As Lisa sucked softly on it, Beth shuddered all over and a small whimper escaped her lips. She was so close now. A shiver of excitement raced through every limb. Lisa sucked harder, while one hand pushed the vibrator back and forth in Beth's vagina and the other hand caressed her own swollen clitoris.

Beth stiffened, sobbing incoherently as another powerful orgasm rushed to overwhelm her.

'Oh Jesus,' she gasped. She heard Lisa moan softly in response and felt her slump forward over her stomach.

Beth was not sure how long it was before she recovered enough to move again. She opened her eyes and gazed down at Lisa's head still resting on her lower body. She smiled contentedly and ran her fingers through the other woman's blonde hair.

Lisa sat up and smiled at her. 'Well? It wasn't so bad, was it?' she questioned teasingly.

Beth grinned sheepishly and shook her head. She could hardly believe how much she had just enjoyed herself, or remember why she had been so apprehensive about it. It hadn't been anything like she had imagined it would be. The whole experience had been so different from sex with a man. Very slow, very sensual. Not better, just very different and very, very good.

Lisa patted her on the leg. 'I'll make us both some coffee.' She got up and slipped on the robe that was

622

hanging over a chair. 'Come on through when you are ready.'

Beth stood up and glanced down at herself. She was covered in sweat. 'Would you mind if I took a shower?' she questioned.

'Of course not. I should have offered. It's through here.' Lisa began walking across the room towards another door on the far side. Beth followed her. As Lisa opened the door into the bathroom, Beth put her hand on her shoulder.

'I don't suppose you would like to join me?' Beth suggested softly.

Lisa's face lit up. 'I was hoping you might suggest that,' she whispered as she pulled her robe from her shoulders and dropped it to the floor.

As they stepped into the shower and Lisa turned the water on, Beth picked up the sponge and soaped it thoroughly. She ran her eyes over Lisa's trim figure then reached out excitedly to caress her puckered nipples.

Chapter Seven

*B*eth ran her eyes carefully over the example financial plan she had just completed, double-checking to ensure she had missed nothing important. She wanted it to be as good as possible. Lisa had just told them that Geoff Stevens was taking the final lecture session the following morning, and that he would probably want to review some of their best work. Beth was determined hers would be one of those selected.

Geoff Stevens! His name was spoken almost in the same breath as that of God in the financial world. Simon worshipped him in an envious, greedy sort of way. Beth knew that he would die for an opportunity to spend a few minutes fawning at Geoff's feet in the hope of learning something useful. She doubted he would have sent her on this course at all if he had realised that she would get to meet the great Geoffrey Stevens.

Beth rubbed her eyes and suppressed a yawn. The week's hectic social activities were really beginning to catch up with her. Thank goodness she had made no plans for the coming evening. All she wanted to do was curl up in bed with a good book and then sleep for at least eight hours. One could definitely have too much of a good thing.

Sensing a presence hovering nearby, she looked up. Lisa was standing behind her. Beth had been both amused and flattered to find Lisa wearing a dress that morning. Considering how she obviously felt about it during work hours, it was the highest compliment the young woman could have paid her.

'OK, Beth?'

'Yes, fine, thanks. I'm just about finished.' Beth was surprised and pleased to find she felt no embarrassment about the previous evening. They had done nothing to be embarrassed about. They had just been two good friends enjoying each other's company.

'Good.' Lisa patted her shoulder gently. 'I'm sure I can see to it that your work is one of those Geoff Stevens gets a look at. He's a wonderful man, Beth, with a brilliant financial mind. What he doesn't know isn't worth knowing. Make sure you take full advantage of him.'

Beth nodded. Even if she didn't learn anything from him, she would still enjoy Simon's professional jealousy over the meeting. She wondered what Geoff would be like. Lisa was obviously more than impressed. She smiled, realising that he was the first man Lisa had ever expressed an interest in, albeit purely professional.

Suddenly, she spotted John watching her with an amused twinkle in his eye. Lisa was still resting a hand on her shoulder and Beth drew a sharp breath and forced herself to return his stare. Her eyes dared him to make anything more of it. John flashed her a knowing grin and lowered his head. In spite of herself, she experienced a brief rush of longing as she remembered his submission to her in the storeroom.

Brian and Steve had both asked her out again, yesterday and today. If it hadn't been for her evening with Lisa, she might have been tempted the previous day. She loved the longing look in their eyes and it was flattering to be so in demand. Today, however, she was less tempted. She needed a rest. She had to be at her very best the following day, both mentally and physically, in order to impress Geoff Stevens.

Lisa patted her shoulder again and moved on. Beth finished a final check of her work and decided that it was time to call it a day. Lisa had already told them they could leave as soon as they were finished and several of her fellow students had already handed their work in and left. She glanced at her watch. Twenty past four. She had plenty of time for a long soak before dinner. Then she planned to curl up in bed with the crime thriller she had bought herself during the lunch break.

'Sure you won't at least come out for a quick drink later, Beth?' Steve caught her as she headed for the door. 'It's our last night. This time tomorrow, we'll all be on our way home. We may never see each other again,' he added mournfully.

Beth grinned. In their closed little world that wasn't very likely. There was a good chance that they would all bump into each other again sooner or later at some conference or other.

'Honestly, Steve. I've already got plans for this evening. Sorry.'

There was no way she was going to admit that she was staying in, too exhausted to take any more excitement. She wondered if he would assume that her plans were with Lisa, then shrugged. Who cared what he thought?

Steve put an exaggerated expression of despair on his face and shrugged his shoulders at Brian. 'Well, I tried,' he muttered. Beth laughed.

Brian looked round for John and shook his head. 'We'll just have to drown our sorrows without her,' he called. 'Unless you can talk her round? See you down in the bar around eight.' John stared at Beth thoughtfully, then nodded silently.

Brian squeezed her hand. 'Don't forget. If you change your mind, we'll be in the bar of the St Anne's.'

'Not tonight, Brian.'

'We could always come and tuck you in later, if you want,' he added with a wink.

'In your dreams,' Beth laughed. 'See you all tomorrow.'

When she asked for her key at the desk, the receptionist shook his head. 'Are you sure it's not in your bag, madam? You didn't hand it in this morning.'

Beth frowned. 'I'm sure I did.' She rummaged hastily through her handbag. She was certain that she remembered dropping it on the desk that morning as usual. Or was that yesterday? She must have had it last night, or rather early that morning, when she got back from Lisa's. Damn!

'Perhaps you left it in the room? I'll get the spare key for you, madam.' Beth noticed that his eyes were focused on her chest again. She felt too foolish about the missing key to pay it much attention. She took the spare key with a nod of thanks and hurried to the lift.

After a long, hot bath, Beth decided to take advantage of room service again, too weary to be bothered with dressing to eat in the dining-room. She couldn't resist another feast of prawns at Simon's expense and she also indulged herself in a slice of raspberry shortcake with whipped cream. It would do her good to get to the gym the following week.

After she had finished eating, Beth hunted for the missing key in vain, then gave up and spent an hour or so making a list of things she would like to discuss with Geoff Stevens, should she be lucky enough to get the opportunity. She couldn't help feeling excited about meeting him face to face. He was such a legend.

By eight thirty, she was dressed in a short lacy nightie and tucked up under the duvet with her murder mystery. It was ages since she had read a good book and she was soon engrossed in the twists and turns of the complicated plot. Exciting as it was, however, by ten o' clock, her eyes refused to stay open any longer and she switched the bedside lamp out and snuggled down sleepily.

She was running across a wide, grassy field in the middle of nowhere. It was dark. The ground ahead of her was illuminated by a huge harvest moon, hanging low on the horizon in a star-splattered night sky. It was clear and balmy and a soft breeze gently caressed her naked flesh. The grass was damp under her bare feet. Someone was following her and she needed to reach the woods just visible on the distant horizon.

She had no idea why. She couldn't even remember where she was or what she was doing there. She only knew it had something to do with solving the recent spate of unexplained deaths in the sleepy little village that lay a mile or so behind her.

Without warning, the scenery changed. Now, she was lying on her back in a bed of rose petals, listening to someone giving a lecture about property investment. She could hear music playing in the distance, and the clatter of dishes. She tried to lift her head to look round but a hand pushed her back down and she heard Lisa's voice telling her to relax and enjoy herself. She jumped as she felt something soft and furry brush up against her legs, purring loudly.

A car horn blared somewhere nearby and Beth heard a clock striking. She counted the chimes. Thirteen. That couldn't be right. Where had Lisa gone? She felt gentle fingers starting to undo the ribbons on the front of her nightie and a shiver of desire tore through her body. Lisa's touch was so sure, so knowing. The nightie came open and Beth felt the material pulled away, exposing her breasts and crotch.

She opened her eyes to look up at her lover. The room was pitch dark. She couldn't see anything except a vague shadow hovering at the foot of the bed. She tried to reach out to turn the bedside lamp on. A hand caught hers and held it fast.

'Lisa?' Beth twisted her head round and strained her eyes. 'What are you doing? Put the light on. I want to see you.' Beth was having trouble collecting her thoughts. She couldn't remember where she was or how she had got there. She wasn't entirely sure she was even awake. There was something about what was going on that seemed more like a dream.

Her unseen lover took hold of her other arm and lifted both arms above her head. She felt a cord being wrapped round her wrists and secured to the bedhead.

'What are you doing?' she repeated, tugging against the restraints.

Somewhere nearby, a door slammed and Beth heard footsteps in the corridor. Of course. She was in her hotel room. She must have closed the heavy shutters over the windows. That was why it was so dark. What was Lisa doing in her hotel room?

'Just close your eyes and relax.' Beth became aware of something caressing her stomach. It was as soft as velvet. A shiver ran down her spine and she felt the goose-bumps springing up all over her body. Unable to help herself, Beth writhed with delight.

'That's it. Just close your eyes and enjoy.'

Where had he learnt to touch her so softly? It took a second or two for that thought to sink in. It was a man's voice speaking to her from out of the darkness. Muffled and indistinct, as if deliberately disguised, but definitely a man's voice. Who was he? Where was Lisa? What on earth was going on? Why couldn't she think straight?

'Who's there? What's happening?' A wave of panic went through her and Beth began to pull harder against the constraints holding her wrists. A velvety touch moved up her body and brushed lightly across her nipples. Beth gasped with shock and pleasure. Jesus! How was he doing that?

'There's nothing to be frightened of. You're just dreaming. That's all. Relax.'

The words were almost hypnotic. The soft velvet continued to tease her breasts. It was the most incredible sensation she had ever experienced. Tingles of pleasure were running down her writhing body. Every caress sent ripples of longing deep inside her. Her clitoris was throbbing as if she had been using her vibrator, yet, incredibly, nothing had touched her there yet. The voice was right. She had to be dreaming.

'That's it. Close your eyes.' The voice was closer. His tongue ran over her neck and up on to her ear. Teeth nibbled her earlobe and warm breath whispered in her ear. 'Enjoy.'

Beth whimpered urgently. Her body felt as if it was on fire and she couldn't keep still. The soft breathing in her ear was causing the muscles in her legs to twitch. Unseen fingers seemed to be running up and down her thighs. The velvety touch continued to stimulate her breasts. He had to be wearing some kind of fur glove. Her nipples had grown so large and rigid that they were almost painful and her lubrication was already seeping from her engorged sex lips. She had never been so ready.

'Take me. Please.' The words fell from her lips before she could stop them. She rolled her hips again, trying desperately to rub her thighs together. If her hands hadn't been tied, she would have been unable to stop herself from pushing her fingers hard up inside her. Her clitoris and vagina were throbbing urgently. The velvety touch began sliding slowly, so slowly, over her stomach. The lips caressing her neck began to move down towards her hardened nipples.

'Oh Jesus. Please.' Beth was sobbing uncontrollably now. She felt his lips licking her breasts and his teeth nibbling her engorged nipples. Her lower body spasmed and a violent climax rippled through her. It was the first time she had ever come without any stimulation of her clitoris or vagina and the sudden intensity of it took her by surprise. She cried out in pleasure.

'That's it. Let yourself go.' The voice was as soft and

silky as the gloved hand. Who the hell was he? What was happening to her?

'John?' She whispered. 'It's you, isn't it?' Her lower body was still trembling and her legs were as wobbly as jelly.

'If you want it to be,' the voice responded softly. 'What does it matter?'

It could be Brian, she thought. She had always suspected that Brian might be a bit of a dark horse. She remembered his offer to come and tuck her in. On his own, without John taking charge, he might be capable of something like this.

'How did you get in?' She felt his gloved hand beginning to caress her thighs again and found it difficult to believe that she would be able to respond so soon. She remembered the missing key. Had someone deliberately stolen it? Who? One of the three men? When had they had the opportunity? Beth remembered the way the hotel receptionist had been looking at her. Surely, he wouldn't dare?

'Anything's possible in a dream.' The voice seemed to reply to her thoughts. His tongue began to tease her nipples again. They were still puckered and swollen. She sighed gently and closed her eyes, allowing the pleasurable sensations to wash over her. It had to be John. As he continued to caress her with tongue and glove, her clit began to tingle and pulsate with renewed desire. Her whole body had become so sensitive that when the corner of the duvet flopped across her stomach, she cried out as if she had been slapped. She sighed with relief as he pushed it gently away and soothed her burning flesh with his cool lips.

She started to fantasise about him plunging his rigid cock deep up inside her. She longed to wrap her legs around his back and bury his shaft inside her to the hilt. She wanted to squeeze and tease him with her muscles, torture him until he could take no more and had to pump his seed helplessly into her. The idea was so exciting that she hardly knew what to do with herself. As she continued to writhe from side to side, her breath coming in short, sharp pants, she heard herself begging him to take her.

'Please. I want you inside me,' she sobbed.

'Like this?'

Beth gasped as his fingers penetrated her. She immediately clasped her legs around his wrist and tried to pull him in deeper. She felt him begin slowly caressing the ridges of her vagina. Sweat was trickling between her breasts and pooling in her navel, as she burned with need for him.

'Yes, oh yes!' She thrust against him.

'Or, perhaps, like this?' She groaned as she felt his fingers withdraw, then cried out in shock as something icy cold was pushed right up inside her. 'Oh Christ!' She bit her lip to try and stem her desperate sobbing. Whatever it was that he had pushed into her was so cold against her burning flesh that the shock was breathtaking. Helplessly, she felt herself climaxing again.

As she gradually relaxed, Beth could feel liquid running out of her. For an awful moment, she thought she had wet herself. Then the truth dawned. Ice. He had pushed a chunk of ice up inside her. She could feel it melting, feel the water running down her thighs. Then she felt him begin drying her gently with a soft towel.

Beth took a deep breath and shook her head. This couldn't be happening. If her hands had not been tied, she would have pinched herself hard to make herself wake up.

'Who are you? What do you want?' she whispered weakly.

'I am whoever you want me to be and all I want is to make you happy. You are happy, aren't you?' She still couldn't recognise the voice.

He finished drying her. She felt his fingers starting to rub her nipples again and his gloved hand gently caress her mound and clit. It was still so sensitive from her last orgasm that even the soft velvet was more than she could stand.

'Yes, but no more,' she whispered. 'I can't take any more.'

'Oh, but you are wrong,' he responded quietly. 'So wrong. Believe me. We have only just begun.'

Beth licked her dry lips and whimpered softly, partly with fear, partly with anticipation. He was the one who was wrong. He had to be. She couldn't possibly climax again. She was completely sated. Utterly fulfilled. She just wanted to sleep. She sighed with relief as his hands moved off her.

The room was so quiet and so dark that, after a moment or two, Beth began to think she was alone after all. She strained her ears but could hear nothing. Had she imagined the whole thing? No. She couldn't have. Her hands were still tied and her body was still trembling with the after-effects of her passion. Had he sneaked away and left her like this? Panic engulfed her as she imagined the hotel maid finding her, trussed up and naked.

'Where are you? Untie me.' She pulled against the cord round her wrists, straining to sit up.

'Not yet.' Beth jumped as his now naked body pressed down hard against her. She sensed that he was going to take her. Amazingly, despite her weariness, she was already trembling with renewed desire.

She jumped again, then gasped aloud as his prick pushed up hard against her thigh. Automatically, she spread her legs and raised her buttocks up off the bed to meet him. She felt his fingers grasping himself, guiding the tip into her.

'Oh!' After the cold of the ice, his cock felt burning hot. Instinctively, she wrapped her legs around him, pulling him deeper into her and sighing with pleasure. She tensed, waiting to feel the exquisite sensation as he began pumping in and out.

He didn't move, just lay there on top of her with his

633

stiff cock impaling her body. She could feel it twitching and throbbing inside her. The sensation drove her mad. What was he waiting for?

Beth pushed her buttocks firmly into the mattress and forced herself down as far as she could. Thrusting hard, she pushed her pelvis forward and pulled him deeper into her. At the same time, she squeezed her vaginal muscles tightly, then pulled back and thrust her hips again. She heard him sigh softly and felt his body stiffen against her, fighting her. His cock throbbed in response to her movements.

'That's it. Enjoy yourself.' She could hear the intense concentration in his voice as he struggled to keep himself from responding. The feel of him pulsating inside her, yet refusing to react to her desperate efforts, was pure torture. How could he stand it? A few short minutes ago, she had been certain that she could not climax again. Now, she was just as certain she was not going to be able to help herself.

She pulled away and thrust again, then stiffened as his fingers reached down between her legs to seek out her tormented sex bud. With a touch as soft as butterfly wings, he began slowly caressing it. Deep inside her, she felt his swollen penis throb again.

'Oh God!' She was past caring if anyone might hear her cry out. She was past caring about anything but her desperate need to make him respond to her. How could he just lie there like that without moving? He wasn't human. She was being fucked by the very devil himself. She sobbed again and pushed against him with all her strength. The bonds at her wrists were cutting into her skin but the pain only served to intensify her passion. She tried to wrap her legs even tighter around him to pull him deeper into her. His lips ran over her breasts again and his tongue began to circle her aching nipples. His fingers continued to rub her clit and his massive cock pulsed and twitched tantalisingly inside her.

Her orgasm seemed to start at the roots of her hair.

The tingling ran down her neck and spine, spreading out to encompass her chest and stomach. Ripples of pleasure rushed through her womb and down her vagina. Her muscles tightened around his cock as if physically trying to squeeze his seed out of him. Hot shivers travelled down her legs and into her feet, curling her toes.

With a final shudder that shook her body from head to foot, Beth collapsed back on to the bed, her head spinning. She was so weak that she was afraid she would never be able to move again. She was gasping and sobbing, trying to catch her breath.

'Are you all right?' he whispered.

All right? He had to be joking. She wondered whether anyone had ever actually died of ecstasy. If so, she had probably just come as close as it was possible to come and still survive.

'Yes,' she whispered feebly. 'Oh yes.'

She heard him grunt with satisfaction. Suddenly, he began to plunge himself furiously into her, his cock ramming in and out like a giant piston and his breathing harsh and ragged. She realised that his whole body was rigid with tension and sensed the enormous self-control it had taken for him to resist her for so long. She experienced a surge of gratitude at his selflessness. Now, it was his turn.

Fighting her weariness and ignoring the protests of her sated body and super-sensitive clitoris, Beth lifted her body and thrust against him, gyrating her hips. He groaned loudly and increased his pace, pumping in and out of her in a mad frenzy of pent-up passion.

The sweat was dripping off him and running in rivulets down his body on to her own. She could smell his body odour, harsh and musky. His cock was so big and stiff it felt as if she were being split in half. She heard herself whimpering with a mixture of pain and raw passion at the extent of his arousal.

When he came, his release was so powerful, so thrilling, that she felt herself climaxing again as spurt after urgent spurt burst from him. It was as if now that he had finally let himself go he was never going to be able to stop. They were both sobbing helplessly, their bodies trembling and shaking with the intensity of it. When it was finally over he just lay motionless on top of her, too spent and weary even to withdraw.

Beth closed her eyes and gradually drifted off to sleep.

When she awoke the following morning, the sun was streaming in through the open shutters. She was not surprised to discover that she was alone. She must have been dreaming. Sex like that couldn't happen for real. No man could do to her what her dream lover had done. She refused to look at the damp patch in the bed or acknowledge the tender ache between her thighs.

After a long, hot shower, Beth began to dress ready for the morning session at the training centre. She put on her favourite skirt and then selected a long-sleeved blouse with buttoned cuffs that hid the red welts on her wrists.

As she left the room, she checked the door carefully. It was shut and locked. If anyone had been in her room, they must have had the missing key.

On the way down, she shared the lift with a man who had just left room 308. He smiled warmly at her.

'Lovely day.'

'Yes.' Beth flushed. Why was he grinning at her like that?

When he saw her, the receptionist gave her a huge smile. 'We've found the missing key under the desk,' he told her. As he spoke, his eyes began undressing her again. Beth's flush deepened. Had he had the key all along?

As she hurried along the road towards the training centre, it seemed to Beth as if every man she passed was staring at her with a knowing grin on his face.

* * *

Beth sat, spellbound, as Geoff Stevens lectured. She had never heard anyone speak with such passion or enthusiasm. To her, despite her enjoyment of some aspects of the work, the financial service industry was really nothing more than a way to earn a living, a means to an end. Clearly, to Geoff, it was his whole *raison d'etre*. In a way, she realised that she envied him. It must be nice to revel in one's work as much as he so obviously did.

The lecture was a long one, taking up most of the morning and covering a broad spectrum of topics, some of which were rather over her head. As he delved into the more complicated aspects of corporate finance and risk management through the use of derivatives, Beth found her attention wandering.

She was still in a state of shock about her previous night's adventure, which did little to help her concentration. It was almost as if she had lived through some kind of supernatural fantasy; entering a an erotic dream world in some parallel universe, where anything could and did happen. It must have been John, mustn't it? But then, it might have been Brian or Steve. It could even have been the receptionist. It could have been a complete stranger. Beth shivered as she remembered the odd looks she had received that morning.

As the morning progressed, she did her best not to look at any of the three men. She needed time to collect her thoughts. During the coffee break, Beth stood alone by the window, hoping to avoid conversation with anyone. Her efforts were in vain. Within moments, she saw John heading in her direction. She fixed a smile on her face.

'He's good, isn't he?' John nodded towards the crowd gathered around Geoff. Beth nodded silently. Noticing Steve and Brian coming in their direction, she cleared her throat.

'So, what did you three get up to last night?' The question was out before she could stop herself.

John grinned. 'Actually, we went to a strip club,' he

told her. 'It was very good. You should have joined us.'
She noticed Steve and Brian nodding in agreement.

'What did you do?'

Beth flushed crimson and swallowed hard. John smiled knowingly.

'Been dreaming about me, have you, Beth?'

'Excuse me.' Beth pushed past them and hurried off towards the toilet. They couldn't have been at a strip club together. It must have been him.

After coffee, Geoff moved on to a brief discussion about playing the stock market. Beth struggled to concentrate. He was an extremely attractive man; tall, slim and well proportioned. His dark, wavy hair was flecked with silver and his deep brown eyes were framed by lashes most women would kill for. His mouth was wide and sensual and when he smiled, two deep dimples formed either side of his lips. Only his nose spoilt the perfection of his features. Long and narrow, it was slightly crooked, as if it had once been broken and not set properly. Beth decided that it gave him added character. Losing the thread of the lecture again, Beth ran her eyes over his well-tailored grey suit, enjoying the way it hugged his figure and emphasised his broad shoulders and slim hips. She had always liked the combination of grey suit, crisp white shirt and dark red tie on a man. She wondered what his taste in women was like. Was there a Mrs Stevens?

True to her word, Lisa not only made sure that Geoff had an opportunity to review Beth's work, she also made a point of personally introducing them during the buffet lunch afterwards. There were many advantages in being the teacher's pet.

'I must say, I was very impressed with your class work. Your financial plan showed great flair,' Geoff told her as he shook her hand warmly. 'Where are you currently working?'

'Thank you.' His handshake was firm and his skin cool to her touch. 'You are very generous. I'm with a small private company down south. Personal assistant to Simon Henderson.'

Geoff nodded his head without commenting and Beth could not tell whether he knew Simon or not.

'I believe this is the last day of your course,' Geoff continued as he helped himself to another slice of quiche. 'This is very good, isn't it? I adore buffet lunches. Just as well, considering how many I get invited to.' He took a swig of his wine.

'Tell me. Have you got all you hoped for out of the week?'

The colour rushed to her cheeks as Beth reflected on her recreational activities. 'Oh yes. It's been wonderful,' she murmured. 'I haven't been back in finance very long and I've got great hopes and plans for the future.'

'I would enjoy discussing some of your ideas with you in more detail, Beth. You seem to have a keen insight into our business. We must get together sometime. My own corporate headquarters are down south, too. Not all that far from you as it happens.' Obviously, he did at least know of Simon.

'I'd like that.' Beth was sure he was just making polite conversation. She was suddenly conscious of several other people hovering anxiously, waiting for a chance to impress the great Geoff Stevens. She was rather hogging his attention.

'Have you done much consultancy work?' Geoff continued.

'Um, well, no. As I said, I haven't been back in the business for long . . .' Beth tried not to laugh at the idea of Simon letting her loose on her own. Despite her title, she knew she was little more than a clerk or secretary in his eyes.

Geoff smiled at her confusion. 'You should. I'm certain you would be good at it. Besides, it's very lucrative.' His face broke into a broad grin. 'How are you getting home, by the way?'

'Train,' Beth responded. 'It's such a long journey and I'm not very keen on driving.'

'Nor I,' Geoff responded. 'That's why I have a chauffeur. Why don't I give you a lift and make use of the time to pick your brains? For a fee, naturally.'

Beth was startled. It was very tempting. A chauffeur-driven car would be much more comfortable than the train. She hated the underground journey across London. Simon would be green with envy at her spending so much time with Geoff.

'Well, if you're sure it's no trouble?'

'No trouble at all. It would be my pleasure.' Geoff patted her arm. 'We should be ready to leave about two thirty if that's OK?' He looked around and then pulled a face. 'Now, if you will excuse me, I need to go and make myself agreeable to my hosts. If I'm not nice to them, they may not invite me again.' He took another bite of his quiche. 'They do the best buffet I ever get.' He gave her a conspiratorial wink and grinned again.

Beth found herself grinning in response. He was nothing at all like she had imagined. She had expected he would be pompous, stuffy and self-opinionated. In fact, he was one of the nicest men she had ever met. A real gentleman. She was really looking forward to the journey home. There was so much she would like to discuss with him.

'You two seemed to be hitting it off OK.' Lisa came up beside her just as Geoff moved away. 'I told you he was worth getting to know, didn't I?'

'He is fascinating,' Beth agreed. 'He's offered me a ride home so we can continue our discussions.' Beth glanced at her watch. 'I suppose I'd better get back to the hotel and finish packing. I was too lazy to do it earlier.'

'I shall miss you, Beth,' Lisa responded softly. 'It's been such fun having you here this week.'

Beth smiled at her choice of words, then gave Lisa a sudden hug. 'I shall miss you too, Lisa. Thanks again for everything. If you're ever down my way you must look me up.'

Lisa returned her hug. 'I hope you mean that, Beth. I'd love to see you again.'

'Why don't you come and stay with me for a few days in the summer?' Beth found that she really liked the idea. 'We could have a great time. I'll write to you, OK?'

'OK. Take care of yourself, Beth.'

Feeling suddenly sad, Beth escaped quickly before she found herself having to say goodbye to the men, too. She wasn't much worried about Steve and Brian but she would certainly miss John. Miss him a lot. It must have been him last night. Mustn't it?

Chapter Eight

B eth made a last quick check round the room to ensure
she had not forgotten anything. She couldn't help
smiling to herself as she remembered some of things she
had got up to here during the past few days. Was this
room often host to such antics? If so, it was a wonder the
bedsprings stood up to the strain!

Downstairs, she paid her bill quickly, using the business credit card Simon had given her, then picked up her
small case and headed towards the main entrance. Before
she reached it, the door swung open and a tall man
strode in, his eyes scanning the lobby. Seeing Beth, his
lips widened into an amused grin and he headed confidently towards her.

'Ms Bradley?' he questioned.

Beth nodded, puzzled.

'I'm Daniel. Mr Stevens asked me to collect you and
your luggage. I understand we are giving you a ride
home.' He raised his left eyebrow as if implying that
there was something strange or unusual about the idea.
His voice was both deep and sensual and Beth felt an
immediate physical attraction for him.

Realising that he must be Geoff's chauffeur, she examined him with interest. He was extremely handsome in

his black three-piece suit, crisp white ruffled shirt and dark green tie. His short hair was beautifully cut and as black as midnight. His eyes were an unusual shade of deep blue, almost violet, and his features had a roguish, almost Romany look that made Beth think of a gypsy or a pirate.

She could almost see him with a patch over one eye, swinging a cutlass and swigging a bottle of rum. Her heart fluttered and a warm glow spread through her body as she fleetingly pictured herself captured and helpless at his mercy.

As Daniel reached for her bag, he raised his eyebrow again and gave her a slightly quizzical look. 'Mr Stevens is still at the training centre making his final farewells,' he explained. 'We'll pick him up as we leave.' He took her arm. He had a strong but gentle grip. She noticed that his hands were large and beautifully manicured.

'This way, ma'am.' He began to guide her towards the door. As they moved, he gave her several sideways glances, his face clearly bemused. Beth had a feeling he wanted to say something but was not sure how to begin.

'Is something bothering you?' she questioned. 'You seem surprised at the idea of me travelling with you.' Surely, he couldn't be such a snob as to think her not good enough to travel with the great Geoff Stevens, could he?

Daniel immediately looked awkward. Beth noticed his hand had tightened on her arm. She shivered slightly at the strength in his fingers.

'Um, well.' Daniel looked around as if to make sure no one else was within hearing distance. 'It's nothing. Just that, well, Mr Stevens hasn't taken any interest in women since,' he paused, seeming to search for the right words. 'Well, not for a long time, anyway.'

Before Beth could react to this startling piece of information, Daniel let go of her arm and stepped away. He turned to face her and gave her a long glance, starting with her legs and working his way up. Beth automatically drew her breath in and held herself tall and straight. She was almost tempted to give him a quick twirl.

'Finished?' she questioned in an amused yet slightly sarcastic tone. She placed her hands on her hips and hoped he wouldn't notice the slight flush on her cheeks. 'Do I pass muster?'

Daniel licked his lips. 'Yes, ma'am. Very nice. I can see why Mr Stevens is interested. I wouldn't mind a round or two myself.' He winked at her suggestively.

Beth found it difficult not to laugh at his sheer nerve. 'Well, you can both just keep your hands to yourselves,' she replied stiffly. 'I'm acting as a consultant, nothing more.'

Daniel smiled and started to move towards the door again. Beth's curiosity began to get the better of her. 'What do you mean, he's not interested in women?' she demanded. It wasn't the impression she had formed of Geoff from what she had seen so far. She realised, however, that he had done nothing to make her believe he was interested in anything but her mind.

Daniel frowned. 'I've already said too much,' he replied softly.

It was Beth's turn to frown. She couldn't stand secrets or mysteries. 'If you tell me what you mean, Geoff won't find out.' She paused. 'Otherwise, I might have to ask him.'

Daniel swallowed and looked around again. 'He can't, well, you know,' he whispered.

'No, I don't know.' Beth was fascinated. She was also enjoying her position of authority over the clearly reluctant Daniel.

Daniel opened the hotel door and held it for Beth to walk through. He followed and hurried past her towards Geoff's car. Beth stood on the hotel steps and examined it appreciatively. It was a Bentley. It was silver grey; shiny, spotless and quite beautiful. Beth noticed one or two passers-by eyeing both the car and her speculatively, and she experienced a rush of self-importance at their interest. She assumed what she hoped was a suitably haughty expression and started to walk towards it.

Daniel, meanwhile, had already put Beth's small case into the boot. As she approached, he moved round to open the rear door. Beth began to climb in then stopped, poised with one leg slightly forward to pull her skirt tight across her buttocks. She pushed her chest out so that her blouse was clearly outlining her breasts. She noticed with satisfaction that the pose was not lost on Daniel. His eyes were devouring her greedily.

'Well,' she repeated her threat. 'Are you going to tell me, or do I ask him myself?'

'It's all the stress, you see.' Beth was amazed to see that Daniel's face appeared to be red with embarrassment. 'As I understand it, he can't, well, let's just say that he doesn't seem to get in the mood any more these days.' Daniel took her arm and helped her into the back seat of the car.

'Thank you.' Beth realised that he could not be sure if she was thanking him for his help or his information. She wasn't entirely sure herself. One thing she did know, however, was that she loved a challenge. Seducing someone like Geoff, such an expert businessman, could be extremely interesting.

She sat down and glanced around her. The carpet on the floor was even more luxurious than the one in Simon's office. She leant back on the wide beige leather seat and marvelled at how deep and soft the seat was. It was like sitting on a feather bed. The car was fitted out like a small mobile office: television, telephone, fax. There was even a small fridge. She thought about the cramped, stuffy train carriage on the way up and grinned broadly. This was definitely the only way to travel.

As Daniel closed the door behind her, Beth remembered that the windows were heavily tinted. From the outside, she had not been able to see in at all. Inside, looking out, she could see quite clearly. It was a bit like peering through a one-way mirror.

645

She watched Daniel walk round and climb into the driving seat. He had removed his jacket and she enjoyed watching the way his trousers clung to his hard body so that she could clearly see his muscles tightening and relaxing as he moved. For such a big man, his movements seemed remarkably smooth and graceful. He also looked extremely fit and alert. Beth wondered if he was a bodyguard as well as a chauffeur.

It took them less than a couple of minutes to reach the training centre. Geoff was already standing on the steps waiting for them as Daniel pulled up. Beth was busy examining the contents of the fridge, so she failed to notice the slight smile playing across Daniel's face or the thumbs up sign he gave his employer as he leapt out of the car and hurried round to open the door again.

'Everything taken care of, sir,' Daniel muttered as Geoff hurried down the steps and slid inside beside Beth.

'Good. A nice, smooth ride, please, Daniel.'

'I don't think that will be any trouble, sir. No trouble at all.' Daniel was still grinning as he closed the door behind his boss and returned to the driving seat.

Geoff pushed a small button on the control console and the opaque dividing window between the driver and the rear seat slid up quietly. He turned his head and smiled at Beth.

'Comfortable?' he enquired as he sat back in the deep leather seat. 'How about a drink?' As he spoke, he pushed another button and a door slid open in front of them, revealing a well-stocked drinks cabinet.

Beth nodded. 'Please. A sherry, if you have one.'

'Dry or sweet?'

'Oh, dry, please.'

Geoff leant forward and lifted a bottle of sherry and a glass.

Although Beth hadn't noticed them pull away, she realised that they were already moving again. The car was so quiet and smooth that it was almost impossible to feel any motion at all. As Geoff poured her drink, Beth examined him surreptitiously, her excitement already mounting at the thought of the challenge confronting her. Using the old trick, she slid forward in her seat so that her skirt began to ride up her thighs.

'Thank you.' She took the drink from his hand and sat back, careful not to pull her skirt down again. As she turned towards him, the lacy top of her stocking peeped out from under the hem. She watched him carefully as he poured himself a hefty malt whisky and then sat back beside her, placing the drink on a convenient shelf in the door.

'Now, for your fee.' Geoff took his wallet out of his jacket and began to count out a number of fifty-pound notes from a thick wad.

'That's really not necessary, Geoff.' Beth was still uncomfortable about the consultancy idea. 'Why don't we just consider the lift as fair payment? I'm sure I shall learn more from you than you will from me.'

From what they had discussed so far, Beth had a feeling that if anyone could help her find a way to improve her finances and escape Simon's clutches it would be Geoff. Not that she minded Simon's clutches much. In fact, she was quite looking forward to teasing him again. Although she hated admitting it, her experiences during the past few days had only heightened her enjoyment of being a man's plaything.

'That may be so,' Geoff told her, 'but you have got great imagination, Beth, and your instincts are good. I am expecting to get a lot from this trip. More than you realise.' Geoff held a handful of notes out towards her.

Beth shook her head. 'Honestly, Geoff. I can't take it.' She pushed his hand back.

'Listen, Beth. The first rule of success is never give something for nothing,' Geoff told her. 'I always charge for my services. So should you, OK?'

Beth smiled. There had to be at least a thousand pounds in his hand. 'Well, I suppose, when you put it like that.' She took the money and tucked it into her bag. 'It just seems a bit much.'

'Nonsense. You're worth it. Now, I want everything you've got.'

For a moment, Beth wasn't sure what he meant. She turned sideways to face him and tucked one leg behind the other.

'Well, then, I guess I'm all yours,' she responded as she sipped her sherry.

Geoff immediately began to talk about mergers and take-overs, continuing a conversation they had begun earlier. The more he talked, the more fascinated Beth became. She realised that he was very close to the edge with some of his wheeling and dealing. Not exactly illegal, perhaps, but walking a very thin line all the same. The whole concept thrilled her.

As they continued their conversation, Beth grew more animated. She started to ask questions and put forward ideas, responding enthusiastically to his probing. She was soon thoroughly enjoying herself and warming to his sharp mind and dry sense of humour. He laughed easily and was quick to see where her questions were leading.

As she considered her answers to some of his more difficult questions, Beth began to fiddle with the buttons on her blouse, twiddling them round nervously with her thumb and finger. At first, she was unaware of her actions but, as she noticed his eyes watching her, she allowed herself to slip one of the buttons undone in her apparent enthusiasm at their discussion.

Gradually, she moved closer to him and began to touch him lightly to emphasise her remarks or respond to his jokes. She was delighted by both his wit and his astute mind. Simon Henderson might think he was clever and slick but, next to Geoff, he was a rank amateur.

'Would you like another sherry?' Geoff offered. 'You've certainly earnt it. I've never met anyone with such a quick, keen mind.'

'Please.' Beth was terribly flattered by his compliment.

She smiled excitedly as she realised just how much she had learnt from him in such a short time. Far more than she had got from the whole week at the training centre. Much of what he had spoken of was less than strictly ethical but, as Geoff himself had just said, if the law doesn't say you can't do it, it means it's technically legal. It's the letter of the law, not the spirit. Her smile broadened. The financial world was much like life itself really, she decided. Do it to them, before they do it to you.

Beth took her drink and snuggled up closer to him. She had undone a couple of her blouse buttons now, the most she felt she could get away with without making herself too obvious. She placed her glass on the parcel shelf and gently pushed her knee against his upper thigh.

'Actually, after all that wine at lunch, I really shouldn't be drinking at all. I don't have much tolerance for alcohol. I get a bit reckless.' When he said nothing, she continued, 'Do you ever get like that, Geoff?' She placed a hand on his chest.

Geoff smiled tenderly and patted her leg. 'Yes, of course. Everybody does.'

Beth smiled and pulled gently on his arm so that his hand slipped up her thigh and over her stocking top. As his fingers made contact with the silky smooth skin of her upper thigh, she leant forward and kissed him on the lips. His hand slid the last inch to the top of her thigh and Beth shivered as his fingers started to caress the thin material of her panties.

Beth kissed him passionately and pushed herself hard against his arm and chest. She felt a surge of triumph as he responded by kissing her neck and ear. She could hear his breathing quicken and sense the urgency in his response.

If what Daniel had said was true, Geoff hadn't done this for quite a while. The thought excited her further. She moved her leg over his lap and wriggled up on to him until she was sitting astride his legs with her skirt almost up to her waist.

Geoff sighed loudly and increased the intensity of his kisses. Beth lifted her hand, undid the rest of her buttons as quickly as she could and flicked the catch of her bra open. As her breasts fell free she took his hand and placed it on her left breast.

Geoff sighed again and squeezed her nipple with his fingers. His mouth and tongue were still sending little tremors of desire racing up and down her body as he nibbled her earlobes and nuzzled her neck.

Beth slid up his lap as far as she could. Geoff released her breast and placed both his hands underneath her, pulling her even closer. Beth put one hand behind his head and pulled it down towards her. She gasped softly as his tongue ran softly across her right nipple. She rose up to meet him, rubbing her nipples over the rough stubble on his chin.

With another soft moan, Geoff pulled one of her nipples into his mouth and nipped it quite hard with his front teeth. Beth whimpered and pulled away, then whimpered again as he moved across and bit her other nipple. She dropped back down on to his lap and began to roll her hips. She could feel the material around his zip getting taut and was sure that he was beginning to harden.

Thrilled at her success, Beth pulled his shirt free from his waistband and ran her hands all over his slim, muscular torso. As he sucked her nipple back into his mouth, she dug her nails into his skin and allowed another whimper to escape her lips.

She pushed her lower body down harder against his lap. She was now quite certain that his cock was expanding beneath her and she shivered with anticipation as he began to lift himself up off the seat and thrust against her. Quickly, she dropped her hands, undid the button of his trousers and began to unzip him. Her own crotch was so close that she found she was able to caress herself with her fingers as the zip came open. A rush of longing shot through her.

He was wearing boxer shorts and Beth wasted no time in slipping her eager fingers through the opening to grab him. He was as stiff as a board. She rubbed her hand slowly up and down his erection, so excited that she barely noticed he was peeling her blouse and bra off down her arms.

Suddenly, he pushed her away and buried his head in her breasts. She gasped and arched her back, feeling his fingers pinching and tweaking her swollen nipples as he ran his tongue down her neck again. His penis was pushed up against her hand, hard and urgent.

'You are so beautiful,' he whispered. 'So very desirable.'

Beth lifted her head. Her bag was on the parcel shelf and she needed to raise herself up to reach it to get the condoms Steve had left in her room. As she moved, she rubbed her knuckles across her mound, shivering with excitement. She pushed her hips forward, so aroused by the touch that she almost forgot her bag completely. She pushed her knuckles harder against her throbbing clit. As the powerful surges of her lust intensified, Beth forced herself to concentrate. She reached out, pushed her fingers into her bag, and rummaged around frantically for the condoms. She quickly pulled one out and ripped the packet open with her teeth. She let go of Geoff's cock and slid off his lap to kneel on the seat beside him.

To her disappointment, although Geoff continued to fondle her buttocks and breasts, he made no attempt to undress her further. Obviously, he was content to leave things to her. Beth reached into his flies and carefully manoeuvred his rigid cock out of the front opening in his boxer shorts. She leant forward, placed her mouth over him, and started to move her lips slowly up and down while her tongue caressed him softly and her hand stroked his balls through the cotton of the shorts.

Geoff shuffled restlessly in his seat and she heard him groan with pleasure.

'Oh God. Please. Hurry,' he whispered desperately.

With a sudden panic, Beth realised that he might not be able to stay stiff for too long if he had problems. Quickly she lifted her head and slid the condom over him. As she pumped him with her hand to keep him excited, she began trying to pull her panties down with her other hand, cursing her clumsiness and scared his enthusiasm would vanish at any moment.

Finally, in desperation, she put her lips back down around him and sucked as hard as she could while using both hands to struggle free of her underwear. As soon as one ankle was free, she lifted her head, grabbed him in her hand and mounted him again, prising her sex lips open to insert him into her before lowering her hips to envelop him.

As his hardness slid right up into her, a rush of elation shot through her. She had done it! So much for what Daniel had said. All he had needed was the proper motivation. Still gloating, Beth began to move her body up and down, savouring the sensation of his huge cock pumping inside her.

Geoff closed his eyes and groaned loudly as he pushed himself frantically against her. Beth started moving faster, squeezing him with her muscles, her own passion increasing rapidly as she thrust herself on to him. With a final desperate groan, she felt him stiffen and come. Another thrill rushed through her body at the extent of her success; the realisation of her ability to restore his manhood.

'That was wonderful,' she whispered in his ear as she slowly lifted herself off him.

'For me, too, Beth. For me too.' She noticed he had that dumb, self-satisfied look on his face that men always seemed to wear after sex. Beth grabbed a tissue from her bag, peeled the condom off him and threw it into the tiny waste bin. She had the feeling he hadn't even realised that he had been wearing it.

'Don't forget to zip me up.' Geoff smiled.

Beth gently slipped his now flaccid penis back into his

shorts and zipped up his trousers, then leant over to pick up her blouse and bra. Geoff put his hand on her arm.

'No. Don't put them back on,' he commanded. 'You look great just as you are. I like you topless.'

Beth smiled and dropped her clothes on to the seat beside her. She began straightening her skirt.

'Take that off too,' he told her softly.

Beth wriggled out of her skirt and stockings so that she was left wearing a small silk half-slip that only just covered her naked mound. For the first time in ages, she remembered that they were in the back of a car, hurtling along a busy motorway. She glanced out of the window at the other traffic and wondered if the tinted glass was really that good, or if the other drivers could see her. She suddenly felt very naked and exposed.

She snuggled down next to Geoff with her head resting on his shoulder and did her best to suppress the self-satisfied grin stretching her lips. She felt like the cat that had got the cream and the canary.

Geoff pushed another button. 'Daniel. Could you pull in at the next service area, please.'

'Yes, sir. About five minutes.'

Daniel's disembodied voice made Beth jump. She glanced up at the thick, dark glass between front and rear. Thank God he couldn't see or hear what was going on!

'Perhaps I had better get dressed?' she suggested.

'No. Please don't. I want you to stay here just like you are,' Geoff told her. 'I won't be long.'

Beth smiled and snuggled up against him again. 'Anything you say,' she whispered, closing her eyes. Was he planning to have another session with her later? Maybe, now that they had done it once, he had completely regained his confidence. Had she, perhaps, awoken some kind of ravenous sex monster? Well, there was no harm in hoping!

As they pulled into the parking area of the service station, Beth sat up and stared out. It took all her self-control not to cover her breasts and sink down into the seat. She knew nobody could see in, but she could see out quite clearly.

They pulled up close to the building. Geoff was humming contentedly to himself and Beth stifled another grin of triumph. So he should be happy, she told herself smugly, remembering what she had done for him.

'Just stay as you are, Beth. I won't be long,' he told her again as Daniel opened the door for him and he jumped out of the car. Beth noticed several people walking past and her heart leapt into her mouth. Surely, they must have seen her through the door? She watched them carefully as they continued walking towards their car, without so much as a backward glance. With a sigh of relief, she moved her hands away from her exposed breasts.

She watched Geoff walk off, then gathered up her scattered clothing and folded it into a neat pile. Glancing down, she noticed that her slip had ripped slightly up one seam, exposing even more of her upper thigh. The tear gave her an idea. Beth reached for her bag and found her emergency sewing kit. She retrieved the small scissors and, carefully, slit both seams up to the waistband so that all she was covered by were two pieces of silk at back and front. It felt very sexy; like an Egyptian slave girl.

A group of businessmen walked by the car, glancing casually at the darkened windows as they passed. Beth forced herself to sit upright with her shoulders back, breasts fully revealed and her legs apart. She giggled at their lack of response. If they only knew what they were missing!

She wriggled around restlessly, wondering what pose to take when Geoff returned. She tried sitting upright with her hands on her knees but that felt rather silly. She lay down and sprawled right across the seat, first on her back, then on her side. The torn slip dropped away completely, exposing her mound. Too obvious.

Finally, she snuggled up on her side, with her legs folded under her on the seat. She carefully arranged the silk slip so that nothing was showing and then closed her eyes. She could hear more people walking past and, somehow, with her eyes closed, it seemed even more exciting with strange voices coming at her out of nowhere.

Beth began fantasising about having sex with Daniel. He was so damned good-looking. She couldn't imagine that he had any stress-related problems. She pictured Geoff receiving a phone call – some kind of business emergency that meant he had to get back to his office straight away. 'Sorry about this, Beth, but Daniel will see that you get home safely after you drop me off.' She imagined the chauffeur opening the door of the car for her and finding her in nothing but a torn slip. She would glance down ruefully at herself and explain to him how Geoff wouldn't let her get dressed. She would claim that he had thrown her clothes out of the window on the motorway and ask him to lend her his jacket.

How excited Daniel would be at the unexpected sight of her nakedness. She imagined him licking his lips in anticipation as she struggled to open her front door. As soon as they got inside, he would rip his jacket off her shoulders and force her down on her knees. She could almost hear the sound of his zip opening.

She pushed her hand down under the silk slip and started to tease her clitoris softly as she imagined Daniel's hot cock ramming into her from behind. She was still tingling from her earlier arousal and her outer lips were damp with her juices. She could clearly picture Daniel moaning with pleasure as she squeezed him inside her until he could take no more and began spurting urgently.

Her excitement getting the better of her, Beth pushed her finger up inside her. What if her friend Ann, who was looking after her house while she was away, arrived while Daniel was still thrusting into her? She imagined

Ann watching, wide-eyed, as Daniel slipped his cock out of her and stood up to introduce himself. What would Ann do? What would she say?

She couldn't imagine Daniel missing such an opportunity. Maybe he would tell Beth to undress Ann while he recovered his strength. She had never imagined making love to Ann before, but after her experience with Lisa ... Or maybe she would hold Ann down while Daniel took her over the back of the sofa? Beth moaned softly and increased the pressure of her fingers. She could practically hear Ann begging him not to stop while Daniel's buttocks tightened and relaxed as he pumped himself into her. Maybe she would join in, too.

She was just about to start fondling Ann's breasts in her imagination when she heard the driver's door open and realised that Daniel must be getting out to open the door for Geoff. She had almost forgotten that Daniel was sitting just the other side of the dividing glass. Hastily, she removed her hand and smoothed the silk slip back into place. She kept her eyes closed as the rear door opened and she heard Geoff climbing in beside her.

The door slammed shut with a resounding click and she was aware of the vibration of car engine as they pulled away. She imagined Geoff examining her as she sprawled back, motionless. Although he wasn't humming anymore, she was aware of his eyes examining her closely. She wondered if he was trying to peek under the tiny silk covering protecting her mound, or if he was enjoying the sight of her naked breasts and swollen nipples.

Beth felt the car pull out on to the motorway and increase speed. Her senses seemed exceptionally acute. Earlier, she had been totally unaware of the motion of the car. It had been the smoothest ride she had ever had. She smiled to herself at the unintended pun.

What was Geoff waiting for? Perhaps he needed a bit more encouragement? Keeping her eyes closed, Beth stretched lazily so that her breasts wobbled from side to side. She felt the silk cloth slide off, baring all. She smiled seductively and opened her eyes.

Her smile froze as realisation dawned. No wonder the car wasn't as smooth as before. Geoff must be driving. Quickly, she tried to cover herself while Daniel just stared at her, his wide grin providing serious competition for the Cheshire cat.

With one hand over her sex and the other clutching her breasts, Beth gazed round frantically, searching for her clothes. Daniel must have moved them; they were nowhere to be seen. She huddled in the corner and tried to collect her thoughts. Her faced burned with the memories of her recent fantasy.

Daniel continued to grin and she was acutely aware of the lust smouldering in his eyes. There was no mistaking what he had in mind and a thrill of excitement and desire raced through her. Beth forced herself to adopt a regal expression. If he wanted her, he would have to take her by force. She would do nothing to make it easy for him. In fact, she would fight him all the way. The thought was so stimulating that it was all she could do to contain herself.

'Where's Geoff?' she demanded. Talk about stupid question. She tried again. 'What have you done with my clothes?'

Daniel laughed. 'You don't need them for what I've got in mind.'

'If you think I'm just going to sit here while you ogle me, you're sadly mistaken,' she informed him. 'Now, give me my clothes at once.' As she spoke, she finally spotted them on the floor by his legs.

'Why don't you come and get them?' he challenged her.

Doing her best to forget her nakedness, Beth moved across the seat and reached down. Daniel licked his lips.

'Like I said before, very nice. I wouldn't mind a round or two with you.'

Beth made a supreme effort to look angry as he picked

up her clothes and pushed them out of reach behind him.

'In your dreams. How dare you?' she raged. 'If you think I would so much as let you touch me, let alone anything else . . . Now, just give me my clothes, you big ape.'

'Let me? I don't want you to let me,' Daniel retorted. He paused to let that sink in. 'I take what I want,' he continued. 'So you see, your opinion is not relevant.'

'I'll fight you every inch of the way,' she declared, surprised that her anger was quite genuine.

'I'm counting on it,' Daniel told her. He smiled. 'Although, to be fair, you are bought and paid for, don't forget.'

'What do you mean?' Beth realised that he was referring to her consultancy fee. The bastard had made her a prostitute. Geoff's money hadn't been for her opinions at all. It had been for her body. Her expression changed to a look of horror.

'No. He can have his damn money back. I didn't want it in the first place. I'm no whore.'

Daniel snorted contemptuously and pulled his tie loose. He had already removed his jacket and now he started taking his shoes and socks off.

'What the hell do you think you're doing?' Beth cried. 'You can bloody well put those back on again.' She shrank away into the corner with her legs drawn up underneath her. She used one hand to push the silk down between her thighs while her other hand crossed over her front, protecting her breasts.

Daniel ignored her and quickly pulled the shirt off over his head. Beth smiled as he struggled with the sleeves. In his enthusiasm, he had forgotten to release his cufflinks. She examined his chest, admiring his well-built physique. He was covered in dark, wiry chest hair running across his nipples and down his firm stomach past his navel. He was even more gorgeous than she had suspected.

Still smiling, Daniel released his trouser button and pulled both trousers and pants off in one fluid motion. Beth felt her breath catch as he revealed his bulging cock to her gaze. He was almost as big as John had been. She realised that he was watching her reaction and she knew she was blushing. Her body felt suddenly weak.

'Now, how do you like it?' he questioned. 'On top, doggy-style, missionary, from the back or maybe you'd just like to suck it? How about all of them?'

'How about none of them? Put your clothes back on or I'll start screaming and Geoff will fire you.' It sounded unlikely even to her. Geoff already knew what was going on. She had been well and truly set up. Jesus. Geoff probably didn't have any sexual hang-ups either. How stupid could you get?

'Maybe you'd like to come over here and stroke it?' Daniel proceeded to rub himself softly with his fingers. Beth held her breath. She had always loved watching a man play with himself like that. It drove her wild.

'No. I wouldn't,' she whispered.

Daniel grinned again. 'Think about it, Beth. If you managed to get me off then I wouldn't be able to fuck you, would I? Worth a try, I'd have thought. Or perhaps you want me to fuck you?' He was pumping himself quite hard now and his penis looked dark and swollen. Beth shivered.

Maybe he was one of those guys who preferred doing it in front of women rather than actually taking them? Sort of reverse dominance. Beth changed her approach.

'Why don't you show me,' she suggested coyly. 'I've never seen a man wank before.' Well, not for a couple of days anyway, she added silently.

Daniel shook his head. 'No, Beth. You come over here and finish me.' He stopped pumping and sat back with his legs open invitingly.

Beth realised how much she was burning to take his cock. Her whole body was tingling with desire. She wanted to jump on him and impale herself on his throb-

659

bing shaft. How should she respond? Should she play along and give him a hand job, or should she refuse to do anything at all? She noticed that his eyes were still watching her and saw the amused expression on his face.

She liked the challenge of masturbating him, the power it gave her. She remembered his words. Their journey was far from over. He was fit and healthy. And there would be plenty of time for him to recover. He looked as if he could probably get it up at least twice more before they arrived. Was that his plan? Let her think she was saving herself and then take her anyway?

Beth sighed. The decision would be a lot easier if her treacherous body wasn't dripping with passion just at the thought of him. The thrill of driving him to distraction with her touch would probably be enough to bring her to orgasm, too. She couldn't afford to give him the satisfaction.

'I wouldn't touch you with somebody else's hands, let alone mine,' she informed him bitchily.

'No? Well, in that case, I'll just have to get on and fuck you, then, won't I?'

Beth shuddered with longing at the threat. She huddled back further in the corner and tried to look suitably unimpressed. She failed miserably.

Daniel reached out and grabbed her arm. Although Beth pushed back even further against the door and did her best to resist him, he pulled her easily along the soft leather towards him.

'Don't you dare,' she cried as she struggled to pull her arm free and push him away. 'Let go of me.'

Daniel pulled her across his lap so that his erection was pushing into her stomach. She wiggled from side to side, trying to escape yet at the same time rubbing him with her skin. Daniel grabbed her leg and pulled her even harder against him. She could hear his rapid heartbeat and his shuddering breath. Another pang of longing coursed through her and she increased her struggles.

Beth stretched her arms out until her fingers found the

bracket for the safety belt. She grabbed it and tugged hard to try and pull herself free. She felt Daniel shift along the seat towards the side of the car, trapping her hands with his thigh. All she could do now was kick with her legs. She made the most of this until he reached out and took hold of her thighs.

'Damn you. Let me go,' Beth shouted.

'But I've only just got you where I want you.' Daniel began to stroke her bottom and Beth renewed her efforts to bruise his shins.

'Behave yourself,' Daniel commanded. He slapped her hard.

Beth shrieked with shock and rage and Daniel immediately slapped her again.

'Keep quiet and keep still or you won't be able to sit down for a week.'

Beth stopped wriggling. Her buttocks smarted and a warm glow spread through her bottom as the sting wore off. She could almost picture the handprints on the soft white flesh.

'Much better.' Daniel started to stroke her again. Beth closed her legs as tightly as she could and gave herself up to the sheer bliss of his silky touch.

'Now, how about that hand job you promised me?' he suggested as he pushed one of his fingers between her clamped thighs. Beth tightened the muscles as hard as she could to trap his finger. Undeterred, Daniel began to caress her aching clitoris.

'I didn't promise you anything.' Beth gritted her teeth as his finger delved deeper and deeper into her slit. He could hardly fail to notice how wet she was.

'Well, what if I do you first?' he offered. 'How does that sound?' He relaxed his grip and Beth immediately rolled off his lap on to the floor. She looked up and saw her clothes on the seat behind him. Immediately, she made a grab for them.

Daniel was too quick for her. He caught her hand and forced her fingers over his groin. As she made contact with his erection, Beth automatically opened her fist and then closed it again around him before she realised what she was doing. She could feel him throbbing and couldn't resist giving him a soft squeeze, even as she used her other hand against the seat to try and push herself away.

Suddenly, Daniel let go of her and Beth fell back against the drinks cabinet. Before she could recover he grabbed her arms and pulled her up. Effortlessly, he swung her up on to the seat as if she were a rag doll.

Beth thumped his chest frantically with her fists. She heard him grunt with pain as one blow found its mark. She felt his hand tighten round her wrist and she swung at him with her other hand. He deflected her easily, laughing as he secured her other wrist.

'That's it, Beth. I love it. Especially when you surrender to me. I can already imagine your hands rubbing me.' He pulled her hands together and pushed his cock into them, forcing her fingers up and down over his length.

'Good girl. You catch on quickly, don't you?' He held her still again. 'Not yet, though. I promised to do you first, didn't I?'

Beth rolled her hips urgently and strained against his clasp. Daniel ignored her. Easily holding both her wrists in one hand, he began to slide his other hand slowly down her stomach towards her crotch. With a supreme effort, Beth finally managed to break free and back away out of reach.

Daniel pulled her along the seat, twisted her left arm behind her back and rolled her on to her stomach. He grabbed his tie and looped it round her wrist, then reached for her other hand. Beth buried it underneath herself.

'Stubborn woman.' Daniel knelt on the small of her back and used both his hands to tug her right arm free. This was a mistake. Beth quickly slipped her left hand under her as he pulled her right one back. Her fingers

662

brushed against his erection and, immediately, he pushed himself into her fingers.

'Not yet, Beth. Not yet.'

'Let me go.' Beth emphasised each word. She gasped as he slid his body down her back so that his pubic hair and balls tickled her skin, making goosebumps spring up all over her body. His cock thrust urgently between her buttocks.

'Now, let's have the other arm, shall we?'

Beth laughed. She was quite sure that she could keep this up for hours. She had forgotten the end of the tie trailing from her wrist until she felt him start to tug on it. Helplessly, she felt her arm slip out from under her. Daniel grabbed her wrist and tied her hands together at the small of her back. He sat up and nodded appreciatively.

'Anyone ever tell you what a nice bum you've got? My prick feels great nestled between those soft buttocks. Does it feel good for you?' She felt him prodding her with his cock as he spoke. The feel of it was driving her insane. Frantically, she tugged her arms, trying to free her hands. It was hopeless. She felt him slide off her and start to roll her over.

'Definitely a body made for pleasure.' Daniel stroked her right breast and then ran one finger down her body, smiling as her skin twitched. 'I love shaved beaver. It shows a woman who enjoys being naked.' He trailed a fingertip over her naked mound.

'Open up. It's difficult fingering you with your legs together.' He pulled her thighs apart and pushed his hand between them.

Beth clamped her lips together to stop herself from moaning. She made a feeble attempt to roll away from him then, realising it was hopeless, she lay still. She was determined not to let him get her too excited. So long as he didn't succeed, she wouldn't have to do anything. The very thought of him trying to satisfy her all the way home was extremely pleasant. He had a wonderful touch. She set the challenge.

'You won't make me come, no matter what you do,' she informed him calmly.

'We'll see. If I succeed, then you'll do whatever I want?'

'No, I won't,' she contradicted, 'because you won't succeed.'

Daniel nodded approvingly. 'I thought you'd given up on me for a minute.' He moved his finger over her nipple and caressed it softly. Beth shivered. Daniel grinned and lowered his head over her breasts. His tongue darted in and out, first on one nipple then the other. He wrapped his tongue round one and then slowly ran his finger down her stomach, over her mound and on to her inner thigh.

As he began the return journey, Beth sighed contentedly, savouring her pleasure. She could endure that indefinitely. Although delightful, it was not enough to push her too far. If he wanted to win then he would have to do a lot better than this. She smiled happily as his hand traced an ever-expanding circle over her breasts and stomach. He was wasted as a chauffeur; he should have been a masseur.

Gradually, she felt him moving both hands and tongue down her body. A small shiver of excitement ran up her legs as he tickled the back of her knee and, as he moved his fingers up towards her thigh, she raised her hips slightly to allow him access to her buttocks. His fingers were as soft and delicate as silk.

A small sigh escaped her lips as his tongue circled her navel and glided on down over her mound and outer sex lips. She felt a rush of wetness between her thighs and realised that she needed to concentrate a bit harder. Seemingly oblivious to her reaction, Daniel carried on down her leg and sucked her big toe into his mouth. She jumped with surprise and allowed him to raise her leg as he started to kiss his way gently back upwards.

664

Beth clenched herself ready for his attack, certain he would take full advantage of her exposure. In fact his lips barely caressed her sex before moving on up her body. She lowered her leg back on to the seat as his tongue licked her breasts and then slipped on up to her neck.

Daniel nibbled her earlobe, then blew gently into her ear and started to kiss her eyelids. As he lowered his head, she turned her mouth away. Kissing always turned her on and she was determined to make him work. Firmly, he pulled her head round towards him again and planted his lips on hers.

Beth screwed her eyes tightly closed and did her best not to respond. She sighed as his other hand began to slide slowly down her body towards her mound. She moaned softly as he pushed his fingers into her slit and gently teased her sex bud. His tongue relentlessly probed her, forcing her lips open and darting in and out.

His fingers slipped deeper between her legs, exploring every inch of her. Beth started to panic. He couldn't fail to notice how excited she was. It might not be as obvious as a man's erection but her dampness was still a dead give-away. His tongue pushed harder and deeper into her mouth and Beth felt her desire building. She pulled back against the seat and resumed her struggles.

Daniel let go and began to chuckle. He tweaked her erect nipples with his fingers then rolled her on to her side and ran his hand down her spine. Beth sighed with relief. Thank God he had stopped when he had. Did he realise how close she had come – or had he thought she was making another attempt to get away? She felt his hand fondling her bottom and she took a few deep breaths to steady herself.

Still chuckling, Daniel rolled her on her back and crouched over her head. Looking up, she could see his rigid cock thrust out in front of him as he leant over her and took himself in his hand. She gasped as he pushed his cock against her breasts and started to rub the damp tip round her nipple. He lowered his head, and covered her mound with his mouth. His penis pressed forcefully between her breasts as he leant over her. As his tongue began to circle her outer lips, she felt the urgent thrill of approaching climax. Desperately, she squeezed her thighs together, forcing his head away. Losing his precarious balance, Daniel slipped off on to the floor.

'Now, that wasn't fair.' Daniel grabbed her legs and pulled them off the seat. He pushed her upright and put his hands on her knees to force her thighs open wide. Pushing his hands under her, he lifted her up and pulled her exposed vagina on to his mouth. His tongue flowed effortlessly into her, seeking her G-spot.

'Oh God.' Beth writhed with passion as he sucked and licked her. She knew she was lost. She felt him pushing deeper and deeper inside her, thrusting in and out, varying the speed and the depth. His hands squeezed her buttocks, pulling her backwards and forwards against him. The more she struggled, the harder he held her.

She came suddenly and violently, shuddering uncontrollably at the intensity of her release. Incredibly, he continued licking and sucking her, long after the final spasm of her climax had faded away. On and on until she felt herself beginning to respond again. Finally, he slid his hands from under her and sat back on his heels. He wiped his mouth with the back of his hand and smiled mischievously.

'Well. That wasn't so difficult, was it?'

Beth stared at him wordlessly, her breath still coming in short little pants. Daniel got up and knelt across her lap with his cock pressed against her breasts. He reached round behind her and untied her hands.

'Now it's your turn.' He placed her hands on his cock and stared at her expectantly.

Beth pulled her hands away and placed them at her sides. 'No. I never agreed to do anything.'

Daniel grabbed her hands again. Beth struggled

against him, trying to ignore the feel of his erection pushing on to her mound. She twisted away and slid down off the seat so that her knees were on the floor and her breasts were pushed up against the leather seat. She sensed the smack coming too late to dodge. Her eyes began to smart as his hand slapped her bottom again and again.

'Are you ready to keep our bargain yet?'

'I made no bargain. Ow!' She received another sharp smack. Her buttocks were on fire and hot tears began to trickle over her lids and run slowly down her cheeks. He whacked her again.

'OK!' She gave in. 'I'll do it.'

As soon as he let her go, Beth raised herself to a crouch and rubbed her stinging buttocks tenderly. Daniel sat himself on the seat, directly in front of her with his legs open wide. His erection seemed to have grown even larger. Beth raised her hand and ran her fingers slowly down it, teasing him. His whole body tensed.

She lowered her mouth over his cock and ran her tongue around the tip. As she slipped her hand down the shaft, she cupped his balls in her other hand and caressed the delicate skin underneath them. Daniel writhed with pleasure and tried to force himself even deeper into her mouth. Beth instinctively closed her lips round him and sucked hard. She heard his groan of delight and a tremor of power rushed down her spine.

If this was what he wanted, so be it. She had become quite good at telling just when a man was right on the edge. She would bring him right to the brink, then stop. She would tease and torture him until he was begging her to let him come, then tease him some more. By the time she was done with him, he would be in such a state he wouldn't even be able to remember his own name.

She began to move her head more quickly, pumping him rapidly in and out. Daniel clutched the back of her head and moaned urgently. Beth felt her own juices beginning to flow again.

Chapter Nine

*I*t was quite late by the time Beth arrived home. Another short stop at a service area shortly after dark had given Geoff the opportunity to return inside the car with her, while Daniel resumed his duties behind the wheel.

Beth used the changeover time to slip back into her clothes. Unsure of what to say to him, she had taken the easy option and not mentioned what had happened at all. Geoff had followed her lead and, after an uncomfortable silence that had lasted for a few miles, they had resumed their financial discussions almost as if nothing else had happened.

Despite her comments to Daniel earlier, Beth had found it impossible to openly give Geoff his money back. What would she have said? She opted for leaving the wad of notes in the drinks cabinet. When he found them, she was certain that Geoff would get the message. Damn her pride. A thousand pounds would have come in very handy.

Although she had wanted to be angry with them both she knew, in all honesty, that they hadn't done anything she had not willingly gone along with. It had been fun, even if Geoff hadn't been in such dire need of her services as she been led to imagine! Just the thought of how neatly they had set her up made her smile. Compared to that, what she had done to Simon didn't seem nearly as clever as it once had.

Geoff had been the perfect gentleman for the rest of the journey although, once or twice, she had noticed the hungry way he was looking at her and had wondered if he had been excited by imagining what she and Daniel had been up to. She was only thankful that the dividing window was tinted. It suddenly occurred to her that it might be tinted the opposite way round from the other windows, allowing Geoff and Daniel a clear view inside. She was slightly shocked to discover how excited that possibility made her feel.

When they dropped her off outside her house Geoff thanked her then wished her well with her future career and expressed the hope that their paths would cross again before too long. Daniel just smiled appreciatively as he helped her through the door with her case. He had even tipped his chauffeur's cap and given her one last, lingering gaze before he turned to leave. She was sure that she could detect a hint of amusement in his eyes and she felt herself glowing with a mixture of embarrassment and desire.

As soon as she had dumped her case in the bedroom, Beth ran herself a hot bath and had a long soak. She was too exhausted even to think straight and decided on a light supper of soup and sandwiches, then an early night. While she was waiting for the soup to heat, the phone rang.

'Beth? It's Ann. I thought you must be home by now. Good week?'

'Mmm.' A sequence of sexual encounters raced through her mind, each one more exciting and erotic than the last. How could she even begin to describe it? If anyone else had told her about such a week, she would have thought that they were suffering from a somewhat overactive imagination.

669

'Yes. Very, er, interesting.'

Her voice must have given her away. 'I sense a man,' Ann responded immediately. 'Don't tell me you found time for some romance, too? Honestly Beth, since Jonathan, there's just no stopping you, is there?'

'Not exactly,' Beth replied slowly. Romance wasn't the word that immediately sprang to mind to describe her recent experiences. She remembered a conversation she had had with Ann a year or so ago when she had confessed some of what she and young Jonathan had been up to. At the time, it had seemed quite shocking.

'Thanks for the bread and things.' Ann had been in earlier that day, as arranged, to switch the heating on and leave a few essentials.

'Don't change the subject,' Ann complained.

'I'm not. Look, Ann, it's been a really long day. All I want to do right now is curl up in bed and sleep around the clock. I'm too tired even to think.'

'OK, you win. Keep your secrets for now. I've got to go and see my parents over the weekend but I'll pop round one evening next week, shall I?'

'Fine. Thanks again for the shopping.' As she hung up the receiver, she found herself wondering exactly what she was going to tell Ann when she saw her.

Simon glared impatiently at his watch when Beth walked through the door the following Monday.

'You're late,' he complained. 'We don't keep training course hours here, you know.'

Beth checked her own watch. It was two minutes after nine o'clock. What had put Simon in such a foul mood already? She had expected that he would be glad she was back.

'Sorry,' she responded meekly. 'The bus was late.' She noticed that he was staring at her body and was surprised to feel a slight shiver of disdain. He wasn't going to make a habit of leaping on her, was he? Teasing him until he couldn't help himself had been great fun, but she hadn't really thought about what working with him afterwards would be like. It was fine if she initiated it, but she didn't like the idea of him assuming he had any rights to her body.

'Well, how was the training course, then? I hope I got my money's worth.'

Beth smiled at that. 'Very illuminating,' she replied. 'I even got to meet Geoff Stevens. He gave me a lift home on Friday.'

Simon's eyes narrowed. She had known that name would get to him. '*The* Geoff Stevens?' he said, clearly surprised. 'What was he doing there?'

'He gave the final lecture. What a brilliant mind that man's got!' Beth enthused. His body wasn't to be sneezed at either, she reflected silently.

Simon shrugged. 'He's just been lucky, that's all. Had a few good breaks. I don't suppose you managed to persuade him to put any business our way?' Geoff was renowned for using smaller financial companies to spread the risk of investment or even hide some of his larger deals.

It was Beth's turn to shrug. 'The subject didn't actually come up,' she replied. 'He did admit to having heard of you, though,' she added generously.

Simon brightened. 'Really? How? What did he say?'

'Nothing. Only that he seemed to know your name.' She tried not to smile at his inflated ego.

Simon snorted rudely, then ran his eyes over her body again. 'We don't have any appointments for an hour or so,' he remarked pointedly.

'I'll use the time to catch up on the backlog of filing, then, shall I?' Beth was already on her way to her own office. What had she ever found attractive about Simon, she wondered? He might be a great lover, but that didn't make up for him being a chauvinistic pig. Could she use what she had learnt from Geoff to find a way to escape Simon for good? She would have to give it some very serious thought. She remembered the way Geoff had flattered her knowledge and praised her skills. Could she, perhaps, go in business for herself as a consultant? She almost blushed again at the memory of what else Geoff had used the word to mean.

'By the way,' Simon called her back. 'I have to go to Rome at the weekend. There's a chance for a big deal there if I play my cards right.'

Beth's heart sank. He wasn't going to ask her to go with him, was he? She could just imagine what a trip like that would entail.

'The thing is, the people I'm going to see, they want me to take my wife along too . . .'

'How nice,' Beth interrupted quickly. 'Mrs Henderson must be thrilled.'

Simon frowned. 'I'm not sure that she will be able to go,' he replied slyly. 'We've got a large dog, you see. Marie adores him. She refuses to put him in kennels in case he pines.'

'Well, can't you get someone to stay at your home and take care of him? What about your son?' Beth vaguely remembered that Simon and his wife had a teenage boy.

'Chris is away at college,' Simon replied. 'I don't think Marie will be able to find anyone she trusts in time.' He paused. 'I have to be seen taking my wife with me,' he added.

So, she was right. He was asking her. She was almost tempted. She had never been to Rome and Simon was a wonderful lover. He was also a complete bastard. Besides, if she was going to make a name for herself in the financial world, she needed people to know her for herself, not mistake her for Simon's wife or, worse, his mistress.

'Well, I suppose I could stay at your house, if you like,' she offered. 'I love dogs, so I would be quite happy.'

'I couldn't ask you to do that,' Simon replied quickly.

'Really. It's no trouble. I'd love to do it. I'll get your wife on the phone for you now, shall I? I'm sure she will have lots of shopping she needs to do for the trip.'

* * *

672

As Beth closed her own office door behind her, Simon frowned. That hadn't gone at all the way he had planned it. How had she so easily outmanoeuvred him like that? He wanted her in his bed in Rome, not curled up at his house, petting the dog. Marie wouldn't be any use to him in Rome. She knew nothing about finance. She wasn't even all that good at flirting with potential clients.

There was something strange about Beth today, he decided. What had happened to her while she was away? A week or so ago, she had been practically begging him to take her. Now, she seemed to be deliberately avoiding him.

He felt a slight twinge of doubt as he wondered if she thought he had taken advantage of her. He quickly dismissed it. The way she had been begging for it, she could hardly blame him. Perhaps she thought she was too good for him, just because she had spent a few hours with Geoff Stevens. It was a pity that she hadn't managed to get anything useful out of that meeting. He would kill for a chance to do some business with Geoff Stevens. He found himself wondering what else Beth and Geoff might have got up to.

Simon glanced at his watch again. He could hear Beth in her office and he felt himself stirring as he remembered the way she had whimpered and cried while he had taken her over the desk. She had certainly enjoyed it. She'd been wet and ready for him. Was she playing games again?

He got up and walked across the thick carpet towards her door. When he pushed it open, Beth was leaning over the filing cabinet so that he could just see the tops of her stockings under her short skirt. He shivered with anticipation as he felt his cock begin to stiffen.

'Beth?' His voice cracked slightly and he cleared his throat quickly. 'About the other day . . .'

Beth straightened and turned round on her heels.

'I'm sorry about your clothes. Maybe you'd like to buy some new ones to replace them?' Simon reached for his

673

wallet. Women could never resist the idea of buying new clothes.

'It's not important,' she responded softly, her cheeks colouring. Simon's eyes darted down her cleavage. He could clearly see the outline of her half-cup bra. His fingers itched to rip it off her and run his tongue across those luscious breasts.

'I insist.' Simon opened the wallet and peeled a couple of notes off. 'Buy yourself something really sexy,' he told her.

Beth smiled. 'If you're really serious, why don't you bring something back from Rome for me?' she suggested cheekily. 'Italian fashion is world-renowned.'

Simon hesitated. He liked the idea of picking out something especially for her. It would be difficult to go shopping without his wife, but he might be able to slip away. He would get her something so blatantly sexy that it would make her blush to look at it, then he would make her wear it around the office. His cock stiffened further. He nodded silently and returned the money to his wallet.

Maybe he would invest in one of those new digital cameras. With no film to develop, there were no restrictions on what you could use them for. He could take pictures of her posing for him and look at them on those nights when Marie wasn't being cooperative enough. He could even put them on the computer. Maybe he would design a screen saver of Beth stripping!

He took a step closer and reached out to run his hands down the sides of her body and over her hips. He felt her stiffen slightly and try to pull away. Was this more of her games? First begging for it, now playing hard to get. Did she want him to force her again? The idea inflamed him.

Simon grabbed Beth round the waist, pulled her roughly towards him and ran his lips down her neck. His cock pushed up urgently against her body and he began to throb with desire.

674

The phone rang and Beth slid easily from his arms. She walked over to the desk and picked up the receiver.

'Henderson's. Good morning. Yes, he is. Just one moment, please.' Beth put her hand over the mouthpiece. 'It's Bob Jarvis, calling from Rome. He says it's urgent.'

Simon tried to calm his breathing. His heart was thumping and he could almost feel the blood boiling in his veins. He had wanted her all week. He would go mad if he didn't have her again soon. Perhaps he could get rid of Bob quickly. There would still be plenty of time before his first client arrived.

'I'll take it at my desk,' he told her, his eyes still locked on her cleavage.

Beth lifted her fingers from the mouthpiece. 'I'm just putting you through now, Mr Jarvis,' she said.

Simon sighed heavily and turned to walk back to his own office. As he moved, he pushed his hands down inside his waistband and tried to adjust his throbbing cock. He would just get rid of Bob and then ... Simon caressed his swollen tip softly with his fingers, his imagination running riot.

As soon as Beth had put the call through to his phone, she walked over and closed the door between the two offices. She leant back on it and closed her eyes for a moment. Her body was trembling and her legs felt shaky. Despite her growing dislike for him, she was already damp at the possibility of Simon taking her again. If the phone hadn't rung when it had, she knew she wouldn't have done anything to stop him.

She took a quick, shuddering breath and walked slowly over to her desk. Damn it to hell. This wasn't what she wanted at all. If he thought he could take her whenever he felt like it, he would become even more insufferable. His fingers could do wonderful things to her body, her treacherous imagination reminded her.

Beth sat down and propped her head on her hands. Sooner or later, of course, he would tire of her, just as he

675

tired of all his conquests. The stories about Simon were littered with broken hearts. She had no intention of becoming another of his discarded playthings. Somehow, she had to find a way to string him along, keep him interested in her until she got her own plans sorted out.

Maybe it wouldn't hurt to provoke him again. After she had pushed him over the edge, she would submit to him, do whatever he asked without a murmur. Even better, she could plead and beg with him to let her go. She knew how much he liked that. It would be so easy. The way he had been acting, the problem was more one of stopping him than of letting him. She was in no doubt about how aroused he had been. The idea of it sent a small shiver down her back.

Pushing her thoughts to one side, Beth began to examine the new computer on her desk. She had forgotten until today that Simon was arranging for this new system to be installed. Why he thought that the two of them needed to be networked was somewhat beyond her. If the door was open, as it was most of the time, he only had to raise his voice to speak to her.

She wasn't totally convinced that she needed a computer of her own at all. Up until now, they had managed perfectly well with her using the one in his office when he was out with clients. Still, it was rather fun to have a computer all to herself. It made her feel more important. If only he would let have a few clients to take care of on her own as well. She knew that she had been perfectly capable of handing that much even before the training course in York.

Beth turned the computer on and waited impatiently while it powered up. After her week in York, at least she felt more confident about using it. When she had first started with Simon, she had known next to nothing about computers despite the lessons that had been part of her refresher course. Even so, she felt very wary at the sight of the myriad of complicated and intertwined software packages the new machine boasted. She knew that Simon would be livid if she crashed the system.

'I just don't understand why people find computers so difficult to master,' he had told her a couple of weeks ago when she had expressed concern about what he was proposing. 'They are perfectly simple, so long as one approaches them logically.'

It was all right for him. He had a degree in computer programming to go with his various certificates and diplomas in financial subjects. You could say a lot about Simon, but no one could accuse him of being stupid. Except maybe, Geoff. Simon was a financial amateur next to Geoff.

Finding Windows Explorer, Beth scanned the contents of the system curiously, fascinated to see what Simon had already been up to. She was not surprised to see that hardly any of the client files had found their way on to the system yet. No doubt that boring task had been awaiting her return.

When she spotted that he had already set up his own folder, Beth moved the mouse over it and clicked to open it, curious to see what else he had been doing. Perhaps it was his electronic little black book with the names and phone numbers of all his willing females. She pictured the fun she could have setting up conflicting rendezvous with some of them. That might teach him a lesson.

To her surprise and frustration, she found he had restricted access with a password. She experienced a flash of anger and disappointment. Was he just hiding the names of his girlfriends, or had he got some other secret he didn't want her prying into? Well, secrets were like a red rag to a bull so far as Beth was concerned. One way or another, she would get in.

Beth cocked her head to one side to make sure that he was still talking on the phone, then made a few wild stabs at guessing his password. She was sure it would be something stupidly obvious. He was too contemptuous of her limited computer skills to imagine she would get the better of him. What could it be?

She tried a few obvious things: his name, his wife, his son, even her own name. Nothing worked. She tried to remember if he had told her what their dog was called, although, considering how scathing he had been about the animal, she wasn't too hopeful. Damn! Beth tapped her finger impatiently on the mouse button. What silly word had he used? She wasn't even sure why she was so anxious to get in to his precious secrets. She just had a feeling they might contain something useful.

Outside, she heard Simon making his farewells to Bob. Was the trip to Rome still on or had Bob called to cancel it? She quite liked the idea of spending the weekend at his home. It would be fun poking around, seeing how he lived his private life. She was curious to see what he would bring her back to wear, too. She was certain it would be skimpy, transparent and totally impractical. She strained her ears to hear what he was doing now.

When the door handle to her office began to open, Beth quickly moved the mouse and clicked for the screen saver to appear. She remembered what he had been doing when the phone rang and felt a sudden thrill at the idea of him storming in to ravish her again.

Just as her door began to swing open, the door to the main entrance buzzed. His first client of the day was slightly early. As Beth jumped up to answer the door, she heard Simon curse under his breath and return reluctantly to his desk. The grin on her face as she greeted his client was wider than she normally used to greet even their most valued customers. His diary for the rest of the day was virtually solid. Tomorrow, he was out all day at a conference in London. It would be Wednesday before he had a chance to get her alone again.

Beth wasn't all that surprised when Ann turned up soon after she got home that evening. She knew her friend's curiosity had been aroused by their brief conversation on Friday night. She wasn't entirely sure how much she was prepared to reveal about what had gone on. Some of it was just too private.

'Ann.' She gave her friend a quick hug. 'It's good to see you.' Beth was shocked to realise that she was comparing Ann's body to Lisa. She had never looked at Ann that way before. In many ways, Ann and Lisa were quite similar: slim build, boyish hips, small breasts, fair hair. Ann was older, of course – the same age as Beth herself. She began wondering again about her friend's preferences, and was surprised and slightly shocked to feel a brief tremor of desire at the idea of pleasuring Ann the way she had pleasured Lisa.

Ann returned the hug and then wandered into the living-room and threw herself down on the settee. 'It's good to have you back. It seems like you've been away for more than a week, somehow.'

'It seemed a long time for me, too,' Beth called over her shoulder as she headed into the kitchen to make coffee. 'I've been wining and dining like a glutton. I really need to get to the gym.'

'Gerri sends her love, by the way,' Ann continued. Loud, boisterous, redheaded Geraldine was another of their closest friends. 'She claims to be in lust again. A new instructor at the gym, if you please.'

Pretty and vivacious Gerri, who had just turned forty yet thought she was still twenty, liked to give the impression that she was a real man-eater. Privately, Beth harboured more than a passing suspicion that their friend was actually scared stiff of men.

Coffee mugs in hand, Beth made her way back into the living-room to join Ann. She settled herself comfortably down on the settee beside her friend, curled her legs up under her, and took a sip of her drink.

'I met Geoff Stevens up in York,' she said. 'He's one of the best-known financial wizards in the country. He thinks I've got great potential.'

679

Although Ann stared at her quizzically, she said nothing. Beth knew her friend was burning to ask if there was anything going on, romantically speaking. She was determined to keep the conversation away from that subject for now.

'Anyway, it got me thinking about my future. I don't want to stay with Simon any longer than I have to.'

Ann looked surprised. 'I thought you loved your job?' When Beth did not reply, she added, 'Do you think this Geoff might give you a job, then?'

'Good God, no. I shouldn't think so.' Beth briefly imagined what working with Geoff every day might be like and felt a tingle of excitement. 'He suggested that I would be good at consultancy work. I'm thinking about going it alone.' It sounded exciting but, at the same time, frightening now that she had put it into words.

Ann looked doubtful. 'Do you think you could? I mean, you're only just back in the field. It takes an awful lot of guts to work for yourself. And money. How would you cope with the overheads?'

Beth sighed. Trust Ann to put her finger right on the problem. She had gone to work for Simon in the first place so that she could become financially independent from her ex-husband. Now, she needed to earn enough to escape Simon. Why did everything always seem to come down to money?

'It's not all that difficult to make money in the financial world. All it takes is confidence and know-how.' Beth frowned. 'Geoff manages to make it all sound childishly simple,' she added ruefully.

Ann laughed. 'Money makes money, Beth. I bet this Geoff character is rolling in it, isn't he? When you can afford to take a few gambles and it's not the end of the world if you lose a few thousand here and there, it's a different matter.'

Beth opened her mouth to protest, then closed it again. Ann was quite right. How could she possibly hope to play in the same league as Geoff Stevens? For one brief encounter, he had willingly offered her more money than she had in her savings account. She should have kept it. She would never have spent it, of course, but it would have been a nice souvenir. It excited her to think of how she had sold herself to two men – even if she hadn't realised what she was doing until it was too late!

'Cheer up,' Ann told her, seeing her face. 'Things aren't so bad. At least you're earning better wages now than when you were at the newsagents. You don't need to rely on Tony any more and you seem to be having fun.'

Beth smiled, remembering her week in York. She was certainly having fun.

'Tony called me while you were gone, by the way.'

'What? Why?' Beth had found several messages on the answer phone from her ex-husband but hadn't got around to contacting him yet. Now, she considered the possibility that it might be urgent. 'Did he say what he wanted?'

Ann shook her head. 'Only that he couldn't get in touch with you and was worried. I think he may have had a tiff with his wife and was looking for a shoulder to cry on. I told him you were away on a training course and I wasn't sure when you were due home.'

'Thanks.' Beth felt a rush of irritation at Tony. Ever since she had asked him round for coffee one day about six months ago, he had been pestering her more and more often. She had never regretted anything as much as she regretted leading him on that day. He was more interested in her now than he had ever been when they were married.

'So, what about your week?' Ann changed the subject to one she was obviously more interested in. 'Was this Geoff your big adventure?'

'No, well, not really. Although he did give me a ride home in his chauffeur-driven Bentley.'

Ann's eyes widened. 'Wow! He really is loaded. I don't suppose he's single, too, by any chance?'

'Actually, I think he is.'

'There you are, then. Why not forget about going into business for yourself and just concentrate on marrying into money?'

'Ann! How could you? After Tony, the last thing I'm looking for is another husband.'

'Not even a stinking rich one?' Ann continued to tease. She took another sip of coffee. 'Well, if it wasn't Mr Rich, who was it that put that sparkle in your eye?'

Who, indeed, Beth wondered. Lisa? Her evening with John, Brian and Steve? John himself? Daniel? How could she even begin to come out with a story like that? She had had a more active week than a professional hooker!

'No one thing or person,' she replied. 'It was just a good week all round, I suppose. The course was interesting and useful and I met several fascinating people, male and female. I've asked Lisa, the course lecturer, to come and visit me in the summer. You'll like her, Ann. You two are quite similar in many ways.'

Beth could feel Ann staring at her in surprise. Her friend had clearly been expecting a revelation about a man, not news of an invitation for a new woman friend to come and stay. Would Ann guess what had taken place between her and Lisa? Her cheeks began to glow at the possibility. She had no idea how Ann felt about that sort of thing.

Ann was a great talker. Beth could remember several times when Ann had surprised and even shocked her a little with her revelations about her sexual fantasies. In a way, it had been Ann who had first introduced her to using a vibrator by giving her the idea of looking at sex magazines. Still, she was never quite sure just how much practical experience Ann had.

As she watched her friend watching her, she realised how much she wanted to experiment with Ann, to enjoy her body as she had enjoyed Lisa. How could she possibly broach the subject? It was much more difficult than with a virtual stranger. She had known Ann since school. Maybe Lisa could break the ice?

682

Suddenly, her mind was flooded with images of the three of them naked on her bed together, and a pang of desire shot through her body so powerful that it was all she could do not to pull Ann into her arms and ravish her there and then. Her limbs were beginning to tremble with excitement.

'I suppose I had better go and phone Tony and see what he wants,' she muttered softly as she leapt to her feet and fled from the room.

Chapter Ten

'This is my wife, Marie. Marie, this is Beth.' Simon led Beth through into the living-room and made the introductions. Before anyone could say anything else, there was a loud bark and a large golden retriever charged into the room, its tail wagging furiously.

'Oh, and that's the dog,' he added unnecessarily as he aimed a spiteful kick at its rear end. The animal dodged the blow easily and, coming to a stop, stretched out its nose to sniff Beth's hand.

'He's very friendly, aren't you, Sandy?' Marie assured Beth, giving her husband a reproving glance. 'He'll soon get to know you.'

'Hello, Sandy,' Beth leant down and patted the dog on the head. She was rewarded with a slobbery wet kiss on the back of her hand. Simon pulled a face. Clearly, he was no animal lover.

Marie held out her hand. 'It's very kind of you to offer to look after him like this.' She appraised Beth cautiously, as though unsure about committing herself.

Beth wondered if Marie knew about her husband's reputation. If so, she was probably wondering if Beth was one of his many conquests. The realisation made her feel terribly guilty and she pushed her thoughts away.

Marie couldn't possibly know what Simon was like. If she did, she wouldn't stay with him, would she?

'I'm only too happy to help. I'd love to own a dog but, being out at work all day, it wouldn't be fair. Sandy and I will have a great time, won't we, boy?' Sandy gave her hand another wet lick and both women laughed. Simon frowned and looked at his watch.

'Why don't you get on and show Beth where everything is?' he interrupted them irritably. 'If we don't get a move on, we'll end up missing the bloody plane.'

As Marie led her round the house, Beth examined her surreptitiously. She was quite pretty, in a washed-out, mousy sort of way. Her light brown hair was cut short and probably permed. Her eyes were grey-blue, wide set over a snub nose and narrow lips. She had a reasonable figure, perhaps a little on the plump side, and was heavily but skilfully made up. Her clothes were beautifully tailored and her jewellery looked expensive. She wasn't the sort of woman Beth would have expected Simon to be married to. What sort that was, however, she had no idea.

The house and its contents looked as expensive as Marie's clothes and jewellery. Simon might moan and groan about business all the time but, unless Marie had money of her own, he obviously wasn't doing too badly. The house alone must be worth over a quarter of a million, perhaps more.

She barely had time to take everything in, far less to learn her way around the huge house, before Simon started yelling for his wife to get a move on. Marie gave Beth an apologetic smile.

'I'd better go. Simon gets in such a state. Now, are you sure you'll be all right?'

'We'll be fine. Don't worry.' Beth patted the dog again. 'Just go and have a wonderful time.'

Marie gave her another sideways glance. Her face made it perfectly clear that she was not expecting to have anything close to a wonderful time. Beth felt suddenly sorry for her and wondered again why Marie stayed with her husband.

'Marie. Come on.' Simon's voice was tight with anger and Marie scuttled off towards the door, still calling final instructions over her shoulder as she went.

Beth heard heated words being exchanged and then Simon's voice called a curt goodbye. The front door slammed and she and Sandy were alone.

She checked her watch. It was a little after six o'clock. Simon had closed the office early so that he and his wife could catch an evening flight to Rome ready for a breakfast business meeting on Saturday morning. Beth sighed, wondering what she was doing here. The long, lonely weekend stretched out endlessly before her. She decided that she might as well get herself something to eat.

After a couple of wrong turns, she found her way to the kitchen and retrieved the exotic cold meat and salad platter that Marie had prepared for her. Sandy followed at her heels, his tail still wagging enthusiastically. According to Marie, he had already been fed that evening. Unable to resist his big brown eyes, Beth fed him from her plate. There was far too much for her, anyway.

After she had rinsed the dishes and tidied away, Beth set out to explore. A door leading from the hallway near the front of the house opened in to what was obviously Simon's private study. She gazed around curiously at the heavy wood-panelled walls and expensive leather furniture. It was a real old-fashioned male retreat. She was surprised that there were no animal head trophies on the walls or a gun rack in the corner.

She wandered around behind the huge desk and tried the top drawer. It was locked. What was he hiding here? Excited, she wondered if she could find anything in his study that would reveal his password to the protected folder on the office computer system. Feeling more than a twinge of guilt, she rummaged around the desk looking for a key.

A sudden bark caused her to jump and look round

anxiously, half-expecting Simon to pop out of the wood-work and catch her prying. Sandy barked louder.

'What is it, boy?' Beth hurried out into the hallway, her heart thumping. It occurred to her just how isolated this huge house was, set back from a quiet road in an acre of so of its own grounds and surrounded by thick, tall hedges. No wonder Marie liked to keep Sandy around with Simon away so often.

The dog had its nose pressed to the crack under the front door. He had stopped barking and his tail was wagging furiously, Nervously, Beth pushed the curtain aside on the window beside the door and peered out. It was already growing dark. She saw a shape moving in a nearby bush and her heart leapt to her throat. She tried to remember where the phone was.

The bush moved again and a large cat dashed out and shot up a tall poplar tree. Sandy began barking again and Beth leant back against the wall, laughing with relief.

'I promised you a walk before bed time, didn't I?' She petted the dog under the chin. 'Right then. But, no chasing cats, OK?' Sandy wagged his tail at a word he recognised and dashed off to the kitchen where his lead was kept. Still laughing, Beth followed.

Saturday dawned fine and sunny. By mid-morning it was clear it was destined be the hottest day of the year, so far. After a long walk in the nearby woods with Sandy, Beth stripped off her jeans and jumper and took a cool shower. Refreshed, she donned a matching set of underwear that would have to serve as a bikini and helped herself to a tall glass of gin and tonic. The Hendersons had a large patio beside a small swimming pool. Although it was probably still too cold to swim, a comfortable-looking sun lounger was perfect for making a start on her suntan.

Beth sat down and carefully applied a liberal coating of suntan oil. She looked around to ensure that she was not overlooked and then slipped her bra off so that she would get an even tan across her top. Sprawled out comfortably, she pulled the old sun-hat, which she had found in the hallway cupboard, down over her eyes. The dog flopped down contentedly under the shade of a big old oak tree, his tongue lolling.

Beth closed her eyes. It was very quiet and peaceful. In the background, she could hear the birds twittering and bees humming busily. It was a perfect early summer day. She let her mind wander. Could she really start her own business? It would be wonderful to be her own boss. No more Simon telling her what to do. What was he hiding in the secure folders on the computer?

Sandy started barking excitedly again and Beth smiled lazily. You'd think it would be too hot to chase after cats. The barking changed to an enthusiastic whining.

'Hello. Oh . . . Sorry. I thought you were my mother.'

Beth jumped at the unexpected voice and pushed the sun-hat back off her face. A young man was standing a couple of feet away from her, one hand stroking the ecstatic Sandy. Beth stared.

He was tall and slim, with longish dark hair and a clean-shaven, boyish complexion. Dressed casually in jeans and scruffy T-shirt, yet wearing an expensive wrist-watch and designer trainers, he looked a lot like a younger version of Simon.

'Are you a friend of my mother?' he asked. 'Where is she?' He appeared to be having trouble not staring at her and Beth suddenly remembered that she was dressed only in a pair of skimpy panties. She made a half-hearted attempt to cover herself with one arm as she swung her legs round and sat up.

'No. I mean, yes.' This must be Simon's son, she realised. She noticed his eyes had dropped to her groin. Considering how skimpy her panties were, it was little wonder he was staring.

'You must be Chris. I'm Beth. I work for your father. I'm looking after Sandy while your parents are away.'

She stood up, keeping her arm over her chest and trying to remember exactly where she had thrown her bra.

'I see.' Chris smiled. He took a step closer to her and held out his hand. 'Pleased to meet you, Beth. You say my parents are away?'

'Yes.' Beth automatically lowered her arm to shake his hand. His skin was damp and clammy. She saw his eyes widen at the sight of her exposed breasts and quickly put her arm back to cover herself. Very clever. He obviously took after his father.

'They've gone to Rome for the weekend,' she explained. 'I don't think they were expecting you home.' His face looked quite pale and shaken. She realised that the handshake had not been deliberate after all.

'No.' Chris was frowning. 'We don't communicate much and, anyway, I hadn't planned this visit until the last minute.'

Beth shifted awkwardly from one foot to the other. 'Well, I suppose now you're here, I might as well pack and leave you to it. I'm sure you can see to Sandy.'

Chris looked puzzled, then frowned again. 'What? Oh, no. Don't go. I mean, well, I'm not sure how long I shall be staying. If Mum and Dad aren't here, I might just as well head back to college.'

'Well, if you're sure. I don't want to intrude. Sorry to disappoint you.'

Chris stared at her in bewilderment.

'About your parents, I mean.'

'Oh, I see.' He grinned sheepishly. 'Believe me, you're, I mean, it's no disappointment.' His eyes ran over her exposed flesh yet again.

Beth flushed. 'I was just thinking about getting myself some lunch,' she muttered. 'Would you like something?' It felt awkward, offering to entertain him in his own house.

Chris nodded and swallowed hard without speaking.

'I suppose I should put something on first.' Beth gave

689

up trying to find her bra and reached for the blouse hanging over the arm of the chair.

'No, don't do that.' He flushed. 'What I mean is, I don't want to cause you any trouble or anything.' He was openly staring at her now and a quick glance at his groin confirmed to Beth what he was thinking about.

Beth smiled and slipped her feet into her strapless sandals before pushing her arms into the sleeves of the blouse. It was just long enough to cover her bottom. She pulled it round and did up just one button to hold it over her breasts. She noticed with amusement that Sandy and Chris were both watching her with the same puppy-dog expression on their faces.

As she made her way back towards the house, Beth was very conscious of Chris walking just behind her. Her panties were riding up between her buttocks as she moved and she resisted the temptation to pull them out. He was certainly good-looking. His young, firm body reminded her of . . .

'So, what are you studying?' she asked quickly, determined to keep at bay her powerful memories of young Jonathan. She looked over her shoulder at Chris.

'I'm sorry?' Chris flushed and his eyes dropped to the ground guiltily as if she had just caught him doing something he shouldn't be doing.

'At college. What are you studying?'

'Studying?' He paused. 'Oh, I see.' He paused again. 'I, um, just general business studies.' He was obviously having trouble concentrating on their conversation. She grinned as he hurried forward to hold the back door open for her.

'I take it you're not too keen?' Beth headed into the kitchen and hovered by the fridge. She really ought to cover up a bit more before she got the food. It was so hot. She liked the way he was watching her.

'Dad wants me to join him in the family business.' He made it sound like a life sentence.

'So, what's wrong with that?' she moved slowly, using

690

all her skill to make her provocative poses seem accidental. She forced herself not to look at him to check the effect.

'I want to study medicine,' he replied as he perched himself on a kitchen stool. 'I've got no head for figures.'

Beth looked up and smiled at his choice of words, noticing that he quickly averted his eyes from her.

'Why don't you just tell him, then? Your father, I mean.' It was definitely far too hot for any more clothes. She opened the fridge and rummaged around for a suitable sandwich filler. 'Are beef sandwiches OK for you?'

'Yes. Great.'

Beth turned to look at him.

'I can't tell my father anything,' Chris replied to her earlier question. 'If you work for him, you must know that. Once he's decided he wants something, there's no stopping him.'

Beth hid a smirk. 'I suppose he can be a bit forceful,' she responded. 'Still, it's your life, isn't it?'

'Is it? I'm not so sure.' Chris's words were so soft that she barely caught them. She tried to swallow her impatience. Chris didn't look like a wimp. If he took after his father at all then, surely, he had enough guts to stand up to Simon over his own future?

She fetched the butter and bread and busied herself with the sandwiches. Her breasts swayed gently from side to side with every stroke of the knife and she noticed that his eyes were riveted to them. Perhaps he and Simon weren't so different after all.

'There you go.' Beth placed a plate of sandwiches on the counter and perched herself on an adjacent stool.

'Thanks. They look great.' Chris took a huge bite and munched ravenously, as if he were half-starved. Lads his age always had good appetites. Her thoughts returned to Jonathan. Chris was older, of course. If he was at college, he must be at least eighteen, maybe nineteen. He

691

was unlikely to be an innocent where women were concerned. Not with a dad like Simon!

Beth took a bite of her own sandwich and examined Chris again surreptitiously. He had mistaken her for his mother. Did he find her attractive? He had certainly had a good look at her body. He was still staring at her legs. The temptation to tease him was too strong to resist.

Beth raised her left leg and crossed it over her right one. Her blouse was not quite long enough to cover her groin. She leant forward slightly to take another sandwich, giving him a clear view down the top of her gaping blouse. She knew that her nipples were hardening.

Chris's eyes widened and the colour on his cheeks deepened. She licked her lips as if to clean up stray crumbs and glanced at his crotch. The way he was sitting, it was not easy to tell if he was responding physically to her body or not. She noticed that he was no longer eating, just holding the sandwich between his clearly trembling fingers.

'Are you going to eat that,' she teased, 'or just play with it?' She raised one eyebrow.

Chris jumped and stared at the sandwich in bewilderment. Finally, he sighed and took a small bite. His eyes returned to her chest. Beth felt the first tingles of her own desire prickling the tops of her thighs. The idea of seducing Simon's son was deliciously tempting.

'So. Are you going to stay around this afternoon or do you have to leave straight away?' she questioned. 'It's awfully hot to be stuck in a car,' she added.

Chris shrugged. 'I don't know yet. I haven't thought. When did you say my parents would be home?'

'Not until tomorrow evening.' Beth decided to push him a bit more. 'I'd be very happy if you stayed around and kept me company. It's very lonely here, isn't it? Especially at night.'

Chris looked startled.

'I could cook us a special meal this evening,' she tempted him. 'How about lasagne? It's my speciality. I can make it as good as anything your parents may have in Rome. That's if you like Italian food, of course.'

'I love Italian food,' Chris replied. 'If you're sure it's no trouble.'

Beth smiled sweetly. 'Like I said, I'd be glad of the company.'

To her disappointment, Chris disappeared up to his room as soon as they had finished their sandwiches. Beth washed the dishes and tidied up the kitchen, then decided she might as well return to the sun lounger. As she settled back down and removed her blouse, she pretended not to notice the sound of an upstairs window opening.

Later, when she rolled over on to her stomach, she glanced up at the house and just caught a glimpse of him ducking out of sight from the window. Although she kept a watchful eye, she saw nothing further of him all afternoon. She amused herself with outrageous fantasies about what he might be up to.

Around five, she headed back to the house and wiggled into her jeans and T-shirt to take Sandy for another stroll. She debated looking for Chris to see if he wanted to join them but decided against it. He might resent her intruding on his privacy.

As soon as she returned, she fed Sandy and then began to hunt around in the kitchen for the ingredients to prepare dinner. Thankfully, Marie seemed to keep a well-stocked larder. She soon found everything she needed and busied herself cooking.

By six thirty, everything was coming along fine and Beth hurried upstairs to shower and dress. She stared ruefully at the few items of clothing she had brought with her. She had packed her case for dog walking, not seduction.

With another twinge of guilt, Beth crept down the landing to the main bedroom. Perhaps Marie had something a bit more suitable that she could borrow. She smirked at the thought of seducing Chris dressed in clothes borrowed from his own mother.

When she opened the wardrobe door and saw the long rack of dresses hanging there, she gasped in astonishment. They must have cost a fortune. Any qualms about borrowing Marie's clothes disappeared when she caught sight of a beautiful green cocktail dress at the far end of the row. She lifted it down and held it against her gleefully.

It was difficult to believe that it would fit Marie. It was only a size twelve. Simon's wife would easily take a fourteen. Perhaps it was one she hadn't worn for a long time, or maybe it was bought as an incentive to lose weight. Either way, it was perfect for Beth; short and clingy, with a narrow waist and flared hips. The neck was wide and worn off the shoulder; a style she had discovered most men appreciated. She slipped it over her head and nodded approvingly at her reflection in the long mirror.

Chris appeared just as she was adding the finishing touches to their meal. She looked up and smiled warmly as he entered the kitchen.

'Good timing. I was just about to call you.'

Chris sniffed the air appreciatively. 'It smells wonderful,' he told her. Beth noticed that his voice sounded slightly nervous. 'And, you look, er, fabulous.' She smiled at him again, pleased to notice that he had also dressed for dinner. The casual yet expensively cut black trousers fitted him perfectly. His dark blue, open-neck shirt was made of silk.

'I thought we would eat in the living-room, if that's OK,' she told him. 'Your dining-room is so huge, I'd be lost in it.'

Chris laughed. 'Dad insists we eat in there. I think it makes him feel more important. You know, lord of all he surveys. When Mum and I are alone we always eat in the living-room,' he assured her. 'Do you want me to carry anything?'

As they made their way into the living-room Beth watched him carefully, enjoying the sight of his firm body, the smell of his expensive aftershave and the underlying scent of his masculinity. Her skin prickled with anticipation.

They sat down side by side on the wide leather couch, and Chris poured them both a glass of wine from the bottle she had already placed on the low coffee-table. He took a bite of his lasagne and smacked his lips.

'This is incredible.' He took another large forkful.

Beth made a start on her own meal. She was acutely aware of the warmth of his thigh close up against her own leg. A small shiver ran down her back. She swallowed her food and took another mouthful. As an awkward silence gradually fell between them, she glanced around the room looking for a topic of conversation.

'This really is a beautiful house, Chris. Your father's business must be even more successful than I had realised.'

Chris snorted. 'King Midas. That's what he tells us to call him. Dad has always had a talent for turning money into more money. Especially when he's playing about with other people's money.'

'His rates are quite competitive,' Beth replied. 'Not everyone in the business does as well as he seems to have done.'

'No? Well, not everyone is as willing to take the gambles with other people's dosh that he does.'

'How do you mean?' Beth was intrigued by the implication.

Chris shrugged. 'Nothing. Only that he uses other people's money to make his own and then takes a bigger percentage than they realise. More wine?' He leant forward to pick up the bottle and used the movement to close the gap between his leg and hers. As his thigh pressed harder against hers, a surge of desire shot through her.

'Please.' She turned to hold her glass towards him and

their gaze met. She could see the longing burning within Chris's eyes. Longing and something else. Fear? What was he afraid of? Perhaps he wanted her but was afraid to trespass on what he assumed to be his father's domain? Anger engulfed her. She loathed the idea that he should think of her as belonging to Simon.

'Still, you have to admit that he has done well for you all,' she continued.

Chris frowned. 'Yeah. Well, you know one reason why he's so successful, don't you?' His words sounded very sharp and sarcastic.

'He works very hard,' Beth replied cautiously.

Chris snorted. 'He's not the only one. He also makes Mum be nice to his clients. I've heard him.'

Beth smiled. 'Well. That's not so unreasonable is it? I mean, she can hardly be rude to them, can she?'

'That's not what I mean.' His voice rose an octave. 'I've heard her being nice to some of them – in the bedroom.' His eyes were flashing with anger. 'You know what really pisses me off? He takes all the credit. Never even thanks her.'

Beth was silent. She couldn't help being a little shocked. She knew Simon was a bit of a bastard but – his own wife! No wonder Marie acted like she did. Beth wondered what she herself would have done if her ex-husband had ever asked her to do something like that.

Chris was watching her closely. 'So, does he ever make you be nice to his clients?' he questioned.

Her temper flared. 'No, he bloody well doesn't,' she snarled. Even as she said it, she realised that that was probably why he had wanted her to go to Rome with him.

Chris sneered. 'Really? He will. Sooner or later. You know, I wouldn't even be surprised if he told me to be nice to one of them, male or female, if he thought it would make him some money.'

'Would you like some more lasagne?' Beth decided that the conversation had gone far enough. She hated the idea that Chris might think she was willing to be manipulated by Simon. Under the circumstances, she was on shaky ground denying any involvement with him. Damn Simon to hell.

As she stood up and bent over to pick up Chris's plate, Beth took the opportunity to let her skirt ride up her legs. Although she was rewarded by the sound of his sharp intake of breath, Chris made no move towards her. He certainly wasn't as quick on the uptake as his father.

When she returned from the kitchen with second helpings, Beth accidentally misjudged her seating and fell back so that her leg was pressed tight against his thigh. She heard his gentle sigh. Although he still made no attempt to touch her, at least he didn't move away either.

She picked up her glass, took a sip and licked her lips slowly. 'This is a great wine, isn't it.' Beth placed her glass on the table and put her hand on his knee. 'I'm so glad you decided to stay tonight, Chris. It's nice to have some company.'

She felt him flinch at the touch and saw the colour flow up his neck and cheeks. He held his body rigid, as if afraid to move. Did he find her unattractive or was he really so shy? Beth began to run her finger slowly up his thigh.

'Actually, I was thinking I should be on my way soon.' He glanced at his watch. 'If there's not too much traffic, I should be able to get back before midnight.'

'Surely, you don't want to go at this time?' Beth's fingers continued their journey up his leg. 'Besides, you shouldn't drive after all this wine. It's surprisingly strong.' Her fingers tightened round his upper thigh, giving it a gentle squeeze.

Chris jumped as if he had been stung by a wasp. He slid away from her along the settee so that her hand slipped off his leg. Beth glanced at his crotch and was delighted to see how tight his trousers had suddenly become. Obviously, he wasn't totally immune to her charms.

'What's wrong?'

'Nothing. Cramp.' Chris leant over and gingerly rubbed his leg where she had touched him. Beth grinned.

'Cramp? In your thigh? How strange. Here, let me massage it for you.' She shifted along the settee and put her hand back on his leg. She felt him jump again. He was as nervous as a kitten. Or a virgin. Surely he couldn't be virgin at his age? The idea both delighted and excited her. She squeezed his thigh muscle firmly and sensed his whole body shudder.

'Better?'

'Yes, fine. Thank you.' His voice was tight and squeaky. Beth stopped squeezing and began to slide her fingers upwards again. Chris whimpered softly under his breath. Suddenly, he leant forward and put his lips to hers. His left arm slipped hesitantly around her shoulder to pull her closer.

Thank God, Beth thought to herself. For a moment there, she had been at a loss as to how to encourage him. Bar whipping off all her clothes and leaping on him, she was rapidly running out of ideas. She opened her lips enthusiastically to his probing tongue.

Chris pulled his head away. 'God. I'm sorry. I shouldn't have ...' He removed his arm and sat there looking like a naughty schoolboy. A quick glance at his fly reassured her that his body did not necessarily agree with his conscience.

Beth snuggled against him and rested her head on his chest. She could hear his heart thumping madly against his rib cage. 'Relax, Chris. I don't bite.' Well, not too hard, anyway, she added silently, as she pictured herself sinking her teeth into his firm flesh.

'But what about my father?' Chris whispered hoarsely.

'Let's just leave Simon out of this, shall we? He's my boss, nothing more.' Was that it? Was he frightened, or perhaps repulsed, by the concept of making it with one of his father's women? Her dislike of Simon increased further.

698

Beth undid one of his shirt buttons and pushed her hand inside. Chris gulped as her fingers gently caressed his smooth chest. His arm slipped round her shoulders once more and his lips returned to hers.

He might be a bit slow on the uptake but there was nothing wrong with his kissing technique. She writhed helplessly as his fingers ran across the bare flesh of her shoulder and came to rest on the swell of her right breast. A pang of lust shot through her. She pulled her hand back out of his shirt and moved it down his body until her fingers were resting over his straining groin.

Chris groaned and pushed his tongue harder into her mouth. His fingers started to explore the shape of her breast and she sensed her nipples hardening in response. The tingling between her thighs intensified. She could only guess how damp her thong must be. What was he waiting for?

Impatiently, Beth raised her hand and guided his fingers inside her dress. She sighed loudly as she felt him gently fondle her swollen nipple; his touch was as soft and light as a feather. She was desperate to feel his lips sucking her there.

Beth put her hand back on to his trousers and fumbled with the button. She almost sighed with relief as it came undone. Slowly, she started to slide the zip down, exposing his bulging underpants.

Chris sighed again and tightened his grip on her breast, squeezing it almost painfully. Beth shuddered with desire and felt her lubrication flowing. His shy reluctance, despite his obvious need, was driving her wild. She could hear her own breath rasping in her throat. Eagerly, she pulled his pants down and wrapped her fingers round his hardness.

His whole body shook at her touch. 'Oh God,' he gasped softly as he thrust his hips upward to push his throbbing cock hard into her fist.

Sensing that he was already close to coming, Beth released her grip and pushed her hand down further so that she could caress his balls with her fingertips. They were already tight and swollen. She definitely needed to find a way to slow things down still further.

Beth pulled her hand out, put his cock back in his pants, wriggled out of his grasp and sat up. Chris lay back against the cushion of the settee, his face burning with lust. She stood up and turned her back to him.

Slowly, she peeled the dress off her shoulders and let it fall to the floor, revealing her naked back and the lacy strap of her thong. She placed her hands over her breasts and swivelled round on her heels to face him.

Chris immediately sat forward and stared at her without speaking. Beth glanced down at the way his cock was straining against his pants. She saw that his hands were at his sides and guessed that he was afraid to touch himself in case he lost all control. Smiling provocatively, she moved her hands slowly down her body towards the tiny scrap of lace covering her mound. Her breasts fell forward to reveal her swollen nipples to his longing gaze.

Beth slipped her fingers down inside the lace and ran them softly over her tingling clitoris. His gasp was loud enough to smother her own sigh of pleasure. Slowly, she slipped the thong down, revealing her shaven mound. Chris gasped again and his right hand involuntarily moved round to rub himself.

Beth dropped the thong to her ankles and stepped out of it. Naked, she leant forward and took his hand, pulling him to his feet. Chris stood up submissively with his hands at his sides and his eyes glued to her mound.

Beth put her hands on his hips and hooked her fingers into the waistband of his pants. Gently, she eased them over his erection. It leapt out towards her like an angry cobra writhing its head from side to side, ready to strike. He might be a bit shy, but he certainly had nothing to be ashamed of. She stepped away to look at him.

'Finish stripping,' she whispered huskily.

Galvanised into action by her words, Chris immediately began to rip the rest of his clothes off. In his desperation, he was trying to get his shirt off over his head at the same time as kicking his feet out of his trousers. Losing his balance, he stumbled back on to the settee and fell on the floor. Seemingly oblivious to how he must look, he continued to struggle with his clothing. As he finally lifted his legs clear of his trousers, his fingers tore the remaining buttons from his shirt. He tossed both garments to one side and struggled to get up. Beth could see his balls and cock swaying under him and her fingers itched to grab him. She raised one eyebrow and stared at his socks.

Red-faced from exertion and embarrassment, Chris ripped them off and pulled himself back up on to the settee.

Beth knelt down and ran her tongue down the full length of his penis, savouring the masculine taste of him. With one hand under his scrotum, she slid her tongue back up and wrapped her lips around his swollen tip. Slowly, she sucked him into her mouth. She heard him gasp and felt him push his hips forward, thrusting into her so forcefully that she almost choked. She immediately gripped him harder with her lips, forcing him to slow his pace. Bobbing her head up and down, she continued to slip him in and out of her mouth so slowly that he was barely moving.

'Please,' he begged desperately as he grabbed her head with his hands to try to push even deeper into her. 'Oh my God, I can't . . .'

Instinctively, Beth fought against him, maintaining the slow, torturous speed that she knew was driving him mad. Another rush of excitement shot through her. There was nothing that gave her greater pleasure than holding a man right on the edge like this. The rush of power it gave her was almost as good as an orgasm. She felt her own juices dampening her thighs.

Pulling back, she let him drop from her mouth and

feasted her eyes on the throbbing veins of his swollen erection. His balls were hard against his body and she knew that he would not be able to hold on much longer. She glanced up.

Chris had closed his eyes. His face was screwed up as if he were in pain and every muscle of his body was tight with concentration. She knew he was fighting to control himself and the knowledge of his struggle was almost enough to bring her to climax. She clamped her thighs together tightly and took a couple of deep breaths to calm herself down.

Seeing that he had also relaxed slightly now that she was no longer sucking him, Beth raised her hand and wrapped it round his cock. He was so damp with her saliva and his own lubrication that her fist slid freely down his length. She started to pump him, slowly at first, then faster and harder as he began to thrust against her once again. Unable to help herself, Beth slipped her other hand between her own legs and squeezed her mound and bud. She was very close herself now.

Chris put his hands on his buttocks and pushed himself harder into her hand. Beth immediately tightened her grip, squeezing him as firmly as she could to prolong the moment even further.

'Oh, Jesus. I can't hold it!' His desperate cry was the final trigger. With a last savage pump of her fist, Beth felt her own climax tear through her body. Chris began to spurt violently into her clenched hand, groaning with every convulsion of his eruption.

Beth waited until he had nothing left to give then opened her fist to release him. She slumped back wearily on her heels. Her skin was tingling and glowing with the aftermath of her own fulfilment.

Chris flopped down heavily on to the couch as if his leg muscles no longer had the strength to hold him. His chest was still heaving and she noticed with delight that his sticky wet cock was still partly erect. She shifted forward on her knees and kissed its tip lightly, smiling as his hands began ruffling her hair.

'That was, I mean, well, you're quite something,' he whispered softly.

Beth stood up and sank down on the couch beside him with her head resting on his sweat-covered chest. She ran her fingernail down his chest.

'You're not going to leave me all alone in this great big house tonight, are you?' she whispered in her best little-girl's voice. 'Who's going to scrub my back for me?' She took his hand and pulled him up. Still holding his hand, she led him unresisting upstairs towards the shower.

Chapter Eleven

*I*n the end, Chris didn't leave to return to college until about an hour before Simon and Marie arrived home from Rome on the Sunday afternoon. By that time, Beth and Chris had enjoyed pleasuring each other several more times in a number of imaginative positions and settings.

Chris had proved to be a sweet and considerate man, nothing like his selfish, money-grabbing father. No wonder he didn't want to go into business with Simon. If his bedside manner was anything like as good as his 'in bed' manners, he would make a wonderful doctor!

The more Chris had told her about Simon, the more Beth grew to despise him. Chris might not want to go into the business, but he obviously knew more about what his father got up to than she did. His revelations about some of Simon's underhand practices had made her really angry. Geoff might walk a thin line between what was strictly legal in some of his dealings, but she was certain that he didn't deliberately fleece his clients the way Simon apparently did. As for the way he used his wife like that! By the time Chris left, Beth was absolutely determined to find a way to really fix Simon.

When the Hendersons finally returned, Simon was in

a foul mood. Obviously, his plans in Rome had not worked out to his satisfaction. Marie looked tired and weary and had little to say for herself. She thanked Beth politely for taking such good care of Sandy, then pleaded a headache and disappeared upstairs. Simon offered her a drink but Beth made excuses and escaped quickly before he got any ideas. At Chris's request, she said nothing about their son's visit. She didn't even want to think about what Simon would do if he found out what she and Chris had been up to.

The following morning, Simon seemed to be in much better humour. As soon as he had taken care of the most urgent business, he called Beth through to his office.

'This is for you.' Simon held out a large, flat box. Beth stared at him.

'You did suggest I brought you something from Rome,' he reminded her. 'Go on, open it.'

Beth took the box curiously. She was amazed that he had remembered.

The dress was red and made of a stretchy, lacy material that would hide little. It was long and slit high up both sides; the neck was wide and the back so low it would probably reveal the crease of her buttocks. It was just the sort of thing she would have expected him to choose, but she had to admit that she loved it.

'Thank you, Simon.' She held it against herself. 'It's lovely.'

Simon smirked at her. 'You can wear it next weekend,' he told her.

'Next weekend?'

'Yes. Marie and I have been invited to a weekend party. It will be a great opportunity to make some useful contacts. I want you to come with us.'

'Won't your host object?'

'No. You're already expected.'

Beth frowned. She didn't like to be taken for granted.

Especially by Simon. 'I'm not sure that I'm free,' she began.

'Make sure that you are. I need you to be there and I expect you to make yourself useful by being nice to the host. Very nice.' He leered suggestively and Beth flushed angrily at the implication behind his words. It was exactly what Chris had warned her would happen. She gritted her teeth.

'Like I said, I'm not sure . . .'

'It's not open to discussion,' he told her firmly. Beth's temper flared.

'How dare you treat me like some woman you pay for by the hour,' she yelled.

Simon grinned. 'Actually, I never do pay. Why pay for something when you don't need to?' He reached round and patted her. 'If you still want a job next week, you'll do as I say.' He grinned again. 'Don't look like that. I don't think you'll find it any great hardship. You already know the host; Geoff Stevens.'

By Friday night, Beth was so keyed up that she couldn't sleep. Although she was still furious with Simon, she couldn't help being excited. As she lay tossing and turning in her bed, she tried to imagine what the weekend might hold in store.

Geoff Stevens' wheeling and dealing weekend parties were infamous in financial circles. She had never expected to find herself among the guest list and she wondered how Simon had managed to wangle the invitation. Although she really wanted to see Geoff again, she had not forgotten how easily he and his chauffeur had manipulated her. What had Geoff thought when he had found the money she left in his car? She wanted to see Daniel again too, but was even more nervous about that as she recalled what had happened between them.

Still, Simon had no right to treat her like this. She remembered his conceited words. Just you wait, she vowed silently. You will pay, one way or the other.

706

Simon and Marie picked her up at nine thirty the following morning. She was so nervous that she hadn't managed anything for breakfast and the thought of the coming buffet lunch was already making her stomach churn.

Marie was beautifully made up and her dress and jacket superbly tailored. Beth couldn't help noticing that her eyes seemed unusually red, as if she had been crying. Marie said little during the two-hour journey and, occasionally, when she thought no one was looking, she shot venom-filled glances at her husband. Beth wondered what he had been up to this time. Had she, too, been given her instructions? Perhaps Simon imagined that, between them, they could be especially nice to Geoff.

Simon, she noticed, seemed to be in fine spirits and totally oblivious to his wife's angry stares.

'I expect great things from this weekend, Beth. I'm sure that Geoff can be persuaded to put a little business our way and I'm relying on you to do whatever it takes to persuade him.'

Beth frowned but chose not to respond to this repeat of his earlier demands. Not that she would really mind persuading Geoff! She noticed the look on Marie's face but couldn't decide what it meant: surprise, suspicion or maybe pity?

When the car finally turned into the sweeping driveway and Beth caught sight of Geoff's rambling mansion and immaculate grounds, she gasped aloud. This place made even Simon's luxurious house seem little more than a hovel. For the first time, she started to appreciate just how rich and successful Geoff Stevens truly was.

As the three of them mounted the wide steps leading up to the imposing oak doorway, the front door swung open to reveal a smiling Daniel. Obviously, he also played the part of butler when he wasn't driving. Beth felt her breath catch at the sight of his muscular body and roguish good looks. She had forgotten just how attractive he was.

'Good morning. Please come in. Sarah will show you to your rooms, then drinks are being served in the library.' As he spoke, Daniel stared at Beth and gave her a quick wink that brought a sudden glow to more than her cheeks. She could sense his eyes burning into her as they followed a pretty maid up the wide staircase.

Her room was at the end of a long corridor, whose walls were covered with expensive-looking paintings of racehorses. Its fittings and decor would have put most five-star hotels to shame and Beth grinned with delight as she bounced up and down on the huge four-poster bed. With any luck, she would get the opportunity to test it properly later.

As soon as she had hung her clothes in the massive oak wardrobe and splashed a little cold water on to her flushed cheeks, Beth hurried nervously downstairs, excited at the idea of seeing Geoff again. On the way, she met several other guests, including Simon and Marie, all heading for drinks in the library.

In the library, Geoff was standing beside a huge, horseshoe-shaped bar, talking with a serious-looking Asian man. He looked across when they came in and Beth shivered with pleasure at the tiny smile that played across his lips when he spotted her among the latest arrivals.

She moved into the room and accepted a glass of sherry from a tall, redheaded waitress. Sipping the drink, she moved over to the french windows and gazed out over the park-like grounds, wondering just how many acres Geoff owned.

'Dreaming about me again, Beth?'

Beth jumped at the familiar voice and spun round on her heels. John was standing behind her with that infuriating grin of his. Her heart flipped and her mind immediately began to relive some of their recent antics.

'John. I didn't know you were going to be here.' She looked round quickly. 'Are Steve and Brian here, too?'

'Not that I know of,' he replied, moving closer so that his thigh was touching hers. 'Still, speaking for myself, I can't say that I shall miss them too much.' He ran his hand lightly down her spine and nodded out of the window. 'Nice view, isn't it? Would you like to take a walk?'

Beth shivered at his touch, remembering the way he had played with her body that night in her hotel – if it had been him. She felt her face start to burn.

'I, um, well, yes, I suppose we –' She broke off as Geoff came up behind them and took her hand.

'Beth. How delightful to see you again so soon.' He raised her hand to his lips and kissed it lightly. 'I'm so pleased you could join us. It should be an interesting weekend.'

Beth smiled as her eyes moved from John to Geoff and then back again. She felt quite weak at the knees being so close to two of her recent conquests at the same time – although, perhaps, conquest was not quite the right word.

'Hello, Geoff. Thank you for asking me. Your house is absolutely breathtaking.'

Geoff took hold of her arm. 'Come on. There are several people I want you to meet. If you will excuse us, John?'

John nodded politely. 'I shall see you later then, Beth.' It was a statement rather than a question and Beth experienced a thrill of desire and longing as she saw the hungry look in his eyes. She could almost picture him beside her in that huge four-poster bed. She nodded without answering and John flashed her another knowing grin. He seemed to have an uncanny knack of reading her innermost thoughts.

'By the way. You left something behind in my car the other day,' Geoff told her softly as her led her across the room towards the Asian man he had been talking with earlier. 'I must make sure to return it to you before you leave.'

Beth opened her mouth to argue, but Geoff squeezed her arm. 'I meant what I told you that day, Beth. The money was a consultancy fee for your business knowledge and was well earnt. To suggest anything else insults both of us.'

Beth closed her mouth again. There was obviously no point in arguing with him. If he was really that determined for her to have the money, well, why not? She had made her point. Not that she would ever spend it. Maybe she would frame it as a memento of her first consultancy fee. When she felt naughty, she could look at it and remember just how she earnt it.

'Here we are. Beth, I want you to meet Ho Chan. This is Beth Bradley. A very promising newcomer to our ranks.'

The rest of the day passed in a whirl of new faces, good food, liberal amounts of alcohol and stimulating discussions. By five thirty, Beth's head was swimming and her feet were aching. Making polite excuses to those around her, she escaped gratefully and headed for her room to shower and rest before dinner.

Without paying attention to where she was going she took a wrong turn out of the library and found herself in a long dark corridor with several doors on either side.

She opened one at random and smiled when she found a narrow staircase leading up. Thinking that it was probably a servants' staircase to the upper floor, she hurried up the steep steps and through the door at the top. It opened out on to a landing that looked vaguely familiar and Beth turned left and hurried along it, looking for her room.

Although she had no idea how many rooms opened out on to the landing, she remembered that her own room was the last one on the left before the landing ended at a huge stained-glass window. She was too weary to notice that the paintings on the walls were of hunting dogs rather than racehorses.

When she finally reached the end of the long corridor,

Beth opened with a sigh of relief what she thought to be her own door. She couldn't wait to take a hot bath.

The room she entered seemed to be some kind of huge games room with a snooker table and table tennis. Through a wide arch at the far end, Beth could see a fully fitted gymnasium with treadmills, step machines and several kinds of weights. She sighed with frustration, realising that she was now totally lost.

She was just about to retrace her steps when she heard a sound coming from the gym. Hoping there might be someone in there who could give her directions, Beth hurried across the room and peered through the archway.

Daniel was standing in the far corner of the gym with his back against the mirrored wall. He was dressed in training shorts and a T-shirt so tight that every muscle was clearly outlined. As her eyes travelled downwards she noticed the obvious bulge at his groin and suddenly realised that he was not alone.

She glanced curiously at his companion. She was obviously one of the housemaids, dressed in the short black skirt and white frilly blouse all Geoff's maids seemed to wear. She had her back to Beth and she had untied her hair so that it was cascading loosely round her shoulders.

Before Beth could move, the maid stepped in front of Daniel and bent forward to slip her hand down the front of his shorts. Daniel sighed loudly as he leant even harder against the wall, thrusting his hips forward to give the maid full access. Beth was close enough to see that his eyes were closed and to notice the look of intense concentration on his face.

Beth involuntarily stepped back into the shadow of the archway. A tingle of excitement swept through her as she saw Daniel put his hands round the maid's waist and undo the zip holding her skirt. The skirt slid down off the maid's narrow hips and Beth could just see the straps of her suspender belt peeping out under the

711

bottom of her blouse. Daniel's hands lifted the blouse and slipped down inside her panties to fondle her taut buttocks.

Beth held her breath as the maid began to lower Daniel's shorts. He wasn't wearing anything under them and she just stopped herself from sighing aloud as his swollen cock fell free. The maid ran her hand slowly down its length and cupped his balls. Beth could feel her own nipples rising with desire. She pushed her legs together tightly as the tingle between her thighs grew more urgent. She knew she should leave. She had no right to spy on him like this.

Daniel removed his hands from the maid's panties and spun her round on her heels until she was standing with her back to him. With his arms around her shoulders, he guided them both round so that they were facing the mirrored wall with their backs to Beth.

Beth examined the maid's firm buttocks, thinking how sexy they looked framed by her panties and the bottom of her blouse. The sight of Daniel's rigid prick waving back and forth with its shiny tip almost caressing the maid's cheeks was even more exciting. Remembering how she had struggled against him in the car, Beth felt a slight twinge of envy for the maid's position.

The maid raised her hands and put her flattened palms on to the mirror as Daniel forced his hands under the bottom of her blouse and pulled her buttocks hard against his cock. Beth looked at the mirror and could see Daniel's hands moving under the maid's blouse. She could almost imagine the way he was teasing her pubes and clit with his fingers and she squeezed herself even harder as another pang of desire raced through her.

His breathing laboured, Daniel grabbed the elastic of the maid's panties and started to peel them down. Beth took a sharp breath and almost choked in her effort not to gasp as the maid's huge penis fell forward over the top of her – his – panties and stuck out proudly in front of him with its tip touching the mirror. Her legs were

712

suddenly much too weak to hold her and Beth swayed, then grabbed the wall with her left hand to stop herself falling.

Huddled in the archway, she looked more carefully at the maid's reflection, for the first time seeing the broad shoulders, the narrow hips, the dark shadow on his cheeks and, of course, the urgent erection. Her eyes dropped back down to the reflection of his groin in the mirror and she had to fight to stifle another gasp as she saw Daniel reach round from behind to fondle his companion's stiff cock.

Beth shuffled back further and crouched down, trying to make herself as small as possible. She had never seen two men together like this, not even in films. Her heart was hammering almost painfully and her emotions were in complete turmoil. She couldn't take her eyes off them.

Daniel's companion – Beth couldn't keep thinking of him as a maid – shifted his feet backwards and arched his back, pushing his buttocks up into the air. He slid his feet apart and lowered his buttocks into Daniel's groin.

Daniel whipped his own shorts down to his ankles and then grabbed his friend's buttocks with his hands, prising the cheeks apart. She could clearly see the other man's thighs and calves quivering as he tensed his muscles, ready.

Beth held her breath as Daniel wet his index finger and pushed it gently into the man's crack. She saw his other hand grasp his own cock firmly to begin guiding it forwards. Jesus Christ! Daniel was going to penetrate him! He was actually going to – She couldn't help the small gasp that burst from her lips.

It didn't matter. Daniel and his friend were obviously too engrossed to notice her. They were both breathing raggedly and she could see the sweat beading on their firm flesh. She whimpered softly as Daniel thrust his stiff cock deep into his friend's anus. Both men grunted and Beth whimpered again as she heard Daniel's groin slap against the other man's buttocks.

She glanced in the mirror and saw the man's face tighten with passion as Daniel began to pump firmly in and out. She lowered her eyes and watched, fascinated, as his own cock twitched and throbbed in response. She experienced an almost overwhelming urge to walk over and grab it in her hand.

Almost as if she had forgotten where she was, Beth slipped her hand under her skirt and up between her thighs. She ran her finger over her mound and on to her sex. Her clit was hard and swollen with her passion and her panties were already dripping wet. With a small sigh, she pushed the damp material aside and pushed her middle finger up into her moist vagina to rub herself. Her eyes never moved from the mirror.

Daniel pulled his friend further away from the mirror and pushed him down until he was bent over, supporting himself with both hands, spread-eagled on the mirror. She saw the man push back with his buttocks as Daniel began to pump harder and faster, grunting loudly with every thrust.

Daniel leant over his friend and pulled him down even harder on to his cock then reached round with his right hand to grasp the other man's erection in his fingers. Tightening his fist round it, Daniel began to pump it in time with his thrusting. His friend groaned and stiffened the muscles in his legs to stop himself falling. His face twisted and darkened and Beth realised that he was about to come.

She started to push more urgently with her own finger, using her thumb to caress her already desperate clitoris. A long tingle of excitement raced through her and her nipples burned. She was almost there, too.

Daniel reached round with his left hand and pushed it under his friend's balls. He squeezed gently and thrust even harder with his buttocks and thighs. The other man cried out and jerked his hips. His spunk began to pump from his cock in violent bursts, splattering the mirror and dripping down Daniel's fingers. Daniel thrust his own hips again, then stiffened and groaned as he climaxed.

Beth bit her lips as she imagined his hot semen bursting from him. With a small cry, her whole body shuddered and a massive orgasm rippled through her so powerfully that she lost her balance and collapsed in a heap on the floor. Realising she was in imminent danger of discovery, she crawled across the floor until she was hidden from view round the corner.

As she huddled there, panting, she could hear the sounds of the two men moving around and talking together in low voices. She felt a tinge of panic. If they came through the arch, they would find her and know that she had seen them. She held her breath, shivering with fear and emotion.

Finally, as her breathing slowed and the strength returned to her shaking limbs, Beth pushed herself up on to all fours and crawled forward to peer round the archway.

Daniel and his lover were lying side by side against the mirror, talking softly. She glanced down. Their damp, limp cocks were both totally exposed to her gaze, pointing towards each other as if joining in the conversation. As she watched, Daniel reached across to his friend's groin and ran his fingers slowly down his cock.

Beth's eyes widened as the man's cock twitched feebly. Daniel repeated the caress and his friend's cock twitched again. He reached out and took Daniel's penis between his fingers, squeezing him softly. Gradually, both cocks began to swell again.

As she watched, the two men continued to pump and fondle each other. Within minutes, they were both semierect again. Daniel turned over on to his stomach and raised his buttocks invitingly. His friend got up and crouched over his legs. Taking his rapidly hardening prick between his fingers, he leant forward and used his other hand to part Daniel's cheeks.

Beth began to tremble. They were going to do it again.

She could hardly believe it. She pinched herself to see if she was dreaming as the man slowly thrust himself deep into Daniel's bottom. She heard both men sigh urgently as he began pumping in and out.

It was too much. With a small whimper, Beth pushed herself back and forced herself to her feet. As the men's passionate moans grew more urgent, Beth lowered her head and fled, trembling, out the door and down the corridor.

'Whoa!' She almost screamed as she felt herself crash headlong into someone. As she lost her balance, strong arms wrapped around her body and helped her up on to her feet.

'Where's the fire?' John still had his arms around her shoulders, bracing her. 'What's wrong, Beth? You're trembling all over.'

'John.' Beth's legs sagged as she swayed against him. 'I'm sorry. I didn't see you. I was trying to find my room only I took a wrong turning and got lost and –' she broke off as she realised that she was rambling incoherently.

John laughed. 'You look as if you've seen the resident ghost.' He held her tight. 'You're in the wrong wing, that's all. This bit's reserved for Geoff's bachelor guests. Women and married couples are housed in the south wing.'

Beth felt his hand slip easily around her waist. 'Not that I'm complaining, or anything, You are welcome to visit us as often as you like.' He stared at her pale face. 'What's got you so spooked?'

'Nothing.' Beth shook her head and pulled herself out of his grasp. 'I just panicked a bit when my room wasn't where I thought it was. Silly, really.' She swallowed hard and tried to block out the vivid images of Daniel and his friend that were still flooding her mind.

'Perhaps you've had a bit too much to drink and not enough to eat.' John suggested, patting her arm. 'Come on. I'll escort you to your room. Unless you would like to take that stroll now? It's a lovely evening.'

Beth hesitated. The fresh air would do her good. She needed to clear her head. She wondered if Daniel and his friend were still pleasuring each other or if they had finished. Her knees began to tremble again. She needed a shower. She could smell the sweat of her arousal and excitement on her body, and her underwear was cold and wet against her still throbbing bud.

'I'd love a walk,' she told John. 'But, first, I really need to shower and change, if you don't mind waiting.'

'I don't mind at all,' John told her with a small grin. 'I'll even help scrub your back if you want.' He began to guide her gently along the corridor. 'This way.'

Beth leant against him gratefully, enjoying the heat of his body through his suit and his warm masculine odour mingling with his aftershave. It would be useful to have someone to scrub her back. Her own hands were still shaking too much to be any use.

'It might take us a bit longer,' she whispered.

'There's no hurry,' John replied. 'We've got all night.'

Before they reached her room, however, they met Geoff coming along the corridor in the opposite direction. His face lit up when her saw her and Beth had the feeling that he had been looking for her. She noticed his eyes narrow slightly when he saw who she was with.

'Beth. I was hoping to find you. I've got a couple of things I want to discuss with you in private. I don't know when I shall have another chance.' He looked pointedly at John. 'I seem to keep coming between you two, don't I?' He didn't sound as if it bothered him. John shrugged philosophically.

'Our plans will keep, won't they, Beth?'

'Fine. In that case, perhaps you would like to come down to my study.' Geoff took her arm.

Beth nodded dumbly and allowed herself to be guided along the corridor. She was feeling light-headed and dreamlike, as if she were watching herself from a distance. Everything was moving too quickly, and she seemed to be having trouble keeping up with what was going on. Her head was still full of pictures of Daniel and his friend and her body had been keyed up with the promise of being alone in her room with John. She glanced over her shoulder at him and John raised his right hand in mock salute.

'Later, Beth.' His words were so faint that she only just caught them. A shiver of anticipation ran down her spine as she turned back and tried to focus her attention on what Geoff was saying to her.

She could feel his hand burning into her skin. Her head was spinning. She had believed herself to be virtually shockproof. She could still hardly believe what had happened or that she had just stood there, watching. Worse, she had actually . . . She shuddered helplessly as the memories washed over her.

Chapter Twelve

Geoff's study was every bit as luxurious and impressive as the rest of his home. While Geoff poured her a drink, Beth perched herself awkwardly on one of the deep leather armchairs that were scattered around the room. She shifted uncomfortably at the cold dampness of her underwear and wished she had insisted on showering first. She hadn't even found her way back to her room.

'Oh. Before I forget, here's your money.' Geoff handed her the wad of notes with her glass of wine. She took both without comment and held the money awkwardly in one hand.

'I'll come straight to the point,' Geoff told her as he eased himself down in a second comfy chair. 'I've an opening at my head offices. A sort of public relations-cum-personal assistant. I was rather hoping that you would be interested.'

Beth stared at him in surprise. It was an incredible opportunity and the prestige of working for Geoff Stevens would do her own career nothing but good. Simon would be livid.

'Why, thank you,' she stammered. 'I'm very flattered . . .'

'But?' He interrupted her. Beth's cheeks coloured.

'No. It's just a bit unexpected, that's all.' What was it that was bothering her, she wondered? It was a great opportunity. One that she would be mad to turn down because of some crazy whim to become her own boss. Ann had already pointed out how difficult that would be.

'Would you give me a little time to think about it?' she asked. Perhaps a year or two with Geoff might be exactly what she needed to give her the knowledge and confidence to make the final step to go it alone.

'Of course.' Geoff reached across and patted her arm in a fatherly way. 'There's no immediate hurry. Don't take too long, though. Your talents are wasted on a man like Simon Henderson.'

Beth's flush deepened, as if Geoff were referring to talents that had little to do with finance. Was he? If he knew anything about Simon at all, then he must know about the man's philandering reputation. She felt another rush of irritation at the way everyone seemed to assume that she was one of Simon's many conquests.

She opened her mouth to defend Simon's business, then closed it again. Chris probably wasn't the only one who knew what his father was up to. Someone as knowledgeable and well-connected as Geoff would be bound to know all about him and his unscrupulous business practices. She remembered that she was supposed to be here to help convince Geoff to put some business Simon's way. Suddenly, it was important to her that he should know she was not a complete innocent where Simon was concerned.

'I suppose Simon is a bit of a rogue,' she laughed. 'His intentions are in the right place but, somehow, he lacks your finesse.'

Geoff pulled a face. 'I certainly wouldn't trust him with my money. As for his intentions, well, they are debatable. There is a clear line between what's acceptable and what's not. Simon crosses it.'

So much for Simon's ambitions, Beth smiled to herself. She wondered why Geoff had invited Simon here at all. It couldn't simply be an excuse to get her here. There had been nothing stopping Geoff from inviting her personally, if he had wanted to.

'Mind you,' Geoff grinned, 'he does provide a little light entertainment. It amuses me to watch him fawning all over everyone. And it did give me an opportunity to try to poach you from him without being too obvious about it.'

Geoff picked up the wine bottle and refilled her glass. 'Drink up. I've got a lot to celebrate this evening. Ho Chan and I have just completed a deal that should prove extremely lucrative for both of us.' His eyes twinkled as he leant closer and put his hand on her knee.

'It's rather clever, actually, if I do say so myself. Would you like to hear about it?'

Beth couldn't help smiling in response to his enthusiasm. She had a feeling that whatever it was he had just pulled off, it was probably only just on the right side of legal. Her smile deepened. He and Simon were not so different really. As Simon once said, Geoff had had a few more breaks.

As she sat back to listen to him talk, Beth enjoyed the feeling of his hand resting on her knee. As she moved her legs slightly, she noticed the way his eyes brightened. It would not take much to distract him from finance as she had done before in his car. It wouldn't take much to distract herself, either. She was still on edge from what she had witnessed earlier and from the idea of enjoying John again. She parted her legs slightly, so that his hand slipped on to her inner thigh.

Gradually, through her growing arousal, she began to register that he had changed the subject. As she focused on what he was now saying, all thoughts of seducing him fled from her mind. She shifted in her seat so that his hand could no longer reach her and concentrated all her attention on his words. She found her mind racing ahead of him at the mention of a company that was gaining power rapidly. Another company she had heard of was in a similar position and she realised that they could dramatically increase their hold on the financial world if they worked together as one company.

'Are they going to merge?' she blurted out excitedly.

'Merge? Did I say anything about a merger?' His eyes sparkled mischievously.

'No, but you obviously think it's on the cards. The benefits to both companies and their stockholders are obvious.'

'Um. In what way?' Geoff was staring at her intently.

'Well, Donald has recently taken over as chief executive at Torrins. He's been looking to protect his market share and increase it.' Beth was thinking aloud. 'A merger with MM would not only cut his closest competitor out of the market but, by rationalising, he could reduce overheads and increase potential. MM have several factories not working at maximum capacity, whereas Torrins factories are . . .' she stared at Geoff questioningly ' . . . are they old? I seem to remember that they had problems not too long ago?'

'Health and safety inspection,' Geoff prompted her.

'Right. So, if the buildings can't easily be salvaged then it might be cheaper just to merge with Torrins and use all their capacity.'

Geoff smiled.

'Torrins's company report is due out soon,' Beth continued thoughtfully. 'The shares are already dropping. With a year like the one they've just had, they're bound to fall even further.'

'Next Thursday,' Geoff nodded. 'The report is due next Thursday.'

Beth stared at him. That information was worth a small fortune. Why did he mention it? 'Are you involved with this?' she questioned softly.

Geoff shook his head. 'No, sadly not. If I tried to take advantage of it, my actions would be spotted immediately and any element of surprise would be lost.' He smiled ruefully. 'Besides, the truth is I can't release sufficient funds at the moment to make it worth my while.'

'Is that why you invited Simon here?'

Geoff looked startled. 'Good God, no.' He patted her hand. 'No, I just wanted to test you. Up until now, your deductions have been spot on.'

'But –' Beth prompted.

'You've got great instincts, Beth.' He paused and his face grew thoughtful, as if he was searching for the right words. 'It's difficult to explain. Once in a while, you find someone special. I could have mentioned this information to half a dozen people here today. Indeed, I have brought the subject up with one or two. Although they had a few good suggestions, none of them considered a merger or remembered the annual report and its consequences.' His fingers began to play with hers. 'You, however, came to the point straight away without any prompting. I want you to think hard about my offer. I really could use your talents.'

When Beth didn't respond, he continued, 'You would be welcome to stay here during the week if it's too far for you to travel. I've got some property in town that you could use, if you prefer. I'd pay a very competitive salary. Better than most.' He smiled again. 'Well, I won't push anymore. Take a few weeks to think it over and make use of what we have just discussed if you can.'

As Beth continued to stare at him, her mind was already running on overdrive. She was suddenly certain what Simon's secret computer file must contain and equally certain of how she was going to make use of it for herself. If only she could figure out what his password was. There must be some way to make him reveal it to her.

Geoff stood up and held out his arm to help her to her feet. 'Well, it's nearly seven thirty,' he told her. 'Much as I hate to break this up, we both need to change ready for

723

dinner. I can't completely ignore my other guests.' He squeezed her arm. 'I can see your mind is already hard at work,' he told her as he patted her gently.

Impulsively, Beth turned and wrapped her arms around him. Hugging him tight, she gave him a big kiss. 'Thank you,' she whispered. 'For everything.'

Geoff grinned. 'Oh, being nice to a beautiful woman is one pleasure I'll never tire of. Would it also be helpful if I arranged to get Simon out of your way towards the end of next week?'

Beth thought quickly. Even if she could break his password and did find what she expected to find, she would still need some time to set everything up. She nodded. 'How about Friday?' she suggested.

'Done. And now,' he guided her towards the door, 'duty calls.'

Beth nodded, her mind barely registering his words as her plans chased each other round her head. If she could pull it off, she wouldn't have to work for Simon or Geoff. She felt a slight twinge of guilt so far as Geoff was concerned but none at all about what she hoped to do to Simon.

'I know this sounds a bit silly,' she confessed,' but I can't remember how to find my room. I was lost earlier when you found me.'

Geoff laughed. 'I can't imagine you ever being lost for anything,' he replied. 'Come on, I'll escort you.'

After a hot shower, Beth dressed carefully. Since she was only wearing her red dress that Simon had bought her in Rome and a pair of sandals, it didn't take her very long. The dress was so skimpy that she couldn't resist the temptation not to wear anything under it. She would have to be very careful how she moved or she would expose a lot more than just a bare thigh.

She practised parading around the room and soon discovered that if she took small steps, she could just about get away with it. She lengthened her stride and was rewarded with a perfect view of her newly shaven mound in the mirror. She would certainly have to save the longer strides for special moments!

By eight thirty, Beth was moving slowly down the wide staircase. She was well aware of how striking she looked and not surprised to see heads turning to watch her descend. The red of the dress was perfect for her dark colouring and the cut looked like it had been made especially for her. It clung in all the right places, then fell gracefully to the floor, emphasising her figure and poise. The material was so thin and light, it felt as if she wasn't wearing anything. It was a wonderful choice. At least Simon wasn't completely useless!

She had been so shaken by Geoff's business proposition that she had completely forgotten about Daniel and the maid until she spotted some maids serving drinks. Suddenly, it all came flooding back and, between the erotic images in her mind and the soft caress of the sexy dress on her naked body, she found that she was feeling incredibly aroused. She watched the maids closely, wondering if Daniel's friend would dare to appear among them.

Beth jumped as Simon appeared beside her out of nowhere and took her by the arm. As he steered her towards a quiet corner, Beth managed to grab a glass of champagne from a passing tray. She took a big gulp to steady her nerves and felt the bubbles stinging the inside of her nose.

'Where the hell have you been?' Simon hissed as soon as they were out of hearing. 'I've been looking for you for hours.'

'I was with Geoff Stevens.' Beth took another sip of her drink.

Simon looked surprised, then pleased. 'And?'

'I . . .' Beth paused for effect and took another sip. She realised that Simon was hanging on to her every word and growing more agitated by the second. She suppressed the urge to giggle and gulped hard. 'I, I, let him be nice to me,' she confessed breathlessly.

Simon's eyes widened. 'What did he do?' He was obviously fascinated by the idea of Beth obeying his instructions. She could almost see the feeling of power it gave him.

'I can't talk about it.' She gave him a pleading look.

Simon leered crudely. Before she could react, he stepped even closer, pushed his hand inside the slit of her dress and started to stroke her mound. Beth gasped with surprise and shock.

Her first instinct was to slap his face. She hated the thought of making a scene. Her treacherous body writhed with delight at his knowing touch; she was already so keyed up that it was enough to send her wild. She took a deep breath and prayed no one was watching. The look on her face and the way her body was squirming helplessly would have been a clear indication of what was going on.

Simon's quickened his caress and the breath whooshed from her before she could stop it. She could sense her orgasm building urgently and wasn't sure whether to try and stop him before it was too late or let him finish her. As a small whimper burst from her swollen lips, a loud gong sounded, making them both jump.

'Ladies and gentlemen, dinner is served.'

Simon slowly and reluctantly slipped his fingers out from her dress. Beth swayed slightly, her knees buckling with the intensity of her need. Simon held her arm to steady her.

'You know what I like about you most, Beth?'

She shook her head, not trusting herself to speak.

'I like the expression on your face when I take you. The way you submit to my will. I want you bent over my desk, waiting for me at the office on Monday morning.'

With supreme effort, Beth found a little spark of resistance. 'I can't. It's the wrong time,' she informed him.

726

Simon shrugged. 'Nevertheless. I want you without any knickers. After you have shown me what you've got, we'll find a good use for those hot lips of yours.'

Beth put on her most submissive face and nodded silently. She bit her lips and blinked as if trying to hold back the tears. Simon grinned.

'Excuse me.' As Simon moved across the room to join his wife, Beth felt another shiver of lust tear through her body.

Much as she loathed Simon, she couldn't resist the opportunity to torment him. Jesus, how she loved to tease men that way, provoking them until they didn't know whether to beg her to stop or beg her not to! She remembered how she had played with Daniel and the way his body had shuddered and writhed at her touch. Monday morning promised to be very interesting. By the time Beth was through with him, Simon would be so desperate for release that he would be forced to push her away and wank himself.

As she followed Simon and his wife, Beth took another deep breath. She realised that she was dreading dinner. If she didn't find a way to calm herself down, she was going to have trouble sitting still. She started to wonder if it were possible to bring herself off by squeezing her thighs together under the table without anyone noticing. The thought made her even more excited.

As she walked into the dining-room, she spotted John. To her astonishment, he was dressed in a kilt and sporran. She stared at him in amazement, realising that she had never thought about the significance of his slight Scottish accent before. She had to admit that he looked fantastic.

John's eyes lit up when her saw her. He walked confidently over to her. 'It seems I get the pleasure of your company again for dinner,' he told her.

Memories of their last meal together rushed into her mind. She forced a smile. 'How so?'

'I'm seated right next to you.'

Beth remembered how he had arranged the seating at the restaurant. 'How did I manage to be so lucky?' she questioned.

'Oh, just fate,' he smiled. 'Besides, I happened to nip in earlier and rearrange the seating cards.' He grinned. 'Hell, you didn't want to sit next to that prick Simon, did you?'

Beth laughed, loving the sheer audacity of the man. 'Well done, John.' She reached out and pulled him closer. 'I've still got those photocopies,' she whispered impishly.

John shrugged. 'And I've still got your knickers,' he replied quickly. 'I even wore them to work one day.'

'Only once?' Beth shammed disappointment.

John nodded. 'The trouble was that all I could think about all day was you. I had such a hard on they couldn't contain me. Most uncomfortable.' He grimaced. 'Shall we sit down?'

Beth laughed as he guided her over to the huge table. She was surprised and pleased by his confession. The thought of what he must have looked like in her panties with everything poking out was both amusing and thrilling.

John held her chair as she sat down cautiously and carefully arranged her dress over her legs. As he sat down beside her, he shifted his own chair closer to her and casually moved his place setting across.

Beth glanced around curiously at the other diners. She couldn't help noticing that, although attractive, many of the other women looked overdressed with their jewellery, frills and complicated hairstyles. She saw several men examining her appreciatively and felt even more pleased with her own simple dress and loose hair. She knew that she looked stunning.

As their wine glasses were filled and the first course served, Beth turned towards John. 'So, how have things been for you since York?' she asked him politely.

'Very quiet,' he responded. 'The excitement went out of my life after you left.' As he spoke, she felt him put his hand under the table on to her thigh. 'Still, I'm hoping that will soon change for the better.'

His fingertips began to trace small circles on her leg and Beth felt the goosebumps rising over her body at his soft touch. One of the waiters came over to serve the soup and she sighed with disappointment as John moved his hand away.

Beth looked up to thank the waiter, then froze when she realised that it was Daniel's friend, this time playing a more masculine role. She wondered what he would do if he realised that she knew his secret. Would he dress as a maid for her, if she asked him? Doing her best to ignore her urgent arousal, she forced herself to concentrate on what John was saying. The last thing she needed at the moment was to let herself become even hornier than she already was.

As soon as the waiter moved away, John put his hand back on to her leg. She felt him slip his fingers underneath the slit of her dress. He began to softly stroke her bare flesh, his fingers gradually moving higher. She gritted her teeth and hoped he could not see the effort it was costing her to keep still. Did he have any idea how much she longed for him to put his hand between her legs and caress her already throbbing bud?

She almost groaned with frustration as he moved his hand away and resumed eating his soup. She glanced at him surreptitiously, trying to assess how excited he was, but his face gave nothing away. Damn his self-control. This thought reminded her of her hotel lover and it was on the tip of her tongue to ask him outright if it was him. What if he denied it? How he would revel in her admission of an unknown man possessing her so completely! She couldn't risk it.

As she finished her soup, it occurred to her that she had the ideal opportunity to discover for herself the truth about what Scotsmen wear under their kilts. She quickly dropped her hand under the table and placed it on John's knee.

Although his face showed no obvious reaction, she noticed with delight the way his muscles were stiffening as her fingers travelled slowly up his leg. As she moved higher and higher, his hand started to tremble and his breathing quickened. Resisting the urge to go all the way, Beth changed direction and began sliding her fingers back down towards his knee.

She felt him relax slightly and watched him lift his spoon to take another mouthful of soup. Quickly, she slipped her hand back up and grinned as half the soup slurped messily into his bowl. John grabbed his napkin and wiped his mouth. His hands were trembling again.

'Wonderful soup,' she commented conversationally as he tried to take another mouthful. Her hand moved even higher and he quickly put his spoon down. 'Or don't you like it?'

'I like it very much,' he assured her tightly as he carefully took a smaller amount and raised it to his lips. 'I'm just taking my time, so that I can savour every second.'

By the time he had managed to finish the last mouthful, his face was quite flushed. As the waiters began clearing away, he placed the spoon carefully back in the bowl and turned his head towards her. 'Touché.' He smiled.

Beth saw beads of sweat on his forehead as he ran his finger round his collar. 'It is rather warm in here, isn't it,' she commented wickedly.

Before he could reply, she turned round to respond to a question that the elderly gentleman on the other side of her had just asked about where she worked. She shifted her chair around slightly so that she could talk to him, at the same time managing to move it even closer to John. The waiters began serving the next course.

When she turned back, she felt the warmth of John's knee next to hers. Although the food was excellent, she ate without noticing what she was putting in her mouth. John's thigh continued to burn her and, finally, she could no longer resist the temptation to continue her exploration. As she began to run her fingers slowly up his leg, she found herself hoping that he was wearing something so that she could take it off. Her fingers drew closer and closer to his cock and John swallowed loudly and reached for his wine.

Beth grinned at the pained expression on his face as he chewed each mouthful of food slowly and washed it down with the wine. She slid her hand between his legs and jumped as she discovered his nakedness. John shifted his buttocks, trying to move her fingers closer to his penis. She pulled away teasingly and turned back to resume her conversation with the man on the other side of her.

John finished his food and leant across her to join in. He placed his arm casually on the back of her chair and turned round so that his thigh was pushed firmly against her buttocks. Suddenly, his hand dived under her dress, homing straight in on her swollen bud. She gasped with shock and quickly covered her mouth with her hand.

'Oh, excuse me,' she apologised to the elderly man. She felt John push the flap of her dress over her leg until she was completely exposed. She could only pray no one would drop anything and bend down under the table to look for it.

'It's probably the garlic,' the man told her. 'It always gets to me, too.' As he launched himself into a long and rambling diatribe about his digestive system, Beth gritted her teeth and tried to cross her legs to stop John from overexciting her.

She felt him shift his hand so that he was stroking her thigh and buttocks. Every now and then, he pushed his fingers higher and caressed her clit from underneath. She realised that perspiration was running down between her breasts with the effort of maintaining a straight face. She didn't dare let him push her over the edge. She knew that she would cry out and then everyone would know.

As another course was being served, she managed to

sit back straight in her chair but could not stop John from sliding his hand between her thighs again. She clamped them together as hard as she could so that his fingers could barely move, but the pressure was almost as exciting and dangerous as his caresses. She was almost swooning with the effort of controlling herself by the time the final dishes were cleared away and the men began to light cigars and call for brandy.

'I need some fresh air,' she whispered huskily. 'Would you like to take that walk now?'

John raised his eyebrow and, to her relief, finally pulled his hand away. 'I was rather hoping for something a little more strenuous than a walk,' he replied.

Beth carefully rearranged her dress before she stood up, swaying slightly on legs too shaky to work properly. John grabbed her arm to steady her as he escorted her round the furniture towards the french windows on the far side of the room.

Beth looked round at the other guests and noticed several flushed faces and hungry looks. She wondered if she and John were the only ones playing games under the table. Simon looked as if he had had too much to drink. He was talking to Geoff and had pulled Marie's chair out from the table so that he could put his hand on her knee.

Marie looked slightly embarrassed as her husband pushed her skirt upwards, revealing more of her leg. Geoff had an amused expression on his face and Beth was sure that he knew what Simon was offering him and was enjoying the view. She realised that it wouldn't take much to turn the party into an out-and-out orgy.

John steered her out the door and she breathed in deeply to help calm herself down. The air was thick with the scent of honeysuckle and there was a slight dampness as if it had been raining. Beth realised that the gardeners must have been watering not long ago. She wondered if they used automatic sprinklers and thought how pleasant it would be to strip off and run naked through the icy spray.

Without saying anything, John continued to guide her purposefully along various twisting paths and Beth had the feeling that he was leading her to some quiet, secluded spot he had already scouted out. His arm slipped down her back until it was resting on her bottom, squeezing it gently in time with his steps. She placed her own hand on his buttocks and considered flipping up his kilt the way the boys at school used to flip up the girls' skirts.

They turned another corner and Beth saw that they had arrived at a secluded alcove with tall hedges all around and a wooden bench in the centre. John tried to lead her over to the bench but Beth stopped short and pulled him round in front of her, then manoeuvred him until he was standing behind the bench.

As soon as she placed his hand on the back of the bench John seemed to understand her intention. As she pushed him gently between the shoulders, he obediently bent over. Beth stood behind him and took hold of the hem of his kilt. Slowly she raised it, gradually revealing the top of his thighs and the curve of his bum. She tucked the hem into the waistband and stooped down to examine him critically.

'Very nice.' She ran her hands down the outside of his thighs then pulled his legs back, forcing him to bend even lower. She slid her hands over his buttocks, smiling as he tensed his muscles. She moved down to his inner thighs and pushed them apart until she could see his balls dangling under him. She crouched even lower and shuddered at the sight of his enormous erection thrust out hungrily in the air. She pushed her hand under him, palm upwards, and wrapped her fingers round it.

John shivered and moved his legs wider apart to give her better access. Beth let go of him and stepped away. 'I didn't tell you to move,' she scolded as she lifted her arm and slapped his left buttock. It made a beautiful sound but she wasn't sure if his bottom stung as much as her own hand. She flexed her fingers and slapped the other cheek.

'Forgive me, Mistress Beth. I won't let it happen again.' Although she could hear the amusement in his voice, she thought she also detected a note of desperation and longing. It sent a rush of desire coursing through her.

Beth grabbed him roughly by the ear. She pulled him round to face her, then tugged him slowly downward until he was kneeling on the ground in front of her. Her eyes lingered over his hardness and she licked her lips as she pushed his knees apart with her foot.

God, he looked fabulous. She ran her eyes up his strong, muscular legs, noticing the way the dark hair gradually grew thicker around his crotch. His cock stuck out like a pole; hard and swollen with its single-minded desire to pleasure her body.

Beth stood in front of him with her legs slightly apart. She lifted the flap of her dress with one hand and then pulled his head towards her. John immediately put his hands on her legs and gently kissed her inner thighs. She thrust her hips forward and mewed softly as his tongue found her engorged sex. As his hands moved round her waist and began to slide up towards her breasts, she grabbed them roughly and pulled them back on to her bottom, forcing him to pull her harder on to his tongue.

John pulled her legs further apart so that his tongue could push right up inside her. Beth whimpered louder and lifted one leg over his shoulder. She dug her heel into his back to steady herself and moaned again as he thrust his tongue even deeper inside her. As she swayed, John put one hand on the small of her back to hold her. His other hand was already fondling her bottom, his fingers gradually parting her cheeks.

Beth jumped then gasped with surprise and pleasure as his fingers eased into her crack and his fingertip began to push gently on her anus. His tongue continued to slip in and out of her, moving faster and faster as he felt her responding. It was all she could do now to keep her balance. If John had not been holding her so tightly, her legs would have collapsed completely.

She started to pant desperately as his tongue relentlessly devoured her. She could sense her orgasm swelling up inside her, like a rain cloud ready to burst. Her vaginal muscles flexed violently, pushing against his unrelenting caresses. She felt him automatically thrust even deeper inside her and she shuddered and cried out as a powerful climax overwhelmed her.

Breathing hard, Beth finally untangled her leg and stepped back. John started to get up.

'I didn't tell you to move, did I?' Beth stopped him with her hand. 'I haven't finished with you yet.' She was so weak from pleasure that she wasn't quite sure what to do with him next. She stared down at him, noticing that his kilt has fallen over his groin again.

'I didn't tell you to cover yourself, either,' she complained as she took hold of his ear again and forced him down on to all fours. With her foot, she pushed his head down until it was almost resting on the ground.

'Now, pull your kilt up slowly,' she commanded as she moved round behind him to watch. Her breathing had slowed and the strength was already flowing back into her limbs. The sight of his kilt gradually rising up over his rump, revealing all, sent a little tremor of renewed desire rushing through her. She crouched down and stroked the soft skin behind his balls.

'Oh, Jesus!' John groaned with desperation and raised his buttocks into the air so that the base of his cock was completely exposed to her. It didn't seem possible that he could be so big.

'Stand up and turn around,' she whispered.

He obeyed her instantly, his whole body trembling as he stood in front of her. Beth took his hands and placed them on the hem of his kilt. She gestured upward with her hands and then held her breath as he lifted the material up to his shoulders, revealing all. She was consumed with an almost overwhelming urge to watch him pleasure himself.

'Strip,' she commanded urgently.

She watched breathlessly as he obeyed her. Naked, he stood in front of her with a slight smile on his face, making no attempt to cover himself. Beth shivered in anticipation.

'Take yourself in one hand. That's it. No, don't move your fingers. Good.' The sight of him holding his bursting cock between his fingers was so exciting Beth could barely contain herself. She slipped the straps of her dress off her shoulders and down her arms, wriggling her hips so that the whole garment slid slowly down her body.

John stared at her eagerly as his hand glided slowly up and down his shaft. Beth frowned and shook her head. He immediately stopped and gripped himself tighter, squeezing himself urgently. She saw his knuckles flexing slightly as he tried to tighten and loosen his grip without her noticing. His whole body was trembling with his passion.

'Don't tell me you need to pee?' she teased, grinning at the way his eyes silently acknowledged her revenge. His hand stopped moving.

Beth stepped out of her dress. Naked apart from her sandals, she walked slowly round him a couple of times, trying not to smile at his unblinking eyes or the way he twisted his head to follow her. He reminded her of an owl. She noticed the way his fingers were gently squeezing his cock again as he slid his hand up and down as slowly as he could.

'Eyes front,' she snapped like a drill sergeant. She whacked his buttocks with the flat of her hand. 'And keep your hand still.'

John spun his head round and did his best to stand to attention. His penis was doing a better job of it. Beth couldn't remember ever seeing anyone so big and stiff.

'Now, lie down on your back,' she told him.

As John lowered himself to the ground, she was delighted to see that he continued gripping himself. She stood over his head with one leg on either side and then crouched down, lowering herself on to his mouth. John obligingly opened his lips and started licking her thighs and mound.

Beth sighed and leant forward to rest her hands on his stomach. She used one hand to push his fingers away and then began to examine his penis inch by inch with her fingertips. She heard him suck in a deep, shuddering breath and then felt his tongue prising her sex lips apart. As he pushed it up into her, she tightened her fist around him and felt his hips lift as he pushed himself urgently upward.

Beth let go of him and deliberately moved his own hand on to his penis. John sighed with disappointment and stopped tonguing her.

'You do it,' she commanded him.

As he began to pump himself, his tongue slipped into her again. She whimpered with longing and pushed down against him, so that her breasts were hard against his chest. She watched, fascinated, as his hand started to move harder and faster.

John moaned and pushed his hips up into the air, his whole body shuddering. She could see the tip of his penis glistening and feel the urgency of his tongue as his climax approached. He was groaning uncontrollably now and writhing helplessly from side to side. His hand was moving up and down almost too quickly to see.

'Christ, Beth. I can't hold on. Don't you realise what you're doing to me? Oh Jesus!'

Beth lifted herself up and pulled away. She was not quick enough. With another frantic grunt, John exploded. His come shot out of him like a firehose, shooting up into the air and splattering over his stomach. A few drops sprayed across her left breast.

Gradually, his hand slowed and stopped. He lay back, panting, with his eyes closed. Beth knelt down beside him and pushed her knee against his chest. John opened his eyes and smiled up at her. She pouted and pointed at the small white patch of come on her breast.

John stared at her for a moment, his face puzzled. Beth frowned and pushed her chest closer to him. Slowly and reluctantly, John raised his head and started to lick her breast clean. Beth sat perfectly still, savouring the soft caress of his tongue. Finally, she stood up and picked up her dress. As she wiggled back into it, she smiled and nodded her satisfaction.

'Very good. I shan't need you again tonight.'

She walked away quickly without looking back. By the time she reached her room, she was having trouble keeping her eyes open. She was asleep almost before her head touched the pillow.

The following morning at breakfast, Simon announced his decision to leave early. Beth smiled to herself at his sour face, knowing that the weekend had proved a big disappointment to him. He was in such a hurry to leave that she barely had time to say goodbye to Geoff. She did not see John at all.

On their way home, she did her best to draw Simon and Marie into conversation, trying desperately to get one of them to say something that would give her a clue to Simon's password. When they dropped her off outside her house, however, she was still none the wiser.

After a lazy afternoon and evening in front of the television, Beth went to bed early. Her sleep was restless and filled with confused and erotic dreams of John, Daniel and Chris. At three thirty, she woke with a start and sat up straight, her heart pounding. Had Simon's son inadvertently given her the information she needed?

Beth was so excited that it took her a long time to get to sleep again. She awoke early and was in the office an hour before Simon was due to arrive. As she sat at the keyboard, her fingers were shaking so much that she could barely find the right keys.

'M, I, D, A, S.' She mouthed the letters as she typed. She almost shouted with joy when she was rewarded with a small beep and the message 'PASSWORD ACCEPTED' flashed on to the screen. Yes!

As soon as the file opened, Beth knew her guess had been correct. It was Simon's private little slush fund. Wouldn't the tax office like to have a look at this little lot?

Beth quickly closed the file again. Well, that was it. All the pieces were in place. She simply had to make a copy of the file so that Simon wouldn't see any evidence of her tampering, punch in the transaction and wait. She started to open the morning mail. Would Geoff keep his promise to get Simon out of the way on Friday? Would she have the guts to go through with it?

As soon as he arrived, Simon hurried across the office and stood in her doorway.

'Well, well,' he said. 'Caught you.'

Beth froze in panic. Oh God! He had guessed what she was doing. She opened her mouth to try to defend herself, then stopped. He couldn't see her computer screen from where he was standing. Of course. She was supposed to be ready and waiting for him without any knickers on. In her excitement, she had completely forgotten about that. She looked back up at him.

Simon frowned and pointed over his shoulder. Beth walked through the door into his office. Simon pushed her over to his desk. Before she could say a word, he pushed her down over it, whipped her dress up and ripped her panties off.

Roughly, he reached round and pulled the front of her dress apart, then pushed her bra up. Cupping her breasts in his hands, he started to kiss the nape of her neck. As he reached down to release his trousers, she could feel his erection pushing firmly into the crack of her buttocks. She gasped with pleasure and then sighed as she remembered she had told him it was the wrong time of the month. Jesus! Was he going to take her in the bottom instead? She felt a thrill of excitement and clenched her buttocks around his erection as he pushed against her.

Suddenly, he stepped away and spun her round to face him. He put his hands on her shoulders and pushed her down on to her knees. As he grabbed the back of her head with one hand, he took his hard cock in the other.

Before she could do or say anything, Simon shoved his cock into her mouth. Using both hands to pull her head harder on to him, he thrust himself right to the back of her mouth and began to push her head back and forth, pumping himself.

Beth swallowed hard and tightened her lips around him. He thrust once more and then climaxed abruptly. She heard him groan with ecstasy and felt him spurt powerfully into her. As soon as he was completely spent, he pulled back and looked down at her.

'Now dress me,' he demanded.

Beth took a shuddering breath and swallowed. He must have been thinking about her all the way to work to have been in that much of a hurry. She reached up and took his now flaccid penis in her fingers. She pushed it gently back into his pants and pulled up his trousers, then stood up and looked down at her gaping dress and lowered panties.

As Beth bent down to pull them up, Simon grabbed her hand and shook his head. Beth tried to look submissive and kicked her panties off. He raised his eyes and stared meaningfully at her breasts. Slowly, she pulled her arms out of her dress and undid her bra.

Her clothes fell in a heap on the floor. Beth stepped over them and stood, naked and shivering, with her arms crossed over her chest and her head hanging down like a young virgin slave girl. She began to fantasise that she was being displayed for sale at a slave market and that Simon was a prospective customer. The urgency of her growing passion blazed deep within her.

Simon stared at her without comment. Beth let her hands drop to her sides and looked up at him hopefully.

'What appointments do I have today?' he questioned.

'Um?' The question took her by surprise. Disappointment rushed through her at the realisation that he wasn't planning anything more. 'Just Mrs Brown at eleven o'clock, I think.' She picked up her dress and slipped it back on.

'When she comes in, I want you hidden under the desk sucking my dick,' he informed her.

Beth stared at him and then shook her head.

Simon turned her round and lifted her dress. She jumped at the sudden sting of his hand on her naked skin. He slapped her again, then again.

'All right,' she said quickly. By the time she was finished with him, this would be one idea he was definitely going to regret.

The following Friday, Simon disappeared from the office soon after arriving. He had a conceited, confident look on his face and Beth wondered exactly what Geoff had offered him by way of incentive. Whatever it was, she had a feeling that he was about to be disappointed again.

As soon as he was gone, she copied his private file on to a separate disk and then called her stockbroker and purchased as many shares in Torrins as she could get hold of. She set the amount the shares were to be sold at just prior to close of market for the weekend, then watched anxiously. To her relief, after an early fall, the shares began to rise steadily around midday.

All she could do now was wait and pray. It was likely to be a very long weekend.

Chapter Thirteen

Beth arrived at the office very early. She quickly logged on to the computer and typed the password. Simon wasn't an early riser on Mondays. Beth could only pray that today would not be the exception.

As soon as the data appeared, she scanned the account anxiously. The figures took a few seconds to sink in, then her face split into a broad grin. It had worked! Swiftly, Beth transferred Simon's money back to where it belonged and diverted the gains to her own, newly opened private account.

Her heart was in her mouth as she watched the screen flickering. She was terrified that Simon would walk in at any moment and catch her. She raced over to the safe and took out the backup disk she had made, then hurried back to the computer.

Finally the message she was waiting for, 'TRANSACTION COMPLETE', came up. Beth quickly closed the account and loaded the backup disk. If anything, this seemed to take even longer. Beth glanced at her watch. Eight fifty. Simon could come through the door any second. She looked up at the screen. Eighty per cent complete. Jesus! The last ten per cent had taken longer than the previous seventy. She watched the figure move to ninety per cent, then ninety-eight. It hung there, without changing. Oh God, hurry!

As the words 'BACKUP RESTORED – DO YOU WISH TO REBOOT?' flashed on to the screen, Beth sighed with relief and slammed her finger on to the return key. The computer started to shut down. Still shaking, she pushed the eject button and made a grab for the backup disk. Her fingers slipped and the disk shot across the room.

Beth cursed aloud as she raced across the room to retrieve it. She pushed it back into its box and moved towards the safe. By the time she had slammed and locked the safe door and returned the key to Simon's desk, the computer had finished rebooting. Trembling from head to foot, she logged on.

She needed a drink. She couldn't stop shaking. Beth took a couple of deep breaths to try to steady herself, then hurried into Simon's office again. Without bothering to find a glass, she grabbed a bottle of scotch from his private supply and took a large swig. The fiery liquid made her gasp. She forced herself to swallow it and took another mouthful. Gradually, she felt her pulse steady. She put the bottle back in the cabinet and returned to her desk to make a start on opening the mail.

She had done it! There was now a very large amount of money safely stashed away in her off-shore account. She didn't need this job and didn't need to take the job with Geoff. She certainly wouldn't need anything from her ex-husband anymore, either. She was free!

Coffee. Shit! She had forgotten to make his morning coffee. Beth was just getting up when she heard Simon walk through the door. She waited, listening to him stomping around.

'Late in this morning, were you, Beth?' he called. Obviously, he had noticed the missing coffee. She heard him typing something at the computer. 'You really shouldn't take advantage of my good nature like this, you know,' he called.

Beth cringed. Had he discovered what she had done?

'I shall have to punish you.' Simon stuck his head round her door and examined her greedily. When she said nothing, he went towards her and grabbed her arm. Beth allowed herself to be led, unresisting, through to his desk.

Simon sat down and pulled her across his knee. He lifted her skirt and pulled her panties down slowly. She barely flinched as he slapped her buttocks, then rubbed her smooth skin gently.

'That will teach you to forget my coffee,' he told her. Beth sighed with relief. He didn't know. As he pushed her up on to her feet, she lifted her skirt and stared at her panties round her thighs.

'Put them back,' she commanded. 'You took them down.'

Simon smiled. As he pulled Beth's panties slowly back up over her still smarting rump, he leant forward and gently kissed her thighs and mound. Finally, he stopped and began to lower the panties again, his fingers gently caressing her legs.

'No.' Beth pulled away. It was time to set the final phase of his lesson in motion. 'Not here. Somewhere else. Somewhere with a bed. Somewhere where we won't be disturbed.' She moved closer. 'Somewhere where we can really let ourselves go.' She bent forward and deliberately stroked the bulge in his trousers.

'Your place,' Simon blurted out.

'No, somewhere else.' She smiled. 'I know a very discreet motel not far away. I could get us a room and then phone you.' She gave his bulge a gentle squeeze. 'While I wait, I could get ready for you. Dress up in something really sexy.' She could tell that Simon was going for it.

'I could pretend to be one of those women who visit lonely businessmen. No, better still, you could pretend to be one of those men who visit lonely businesswomen.' She gave his erection another squeeze.

'I'm very demanding, you know.' She pushed him

744

down into the chair, lifted her skirt and sat astride his legs with her hands still caressing him. 'I expect my men to pleasure me until I beg them to stop. I only take the best. You are the best, aren't you?' She ran her finger down his groin.

Simon shivered. 'Now. Let's go now.'

'Not yet. You've got a ten o'clock appointment. We'll go at lunch-time. I'll book us a room and then you can satisfy me all afternoon.' Beth pushed her tongue into his ear.

'You'd like that, wouldn't you?' she whispered. 'I've never been properly satisfied yet.' Beth stood up, stepped away and slowly pulled her panties back up.

'OK, we'll do it.' She almost laughed at the lust in his eyes.

'You'll be begging me to stop before I'm finished with you.' Simon grinned wolfishly.

Beth smiled. 'I do hope so,' she replied in a voice filled with anticipation.

Although the rest of the morning passed slowly for Beth, she consoled herself by imagining how much more slowly it must be passing for him. At one o'clock, she picked up her coat and went into his office.

'Don't forget to bring some cash with you to pay for the room.'

Simon nodded. 'Don't take too long to call,' he told her excitedly.

For once, Beth had used her car. She drove quickly to the motel. On the way, she stopped at a post box and, with a self-satisfied grin, posted her letter of resignation to Simon. Knowing how angry he would be, she had no desire to be there when he learnt she was deserting him. A surge of elation rushed through her as she allowed herself to think about her future prospects with her newly acquired wealth.

As soon as she had registered at the motel reception, she found her room and unpacked the small suitcase she had put in the car that morning. Then she took a quick shower. Wrapped in a bath towel, she sat on the bed and phoned Simon to tell him exactly where she was. He answered it on the first ring and she smiled at the enthusiasm in his voice.

Quickly, she finished drying herself and then dressed to kill. After she had pulled the boob tube down over her breasts, she stepped into lacy panties and wriggled into a PVC skirt. Finally, she pulled on fishnet stockings and stepped into a pair of heels much higher than she normally wore.

Beth moved over to the mirror and applied a heavy coat of lipstick, then emphasised her eyes with eyeliner, dark-grey shadow and black mascara. She stared at her reflection in delight. She spun round and examined herself critically from all angles. Heavily made up, she looked just like a prostitute. Her stockings only just reached the bottom of her skirt, the boob tube was virtually see-through and the outline of her nipples was quite clear. It was perfect for the role she intended playing.

She was brushing her hair when the knock came. She moved over to the door.

'Who is it?'

'Me. Simon.'

Beth opened the door wide. Simon walked in quickly and his eyes widened when he saw her.

'Well, hello.' Beth smiled. 'Have you come for me?' she enquired with a slight lift of one eyebrow.

'Any second now,' Simon responded as he scanned her from top to toe. His eyes lingered on her breasts and the tops of her stockings.

Beth let him look for a few seconds then pushed the door closed, allowing her body to rub against him. The door clicked shut and Simon grabbed her from behind. As he kissed her neck, she felt his hands running all over her body. She let him fondle her for a while longer, then broke the embrace.

'Did you bring the money?'

'Yeah. How much?'

'Fifty pounds should cover it,' Beth replied.

Simon took out his wallet and counted out two twenties and a ten. Beth took the money and put it on the table. She took his hand and guided him towards the bed. Simon tried to grab her again but she moved nimbly out the way.

'No. This is my treat. You don't need to do anything. Just allow me to pleasure you.'

His face broke into a huge grin.

'I'm all yours.'

Beth smiled and stepped closer. She removed his jacket and hung it over the back of the chair. Standing in front of him, she loosened his tie and undid the buttons of his shirt. She placed his hands on each of her breasts while she carefully removed his cufflinks, then she opened his shirt and started to kiss his chest. Slowly, she peeled the shirt off his shoulders and down his arms. Then she knelt in front of him on the floor and removed his shoes and socks.

Simon put his hands on her shoulders to steady himself and Beth reached up and undid the catch on his trousers. As she slowly unzipped his trousers with one hand, her other hand slipped inside behind the zip so that her fingertips were caressing his erection.

Simon shuddered and took a deep breath. He let it out slowly as his trousers dropped round his ankles and Beth removed her hand. She ran her fingers up the inside of his leg and gave his balls a gentle squeeze. Simon sighed urgently and Beth smiled again as she pushed him backward on to the bed.

Leaning over him with one leg either side of his, Beth ran her hands down his chest. As they passed over his lean stomach and on to his pants, she traced the outline of his penis with her finger. She was fascinated to see that he had grown even bigger, so that the tip of his erection was now sticking out of his pants.

Beth moved on down his legs and removed his

747

trousers from around his ankles. She folded them neatly before placing them with his other clothes. When she turned around, Simon had moved up on to the bed and was lying back, waiting for her.

Beth pulled her panties down under her skirt and kicked them aside. She walked across to the bed and ran her fingers up his right leg, enjoying the way his body stiffened at her touch. She climbed on to the bed and swung a leg over him so that she was sitting across his chest with her back to him. She shuffled back slightly and raised her buttocks so that her sex lips were just above his mouth. She saw his cock spasm as she placed her hands on his stomach and pushed her fingers under the elastic of his pants to lift them up over his erection.

Simon sighed heavily and raised himself up so that she could pull them down over his buttocks. Beth slipped her hands round under him, allowing her nails to scratch his cheeks as she slid his pants down. Simon collapsed back on the bed, almost trapping her fingers underneath him.

She heard him moan urgently as she played with his hardness. When she started to make small circling motions round the tip with her fingers, Simon groaned and reached up to pull her down on to his mouth.

'Come here, you witch,' he whispered. He forced her sex lips open and drove his tongue deep into her. His hand slid under her and his fingers expertly sought out her swollen bud.

Beth closed her eyes for a moment and allowed the waves of longing to build up then, before she lost control, she moved off him.

'I see you are not going to behave.' She pulled the piece of cord out from where she had hidden it under the pillow, then climbed up over him again so that she was facing him. She lowered herself on to his mouth and began to rock back and forth as he licked and sucked her.

When she could take no more, Beth reached out,

grabbed his arms and raised them over his head. Simon ignored her, his tongue still busy probing her. Beth whimpered with excitement and struggled to contain herself as she tied his wrists together and attached them to the longer cord she had already secured to the headboard.

She put one hand behind his head, grabbed a handful of his hair and tugged him harder on to her. With her other hand she gently teased her puckered nipples.

Simon forced his tongue deep inside her and started to flick it in and out. Beth gasped with delight and started to caress her throbbing clit. She was so close to climaxing that she barely stopped herself from yelling aloud. She increased the pressure of her own hand and pulled his head even harder against her so that his tongue was deep inside her. She moaned loudly as she felt her climax flooding through her. Gradually, she relaxed and her movements slowed to a gentle rock. She gulped noisily, let go of his hair and moved off him.

'Well. I certainly seem to have caught myself a wild one here, don't I?' she whispered shakily.

'You'd better believe it.' Simon's grin seemed to cover his whole face. He tried to move his hands and, for the first time, seemed to realise that he was tied up. He pulled against the restraint, testing the strength of the knot and the length of the cord. Beth smiled.

'Now I shall be able to play with you without fear of you grabbing me,' she told him.

Before he could reply, Beth leant over and licked his now only semi-erect penis. She continued to tease it gently until it began to grow again. She loved watching a man growing like that in response to her touch. When he was completely stiff again, she reached under the pillow for a condom.

As she unrolled it down his length, she continued to play with him, pushing him from side to side and stroking him under the balls. She felt him gradually become stiffer and stiffer until he was as rigid as a board and his penis would no longer bend in her fingers.

Simon groaned and twisted in his pleasure, raising himself up off the bed as he tried to thrust into her hand. Beth teased until she felt sure that he couldn't take much more, then quickly mounted him, lowering herself down over him as Simon tried to push up into her.

Firmly, Beth pressed him back down on to the mattress and continued to lower herself on to him until he was fully enveloped. She began to stroke his chest with one hand and reached behind her to caress his balls with the other.

Simon grunted and tried to thrust up into her again but Beth was using all her weight to hold him down. She leant forward and bit his nipples again. Simon jumped and, with a desperate lunge, arched his back so that she was almost thrown up into the air as he pushed himself upwards. As they fell back, his cock rammed up so far into her that Beth gasped with shock, then cried out as he did it again. Instinctively, she tightened her vaginal muscles around him, squeezing him.

Simon's whole body went rigid and Beth noticed a tiny nerve on the side of his jaw begin to twitch as he struggled to keep himself under control. As he arched his back to thrust into her again, Beth dug her nails into his chest.

'Keep still,' she commanded as she increased the rhythmic caresses of her inner muscles.

Simon moaned softly and began twisting from side to side. She watched the droplets of sweat beading on his face as he drew his knees up and used his legs to push his whole body up, lifting them both off the bed. Even though she wasn't all that heavy, Beth was impressed by this desperate show of strength. For a while she allowed him to enjoy his success, losing herself in the enjoyment of the deep penetration.

As his gasps became more urgent, Beth reached round

with both hands and cupped his balls, squeezing them harder and harder to get his attention.

'Stop that. Keep still,' she repeated.

'Christ. I can't.' Simon gasped again and started to climax violently. As his seed pumped from him, he fell back on to the bed, moaning with pleasure. Beth continued to squeeze him as if trying to force every last drop out of him.

Completely spent, Simon lay still and closed his eyes. Beth lifted herself clear, peeled the condom off and wrapped it in some tissues. While he was still recovering, she picked up another piece of cord and tied his ankles so that his legs could only open about eight inches.

Simon opened his eyes and lifted his head. 'What the hell?' he tried to sit up but could only partly raise himself because of the cords on his wrists. 'What do you think you're doing?'

Beth smiled. 'You need to be restrained,' she replied as she used a final piece of cord to secure his feet to the end of the bed. She was careful to leave him enough slack to move around but not enough to leave the bed.

'If you're not careful, I'll tie you down completely so that you can't move anything but this.' Beth flicked his limp penis from side to side. 'Now, lie there and be a good boy while I go and freshen up.' She gave him another little stroke under the balls.

'I hope you're feeling fit,' she told him. 'You've got a lot more to do yet.' Beth stood beside him and, realising that her skirt was still right up over her bottom, pulled it down to cover her nakedness. Simon looked disappointed.

'Don't cover yourself. I like looking at your shaved snatch.'

Beth knelt on the bed beside him and lifted the front hem of her skirt to expose her mound. She opened her legs as far as her skirt would allow, then licked her finger and pushed it between her thighs. Simon's eyes bulged as she played with her clitoris. Using all the freedom

751

Beth had allowed him, Simon wriggled closer and put his head between her legs.

'So. You like me shaved, do you?' she questioned.

'Yeah!' Simon licked his lips.

As Beth continued to caress herself, she glanced round and was pleased to see that he was already partially erect again. She smiled and stood up.

'No. Don't stop. I want to watch you come.' Simon strained against the cords. 'I want –'

'I want,' Beth interrupted, mimicking him. 'What you want doesn't matter. It's what I want that counts now.' She put her damp finger to his mouth. 'Lick it,' she commanded.

Simon pulled her finger into his mouth and started to suck greedily. She looked down and saw his cock stiffen further. She smiled and pulled her hand back.

'Don't go away,' she told him as she headed for the bathroom, adjusting her skirt as she walked.

When she returned, she was carrying a bowl of warm water, a bar of soap and a towel. She placed the towel under him and started to wash his genitals thoroughly. At first, Simon thrashed about, trying to get free but, gradually, as she caressed his penis with soapy fingers, he stopped protesting and lay back contentedly.

Beth pushed a pillow under his buttocks so that she would be able to reach right under him, then sat across him so that his tongue could satisfy her again. She quickly worked up a rich lather and was delighted by the ease with which her fingers slipped up and down his soapy cock.

She sighed with anticipation as he started to probe deeper and deeper into her. King Midas certainly did have a golden tongue. She was sorely tempted to let him bring her off again, but reminded herself how draining multiple orgasms could be. She still had a lot to do. Reluctantly moving off him, she used a flannel to remove the soap from his penis and then began to pat him dry with the towel.

His cock was already rigid again and she pictured him standing in the shower, covered with soap, masturbating while she watched. It was very tempting but she couldn't afford to untie him. Not yet.

When he was as dry as she could get him, Beth stood up and dried her hands while she admired her efforts. His pubic hair was soft and fluffy, surrounding his rigid cock like a halo. It was a pity, but . . .

Beth returned the bowl to the bathroom and picked up the scissors. By the time she returned, Simon had closed his eyes again and was lying there with a self-satisfied smile on his lips. She sat over him with her back to him and took his cock in her left hand.

Simon strained forward. 'I can't reach you,' he complained, eyes still shut. Beth ignored him. Although his tongue was very tempting, under the circumstances she felt it was probably safer if he couldn't touch her. She raised the scissors and proceeded to snip his pubic hair away.

'Hey! What the hell do you think you're doing?' Simon struggled to sit up and tugged angrily at the wrist cords. Beth continued to ignore him as she carefully cut his pubes and dropped the bits on to the towel. Simon started to thrash his hips about. Beth stopped.

'Careful,' she laughed. 'You might make me cut the wrong thing.' She ran a finger up his rapidly shrinking prick. 'That would certainly ruin the rest of my afternoon.' She took another snip.

'Stop it, you bitch. Let me go. Bloody whore.'

'Bitch?' Beth questioned. 'Whore?' She pushed herself hard on to his face. 'I didn't notice you complaining earlier. Go on, lick me.'

Simon twisted his head angrily to one side and tugged furiously on the cords again. 'Let me go, damn you.'

Beth curled her fingers into his now short pubes and tugged hard. Simon grunted in shock and pain. 'Lick me.' She gave another tug, then moaned as he pushed his tongue deep inside her. 'That's much better,' she

753

sighed. She squeezed his cock gently between her fingers and felt it twitch.

She moved off him again and examined his remaining hairs carefully, using the scissors to snip away the remaining strands on and around his balls. Simon watched in silence, holding his breath whenever the scissors touched his skin. His penis seemed to get smaller with every snip and she had to stretch it tightly in her hand so that she did not snip the skin.

As she gave the area a final inspection, she saw he was staring down at himself in horror. She heard him whimper softly and couldn't help laughing.

'Don't worry. I haven't finished yet. It will look much better after it's been shaved.' Simon whimpered again and Beth giggled. 'What a fuss over a little haircut. You men are so pathetic. It will grow back again.'

'When?' Simon whispered miserably.

'Oh, a few months.'

Simon gulped. Still laughing, Beth threw the clippings into the bin and went back into the bathroom to fetch another bowl of water, shaving cream and a razor. When Simon saw the razor, his face went white.

'Please don't, Beth. What am I going to tell Marie?'

'It's a bit late to worry about that now. You don't want me to leave it like that, do you?' She ran her hand over the stubble. 'You can always tell her that your barber got a bit carried away.' She knew it wasn't funny, but Simon was too busy staring in terror at the razor to notice.

When she placed the blade on his chest, Simon tensed as if it were a poisonous snake. Beth soaked his tackle again and began to cover it in shaving cream. She shivered at the way the cream spurted out of the can like a shower of spunk, and she rather overdid it in her excitement. When she realised what she had done, she scooped the excess off with her fingers and rubbed it into his tummy. She couldn't resist pumping him a few times with her slippery hands as well, enjoying the feel of it, even if he was too nervous to respond.

As Beth wiped her hands on the towel and then picked up the razor, Simon finally found his voice again.

'Please, Beth. I'll do it while you watch.'

Beth hesitated, almost tempted. She really didn't want to untie him. She shook her head and took hold of his prick to pull it tight. Her fingers slipped and Simon let out a terrified yelp. She wiped the tip of his cock with the towel and took hold of it again. Gently, she pulled him out to full length and began to shave the sides.

As she moved down, she pulled the skin of his balls tighter and ran the sharp blade over them, slicing the stubble away. Giving it her full concentration, Beth moved around him carefully, climbing on and off him to get into the best position. Simon barely seemed to breathe. Every time the blade touched him, his muscles tensed and his whole body went rigid.

When she had finished the crotch, Beth moved down and shaved under his balls, then moved up to do the base of his stomach. By this time, she was feeling so confident that she carefully shaped the hair at the base of his shaft into a heart. She put the blade down and washed the foam away, smiling with delight. Well, it almost looked like a heart if she squinted her eyes.

She dried her hands and ran her fingers over his hairless balls. She could hardly believe how smooth the skin felt. It was as soft as satin.

'Jesus Christ!' Simon took a long, shuddering breath. Beth grinned and ran her hand up his cock. He obviously hadn't suffered all that much. She could already feel him hardening again in response to her caresses.

She gathered up the shaving things and took them back in the bathroom. After she had rinsed them, she put them in her case and then stood at the end of the bed and stared down at him in silence.

It was quite a shock to see his cock and balls as naked as her own mound. His cock was so exposed; it seemed even bigger than ever. She shivered. It looked so rude, so sexy. No wonder men liked women to shave.

Beth moved round beside him. She took hold of his cock and pumped him until he was fully erect. As she put her other hand down between his legs and caressed the soft flesh of his balls again, another shiver of desire rushed through her. Simon lifted his head and stared at himself in silence. He seemed even more fascinated by his nakedness than she was.

'Now, how shall I pleasure myself next? Perhaps a hand job?' Beth pumped him harder and heard his sharp intake of breath as his cock twitched against her. 'Maybe I should suck it dry?' She bent over him and licked the tip with her tongue. Simon sighed and lifted his buttocks up eagerly.

There was a heavy knock at the door and Beth froze.

'Who the hell is that?' Simon hissed. 'Quick. Untie me.'

Beth stood up and pulled her coat around her shoulders. Before she could walk across the room, the outer door opened and someone entered the little passageway. A woman came into view and she heard Simon gasp in horror at the police uniform. Beth put her hand to her mouth in mock horror and dropped her coat as the policewoman stood in front of her.

The policewoman scanned the room quickly and her eyes widened. 'I see.' She bent down, picked up the coat and placed it round Beth's shoulders. Then she turned towards Simon, her face expressionless.

'It's not what you think,' Simon blurted out. 'She's my personal assistant. She works for me.'

'Yes, sir. I know. By the hour, I expect.' The policewoman moved over to the table and picked up the money that Simon had brought earlier. She counted it out slowly. 'Fifty pounds. Not bad for a hour's work.'

Beth opened her mouth as if to argue, but the policewoman waved her quiet. 'Don't bother. I've heard it all before. Your husband makes you do it. You've three children to feed and clothe. Your rent is due and you are going to be thrown out into the streets.' She glared at Beth.

'I really don't care why you do it.' The policewoman

moved closer to Beth and leant forward to run her hand up Beth's leg under her skirt. Beth and Simon both gasped.

'I suppose you always wear a short skirt and no knickers when you and your boss are working?' The policewoman grinned. 'Don't worry. I'm not going to run you in. It's not worth all the paperwork. The motel just wants me to make sure you don't come here again.'

She removed her hand from under Beth's skirt and gave her left breast a quick squeeze. 'I should have thought you could have done better than this, an attractive woman like you.' She put her hand back on Beth's leg and both women heard Simon gulp.

Beth glanced at Simon's reflection in the mirror. Despite the compromising position he was in, he was clearly enjoying watching what the policewoman was doing to Beth. Her eyes moved down his body and she saw that his cock was rapidly swelling. She swallowed hard and turned her head away quickly. She was having trouble stopping herself from laughing.

Ann was doing a marvellous job. Better than Beth had dared to hope. The uniform seemed to be giving her added confidence. It was almost as if she were a completely different person. Beth remembered the thoughts she had had about exploring Ann's body after her experience with Lisa. She felt a sudden shiver of longing as Ann's fingers continued to squeeze her breast.

'Do you understand?' Ann emphasised each word.

'Yes.' Beth's voice was squeaky with her growing passion.

'OK. Get dressed and go.' Ann watched in silence as Beth slammed her case closed and pushed her arms into her coat.

'What about these?' Ann picked up Beth's panties. 'You wouldn't want to go without them or I might have to arrest you for indecent exposure.'

Beth stifled another giggle, grabbed the panties and stuffed them into her pocket. She moved her head and saw Simon staring at Ann, wide eyed. 'What about him?'

'Oh, don't worry. I'll take care of him for you.' Ann licked her lips and walked across the room to the bed. Beth felt another pang of excitement.

'So, you like being punished, do you?' Ann asked Simon as she examined the cords at his hands and feet.

'Look, this is just a misunderstanding,' Simon began. He stopped abruptly as the policewoman ran her hand across his newly shaved groin.

'I've never seen a man with a bald cock before,' Ann told him. 'I can't remember if there's a law against it or not.'

Simon flushed from head to toe. 'Look, just let me go, will you?'

'What's your rush?' Ann caressed his naked cock again. 'I think you and I need to have a little chat about law and order first. Turn over.'

Simon stared at her in shock. Ann flicked his cock with her fingers. 'You're not going to disobey an officer of the law, are you?' She flicked his cock again. Simon strained against the slack of his wrist and leg ties and managed to half-roll over to protect himself.

'Nice bum. I'm going to enjoy this.'

Beth put her hand over her mouth to smother her laughter and backed out into the passageway. She could hardly believe that Simon was putting up with all this. Mind you, given the circumstances, what choice did he have?

Ann gave his backside a resounding slap and Simon flinched. She raised her hand and slapped him again, then again. His buttocks turned red.

'Turn over again.'

As Simon rolled over on to his back, Ann put her hand up her skirt and pulled her pants down. Beth looked down at Simon and saw how excited the spanking had got him. His cock was fully erect and twitching up and down. Or perhaps it was the uniform. She knew that some men got a kick out of that. Whatever the reason,

Beth was certain that Ann had now got him right where she wanted him.

Without a word, Ann climbed on to the bed and sat over him. She pulled up her skirt, revealing her suspenders, and wriggled up so that his tongue could lick her mound. She leant over and pulled his head on to her, then reached behind her and grabbed his throbbing cock in her fist.

Beth gulped at the sight of her friend and her boss together. In some ways, it was even more exciting than watching Daniel and his friend had been. She leant against the wall and lowered her hand down on to her mound. She was already dripping.

Ann climbed off Simon and put her mouth over his cock, licking and sucking it like a lolly. Simon writhed helplessly from side to side, straining against the cords at his wrists.

Beth slipped her hand up under her top and teased her nipples as she watched Ann pick up a condom and peel it down over Simon. She felt her clit tingling with anticipation and she pushed her fingers up hard inside herself.

Ann lifted herself up and crouched over Simon's groin, using one hand to guide his tip up into her. She put her hands on his chest and started to push herself up and down as if she was working out. Beth could see her friend's white buttocks bobbing up and down faster and faster as she got into her rhythm. She was consumed with the desire to go over and fondle her. Simon's balls bounced with every stroke and Beth could hear his urgent grunts as he raced towards his climax. She pumped herself harder with her finger and slid her other hand down to rub her engorged bud.

Simon groaned loudly and Ann's police hat fell from her head and bounced across the room. Ann whimpered with enthusiasm and thrust herself even harder down on to him, so that Beth could hear her friend's thighs slapping against Simon's groin. Simon groaned again and

759

came. Beth gritted her teeth to stop herself crying out as her own orgasm enveloped her. Her ecstatic whimper was masked by the loud cry of release that burst from Ann's lips as she reached her own peak and slumped down on to Simon's stomach.

By the time Beth had recovered, Ann had already climbed off Simon and was pulling on her panties again. Simon was sprawled back on the bed, clearly exhausted by his experiences. It was only as Ann turned to leave that he seemed to remember he was still tied up.

'Wait. You can't leave me like this.'

'Oh, don't worry. I'll call room service for you.' Ann picked up the phone and pressed one of the buttons. Beth grabbed her case and slipped quietly out of the room. She was certain that Simon hadn't seen her. He seemed to have temporarily forgotten about her altogether. As she pulled the door to behind her, she heard Ann's voice on the phone:

'Could I have coffee for two in room 33, please. Thank you. Just let yourself in, will you? We are a bit tied up at the moment.' She replaced the receiver.

'I'm sure the waiter will sort you out,' Ann told Simon as she picked up her hat and headed out of the door. Beth giggled as she heard Ann's carefully planned final words: 'Of course, you may have to be nice to him.'

The two women hurried down the corridor and into the room Ann had already booked. Beth gave her friend a big hug.

'You were great, Ann,' Beth told her. 'Absolutely fantastic.'

Ann flushed with pleasure at the compliment and began to strip off her hired uniform. 'I can't remember when I last had so much fun,' she confessed. 'And, it's not over yet,' she added as she wriggled into her own clothes and stuffed the uniform into Beth's case.

The two women went back out into the corridor. A tall man carrying a tray was just knocking on Simon's door.

'Room service,' the man called as he opened the door. They hurried after him and positioned themselves just outside the open doorway.

'Oh my God,' the waiter – actually a friend of Ann – cried in surprise as he stepped into the room. 'Oh, sir. I didn't realise that's what you meant when you said you were tied up.'

Beth and Ann covered their mouths and peered round the door. Ann's friend had put the tray down and was standing by the bed, eyeing Simon up.

'Oh,' he twittered. 'I really like that shave. Very sexy. Especially the little heart.' He ran his hand up Simon's leg. 'I shall go straight home and shave myself just like that.'

Beth glanced at Simon. His face had gone completely white. 'Just let me go,' he whispered, so faintly that she only just made out his words.

'Oh, but sir. That would be such a shame.' The man's hand moved further up Simon's leg and Simon quickly rolled over on to his stomach. The man grunted with obvious delight and ran his hand over Simon's buttocks.

Beth turned to Ann. 'Your friend's gay, isn't he?' she accused. 'You never told me about that.'

Ann sniggered. 'Don't worry. He promised that he wouldn't take any real liberties. Well, not unless Simon encourages him, of course,' she added cheekily.

Beth started to laugh helplessly. There could be no doubt that Simon had been taught a lesson he wouldn't forget in a hurry.

'Come on, let's leave them to it. We've got some serious celebrating to do.' Beth grinned as she remembered her swollen bank account and her exciting future.

Still laughing, the two women turned away and headed out to Beth's car. They were already outside before Beth remembered that her panties were still in her pocket. She glanced excitedly at her friend's trim figure, already anticipating taking a few more liberties of her own.